MOLOKAI

MOLOKAI

O. A. BUSHNELL

THE UNIVERSITY PRESS OF HAWAII

HONOLULU

Pacific Classics Edition 1975
Published originally by The World Publishing Company

Library of Congress Cataloging in Publication Data

Bushnell, Oswald A
    Molokai.

    (Pacific classics; no. 4)
    Reprint of the ed. published by World Pub. Co.,
Cleveland.
    I. Title. II. Series.
PZ4.B979Mo6 [PS3552.U823] 813'.5'4 74-31402
ISBN 0-8248-0287-X

CONTENTS

I. NEWMAN

1

WITH THE Prime Minister of the Realm to present me, I went to ask the King for a boon.

Silent in his open carriage we sat, the Premier and I, as we were driven across the muddy plaza which kept the Government Buildings of Hawaii at their distance from the opulent pile of Kalakaua's new palace. I was silent because, after months of unrelieved disappointment in my research, I was discouraged and, I must admit, hurt in my pride. My hurt made me defensive; and, suspecting laughter and sneers from my associates in medicine in Honolulu, I hid behind a wall of reserve.

My companion was quiet because he did not like the errand on which we were going. "This is a strange thing to ask for," he had said once again, just before we set out for the palace. "And I am not at all sure you'll get it." He disliked asking the King for anything he was not certain the King would readily grant: many years of pleasing whimsical majesty had made him sensitive to the King's humors. With all his power he himself could have granted me in an instant the favor I sought. But "No, I cannot do it. I will not," he maintained, as stubborn as a goat. Only after I threatened to go alone to the King did he finally consent to call with me upon his master.

I looked at him, the unbelievable man who was my sponsor, my guide, my employer, and, I was beginning to suspect, my enemy. Long and lean and elegant, he lounged in his corner, his legs crossed at the knee to accommodate them in the well of the carriage. His eyes were closed against the brilliance of the tropic day; he appeared to be dozing in the shadow of his silk hat. One thin-fingered hand resting lightly on his breast kept the soft white beard from blowing about his face. The other hand, pallid and empty, lay upon the seat of the barouche. He carried no portfolio or sheaf of papers or any sign of his office. The patrician head, with its piercing eyes and long curved nose and aureole of white hair, held everything he needed to know in his tireless mind. In any country on earth this man would have been outstanding. But in the Kingdom of Hawaii, surrounded as he was by natives only a generation removed from savagery, or by white men stamped with the dullness of their Calvinism, his virtuosity made him conspicuous and, in consequence, somewhat ridiculous.

Who else but Walter Murray Gibson could have been the Prime Minister of the Nation, Minister of Foreign Affairs, Minister of the Interior, President of the Board of Health, President of the Board of Education, holder of a dozen other lesser offices, all at one and the same time? The "one-man Privy Council" he was called in Honolulu, by some in admiration, by most in execration. Equal to any task the King put to him, insatiable in his ambition to serve both the King and himself, Gibson gradually had supplanted most of the members of the Government. By the time I arrived in Honolulu, Kalakaua, it was being said, was having no difficulty in filling any vacancy in his kingdom "with a good man": he simply named Walter Murray Gibson to the post. As owner and editor of the *Pacific Commercial Advertiser*, the Government's newspaper, and as the richest white man in the kingdom, Gibson extended his power to those parts of the islands which were not under his control as a member of the Privy Council. But, in the *opera buffa* Kingdom of Hawaii, this factotum, this busybody, held one other office of supreme importance which outweighed all of the others together: he was Master of the King's Revels as well, and in this way he completed his domination over the King and the kingdom. The man was a mountebank as well as an opportunist.

To confirm my opinion of him, the elongated figure opened one glittering eye. Of astonishing brightness and blueness, it examined me, upright in my corner. It winked slowly, insolently, at me. "Sun's bad for the eyes, you know," the oracle murmured. A faint smile played about the thin lips, implying that my head as well as my eyes were in danger of the August sun. Then the eye was closed, the smile vanished, and he appeared to doze again. But I knew the clever mind was not idle: behind the closed eyelids that agile brain was juggling a dozen different schemes. He might be a mountebank, but he was no fool.

Fretted by his jeering—he could make me feel so small, so much like a child!—I turned away from him. He was right, however: the glare from my white uniform was blinding, and the sola topi I wore did nothing to protect my eyes from the reflected sunlight. I must make a note, I reminded myself, respectfully to inform the *Gesundheitsamt* at home that the uniform they designed so carefully in Berlin had its limitations in the sunny lands where it was used. It was a handsome uniform, high at the collar, slim at the waist, and I was proud to be seen in it. But perhaps—I hesitated over the proper wording of my memorandum—perhaps some other color than white might be more practical? I would offer it as a suggestion, with the correct degree of diffidence, of course, when I reached home next spring. With a sudden longing for Berlin welling up within me, I looked beyond the blur of my uniform to the dirty alien world beyond the carriage.

We were being driven along King Street, the shabby main road of Honolulu. On our left the naked statue of Kamehameha, the barbarian first king of Hawaii, leaned upon its spear, lifting its right hand like a beggar to the spendthrift successor who lived in the new palace across the street. On our right stretched the high coral wall which enclosed the great square of the palace grounds. Eight feet high, a solid rampart of hewn reef-rock, it was interrupted once upon each side, where a wide gateway permitted access to the palace. Above the wall the crowns of exotic trees, with names unknown and unknowable to me, tossed and bowed in the wind from the mountains. The pendulous leaves, unaccountably greedy for sun in this land of sun, glistened as though they had been freshly washed in a rain of oil. They were all so lush, so foreign, those trees. I didn't like them. I prefer the more restrained, the more symmetrical vegetation of my northern homeland.

Because ours was not a visit of state, we were driven past the Kauikeaouli Gate on King Street, its wrought-iron barrier closed, the two native sentries, drowsing in their narrow sentinel boxes, not even noticing our passing. We were required to go halfway around the wall, to the Kinau Gate on Richards Street, before we could turn into the palace yard.

In the meantime I was free to vent my irritation upon Kala-kaua's folly. What a crazy thing it was, to be set down in that miserable dirty town, on that windswept island, in the middle of that vast and monstrous sea! A rococo concoction of stone and wood and glass, it rose like a Frenchman's wedding cake, tier upon tier, beyond the barricade of wall and the jungle of trees. Newly finished, it gleamed and sparkled like a parvenu bedecked with both true diamonds and jewels of paste. It might possibly have been at home in Florence, or in Paris, with its colonnades and balconies, its florid Corinthian pillars, its square towers and mounting turrets with their mansard roofs; but there, in a setting of fantastic vegetation and acres of vivid green grass, against a backdrop of violent mountains and brilliant blue sky, it was bla-tant and vulgar. Like everything else in the tawdry town, it was ridiculous. It had no right to be there.

It was like Honolulu, raw, presumptuous, and false. Honolulu had no right to be there either. I had summed it up very well, when I wrote my first impressions of it to Luise, waiting for me in Berlin:

> A village so new that it has no history, it sprawls like a pimpled adolescent beside the dirty pond its people call a harbor. The earth upon which it lies is raw and naked, not yet clothed either with buildings or with verdure. Here, for the first time, a street is forming, following the aimless path of a pig. There, upon the sur-rounding waterless plains, no tree has ever grown, and on the nearby foothills only the scrawny striving grass has managed to gain a hold. Palaces of princes spring from coral reefs, where the stinking seaweed has not had time to dry; and between them clapboard cottages and grogshops and churches—so many churches!—are rising to milch the commoners. I do not like this place, and I shall not be happy until I leave it, on my way home to kiss your hands again.

Nine months of hard work in the primitive place did not lead me to soften my opinion of it. *Mein Gott!* I could no longer deny it: I hated the place!

No sentries barred our way at Kinau Gate, and I looked about with interest as we drove into the enclosure. This was my first visit to the palace. I had not been honored with an invitation since soon after my arrival, when I was served with a bid to attend a Court Ball. I could spare no time for dancing, busy as I was with my research, and I did not even bother to send my regrets to Their Sable Majesties. I supposed they were pouting still, for no further claims were made upon my time.

Ahead of us, at the center of the vast yard, was the flamboyant structure itself. To our left, tucked away in a bower of trees, squatted a low frame building, with latticed verandas and the comforts of a dwelling place. This was "The Bungalow," where Kalakaua spent much of his time, even now when his fancy palace was built, and where, it was rumored, many of the revels were held at which my lolling companion presided so efficiently. To our right, less obscured by vegetation, was the octagonal pavilion where Kalakaua's private band played in concert to please the Court. The pavilion, as every visitor to Honolulu is soon informed, is a relic of the ceremonies of the King's coronation. He had been King for ten years already at the time of his crowning. After his ridiculous Royal Progress around the world, and his discovery of the pomp and splendor which the world's great rulers enjoy, he came home determined to have a palace and a coronation of his own. And—protests from his government, the poverty of his people, the foolish extravagance of it all, notwithstanding—he was given his coronation when the palace was finished. It is common knowledge that Mr. Gibson owes his power, and the enjoyment of the King's favor, to his parliamentary skill, which forced both palace and coronation upon the country without the King's having to lift a finger to acquire them for himself.

The coachman called to his horses, flicking at them with the reins. They quickened their pace as we drove along the short *allée*, between rows of young royal palms. The fanciful edifice, its towers soaring above our heads, its kingly standards flying bravely in the wind to announce that His Majesty was in residence, impressed me in spite of myself. Ornate, impossible as it was in this setting, it did have an airy sort of grace about it to save it from being a complete fraud. I was forced to admit that there are worse examples of architecture and of princely taste in London, even in Berlin. As for Birmingham, the city of my birth and of my youth— *ach!* the less I thought of its monstrous smoky ugliness the happier I would be. I do not think of it as home, any more, or of the sinister merchant prince in it who is my father. I do not intend to go back to Birmingham again, ever. Berlin, in the new German Empire: that is where I belong.

As we rolled smartly toward the grand staircase of the palace, the Prime Minister rearranged himself in more decorous order. The long legs were uncrossed, the narrow feet with their toothpick-toed shoes were placed on the floor, the slouching torso imperceptibly stiffened and straightened, the head rose above the folded carriage top, and, when we drew up with a flourish, amid a great stir of native footmen running down the cascade of stairs to greet us, there he was beside me, erect and composed, the very model of the dignified statesman. Oh what a rogue he was! I all but laughed in his face. Somehow, the knowledge of him, a rascal in power, combined with my sense of expectancy to lighten my humor. I shrugged. If this is the way the kingdom is managed, why should I try to change it? I was almost free of care and light of heart when we stepped from the carriage.

In the distance, as we began our ascent of the palace stairs, the bells of Kawaiahao Church were ringing the hour of eleven.

Briskly we climbed the stairs and entered the darkness of the Reception Hall. The change from the bright daylight dimmed my vision, and I stumbled over the threshold, making an awkward entrance. When I could see again, I found Mr. Gibson waiting for me, flanked by dark attendants in flamboyant livery. One of these, judging by the abundance of gold worked into his close-fitted uniform, I took to be the Royal Chamberlain. Thin of frame, with a narrow drooping mustache to complement the lines of his saddened mouth, he barred my progress with a tired hand. One felt fatigued just to see the mournful man.

"You will leave your hat there, sir," he said languidly, his flaccid arm directing me to the side table against one wall of the room. I went obediently to place my topi beside Mr. Gibson's silk hat. On the wall above the table hung a small round mirror, borne upon the intertwined initials of Kalakaua and of Kapiolani, his Queen. Hurriedly I peered into the mirror, to check upon my presentability. The thin nose and fair skin of the Neumanns were there, and the flaxen hair and the wide blue eyes of the Heywoods. The mustache was my pride: blond and arrogant, following the curve of my lips, held tight in the self-contained sneer I had developed since my arrival in Honolulu, it was my protection against comments about my youth and testimony of my arrival at man's estate. My chief trouble lay in the fact that although I was almost thirty years old I still looked to be only twenty. Most of my diffi-

culties, wherever I went, could be traced to this persistent youth-
fulness, in which people never accorded me either the wisdom of
my years or the honor of my rank. Mr. Gibson, worst offender of
all, continued to think of me as a boy still in the *Gymnasium,*
of whom he held no high opinion.

He was arranging the hang of his frock coat and talking with
the Chamberlain when I turned away from the mirror on the
wall. The Reception Hall was long and narrow, running the width
of the palace, and it was illuminated only by the daylight coming
through the doorways at either end of it. The high ceiling, done
in regal gold and purple, rose at least twenty feet above the smooth
sandstone floor. From the ceiling six unlighted crystal chandeliers
wept their tear-shaped lusters. The walls on either side were
pierced at regular intervals by tall Gothic doorways. Between the
doors hung enormous portraits in oils of royal personages from
several of the reigning houses of Europe and, by the presumption
of the newly arrived, of some of Kalakaua's forebears. Below the
portraits ran a low wainscoting of carved native wood. Potted
plants, sprouting from bulbous Oriental jardinieres, alternated
with stiff-backed chairs and uncomfortable benches. The portraits
were bad, the woodwork was skillful in its fashioning but unfortunate in its orange color, the jardinieres were too gaudily Chinese. . . . It was all of a piece with the rest of this vulgarian's
plaything.

My observations were achieved at a glance, of course, and I
turned back to the Chamberlain and the Prime Minister. With a
gesture I let them know that I was ready to see the King.

"No need to accompany us, Kapena," said Mr. Gibson breezily,
clapping a familiar hand upon the Chamberlain's sloping shoulder.
"I know the way."

The Chamberlain smiled wanly, permitting himself to subordi-
nate his natural sadness to the Premier's hoary jest. "You better
than anyone, sir. Go right up. His Majesty is expecting you."

The Premier raised an eyebrow at me. "Ready for the bearding?"
Without waiting for my answer, he was off, striding toward the
staircase rising beyond the knot of grinning footmen, splendorous
in white teeth and gold braid. He climbed the stairs, three at a
time, forcing me almost to trot after him. I dared not call to detain him, much as I wanted to stop to examine the staircase
more carefully.

For it was a beautiful thing! Springing from the center of the

Hall, it vaulted effortlessly and with unerring grace toward the second floor of the palace. When, in its sweep, it had almost reached its goal, it divided into two exquisite parts, each one curving toward the front of the building, to complete the ascent to the second floor in another easy flight. Made of a native wood happily darker than the rest employed in the room, simply carved and masterfully designed, it was the most noble work of man I had yet found in Hawaii. It would have done justice to any palace in Europe. Delighted with my discovery of it, running my hands admiringly over the smooth curve of the handrail, I did not hurry to catch up with the Premier.

He was waiting for me at the head of the staircase, a sardonic smile upon his lips. "Why, I believe you've found something to like in Honolulu."

"It's beautiful," I conceded, unwilling to express my enthusiasm too openly. I knew him well enough to be sure that he did not like interests which he did not share.

"Aye, that it is. Designed it myself."

My irritation at this artfully baited trap for the display of his talents was checked almost as it began by the sound of a door closing softly. Turning to look, we saw a young woman, weeping quietly into a handkerchief. The bend of the head, the droop of her shoulders, confirmed the evidence of her tears: she was in great distress of spirit.

"What's the trouble, Malie?" asked the Premier, stepping to her side.

Startled, she looked up at him, tall and gaunt beside her. Even in sorrow, with eyes reddened and swollen, her mouth half opened with the need to breathe, she was remarkably beautiful. The complexion showed her to be a half-caste, a *hapa-haole* as the expression is in Hawaii, but she was richly dressed in the latest mode. The tight bodice of the day dress, made of natural shantung, set off handsomely the dusky color of her skin and the blackness of her hair, the while it revealed the charms which by clothing women pretend to deny the existence of. The upper skirt, of plum-colored silk, draped and looped up over a gored underskirt of golden brown silk, fell in the fashionable waterfall back which just then was being affected by the women of Europe. Obviously she was a person of some station at Court.

Eyes brimming with tears, she gazed up at the Prime Minister and then at me. Overwhelmed by her woe, she shook her head and raised the handkerchief once more to her face. Without a word, she curtsied gracefully before him, gathering the train of the dress in her free hand as she did so. Then, quietly, save for the rustle of her skirts as she moved, she went away from us, hurrying down the Grand Staircase to the Reception Hall below. Even in flight there was loveliness in her carriage, in the slimness of her waist above the bobbing bustle, in the flicker of the narrow shoes amid the froth of underskirts. She disappeared around the curve of the staircase, leaving only the faint scent of herself in the air about us.

"Poor Malie! She seems to be very unhappy," laughed Mr. Gibson. "A scolding from the Queen, no doubt, for being too flirtatious at the Ball the other night." With the silly smile upon his lips, the fond look he sent after the departing girl, it was impossible for me not to wonder if there were not some connection between Malie's present distress and the Premier's staircase reminiscences. It was a logical conclusion for me to draw. Was he not the man who said, upon every pertinent occasion, "My hair may be white, but my heart is still green," and who often proved the boast with an impertinence which made the occasion? Poor Malie indeed! I shuddered with disgust at the thought of her submitting to the attentions of this satyr. He even resembled one, with his straggling beard and the long curve to his nose.

My revulsion was cut short by the opening of the same door. Ah ha, I found myself snickering, even as I bowed low before Majesty. Where does Malie lie in this game? Tales of the infamous Ball of Twine Society popped into my head: of the revels Gibson arranged for the King in the Boathouse down in the harbor, or in the cottage, far removed from town, on the distant beach at Waikiki. I became almost as entangled in my recollections of them as those skeins of twine would have been, tossed across the Boathouse floor, when the merrymakers at those orgies chose their companions of the night according to the roll of the balls of twine.

The voice of the Prime Minister assumed an official tone, he drew his lank form into something resembling attention. "Good morning, Your Majesty." Then, more suavely, "Sire, may I present to you Doctor Arnold Newman, a member of my staff in the Board of Health." Again I bowed low before the King of Hawaii.

"Good morning, Your Excellency. Welcome, Doctor Newman. I have wanted to have a chat with you." The voice was soft, cultured, almost feminine in its languor. "Do come into the Sitting Room, where we can be comfortable." With a plump hand he indicated the farther end of the large room extending from the head of the staircase. His manners were impeccable.

We were moving off at his suggestion when from the room beyond the open door we heard a woman's voice. "Kawika . . . Please shut the door." The request was followed by an unmistakable sniffle.

"Yes, my dear. I'm sorry—I forgot." With surprising speed for one of his portliness, he closed the busy door, then returned to shepherd us into the sitting room.

"How is Her Majesty this morning? Is she ill?" inquired the Prime Minister, all solicitude. With my lesson in palace geography thus driven home, and with the Queen's dominion so evidently established for me, I should have had the grace to blush at the naughtiness of my thoughts about who had lain behind that mystifying door. But, alas, I have weaknesses, as have other men, and I did not profit by the lesson.

"Oh, she is quite well, thank you.—We've just had an unhappy parting with one of her Ladies-in-Waiting.—Malie, you know.—We were bidding her good-by. She's having to leave us . . ." The soft voice paused frequently in our progress, as we rounded settees and tables and potted plants in our course toward the cluster of chairs where he wanted to seat us. Passing under a large skylight designed, in a naive conceit, in the form of a crown, we skirted an enormous round table made of the same orange wood used so liberally in the walls of the palace. Neatly arranged on the table were stacks of foreign magazines, piles of foreign newspapers, all of them in English: *The Times* of London, the *New York Herald*, the *Edinburgh Review*, the *Atlantic Monthly*. As I saw the familiar names I wondered how well those publications were read. The dog-eared copies of *Punch*, lying among the pristine monthly reviews, gave me my answer.

"Here we are. Let us sit down. Doctor Newman, please, here.—Walter, you here.—The Queen is very unhappy about losing her. A lovely girl, you know. Very lovely." He stopped the disjointed talk while he eased himself into his chair. Only when he was installed in it did we seat ourselves.

I had seen him before, of course, but only at a distance, riding in his carriage, and this was my first view of him at close range. Dressed in a loose navy-blue sack coat and comfortably baggy white linen trousers, he looked heavier than he actually was. The slowness with which he walked, the frequent pauses for breath, the occasional fits of asthmatic gasping, all indicated a certain discomfort of the body. Sitting as portly men so often must, on the edge of his chair, with his feet set firm upon the floor, his rounded belly filling the space between his legs, he rested his arms upon the rails of the chair, letting his hands hang limp.

"Please be at ease," he said to me, perched stiffly on the edge of my seat. "We have no ceremony here." The First Minister of the country needed no such encouragement: his long bony body was already settled in his usual posture, with the legs crossed at the knees, almost on a level with his head.

From a table beside him the King lifted a carved wooden box. "A cigar, Doctor?"

"Thank you, sir. I do not smoke."

"Walter?" As with all *kanakas*, he had difficulty in pronouncing his *r*'s. The Premier's name, as he said it, sounded like "Waltah." Mine, inevitably, was "Doctah." This softening of the harsher letters of our English words makes the language gentle and fluid when the Hawaiians speak it.

While they lighted their cigars, filling the quiet air with blue smoke and the stench of tobacco, I examined His Hawaiian Majesty with a physician's discernment. His wide face was sallow: the color beneath the brown skin was not a healthy one. Too much easeful living, not enough exercise, was too simple a diagnosis to make. Something else—a sluggish liver? an overtaxed heart?—would need to account for the pallor, the puffiness about the eyes. The jet-black curls of his Dundrearys and the full, flowing mustachios were still untouched with gray, as were the waves of glossy hair combed back from his high forehead. But the great brown eyes, which in *kanakas* are so often the most attractive of their features, in him were weary and puzzled, as though, despite his rank, he had been rebuffed by fate and had known little but sorrow. Bloodshot and heavy-lidded, they frequently strayed from me or from Gibson, while we talked, and always they came back to rest upon us with a suggestion of surprise at finding us still there.

But the Prime Minister was not inhibited in the least by the royal vacancy. "Your Majesty," he began at once. "Doctor Newman, as you know, came at my invitation to make some inquiries upon leprosy as it is found in these Your Islands." It is characteristic of Gibson that, for his vanity's sake, he must squeeze every ounce of credit out of every one of his creditable actions.

The King's gaze turned upon me for a moment, he nodded his awareness of the self-evident fact.

The eyes of people fascinate me: I am so sensitive to them, and to the revelations they can make of the person who wears them, that they are almost an obsession with me. I look first at them, in my estimation of people, placing much faith in the signs I read in their eyes for the judgment I make of them. I was still a boy when I discovered this power, and discovered also the distressing corollary to it, that through these unguarded windows I could perceive, even without the guidance of words, the nature of a mind and the anguish of a heart.

The eyes of Kalakaua were like those of a dissolute bull, jaded of his servicing, and I expected little in the way of thought to issue from the unoccupied mansion of his mind.

"Since his arrival last November," continued Mr. Gibson, "he has been pursuing his investigations with great devotion and most commendable vigor. I can vouch for this, for I have seen him working, at all hours, when less diligent folk were taking their rest." Here he rewarded me for my months of labor with a regal nod of his own and a frosty sort of smile.

"But," he hastened on, before I could grow warm in the sunshine of his approbation, certainly before the King (if he had conceived the thought) could ask him how he could know all this about me when he was noted more for his relaxations than for his diligence, "despite his efforts, and despite the most scientific of approaches to the problems of the disease, he has not yet succeeded in discovering the answer to some of the most profound— if not the most pressing—of the questions he came here to investigate." The orator in him was taking hold. The full flatulent phrases were beginning to roll, the long-fingered hands to wave. If he were not stopped soon, the King and I would be in danger of hearing an hour's flowery disquisition upon the evils of leprosy in Hawaii, in Polynesia, in the whole Orient and Occident, and of Mr. Gibson's efforts to exterminate it, single-handed, at home and abroad. The old humbug! But how could I stop him?

"He has examined, with his microscope, and by technical procedures wondrous to behold, preparations from the skin, the pus, the blood, the internal organs, yea, from the very urine and excrement of lepers, and from their food, their garments, their possessions—" He stopped for breath, choked on his verbosity. "And in all of these, Your Majesty, he has found, with his microscope, the tiny little germs, each about one thousandth the size of the eye of a louse, the devilish little bacilli, which the foremost medical scientists of Europe say are the cause of this scourge of leprosy."

Kalakaua Rex, mouth slack, eyes dull, was unhappy. I was sure that he did not understand a word of his Prime Minister's learned lecture and was merely offended by its catalogue of intimacies. In his hand the cigar hung forgotten, a thin wisp of smoke rising from it in an unwavering path.

"He has attempted," the clarion trump of the Educator went on, "in the approved manner of his fellow scientists, to grow these foul microbes in captivity, in foodstuffs, or artificial soils, prepared for the purpose from meat and eggs and blood, from fish and vegetables and even from our native *poi*." Here, the Mentor's proficiency as a lecturer in bacteriology being sorely tried, he broke off suddenly. I glared at him, wishing he would choke or shut up.

"He has attempted to cause leprosy in animals, by introducing into their healthy systems some of the nefarious microbes which he has descried lurking in the purulent sores of lepers, by transferring to these animals some of the diseased flesh of lepers. For this purpose he has used dogs, cats, pigs, chickens, rabbits, mice, pigeons, a monkey—even animals but recently introducd into Your Kingdom, Sire, guinea pigs from South America."

The King looked ill. This is not an uncommon effect upon people hearing for the first time of the work a bacteriologist must do.

"In all these efforts, and in others it were tedious to mention," intoned the Prime Minister, "he has failed to achieve his grand purpose—" How he drew out that word *failed*, dwelling on it, dragging it out, prolonging the sound of it with lingering affection, as though it were a word his tongue had fallen in love with and was unwilling to release into the air beyond the reach of his lips. But with my frown of disapproval at this turn in the flow of his discourse, he hurried on. "—that of growing the germs of leprosy in his artificial soils, or in the animals he has subjected to his experimentation. *Now* he wants to—"

The clever fiend! In my very presence he was maligning me and my work. Before I was given a chance to utter a word he was undermining the purpose of my call upon the King.

"Your Majesty! Permit me to speak." The bull-eyed gaze turned upon me. Without waiting for more permission than that, I rushed on, fighting to hold my anger in check. "Mr. Gibson does not say —I hope because he does not *know*—that exactly this same failure to grow the leprosy organism in experimental animals or in artificial soils has been the sole fruit of all investigations of leprosy in Europe. This failure is one of the most baffling of all the puzzles relating to this strange disease. This failure is *exactly* the reason why I came to Hawaii, all the way from Berlin, to make my studies here." How could I make him understand, this benighted man, this king of ignoramuses, so far removed from learning and from science, with its amazing discoveries and its astonishing revelations? I could only plunge on, sitting forward on the edge of my chair as though to prevent the Premier from reaching the King's mind before I could.

"The question of the *cause* of leprosy is the most essential part of my investigations here. It is the most subtle and delicate of my tasks, because upon the answer to this question depends all else. Until we know with certainty what the cause of leprosy is, we cannot with certainty know what the disease is. When I have proved its cause, then will we be aided in the detection of the disease, in our understanding of the manner in which it is spread from old victims to new, in our discovery of medicines with which to treat it."

In my eagerness to make myself clear to him, I laid my hand for a moment upon the sacrosanct arm. "Your Majesty. I am not yet discouraged. My work has only begun. The results of all the work I have done until now are not valueless, even though they have not been as successful as I hoped. Nor do they mean that my work must come to an end. On the contrary, they must act as a stimulus to further research. I must continue my investigations until I prove beyond a doubt what the cause of leprosy is."

"And how do you propose to do this, sir," asked Mr. Gibson coldly, "if all the work you and these other investigators have done has met with this—this absence of success?"

Patiently I answered him, more certain now of my hold upon my temper. "No one who has not tried this kind of modern research is able to judge of its many disappointments, its dependency upon apparently insignificant particulars, and"—I thought I might as well insert an innuendo of my own about his damned obstructive and inefficient Board of Health—"and the difficulties which crowd upon one when one is working outside of his accustomed laboratory with its intelligent assistants and its never-failing supply of the equipment he needs." I wished these critics of my work could see my splendid laboratory in Berlin, in the Imperial Bureau of Health. Compared with it my dusty hut in the Leprosy Hospital in Honolulu was less than a German peasant's pigsty.

The President of the Board of Health grinned, knowing well what I was getting at. "You are straying from the point, Doctor. I repeat: how will you—or anyone—prove the cause of leprosy?" The sneer was the insult of a politician, offered to all scientists, not only to myself. Eagerly I took up the challenge, for now we were on familiar ground for me. Not for nothing was I a pupil of Doctor Koch.

"By following a set of rules, sir, laid down by my respected teacher, Doctor Robert Koch." I turned to the King, wondering if he would be able to follow me in the logic of discovery. He appeared to be half asleep, his mouth open, his eyes partly closed, the breath so audible between the thick lips that it sounded like snoring. Gibson, the old fox, could understand me perfectly well, I knew. His years as President of the Board of Health, coupled with his own quick intelligence, had made him sufficiently familiar with all of the new theories about disease.

He could devote his money and his labor, as well as the nation's, to the safeguarding of the Hawaiian people; he alone of all the officers of all the Boards of Health throughout the world, had the foresight to invite an investigating bacteriologist to come to his country from the font of bacteriology in Berlin. And yet, now when I was here, a member of his staff, doing my very best to solve the problems I had been invited to Hawaii to work upon, I was finding him impatient, obstructive, far from the intelligent and co-operative statesman whom I had expected to find in Honolulu when in Berlin I read his enlightened letters to Doctor Koch. This disappointment in my expectations of him baffled me.

But now, while I pondered how to explain Koch's Postulates to the King, Gibson did not bother to hinder me or to help me. A malicious glint in his eye, he left me to myself, while he puffed easily on his cigar. Hopefully I addressed myself to the King.

"In order to prove that a specific bacterium is the cause of a disease, the bacteriologist must first show that this bacterium is present in every case of the disease. Then he must take a specimen from the diseased body of such a case, and from it he must grow the suspect germs in an artificial medium." I spoke slowly, patiently, precisely, as though I were explaining something to a student. But even these simplifications of a complicated subject seemed to be too difficult for the dullard who sat opposite me.

"He must grow these germs in what is called 'a pure culture'— that is to say, in a growth in which all of the germs are of one kind, unmixed, or uncontaminated, as we say, with living microbes of any other kind. This is not always easy to do—"

"An understatement," snorted Mr. Gibson, "if ever I heard one."

"But it is possible to do so," I flared back, "and there are ways of doing it. When this pure culture has been obtained, a portion of it must be introduced into a healthy experimental animal. The animal, of course, must be of a kind which can show visible response to the germs being studied. The germs must cause the animal to show responses—we call them symptoms—which are identical with those shown in natural cases of the disease, or which are similar to them, at least."

I was treading on thin ice here, because of course laboratory animals do not show the same symptoms as humans do. But I did not want to make my explanations too complicated for the mind of the monarch who read *Punch*, and I skipped lightly past one of the chief pitfalls in the proving of Doctor Koch's Postulates.

"As a last step in the proof," I went on, feeling defeat before the battle was done, "the bacteria must be grown again in pure culture from the animal which received them. And they must be shown to be the same kind of bacteria as those which were cultivated in the first place from the original cases of the disease. Only when all of this has been done, and redone, beyond all doubting and all possibility of error, can the bacteriologist say with certainty that he has proved the etiology of a disease." Finished at last with my exposition, I sat back, exhausted. Why had I bothered? My plea was lost for lack of a listener.

His Majesty stirred, opening his heavy-lidded eyes. Panting with the effort, he reached into a pocket of his jacket for a handkerchief, into which he coughed delicately. Now the mountain labors, now let us observe the mouse of which it will be delivered.

The kerchief was applied gently to the royal forehead, to the kingly cheeks, to the pink palms of the soft moist hands. I watched in fascination, wondering how long fatuous ignorance could pretend to be learned deliberation. At last the royal lips parted for speech.

"How interesting.—How fascinating must be this microscopic world in which you work.—Is that how Doctor Koch established the cause of tuberculosis?"

I could scarcely believe my ears. I was expecting a belch. The gentle voice went on, to complete my routing. "I have read of your teacher's investigations with great interest, Doctor—although with somewhat deficient comprehension."

I could not find a word to say. Not daring to look at Mr. Gibson, who would know full well the extent of my surprise, I sat there, watching the King restore his handkerchief to its place in his pocket.

"More recently I have followed in the foreign press his studies in Egypt, about the cholera. Fortunately, the cholera is not one of our problems of health here—at least not at the present time. —We enjoy so many importations from the great world beyond our horizons, however, that it too will undoubtedly join our list before many more years have passed."

Unhurried, for he was accustomed to being listened to, he continued. "But we do have the leprosy in Hawaii Nei, and it is a terrible problem. A terrible thing. Perhaps our worst.—Would you believe it, Doctor Newman? When I was a lad there were no lepers in these islands. I was about ten years old when the first case of the leprosy in a Hawaiian was discovered—by old Doctor Baldwin, of Lahaina, I believe. He was a friend of the chiefs, this first leper, and the husband of Queen Emma's mother. I knew him well. Naea was his name.

"In twenty years there were so many lepers among my people— some say a thousand, some say two thousand—that the King of the time felt it necessary to ask his Legislature to pass an act providing for the segregation of the lepers. That is when our Settlement at Kalaupapa began.

"Today, after twenty more years—who knows?" He lifted a hand, opened it to show its emptiness. "Who knows how many lepers there are among my people, or whether this cruel isolation of them at Kalaupapa does the nation any good—any good at all? Who can say? Not Mr. Gibson's Board of Health. Not, if I have heard you aright, your learned self." Though I searched for it, there was no sarcasm in the mellow voice.

"But we are interested in finding out, Doctor. Our hearts are full of sorrow over this blight which has fallen upon the nation. And we are trying to combat it with all the means at our disposal. We have built hospitals, we have called in physicians, we have tried treatments new and old, brought in from the ends of the earth. This little nation, Doctor, devotes a greater portion of its income to the care of lepers and to the combatting of the disease than does any nation on earth."

"Sire, this is why I came to your islands."

"Yes, Doctor Newman, and we are grateful for your help in this discouraging conflict. It continues to be one-sided, with all of the victories going still to the enemy. But I hope that soon there will be a change in our fortunes. The foul plague cannot always win."

"And the first triumph against it will be achieved when someone shows what the cause of the disease is. I am hoping that this proof will be achieved here, and that I shall be the one to do it."

"Bravo!" applauded my employer from the depths of his chair. "A most laudable service—if only it can be rendered."

"What do you want in nine months?" I snarled. "Cause, cure, —and immortality?"

His complacency was unshaken. He laughed good-naturedly. "Any one of these would be enough. Give us the first two, and you may keep the third."

"I've told you that I've just begun upon my work. These things take time"—I hated the high pitch of earnestness creeping into my throat, the nervous hurrying which made me sound peevish when I wanted only to be explicit—"and more time, more facilities, more help, more of *everything*, are what I need to bring it to a successful conclusion."

"Ah, yes, the guinea pig."

"I thought that you were unsuccessful with the guinea pigs," said the King, turning from Mr. Gibson to me.

"He is being facetious, sir. He knows very well that I would not bother you with a request for guinea pigs."

"What is it, then, that you wish from me?"

And there we were, thus suddenly, and thus slowly, in the most roundabout fashion, at the purpose of my call upon the King. The ease with which he invited it combined with the sensibleness of his conversation to make me state my request of him blandly, as one scientist speaking to another.

"One of your subjects, Sire. A murderer condemned to die."

"One of my people?—But why?"

"I want to experiment upon him, Sire. To see if I can give him leprosy."

2

SITTING IN HIS CHAIR like a corpulent doll, the King remained motionless for a long time. The color drained from his face, the fat cheeks sagged, the tears filled his eyes, which no longer looked upon me. At last, in a strangled whisper, he said, "How can you ask this of me? How can I do this to one of my people? How can I do this to any man?"

I was appalled by his absurd response to a perfectly logical request. I had not dreamed that I would see anguish of this unkingly kind. The worst I had feared was a grunt of refusal, a quick rebuff. Slouched in his chair, Gibson watched us, enjoying my dismay.

"Doctor Newman. I—I cannot do this thing you ask of me."

"But why not, sir?" The swift refusal angered me. There was no chance here for reason, for the exercise of logic and the gradual conversion of an opponent to an intelligent and dispassionate conclusion. He was a creature of emotion, as all *kanakas* are, and his retreat into emotion annoyed me. "Why not?" I pressed the question, almost insultingly for Majesty.

"Doctor . . . You have seen a leper. Indeed, you have seen more lepers during your short stay here than I have looked upon during my entire life.—I cannot endure to see them: my sorrow for them is too great." He looked straight at me, censuring me with those great eyes, now grown hard and cold. "You have seen them in their dreadful disfigurement and in their long dying. You have seen how ghastly is their fate, how hopeless is their lot.—And yet you would deliberately try to make one of these living dead out of a healthy person? Deliberately, without pity, you would condemn him to—" He broke on the long question, staring at me in disbelief.

I could have taken issue with him on some of his assumptions. The accusation, for example, that I was a man without pity. What evidence did he have for this sweeping conclusion? What man is there who does not know compassion? But I would not quarrel with him over small things. The greater cause was at stake.

"I would, if by doing so I should gain evidence that would save other men from contracting the disease."

"Ah, yes. There is your justification.—I see. It is a point. But I cannot accept this reasoning for myself. I cannot be the instrument by which a man becomes a Lazarus. I have seen too many lepers to be willing to lay their awful fate upon one of my fellow men."

"Your Majesty's Kingdom has shown the world its concern for the welfare of its lepers. Why can it not show the world its interest in the scientific research which must be done before the disease can be vanquished? Here, in your own land, is the ideal place for studying this disease. With your sanction of this experiment, a great step forward will be taken. Humanity will bless you for your foresight, scientists will acclaim you for your wisdom." I spoke foolishly, playing upon his vanity as Gibson would, yet knowing all the while that one man, one guinea pig, would not give me the evidence Science needed. One man was only the beginning: insatiable Science would demand a hundred, a thousand men, men in their hecatombs, before it would yield up its verdict. One man was only the beginning—and I wanted Kalakaua to give me this beginning.

"This may be so, Doctor, but I could not do it. I must live with myself, and with my people. I could not willfully hurt the *mana* of one of my people: to hurt his *mana* would hurt my own. —How could I, dedicated as I am to the increase of the nation, commit one of them into your hands and perhaps into a living death?"

"Is this not better than killing a man outright—as the judges and the Courts of your Kingdom are permitted to do in your name? There is no certainty that my experimentation upon him will succeed. Indeed, there is every chance that he will not become a leper. But what certainty does one of your prisoners have, a murderer condemned to death, that he will escape your hangman?"

I had him there: he did not like the truth of my argument. He searched for words with which to answer me, but he could find none. At last he fell back upon a device of the defeated everywhere, perhaps of Kings everywhere. "The laws of the Kingdom are not of my making. They are the laws of the *haoles*, who tell me and my people what we must do. It is their laws, not mine, which exact an eye for an eye, a tooth for a tooth—a life for a life." The heavy head shook despondently; moodily he studied the floor at his feet, not wanting to say more.

His venomous Prime Minister filled out his thoughts for him. "His Majesty and his people have long been learning what so many other *heathen* people have learned at the hands of good Christian folk: how the teachings of Christ are not practiced by Christians, and how Christians are in greater need of missionaries from the heathen than the heathen are in need of missioners of Christ." This is a philosophy with which I am in hearty agreement, and I laughed not so much at the epigram, unoriginal as we knew it to be, as at the manner with which the Premier delivered himself of it. He had all of the attributes of an aged Mephisto very much pleased with his role.

"If only," groaned His Majesty, falling into the humor of the moment, "if only all the *haoles* would go home. How much simpler life would be."

"I fear they're here to stay," mourned Gibson, choosing to ignore the fact that he was the foremost *haole* of them all.

"With their confusion of preachments and laws, their pride and their grasping and their prejudices," continued the King, "all mixed up in the same person with good will and great concern for our well-being and an overgenerous heart. Such bewildering people these *haoles* are."

Grinning wickedly, the Premier became particular. "The same man who calls me a sinful monster in the Legislature on Friday will get drunk on my whiskey—with his arm over my shoulder—on Saturday night."

Kalakaua lifted a cautionary hand. "And on Sunday he will pray for both of you sinners, on his knees in his church.—Oh these *haoles!* They do not know how to hate, but they do not know how to love, either.—Their souls are too *thin.*"

I was on the edge of understanding the bewilderment of the native confronted with all of the conflicts of the white man's chaotic world. Here was Kalakaua, a King enthroned, sitting in his palace, with all of the trappings and much of the sophistication of a great monarch. But beneath the royal crown, made in England, behind the fashionable Dundrearys, borrowed from America, behind the façade of worldliness and courtesy and gravity imposed upon him by his estate, hid a frightened confused savage, half longing to return to the ancestral freedoms of his people, half in love with the easeful life of a king at peace with the world and thoroughly captivated by its pleasures. This insight into his dichotomy bored me and I turned away from it. I should have pitied him for it, and left him alone in his turmoil. But, because I was one of those *haoles* about whom he was protesting, I pushed on to my goal.

"But some *haoles* have come to your islands to help you, Sire." Can I be sure, even now, that the hissing of serpents was not in my speech, that a sinister glitter to match Gibson's own was not in my eye, as I mouthed the unctuous phrases? I had a purpose in speaking them, and it is my only excuse.

"You are right, sir. My country has reason to be grateful to so many of its—its visitors. What would my country be without great men like Captain Vancouver and Don Marin, like Admiral Thomas and Doctor Judd, and almost all of the missionaries who have come to help us? They gave us so much, they took so little in return from us, and they are the ones we should remember when we speak of *haoles*. Not the diseased sailors and the licentious whalers and the greedy merchants who stole from them as they stole from us, too.—The good *haoles* have saved us from dying out, of this I am convinced; and a good Hawaiian will always be grateful to them for their help."

"Does this gratitude not extend, then, to more positive deeds? To a more active participation? Will not Hawaiians help *haoles* in the good works they are performing for the nation?"

"You are very clever, Doctor Newman, to fix upon the one argument to which I can make no good answer. But I cannot do what you ask."

"Not even to give me a murderer? What difference if your

hangman kills him with his noose, or I with my experiment? If he must die, then let him die usefully!"

"You treat life so cheaply, sir!"

"I say again, Sire, what I've said before: the spending of one life now, of a hundred lives, is a small price to pay for the saving of thousands of lives later. Give me this murderer, Sire, this miserable useless murderer who lies now in your jail, condemned to death under the laws of your government. Give me this man, this—" Because I could not remember the barbarous name, I turned to Gibson for help.

"Keanu."

"Give me this Keanu for a guinea pig, and I'll not ask you for anything else in my—"

"David! What does he want with Keanu?"

The King heaved himself to his feet before Gibson or I could realize what was happening. "My dear, you should not have heard. You should not be here!" he cried to the woman who stood in back of me. "This is not for your ears." Despite his protest she came forward and entered the circle of our chairs. The Premier and I rose quickly.

Massive and formidable, she stood before us, questioning with her glance each of us in turn. Arrogant and regal, she was no imitation queen. She was not tall, but she gave the effect of masculine strength and hardness, as Kalakaua gave the effect of feminine softness. Her heavy rounded jaw was that of a man. It was not improved by her mouth, twisted now in anger. Above it a finely cut nose and astonishingly lustrous eyes tried to give a woman's beauty to her face. But her black hair, arranged as it was in the most recent mode, immediately dispelled this lapse into womanliness: drawn tight over her ears and swept into a high mound at the top of her head, it accentuated the hardness of her unwomanly body. The fringe of curls combed low over her forehead did nothing to soften the severe coiffure. And the circlet *lei* of royal yellow feathers which held the mound of hair in its place was not, one knew at once, a woman's concession to femininity: for Kapiolani it was worn as a crown.

Brusquely she turned on me, her earrings, made of tiny polished seeds, dancing at the ends of their golden chains. "What will you do to Keanu?"

"Madame," I said in my politest manner. "I need him to help

me to learn how the disease of leprosy is given by a leper to a healthy person."

"And how do you do this?"

"By placing some flesh taken from the body of a leper directly in the body of Keanu."

"And if you do this—this thing? He will become a leper?" The eyes had lost their hardness. There was unbelief in them, as though what I said, and what I was about to say, was beyond crediting.

"Perhaps, Madame. I *hope* that he will. But his—" I was wanting to say that his sacrifice, if they wanted to dramatize it as such, would not be in vain, but she gave me no chance to continue. With a cry of horror she turned upon her husband.

"Kawika! No! This he cannot do! Not to Keanu. Not to anyone."

"Yes, my dear. I know it. I have already told Doctor Newman so."

"Oh, thank God! I cannot bear to think of us letting anyone to be hurt in this way." Facing me, she asked, "Do you hurt yourself the way you want to hurt Keanu?" Her English was by no means as good as her husband's. She did not have his command of words, or the easy flow of his speech; and her pronunciation was much more like that of the natives in the street than of a queen in her palace. Yet, like any woman in this, she used what speech she had with remarkable effect. Seeing me hesitate, she stamped her foot. "Well?"

"No, Madame, I would not. Because my work is a greater thing than either myself or Keanu. I cannot waste my training, my learning as a scientist. To put it bluntly: Keanu can be spent, but I cannot be."

"He is right, my dear. His learning can save many lives. It must not be misspent."

"Then let him find another way, with his learning." Ceasing to be a queen, she became a woman again, as lost in the modern world as her husband was. Seating herself on the edge of a chair, she tugged impatiently at the folds of her skirts, to get them, and the cumbrous bustle, out of her way, so that she could sit as she had been taught a lady should sit. Her taste was not equal to her station: the ensemble of black and gray was badly chosen, considering the chocolate richness of her skin.

Attentively we waited for her to continue, I standing bowed

before her, Mr. Gibson leaning against his chair, one hand tucked in the breast of his frock coat.

"It is all so mix' up, what these *haoles* tell us," she burst out, shaking her hands at us. "One time they tell us, reading in a black book, 'Do to others what you want them to do to you.' 'Ah, that is good,' we say, and we learn the lesson in the heart. Then another time they say, 'Give us land, or we burn your houses,' or, 'Give us *wahine*, for making *pani-pani*,' or, 'Kill this man, because he killed that man.'—How does this follow their teaching from the black book? They are like *kolea* birds in their coming and going, these *haoles*. But in their thoughts they are like the winds that blow upon the desert of Kau: uncertain is their direction, and dust in the eyes is their only effect."

She looked up at me, no longer in anger. "The missionaries tell us how the soul of a man is eternal, how the life of his body is precious. 'This is good,' we say, 'this we will believe.' They teach us new ways, that our people might live, rather than die, in this land of Hawaii Nei. And we are thankful for this, for the life of our people is short, their number grows smaller with each year. But now you come. And you ask for the life of a man to be put in your hands. We have learned the lesson that his body is not the King's to give, because it belongs to the man, and to God, not the King. Yet you say, 'Give him to me, to be my plaything, to be my animal, to do with as I wish.'—Who are we to believe?"

Damn their ignorant benighted minds, I swore to myself. If they can't see the value of my work, if they can't see how much more useful would be Keanu as an experimental animal than Keanu hung, then why should I stand here any longer, urging a petition they refuse to grant? Furious within, but as courteous as I could be, I said, "Madame, you raise dust in our eyes, as do the winds of your desert Kau. There is only one question here: which is the more important, the safety of the nation, or the safety of an individual person in the nation? Which is the greater evil: by sacrificing the welfare of the individuals in it, to preserve the welfare of the State? Or, by permitting the liberty of individuals, to disregard the needs of the State? Which to choose: the Nation? Or the person? It is this simple, Madame."

But in elevating our argument to such an abstract plane I lost her—and I think I left the King behind as well. *Kanakas* do not take well to philosophy. They stared at me, frank bewilderment in her expression, a careful blankness in his. Only the Premier followed me to my metaphysical heights.

"Ah, yes, the eternal conflict," he drawled. "The rights of man as opposed to the rights of the State."

"Precisely."

"It is quite apparent on which side you stand, Doctor."

"I am on the side of reason, sir, of system and efficiency. I have seen such a system at work, in Prussia, in the new German Empire. In my opinion, all other nations suffer by comparison."

"I wish you long life and happiness in it, my boy, upon your return. As for me—and I am sure I speak for Their Majesties in this—I prefer to fumble along in the inefficient way we seem to have found here in Hawaii. It may be illogical, I know it is unsystematic, but I thank God it is not yet so monstrously efficient that its King and Queen cannot be concerned about the personal fate of every individual in it. Do I speak aright, Your Majesties?"

The Queen contented herself with a nod. The King muttered, "Aye."

"And am I correct, Sire, in concluding that Doctor Newman's petition for the person of Keanu is denied?"

The King was very unhappy. For a long time he could not find his voice. Mopping his forehead with the sodden handkerchief, he looked from one to the other of us, reluctant to commit himself yet knowing very well that he must. At last he exploded. "Yes, yes, of course!—But damn it!—excuse me, my dear—I don't like to see Doctor Newman made unhappy.—Isn't there something else we can do to help him in his work?" Eagerly he turned to me, hoping to find a sop to appease me with. "More animals, perhaps, for your experiments? More assistance in your work?" What a fool he was, standing there, fat arms outspread, offering me bribes I did not want. For a moment I thought he was going to rush on, as fat foolish kings do in fairy tales, offering me the half of his rocky kingdom and the hand of a fat ugly daughter, if only I would withdraw my petition.

The Champion of Health in the Pacific saved me from such a fate. "The Doctor has only to ask for anything he needs," the Spokesman for Inefficiency said, "and he will get it from the Board of Health." It was an unmitigated lie, as anyone who has ever tried to get anything at all from the Board of Health has always found out, and he knew it for such, as the smirk with which he finished his speech told me. But it served to soothe the

King, while it warned me that I had lost not only my appeal to the monarch but also all hope of further aid from the satanic Gibson. The Black Devil had baited me and beaten me, in a trap of my own fashioning, and I knew that there was nothing more I could say.

"I am sorry, Doctor Newman, that we are not as enlightened as are the people of your country," His Maundering Majesty said. "But we are a nation new to the ways of the civilized world, and we are slow to learn them. Perhaps someday we shall reach the point where great nations like your own will not find us lacking in—"

"I sincerely hope so, Your Majesty," I cut him short, thoroughly weary of his whining. Apology is not for kings! Why must this ordeal be prolonged? I had lost my case: it was time for me to go. Why did he not dismiss me? Or was he so unaware of Court Protocol that he did not know what to do? It would be just like him, to escort me to the door now, like any portly burgher.

"Then good luck in your work, Doctor, and God's blessing on it. My people and I will be grateful for anything you may learn about the leprosy that will help them to free themselves of it." He put out his hand. In his country, overrun as it is with Americans, I knew that the hand was to be shaken, in their germ-passing custom, not kissed, as in ours.

"Your Majesty, I bid you good day." With a click of the heels such as he could never have heard in his slovenly Court, I bowed over the soft hand and shook it, once.

"Your Majesty." With another click of the heels I bowed toward the Queen, sitting stiffly in her chair. A curt nod was all the farewell she offered me.

"Sir," was all I thought the perfidious Premier was worth. He had betrayed me in more ways than one, but most of all by leading me into this nest of sentimentalists. Henceforth my contempt would fall upon the King, but my hate would be reserved for Gibson. I could feel it bursting into flame within me, even while I returned his icy stare.

Then, furious with them at their blindness, their irresponsibility, their stupidity, I turned away from them and fled among the maze of chairs and tables and potted plants.

Down the curving sweep of the staircase I stormed, not seeing it this time, not feeling the smooth rail of the banister as it passed under my unheeding hand, nor hearing the clatter of my boots as they fell heavily upon each resounding tread. All I could feel was the pressure of my rage growing within me, the maniacal rage of disappointment, of dashed hopes and shattered ambitions, of absolute and helpless frustration in the face of official apathy. Tears of anger crept unwanted into my eyes, and I was almost blind with them and with the brilliance of the sunshine from beyond the open doors when I reached the foot of the staircase.

"Your hat, sir," the humble voice of a footman stopped me. Gently my topi was placed in my hands. "May I help you to the door, sir?" It was the kindest voice I had heard all morning, and gratefully I accepted the offer of his assistance, hardly able to see who my Samaritan was. His kindness was on the point of comforting me when, out of the ranks of waiting petitioners seated at the side of the Reception Hall, I heard a vulgar voice: "*E!* Wat band dat falla plays een?"

I knew at once that he was asking about me, pointing his dirty finger at my tropical uniform. The burst of laughter which answered his question told me that the commonalty were ridiculing me as openly as their rulers upstairs had ridiculed me in private.

This was the last straw in my load of frustration. Freeing myself from the footman's arm, I pushed him away, and, with the echo of that laughter in my ears, I ran out upon the broad veranda of the palace. Down the great flight of stairs I stumbled. Fortunately I did not fall.

In the blaze of midday I made my escape from the mocking place. While I staggered through the loose gravel of the driveway toward Kinau Gate, the bells of Kawaiahao were ringing the hour of noon.

3

FOR MORE THAN A MONTH after the day of insult I tried to forget my disappointment by devoting myself entirely to my research. Early each morning I went to my laboratory, a misshapen hovel set down in one corner of the Lepers' Branch Hospital at

Kakaako. There, on the mud flats near the entrance to Honolulu's dirty harbor, behind a palisade that was intended to separate the patients from the world which had expelled them, a hundred or so suspect lepers were held in restraint. They stayed there, sometimes for months, until the examining physicians were able to decide whether or not the symptoms they showed were those of leprosy. Sooner or later most of them were proved to be lepers, and when this diagnosis was reached they were sent by an early boat to the Leper Settlement on the island of Molokai. A few of the inmates, however, were shown to be suffering from diseases other than leprosy: they would have the itch, for example, or tuberculosis of the skin, or a late stage of syphilis; and when their condition was recognized for what it was, they were sent home rejoicing—but just as dangerous to their relatives and neighbors as though they suffered from the leprosy.

For the inmates of the dismal lazar-house life was anything but pleasant. Penned up in a hot treeless waste, living in dirty frame huts set high on posts—because when the winds blew from the south the sea would come rolling in across the mud flats into the hospital grounds—they spent their time of waiting in squalor and in idleness. Maintained by the Kingdom, nursed by Franciscan nuns, they did nothing to help themselves. By day they sat in what shade the drab houses could provide, pretending to a decorum they did not possess. By night, after the nuns went home, most of the lepers prowled from bed to bed, like licentious cats, making up in lust what they were denied in hope.

In this idyllic Polynesian setting I labored each day, shunning the company of everyone. I spoke only with the nuns, or with the lepers as they presented themselves to me for the tests I wanted to perform on them.

Except for one of them, the nuns were faceless nonentities to me, shy fluttering things in swirling black robes and dazzling white coifs. All of us had come to Hawaii in the same steamer, almost a year before, but I had avoided them aboard ship as I did on land. Englishman and anti-Papist I had been raised, German and rationalist I had become; and I mistrusted them and their religion.

Late each night I was forced by fatigue to return to my empty cottage in the town for the few hours of sleep my body needed. Work by day, sleep by night—this became the pattern of my life. If I had departed from this self-imposed rhythm I think that I would have left Honolulu by the next vessel for San Francisco: I would have seen how meaningless were my labors.

The time came at last, however, when I was forced to admit that Gibson's condemnation of my studies was in fact correct: they were failures. Not a single one of my hundreds of attempts to grow the leprosy bacilli was successful. Whether I tried to grow them in artificial soils or in the bodies of living animals, the bacilli of leprosy simply would not grow for me. Something was missing from those menstrua which Hansen's bacilli needed for their growth.

Hansen's bacilli. *Pfui!* How his possessive name irked me! I wanted to show the world that they could be grown by Newman's technique, in Newman's medium. I wanted to have *my* name attached to those deadly elusive unco-operative cells, to have them known henceforth as Newman's bacilli. But still they escaped me.

Burning with chagrin, I imagined the snickers and the bursts of laughter being directed at me by my colleagues in the enlightened village of Honolulu. The sound of Doctor Hook's laughter, for example, as once more he would vaunt the theory which most pleased his coarse mind: "Why, suh, 'tis evident this abomination of leprosy is nothin' more than the disgustin' late stage of the syph'lis. What else you expec' from a people so addicted ta venery?" Thumbing his braces, his face red under its fat, he would go on to bawl, "The whole nation is eaten away with this rottenness. Soon—I give 'em 'nother fifty yeah at the mos'—they'll not be one single *kanaka* lef' in these misable isles." He did not seem to be especially disturbed about their disappearance as, from the profits of his practice upon the same vanishing *kanakas*, he bought up acre after acre of their land, preparing for the time when "the *haoles* will take ovah these islands, suh, and make somethin' of 'em, by Gawd."

Others of my eminent colleagues were not so advanced in their thinking. Most of them were as ignorant of modern medicine as were the patients they tried to treat. Few of them had even heard of the Germ Theory of Disease before I arrived to tell them of it; and even fewer would accept the unnerving fact after I had done my best to enlist them among the disciples of Koch and Pasteur.

"The leprosy," some of them maintained, "is a morbification of the humours, to which the lascivious Hawaiians have a peculiar propensity." Or, "This disease comes from too much bathing in the sea: an excess of saline corrodes the flesh, especially if it remain unwashed by water that is fresh." One of them, long of nose, sharp of finger, and short of brains, impaled me on a fanatic glare. "The leprosy," he pronounced with absolute finality, "is a punishment from God, sent as castigation for Sin."

They couldn't distinguish a chancre from a cold sore, a leproma from a boil; but, by grace of an inscribed diploma, usually from America, they were physicians, and therefore something near to gods, in their own esteem. They prescribed mercurials, or housewives' simples, for the treatment of leprosy, being careful to leave the medicines on a post outside their office doors, to keep the lepers at a distance. And they managed comfortably to ignore the fact that infants, virgins, and celibate Christians who had never been bedded with more than a sheet could still acquire leprosy without benefit of lechery.

Some of the physicians in Honolulu were intelligent, of course, and were well informed in the latest developments in medicine. But their quiet voices were drowned in the flood of jeers directed at me and my "Noah's Ark" upon the reef at Kakaako, and I could not hear them. I heard only the sound of laughter, rude and malicious, like the laughter I heard that day in the palace.

Damn, damn, damn! If it were not for the ill-placed sentimentality of fools in power—

I racked my brain to find a way by which I could gain my experimental animal. Day and night I worried over it, until there was no other thought in my mind.

A man, a woman, a child—it made no difference. I must have one human animal, to begin with. After that, the others would come easier: a dozen, a hundred, before my grand design would be accomplished.

I thought of stealing one, kidnapping it in the dark streets of Chinatown, as ships' crews are shanghaied in every port; and of caging it in a house somewhere, just as I kept my guinea pigs in a cage. But I saw soon enough that the scheme was impracticable, if not impossible. Where would I keep it, how could I take care of it, without assistance? And even if I could arrange the means of confining it, the plan was too dangerous. What if Gibson and the King should learn of it?

Then one night, while I lay sleepless in my bed, the way opened up before me. Why should I not ask for a volunteer?

The idea appealed to me for more reasons than one: it was lawful, it was honorable—and it was perfectly calculated to bring the utmost annoyance to Gibson and the King when they learned how I was outwitting them.

With the cleverness of a diplomat I went about the Kakaako Hospital the next morning, planting my idea. I put them all to work for me, patients, guards, especially the *kokuas*—the helpers—those healthy ones who assisted the physicians and the nuns in the Hospital. I used the best method of advertising yet discovered: the talk of people. Their gossip, their delight in circulating rumor and innuendo, would be doubly effective if I put it to work in spreading an idea so appealing to their need as mine was. To help my cause, I reminded them of the lifetime of security a leper received as a ward of the State, with free food and a free home awaiting him at Kalaupapa; and I assured them that my volunteer, if he should contract the disease as a result of my experimenting, would be accorded the same privilege. I hinted at monetary rewards—although I was very careful not to mention the fact outright, or to name any specific sum or from whom it would come. I certainly had no intention of using any of my money to purchase equipment for my research that the Board of Health was supposed to provide.

The only thing I specified was that the volunteer should be free of the disease, and—as well as he could tell—free of contact with anyone who had already contracted leprosy.

But I did not speak of my idea to the Catholic sisters, fearing that their medieval religion, with all its superstitions and delusions, would set them to buzzing around me like a swarm of bumblebees, trying to keep me from claiming my prize.

Nor did I mention my thought to my fellow physicians. My instinct warned me to avoid stirring up both their ignorance and their ill will.

Having planted my idea so carefully, I sat back to await its harvest.

To my surprise, no one came forward. Not one of the lazy guards, not one of the water-front bums or drunken derelicts of Honolulu jumped to my bait. After two weeks of expectancy I was in despair once more. And only at the last did I become aware that I was being avoided and forsworn more than any hideous leper. Patients and *kokuas* alike turned their faces from me when I went past, on my way between the gate and my laboratory. They did not fear leprosy nearly as much as they feared me.

It was then that I decided to go home to Berlin. To hell with these stiff-necked *kanakas*, these obstructive *haoles!* For all I cared, the whole lot of them could rot with leprosy.

But before I went away I thought I should see the Settlement at Kalaupapa, if only to say, when I got home, that I had been there. A few days there, I promised myself, observing the grim place and its gruesome inhabitants, and then I'd be off. I was sick to death of Honolulu, of its dirt, its invincible ignorance, its lepers. My work was at an end, and whether Mr. Gibson and his Board of Health liked it or not, I was finished with them too. Let them wave their stupid contract at me, they had no hold upon me other than my interest in their damned disease.

The thought of being in Berlin by Christmas overwhelmed me. The thought of seeing my Luise again, of taking her lovely hands in mine, of kissing her at last—*Ach!* I grew faint with longing.

The respite Kalaupapa offered was irresistible. Within a day I made my plans to go to Molokai. By the evening of the second day I was on my way.

A shipment of lepers was being sent to Kalaupapa by the steamer *Mokolii*. "You wanna go with 'em, 's all right with me," growled Mr. Harrison, the Secretary of the Board of Health, when I talked to him over the telephone in the Hospital office. "It's your skin, not mine," he went on, very much aware of the relevancy of his idiom. Harrison was the son-in-law of Mr. Gibson, and the one who really managed the Board of Health for his busy kinsman. Since the day of perfidy I would not have a thing to do with Gibson, and I preferred to deal with his minion rather than seek any favors of the old devil.

I asked what arrangements I needed to make for the passage. "This on official business?" He sniffed, with the perennial suspicion of bureaucrats. "O.K., O.K. Just go aboard when you get to the wharf. Wilder's wharf. Any hack driver knows it. I'll tell Cap'n MacDougal you'll be going.—Naw, naw, you don't need a ticket. She leaves five-thirty, six o'clock," he concluded, with an annoying casualness about the time.

I was at the *Mokolii's* side by half-past four. My instrument case and clothes hamper were carried aboard by a young *kanaka* sailor. Still half drunk from his session ashore, he smiled widely and chattered incessantly in his native tongue. Not a word of his gibberish could I understand, but his good humor joined with my own expectations of the trip to put me in a happier state of mind than I had enjoyed for many months.

The *Mokolii* is one of the ancient and outmoded vessels which plies among the larger islands of the archipelago like water bugs among lily pads. Smaller than most of the ships—it is scarcely larger than a tugboat in the Bremerhaven—it must have been one of the first coastal steamers ever made. Heaven knows what its history was before, old and worn, it arrived in Hawaii to end its long career.

To forestall the possibility of seasickness from the heaving ship and from the smells of bilge and paint and harbor water dirtied with filth from half the town, I stepped back upon the pier. In a corner of the shed, among tiers of sacks filled with raw sugar, crates of tinned foods, barrels of flour, I made a place for myself, watching the half-naked sailors, their brown skins wet with sweat, loading the last pieces of cargo aboard the ship. It was a pleasure to watch them. After my months of looking only at lepers, I had all but forgotten that healthy skins and unbroken bodies still existed.

Swiftly the sun sank toward the horizon, mysterious beyond the muddy reef closing in the other side of the harbor. The forest of masts and spars on the merchant ships rose in a thin and rigid geometry, black against the western sky, as drained of color as an etching. Upon the planking of the wharf the *Mokolii* cast its lengthening shadows. Through the gaps between the planks the restive water gave off tremulous reflections of the bleak sky. Then the sun sank behind a bank of clouds, taking all life and light with it, plunging the world in mourning. The sailors, as though drawn with it, finished their loading, and disappeared into the belly of the ship, leaving me alone.

The world waited in melancholy, as a woman in grief waits for night before she will weep her tears.

It was too contrived to be honest, and in a mounting tide of irritation I awaited the orgy of tears about to take place. Why the devil can't these sailings take place at high noon, under a cheerful sun?

We were supposed to cast off at six o'clock, but not until long after the hour did my fellow passengers arrive. And then, just as I feared, they arrived suddenly and all at once, borne in on a flood of tears, complete with hordes of snuffling relatives and the funereal scent of flowers.

One affront to my nerves I was spared, however: there was very little noise.

In an almost wordless silence, broken only by the sounds of weeping, the people in their little clusters bade farewell to the lepers. With murmurings of *aloha*, with kisses upon the tainted lips and swollen cheeks, with handshakes and the graceful motions of giving a *lei*, the healthy said good-by to the dying. With murmurings of *aloha*, with tears streaming down their cheeks, with the tender voicelessness of sorrow, the dying received for the last time the ministrations of love. In the darkness of the pier, touched now only by the last hint of light from the dead sun, the terrible ordeal of farewell was like a ghostly dance in limbo, where forgotten souls touched hands and bowed to faceless figures and moved to unheard music, in a desperate endeavor to be remembered.

Alone in my corner, horrified by the unwanted acquaintance with grief, I felt a tug of pity at my heart. And, as is usual with me in such regrettable lapses of sentiment, I blamed the others for my weakness. *Fools*, I called them under my breath, *Fools!*—as the tears came unbidden to my eyes.

At last even they, in the kind darkness, could shed no more tears. And I, in my darkness, blessed the darkness, as I understood at last why the *Mokolii* did not sail before sunset. On the patient vessel the bronzed sailors, with long tapers in their hands, began to light the paraffin lamps. At the far end of the pier, near its entrance, an attendant began to light, slowly, one by one, the great lamps of the cavernous shelter. In their warm glow the scene lost much of its grimness, and clothes, faces, flowers began to resume their rightful shapes and colors. Even the livid splotches of red upon a leper's brow, the convoluted waxy swellings upon his cheeks, became visible as the reflectors of the lamps cast their brilliance upon the throng.

At sight of those evidences of infection, and of risk to the healthy people who pressed around them, heedless of their peril, my heart regained its hardness. I wanted to chase them all away, those careless healthy ones, shouting of the dangers they exposed themselves to, cursing the Board of Health for its laxity.

While I looked with rising impatience at group after group of them, closing in toward the gangway, I saw for a moment a remembered face. A young *hapa-haole* woman's face, beautiful even in sadness, her eyes filled with tears, her head bent upon the slender neck. I could not recall where I had seen her, or who she was, and in an instant the shifting figures in the crowd hid her from my view, and I could not use her present self to help me to remember how I had come to know her.

A strained and tortured hymn began, the voices trying to bear their joyless tune above the whispering throng. I found the singers in a knot of *haoles*, somber in their black garments, kneeling in the dust. In their midst, bewildered by the phantasmic scene, was a thin frightened boy, his long blond hair framing his head like a halo. But his face was not that of an angel, and his mourners averted their gaze from him while they raised their song to comfort him. Who can comfort him now? I wondered, sneering alike at their helplessness and at their faith. He was doomed, and they would have been better advised to sing his requiem than to raise their voices in prayer for his salvation.

The brutal blast of the ship's whistle broke into the farewells. Surprised by it, the people started with fright. Many threw themselves into each others' arms. Children who had not been touched by the anguish of parting wailed now in terror, their voices drowned in the roar of the whistle. The missionaries continued to sing, their mouths working to shape the words no one could hear, not even their remote Jehovah. The boy in their midst whirled in panic, seeking his mother's bosom. She did not deny him this last comfort, and, kneeling still in the dust, her face wet with tears, she ran her fingers through his golden hair, kissing him again and again upon the crown of his head, upon the nape of his neck.

When the whistle ceased its bellowing I made ready to leave my place among the bags of sugar. Fretting still over the stupidities of humankind, the inefficiencies of government in this disorderly country, I was about to make my way toward the ship when suddenly, at the entrance of the wharf, a tremendous burst of sound arose: the clatter of horses' hoofs, the crack of a whip, the shout of a coachman urging on his team.

Erupting into the pier, thundering toward us across the resounding planks, came a carriage—a long low barouche drawn by a pair of splendid black geldings in perfect gait, heads forward, hoofs high. Without slowing their pace the coachman turned the dashing pair toward our end of the wharf, until it seemed that he would hurl them among us. Shouts of warning rose from the men, shrieks of fright from the women. The missionaries stopped their singing, rising in alarm from their knees. All eyes, all thoughts, were turned upon the violent furious equipage bearing down upon us, as if the Devil himself were come to fetch one of us away.

As we watched, too stunned to move, the coachman maneuvered the carriage in a wide arc and, drawing back upon the reins, brought the team to a prancing, jingling, unwilling halt within a few paces of me. The body of the coach itself was not five feet away from where I pressed against a whole citadel of sugar bags. Looking down upon me was the Prince of Darkness himself, disguised in a flimsy white beard and a headful of white hair. Beside him sat a fat *haole*, puffing out the uniform of the King's Guards, his burnsides falling over the high collar of the tunic.

Opposite them was a *kanaka*, a short beard dark upon his cheek, the long black hair blown forward to cover his face.

"Good evening, Doctor Newman," said the Prime Minister, most suavely. "About to make a trip, I hear."

I could not answer him for rage, for a sickening sense of fury because this Arch-Fiend of mine was informed of my every move. I could not have answered him, I think, for surely if there had been something in my throat it would have been purest venom.

With the hint of a chuckle, he addressed me again. It was plain that he was quite pleased with himself, after such a grand entrance, such a diabolical evocation out of the very night itself. "Have no fear, Doctor. I shall not interfere with your—voyage." There was the slightest of intimations that he really did not mean my voyage. Still I did not trust myself to speak.

"As a matter of fact, Doctor, concerned as I am for the success of your research here, I have brought you something you have been in need of. Something you've wanted very much." He was playing with me. I could tell by the way he looked from me to the hushed throng beyond me and back again to me that he was delighted to have an audience to hear him manage my humiliation. I refused to be trapped, I was about to turn away.

"Here is Keanu . . ." The slow drawl, the dying away of his voice—it was the most sinister sound I have ever heard. It was the Voice of the Tempter. And I listened to it, to the evil, mocking sound. Instead of turning away, I listened to it: I heard with a shock of joy the sound of that name, the promise it offered, the bargain it implied. With a lift of the heart, a turn of the head, a wild quickening of the pulse, I heard the bewitching name dropped softly into my ear.

"Keanu?" In my surprise and delight I could not help but echo him.

Behind me the crowd took it up—"Keanu," they breathed. "It's Keanu," they whispered. "Keanu . . . Keanu . . . Keanu . . ." until the magical name was carried to every waiting ear. Under the mop of black hair the eyes of Keanu were turned upon me.

"Yes, Doctor. Keanu offers himself to be your guinea pig, for your testing."

"But how did he? Who told him?"

"Your advertising is extremely effective, Doctor. Even without benefit of newspapers. Word of your search reached him, even in the depths of his prison cell." He who had once been a prisoner himself, in Weltevreden, the infamous Dutch jail in Java—I have wondered since if he himself did not bring the word of my bargain to Keanu.

"And the King? Does he permit?" I was looking at Keanu, motionless under the shadow of his hair. I could not yet see his dark face.

"Aye, under these terms: that Keanu submits to your testing willingly, of his own free will. If this be so—and Keanu agrees that it is so: he has put his mark upon a paper to this effect— then, whether or not your experiment with him succeeds, Keanu remains forever, for the rest of his days, a resident of Kalaupapa. To these terms, also, Keanu agrees. Whereupon the King—long may he reign!—tomorrow, upon the recommendation of his Privy Council, will decree a commutation of Keanu's sentence, from one of death by hanging to one of imprisonment for life. At Kalaupapa."

My spirits soared. These were excellent arrangements on Mr.

Gibson's part. I could not understand what his motives were, but I could imagine his subtle tongue at work upon the King, persuading him that there was no harm in letting Keanu be my guinea pig, if Keanu chose his own fate. "Then I am grateful, to the King and to you, for assisting me in my work."

"Anything to oblige, Doctor. Remember, you have only to ask." His sarcasm no longer stung. I was so happy that I was ready to laugh with him over the remembered phrase.

With great gentleness, as though he bore a father's love for the prisoner before him, the Prime Minister said, "Ready, Keanu? You may go with the *Kauka* now."

Slowly Keanu rose to his feet. Before our very eyes he seemed to grow from a mere man to a god until, like a god in his chariot, he towered above us who stood in the dust of the pier. Gasps of admiration, little exclamations of pleasure, came from the throng at sight of his superb body, little hisses of fright from the few who remembered his crime. They all knew him, as all Hawaii knew him, who committed the most titillating crime of passion the Kingdom had experienced in a generation; and they turned to him, faces uplifted, like worshippers before a dark Phaëthon readying for the dawn.

Like a god among men he stood there for a moment, as if challenging us to look upon him who for so long had been hidden from the sight of men. Proud, disdainful of us, he flaunted his health and his virility. In the haughty lift of his head, in the magnificence of his shoulders, taut against the prison shirt, in the flat hardness of his belly and the brazen bulge of his manhood, where the dungaree trousers divided to show the columns of his legs, we saw revealed, naked as if he never knew the touch of clothes, the triumphant unregenerate male. Unrepentant (why should he repent a murder committed for love?), unpunishable (who could punish an instrument fashioned for love?) he looked down upon us, challenging us to question his supremacy in love, daring us to deny him the right to live.

It is not for his one crime that he should be imprisoned, I knew, not for the one murder that he should be murdered in return: it is for all those crimes which in the future will be committed in his name that he must be hidden from the sight of men. Not for his ugliness must he be hidden away, but for his beauty, a thing unbearable to all other men.

Struck with terror at my part in unleashing this demon among us, I turned to Mr. Gibson, shouting in my urgency. "But does Keanu understand? Does he know what he is committing himself to?" Gladly would I give him back to his keeper.

"Ask him," the Prince of Darkness answered, with horrid indifference. The shifting of responsibility from his shoulders to mine was almost done.

My senses whirled. In the incredible evening I could not think: I did not know what to think. I looked up at Keanu. I did not dare ask him to speak. In the strange lurid light coming from on high, in the expectant silence, more than ever he seemed to be an incarnate god about to step forth from his newly opened heaven.

His voice came down to me, deep, strong: "Bettah to live dan die." The sound of that voice set me to trembling with despair and delight, as it set the shades behind me to their counterpoint of sighs and whisperings. Hearing him, I had my judgment: my future, and Keanu's, was taken out of my hands. From now on all of the gods in all their different heavens would decide what happened to us here on earth, not I—

An old man's cackle woke me from my vision. "And I agree with him. He's much too fine a fellow to hang."

Keanu held out his wrists to the jailer at Mr. Gibson's side. Only then did I see the prisoner's manacles, the iron chain hanging between them. Swiftly the officer unlocked the handcuffs; bending low, he removed the shackles from Keanu's legs. The chains fell heavily to the carriage floor.

The door of the carriage swung wide, the little folded steps fell into place, inviting Keanu to descend by them to earth. Unhurried, Keanu accepted their invitation and, placing his foot upon the first of them, he stepped from the King's care into mine. Without a thought for me he turned to the Premier, and gave the great man his thanks.

"Good luck, Keanu," said Mr. Gibson, touching him on the shoulder. "For your sake I hope Doctor Newman fails in his experiment."

"*Mahalo nui loa.*" The wide full lips parted in an easy smile of thanks. It revealed teeth dazzling white against the brown skin, the black beard. There was no pride in him now; and he was not as gigantic, nor as godlike, as I had thought he was. Still more than six feet tall, he was a good head higher than I, but somehow his descent to earth had robbed him of his awesomeness.

He was younger, too, than I had thought: the smoothness of his skin, the self-consciousness with which he brushed the long hair from his face, showed that he was not much more than twenty years old. His youth gave me another hold upon reality, another claim upon superiority. And those enormous bare feet, with the mud of the prison yard caked thick upon them! How could I stand in awe of this savage? Swiftly the relationship between us was adjusted: where first I saw a god, I was quite able now to see not even a man. A savage, perhaps, with some claim to handsomeness. Or, better still, a superlatively handsome animal—exactly the animal I needed.

"He has no other clothes, Doctor," the Premier called. "We did not have time to fetch his things from the prison wardroom. Captain Parke, here, will send them up by the next boat." He held out his hand to Keanu. "This will help take care of you until then." Into Keanu's outstretched hand he dropped a gold coin. Gracefully, with no trace of resentment at the public offer of charity, the youth accepted the gift, flashing a brief smile of thanks.

"Now you'd best be off. I fear we've delayed you." The Premier waved us toward the waiting ship. "*Aloha* to you both: I give you each into the other's care." With a nod and another wave, he settled back into his corner, as benign as a grandfather.

The people opened their ranks to let us pass through them to the *Mokolii*. Keanu, in his prison rags and bare feet, I in my gleaming white uniform and polished boots, walked between them, seeing their expressions of wonder, of curiosity, of fright, even of rapture and of lust, as we passed. The faces of the healthy, the faces of the lepers, were no different in their responses to Keanu. But none of them, I noticed, had any thought for me. The handsome youth walked heedlessly among them as though he walked alone, indifferent to the stares, the smiles, the winks of the *kanakas*, and to the backs of the missionaries, trying to pretend that he was not there. He had all the dignity and poise of a king, and I could only hurry along at his heels.

Aboard the ship I rushed him into the tiny cabin. Fortunately it held two berths. Soon Keanu was lying in one of them, dirty feet and all. "Long time I nevah had a bed so good," he remarked in the strange syntax and rude inflection of the uneducated native. His face was shy and innocent as he confessed this, dismissing with the comment his entire experience of prison. And so did he look, very soon, when he fell asleep, indifferent to me or to the light of the wall lamp warming the little room. I put out the light and climbed into the upper berth. I had forgotten to bring food with me and I was hungry, but I did not want to leave the cabin.

Outside I heard the last farewells of the lepers, the last *alohas* of their friends and relatives, calling across the gulf between them. The missionaries began to sing a hymn, first in hard English words, then in soft Hawaiian—and rigorously I suppressed the thought of the missionary mother bidding good-by to her leprous son. The slow throb of engines warned me that we were about to begin our journey. Only the sudden rise in the calling of farewells told me when the gap between ship and shore began to widen, to widen forever for some of us on board.

In my berth, in the dark, I was strangely happy. Forgotten were my plans to return to Berlin. I thought once more of my work, eager to take it up with renewed vigor now that I'd gained my volunteer. I planned what I should do when we got to Molokai, the observations I should make, the tests upon the lepers I must run. I knew exactly how to proceed with the experiment upon my volunteer. But now that I knew who my guinea pig was going to be, I planned how Keanu would assist me in my studies, and how I must keep him from being bored in the time of isolation which lay ahead of us, before my experiment upon him would be concluded.

Not once did I remember that I was sharing my cabin, and my life, with a murderer.

4

Long before dawn we were lying off Kalaupapa. The *Mokolii* rolled lazily in the low swells coming in from the north to spend their force upon the cliffs of Molokai. The ship's engines were stilled, there was no movement on deck. The lamps had been put out, and the space framed in the window of the cabin was dark with night. The tired crew slept, the lepers slept, and the little ship lay in peace.

When next I woke the sky beyond the window was gray. Against it I saw the head of Keanu. He was looking toward the desolate shore. Yawning noisily, in order not to startle him, I asked, "Can you see anything out there?"

Without turning his head he answered, "Torches. On da shoah."

"How is the sea?"

"No trouble."

I was relieved. The landing at either of the Leper Settlement's two approaches is hazardous, even when the sea is not running high. There is no harbor, nothing but the open roadstead off the curve of the shore, where the promontory joins the body of the island. In the deep water offshore the steamers make their uneasy stop, sending in passengers and cargo by rowboat. It is not unusual for everything being set ashore, lepers and cargo alike, to become thoroughly soaked in the transfer.

Lying warm in my berth, I shuddered at the thought of being plunged into the inhospitable sea. It was not the fear of drowning which worried me. It was the discomfort of the wetting, and the indignity of it. Fervently I hoped for a dry landing, and a dignified one.

But before we left our cabin I needed to warn my volunteer. "Keanu," I said, "from now on you must not touch a leper—or let a leper touch you. This is very important. You understand? Everything depends on this." He stood so quietly, looking beyond the ship to the land, that I wondered whether he heard me. Fearing that I'd been saddled with a dullard, I was about to speak sharply to him, to remind him who was in charge of our little enterprise, when he spared me the need.

"Aye. We bettah go firs', den."

Unwilling to acknowledge, even to myself, how in this instance his understanding seemed to be in advance of my own, I muttered, "Good," and hurried to ready myself for the landing. Because we had slept in our clothes the preparation did not take long. In a few minutes we were on deck, I with my clothes hamper, Keanu with my heavy instrument case held in one hand, as though it were as light as a birdcage.

About a mile away lay Molokai. Shrouded by a great covering

of cloud, it still clung to the night. There were no stars overhead in the murky sky. Sensing the land there, more than seeing it, I felt that we were wanderers about to be shipwrecked upon an uncharted shore.

Low in the black shadows were the torches. Their orange-yellow light came to us across the water, the only sign of life upon the forbidding coast. They did not move. Fixed in place, they stared at us like the eyes of animals, unblinking, feral, evil.

"How soon can we go ashore?" I asked the nearest sailor, a small thin wrinkled *kanaka* struggling to pull the heavy canvas cover from one of the rowboats. "Half-houah, maybe," he barked at me over his shoulder, then went back to his work.

"We like go in 'a firs' boat," Keanu said softly, with his free hand flicking the cover from the boat to the deck of the *Mokolii*. "—Befoah we catch de Kalawao sickness heah."

The scrawny sailor grinned, revealing a most impure set of teeth. "O.K.! O.K.! Put yo' stuff in 'a bottom. I covah heem up wid *kalo*, and rice, and flouah. Den he no can get wet." Like most *kanakas*, like Keanu himself, he spoke in a horrid patois, in which the English words were debased into a rude resemblance of themselves which, by careful attention, the cultured ear might sometimes recognize. It was a long time before I could begin to understand their barbarous lingo with any certainty. Of course I would never speak it, but I never heard it without annoyance at their unwillingness to learn to speak English properly.

At a roar of command from the bridge, the ship came to life. A veritable aria of oaths, with a strong Scots burr to them, roused everyone in the vessel. Captain MacDougal, we had no doubt, was awake and taking charge of his ship. Its engines began throbbing almost the second his vituperation ended, as though his energy was going directly into their reviving. Slowly we moved in toward shore.

Soon the patients began to emerge from their cabins, gathering in a silent group at the rail, peering into the darkness for their first glimpse of the isle of exile.

There, in the shadows toward which they were being borne, they would spend the few months or the few years which were left to them. And there, when the time came, they would die.

Or had they died with yesterday's eve, at the time of their parting from families and friends? That had been the true death for them, it seemed, for this morning there were no tears. The farewell of yesterday was like the Mass for the Dead said in ancient times over the person of the leper. Lying before the altar upon the mort stone, covered with a black pall, he heard the pronouncement of his own death, the denial of his own life. Sentient, feeling still, despite his foul breath and hideous aspect, despite the claims of life and of the world, he heard himself mourned as dead. Breathing still, he was declared buried as, the Mass ended, he was proscribed the company of his fellow men and was banished to the company of the living dead. After such torment how can a heart suffer more, how can a man feel grief?

The lepers stood at the rail like shades, gray themselves like the gray world around them, being ferried in a barque of death across the gray waters to the isle of the dead. Their faces, not yet ravaged by their malady as one day they would be, showed only traces of yesterday's sorrow and much more of the marks of sleep. But something had gone out of them since yesterday, something which had showed in their walk, in their carriage, in the hang of their hands. Until yesterday they had lived in hope—in hope of cure, in hope of miracle, in hope, perhaps, of the salvation of death. This morning, confronted with this finality, they had abandoned hope: and hopeless they stood now, side by side at the rail, a little company of the dead, waiting for the last link with the world to be broken.

The sun brought no cheer. Hidden by the mass of clouds that covered the sky from horizon to horizon, it rose wanly over the eastern sea. With its coming the darkness was a little less gray, but the light which showed us our destination was as somber as the funeral passage that was about to begin.

When the *Mokolii* was close in, no more than a quarter of a mile from shore, Keanu's sailor friend summoned us to the rowboat. The cliffs of Kalaupapa appeared to rise just beyond the side of the ship: their wet black faces sprang abruptly from a narrow shore, upon which the waves fell in surges of foam. Overhead, the tops of the cliffs were lost in the rack, cut off by the flat underside of the layer of cloud poised at one exact level along miles of vertical coast. Where the black cliffs met the black beach the torches still burned. A number of people huddled around them; and, toiling across the beach from the shelf of higher land at our right, other people came in small groups. Most of them were on foot, a few rode on horseback.

The shelf of land from which the people came thrust itself into the sea, like a leaf of rock, for about a mile from the line of its juncture with the island. At the apex of the promontory the land descended almost to the level of the ocean; but as the leaf broadened to its base the cliffs grew higher, and in some places rose thirty or forty feet above the water. Beneath them the incoming waves foamed and splashed, rushing in until they fell upon the beach.

This tiny promontory, this infinitesimal afterthought to an island, this ink spot upon the broad expanse of the Pacific Ocean, is Kalaupapa.

"Which side we landing?" asked Keanu of the ancient mariner.

"Kalawao side. Lucky."

The triangular cape held two villages, one at either angle of its base. At the far side was the huddle of houses known as Kalaupapa, where a few of the lepers lived and those of the original undiseased inhabitants of this godforsaken place who had not yet followed God's sensible example. Facing us was the corner where the village of Kalawao was supposed to be, but from our position, beneath the level of the sea cliffs, we could not see much evidence of it. Only a thin steeple rose above the line of the cliffs to show us where the village lay hidden behind jagged rocks and scraggly trees.

Captain MacDougal favored his crew with another bit of polyglot vilification. "O.K.! O.K.!" sang out our *kanaka* Cicero. "Firs' boat away!" Four shirtless members of the crew came hurrying up from the stern, each of them three times the size of the little sailor. He was, I discovered, the bosun of the *Mokolii*. The four sailors swung the small boat out over the water, in the lee of the ship. They held the boat at the level of the rail, while everybody shouted at once for Keanu and me to climb into it. Keanu stepped into it as though the high rail did not exist. Keeping his balance amid the bundles of freight, he reached down for me and pulled me in beside him. While we settled ourselves on the cargo itself, the four oarsmen swarmed in.

While they were taking up their oars the bosun loosed the ropes and dropped us to the water. With a splash we hit, with a cry the umbilical lines were unfixed, and we were set free. The

Mokolii, moving on its course, left us exposed in its wake, and in the same instant the steersman turned our bow toward the shore. An inrushing wave, enormous now when we looked up into it from below its crest, rolled in upon us. With another shout the sailors pulled in unison upon their oars, and the boat took a great leap forward. "Row!" they shouted again, pulling mightily, and we gained momentum with a rush. A third shout, a third immense pull, and the curling wave caught up with us, lifting the rear of the boat in its advancing slope. The rowers raised a yell and I turned in alarm to see what was amiss. But I was assured by their whoops of glee. They were exulting at having put the wave to work for them.

With the heavy oars lifted above the water, the boat swept in, like a bird skimming the sea. The wave bore us in with amazing speed. As we rushed down the front of the great swell the water hissed and curled past our bow until I thought surely there was no more of it to pass us by. But always the surge at our stern pushed us forward, and always there was more green water to prevent our darting down into the very floor of the bay. The effect of speed and power was thrilling and, almost gaily, I was enjoying the ride—when suddenly I saw those rocks upon the beach, those awful cliffs rushing up to meet us.

There was no sand upon the landing place! Only rocks, black rocks, wet and smooth and shining, waited there in their adamantine millions for us to crash down upon them. Already I could see the lepers upon the shore laughing at us, the black circles of their mouths rounded with laughter and brutal delight in our impending doom, doing nothing to help us while we drowned before their very eyes. The more I tried to tell myself that surely the ride would end in good order, the more certain I became that it could end only in disaster. I thought to throw myself from the onrushing boat, but my hands, gripping its sides, would not let go. I wanted to cry out, "Stop! In Heaven's name, stop!" But my teeth would not loose their hold upon my lips. I could only sit there, waiting for death, wet and ignominious death.

Keanu's hand touched my shoulder. "No worry. We O.K." My panic ceased. I could not look at Keanu to thank him for his comforting. I contented myself with nodding, as if, of course, I had known all the while that we were safe from the monster sea.

We were close upon the shore now and, in the curve of the bay beneath the stupendous cliffs, the waves as they crashed upon the land made a deep-throated roar. Mingled with it, underlying it, an ominous pedal point to the unending rage of the sea, was the rumbling and booming of those millions of rocks being rolled each upon the other, up toward the land as the waves swept in, back toward the sea as the waters fell away. Rolling hollowly, dully, those restless wallowing rocks, endessly condemned, like the rock of Sisyphus, to the endless torment of motion, were the dirge of Kalawao, the sound of doom.

When we were only a few feet from the appalling beach the wave slipped out from under us, to take its turn in casting its life upon the groaning land. While we were in the trough between our wave and its successor, the rowers slipped over the sides of the boat. Wet up to their bellies, stumbling over the treacherous rocks underfoot, they pulled and lifted the boat upon the shore as far as the water would float it, shouting at us to jump. Keanu was out immediately, helping them haul the boat. But I was slower to leave, and the next wave, rushing past, managed to wet me up to my waist. Beside me the five muscular *kanakas* lifted the heavy boat and carried it over the rocks to a place beyond the reach of the sea.

Looming above us was the cliff, covered with dripping mosses and lacy ferns for scores of feet before, high above, it began to lean away from the bite of the sea and the small shrubs and dwarfed trees began to grow. Beyond them the pall of mist lay thick upon the mountain, hiding the upper reaches of the cliff.

At the foot of the dank wall the lepers huddled, safe from the waves and from the falling rocks which every now and then came tumbling down. It was also a refuge from the chill wind sweeping in from the ocean and up the face of the cliff.

The rowers began to unload the cargo, heaping it upon the rocks at either side of the boat. Without waiting to be asked, Keanu helped them. Only then did the nearest lepers leave the shelter of the cliff. Walking over the loose stones was difficult at best, but their infirmities of limb and of eye made their passage even more awkward.

They came up to us, smiling painfully, as lepers always do, terribly conscious of their disfigurement and always hoping that one will not notice the signs of their affliction. "*Aloha,*" or

"Hello," they said, their voices rasping as though rust had settled in their throats. Our sailors answered them in the same futile words, with the false heartiness of healthy folk who are trying too hard not to observe the stigmata of the disease. Some of the *kanakas* had tried to hide the sores on their faces beneath beards or full mustaches, with varying degrees of success. But the wispy beards of the Chinamen were not any more effective as masks than were the pigtails dangling down their backs.

"Get *poi?*" one of the Hawaiians called hopefully.

The steersman laughed. "Plenny. Nex' boat. Coming soon."

The lepers stopped in a half circle a few paces away, looking hungrily at the bags of taro, the packages of food.

"Any new patients?" wheezed another. The destruction of his vocal chords was almost complete. He stared at me, not quite certain how to place me.

"Aye. Seexteen. Five *wahine*, ten *kane*—and one small *haole* boy."

"Too bad, too bad," said the inquirer, shaking his death's-head.

They were joined by a short, thickset, very dirty white man. "Any mail?" he called officiously. Hatless and collarless, he was dressed in an ancient black suit, so old and so filthy that it was more brown than black. His face, rough with half a week's growth of beard, was brown as a *kanaka's* and stained, like his clothes and the whole of his person, with sweat and dirt which the color of his skin did nothing to disguise. He was vigorous almost to the point of offensiveness.

The steersman answered the *haole's* question with the same cheerfulness he served up to all the lepers. "Aye. Liddle bit. Coming bimebye, dough."

"We can wait. We get plenny time," said one of the other patients. The others laughed mirthlessly. One easily got the impression that this same useless conversation, this same wan show of unfelt humor, attended every landing of the *Mokolii's* boats upon the hellish beach.

"What else you brought?" interrupted the dirty *haole*, pressing in closer to the unloaded cargo. He wore eyeglasses, one lens of which was thicker than the other. They made him appear to have one enormous eye glaring upon the world, and a smaller one peering at it.

Aggressive as such types often are, he did not keep his place with the other lepers. Angered by his presumption, I wondered how to stop him from coming right up to us. But even I, sharp-tongued as I can be, could not think of anything to say that would not be downright rude—until I saw him veer toward Keanu.

"Here, let me help you with that," the dirty fellow said, reaching out to take my instrument box from Keanu.

The thought of that loathsome hand meeting Keanu's hand, of it touching the instrument case which my hand would soon touch, infuriated me. "Don't touch him!" I shouted, springing up from my seat. "Don't touch that box! Get back where you belong, you damned leper!" If I could have overcome my revulsion for him, I would have pushed him away with my own clean hands.

At my shout the waiting lepers looked toward me, their scarred mouths opening. Let them stare, I consoled myself. This pig should know better. The sailors stopped their work, straightening up to learn what was amiss. From the boat Keanu looked down upon the leper with an expression which, slowly, before my very eyes, became a smile of apology for my behavior.

The leper stood motionless, his hand still reaching out toward Keanu. For a long moment he looked up into Keanu's face, as Keanu, gazing intently down into his, lost his foolish little smile and stared as though mesmerized at the hidden countenance.

Then he started to turn to me. And I, the words of my abuse of him still ringing in my ears, I wanted inordinately to call them back to me, to expunge them from the tainted air and the re-cording ears of the victim of my anger. The others who had heard did not matter. It was this one dirty old man who, with his back still turned to me, had the power to remind me of my pride and to make me ashamed as I had never been ashamed before. I knew, even as he swung to face me, that I would regret those words as long as I lived, that I could never forget the sound of them, shouted into the winds of Kalawao at an old man who was doing his best to help.

I was framing the words of my apology, shaping them in my mouth, when I saw his face again. Behind the green circles of pitted metal, behind the thick lenses, I saw for the first time those eyes. Brown and clear and deep, they were filled with an inexpressible gentleness.

One of the sailors recovered his tongue. "Nem mine heem."

Spitting his contempt for me among the rocks near my feet, he hit the side of the boat with his fist.

The lepers, too, muttered their protests. "Stupid buggah!" they said. "Sassy *haole!*"—and other epithets I could not understand. Their hostility did not touch me one whit as much as did the powerful goodness of the man who stood silent before me, looking down at me.

Their discontent grew louder. "Le's go. Let 'im carry his own stuff, if he too good for us."

Only when he himself raised his hand, in the unmistakable imperious gesture, did I know who he was.

They obeyed him immediately. I listened, as they did, for his voice above the clamor of the waves and the wind, above the ceaseless rumbling of the rocks, rolling and grinding and groaning against each other in the rush and the ebb of the surf.

"No, he is right," he said, pointing to me. "We must forgive him. He did not know." A smile of apology softened the rugged face, making me forget the dirt, the stubble of his beard. "I should remember to introduce myself."

But now I did not need to be told that I was being given a lesson in Christian charity by Father Damien.

5

"I'M SORRY," I said. "I did not know who you were." Rarely have I been so meek. "You see, you are not as I expected you."

"No wonder, that. I am a gravedigger this morning. There was no time to change. Now it is your turn. Who do I have the honor to welcome to Kalawao?"

"I am Doctor Arnold Newman. I have Mr. Harrison's permission to land here. As a matter of fact, I am employed by the Board of Health."

"A doctor! To stay with us? A doctor at last, to care for us?" He became as excited as a boy at a feast.

"For a short while only. I am not the Government physician

you have been asking for. I don't believe Mr. Gibson has found one yet."

The eagerness faded. He shook his head. "Not yet, not yet. Always tomorrow!" The voice was harsh now. It did not have the magic in it that his eyes held. A good sturdy peasant's voice, neither did it have the unctuousness of a priest, and I was grateful for that small relief.

"We must have a doctor to stay with us. Our people need doctors too. They have their wounds, their broken limbs, their childbirths and sicknesses, just like the people in Honolulu." Impatience broke out in a testiness of speech, an excitement of his hands, used like bludgeons against barriers of paper. "They die here, too—not only from leprosy but from a dozen lesser illnesses." Studying me closely, he asked, with a peasant's shrewd pursuit of a bargain, "You will see our people while you are here? You will help them?"

This was not exactly the employment I was planning for myself, but it held the advantage of winning for me the immediate assistance of both the priest and his lepers. Perhaps the unfortunate first impression of my arrival would be forgotten if I tended a few patients, delivered a child or two, during the weeks of my stay. The surest way to gain the confidence of lepers, always a proud and stubborn lot, is to pretend a devoted interest in their loathsome persons. I had nothing to lose, everything to gain, by pretense of this sort, much as the priest must have won their friendship by his life of pretense. "Of course," I assented. "Of course. Anything to help."

"Oh, I am glad!" He clapped his hands together, interlocking his fingers in a contorted expression of joy. What a simple rustic he was! Turning to the lepers standing around us, he shouted, "We have a doctor now. A *kauka!*"

They were not as overjoyed by my presence as he was. No one jumped for glee, or sped to shout the loud hosanna through the Settlement's streets. A couple of them managed a pout of acknowledgment, more for Damien's sake than for my own. Most of them merely stood there, morose and unmoved, as if, having heard, they just didn't care a tinker's curse about me or about anything else that could possibly happen to them.

"They are still mad with you," Damien informed me soberly. "But they get over this, when they see how you will help them."

He stopped, obviously searching for something to put me at my ease. "They did not like me, too, when I came," he went on. This was hardly the essence of tact, but at least it was forthright. Honesty I like in anyone, even in a dirty old priest in whom I expected to find nothing more than hypocrisy, sweetened perhaps with a bit of loving-kindness. Perhaps this priest—properly washed, of course, and properly dressed—had more to commend him than I had thought.

"And who is this young man you defend from my touch?"

"This is Keanu," I said casually. "He is my—my *kokua*." If it was not exactly the whole truth, it was enough of the truth for him to know for now.

"Then *aloha* to Kalawao, Keanu. And let me help you, like I started to do."

Without a word, as though mesmerized still, Keanu gave the heavy case into the priest's keeping. Effortlessly the vigorous old man swung it from the edge of the boat to a place on the rocks.

A shout from the sea interrupted us. It came from the second boat, arriving with its burden of lepers from the *Mokolii*. Six of them rode in the weighted craft, and four sailors pulled wearily upon the long oars. Not fortunate enough to catch a wave to bring them in, they had rowed the long haul from the ship. Now, close to the shore, where the swells curled to their crest and broke with a rush, the boat was in danger of being trapped in the confusion of incoming waves and receding ebb.

Perceiving the situation, our sailors dropped their bundles and ran down the treacherous beach. Keanu started to run with them, but I threw myself after him, catching him by his shirt. "Stay away from them!" I cried. He looked down at me, annoyed at my interference, until he remembered what I meant by it. "I forget," he mumbled sheepishly, stepping back beside me.

The four sailors reached the water just as a huge wave rising under the boat seemed about to overturn it. The rowers looked helplessly over their shoulders, frantically pulling upon their oars to turn the craft toward shore. The passengers clung in fear to each other and to the sides of the vessel.

Shouting their concern, the lepers around us began to hobble over the rocks toward the water's edge. The priest stood with his hands clasped, praying at the top of his voice, as though prayer alone could save the little boat from its peril.

But the wave slipped under it and crashed upon the shore. Broadside now to the beach, the boat was in danger of being swamped by the next breaker, while our four sailors were still an arm's length away from it. They reached it just in time, and, pulling it to them, pointed it to shore as the enormous wave pushed past it and broke upon the land.

Cries of relief went up from the lepers around us. *"Deo gratias!"* shouted Father Damien, making the sign of the cross in the direction of the rescued boat. In the water, our four sailors held the vessel steady while its exhausted crew jumped overboard to help lift it ashore. The six new arrivals looked longingly at the land, their faces sick with fear. It was grotesque to see how those people, already near to death from leprosy, shrank in fright from drowning.

They were too heavy for the sailors to lift the boat very far, and soon they were ordered to jump out upon the rocks. Soon they too were being wetted up to their waists by the rushing waves. Tottering over the rocks, they came with the boat up the rise of the beach, surrounding it like mourners about a bier, hindering its progress by their awkwardness. But the patient sailors did not curse them, as sailors in any other land would have done.

Making little cries of encouragement with each step, their bodies straining until their muscles stood out as hard and dark as the stones underfoot, the sailors reached at last the level where we stood. Only then did they lower the boat to the ground and take their rest. Only then did the lepers, pale and weak, sink to the stones beneath them.

The four men sat some distance away from us. The two females huddled in each other's arms. One of them wept without restraint. The younger one tried to comfort her, gently patting the back of her companion, uttering the meaningless noises a mother uses with an infant. Her thin figure showed under the stuff of her Mother Hubbard, pulled tight against her by the weight of the old woman.

Father Damien was among the men almost as they fell upon the shore. Taking off his filthy coat, he used it to wipe their hands and their wet clothing, trying to brush off the coarse black sand and the fine seaweed. He left them rather the worse for his care, streaked with mud from the accretions of his coat. Soon the other lepers from the Settlement gathered around the newcomers, watching while Damien worked. There was no attempt at conversation. Why should they bother? their silence seemed to ask. Or perhaps it was shyness; perhaps they've not been introduced? No matter, the busy priest would soon take care of that. At the rate he was going, a bustling reception committee of one, he'd have them all hobbling a ridiculous rigadoon before breakfast, if they weren't careful.

The new men looked to be annoyed at his attentions, obviously wondering, as I did, who this intrusive *haole* was. But the women, when he reached them, responded more graciously to him. They spoke briefly to him, on his knees before them, nodding to some of his questions, shaking their heads to others. Then the old woman did a silly thing: she seized his hand in her claws and lifted it to her lips. He looked down with horror for a moment, before he sprang to his feet and fled. The poor fellow! I wondered, while he scuttled off, what penance he would impose upon himself for that feminine affront to his priest's virtue, that attack upon his celibate flesh.

He was rushing past us in his flight, an insular Saint Anthony running from his devils, when I stopped him. "Where do we go now?" I cried, waving him down. "What do we do?"

In confusion he stopped before me. Breathing heavily, he stared at us, his face as white as the blank glasses in his spectacles. "Come with me," he said with effort. "Come with me. I will show you the way." Reminded of his duties, he called to the Settlement lepers squatting nearby. "Opae! Makapuu! Kewalo! *E hele mai.*" The three men came at once to his side.

"Opae, I go back now. You be *luna.*" Opae, a burly native whose face was more disfigured by the scars of smallpox than by the erosions of leprosy, went to his task of supervising the loading of the pack horses. "Makapuu, you help Opae, please. Kewalo, you take care of the new patients." With something of his own efficiency they began to summon others of the lounging lepers. Makapuu put his fingers to his mouth and, with a succession of whistles, attracted the attention of the men who sat with the pack horses in the shelter of the cliffs. Hobbling with stiffness, they moved among the horses, preparing to bring them down to the piles of cargo.

"What are your things?" Damien asked.

"These two."

"No food? No taro? No meat?"

"No. Do I need to bring my own?"

"There is never enough of fresh food here. Almost everything we eat is brought in from outside."

"I'm sorry. I was not told."

"Of course. In Honolulu they say we should grow our own food here. They do not know, in the Board of Health, how hard is the life of a farmer, even when he feels well. They do not believe that a sick man, even when he walks around, cannot do a farmer's work. They send us always a little less than we need, thinking to make us grow more. So always do we live in hunger, and the sick ones have not the comfort of dying with a full belly."

Once a peasant, always a peasant, I thought, remarking the landsman's dirty hands, the morose countenance, as he ruminated on the peasant's favorite subject of food. I am well acquainted with the breed, and with the readiness with which they worry over every rainfall or every drought, and predict famine at the height of every summer and disaster at every visit of the tax collector. Yet always they manage to endure, usually in somewhat better fashion than do city folk; and I was willing to wager that, in Kalaupapa, as in his native country, the situation was better than he claimed it to be.

"But we do for you the best we can. You have money? If you have money, we buy for you tinned foods in the Settlement Store."

"We are saved from starvation, at any rate," I laughed. The old fraud!

"Where are Keanu's things?"

"He has only the clothes he is wearing. His things will be sent up later."

"Well, then, let us start on the way," said Damien. "Keanu, you carry the *kauka's* box, please. Doctor, will you carry your clothes hamper? I take a bag of taro. The patients in the hospital will be glad to have it."

Flinging the battered coat over his right shoulder, he reached down and picked up a bag of taro. It must have weighed at least fifty pounds. Lifting it with both hands to his shoulder, he rested it upon the pad made of his coat. Then, swinging around to observe us, he asked, "Ready?"

"Ready," said Keanu, thrusting my hamper into my hand with one motion, picking up his burden with another.

"Kewalo. Your people are ready?"

"Aye," responded the bull-bodied Kewalo. The six new arrivals were on their feet, awaiting Damien's signal.

"Then let us go," he said, starting across the dreadful beach.

6

THE BEACH WAS NO HAZARD to Keanu. He stepped upon the slippery rocks as though they were no more than the finest of white sand. Damien, too, was as sure-footed as a mule. But for the rest of us who were newly arrived it was a harrowing course, in which frequently we tripped upon the shifting stones and were thrown to our hands and knees. My white trousers, already wet by the sea, were soon dirtied and stained; and my tunic, as time after time I wiped my hands upon it, quickly became as soiled as my trousers. After a while there were bloodstains also upon my clothes, mixed with the green slime of seaweed, as my fingers began to bleed from the scratches and the cuts they received when I fell.

The new patients, unaccustomed to exertion after their weeks of inaction in the Hospital at Kakaako, were in much greater difficulty than I was. The two women, clinging to each other in ungainly dependence, were left far behind, staggering along in our wake like drunken harlots. Their long skirts, heavy and wet before the start of our walk, were quickly stained, and their lacy petticoats lost their whiteness forever among the slimy stones.

Out to sea the *Mokolii* kept its place, rising and falling with the swell of the waves. The rowboat which had brought me to shore was on its return trip: we could see its white hull and the long bleached oars against the black bulk of the ship. Upon that background the dark bodies of the rowers were invisible, and the tiny boat looked as though it were being rowed by ghosts. The gray sky, the gray sea, pressed in from all sides, the color of desolation. Like damnèd souls in one of Dante's circles of hell we made our slow way, while the keening wind and the groaning rocks gave tongue to our despair.

Keanu and the priest were the first to arrive at the end of the beach, where it met the flank of the peninsula. When I caught up with them, they were sitting on the huge black boulders which littered the sheltered angle of the bay. The waves were not able to get at those enormous rocks, to grind them down to sand. Here, too, the force of the wind was lessened, and the roar of the sea: it was almost quiet, and the hush lay heavy in our ears.

I sank wearily beside Damien, near the sack of taro deposited on the ground. The priest was lighting a battered pipe, fetched from one of his sagging pockets. Crouching, to shield the pipe from the wind, he lighted it with one flaring lucifer. His big hands, with their earth-stained fingers and dirty nails, managed the action with a strange precision, as though he had trained them, by an act of will, to do with dexterity the work that, left to themselves, they would have done more clumsily.

The match box put away, the pipe drawing well, he turned to me. "Ahh, tobacco. One of man's great comforts." Taking the pipe from his mouth, he offered me the malodorous thing. "Smoke?"

"No, thanks—not for me. I—I don't smoke."

"Keanu?" He held the pipe toward the lounging youth.

The sharing of pipes, of *poi*-bowls, of clothes and beds, of everything, even of mates and lovers, is a commonplace among the *kanakas*, of course, and the priest's offer was neither surprising nor revolting to Keanu. He was putting out his hand to accept the pipe when I cried, "No, Keanu!" and pushed the priest's arm aside. Once more I offended by trying to protect. Keanu was annoyed. He wanted a taste of the tobacco, the scent of its smoke delicious in his nostrils. Damien was startled, more by my intervention in Keanu's affairs than by my bad manners. And I began to feel an irritation of my own, that this bumbling interfering old man should always be placing me in a position of being rude. An hour ago, moved by some emotion I could not control, I wanted to beg his forgiveness for my rudeness to him. But that had been an hour ago, a whole lifetime ago, and now that I knew him better there was little of contrition left in me.

He hunched his shoulders, like any peasant, and put the stem back to his mouth, drawing on it thoughtfully before he spoke. "Why do you protect the boy?"

"Because," I barked, no longer worried about giving offense, "I don't want him to have any contact with lepers."

The priest looked sharply at me. "But I am not a leper."

"I know you're not. But I am trying to teach him not to accept things from anyone here except myself. We have just begun this instruction, and he is still not accustomed to it. This is why I watch over him like a mother hen." I hoped by this comparison, and by the forced laugh which followed it, to return the conversation to a quieter tone. After all, I am a moderate man in most things, and I did not want to go out of my way to hurt him.

He was not at all interested in my attempt to mollify him. "Then why do you bring him here?"

This was the great question, as it was the great weakness, in my whole plan. How was I going to keep Keanu away from all contact with lepers, while he was set down in the midst of one of the most dismaying concentrations of lepers in the whole world? How was I going to keep him a prisoner, in a prison without walls, and at the same time leave him a free man, in spirit and in body? A free man? He was an animal, wild and untamed. I did not need to look at him, lying sleek upon the smooth rock beyond Father Damien, to know that he was like some jungle cat taking his ease in this moment of respite, but ready to spring, to run, to hunt, perhaps even to kill, when he felt the instinct rise in him again. To cage him would be to kill him; and while I felt no special affection for him, or any compulsion to spare him the caged panther's long pining and slow dying, neither did I want to jeopardize the success of my experiment upon him.

It was a problem I had not yet resolved, and, from what I had seen as yet of Kalaupapa, it was a problem I was beginning to wonder if I could ever resolve. I was determined to find a way, but in the meantime I could only lament my fate for having presented me with my guinea pig under the most unfortunate circumstances that could be devised. Damn Gibson anyway, for thrusting Keanu upon me at the very instant of my departure for Kalaupapa. Why couldn't I have got him a month ago, when I first asked for him? In a secluded house in Honolulu, completely out of touch with lepers, I could have placed Keanu under absolute control, and my chance of succeeding in my work there would have been almost warranted. If only I'd had the presence of mind, last evening, to return him to Gibson's care until I came back from Kalaupapa. Or, better still, if only I'd not come at all to Kalaupapa. But no, my memory reminded me, I couldn't have done that, with Gibson watching us depart, with the King's decree banishing Keanu to Kalaupapa in my care. Oh, that evil genius planned things well. What a vicious circle he had trapped me in!

"Later, Father, later, I will tell you. Right now it is enough for you to know that he must be kept away from the lepers. They must not touch him: they must not even go near him, not even breathe upon him. And he must not touch them, or anything they have touched. He must be segregated from them, even in Kalaupapa, as the lepers themselves have been segregated from the rest of the people in this country."

"Will you keep him a prisoner?" Beyond him Keanu listened, intent upon my answer.

"No, not really. Just isolated from them."

"Does he fear the leprosy so much? Or do you fear it for him?" The old man shook his head reprovingly, pointing the moist stem of his pipe like a finger. "Keeping him apart will do him no good, or you. You will see. It is by God's will that Keanu will catch the disease, or that he will remain free of it. Nothing else." He was the churchman now, dogmatic, as full of certainty as the Pope of Rome himself, and as convinced of his infallibility.

"I do not agree," I was saying when Kewalo arrived, followed by the first of the new patients. They dragged themselves to the lesser boulders disposed around us and lay in exhaustion upon them. Still fifty feet away from us, the two women toiled on their way. The brisk wind had blown the hats from their heads, the hair was being whipped free of the careful arrangements in which they had worn it. They tried to hold their hats, to keep their hair in place, to support each other, while they staggered toward us.

Damien slipped from his rock. "E, Kewalo," he called. "You like finish my pipe?" The old leper, less weary than the new-comers, reached out a red and swollen hand, upon which golden crusts of scabs floated in lakes of bloody fluid exuding from half-open sores, and took the pipe from the priest. I watched with horror while he put its stem into his mouth. Keanu rolled his eyes at me, and pretended to be sickened.

Once more I challenged the priest's insuperable ignorance. "You shouldn't do that! It's dangerous."

Shrugging, he smiled down at me, tolerant of my intolerance of him. "I do not fear. I, too, am in God's hands. If he wishes me to be a leper, then I will be one, and nothing I do or do not do will prevent me from being one of them. And if God does not wish for me to be a leper, why should I walk in fear of it?" Then he hurried to the aid of the two women.

The older one was gasping for breath. Her hair blew in wisps of white about her face, now grayer than the clouded sky. Even with the support of the younger woman, she was so weak that she could hardly move.

When he reached them the priest picked up the old woman, laying her hideous head against his shoulder. She hung there, wheezing into his face, while he spoke words of comfort to her. She had lost her shoes, and her feet and legs were green with muck.

Leaving the girl to her own pace, he started back to us. "Water, Kewalo, water," he called when he came near. Smoking the pipe still, Kewalo limped to the bushes at the foot of the cliff and drew from them a slender green bottle. Instead of sacramental wine this one held clear cool water.

Damien placed his burden upon a flat boulder, laying her out upon it as though on a bier. When Kewalo brought the water to him, the priest held the bottle to the old woman's lips, urging her to drink. She tried to obey, but the water rolled from her mouth down the sides of her ravaged cheeks.

The younger woman came up to them. Without pausing for rest, she knelt beside the old hag, lifting the gray head to support it in the bend of her arm. As Father Damien poured small measures of the water into the old one's mouth and applied some of it to her brow, the young one knelt motionless, too weary even to weep for her own distress.

With a start I recognized her. She was the one I had glimpsed for a moment in the crowd at the wharf. She was the young woman I had seen at Kalakaua's palace, the morning of my call.

There was nothing elegant about her now: the hair hung full and thick down her back; the tattered Mother Hubbard, falling in loose folds about her like a filthy sack, had nothing in common with the morning dress of latest style in which I saw her weeping at the Queen's door. But her face was the same, looking down at the old woman in the same saddened way as once it had gazed upon the palace floor. The smooth curve of the brow, the fine line of the nose, the black eyebrows and the curling lashes upon the smooth skin, the slender neck—ahh, there was no doubt of it: this was the Queen's Lady-in-Waiting, this was— Fretted by my forgetfulness, I tried to remember her name, the while I attempted to explain her presence in Kalawao.

"*Auwe, auwe,*" the old woman quavered. "Let me die, let me die." Tears coursed down the sunken temples, to lose themselves in her hair. The younger one crooned her comforting formula: "No cry, *Tutu,* no cry. We almost home now." Her voice was soft, her smile was tender, as she looked down into the monstrous face.

Could she be a leper? She did not look it: there was not a flaw upon the chaste countenance. But why else should she be here? As a *kokua,* the devoted attendant of the old hag who was gasping for her life upon the bed of rock at which the maiden knelt, willing as Iphigenia at her sacrifice? This was possible. But what a terrible price to pay for devotion!

Whatever the reason, her presence here explained her sorrow on that morning in the palace, and the King's talk about her "having to leave us," and the Queen's sniffling beyond the open door.

Oh what a stroke of bad timing that was, what a veritable plaything of ill luck I am, I groaned, as I looked upon the cause of my failure. *She* was the reason for my humiliation! And yet, if I were honest, how could I blame the girl for her role in a drama in which she could hardly have known she was taking part? Like a dog gnawing a bone I worried this question in metaphysics, seeking how far back in the network of interrelationships I could trace her responsibility for my defeat. But in this, as in all of my other inquiries into the event, I soon concluded that I could not easily place the blame for my disaster. If anyone was to be blamed, it was the malignant maleficent Premier. And yet, I was forced to admit to my most secret self, time having done something to heal my hurt, I couldn't be so certain that even Gibson deserved all of the blame. With a sigh I concluded that perhaps the *Zeitgeist* was against me, and that I was too far in advance of my fellow men to be understood.

My revery was interrupted by a touch from Keanu. Leaning over me, he asked, "She's a leper?"

Once more I looked at her with a diagnostic eye. Keanu was right to ask: she did not show any sign of the disease upon her head or hands. But I was not a student of leprosy for nothing: underneath the virtuous envelope of clothing could lurk a thousand loathsome sores, each weeping, each encrusted with golden scabs, like those on Kewalo's hands, each shedding millions of bacilli into every serous tear they wept upon her body. Or, if there were no sores yet, their precursors could be there: the scaling of dead skin, to make a white powdery scurf, would be the most innocent. Or she might show the little red swellings which grow up out of those bland areas of menald whiteness. Or the evil heaps of livid and rugose flesh, insatiable tumors, growing out of the smaller swellings. She could present any one of a dozen variations of the disease, without showing a sign of it in her face. "She does not look like one—but she must be," I answered him. "Why else would she be here?"

"*Kokua*." Keanu, I was beginning to be aware, was a man of very few words.

"Yes, she could be." But I had to keep him away from her, else he would be after her like a tomcat chasing a puss in heat. The nature of his interest was all too obvious: the tongue flickering over the parted lips, the peacock's vanity with which he displayed his body, hoping to catch her attention. "But I doubt it. The Board of Health doesn't usually let young girls come here as *kokuas*. She's probably a leper, all right, underneath her clothes"— in the event that this was not clear enough for Keanu, I completed the picture—"with sores between her legs and under her breasts and in all the secret places of her body."

Aghast, he drew away from me. Turning abruptly, he ran across the rocks toward the reef, where the sea and the sharp coral brought him to a stop. Smiling like a sphinx, I stayed upon my throne.

The ministrations of Damien and the girl had their effect. The old woman sat up, supported by the girl's arms. The marks of the leprosy were most evident on the old hag: the eroding nostrils and the sunken nose, the falling eyebrows, the patches of red upon the forehead, and the thickening of the flesh upon her cheeks showed that she should have been sent to Molokai long before this time.

Damien, no longer needed at the old woman's side, went among the male patients with the water bottle, inviting them to drink. Among these men was one who stood out from the rest.

The three others were middle-aged *kanakas*, graying of hair, stooped of shoulder, nondescript. They were in assorted stages of the disease, although none was as advanced a case as the old hag. But this fourth man was young, appearing to be in his middle twenties, and was almost untouched by the infection. Slender, of middle height, he was extraordinarily handsome, with a strong lean mouth, a thin beaked nose not entirely Hawaiian in its curving, and the olive complexion of a *hapa-haole*. But the most remarkable feature about him was his eyes: bright green in color, unmistakable bequest of some *haole* ancestor, they looked out upon the world from under hooded eyelids in the cold appraising stare of a hawk.

He stood a little apart from his fellows, watching the girl as she attended the old woman. His clothes were of excellent cut and fine cloth, although his gabardine trousers were much the worse for the traverse of the beach. His derby hat he wore like a helmet, set firm upon his head.

I had seen his like before: a man in rage against the world. Finding it difficult, still, to think of himself as a leper, he held himself aloof from the other lepers. Angry and unhappy—look at the sullen mouth, look at the lines of protest graven into the cheeks, sweeping from the sides of the nose past the turned-down corners of the mouth to the stern chin—he was seething with rebellion against a fate which struck him down in the bloom of his manhood. Sour with hatred for a society which condemned him to an exile he felt he did not deserve, he hated his fellow exiles even more, refusing to see in them the prophesy of the thing he himself was to become. When the priest lifted the water bottle to him, he spurned it haughtily, refusing to touch it. Damien did not mind the rebuff: he moved to the next man in the group, offering the half-empty bottle to him.

I had to look closely at the green-eyed fellow to see why he should be banished to Molokai. The skin on his forehead and on his clean-shaven cheeks did not show any sign of the disease. But the telltale ulcers on the margins of his ears, red and un-healed, marked him for a leper. I felt sorry for him, for his lost happiness, for all the opportunities he was forever denied.

I tried to catch his eye, to send a consoling greeting to him, but he would not look my way. The thought occurred to me that perhaps he was a man worth knowing: he had the look of intelligence, the dress of a man of taste, and of means. Perhaps his company would help me to pass the time of waiting at Kalawao. But then, I argued, not knowing how to decide, to become friendly with him would only lead to complications. Not the least of these was my need to keep Keanu sheltered from everyone who was a leper.

I turned to see where Keanu was. He was throwing pebbles into the sea, as a boy does at the seashore. I sighed, wondering if there was a man's mind awaiting discovery in that man's body. How was I going to survive being shut up with Keanu, conversing in monosyllables babbled in pidgin English? To my credit, I thought of Keanu too. How was he going to endure being shut up with me? Especially after I had done what I planned to do to him? The prospect of our future on the little peninsula of bleakness was suddenly frightening. I did not have the courage to face it.

Dreading the approaching loneliness, which I could foresee coming upon me as, in England, when the weather is changing, one can see the great banks of fog rolling in from the sea, I made an unprecedented effort to win myself a friend. Rising from my rock, I went toward the proud young man, in the place where he stood alone, like a falcon leashed to earth. Hardly knowing what to say—what does one say to a leper whose spirit is corroding away faster than is the flesh of his body? How does one start such a conversation? By inquiries after the state of his health? By the conventional absurdities upon the weather? By vacuous commentaries upon a place we had not yet seen, or about people we did not know? I approached him almost timidly, as if I were a petitioner and he were the great one about to hear my plea. When I stood beside him, I did not yet know how to begin.

But he saved me the need. Turning upon me in a fury, his mouth tightening in scorn, those astonishing green eyes piercing me with their glittering coldness, he assailed me in excellent English. "You are a doctor. Why, then, do you not take care of your patients?" With an emperor's hand he pointed to the old woman lying on her rock.

I was overcome with surprise. Not once had it occurred to me that I should treat her. But the angry man was right: I should have remembered my duties, and at least offered her my services. Yet how could I explain to this acidulous fellow that I had been busy being a bacteriologist for the last four years, that I had all but forgotten I was a physician as well? Or tell him that Damien and the girl were doing all that I could do, and that there was no need for me to intervene? I did not try to explain. Hurt by his accusation, stung by his scorn, I turned and left without having said a word to him.

I went down to the seaside, to Keanu and his monosyllables and his inarticulate mind. At least he did not have a serpent's tongue, or a serpent's eyes. The naked hate in those green eyes had wounded me beyond hope of healing.

Keanu looked down at me, offering me a grin of welcome and a pebble to throw.

"Time to go," I snarled, passing on to him some of the hurt which had been dealt to me.

"O.K., boss. You say. We go."

At the foot of the trail we took up our burdens once more. This time Father Damien carried the old woman, cradled in his arms. The girl followed them, carrying the priest's coat over one arm. Her free hand held the remnants of her muddied skirts above the level of the trail. In exactly the same way had she held the skirt of her morning dress, when she vanished down the palace stairs. When she went past us, her eyes lowered modestly, Keanu averted his gaze, as if my description of her were being realized in his very sight. I did not turn away. I saw the pallid face of a young woman near exhaustion, beads of sweat upon her brow, lips pressed tight to keep her from sobbing out her weariness and her fright.

I followed them with Keanu. He carried the priest's sack of taro on his shoulder, and my instrument case in his other hand for balance. The new male patients fell in behind Kewalo, my castigator coming last of all.

The trail doubled on itself twice before it emerged upon the plain of Kalaupapa. About halfway up the face of the cliff it entered a small grove of wind-swept trees. From the trail we could look out upon the curve of the deep bay. In the distance, beyond the sugar-loaf islands and the fallen mountain which formed the opposite side of the bay, the black cliffs of Molokai marched in grand procession along the receding coast, until in the distance they were lost in mist. In the bay the dutiful *Mokolii* rode at anchor. The rowboats were making their way: one, just loaded, was on its second voyage to shore; the other was leaving the beach, on its journey back to the ship. On the beach the work gang of lepers was loading the pack horses with the supplies for the Settlement. It was a tranquil scene, melancholy perhaps, but full of quiet grandeur.

We emerged from the head of the trail into a scene of unmitigated horror.

The lepers were waiting to greet us.

In a vast carnival of hideousness, the people of Kalawao were gathered by the hundreds upon the plain lying between the brink of the peninsula and the village. This immense space, covered with the brightest greenest grass, was their playing field, their promenade, and their market place. It was also their City Gate, through which the new arrivals must make their terrible way, running a gantlet of torment such as the most cruel of Swedish garrisons could never have contrived.

The first ones to see us were the children, playing noisily at a game of ball. "*Kamiano!*" they shrieked. "*Kamiano!*" abandoning their sport to run toward the priest where he stood at the head of the trail. They looked to be healthy youngsters, at first. Then the dismayed eye began to pick out, among the unspoiled visages, the faces of those who had no lips, whose noses were eaten away, whose ears were swollen thick as sausages. Behind them came the cripples, running on stumps of feet, shouting as merrily as the rest.

Father Damien set the old woman down beside him. Holding her with one arm, he waved with his free hand at the advancing horde. "*Aloha*," he bawled. "We're back. We're here."

At a slower pace came the elders—or those of them who could walk. Here, too, many appeared at first glance to be quite healthy, but among them were others who were monstrously disfigured in feature and in limb. Hideous with their smiles and laughter, looking like masks of death brought living out of a witches' sabbath, they came toward us, a legion of ghouls, rank upon rank of them closing in.

Assailing our nostrils, borne ahead of them by the wind, came the stink of their sores. Assailing our ears came the horrid babble of voices, rising through throats which had lost their vocal chords, through mouths which had lost their palates, through faces without lips, calling "*Aloha*" or "*Kamiano*" or "What news?"

Ahead of me the girl stopped still with shock. ·

Keanu, horrified by the surging mob, cried out "*Auwe! Auwe!*"
He turned his back upon the sight, not wanting to admit that
such things could be. His great body cringing in fright, he
crouched for safety behind the bundle of taro on his shoulder.

Even I was not prepared for that ghastly mass of corruption.
Even while I looked with a doctor's experience upon all of the
symptoms of leprosy ever disclosed to the gaze of man, my stomach
revolted at the sight and smell of them. The patients at Kakaako
were for the most part in the early stages of the disease, and the
few who were advanced cases kept to their beds out of a sense
of delicacy or, perhaps, out of a sense of shame. But at Kalawao,
where everyone was a leper, there was no need for delicacy, it was
meaningless to feel shame. Here the lepers were the proper residents of the place, and the healthy were the intruders, tolerated
only for the comforts they could bring.

With the effervescent joy of a mob on holiday the ragged,
tattered, putrefying crowd came to a jostling halt before us.—

"*Kamiano!*" the hoarse voices called. "Any *poi* today?"—"Any
mail?" One wit, seeing the old crone standing so close to the
priest, bawled, "E, Fadda! You get one sweetheart for you?" The
mob shrieked with laughter. The clown, a tall gangling *kanaka*
with a shock of black hair and a wildly ribald cock to his eye,
slapped his knee, looking around him at his companions in red-
mouthed pleasure at their delight in his charge.

Not at all embarrassed, Damien laughed with them, his shoulders shaking, his head bobbing like an actor's in acknowledgment
of applause. As expert in timing as a stage manager, he let them
enjoy their joke just long enough to avoid wearying of it, then
he held up his hand for quiet. It was a long time before he gained
it, and only after much help from the self-appointed silencers
who, as usual, made as much noise as the people they were trying
to hush.

"Good freight," he called. "Plenny *poi*, plenny beef." The mob
roared its approval. "Plenny mail. Some packages. Some books
and papers." After each accounting there were more shouts, more
cheers. "And medicine for the Hospital, lumber for the houses,
some more pipes for the water." They were silent.

Damien laughed, "O.K. O.K. Today you rest. But tomorrow
Ambrose and I, we chase you to work."

This would seem to be the funniest remark ever made. Clapping with merriment, shouting with glee, the incredible mob literally danced in the meadow with joy. Were they maniacs, I wondered, witless with their disease and their isolation? Or were they light-hearted as children, even with their affliction, because they were *kanakas* and *kanakas* are always children at heart?

Who can understand these alien people? I asked myself, looking out upon them cavorting on their village green. Although a few sinister Chinamen were mixed among them, and a rare white man, most of them were Hawaiians, dressed in the oddments of their confused country's confusion of styles. The men wore trousers, not invariably of trouser length. Many of these were cut off, or torn off, at the calf or at the knee, but all of them were recognizably the remnants of trousers. Above these they wore shirts, or portions of shirts, or jackets, or nothing at all, exposing their chests and shoulders with indifference, whether they were diseased or clean.

But the women! They were clad in a bewildering variety of garments. Most of them wore the loose shapeless Mother Hubbard, but some were garbed in fashionable street clothes, complete with bustle. Others wore dressing gowns, nightgowns, castoff men's clothing, even—and at these I had to look twice—blankets and *lauhala* mats wrapped around them in the manner of Red Indians. Their headgear was as riotous as their clothing: *chapeaux* from Paris (or at the least from San Francisco), their feathers and flowers and laces ruffled in the morning breeze, were as much in evidence as were the native hats, woven from ferns and *lauhala*, or sunbonnets of the kind American missionary women wear.

Only the utter grotesqueness of their bodies reminded me that the grotesqueness of their costuming was not the result of some fantastic masquerade.

As the laughter died away I heard behind me the sound of vomiting. It was the proud young man, in the bushes at the end of the trail, brought to his knees by his revulsion, coughing up his chyme, sour in his mouth, because he rebelled against becoming like those things out there. Under my breath I spoke to him, reviling him: Puke, you proud son-of-a-bitch! Puke! In another year you will be as they are. . . .

I shuddered when I realized what I was thinking. Ten minutes ago I was wanting to bring him comfort; now I rejoiced in his humiliation, in the torment that his living death was going to bring him. Who could understand my alien ugly self, I wondered, as with horror I heard the sound of lepers' laughter and with cruel joy I listened to the agony of that sickened one.

"Sixteen new patients today," Damien was saying. "Six here, ten more bimeby."

"You get eight dere, Fadda," someone called.

"Only six patients. Two healthy. From the Board of Health."

"Tell 'em go back. We don' need 'em heah," another man shouted. I found him: a short solid bull-necked man with a face that looked as if it had been seared over a fire. He had no ears at all: they were rotted away. From the hoots and jeers, the hostile glances and vehement spittings, I gathered that Mr. Gibson's Board of Health was not very popular with the patients. Somehow the discovery pleased me.

"Now, now," the priest said, "do not be mean to the Board of Health. They do the best they can."

"O.K. O.K." they chanted back, using the stupid American-ism like some acknowledgment of mystic understanding. "O.K. We know," they shrugged patiently, full of the wisdom of fools.

The priest beckoned to the girl to help him with the old woman. With another wave he invited the rest of us to follow him, out from under the trees where we hid from the amassed horror. See-ing that the priest was ready to leave, the mob began to open a path before him.

"Keanu," I whispered. "Ready?" Gently, I took his arm and faced him in the direction of Kalawao. But he did not raise his glance from the ground.

The multitude of lepers opened up before us, arranging them-selves in a ragged file upon either side of a wide path stretching across the greensward toward the village. Was it only I who noted the justness of the symbols revealed to us at the far end of the parted horde?

A minute church was there, its long slender spire rising high against the morning sky. It ended in a cross, black against the lowering clouds.

My eye followed the lines of the church to the ground upon which it rested. And there were the graves. Hundreds of them, each with its cross of iron or of wood or of rock, thrust their re-minders of mortality out of the green grass of the plain.

We began to walk toward the distant sanctuary of death. We, the living, walking in our own funeral. Our dreadful parody of a funeral procession set me to cursing, muttering my protests to unhearing Keanu, while we walked side by side.

We had walked only a little way when the singing began somewhere ahead of us. Was it among the older patients, the sicker ones lying on the ground, on their pallets in the sickly morning light, that the singing began? Was it among them, less active and less subject to the frenetic humors of our mad greeters, that the imminence of death spoke so urgently that it could triumph over morbidness with song? Somewhere ahead of us, around us, for us, the singing began.

The words were beyond my ability to hear. But the tune, sweet and plaintive, was like a grieving farewell. The voices, of men and women and children, rose high and tender in the morning air, carrying the burden of the song. There was no resisting it, or its message: this was not a song of welcome, this was the lepers' song of farewell. The music was the sweetest, saddest music I have ever heard; and the voices singing it were the voices of the angels of death.

The ordeal of Kalaupapa had begun, for all of us who arrived there that day.

7

WE MADE OUR ENTRY into the world of the Settlement through the graveyard.

Beyond the cemetery, on the left of the path, which widened to become the single street of the village, were the first straggling houses of Kalawao. Built of cheap rough lumber, they had been whitewashed at one time, but now they looked as leprous as did their occupants. Separated from the public street and from each other by walls of field stones, they moldered away in their unkempt yards as if they too were ill with the morphew and could not survive many more of the dreary days and miserable nights of Molokai.

At the edge of the graveyard squatted the little church with the impossible spire. The steeple belonged upon a building the size of a cathedral, and it was attached to a box about as big as a cracker tin. The church itself was painted as gaudily as a joss house, with vermilion cornices and bright green trim bedizening the buff-colored walls. With relief I noted that the streaks of color stopped short of writhing up the sides of the spindly steeple.

Knowing my concern for Keanu's safety, the priest took us to his house. It lay toward the sea, at the end of a narrow path between the graveyard and the rear of the church. Raised high above the ground, in an inescapable resemblance to the stilt-like roots of the large *hala* trees growing in the cemetery and the church-yard, the cottage was little more than an aerial room with a flight of stairs leading up to it. In the yard beneath it, unprotected from the weather, were pieces of rough lumber, assorted tools, and a pair of carpenter's horses on which rested a half-finished coffin. Wood shavings danced and whirled in the freshening breeze, uninterrupted in its course by hedge or fence.

At the foot of the stairs the priest stopped the cortege. Behind us dozens of curious lepers came to a shambling halt. Turning to me he said, "Here is my house. I think you and Keanu should better wait here, while I take the new patients to the Office. When I am *pau* there"—he reached into one of his pockets and, after considerable searching among its hidden treasures, pulled forth an ancient watch—"I must say Mass. After this I fix you some breakfast, and then I take you to the Doctor's House. O.K.?"

"Thank you. We'll wait for you here. What is the time now?"

"A quarter till seven." I heard him with unbelief. The day was not really begun, and already I felt that I had lived a lifetime on the accursed isle.

I had no idea how many hours all his duties would take, but I did not care. Tired, and ill from the sight and smell of the lepers, I wanted only to rest, to be freed of their nightmarish presence. Although I had not eaten since yesterday's noon, I was not hungry, and the thought of food in such a place was nauseating. Keanu felt as I did, I was sure, after one swift glance at him, still hiding behind the bulwark of taro. "Send them away," I said to the priest.

"Everybody go home!" he shouted. "Errybody *vamoose!* Almost time for Mass." With shrieks of merriment and much happy tugging and pushing, they scattered, running and hobbling in all directions, even dodging past us and among the forest of tomb-stones to reach their homes.

Relieved, I sat down upon the dirty steps.

"You come with me now," Damien said quietly to his six charges. "Not far. Just across the road from the church." The newcomers turned in their places, and went with him up the path to the village street. The young woman looked as if she were about to faint: her eyes were closed, the long lashes lay wet upon her cheeks. Yet she walked as well as the priest did, her shoulders erect, her head high, in a final exertion of her will. It was the arrogant young man with the green eyes who was in collapse. Two of his graying companions almost carried him away, his feet falling like a drunkard's upon the grassy path. This time I did not jeer at him.

When they were gone the stillness of the morning was left to us. For a long moment we heard the beautiful solace of silence, before our ears, deafened too long by the violence of the beach and the clamor of the lepers, could detect the rustle of the wood shavings in the cottage yard, the call of a distant bird, the burbling of a nearby brook. The warm breeze was gentle, giving the promise of a fair day if ever the coluds were burned away. The comforts of the good things in life moved in upon us, to remind us that they existed still, even in Kalawao.

With a great sob Keanu began to cry. Blinded by his tears, he dropped my instrument case upon the ground beside his feet. Bending over, he let the bag of taro tumble to the earth. The tears fell like rain drops into the dust, upon his feet, upon the unfeeling cover of my instrument case. Stumbling away, weeping almost soundlessly, he fell against the unfinished coffin for support in his time of agony.

I left him to his tears. What could I say to comfort him?

At last he ceased his weeping. For a long time we remained silent. Only once was the quiet broken, by the brassy clangor of the church bell summoning the faithful to Mass.

Much later, with the deep sighing intake of breath, the delicious release of tension which marks the end of weeping, he rose to his feet. He found some old newspapers under the priest's house. With them he dried his face, blew his nose, made himself into a man again. Then he came to the railing, across the stairs from where I huddled, miserable with what had passed but shrinking more from what was about to come.

"I going look like dem?"

I did not dare to face him as I told him what he dreaded most to learn. "Yes, Keanu," I said, as kindly as I could. "You will look like them—*if* the experiment succeeds."

"An' eef not?"

"Then you will remain well. As you are now."

The slap of his hand upon the railing made me jump. I looked up at him, leaning over me. His eyes, red from weeping, were fixed fiercely upon me; his head was thrust forward over the rail as if he meant to do me violence. With a surge of fear I understood for the first time that he was a murderer.

"Wat chance I get? I mean, fo' stay well?"

"Very good! Very good indeed! Nobody knows for sure, but I think perhaps ten to one, maybe even one hundred to one—" He would never know how I drew those figures out of the very air: I would have run them up to a million to one to escape his wrath. He was a fool to ask for statistics which do not exist, but I would have been the greater fool if I did not invent some for his comfort.

"Ahh, dass good. I get a chance, den. Dass all I ask. A chance fo' ween—an' fo' keep my promise, too." He thought over his plans, heedless of me. "Maybe I run away . . ."

Now I knew how trustworthy was the sportsman's promise. "Where would you go? How would you get away?" Beyond him the cliffs rose, black and topless in the clouds, an insurmountable prison wall. Behind me stretched the open sea, unbroken to Alaska. "Can you climb those mountains? Can you swim back to Oahu, across the sea?"

"Aye. You right." Lifting his head he looked beyond me to the sea. "Dey trap me heah. Jus' like in jail."

The undisguised hatred made me draw away. "You want to go báck? To jail? To be hanged?"

"No," he shook his head meekly, his brief rebellion past. "No. I have said it: to live moa bettah dan die. I take my chances heah. Maybe I get use' to it." Staring at the sea, he summed up his philosophy. "Eef I no like it heah, I go sweem one day, 'way out. An' I no come back . . ."

I shall never know whether it was compassion for Keanu or concern for myself that brought the thought to my mind, but all at once it was there, the perfect armor against the murderer's hand. "Keanu," I said impulsively, putting all the sincerity I could summon into my voice and into my face as I looked up at him, "Keanu, I promise you this, upon my word of honor. If the test does not work, I shall do everything in my power to get a full pardon for you from the King. I think you will deserve it. And I think the King, too, will feel that you should have it."

"Dose are good words. Dey make me feel good." The hate fell away from him. He smiled, his face was young gain. Straightening up to his full height, he put out his huge hand toward me, taking my hand in his. "You a good man, *Kauka*. I do wat you say."

His words, his trust, made me feel better, too. An almost unknown warmth of pleasure welled up within me, a surge of good will not only for Keanu but also for myself.

The bell began to ring joyously then, from Damien's gay and festive church, like a messenger of happier times to come.

In a few minutes Father Damien came to join us. At first we did not recognize him, striding toward us in his womanish habit. He had found time to wash his hands and face and to change his gravedigger's clothes for a priest's soutane. Although the stubble of beard still smudged his cheeks, the parts of him which showed were clean; and the full-skirted cassock and the broad-brimmed hat were in good order. He was taller, thinner, less of the peasant in this dress than in his workman's clothes.

"So," he peered from one to the other of us. "The rest has been good. for you. You look better." He winked at Keanu. " 'A good crying cleans the spirit as well as the face.' This is what my grandmother would tell me, when I was *pau* with my crying." I was able to detect now, as I could not earlier in the noisy day, remnants of the languages of Europe in his accent. He spoke English well, choosing the words with ease; but the thickness of his native tongue still affected his pronunciation and often arranged the order of his words.

Resting one foot on the lowest step, he leaned on the railing next to Keanu. "This is a terrible place to see for the first time. You will think that Hell itself has nothing to compare with this. But you should see it ten years ago. Or even five years ago. It is like a Paradise now. But we talk of this some other time. Now you are hungry. Come upstairs. I find us something to eat."

By the time we reached the porch he had thrown open the

doors to the two rooms into which the house was divided. To the left, on the seaward side, was his bedroom. A monk's cell it was, even in this Hawaiian Paradise: it contained no more than a low cot, a sea chest, an ugly crucifix for him to gaze upon when he lay in his bed. The walls were whitewashed, the floor was bare of mat or carpet. The room was so neat that one wondered whether he spent any time at all in it.

"Make yourself comfortable," he called from the room on the right. "Here are chairs." The cubicle on the inland side of the house was his office. It became, of necessity, his living room and kitchen as well. While I looked surreptitiously into the setting for his private life, in the strange mixture of curiosity and embarrassment which overcomes one who is thrown among strangers he does not especially like, the priest was busy lighting a paraffin lamp. What the devil does he need light for, in the middle of the day? I questioned, as, with his precise motions, he removed the squat chimney from the lamp and set the match to the wick.

He did not share my embarrassment at exposing his private world to our view. Yet I was ashamed of it for him: it was a poor and graceless house, even for a priest. A homemade desk, fashioned of the same cheap lumber as that from which he made coffins, stood against the central wall, a heavy homemade chair before it. The desk held his hat, a few churchman's books, and some loose papers weighted down with a smooth stone. Above the desk, nailed to the wall, was a dreadfully garish chromolithograph of the bleeding heart of Jesus, and the inevitable misshapen merciless crucifix. Two ungainly chairs and the narrow kitchen table completed the furniture of the room. One small glassless window brought air and light into it when the door was shut.

"You like *kokua?*" asked Keanu. He could not have stood upright in the minuscule room if the priest had accepted his offer. Damien realized this even if the slow-witted youth did not. "Thank you. No need. Maybe later." Reaching through the window he filled a pot with water scooped from a rain barrel. "Seldom do I cook here: I do not have the time. Usually I eat in the Hospital, or with the people in their houses—wherever I am when I am hungry. Sometimes I do not eat. I forget. I am a very forgetful man."

He took down a rusty tin canister from a shelf, deftly poured water into it from the pot, and then hung the can from a well-placed nail in the wall above the table. Moving the lighted lamp, he put it beneath the can.

"Is that your stove?"

"Yes. Do I need more? This makes all the heat I need. A wonderful invention, the paraffin lamp. You like eggs? Coffee? So, in a few minutes we shall have a grand feast." He crossed the room to the desk. Carefully pulling open a drawer, as though he were about to discover an angel asleep in it, he reached in and drew out five eggs. "Ahh, Panui has been good to us today. Sometimes I find one, sometimes six. Today we have a happy dispensation." The eggs went into the warming water.

He sent us down into the yard, to wash the beach slime from our hands and faces, with water drained from the rain barrel and a very small piece of soap. "I am sorry I do not have more soap. It is very hard to get here. But I have towels. When you are ready for them, I drop them to you from the window."

During our absence he moved the desk and the chairs to the veranda, at the head of the stairs. When we returned, feeling and looking the better for our ablutions, he was in the doorway thrusting the tableware at us—thick mugs of cheap china, such as soldiers in barracks use, and spoons of dull pewter. We laid them on the bare boards of the makeshift table.

"Sit down, sit down," he begged us. "Soon it will be ready." Keanu and I settled in our chairs, I taking the one in the bedroom doorway. From my place I could see the back of Damien's church and the clutter of houses across the road from it, but the line of the roof cut off the cliffs rising beyond them. My view of the sea was unimpeded, however, and in the distance, beyond Keanu's dark profile, beyond the descending fields of green grass and black rocks, I could see the gray ocean rolling in and the startling flashes of white spray where the waves fell upon the shore. It was an Arcadian scene, touched with an austere loneliness; and it was made all the more restful because in all the expanse of land and sea not a leper was in sight to remind me of where I sat.

Sooner than I expected the priest came with portions of our breakfast. "I have only one dish. We use sea biscuits for plates." On his one dish he had laid out three large round crackers, flat and dry as shingles. Upon them, arranged just as they must have fallen from the sugar loaf as he chipped at it, were the moist nuggets and crumbs of raw brown sugar. Never in my life had I been served such poor fare, but all at once I was hungry. The aroma of boiling coffee completed the restoration of my appetite.

"Smell good, yeh?" Keanu observed. Leaning forward, his left arm resting on the table top, he began to pick up with his right hand the grains of sugar scattered over the serving plate.

Back and forth, from plate to moist lips, the long supple hand went, salvaging the crystals of sugar with his spit-moistened finger. In fascination, suppressing my horror of germs in my pleasure in the moment, I watched the large hand, the slender fingers, with their long well-shaped nails, each nail rimmed most delicately with dirt. Seeing the deftness of those fingers, the grace with which they flexed and crooked and deferred in exquisite careless-ness to the demands of the single searching one, I wondered why those elegant fingers and that beautiful hand had conspired to-gether to commit a murder. What have they done? I tried to re-member. Have they choked a man to death? Have they lifted a knife against a woman? Or did they, in response to a rage that drove a savage brain into a frenzy of unleashed anger, did they hit out in fury at some offending intruding face and find themselves, before they realized what they were doing, shattering into lifeless pulp the presented teeth, the unwary flesh and eyes and bone? I could not remember what that hand had done, because when Keanu came to trial for his life I was not yet interested in getting him for my experiment and I had not bothered to acquaint myself with his past.

But now I sat within inches of his dangerous hand, examining it with an anatomist's perception, wondering what it had done to so affect its fate that now it turned and flexed and flaunted its per-fection of shape and function before my possessive eye. This handsome hand—how I enjoyed the alliteration—this perfect hand belongs to me now, whatever it has done. And because it belongs to me, soon, if my premises are correct, soon I shall see it swelling and stiffening, with hungry ulcers opening up the flesh of these shapely fingers, and the bones within these slender phalanges melting away. The nerves will die, no longer performing their duty, no longer recognizing pain; the dying flesh will tighten, drawing these fingers into the aspect of claws. They will not be able to pick up errant grains of sugar, then, I promised myself, for—and I smiled at the delightful conceit—the murderer's hand will itself have been murdered, by a killer that he himself will never see . . .

"Here they are, at last." I sat up with a start. Keanu's hand withdrew from its hunt. On the bare desk top, before each of us, the priest placed two eggs, brown and wet and steaming. The water draining from the eggs stained the soft wood in little whorls of darkness. Unaccountably, it held the fragrance of coffee. At his place Damien set down the fifth egg, leaving it to roll in an eccentric path until it came to rest against his cup. By then he was back with the coffee, pouring it, hot and steaming, from the same can in which he had boiled the eggs. My immediate thought of spurning the coffee, however efficiently it was made, weakened at the scent of it. I consoled myself with the knowledge that, anyway, the boiling would have killed the germs.

"Ahh, this smells good," the old man said, coming to sit with us. "Coffee—this is the other of my vices. If I have to choose between coffee and tobacco, I will be very sad." Quickly he crossed himself, said a silent grace, repeated the sign of the cross. "Now let us eat. Please—"

Never did food taste so good. When the edge had been taken from our hunger and the piles of eggshells on the table had been brushed by one of Damien's calloused hands into the open palm of the other, he brought us another round of sea biscuits with sugar and another filling of coffee. "If I have some tinned milk we could make us *kanaka* pudding—a real celebration."

" '*Kanaka* pudding'?"

"You do not know what it is? It is the people's favorite dessert. Keanu, tell him what is *kanaka* pudding."

Keanu looked as unhappy as though he'd been called upon to address the *kaiserliche Gesundheitsamte* in full and formal session. Shifting in his seat, swinging his head from side to side, often wiping his mouth with his hand, he tried valiantly and inarticulately, a vagrant foolish grin upon his face, to tell me how to make the impossible confection. I do believe it was the first time he'd ever been called upon to explain anything to anyone.

"Tea!" he exploded, when at last he was able to start. "Got to have tea. Coffee, too, maybe. I dunno."

"That's right, either one." The priest nodded.

"You soak um—da beeskeet, I mean—all crumble' up—you soak 'um in da tea." He looked imploringly to Father Damien for confirmation of this complex recipe.

"Right, right." The priest was encouraging him with almost

every word he said. "Tha's right." Hoisting his skirt, Damien reached into his trousers pocket for pipe and tobacco. It was the communal pipe, still partly full of ash. Calmly he loaded it with tobacco, while Keanu stumbled along in his account.

"Da cracker—when he get all sof'—you squeeze 'um—squeeze out da tea—" His facile hands spoke more clearly than his tongue did, showing me how the tea was expressed from the soggy biscuit, how the sopping mess was compressed into some sort of pulpy cake.

"Hygienically, on a plate," Damien explained to me in a professional aside, blowing a cloud of smoke across the table. I could scarcely control my laughter over Keanu's antics and the revolting dish he was describing with such lucidity.

"An' den, s'pose you get sugah, can-creem—you poah 'um on top da sof' beeskeet." With a great smile and a flash of teeth Keanu brought his recital to a triumphant conclusion: "You get *kanaka* pudding."

"Good boy, Keanu," the priest applauded, while I seized the chance to laugh at last, hoping they would think I laughed with pleasure at my enlightenment.

But Keanu thought I scorned the national dessert. "*Ono*, boy! Tas'e good!"

"I wish I could make you some today," said Damien. "If sometime I have a tin of cream, I invite you to have pudding with me."

"*Mahalo*. I come."

They were planning their exchange of courtesies when a native boy came running down the path from the road. "Fadda! *Kamiano!*" he called, long before he reached the yard.

Damien was halfway down the stairs when the boy reached them. His dark face was lifted toward the priest, the whites of his eyes showed large and round. The marks of the plague were on his forehead and cheeks, great splotches of raised red flesh which stained them to a darker hue than the rest of his skin.

"Fadda! Makaio say come queeck. Kenahu dying." At the sound of the word, as though by speaking it he was committing Kenahu irrevocably to death, he began to wail. The tears spurted from his eyes. He was old enough to put his hands to his face, to hide his shame. Kneeling in the dirty yard, the priest drew the hideous child into his arms, comforting him, wiping away the tears with his hands.

I looked down on him in anger. What risks the damned fool took!

Gently he checked the child's sobs. "Tell Makaio I come at once. Tell him I bring the Touch of God to Kenahu." Not trusting himself to speech, the boy ran off the way he had come.

Damien called up to us. "Kenahu's time is near. I must go to her. Do you wait for me here? Or do you want that I take you now to the Doctor's House. It is on my way."

"Take us now, please."

"Good. I meet you in five minutes, by the road up there. Please: leave the dishes. Somebody will come after a while and clean them." He hurried off toward the church.

Keanu and I gulped the last of our coffee, too aware of its value to let it go to waste. Then, hastening down the steps, we picked up my possessions, leaving the bag of taro where Keanu had let it fall.

8

THE DOCTOR'S HOUSE was perfect for my needs. Placed at the upper end of the Hospital yard, as far away as it was possible to be from the village street, it was remote and quiet. It was furnished with beds and bedclothes, firewood for the stove, and some ancient books and newspapers left behind by our itinerant predecessors. We even had our own private outhouse in the back, among the trees and shrubs at the foot of the scree tumbling down from the foot of the great cliffs.

The smell of mold and of stale air was heavy in the dark rooms when we walked into the house. "Go right in," said Damien, when he brought us to the veranda. "It's not locked." Somber in preparation for his errand, he had not spoken a word since he joined us at our meeting place.

Often enough, in Catholic Austria and in Bavaria, I have seen the processions of priests and acolytes carrying the Last Sacraments to the dying, with candles to light their way and bells to warn the living of the nearness of death. But here in Calvinist

Hawaii, I noted with approval, the Catholic Church was not so powerful, and the Viaticum was borne abroad with more circumspection. No acolytes accompanied Damien, no bells or candles cleared his way. The Sacrament was hidden in the bosom of his cassock, and only his biretta, perched upon the graying head, and the haste with which he rushed us up the pathway to the Doctor's House, would have told the knowing that he was on a priest's mission rather than a guide's.

"When I am *pau* I come back, if I can," he said, as he strode away.

Keanu and I spent the rest of the morning airing out the house, cleaning it of its deposits of dust and mildew, drying out the bed-clothes in the kitchen, above the roaring fire we made in the stove. The thin straw mattresses on the beds were hopelessly musty. "Nemmine," said Keanu. "Maybe someday I get *pulu* fo put inside." I hadn't the slightest idea what *pulu* was, but I agreed that anything would be better than moldy straw.

The house held one modern convenience which impressed Keanu more than anything he had ever seen. This was a kitchen sink, with a rusty faucet from which cold water would flow whenever we needed it. Where did the water come from? How did it get there? he wanted to know, marveling at this invention of *haoles* which made housekeeping so easy. I didn't know myself where the water came from, so we went outside to see. We traced the exposed lengths of pipe a short distance into the shrubbery, before they disappeared into a mound of dirt. The chatter of a nearby brook gave me my clue, and we set out in its direction, following the general course of the pipe line. After a few minutes of search we found the pipe again, and it led us straight to the stream. There a small dam had been raised, of mountain rock and mortar. The impounded water stood still and clear to a depth of three feet or more. Its overflow fed the brook which splashed and gurgled its way down the hill, past the Hospital and Father Damien's house, on its way to the sea.

The miniature valley was cool and dark in the shade of ancient *kukui* trees, and the tangle of ferns and native ginger was thick upon the ground. It was a mysterious place, brooding and withdrawn, but beautiful, as some ruins are, or shrines of ancient times which have survived into the present day. "*Lapu,* dis place," whispered Keanu, looking around unhappily. *Haunted.*

He plucked fern fronds and a fresh leaf from a ginger plant, placed them upon a large rock at the side of the brook, weighted them down with a small stone. His offering to the resident gods completed—or were they ghosts?—he said abruptly, "We go." Without waiting for me, he hurried back to the house. I followed at my own pace, thinking about the strange youth. What was I going to do with him?

When I emerged from the forest I saw for the first time the whole of Kalaupapa laid out before me. At my right was the bay in which we landed. The *Mokolii* lay as small as a toy upon the flat expanse of sea. Below me, beyond the top of my house, the roofs of the Hospital buildings showed, weather-beaten in the treeless space which had been cleared for them. Across the street from them lay Damien's church, and his spidery house among the tombstones. Beyond, in a great curving arc bearing off to the left, stretched the coastline of the peninsula.

The leaf of land, sloping down to the sea from the cliffs beneath which I stood, lay treeless and barren for most of its course, covered only with thick green grass blighted by scattered outcroppings of jet-black rock. At its edge the peninsula broke off abruptly, baring in upright cliffs the black lava of which it was made. The sea fell voraciously upon the land, the white foam and dashing spray looking like teeth bared in hunger or in rage. As in the haunted forest grove, there was beauty here, too, but beauty of an evil kind. Here violence was too closely allied to indifference, as in a beautiful woman who is mad.

Inside the prison of our house, set down in the prison of Kalaupapa, Keanu was moving from room to room, his feet clumping noisily upon the uncovered floors. Once more the thought came to me, nagging as a headache: What shall I do with him? How can I prevent him from becoming mad, as this place is, in his loneliness? And—here was the tug of fear again—how can I prevent him from doing me harm, in the months of waiting which lie ahead?

The thought had occurred to Keanu also. When I stepped into the house he challenged me immediately. "*Kauka*. Wat I going do heah, alla time?"

"Well, Keanu," I said easily. "There are many things we can do. We'll get books to read, and—"

"I no can read."

"Then I'll teach you. This in itself will help you to fill many an hour."

He was thoroughly unimpressed by the pleasures of learning to read. "Well, what do you like to do?"

"I like work wid my hands. Plant taro, make house, ride horse. I like go sweem, I like feesh . . ." He didn't say it, but I knew what he was thinking: I no like read.

This is just wonderful, I groaned to myself, an outdoor type of man, the hunter rather than the scholar. Why couldn't I have got a lazy, good-natured, stay-at-home type of fellow who would have been delighted with the chance to do nothing for the rest of his life? Why do I have to be afflicted with a wild man like Keanu? The picture of Gibson, smirking over my predicament as he sat in his princely suite of offices in Honolulu, while I, trapped in this moldy shack in this wretched sinkhole of lepers and outcasts, was vexed with the problem of entertaining a murderous boor: *Zum Teufel!* It was almost enough to make me as violent with anger as I feared Keanu would become out of constraint. Damn that Gibson, again and again and again, damn his black and scheming soul!

"Well, then, Keanu," I fought to keep my composure, "I think we can arrange for you to do those things here. You won't have to be locked up in this house, you know. This is not a jail. You can ride. We'll get you a horse, if they have any here. You can go fishing, or walking, do almost anything you want, as long as you stay away from the lepers. At first I think it would be better if you stayed away from everybody, even the *kokuas*, even Father Damien. Later on, when we know better how the test is going"— I took a deep breath before plunging into the lie—"maybe then we can let you visit the *kokuas*."

"O.K., da's faih enough. I hate be lock' up. Oney, wat I going do fo *wahine?*"

"No *wahine!*" I slapped the table with my hand. "You stay away from the women, you hear me? You are in greatest danger from them. *Stay away from them.*"

"How can? Even in jail I get *wahine*. Any time I like."

"I don't doubt it, this country being what it is." I cut short my indictment of things Hawaiian. What good was it, if he had no knowledge of any other country, of any other way to live? I decided to start all over again, from the beginning. "Look here,

Keanu. How much of this bargain that you made with Mr. Gibson did you understand?"

"If I let you poke me wid da *lepera*, dey no hang me." His hands sketched the placing of a noose around his neck, a rope hanging from some imaginary gibbet above his head. "I t'ink I radda take a chance on you dan on dat rope."

"Did Mr. Gibson tell you why I needed you to 'poke with the *lepera*'?"

"No. He jus' talk like it was one damn'-fool *haole* idea." The grin invited me not to be disturbed by his frankness. He need not have worried for himself. My rancor was reserved for Mr. Gibson, and I put another tally back of his name in the growing account of his misdemeanors.

"Then let me tell you now, so you will understand. Sit down." He slid into a stiff-backed chair, while I sought for simple words with which to make clear to him, once and for all, his role in the experiment.

"No one knows for sure what causes the leprosy," I began patiently, taking a seat opposite him. "Doctors like me think that it is caused by germs—those are tiny little things, so small that our eyes cannot see them: we must look at them with a microscope—" How does one explain a microscope to a savage? It was as easy to tell him about a germ as about a snowflake. He who had seen neither, had never thought of either, sat calmly in his chair, not at all enthralled by my revelations about microbes. "Some day I will show you a microscope, and germs, too." He nodded his acceptance of the promise, with all the enthusiasm of a sleepwalker.

"But we don't know where the germs come from, or how these germs are spread around. We don't know for sure if any person can give these germs to another person, or if the germs just happen to grow in the bodies of the people sick with the *lepera*, and really do not cause the disease at all. Do you understand me?"

"Yeah, O.K. so fah—I t'ink." Raising one long leg, he put his foot upon the seat of the chair and began to play with his toes.

"The only way we can be sure just what the germs do"—I stopped, wishing that I could tell him to put his damned dirty foot back on the floor; but I didn't dare offend him—not yet, at least, not yet—"is to take some of them from the body of a person who has the leprosy, and put them inside the body of a healthy person who does not have the sickness."

"Dass me?"

"Exactly. That is you."

"Den wat? How soon I get seeck—or no get seeck?"

"That's something we don't know yet, either. I think that maybe in three months, maybe in six, we will be able to tell if the germs will grow in you."

"T'ree mont's! So long?"

"As I say, I do not know with certainty. But I am guessing that it will take at least this long."

"But I still get a good chance? Like you wen' tell me dis morning?"

"Dass right. I mean, that's correct. There is a much greater chance that you will not catch the leprosy than that you will." Did I need to go on to tell him the evidence which supported my statement? To tell him, for example, of the dozens of similar attempts made in other parts of the world, even before the discovery of the relationship between germs and diseases, in an effort to show that leprosy was contagious? Would I encourage him by telling him how every single one of those attempts had failed, even those undertaken by Danielssen, the father-in-law of Hansen himself? Or would I, in revealing all this to him, make him wonder why it was so necessary that he lend himself to the experiment at all? Carefully I watched him, waiting for any sign of questioning.

He shrugged. "I try fo dat chance. Hope fo da bes'."

Relieved, I rushed us past the delicate point. "So you see, now, don't you, why you must stay away from *everyone* during the time that we are waiting? If you touch a leper, or a leper touches you; if you touch something a leper has touched, or breathe the air he has breathed, then we'll never be sure how you got the leprosy, *if* at the end of our waiting we find that you have caught the disease." I had his full attention now: toes forgotten, he listened to my every word.

"Remember, then, the only way we can be sure of our test is to make certain that the only way the germs can get into you is because *I* put them there. If you give somebody else the chance to give them to you, our test will be useless. You understand?"

"Aye." Nervously he plucked at the lobe of his ear.

"Good. But the best reason of all for you to stay away from everyone is the promise I made to you at Damien's house—about asking the King to pardon you. Is this a good bargain with you?"

"It is good. I do wat you say."

"Even stay away from the women?"

"Going be hard, but I try."

"Fine. Then I think we'll have no trouble."

"Wen we going staht?"

"Tomorrow. Tomorrow morning."

9

MY HASTE WAS UNREALISTIC, my prediction rash. Not until a week after our arrival was I able to begin my experiment upon Keanu.

Establishing ourselves in that mildewed cottage proved to be more difficult than I expected. Obtaining food was the worst of our problems, and I learned very quickly why on the beach Damien showed such concern over our lack of comestibles.

There was not a scrap of food in the house. For half the day we had been wondering, quite aloud, where we were going to find our next meal when, late in the afternoon, Damien appeared at our door to ask if we were settled. Like everyone else in the sprawling lazaretto, save perhaps the priest himself, we began thus early our participation in the institutional game of the place.

I gave the old man little more time than he needed to say his *aloha* and to take a seat before I brought up the subject of food. As I should have known, he had already solved the problem.

"We borrow some for you from the Hospital, I think. They have plenty there today. Tomorrow I drive you with William to the store in Kalaupapa, where they have tinned foods and other things to make you comfortable. Also shoes for Keanu, and milk for the *kanaka* pudding." It was plain that he had taken a great liking to Keanu, and the boy's grin showed how pleased he was with the old man's notice of him.

"Do you stay here long? If I may ask?"

"Three months, perhaps. Perhaps longer."

"So? Then, if I may advise?" He sat on the edge of his chair, the flat-crowned hat balanced on his knees, his eyeglasses reflecting the pale light of a day about to end in rain and storm. "Please to write your friends in Honolulu, to arrange with them that each steamer brings you food. The Settlement Store cannot furnish all the things you need—and it is so expensive!"

"I know no one in Honolulu I can ask to do this for me."

"No one? You have no friends there?"

"None. I have no time for friends. I am busy with my work."

"But this is a pity. A man should have friends." He broke off at sight of my frown. I wanted no lecture from him on the value of entanglements I endeavored to avoid. "Then the Board of Health? In your official capacity?"

I could see myself writing to the President of the Board of Health: "Dear Mr. Gibson: Please send me, as per attached list, by next *Mokolii*: 1 bbl. flour; 1 bag potatoes; 1 side beef; 1 cwt. sugar, raw . . ." Oh yes, "and 1 pr. shoes, to fit feet the size of accompanying pattern." If I could be sure that the whiskered old devil himself would be burdened with the chores of going to market for me, I would have sent the list gladly. As it was I knew him well enough to be certain that he would turn the whole business over to Harrison, who would turn it over to one of his minions, grumbling as he did so. Harrison, the close-mouthed bureaucrat, could have spared me all this bother!

Pfui Teufel! Let him make up for it now. "Yes, I suppose Harrison would do it for me, although I do not like to ask anyone at the Board of Health for favors."

"This is not a favor: this is a need. Not only for you but for the others here who have less than you. What you take from them cannot be replaced."

"Yes, I understand. I have no wish to rob them."

"Good. Then you will write to Mr. Harrison? The mail bag is sent to the *Mokolii* at five o'clock tonight, from the Hospital. You will write your letter before then?"

"I'll do it right away. It won't take long. I have a few other things I might as well ask him to do for me, too."

"Excellent. So, if you send Keanu with me, I will give him the *kaukau* from the Hospital."

Keanu was halfway to his feet, and I was halfway to anger, when the thought finally hit him. Still in his awkward posture, he looked at me. "I no can go—"

"That's correct, Keanu." I sounded far more withering than I meant to be.

The priest turned his opaque lenses upon me. "Does he not leave the house?"

"Yes, Father, he may leave the house. But only by himself, or with me. Remember, I told you this morning? I don't want him to go near the patients, or the *kokuas*. As a matter of fact," I went on, as kindly as I could, but knowing even before I spoke the words that I could not free them entirely of offensiveness, "I don't want him to go near you, either, for a while. I want him to stay apart from everyone. If it were possible, even from me."

The priest jumped to his feet, shaking his hat at me. "But this is no way to treat the boy! This is no way to treat anyone, especially here. He will go crazy!"

"I will try to keep it from happening," I said icily. The meddling old fool! I needed to shut him up before he gave Keanu any ideas. "I shall keep him busy, and entertained, and—"

"And happy?"

Rising from my chair, showing a calmness I did not feel, I said quietly, "Come. I will go with you for the food."

The old man groaned. "There are things here I do not understand. Someday I hope you explain them to me, so I know."

"Someday, perhaps." I smiled politely. But falsely, I knew: the teeth showed in the smile, and the priest was not fooled by it. "Come, sir," and I opened the door.

We left Keanu alone in the darkening room, his jaw slack with wonderment at our arguing.

Without a word Damien led me to the Hospital. The storm clouds were moving in, and great curtains of rain were falling upon the smooth plain of the sea. There was no wind, and the waves seemed to be appressed by the weight of the approaching storm. The land lay quiet, waiting. Smoke from scores of cooking fires rose, steady in the air.

At the door of the grimy kitchen shack the priest left me. Drawn by the smell of food, I peered through the open doorway, careful not to touch any part of its dirty frame. In the low shed, its walls blackened by soot from open hearths, a number of people were preparing supper for the hospital patients. They worked like trolls in an underground cavern, and I could only hope that they were *kokuas*, not lepers. The aroma of meat stewing in huge caldrons, the bland scent of rice being steamed, were irresistible. I was hungry enough to eat food prepared even in that suspect kitchen.

The priest was angry with me, I knew, by the way he stamped through the shack, by the way he threw the foodstuff he was collecting for me into a large wooden bowl. I was expecting cooked food, ready for us to eat, but he chose only raw things for our supply. A handful of small potatoes, two purple onions, a small head of cabbage, two handfuls of rice, thrown into the bowl, a bundle of something wrapped in green leaves. I was amused that he could show anger in such a human fashion. He was far from being the sickeningly noble and self-sacrificing saint certain folk in Honolulu made him out to be.

He came back from the far end of the shack with a large tin of sea biscuit, a small canister of tea, and a loaf of sugar wrapped in heavy brown paper. Meekly I stood at the door, waiting like a beggar, or—the thought struck me with a sudden chill—as a leper at home in Europe would have waited, once upon a time, outside a monastery kitchen.

Last of all, he brought a chunk of raw meat, dripping still with blood. His hands were bloody from his butchery upon the hanging carcass. Pulling some long green leaves from a gaunt stalk growing like a feather duster near the door, he wrapped the meat in them and placed the neat package on the top of all the other edibles in the bowl.

When he brought the full bowl to me his anger was spent. "*Bon appétit*," he said, as I took it in my outstretched hands.

"*Je vous remercie, mon Père*," I said, with a shyness I had not known for many years.

"*Pax vobiscum*," he said gently, as I turned to go.

We supped that night only because Keanu knew how to cook. While I wrote my letter to Harrison, Keanu prepared the first of the many meals he was to make for us in the Doctor's House.

The smell of it was enticing, as the products of his chopping and peeling and slicing underwent their transformation over the flames of the cookstove. The storm broke upon the Settlement while we were busy at our tasks. As I sat in the living room, writing by the light of a single unsteady candle, with the rain falling in torrents from clouds tearing themselves open upon the mountain peaks above us, with the pleasing aroma of cooking food filling the house, I felt a sense of security and of peace. Is this the meaning of the priest's blessing? I wondered, and I thought of him, of where he would be in this wet evening, of where he would take his supper and find his rest.

When it was almost dark Keanu summoned me from my musing to the warm dry kitchen. Hunger, and my disinclination to get wet for anybody, were excuse enough to put my letter aside and to forget it. We were sitting down to eat when we heard a knocking at the front door. It was Father Damien, dressed in an oilskin coat and cap, huddling against the wall of the veranda. He refused to come in, pointing to his wet trousers and sodden shoes. I could scarcely hear him above the drumming of the rain. At last I caught his meaning. Snatching up the letter from the table in the living room I handed it to him. Before I could thank him, he ran back into the rain.

"He's one good man," said Keanu when I explained the interruption. "He give us plenty *kaukau*."

"How have you fixed it?"

"Stew and *poi*. You like?"

"The stew looks fine, smells delicious. But I'm not so sure about the *poi*."

Which is a verdict upon the national dish of Hawaii that I have had no cause to change since the day I made it. Keanu, of course, disagreed with me, and devoured my share as well as his own.

The happy beginning to our stay in the Doctor's House did not outlast the evening. The roof leaked, naturally; and naturally it had to leak above my bed as well as in half a dozen other places of less importance. Not that I was getting much sleep, plagued as I was by mosquitoes swimming through the watery air to reach me. They didn't bother Keanu, in the room next to mine, nor did the roof leak above his bed. Worst of all, from moving around in the drafts of the night, when I shifted my bed, and from having to spend most of the night in damp bedclothes, I caught a cold. For the next four days I was too miserable to do more than sit beside the warm stove in the kitchen. Keanu took care of me and, outside the house, Father Damien took care of both of us, bringing us gifts of food which he left upon our doorstep.

On the fifth day after our arrival I was able to leave the house, to begin my search for the material I needed.

Under the pretense of observing the lepers I went with Damien to the Infirmary in the morning, after his church service, while he dressed the wounds of the more decrepit patients. They did not ask me to minister to them. For this I was relieved, and Damien's apology that they were frightened of me because I was new to them was not at all necessary. I could not have endured to touch a one of them, the stench of their sores was so offensive, the sight of their deformities so revolting. He remained with them for hours, changing their bloody rags of bandages, washing their foul ulcers, anointing them with salves and unguents, giving them advice and attention, until at last every one of them was done. But among the score of patients who came for this service I did not find the one I was seeking.

In the afternoon I went with Damien and his William to Kalaupapa, to the Settlement Store. William, it turned out, was a reluctant old horse, who pulled us in an ancient buggy at a pace we could have exceeded if we had gone afoot. Damien said as much. "But I do not dare to go to Kalaupapa alone, for fear I hurt his feelings. He likes to visit the other horses." Besides, we needed both William and the buggy to haul the supplies I went to buy.

The dunce of a clerk at the store refused to sell me anything from his shelves "because this store is only for patients." When, angrily, I asked if he didn't sell things to *kokuas*, to Father Damien, to other visiting physicians from the Board of Health, he resorted to the answer of bureaucrats everywhere: "Yes, but they are different—they are authorized exceptions. You, sir, are not. I do not have your name upon my list." He had the effrontery to look me straight in the eye while he gave me this most ancient of subterfuges. His were hard eyes, yellowed from his jaundice. The man's liver was as rotten as his logic. Wasted and round of shoulder, his dark face drawn and haggard, he glared at me across the empty counter at which I stood like a prisoner before a judge.

In a fury of bedevilment at his argument, I was ready to pull down the store about his leprous ears when the priest interceded, asking the surly clerk if he could not make an exception for me if Damien himself assumed responsibility for the account. The loungers around us watched with interest to see how the clerk responded. Unwilling to be too agreeable, yet not wishing to oppose the priest, the idiot relented to the point of selling me "necessaries." These did not include shoes for Keanu, or tinned milk for *kanaka* pudding. The miserable minion took a subtle pleasure in denying me such "luxuries." But even he couldn't deny me two great mosquito nets, one for me and one for Keanu, which I insisted were "necessaries" to me if not to them.

William was not overworked on his return journey to Kalawao. "I cannot understand," said Damien, as we ambled home. "Never before has Kuoo been so *paakiki*." But I knew why he went to such trouble to obstruct me: the arm of Gibson was long, the mind of the Prime Minister was ingenious in ways to annoy.

The next morning I forced myself to go again to the Infirmary with Damien. Once again I was disappointed: these patients also were too far gone in their decay to provide me with what I needed.

That afternoon I went to the meadow above the bay of Kalawao. There the children were, playing their endless games with their endless energy, not yet sapped by their illness, not yet so filled with despair that they could not romp as children everywhere will run and shout with joy at being turned loose on a grassy field. Few of their elders were near on this occasion.

It was a clear day, as much a contrast to the day of my arrival as it would be possible to find. The sea lay flat and sparkling on three sides of us; and on the fourth the tremendous palisade of cliffs raised its barrier for thousands of feet, stretching its grim height along the coast of Molokai for as far as the eye could see.

Among the children I found exactly what I was seeking. She was a young native girl, about twelve years of age, romping like a tomboy with a horde of boys, most of them younger than herself. A boy would have done just as well for my purpose, but I saw her first, conspicuous by reason of her sex and age, and when I saw her I did not search any farther.

Her face showed several of the swellings which, as they progress, develop into those tumescent lumps of flesh called lepromata. Tender yet, the child's cheeks were just beginning to swell unevenly and uncertainly under the effects of the disease. These lepromata, I knew from my investigations in Honolulu, would be teeming with Hansen's bacilli. And they were young enough, in that girl, to be filled with microbes which were viable enough, I hoped, to continue in Keanu the process they had begun in her.

She felt my eye upon her, and moved away. I followed, not wanting to lose her. She must have spoken to the boys for suddenly they all stopped playing and stared at me.

"*E, haole!* Wat you like?" one of them, an insolent brat, called to me. A scattering of dark brown freckles spotted his light brown skin. The wide-spaced teeth, bared as he squinted up at me, the close-cropped black hair, were expected in a street urchin; his swollen ulcerous ears were not. "You like young girl?" he asked. He was just about the age, I judged, when he himself would be taking a beginner's interest in the subject. They all shouted with glee, as knowing as Satan's imps, when he put his question.

"You like *pani-pani* wid Akala?" called another one, hardly more than eight years old, delighted with his bravado and his indecency. His face was so swollen that the eye sockets were mere slits, through which the enclosed eyes glinted merrily. His legs were so wrapped around with dirty bandages that he appeared to be wearing gaiters.

"Akala no like you! You too *old!*" another one shouted, where-upon they all shrieked again and ran away as fast as they could go, scampering like colts in a pasture. They ran so swiftly, so joyously, after their freckled leader that I could not feel embarrassed by their insults. Such vigorous, if obscene, merriment was something to be admired in them, and I watched them go, with a laugh.

I was sensible enough not to follow them. At least I had her name: Akala. I wrote it down in my pocket notebook, lest I should forget it, but knowing that I could not. I walked slowly homeward, wondering how I could find her again in the Settlement.

It was one of her playmates who, in effect, sold her to me. The knowing brat, he of the snaggleteeth and the freckles, accosted me among the tombstones in the graveyard. "Psst!" he hissed at me from behind a tipsy cross. I stopped, half knowing already what he had in mind. I have seen pimps enough in Berlin (if not in puritanical Birmingham, where I was not permitted to know about such things), and this dark diseased scamp was a pimp born to the profession. He came out from behind Halehua's pious memorial, leering splendidly as he sidled up to me. "You like *wahine?*"

I was disturbed by the fear that I might have given more people than this natural pander the impression that I was hunting a bedmate, but I could not help being amused by his style. He would have been a successful entrepreneur in Honolulu, or in any town.

"No, I no like *wahine*." A week of association with Keanu had made me almost proficient in the *kanakas'* bastard tongue.

The urchin raised what was left of his eyebrows, cocked his head. "You like boy?"

"No! I no like boy either!"

He was mystified. "Wat you looking, den?" He forgot to whisper.

"*E*," I said, "*E*, what's your name?" I was curious to know what title this thing of scabs and tatters bore. His clothes, castoff garments from older folk, scarcely covered his sturdy frame. His bare arms and legs, and the dirty feet, were covered with flea bites and with the abrasions of his active life.

"Eleu. Means 'lively.' " He was proud of the name, in both languages. It was singularly appropriate to him, as the *kanakas*' names usually are. "Udda keeds call me Elelu—'cockaroach.' " He laughed, a merry sprite, and I could not help but join him.

"What's your name?"

He was amazed when I told him. "You one *kauka*? So young? I t'ought *kaukas* mus' be ol' an' fat, wit' beard." He gave me a demonstration, complete with stiff knees and paunch and shortness of breath, and I knew at once which one of my associates in Honolulu had left a lasting impression upon Eleu-Elelu.

I thought it best to avoid comparisons, even though I enjoyed his miming. "I'm a *kauka* all right. I have come here to study the *lepera*. To make tests upon the sick ones."

"Why?"

"To learn what makes the people sick. To tell how the *lepera* is spread, from sick person to well."

"To make a cure?" Wide-eyed, with all of the suppressed dread in his frightened little heart coming to the surface, he looked up at me hopefully.

"Aye, Eleu. Perhaps for this, too. When the *kaukas* can learn about the disease, then they can try to make a cure for it."

"This is good. I like help you."

"Thank you. It is good of you." And why should I not enlist his aid? Who else could I turn to? "I—well, I was going to ask you to *kokua*."

"Wat I can do?"

"Help me to get sick people to test: old people, young people, boys, girls. I need some of every kind."

"Me too?"

"Yes, you too. You can be my number-one boy."

"An' Akala?"

"Yes. Akala would be a very good patient for me to start with. She is in a special stage of the *lepera*: I need her for a very special test I want to make. That's why I was looking at her over there."

"Wen you want her?"

I pretended to think over a very busy schedule. "Tomorrow? Could you bring her to my house tomorrow?"

"Sure. I bring her."

"Thank you, Eleu. That's very fine." He was pleased by my commendation. His eager face opened up in a wide smile. It is safe to say that he had one of the worst sets of teeth I ever saw among the *kanakas*, and one of the quickest minds.

"Wat time you like us fo come?"

"Early, I think. About eight o'clock in the morning. At the Doctor's House, you know, not the Hospital. Can you do this?"

"Easy."

"And, Eleu, another thought occurs to me. Perhaps you'd better not tell anyone else about my work, or my tests, until we've made the first test on Akala. You know. Let them get used to the idea first."

He winked. "No scare 'em, *e*? O.K., I go slow. I no talk until you tell me."

"Fine. That's the idea. You know how funny people can be."

"O.K., O.K." He was suddenly bored. "I see you tomorrow." With a mocking salute, he ran away, leaping over the graves, vaulting over headstones, in a scandalous disdain for the brooding dead. I was almost sorry when he left me alone.

Then I went home to Keanu, sulking in his kitchen, to tell him that tomorrow was the appointed day.

10

THAT FATEFUL DAY, as my notebook reminds me, was the thirtieth day of September, in the year 1884. I have it before me now, the notebook with Keanu's name on its cover, lettered in my own neat hand. It is a small thin copybook, of the kind used the world round by school children and by scientists, those disparate students intent upon preserving their lessons as they learn them. I bought it in Honolulu, soon after my arrival there. In notebooks like it I kept the data from my research with hopeful cultures, with microscope preparations, and with experimental animals, during the time of my work at Kakaako; and in this special one for Keanu I proposed to record, in the necessary detail, the nature of the experiment I was to perform upon his body. In it I would enter my observations upon his health, his well-being or his sickness, the course of his response to my experimentation; and, I fatuously imagined, its pages, as they unfolded, would gradually reveal the progress of my achievement, the documentation of my triumph over disease, and ignorance, and time.

Keanu's life, as I wrote it down in my schoolboy's notebook, was to be my forfeit for a scientist's immortality. I knew it then, as, on the morning of September thirtieth, I put Keanu's name upon the cover.

Yet this notebook, which was to be devoted so exclusively to my observations on the health of his body, held no room in it for my observations on the health of his soul. This notebook, which was to receive so much into it, would tell so little when at last it was filled, because it held no pages in it for the histories of other people, and because it made no mention of the story of their interwoven lives. Why did I think that, in this bookkeeping, only Keanu mattered, and only Keanu's body? Why did I not keep a journal on myself, in which to record my progress along the future's unplotted path? Or one for Damien, who had his road to walk? And one for lively little, cocky little Eleu-Elelu, and another one for the man with the green eyes?

A scientist's notebooks are sterile, terrible inhuman things— preoccupied with the dispassionate remembrance of things done, of things weighed, measured, seen, observed, they leave out so much that, given in detail, would fill out the portraits of the things observed and of the sentient being who observes them. To a scientist there is no other way, of course, than to leave emotion out of his method. But to deny the passions their expression, in science and especially in scientists, is an invitation to disaster, as I have learned.

The first entry in my notebook on Keanu is an illustration of my argument: it is not even true, because it does not tell all that

happened that morning at the Doctor's House in Kalawao. And
yet an investigator, reading it in some other time and place,
would have no doubt but that it gave him all of the information
he needed to know about the beginning of my experiment upon
Keanu.

It is correct in fact, but the entry gives no hint of the drama
which took place high on the slope above Kalawao. It does not
explain the strangely unscientific imprecision of the time, the
figure 9:00 crossed out, the hour of 10:30 put in its place. Nor
does it explain the great smeared stain, brown now with age and
drying, which, spoiling the neatness of the entry, blurring the ink
of the fine blue lines, spreads over the bottom of its first pages,
wrinkled still because once they were wet. Only I can know how
this stain was made, and that it was made by blood.

I was so sure of myself, in the morning of my pride, when I
wrote my first entry, neat and presumptuous, even before Eleu
brought Akala to my door. For many months before the day I
had known the exact technique by which I would perform the
operation which was to prove forever whether or not leprosy is
transmissible direct from one human being to another. Wanting
from my protocol was only the recipient of the inoculum, the
donor of it, and, of course, the time. After my meeting with
the lively Cockaroach the last detail fell into place, down to the
minute, and there was no more uncertainty.

In my certitude, I did what no scientist should ever do: I made
a series of assumptions and drew from them a conclusion, without waiting to be sure that my assumptions were established upon
facts.

In the few minutes before eight o'clock, when all of my preparations had been made and Keanu and I waited for the footsteps upon our stairs, I wrote the entry in my notebook. My
preliminary examination of Keanu's body, as I made my belated
check to be sure that he showed no taint of the leprosy on him,
was quickly finished. He was the healthiest animal I would ever
see. After this was done I could not bear to look at him, wandering nervously from one room of the house to another without
being able to find anything to do in any of them. Neither of us
had eaten much for breakfast, and in the hour since I had risen
from the kitchen table to prepare my instruments, while he

washed the dishes, we had not exchanged a word except during my examination of him. I was nervous, too, although I would not admit it. The entry in my notebook was performed in the interests of efficiency, I convinced myself, not as a concession to nerves.

I waited in increasing tenseness until eight o'clock had come and gone. Bitterly I began to suspect that I had been fooled by a wicked irresponsible child. The little monster! *Verdammt noch einmal!* If I ever lay my hands on him— With pleasure I was devising means for punishing him when I heard the soft voices, the crunch of boots upon the gravel path leading to our door. Boots! At a time like this, when I was expecting the stealth of bare feet. I leaped from my chair to chase the booted visitor away.

To my surprise there was the Lively Cockaroach, about to set his bare foot upon the stairs. Beside him was Akala, also bare of foot. Both of them were grinning crookedly, with an embarrassment which suggested that they had been found out in some secret exploratory sin.

The boots belonged to the man with the green eyes. He was unsmiling. Beneath the hat his face was hard, his eyes glittered, cold in the lean brown face. He looked quite ready to be troublesome, and I was not at all happy to see him there.

"Good morning," I turned my attention to the children.

"Morning," said Eleu, tongue-tied to a degree I had not thought possible for him. "Morning," echoed Akala in an almost inaudible squeak. They were freshly scrubbed, even Eleu; and they were dressed in their best clothes instead of their playtime rags. Akala wore a blowzy frock of pink calico several sizes too large for her, which she pulled and pinched and tucked about her dumpy body in an effort to make it fit more becomingly. Poor Cockaroach suffered from the other extreme: he was stuffed into a pair of short black woolen pants, most obviously outgrown, which would itch him mercilessly a little later in the morning, when the heat began to rise. His white sailor blouse bulged alarmingly over his chest and shoulders, as did his breeches in certain places. He was very unhappy, trapped by the superior forces of too many demanding elders.

"And who is this?" I asked, not able to put off any longer an acknowledgment of the guardian behind them.

"Caleb," said the Cockaroach, with a jerk of his thumb and an agonized roll of the eyes.

"My name is Forrest, Caleb Forrest," said the young man. "I live near Akala. We are not related—but her grandmother has asked me to"—he hesitated slightly as he chose the right word —"to inquire into the purpose of this invitation to your quarters." As I had good reason to remember, his command of English was perfect. But the undertones to certain of his well-chosen phrases were insulting: there was no doubt in his mind about the purpose of my invitation to his nubile neighbor. If I had not been so relieved by this explanation for his visit, I would have been furious with him for his insinuations.

"You misjudge me, sir, with your suspicions," I said, drawing myself up with all the hauteur of an aristocrat. I have not been to the best watering places of Europe without learning something of the manners which distinguish the upper classes from the underlings who serve them. "If I wanted to go to bed with someone, I am sure that I wouldn't choose a girl Akala's age— and a leprous one at that."

Between us the ravishing object of our contention stood sway-backed and knock-kneed, gnawing at the tip of one of her frazzled pigtails. My God! How could the man accuse me of lusting after a thing like this?

Unbending a bit, he permitted himself a tight smile, a haughty gentleman's concession to another gentleman's word. Putting his hand to the lapel of his dark-green jacket, in a pose I have seen many an arrogant blood assume, he showed me the mettle of his mind. "I am relieved to hear you say it, sir. You will forgive us, I am sure, if in Hawaii we feel we have had too much evidence of the unchanging inclinations which visitors of less discriminating taste than your own have shown."

It was a devastating rebuttal, and, secure as I was in my freedom from it, I appreciated its pertinence. But it also gave me my first clue to the enigma of the man. Was it national pride, in a firebrand of a patriot, which made him the way he was? Or was it personal pride, the vengeful reverse of personal shame, in an abandoned bastard, the neglected by-blow of some *haole* visitor of a generation ago? Was his brown skin the key to the hardness of this man? Or was it those green eyes, the legacy of some casual couching by a member of some other race?

I laughed at his rejoinder, to show that I was not offended by it. "A point well made, sir. But I assure you that my interests are of another sort. As I told Eleu yesterday, I want to do some work here, some research, you know, into the cause of leprosy. I began this work at the Kakaako Hospital, and while I am here I naturally want to do some more."

"Yes, I am aware of your work."

"This means that I must perform some tests upon specimens of various kinds obtained from the patients here. One of the first things I want to do is to take one of these swellings from Miss Akala." I sketched for him not the specific thing I intended to do with the tumor from Akala's body, but the grand generalizations of how the medical arts would be benefitted by investigations like mine, and how Akala's contribution would be a useful one which he would be blocking progress to deny me, and so on, until I ran out of words with which to appease him. Eleu and Akala, quickly lost in my commentary, lost interest in us as well, and took to peeling splinters from the rail of the stairs.

"This is all very fine, Doctor. But why must you have Akala —Akala specifically—for your purpose? Would I not do as well, or Eleu here, or any one of a hundred others? And why must she be delivered here to you, almost in secret, by this—this agent of yours, to use a kind word for him, instead of reporting to the Hospital down there, where all other physicians would be likely to perform their tests?" He was like a lawyer, tenacious and shrewd, and he questioned me with all of the deliberate politeness of a lawyer leading a suspect into a trap made out of his own words.

Stopped short by his logic, I glared at him in annoyance. Only then did I perceive what I should have realized long before. He was looking beyond me, to Keanu lurking in the shadows beyond the doorway.

I felt like a fool. Pimping for Keanu. How else would it appear to anyone who knew only the facts of my bargain with Eleu? I blushed with fury for what he must be thinking of me. "Oh damn! To hell with this secrecy! Listen to me, then. I'll tell you what I want to do with Akala." The children looked up at the change in my manner. Forrest was good enough to discard the expression of scorn for one of noncommittal blankness.

Taking Akala by her long black hair, I turned her toward him.

"You see this lump here, in the flesh of the cheek?" Forgotten was the drawl of the upper classes at Bad Nauheim. I was almost snarling in my eagerness to convince him of my honesty. "I want to remove it. And I want to put it—transplant it, as you would transplant a seedling from a small pot to a larger one—transplant it into the body of Keanu."

"But why?" he gasped.

"To see how long it takes before a healthy man who is given the germs becomes himself a leper. To see—" *Ach, Gott!* I was so weary of explaining all this, over and over again, to ignorant questioners. "To learn many things that cannot be learned in any other way," I shouted at him, to rout him and his objections before they were expressed.

"And Keanu? Will he let you do this to him?"

"He is ready. We are to do it this morning, when you permit us to begin."

Forrest looked past me to Keanu, standing in the shadows within the house. "Don't let him do it, Keanu," he called, *"don't let him do it!"* The scorn was gone from him now, as the pride was gone from me. There were only the two of us, fighting over Keanu, he from the softness of his ignorance, I from the coolness of my reason.

Behind his cry was the warning: Look upon me, Keanu. See me, broken in the bloom of my youth, betrayed in the time of my achievement. Be warned, Keanu! Anything, anything, even death itself, is better than this foul disease, this wasting and corruption of the flesh, this long unending agony of dying even while one walks. He did not say this, he did not need to say it. We knew what anguish lay in the leper's cry.

Vanquishing the contender without a sound, with only a glance, I stood victorious before Keanu. I had my word a week ago, before ever I saw Keanu, and I did not need to say anything more. My claim upon Keanu was one of reason: Hear me, Keanu, my posture invited. Without me your life will cease at the end of a rope, ignominiously and forever finished. Lend me your body, to use as I must, and in exchange for this service from you I will give you another chance at life. Perhaps there will be many more years of it, free of disease and free of pain. Perhaps there will be only a few short months of it, months of sickness full of pain. However they are spent, Keanu, they are moments of life which I will give to you, moments of life, Keanu, which otherwise

would end when you are hanged by the neck until you are dead.
I did not say this, I did not need to say it: we knew, we two, the
bargain Keanu had made.

He did not say it again, but Keanu's silence spoke for him in a
voice as oracular as that he had used on the wharf in Honolulu.
Better to live than to die, it said, and even Caleb heard its
meaning.

From my vantage on the veranda I looked down upon Forrest
standing in the sun. "Now that you understand what I want to
do," I said, not trying to keep the triumph out of my voice, "let
me get on with it. If you will let me use Akala now, as I have
planned, it can be done at once. If you take Akala away, I shall
find someone else. You are right: she is not the only one. She
just happens to be the first suitable one I've found. And this
happens to be the best place in which to perform the operation."

But my conquest of Keanu was not complete. I had one more
champion to contend with.

Into our midst came Father Damien.

He came up to us in a hurry. "You are having trouble?"

"No, Father. Just a little friendly discussion." The last thing
I wanted was to get him involved now. Damn it! For one who
wanted privacy, I had the most unfortunate luck. I might just as
well have scheduled this operation for the front steps of Damien's
church, and sold tickets for the performance.

"I saw your visitors," the priest said delicately, "and I wondered."

"The rule still holds, Father, but today I asked these good
people to make an exception and to visit me."

"That's nice. I am glad you have—well, a change of view now
and then. I know this small fellow here." Grasping Eleu by the
neck, he squeezed him affectionately, while the urchin wriggled
and gurgled with ticklish delight. "Everybody knows Eleu. And
I know Akala. She sings in my choir, with a beautiful voice. Like
an angel."

Blandly he turned to Forrest, withdrawn almost into the shrubs
at the side of the path. "This young man I have seen only from
a distance, since the day he arrived. He avoids me. You do not
like priests?" The question was asked kindly, but I had to admire
him for going straight to the point.

"No, sir, I do not."

Damien chuckled. "Perhaps this is because you do not know them well. What is your name, young man?"

"Forrest. Caleb Forrest."

"Of Kona? I wanted to ask. Ah, that explains it. I knew your father quite well—he did not shun my company—when I had the parish of Puna long ago, before I came here. How is he?"

"He was my grandfather, sir. And he is dead."

"I am sorry to hear it. He was a good man. Forgive me. I know little of what happens outside of Kalaupapa." The stiff-necked Forrest did not deign to answer, and Damien resorted to one of his churchly platitudes. "But when it is God's will—"

"For an old man like my grandfather, sick with age and ready to die, death may have been welcome. It is the young who have the right to resent it."

"This, too, is God's will."

Forrest shrugged impatiently, "I do not need your pity, nor the false consolations of religion. To me they are useless."

"Then I do not impose myself upon you any longer. But if ever the time comes when you need me, I am here for those who do not share my faith, as well as for those who do."

The priest prepared to leave, patting the heads of the children, bidding them *aloha*. I was full of admiration over Forrest's rout of the old man, and waited only for the priest to go before I thanked him for his help.

His snake's eyes were fixed on me, but he spoke to Damien. "Wait. There is a question of morality here, which you can settle for me." The word was ominous, the tone deliberately offensive. My hope sank within me.

Damien peered from one to the other of us. "Of morality?"

"Yes." Carefully, precisely, Forrest put his question. "Where does God's will end, and man's begin?"

The priest was not slow of wit, but Forrest's puzzle meant little to him. He sensed at once that the greater conflict was between Forrest and me. "There is something here I do not understand."

"Nor I." Forrest lifted a casual hand in my direction. "But here is a man who is presuming to interfere with the natural order of things. Or, to put it in your terms, here is a man who is presuming to play the part of God." The hand was pointed now in accusation. "Where does his part end, and where does God's begin?" He turned his beak of a nose, the arrogant glance, upon the priest. "Or am I safe in concluding that both are one, or that each is indifferent to the other?"

"Please! You talk in riddles."

"Then let me explain. Perhaps it is by God's will that Akala here, and Eleu—and I—have got the Kalawao sickness. I do not know, I cannot say. But what of Keanu, after this morning's work is done? Will it be God who gives him leprosy? Or will it be Doctor Newman? What is your answer to this?"

Father Damien turned upon me, ignoring philosophy for reality. "What is 'this morning's work'? What do you do to Keanu?"

Forrest looked at him in astonishment. "You do not know why he came here? Why he brought Keanu here?"

"No, but I have wondered."

"Well, this puts another light upon the matter. Excuse me, Father. I thought you knew, and that you condoned the crime."

"In God's Holy Name, young man, stop these riddles! Tell me! What crime?"

Forrest, you son-of-a-bitch, you stiff-necked green-eyed cold-blooded tattling son-of-a-bitch! Two minutes ago I saluted you as my ally. Now you're turning me over to the priestly Inquisition for trial.

"Doctor, this is your province, not mine. You tell him what you've planned to do."

"It's none of your business—either of you—what I do with Keanu. He's mine to do with as I please. The King has given him to me. But I'll tell you anyway, to relieve your little minds of strain. Maybe then you'll go away and leave us alone."

And once more—and how I hoped it would be for the last time! —I explained what I proposed to do. Impatiently, without trying to hide my disdain for them, I presented my argument with crystalline clarity and the irrefutable logic of a scientist who has accounted for every controllable factor in the establishment of his schema of experimentation. I even threw them the sugar pill of comfort I had given Keanu, acknowledging with complete honesty the possibility that he would not contract leprosy as a result of the testing. When I finished I felt that I had delivered the most brilliant, the most successful lecture of my career.

The effects of my presentation were apparent in my audience:

Father Damien was open-mouthed with wonder. Forrest's countenance was softened by a smile which was one speaker's tribute to
the eloquence of another. Even the children looked up at me
with awe.

The priest was the first to speak. The glasses staring up blindly
at me, he said softly, "You are mad. You are mad."

"I? I never felt more sane in my life."

"No man has the right to treat God's creatures as you do."

"God is for the ignorant. My learning has set me free of him."

"Someday you will feel his force. Your learning will not save
you then."

"What I am about to do I do for the sake of my fellow men:
to learn something about this disease of leprosy, so that I and
others of my fellow men can do something to relieve mankind
of it. What has your God done, in all the years of his rule, to
relieve mankind of a single one of its plagues?"

"Sickness and pain are the will of God. His testing of us. His
punishment for our sins. And man cannot change this."

"Cannot? Or *must* not change this? Which do you mean?"

"It is the same. God's will is the Law, and man is subject to it.
Nothing can be gained by trying to change his law."

"Do you really believe this nonsense, Father? Do you really
believe that we are God's playthings here below, each moved by
him, like a puppet, and only by him? And that there is nothing—
nothing—that you or I can do to affect his will or to change our
lives?"

His head bowed low, his voice meek, he said, "Except for the
help of God's Grace, as in his mercy it is given to us, this is my
belief. I find my comfort in it."

"But for the rest of us, Father? For myself, for Mr. Forrest
here, who do not share this belief: what of us? Are we to sit idly
by, doing nothing to change the world we know, while this world,
unchanged, takes its changeless toll of us? Where are we to find
our comfort?"

He shook his hand at me. "You talk too much! You play with
words, words that mean nothing to me. Now you listen to me:
I am a priest, a man of the Holy Catholic faith, and I am happy
in it. And you—whatever you believe—you have your faith,
whether it is in your science or in your germs or in something
private to you which I do not know. We are different, you and I.
Let us agree upon this, and leave each other to his belief."

"Excellent, Father, excellent! We are much more enlightened, I see, here in lonely Molokai, than Christians have permitted other Christians to be in other parts of the world. Yours is a most generous attitude—"

"You are sarcastic, Doctor, but—"

"And you are inconsistent, Father. You permit me my liberties of faith, but you want to prevent me from testing Keanu?"

"I cannot prevent you, Doctor. But I ask it of you. I beg of you, for your sake, as well as for Keanu's: do not interfere with the will of God. In Jesus's sweet name, I ask it." Clasping his hands before him, he held them up to me.

"In Jesus's sweet name!" I mimicked him. "Jesus and all his promises!—Why doesn't *he* do something for your lepers?"

Damien's cheeks flushed under the stubble of his beard. His peasant's face was stern, as he raised his priest's hand in warning. "Be careful what you say! Do not mock the power of Jesus. Do not doubt it, for it is very great."

Again I laughed, because I could do nothing else. I had no words to raise against the warning, but because I was drunk with pride I could not let him see me silent.

Then he became fearfully angry. Thundering at me ancient words of terrible power, he beat down my laughter. The phrases came rolling from his mouth, awful and frightening. I could not hear them all, his voice was so thick with anger, but as they fell upon me I knew that I was being cursed: "Because I called, and you refused . . . I also will laugh in your destruction and I will mock when that shall come to you which you feared . . . Then shall you call upon me, but I will not hear!"

Then he turned away from me and went striding down the hill, a prophet in his wrath.

Quieted, I leaned for support against the post of the veranda, rubbing my forehead against the rough wood, trying to think of what I must do next. My head ached, the blood roared in my ears. The three lepers standing at the foot of the stairs were forgotten.

At my side Keanu spoke for the first time. "*Kauka?* You a'right?"

"Yes. I'm all right." But the curse of Damien still rang in my mind: the seed of doubt was planted in me. And when I opened my eyes Forrest was there before me, sober and questioning. I looked from him to Eleu to Akala. I saw upon each one the mark of Molokai: in the livid swelling flesh the seal of their doom was stamped. Too late, I felt pity for them flooding through me. How could I put this mark upon Keanu's firm and healthy flesh? How could I endure to sit by him and watch him day after day, week after week, waiting, endlessly waiting, for him to show the first signs of the dreadful mortification, and know, at last, when the indubitable stigmata came, that it was I who had put them there?

And yet how could I not attempt to endow him with this taint and corruption of his flesh, when my whole ambition and entire career were founded upon this great achievement? And when— the paradox made me laugh until I was weak—his very life depended upon my inoculating him with the seeds of death? I was very tired, sick to weariness with the whole business, and I wished that I had never begun upon it.

"Keanu," I said, seeing no other way. "I'll leave it to you to decide. What shall we do? Go ahead, as we planned? Or—?"

For a long time he did not answer me. And I, waiting for his decision, found the time at last to see the sadness in his face, the immense sadness in his eyes, to realize once again how handsome he was. He had trimmed the beard and the long hair, and they framed his strong brown face in their familiar way. Yet he was not familiar: he was like a stranger, a man I was looking upon for the first time.

"I take a chance, *Kauka*," he said at last. "Do it now." The sadness in his face, the sacrificial sadness in his eyes: ah, the remembrance of it haunts me still—

"Very well, then. Let it be so. And let God's will be done." I meant this to be a joke, a last blustering of defiance; but when it was said it sounded like a prayer.

In absolute silence I performed the operations.

I motioned for Akala to sit in one of the chairs upon the porch. She obeyed at once, in complete composure, folding her hands in her lap, tucking her feet under the rungs of the chair. Without being asked, Forrest stepped up behind her. Eleu watched from his place upon the stairs, and Keanu retreated into the house.

After putting on my rubber gloves I felt Akala's cheek, to define the leproma I intended to excise. Following Lister's technique of antisepsis I prepared the field of operation with a wash of soap and water, following by a rub with diluted carbolic acid. Then, while Forrest held her shoulders, I took up my scalpel and made the initial incision. She did not wince: already the disease had deadened the nerves of her cheek. In a few seconds I freed the encapsulated leproma from the surrounding tissues and, much as one squeezes a grape from its skin, I expressed the deadly prize from its place. Catching it in a pad of freshly boiled bandage, I set it aside to await the use for which I had fought so hard to get it, the while I stanched the brief flow of blood from the wound, and sutured it. A touch of ointment, a bit of linen bandage, a patch of adhesive plaster, and she was no worse than before. Forrest helped her from the chair.

I did not think to chase them away. The three lepers watched while I transplanted the leproma into Keanu. Seating him in another chair, I made him rest his right arm upon the rail of the chair in such a way that the volar surface of the forearm was uppermost. While I cleaned his skin with soap, then with the carbolic acid, I marveled at the beauty of the healthy flesh: firm and smooth under the touch of my fingers, so delicately tinted with the natives' brown color, the blue veins showing their tracery through the thin skin, the musculature tapering from the broadened elbow to the narrow wrist and the relaxed hand—I recognized it at last for what it was, a part of a living man's most precious body, and I realized at last the monstrousness of what I was about to do. With a sterile scalpel grasped in my gloved hand, I hesitated over the prepared site.

Keanu looked up at me, his eyes enormous in the pallid face. "Do it," he ordered me.

And I obeyed.

On its first stroke the sharp blade cut open the satin skin. On the second it sliced the corium below. After the moment of affront, the small blood vessels poured their crimson protest into the neat and narrow wound. On the third stroke the knife opened the deep fascia holding the layers of the skin to the flesh below. There, in the space revealed, lay the folds and curves of the interwoven muscles I sought. Different as Keanu would henceforth be from all other men, he was no different from them in this. As I had planned the inoculation, so would it be.

There, on the exposed belly of the *musculus supinator radii longus*, in the fossa lying between it and the *musculus flexor carpi radialis*, I carefully laid the leproma taken from Akala's cheek.

It was larger than I wanted it to be: it was about the size of a pigeon's egg: but Keanu's big arm could encompass it. Quickly I sutured it in position, using a different needle and thread than I had applied to Akala's wound. Keanu was tainted, now and forevermore, by the very touch of that fertile egg robbed from Akala's rotten flesh.

Closing the incision was anticlimax: a few quick stitches, joining each of the lips of layered tissue to its severed twin, and the operation was finished. Ointment, bandage, plaster—my fingers were trembling when it was done. The fate of Keanu now lay in other hands than mine.

He was faint, as he had reason to be. "Go lie down, Keanu," I told him gently, and he fled to his room.

"Thank you for your help," I bowed to the attendant lepers. Eleu was so pale that his freckles shone purple in his yellow skin. Forrest appeared as ready to be ill as Keanu was. Only Akala was unaffected by the operations: as placid as ever, she was more interested in the set of her ugly dress than in the event in which she had shared. Sourly I wondered if all of History's participants were as stupid as this girl was, as oblivious to the meaning of the events they witnessed. There was probably a drab of her kind fingering her dress instead of her beads when Joan of Arc was burned at the stake; and another one, plucking at her kirtle instead of weeping into her kerchief, when Christ was nailed upon his cross.

I was exhausted, my head was ready to burst with pain. I wanted to see no more of the dismal three, and yet they showed no sign of leaving. "I think you'd better go now," I said dully. I could think of no reason to give them, but I could think of none why they should stay.

Without a word they went away, and I was alone. For a long time I stood there, too drained of strength to do more than lean against the veranda post, rubbing my hand upon it, to ease the pain within.

Much later, remembering the notebook, I went in search of it, to correct the notation of the hour. I had no idea what time it was. What difference did it make? Taking the notebook with me to the veranda, I sat down in Keanu's chair.

Carefully I read the first entry. It said all that needed to be said:

I. 30 September 1884.   9:00 A.M. Inoculation performed. Small
leproma, excised from cheek of young
female (aged c. 12), embedded in belly
of rt. supinator radii longus. Transplant
sutured in position, incision sutured
separately.

Wearily I crossed out the 9:00, put in my guess: 10:30.

While I was writing it, bending over the table, the dizziness
came over me. I felt the rush of blood through my nose, tasted
the warm salt flood of it in my mouth, saw with dismay the
bright splashes it made, like red snowflakes, where it fell upon the
page of the notebook I had started for Keanu.

11

THEN BEGAN THE MONTHS OF WAITING.

For the first week, each morning just after breakfast, I removed
the bandage from Keanu's arm and examined my handiwork.
To my gratification, the incision healed by first intention, in the
course of a few days, without a sign of the festering which surgical
wounds so often develop in patients far more carefully treated
than Keanu was. This happy effect I attributed to the use of
Lister's carbolic acid, and to the clean air of Molokai.

After the first day, during which he kept to his room, Keanu
took up his usual duties as my houseboy. Only the clean bandage, the lump of rubbery flesh, and the healing incision showing
red upon the tender skin, reminded us of the experiment we had
begun.

Only the unnatural swelling, deforming the smooth surface of
Keanu's arm, was there at the end of the second month: that ugly,
unyielding, unhurried lump, neither growing nor dissolving away,
but lying in wait in its ambush of flesh, like the time bomb of a
nihilist hidden in a wall, waiting for the predestined minute to
achieve the havoc it was meant to create.

As it waited, so did we, Keanu with a growing air of worry, I
with the mounting tension of uncertainty. In the Doctor's House,

high on the hill above Kalawao, we sat and waited. There was little else for us to do.

No one came near us for two days after the inoculation. I was not surprised, and at first I was content for us to be left alone. But early on the third morning the priest was back at our door. He was clean and freshly shaven for a change, in honor of the morrow's Sabbath.

"How is Keanu?" His solicitude was genuine, and I allowed Keanu to answer for himself, from the doorway. "Fine, t'anks, Fadda. How's you'self?" The polite rejoinder pleased the old man. "*Maikai, mahalo.*" He beamed. "Keeping busy."

His smile was less broad for me, but still friendly enough. "Doctor. We had our difference of opinion the other day. I hope there is no unhappiness in you because of it. Certainly I did not mean to—" Impatiently, he brushed the past aside. "Doctor, if you have recovered from your sickness, the patients and I would be grateful for your help in the Infirmary."

"Of course, Father. I remember my promise. Let me get my things." I hurried to my bedroom, glad for the chance to escape from the house. There was nothing to do in it but eat and sleep, for Keanu and I had long since exhausted our small fund of conversation. He had a mind of sorts, but an unaspiring one. He was content with the world as he knew it, and he did not care to know a thing about mine. My enthusiasms were unknown to him. How could I tell him about a Schumann symphony or a Wagner opera, when never had he so much as seen a violin or heard the sound of an orchestra? How could I describe to him the great paintings in Dresden and Potsdam and Vienna, or the magnificent sculpture in Florence and Rome, when he didn't know there were such things as canvas and brushes, or such materials as marble and bronze? In his poor world, where the most enduring objects were made of coconut fiber and of wood, nothing was fashioned to outlast tomorrow; and the *kanakas'* thoughts were as transient as their sojourn in their dirty, barren, disease-blighted islands in the middle of that vicious sea.

His enthusiasms were tiresome to me, even unintelligible. Half the time I couldn't understand what he was talking about, in his vile English, with its fits and starts, its erratic rhythms, his preoccupations with the smallnesses of life. I didn't give a damn for fishing; nor could I begin to share his recollected pleasures in the chase of *wahines,* if only because I had never known those bestial pleasures. In short, we had nothing in common to talk about, not even teaching him to read and write, for he shrugged his shoulders and raised his eyebrows and said, "No need," when, in desperation, I returned to the suggestion as a way of spending our evenings. We were quite bored with each other's company by the end of the first week at Kalawao; and much more than I dreaded the vengeance of Damien's Jesus did I dread the prospect of those evenings of silence with Keanu in our moldering cottage on the hill.

Quickly I threw my things together, eager as a husband about to escape a tyrannical wife. I could not help but feel the injustice in the comparison, and the unfairness of my being free while poor Keanu remained shut up in the house. Yet what could I do?

Already I had suggested that, when the wound in his arm was healed, he make a garden and grow fresh vegetables for our table. "Good idea," he answered, the appeal to his farmer's instincts as well as to his belly moving him to a ruminative nod. "No worry about me. I use to lying aroun', you know. Not much to do in jail." After half a minute of contemplative withdrawal he finished his thinking for the day. "Besides, I no like look da lepahs." In times of such candor I was filled with liking for the fellow. But when he began to play with the toes of a huge foot; or when, with intense concentration, he whittled a burned matchstick down to a sliver and with it slowly cleaned his teeth—why then I could have screamed at him for being the oaf and the bumpkin that he was. But how does one tell a bumpkin that a gentleman doesn't do those things, when the bumpkin doesn't give a hangman's damn about being a gentleman? And, what's worse, really has no need to be a gentleman? When my use of him was done, and I left him to his fellow *kanakas,* which one of them would appreciate the niceties of his being a gentleman? The best I could do, when he played the boor, was to look the other way, and vow that I'd escape the company of the complacent animal as often as I could.

And here was Damien with the key to my cell. "So long, Keanu," I chattered on my way to the door. "Take care you'self. I come back bimeby." Thus do white men demean themselves among the lazy *kanakas.*

"Nevah worry," he waved me off, amiable as ever, thinking, as always, about the pleasures of going back to bed.

"What can I do to keep him busy?" It seemed natural to turn to the priest, the solver of all problems.

"Yes, he should do something. Very soon. Or else he goes *pupule*."

"He goes what?"

"*Pupule*. Crazy. Insane. A madman."

"Well, I've suggested a vegetable garden."

"Too wet, too cloudy up here," the hereditary peasant said. "Under these cliffs nothing grows well. Or if, by chance, it grows, the bugs eat it up faster than it grows." He spat into the grass, as *kanakas do*. "The Board of Health does not believe me, of course. It demands we should raise more vegetables."

"How about animals?"

"Yes. Cows, pigs, horses—all do well. Have you ever seen grass so green and fresh as this? But they cost money. They need grazing land, far away from the villages. Keanu maybe can manage, but most patients cannot do it." I didn't care a whit about his damned lepers, but he went right on plowing his furrow to its end. "They are too sick for much walking. So the pigs roam loose in the villages, and sometimes the cows and horses, too. What do you think? Should I give him some chickens?"

"Can you get chickens? They would be excellent."

"But they do not keep him busy long. He needs something more." He tugged at my arm, to detain me outside the Infirmary. "Would he make coffins? Always there is a need for them."

The memory came back to me of Keanu fallen in his grief over the half-finished coffin beneath Damien's house. "No!" I pulled away from the priest. "No! Not yet!" The reflection from my uniform lighted up his face, tried desperately to lighten the somber blackness of his garb, and failed. "Perhaps later, but not yet."

He said no more, and led me into the stinking Infirmary.

"You're a fool!" I told him at the end of the second morning. He was cleaning up the filthy room. I would not touch a thing in it, so thoroughly besmirched with leprous matter did it seem to me. I was standing impatiently in the doorway, gulping in the fresh air, while he gathered up the noisome bandages from the floor where he had let them fall and put them to soak in a rusty pail filled with cold water. I could restrain myself no longer.

"You're a fool! You take too many chances, exposing yourself as you do. Now wash your hands—thoroughly!—before you leave." I pointed to the small basins, one containing soap and water, the other diluted carbolic acid, in which I washed my rubber gloves and my hands until the skin smarted. Meekly he obeyed me, but in an aggravatingly perfunctory way. " 'Thoroughly!' I said."

I could not get over the way he sat among the lepers, peeling off their foul bandages, encrusted with blood and pus, washing and dressing their wounds, all with his unprotected hands. Smoking his pipe, talking with the *kanakas,* he subjected himself to constant risk. And they, almost with malice it seemed to me, thrust themselves at him, delighting to take their advantage of him.

"Why should I fear? Eleven years have I been here. For eleven years the good Lord has protected me. I am content with his care."

"Then wash them for my sake, not yours! I don't want your filthy hands to touch the things I touch." It sickened me to think back to our first days at Kalawao, and to the possibility of those unwashed hands having touched the food Keanu and I ate. I could only hope that his other duties, in those days, and his devotion to his papist ritual, led him to wash his hands more than once before he brought the food to our door. But looking at him, in his spotted cassock, none too clean by any standards, hearing his whining claim that God was his carbolic acid as well as his buckler and shield, I wondered if the man ever washed his hands, or took a bath.

The very next day, after another dreadful morning in the Infirmary, I turned on him again. This time he was sweeping the floor with a battered old coconut frond, arranging the few benches and chairs in preparation for the following day's horde. I was more irritated than usual with him and with everything about Kalawao. The weather was hot and humid, and I was tired. For longer than I could remember I had not enjoyed a good night's sleep.

"Why do you do this for them?" *Them*—this was how I thought of the lepers, as creatures not quite human, not worthy of dignity, of names of their own, and identities which marked them as persons named Hamau, or Kaaimoku, or Nakiele, or even

Thomas Birch and João Rodrigues. "Why don't you make them take care of themselves? They're able enough to do it, if you show them how."

He stopped sweeping. "Because they need to know that someone who is clean likes them and cares for them." Leaning on the stump of the coconut frond, he surveyed the ugly room. "I built this house, with my own hands. It was the thing I built first, when I saw it was what these people needed the most."

"I thought you built your church first."

"Oh, no. I did not need to build that." He was so earnest that he did not even hear my jibe. "It was built already when I came here—by Brother Victorin, from the Mission in Honolulu. And Father Raymond used to come here, you know, two or three times a year, from Honolulu, to minister to the patients of our faith. No, I put only the steeple on it, and some of that pretty paint. The natives like color, and I knew that not Saint Philomena, whose church it is, not Brother Victorin would mind if it was made beautiful in the sight of the people who look upon it every day. I let them choose the colors they wanted, before I sent to Honolulu for the paint. But this came later, several years after."

He pushed the coconut frond across the floor, talking as he went. "First I must make them want to come to the church. It was just a house to them, not a church. But before I could make them want to come to church, I must make them want to come to me." He paused in his task, looking at me over the stump of the broom. "This, Doctor Newman, is not an easy thing to do."

In spite of his preaching at me, I was interested. I wanted to hear more about him, to enable me to understand him, and why he lived and worked in this putrescent hell.

"For almost a month after I landed here I was—well, let us say that I was left alone. A few patients who were Catholics were kind to me. Also some of the Calvinists, I am happy to say— there are good people among them, too. They brought me food, they spoke to me, but they did not dare to stay with me. Nor did more than a few of the patients who were of my faith dare to come to my church. Empty it had been for so long, and almost empty it remained."

"But why?"

"Because the most of the patients were unfriendly to anyone who tried to bring order to the Settlement, whether he was a layman or a priest. The father who came two or three times a year, the Protestant missionary who visited on his rounds—these they did not mind. Such visitors they could forget. But I was different. I came here to live with them, and this they feared. That was in the time of the sick King, Lunalilo, the one who died of the consumption. While he was sick the Board of Health, the Government of the Kingdom—all of them forgot the poor lepers they were sending here since seven years. Abandoned here by the people who promised to take care of them, the patients fell into despair. '*Aole kanawai ma keia wahi*,' they said. Do you know what this means? 'In this place there is no law.' And, because they believed this, they sank into the deepest forms of sin." Furiously he resumed his sweeping. Then he stopped abruptly, forcing himself to go on with the tale.

"Vice, not virtue—this was in their hearts. They passed their time with playing cards, with dancing the *hula-hula*, drinking the *okolehao* or the rum, and"—he hesitated, regretting to offend my ears with plain-speaking—"in fornication and adultery, the ugly fruits of their lawlessness." Embarrassed by this kind of talk, he attacked the floor once more with that pitiful substitute for a broom. He did not speak again until he was finished and the coconut leaf was restored to its place behind the door.

"You see, when I came among them I was a sign of the law, of God's law, and they did not like me. I could not blame them. It is hard for most of us to remember, when we are unhappy, that our friends have not turned away from us, that God has not deserted us. How much more hard it was for these poor people, almost abandoned by their fellow men, to remember that God did not abandon them too.

"When I went among them, seeking ways to remind them of God's great love, I found them sullen and vicious. There was no reaching them. 'Go 'way!' they said. 'Go 'way, you *haole!*' Or, 'You black *kolea*: fly away home!' You know what is a *kolea*? It is a bird of passage, which comes here, to these islands, only to rest and to feed, before it flies on its way again to some other place."

"Oh yes, the plover. I have heard of it."

"Yes, the plover. They thought I was like a plover bird." He looked at me across the bleak room, pleading with me for those who had reviled him. " 'You are clean,' they said. 'How can you know what we suffer? Talk is easy for you, who are clean. But do not come among us, who stink, to tell us of God's love.' And they were right, they were so right! In my heart I could not blame them. They saw how I could not go among them without turning green with sickness, without running to the fresh air whenever I could escape from their foul huts. Without trying to avoid the touch of them."

If this were a confession, I did not acknowledge it.

"They were right to dislike me, for I was unknowing then, and proud. And I was afraid of them."

"And with good reason!" I snorted, meaning to take up my lecture at this point. But he went on with his tale, as though he had not even heard my interruption.

"In those days most of the patients were living here at Kalawao —about eight hundred of them. The few who could find an empty bed in the Hospital lived there, in the same small building we have here today. Besides this, there were very few other houses in Kalawao. All of the other patients lived in the outside, or in small huts made from the trunks of *hala* trees, with roofs made of sugar-cane leaves or *ti* leaves or from the branches of castor-oil plants. Very few had the skill or the strength to build such a decent house. Most of them, with their sickness and their sores, lay under the trees, upon mats and blankets wet by the rain and by their own filth, the grass under them rotting in the mud."

From one of his pockets he drew out the battered pipe. "It was a terrible time. That is when I learned to smoke a pipe. It was my only protection against such smells as I think the Devil himself created for my humbling."

"Then where did you live?" Not a little malice went into the question. I wanted to force him to admit that he had bedded down in comfort in his tight little church while the lepers rotted in the fields.

He beckoned me to follow him outside, into the bright sunlight. "There, in the nicest home I ever had." I looked at him twice, to be certain that I was seeing what he intended me to see. Noticing my confusion he said, quite simply, "Yes, there. That is the place."

It was a *hala* tree in the graveyard.

"And why should I not live there? When many of the patients had nothing better? Indeed, sometimes not so much?"

"Then when did you build your own house?" I hid my ugly suspicions behind the innocent new question.

"Oh, not until many years were passed. It was the last house built in Kalawao. But I did not live under the tree all that time. I stayed for a while with some of the patients, when they began to have real houses. I needed only a place to sleep. And then I slept here, after I built this house." An ungainly farm shed it was, a leprous barn, with the dirty whitewash flaking from it like a scurf, and yet he looked upon it with more pride and love than ever did Kalakaua gaze upon his palace.

"They needed a place where I could dress their sores. I could not do it well in their houses. The steps of the church are not good, especially when there is rain. So I built them this Infirmary. And now—do you know?—now it is used also as a schoolhouse, in the afternoons, when we are *pau* with it."

At last he was finished with the long history of the scabby Infirmary. Relieved, I turned to go home to my rest. But he was not yet ready to let me leave.

"A little while ago you asked me why I do not let a patient be their physician. The answer is very simple. They need me, and I need them. They would not come to another leper for their care. Lepers are strange people. Have you not noticed? They are hurt in their hearts, very much hurt. To make up for the hurt, they are proud. The only way to reach them is to love them, and to show them that they are loved, in spite of the ugliness of their bodies, the stink of their sores. I have learned to love them, and I hope that they have learned to love me.

"It was not an easy thing for me to do. The first time I ate with them, dipping my fingers into the same *poi*-bowl where they dipped their fingers, wet with the spittle from their mouths—I could hardly swallow that *poi*. The first time I shared a pipe with them—only an act of the will helped me to close my lips around the mouthpiece of the pipe. But they were watching me, while they pretended not to be watching me, and I saw how they were pleased when I did not refuse their hospitality. The second time was easier, the third time easier yet. Now I do not notice any more."

"Again I ask it: Why do you go through this living hell for them?"

"Do you not see? For their poor sakes, not for mine. Because it brings them comfort to know that they are not forgotten by everyone who is clean. But also for the glory of Our Lord, and the comfort that the knowledge of his love can bring to them. To let them know that if I can love them, weak and human as I am, then God, to whom all things are easy, can love them even more."

I could look at the distant *hala* tree, but I could not look at him. I could think of a million words with which to berate him, but not one with which to honor him.

"But I talk too much," he chuckled, mistaking the reason for my speechlessness. "I keep you too long. Go now, my son, and take your rest. Give my *aloha* to Keanu, and tell him his chickens are ready when he wants them."

I walked slowly up the long path to the Doctor's House, the noonday sun hot upon my shoulders.

After that morning I no longer nagged him with my concern for his safety. Even I could see that only his miracle-working God could preserve him now from the leprosy.

12

THE WEEKS STRETCHED into months. Keanu's body remained healthy, as did mine, after the illness of the first week and the frightening nosebleed on the morning of the operation. But our minds were beginning to be affected. The long weeks of suspense were cruel enough. But the strain of living together, the utter unrelieved boredom of facing each other every morning and every night, with nothing to say and nothing to do, took an even greater toll of us. I was the keeper of a magnificent animal; he was the jailer of a worried mind. At first we tried to be considerate of each other, then we were content to ignore each other; at last we began to hate each other.

In the evenings we would sit in our dim parlor, staring balefully one at the other across the room. Keanu's eyes, bloodshot and sunken with a semblance of inner occupation, would look at me as though he were praying me to death, in the fashion of his native witch doctors. And I would appear to be staring at him, but I would not see him there, as I knew he would not be seeing me. I could loathe him, that keeper of my future, without the need to see him. I had hate for him, and to spare; and what he did not get from me, as his meed for an evening, I would transfer in my thoughts to Gibson, across the channel moat, or to the dirty heedless Damien, or to Forrest, that proudful thorn in my memory. I had not seen him since the day of the inoculation, but this did not prevent me from hating him too.

But I would grow weary of hating after a while, and, to escape Keanu's glare, his monolithic silence, I would go to my room to sleep. Sleep would come instantly, a blessed relief; but it would never last for long. Soon after midnight I was awake again, unable to go back to sleep. In the dark night I would lie awake and alone, tormented by my thoughts, until the morning came. Under the great circular mosquito net I was safe from the buzzing insects, but what barrier could keep out the thoughts swarming into my helpless mind? Thoughts of my work, fantasies of my future, of home, of Luise—of Luise waiting for me there; of Luise, and *was* she waiting for me there?—of my work and when it would be finished, of Keanu and his part in my great experiment, of that taunting haunting man in Honolulu who had given Keanu to me. And thoughts of other things, too, breeding like maggots in the night soil of my mind . . .

Each morning I would rise, more tired than I was the day before, to spend another day of waiting which was no different from all the rest.

Keanu, too, became bored with lying at home alone by day. Cautiously, gradually, he emerged from his hiding place in the Doctor's House, coming at last into the daylight like some nocturnal animal routed from its lair. Sated with sleep, he roused himself to ask for tools with which to make a chicken run and the vegetable garden. I did not tell him of Damien's gloomy prophecy of failure for the vegetables. Instead I borrowed Damien's garden tools, purifying their handles in the heat of a fire before I gave them to Keanu to use.

He was not lazy. In a few days he cleared an enormous patch in the brush and turned over the sod to prepare it for planting. Rich black earth, it looked fertile enough; but the frequent rains kept it wet as a bog, and I wondered if the seeds Keanu intended to sow in it would not rot before they would have time to sprout.

"Need manuah now," Keanu informed me one day, upon my return from the Infirmary.

"How would chicken manure do?" Gravely we discussed the merits of the different kinds of manures, almost loquacious in our joy at discovering a subject of conversation.

"Hoss manuah, cow manuah, bettah," he decreed at last. "Chicken kine burn up da plants, unless you let 'um get ol' firs'. We no get time fo dat." With a lifetime of waiting ahead of him, he must get the garden started at once.

I accompanied him in the afternoon on his first walk beyond the village of Kalawao. He carried an empty gunny sack and a spade, and I went with him to be certain that he did not have any contact with the lepers. Past Damien's showy church of Sancta Phenomena, as I had taken to calling it, we trudged, along the rocky road to Kalaupapa. We passed the Protestant church of Siloama, a Puritan chapel, neatly proportioned and with a proper spire, raising its austere whiteness against the blue sky and the encircling blue of the sea. Larger, and much more attractive than Damien's pillbox, it was also less used. Its doors were closed, its windows were shuttered, where Damien's church was always open.

Beyond Siloama we emerged upon the peninsula. There, where the grass grew green and thick among the scattered rocks and the outcroppings of jet-black lava, the horses and cows of Kalaupapa grazed at will, and the pigs rooted where they pleased; and there Keanu was able to fill his bag with all the manure he could carry. While he sought his treasure I sat upon a rock and guarded him.

We met very few patients, and those we did encounter hurried past us as though we were bandits in search of victims instead of gardeners in search of dung. Keanu turned his head whenever we came close to them, still as unwilling to look at them as he was on the day of our arrival.

Encouraged by his behavior I let him wander free thereafter, glad to be rid of him. "Remember"—I warned the only instinct through which I could reach him—"if the test does not take hold in you, you will not be a leper. Keep yourself clean, then, by staying away from the lepers."

"No worry." The loathing was not pretended. "I stay away."

After that he went for long walks across the treeless peninsula or along its seagirt coast. Sometimes he would fish from the pinnacles of rock hanging over the sea, sometimes he would just sit there, watching the waves come crashing in upon the shore. Or he would go into the mountains, into one of the three deep valleys gouged into the tall cliffs in back of Kalawao. Always he went alone, exploring his prison as though he were the only inmate in it, a lonely barefoot savage, a Man Friday without a Robinson Crusoe, or, better, a gigantic inarticulate Ariel to my Prospero, in an island pledged to a thousand Calibans. There were days when, watching him go forlorn to the sea, I wished that I were indeed Prospero, who, by a wave of my hand, could free him of his troubles, and me of mine.

But then there were other times when I was irked by his slowness to respond to the inoculation. On those occasions I was eager to see the evidence appearing in his body which would have condemned him to a lifetime of imprisonment in Kalaupapa, which would have made him one more among the many misshapen Calibans.

One morning, soon after I turned Keanu loose, I was walking to my hated servitude, dreading the moment when I must step into the Infirmary. The smell of any mortifying wound is bad enough, but the miasma from a roomful of lepers is enough to turn the stomach of a healthy man inside out. There is nothing in nature to equal it, and only the unlikely conjunction of a herd of goats wallowing in a cesspool filled with decaying goose feathers can match the effluvium I was forced to breathe while I rendered my service to the lepers.

Damien was waiting for me outside the Infirmary, already filled with its habitués, buzzing like a cloud of flies feeding upon a corpse. Eager as any gossip, he pounced upon me. "Do you know that Keanu goes out alone, in the Settlement?"

"Yes. I think it's safe for him to do so now."

"Oh, I am glad you let him out. I was worried to have him stay up there all the time. This way is much better. He needs a change from that house, and from—" He stopped in confusion.

"And from me?" I tried to laugh. It was true. I recognized it.

"Yes, from you. To see the same person all the time, and no one else, is not good. Even in monasteries and seminaries, where usually there are many people, because they are always the same people one sees, day after day, month after month—ah, this causes trouble. Monks go *pupule* too."

"I don't think we need to worry about Keanu going *pupule*. He doesn't have mind enough to lose."

"But Keanu is not the only one in that lonely house."

This came too close to home, although I would not admit it even to myself. I certainly would not admit it to him. "Thank you for your concern, Father. I think we have nothing to fear for the other member of our household—at least not yet." The humor was as heavy as my body was, after one more harried and sleepless night.

"Does he have enough to do? Have you asked him will he make coffins?"

"No, I have not asked him. He prefers to work in the garden. By the way, he is ready now for the chickens. When may we come and get them?"

"This afternoon? When I come back from Kalaupapa. I go to perform a wedding there."

"A wedding? *Kokuas?*"

"No, patients." Seeing my disbelief, he said, "Are they not human? Should they not marry, too, as other people do?"

The thought of two lepers marrying shocked me. Never had I thought of such a grisly farce as a wedding between lepers, the bride and groom in their finery but without fingers and faces, the guests singing hoarsely their lascivious madrigals, dancing footless 'round the connubial bed. And when, at the thought of that conjugal bed, my reeling mind imagined the amative play of those horrendous bodies, clasped sweating each to the thrusting other in futile memberless embrace, in a great sloughing of scabs and halluces, in which lipless mouths sought frantically for love's tender kisses, in which the blood of weeping ulcers stood surrogate for the swift bloody tears of missing hymen—I started to laugh, ready to weep at the horror of my thought.

"Stop it! Stop it!" I heard him shouting, felt him shaking me by the shoulders. Startled, I looked up into his anxious face. "There. That's better," he said, removing his hands. "Doctor, you worry me, too. I—I do not think you are well."

"No, I'm all right. I'm all right. It's just that I haven't slept very well lately. I'm very tired."

"You need a change, too, not only Keanu. You must take more care of yourself, or else you, too—"

I saw him, watching his lips move, but I did not hear the sound

of his voice, strangely cut off by my delight in the words he had
just uttered. Smiling, brightly brilliantly joyfully smiling, I studied
the moving mouth as I treasured in my ears' memory the lingering sound of the words he had just said. "You must take care of
yourself," he had said, in his kind voice, out of his Christian
concern. "You must take care of yourself," he had said, and the
compassionate words hung in the golden air between us, in the
convoluted chambers of my ears, in the hollow emptiness of my
mind. Round and round inside my brain they hooted and rattled
and jeered, shouting and whistling with fingers to their teeth, like
unruly schoolchildren, stamping up and down the stairs of bone
and blood that led to my heart, where, in an even vaster emptiness, they glowed and sparkled and exploded in shouts of rocket-
ing racketing laughter. Like echoes in an underground cavern the
words came back to me in all their clangorous changes, "take
care . . . take care . . . take care . . ." And high above them a shriek
soared and dipped, a screaming swooping spreading shriek of despair, shattering me to my very core, as at last I realized that in
all the world there was no one but myself to be concerned over
my self, to take care of my self, to love my self. In all the world
there was no one, not one, to care about me, to care whether I
lived or died. No one—unless I chose to accept this ragged priest
as my father and my mother, my brother and my only friend.

I smiled at him, sweetly, serenely, as, inside of me, my heart
cracked with the discovery.

"We'll come for the chickens this afternoon, Father," I said.
And I went away from him, to the stinking Infirmary, crowded
with its mob of putrid lepers, waiting there for him, but not for
me.

In an evening crisp with masses of pure white clouds and a sky
of Wedgwood blue, Keanu and I walked down the path to
Damien's house, to fetch the chickens home. Physically I was
quite recovered from the morning's fantasy, but the strangeness
of the experience had left me touched with melancholy, and not
a little self-reproach. How could I have forgotten my faithful
Luise, waiting for me in Berlin? How could I doubt my Luise of
the lovely cool hands, of the chaste lips, of the demure glance?
Luise, who promised to wait for me until my return, who called
me her "explorer of science," who was so proud when I was

chosen by Doktor Koch to be sent by the Imperial Bureau of
Health on "an errand of mercy," as she pronounced it, to the
far-away Sandwich Islands—

Luise of the *Gottverdammte* virgin's coldness, too, my mind
tried to tell me (while my cracked heart would not let me listen),
who had not permitted me one single embrace in the two proper
years of our very correct engagement; who had not thought, in
her maidenliness, to give me a farewell kiss as, all hunger for her
chaste lips, I stood bowed over her cool white hand in a most
correct farewell. Indifferent, passionless Luise, who, in the year
I had been away from her had sent me one brief note, written out
of ennui, drenched with *Weltschmerz*, and sent on its way, anyone could see, without a tender thought for its receiver. Yet my
hope insisted on mending my heart, patching it together out of
old ribbons teased from her hair, old programs from our visits to
the opera (where her parents sat watchfully behind us in their
box), and glue from the tiny envelopes in which she would send
me those cold formal engraved summonses to tea, to dinner, to an
elegant ball in their marmoreal mercantile *Palast* in the Tiergar-
tenstrasse. Luise, Luise, can I really believe that you care?

Having nothing to say, Keanu and I walked apart, I in the lead,
he carrying the same gunny sack in which he hauled manure for
the garden to use now for transporting chickens. We were entering the main road at the side of the Infirmary when we almost
collided with a young woman romping in the street amid a crowd
of shouting children.

They were having a happy time, shrieking and laughing with
a gaiety rarely shown at Kalawao. The children were besieging the
young woman, who held a beanbag above her head which they
were trying to take from her. Pushing and pulling at each other,
tugging at her, they tried to bring down her arm so they could
reach the scarlet bag. She was calling to them, in a voice choked
with laughter, "*Pau, pau* now! No more! *Pau!*" growing more
fearful as they began to clutch at the full sleeves of her Mother
Hubbard. Long black hair fell loose over her shoulders, almost to
the middle of her back. Her unmarred face was lovely to see,
flushed with excitement, the white teeth shining against the darkness of her skin, the red of her lips.

When she saw us emerging from the path her arm fell to her
side in the moment of surprise. A boy snatched the beanbag

from her hand and dashed away with it, screeching in triumph. The other children followed him in the instant, and with their flight she was left alone. The hand which a moment before was clutching the beanbag now flew to her throat; the laughing mouth closed primly; the merry eyes hid behind lowered lids. In the transformed creature I recognized the demure young Lady-in-Waiting to the Queen. It was Malie. Unbidden, the name sprang into my mind, which on the day of our arrival refused to recollect it. But it was a Malie happier than I ever expected to see her.

I looked with astonishment upon this Polynesian nymph. Desperately I searched for some pleasantry to say, some remark to overcome her shyness, to keep her near while I talked with her. But she was swifter than my wit. Looking beyond me, she saw Keanu and, with a gasp of fright, she turned and ran away. She lifted the skirts of her *holoku* as she ran, and I could see the slender legs, the dark soles of her narrow feet, the little spurts of dust in the road, as she fled toward Siloama.

Keanu, too, stood watching after her. Once before I had seen him stare at her, with lust in his blood, the blaze of passion in his eye. This time there was loneliness, and yearning, in the unmasked face. With something like annoyance I realized that the animal I called Keanu knew longings which were unappeased, and lonelinesses of which he never spoke, and a heart unfulfilled. He was no different from myself in these respects, unschooled as he was, inarticulate as he remained. Perversely, the discovery of our kinship did not soften my feeling toward him. The pang of jealousy which I felt as I looked upon his handsomeness was easily, too easily, turned into a sneer at his lusting. Inexpert in the ways of love as I was, I did not recognize the bite of jealousy, or the sneer, as symptoms of my own claim upon love. Physician that I was, expert in the diagnosis of leprosy, I was not physician enough to diagnose my own ailment, or to recognize my jealousy as the symptom of my need for the heart and the body of a beloved.

"Come on!" I growled. "Don't stand there like a fool! We're late." This time I was not granted what for so long I had taken as my due. Scowling down at me from his height, his face taut with anger, he put out his arm and thrust me aside with such force that I fell against the stone wall. Without a word he stalked away, down the path to the priest's house.

White with the affront to my dignity, I struggled to my feet, looking around to see if anyone was a witness to his attack upon me. Fortunately no one was there to see it. Boiling with rage, I hurried after him, down the path through the graveyard. "You damned *kanaka!*" I swore. "I'll show you!"

When I caught up with him the priest was already coming out of his coffin factory to greet us. I thought this fortunate at the time, because the presence of Damien gave our anger a chance to subside. But I wonder now if the meliorative presence was really the kindest thing Fate could do for us that evening in the tropical dusk. Perhaps our lives would have been different, our futures less hurt and hurtful, if Keanu and I had quarreled then, in a fine cathartic explosion. We would have shocked the priest, no doubt; and we would have left a few scars upon our individual vanities, but we might also have avoided the effects of those pressures being built up in us because we could not give them release. As it was we kept the peace, he out of his innate good manners, I out of my artificially acquired ones, and the unsuspecting priest swept us into his conversation.

"You know how to take care of chickens, Keanu?" Brushing the wood dust from his arms and his work clothes, Damien gave me a nod of welcome.

"My house had some. Until we went eat 'um." Grinning and ducking his head at the same time, Keanu put a hand to his mouth. All of this foolishness is the *kanakas'* expression of embarrassment, apology, and suppressed laughter, used especially when they are telling a joke upon themselves.

"Why you went eat 'um all? Why you nevah eat some, save some?"

"We had one beeg pahty one time. Plenny people stay come my house."

"Where's your house, Keanu?"

"Kohala. Place name' Makapala. Nice place, dat."

With quick tact the priest turned the conversation away from sentiment to realities. "What kine *kaukau* you gave your chickens?"

"Any kine stuff. Grass, leafs, rice, worms—any kine." The *kanaka* farmer shrugged, surprised at the *haole* farmer's absurd question. "Mos'ly we let 'um run aroun'."

"But you no can do that here, you know. Too many hungry *opus*, which don't care how they get filled. You have built your chicken yard, the *kauka* tells me."

"Aye. By da gahden."

"Good place. You can watch 'um from there. O.K., you know how to take care of 'um. I feed mine the same things. Only I chop 'um up in small pieces, before I feed 'um to my chickens. Not so much waste, this way. You have a big knife?"

"No moah."

"I give you one." He went away to rummage among the tools in his workshop, among the litter of things on the ground, talking all the time. "It came a few weeks ago, in a box of things from Honolulu. I never know where those things come from, but I am always glad to get them. Ah, here it is." He reached up into a crotch of beams above his head and pulled from it a long double-edged knife. The blade, about six inches long, was mounted in a wooden haft. Even in the fading light the knife looked sharp and evil.

"Here, take this one." He wiped the blade on his sleeve as he returned to us. "You will get good use from it."

Keanu was slow to respond. Even after he took the knife from Damien he looked down upon it as though scarcely able to credit his good fortune at receiving such a treasure.

"Now we go get the chickens," said Damien, "down there, past the *Hale o ka Make*." Keanu opened the gunny sack and dropped the knife into it. He did not say thank you, I noticed, cherishing the omission as further evidence of his boorishness.

The House of the Dead was little more than a roof covering a long table, upon which the corpses from the Settlement were washed with water from the nearby brook before they were wrapped in their winding sheets. The carpenter-priest had managed to get rather a good lead upon the dying: four finished coffins, fresh from his manufactory, were stacked at the far end of the shed. They were nothing more than narrow boxes, with lids which were to be nailed in place. They would not last as long as the bodies they held, in the wet earth of Kalawao.

A short distance beyond the morgue, so close to the edge of the sea that we could hear the roar of the surf, lay the chicken yard. It was hedged around by a palisade of saplings with the bark still rough upon them, to which plaited coconut fronds were bound as a windbreak. About thirty ragged chickens of mixed and indeterminate breeds prowled disconsolately about the enclosure, looking hopefully for a blade of grass in the dirt from which everything green had disappeared. A few weather-beaten boxes at the far end of the run gave the birds scant protection against the weather.

"Panui takes care of them by day," the priest explained. "The ghosts of the dead guard them even better by night. But I hope also the needs of the living. The patients know that the few eggs, and maybe now and then a chicken, go to the sick people in the Hospital. They do not steal things belonging to everyone. Only things held in private do they take, if they cannot hold back the temptation. That's why I tell you to watch your flock, Keanu." He chuckled. "But they are better now than they used to be. Before they would steal food out of the mouths of the dying. They would dig up the dead to take from them their shrouds."

Positively cheerful while he talked of ghouls and ghosts, he unfastened the rope of coconut fiber which held the gate shut. "Wait for me here," he whispered, as he stepped into the enclosure.

Turning to the chickens, he called to them in a high-pitched sort of song, a weird ululation of cluckings and gabblings. At the first note of his incantation the chickens ran toward him, cackling and squawking in their own raucous voices. Wings outspread, necks extended, long legs carrying them swiftly to the object of their search, they ran to where he awaited them, with his arms held out at either side, like a scarecrow, or like one of them immobilized. Clamoring excitedly, they fluttered about him, rising in a whir of wings and a shower of feathers and feces to his arms, his shoulders, his bared head. They clung to him with their dirty talons, stained with the mud and manure of the fowl yard. In the cacophony of cackling and the reek of ordure the priest stood happily, a barnyard simpleton with a beatific smile. Nothing I ever saw at Kalawao, not even the foulest of lepers, disgusted me as much as this dumb show of Damien's with his chickens.

The stupid creatures would not end their clamor until he reached into his pockets and pulled from them the grains of rice and crumbs of bread and shards of eggshells with which he rewarded them for their show of affection. Scattering them broadcast, as a farmer sows his grain, he threw the morsels of food to the sides of the chicken run. The greedy birds deserted him in an instant, darting giddily around the yard to quarrel over his bounty.

Brushing the feathers and refuse from his clothes, he now advanced upon them, to betray them as readily as they had forsaken him. Bending low, he swooped upon them, clutching the unwary birds by wing or neck or leg. In a few seconds he held five of them in his grasp, hanging head down, their combs dark with blood, their wrinkled yellow legs bunched in his hands. Four hens and a cock: the continuation of the race was assured.

Glowing with satisfaction at this exercise of his farmer's skill, he returned to us by the wicket. Keanu held it open for him. The chickens hung quiet, resigned to their captivity. He himself lost his cheerfulness almost as quickly as they did. "I feel like a Judas when I do this to them."

Keanu unfurled the sack, shaking it until the knife fell to the grass next to his brown feet. When he stepped forward, holding the bag while the priest carefully lowered the chickens into it, I picked up the knife. It was heavy, and surprisingly sharp. With its double edge and pointed tip it was more a dagger than a kitchen knife. The flecks of rust upon it looked like drops of blood. I wished it had a sheath, to cover the naked blade.

The chickens, plunged into darkness, complained once or twice and then lay inert in the bag. "O.K. Bettah go now, befoah dey *make*," said my single-minded prisonmate. "T'anks, Fadda. Fo erryt'ing."

"You welcome, Keanu. I hope they lay many eggs for you, I hope your flock prospers. Put a *kapu* on them until you have three times this many. Then you can eat some."

"Cheecken stew—tas'e good," agreed Keanu, summing up his whole comprehension of cookery in the statement. Stew and *poi*, stew and rice, stew and bread, stew and hardtack—he knew no other way to prepare meat. And because I knew nothing about cooking, we lived on stewed meats until I was as heartily sick of them as I was of the chef.

Not forgetting, Keanu looked in the grass for the knife. "I have it," I soothed him. "It's safe. I'll carry it for you. You carry the chickens."

"O.K." He lifted the bag from the ground. "No cut you'self."

With a stifled protest from the chickens to start us, we set off on our way homeward. In single file, like a band of foraging Indians, we walked along the narrow trail, our footfalls muffled in the thick grass.

At Damien's house, as we stopped to bid him good night, we heard the singing, of voices rising in unaffected tranquil loveliness, chanting a mournful hymn. Hungry for music, I stopped to listen, turning my head the better to hear. It came from the yard in front of the little church.

My ear picked out the instruments attending the voices in a wistful accompaniment: two violins, a flute, and a bass viol. What an unbelievable grouping! But the 'sweetness of their concert had a haunting ethereal beauty, and in the dusk it was easy to understand why every passer-by must stop to listen to the poignant blending of voices and strings, with the flute hovering like the ghost of life above the rise and fall of the melody. It was a moment too beautiful to be missed—and yet too sad to be borne. How can they sing like this here? How can they hear such music without drowning in their tears?

"The singing societies are having their practice," Damien said softly when the song came to its end. "Will you stay and listen? I fix us some tea."

"No. No, thank you, Father." For once I was not rude to him. "I think we'd better be getting home. With the chickens." I remembered them in time, but it was myself whom I was protecting. "Some other evening, perhaps, I would like to come and listen. But not now, not now." Even as I put him off I wondered if I could ever return to hear more of the unearthly music.

"Good. You come back when you are ready. You and Keanu come. The music is here every Friday evening, when the weather is nice, like today."

"Thank you. We shall. Good night, Father."

"Good night, my sons. God be with you."

As Keanu and I went along the path behind the church the musicians took up their playing, in a short instrumental introduction of piercing unhurried loveliness. As we crossed the road by the Infirmary the voices joined in the song. But by the time we reached the Doctor's House, the distance, and the soft stir of the evening's breeze in the trees, succeeded in drowning out the sounds of the music, and I was no longer a prey to its effect.

13

AN UNEXPECTED RESPITE for me came early in December when
—as it usually does, unannounced and unpreparing—the Board of
Health sent up a Government Physician for as long as he could
bear to stay at the Settlement. He was Doctor Anton Pietsch, a
young Swiss physician just arrived from his homeland, eager to
serve the vanishing *kanakas*. The best the Board of Health could
do for him was to consign him to the hellhole of Molokai.

The first I knew of his coming was when he appeared on our
doorstep, in tow of Father Damien. He wore the wet and dirty
clothes of one who has been landed on the beach of Kalawao,
and the green skin and haunted eyes of one who has just run the
gantlet of the lepers. Damien was in his laborer's clothes again,
and he seemed to have made no better impression upon Pietsch
than he did upon me.

As bumptious as ever, the priest called to me from the foot
of the stairs. "A visitor for you, Doctor. A Government Doctor,
who promises to stay with us for a while."

My immediate thought, when I saw Pietsch standing there,
was to curse him for an interloper, to swear at the Board of Health
for sending him to a place like Kalawao. But in the next instant
the tantalizing hope was born: *If he stays, I can get away!* This
second thought swept all else before it. I rushed to the porch, a
genuine smile upon my lips. "Welcome, Colleague, welcome! I'm
delighted to see you. We can certainly use you here."

The plump young man came diffidently into the shelter of the
veranda. Did I look so young and timid once, so bedraggled and
so sick? "How do you do, Doctor Newman," he offered me a
hand sticky with seaweed and sand. "I haff heardt . . ." He sighed,
swallowing hard. "And I am gladt to be here—at last." With the
formalities ended, he sped down the stairs and was sick in the
shrubbery.

Damien regarded him sorrowfully. "Poor boy. He is almost too

young to go away from home. You will take care of him, please?
I must be on my way." He tossed Pietsch's bags upon the veranda
and, after a compassionate pat upon the back of the wretched
newcomer, hurried down the path. I measured the height of the
sun above the horizon, found the *Mokolii* floating upon the glassy
sea. He would be going to prepare for Mass. How many times had
this scene been enacted, how many more times would it happen,
before no more lepers would be exiled upon this dismal shore?

Keanu was already carrying Pietsch's bags into the house. The
novice, startlingly pale behind the black brush of his mustache,
took to his bed for the rest of the day, groaning at our mention
of breakfast. But by evening, steady again in stomach and in gait,
he was ready to join us at supper. The beef stew he ate with gusto,
but the *poi* he declined, despite our urging that it was newly arrived, difficult to get, and would soon disappear. Politely he murmured that he was not yet accustomed to *poi*. As knowing as a
sophister, I reached for his bowl and put it before Keanu. He
could never get enough of the stuff.

Within a week the priest and I had introduced Doctor Pietsch
to his duties at Kalawao, and I felt that I could run off for a while
to Honolulu without endangering the progress of my experiment
with Keanu.

It was not Honolulu I needed, although I was eager to see how
my experimental animals were getting along, and the cultures I
had put up before I left for Kalawao. It was escape from Molokai
that I must have, and from the boredom of life with Keanu. At
first, it is true, Pietsch helped a little to while away the evening
hours. But I soon picked him clean of his ideas and his news,
and then we settled into our dull routine again, three of us now,
sitting and staring at each other. Yet in some ways Pietsch was
more fortunate than I. Being essentially a dull man, he did not
mind the unending dullness of Molokai; and being a Catholic he
got on so famously with Father Damien that he could find company and solace with the priest in a way which was denied to me.
The two of them were fit company for each other, but I wanted
no part of them together and very little from either of them alone.

One last session with Keanu, during which he assured me that
he had no more desire in December to contract the leprosy than
he had in September; one last conversation with Pietsch, during

which I instructed him anew in the rules of Keanu's segregation, and I was ready to leave the Settlement.

In the cool of a December evening I managed to do what most of the inhabitants of the grim place are forever denied: I stepped into the *Mokolii's* rowboat, waiting at the shore of the quieted sea. I was the only passenger, my uniform was my passport. Without a backward glance at the accursed island I went immediately to my cabin. For the first time since the beginning of my experiment upon Keanu, I slept the whole night through. I did not know when we left the bay of Kalawao, or when we arrived in the harbor of Honolulu.

The new year was only two days old when I received an official communication, complete with sealing wax and seals, plastered with a lot of cheap postage stamps displaying the inky visages of a batch of savage kings. Tearing the envelope apart, I tossed it into the rubbish, while I sat down to read the document it brought to me:

OFFICE OF THE BOARD OF HEALTH,
KAPUAIWA, HONOLULU, H. I.,
January 1, 1885

ARNOLD NEWMAN, M.D.
SIR:

By instruction of His Excellency Mr. Gibson, the President of the Board of Health, I have the honor to request at your earliest convenience your report as to the course of investigations carried on by you with regard to leprosy during the interval since your arrival in the Kingdom of Hawaii, November, 1883, and December 31 of the year just ended.

It is reasonably considered that after the year you have spent on these Islands in the service of the Board of Health with liberal endowment, combined with your high recommendation to the Board as an honorable scientist and close and faithful student, and the facilities and opportunities it has placed at your disposal for experiment and observation, you have been enabled to acquire knowledge and information in regard to leprosy, of great value and importance to the Health Authorities of the Kingdom, and to all interested in the study of the disease. The impression is therefore felt that it is within your power to present a report of value and benefit to those engaged in battling with the disease abroad; creditable to this State and honorable to your talent and position as the Government's Special Medical Representative.

Having outlined the views of His Excellency the President for
your consideration,
I have the honor to be, Sir, your most obedient servant,
S. M. HARRISON,
Secretary, Board of Health

The secretarial hand of Harrison's amanuensis was so neat and
flowing and mesmerizing that at first I did not detect beyond it
the Machiavellian hand of Gibson. But on second reading the
unmitigated insolence of the letter, and of its instigator, began
to sting me. The tone of it was offensive enough. But the claims
it made were insane. *Liberal endowment,* indeed! The hundred
and fifty Hawaiian dollars I was receiving for each month of my
servitude might be liberal in Hawaii, but they were not a sixth
of the sum I would be receiving in Berlin if I were following my
profession there. *The facilities and opportunities it has placed at
your disposal*—Damn their eyes! When I thought of the money
I spent out of my own pocket! And the blandness with which
Gibson took credit for providing me with all of the Kingdom's
lepers for study—*Was zum Henker!* The man was mad—crazier
than any *pupule* thing that Damien could conceive of!

I could see him, lolling in his office of the moment, one lean
hand fondling the shark's tooth he wore upon his watch chain,
grandly discoursing to the world upon the enlightened policy of
his regime: "Leading the world, ladies and gentlemen, in the
sums of public and private monies it expends upon its unfortunate
brethren smitten with the leprosy, leading the world, I reiterate,
in the facilities and opportunities it has placed at the disposal of
Science for the study—nay, the conquest—of this most dread, this
most fell, this most fearsome of afflictions." Turning his head, to
show the caprine profile, he would go on to tell them (oh, the
picture was so vivid!) how he had persuaded "several healthy
convicts from the prisons of His Majesty's Government to volunteer their bodies, their very lives, to the service of this Great
Cause," how he had "petitioned His Majesty the King graciously
to permit these convicts to make their Noble Sacrifice . . ." Oh,
if I knew Gibson, he would make a fine story, to his credit, out
of my fight to gain Keanu; and I knew him well enough to be
sure that neither Keanu nor I would ever be named in the account. Walter Murray Gibson, unaided, single-handed, stalwart,
alert, relentless, would be waging the war against leprosy. *Verdammt, verdammt noch einmal!*

But the portion of his letter which really infuriated me was the sentence wherein he revealed his greed for the results of my work, which he could then proclaim as his own, "creditable to this State," to "those engaged in battling with this disease abroad."

"Hah! And to the greater credit of Walter Murray Gibson!" I screeched at the offending sheet of paper, cursing it, beating it, in my rage at the black fiend who wanted now to take my work for his own. "I'll be damned if I let you have my results! I'll be damned if you ever so much as see the notebooks with my data! I'll write you a report, by Heaven. One that will tell you absolutely nothing. A report such as you've never seen. I'll fill it with words, with fine Gibsonian frothings and foamings. It will have tables and charts and protocols. It will give you figures and statistics which any fool can find in the reports of your stupid Board of Health. It will tell quaint stories about your *kanaka* lepers, and naive descriptions about the most simple of bacteriological tests. Words, words, words! I'll fill it with so many fine useless words that it will make you the laughingstock of every scientist who reads it over your name, you thief, you scoundrel, you—"

Gleeful with my plans for the beautiful hoax with which I should take my revenge, I dashed to my workbench and drew from it a writing tablet. "Nothing like the present," I announced to the listening rabbits, to the squeaking rats, "for getting a good report begun."

I began, going directly to the source of all my troubles in one breath and reaching past him with the next. Hah! This will show them what he's trying to do to me—

To His EXCELLENCY W. M. GIBSON, PRESIDENT,
and Members of the Board of Health,
SIRS:

At the request of the President of the Board of Health, I have the honor to furnish you with a report as to the course of investigation carried on by me with regard to leprosy.

The general headings under which the work is being conducted may be classified thus. . . .

If theirs was the clumsy style those bureaucrats wished me to emulate, I could write it as thick as any of them.

Tongue in cheek, pen flowing smoothly, at a pace designed to keep us all busy for many a page of fools' talk, I was just beginning to capture Harrison's ponderous jargon when I was interrupted by a knock at the door. I turned in annoyance to drive the unwelcome visitor away. To my great surpise, it was Sister Marianne.

"I am sorry to disturb you, Doctor." The stern beautiful face, bound by its white coif, was composed in the lines of polite regret with which she confronted any situation not to her liking. Her voice was low, unhurried, supremely confident of its effect; and I believed her, at once, as the nuns of her company and the patients in her care obeyed unquestioningly her every word.

"It's quite all right, Sister. I'm not doing anything important."

The magnificent gray eyes with which she looked calmly out upon the vineyard of horrors wherein she labored were shielded against the sun by a long-fingered hand. The hand was rough with calluses, red with the attrition of the soap and water with which, for hours on end, she washed clothes, washed dishes, washed the loathsome bodies of lepers, even the dirty floors under their unheeding filthy feet. Eighteen thankless hours a day she labored in the lazar house, a living sacrifice to her demanding God; yet her face was serene, her eyes, her spirit, and, one knew instinctively, her body were as pure as the great white collar which fell from coif to waist, never showing a speck of dirt, a hint of sweat, despite the indignities to which she exposed it as she exposed herself to them.

"Doctor Trousseau has sent you a message by the telephone. He asks you to join him in his consulting rooms in Fort Street, as soon as you are able. There has been an accident, he says, and he needs your help."

"Oh, so. Did he say to whom?"

"No, Doctor. He did not."

"Thank you, Sister. I shall leave at once."

"A carriage is ordered for you, Doctor. It will be waiting for you at the main gate." With the briefest of nods, which held little of humility in it, she left. Tall in her black habit, the long veil flowing behind her, she walked down the wretched road, not seeing the mud and the ugliness, not seeing the lepers lounging on the narrow verandas. Her vision was fixed on Heaven, her love was for Christ—and all this misery around us, I thought enviously, is as if it does not exist. The knotted cord around her waist had no meaning for me then.

I went back into the cluttered hut, the report to Gibson forgotten. Swiftly I gathered up my things: tunic, topi, instruments in their leather bag, although I did not expect to need them.

All the way, as the cab dashed through the dirty streets along the water front, I wondered why Doctor Trousseau should summon me. Who could this mysterious patient be? I was flattered at being called, for Trousseau was one of the few physicians in Honolulu whom I considered competent in the practice of his profession. When, twenty minutes later, in clouds of dust and amid a rearing of neighing horses and the shouting of street boys, we drew up before Doctor Trousseau's elegant rooms in the heart of Honolulu, I still did not know what to expect.

He himself met me at the curb, as pallid as the panes of frosted glass in the doorway to his house. "Come in, come in," he took me by the arm and guided me into the passageway. "I am grateful you come so quickly." His long sallow countenance showed his worry, despite the Mephistophelian Imperial he wore even now, even in this remote Pacific backwater, so long after the defeat of Napoleon the Devious. Usually he had a Frenchman's jollity to share with his company, but now he shook his head while he guided me into a parlor just inside the door. "Tch, tch. This I do not like so very well." Taking my hat and bag, he flung them on a low table. "These you will not need. But come in and see it for yourself."

More mystified than ever, I followed him into the passageway. At the far end, in the rear of the house, he drew aside a heavy tapestry hanging and ushered me into his consultation room.

It was flooded with sunlight pouring in from a tall window opposite the entrance. Standing at the window, looking out into the garden court beyond the glass, like a prisoner gazing with longing at the world beyond the bars of his cell, stood a man, a stocky broad-shouldered man dressed in black.

"Father Damien!" Before I could restrain it the cry was out. And so was the fatuous question: "What brings you here?" Turning to Doctor Trousseau I said in bewilderment, "I thought there was an accident?" The priest smiled a vague welcome at me, as a blind man would smile at the sound of voices.

"But yes, there is an accident," said Doctor Trousseau. "Come closer to the light, if you please." He pushed a chair toward the window. "Father, do you mind?"

The priest seated himself, looking up at us standing before him.

Wide with questioning his eyes were, and with some other emotion. Was it pain, was it fright, was it awe, or ecstasy? I could not
be sure, as I looked down in amazement at him, so familiar and
yet so changed.

He was clean, of course, and freshly shaven, and not nearly
so tanned by the sun. His clothes were new, and neat and clean.
But the changes lay deeper in him than in these superficialities:
he was thinner, as if he had been ill for a long time—much longer
than the three weeks since last I had seen him—and there were
great circles under his eyes, as if he had not slept for many
nights. But the greatest change of all lay in his terrible quietness.
Where before he was the incarnation of energy, ready to burst
forth in noise and activity of some sort at any time, now he sat
in the most complete stillness I have ever seen a person display.
He was stilled, as though he sat in an immense quietness, waiting, waiting, for a voice to rouse him from his spell.

"*Cher Père—s'il vous plaît?*" Doctor Trousseau touched the
priest's arm. Obediently, Damien took the shoe from his left foot,
placed it neatly beside the chair. Then the coarse black woolen
stocking was removed, with its limp garter. The pale naked foot
was ugly, as all feet are ugly, the toes disfigured and cramped by
shoes, the skin and nails yellowed with the stains of dirt and sweat
and age. It was not at all like Keanu's heroic foot, with its splayed
toes, its leathery sole, its tracery of cracked skin stained with mud
and the juices of bruised grass. There was something indecent
about our prying into the private person of the priest, demanding
to see his unclothed foot, his very human foot, which made him
nothing more than another man and robbed him thereby of his
priestliness. Why did I not feel this way about Keanu's exposed
feet? I wondered, until with a shock I realized that for the first
time in his entire adult life another person was seeing the naked
foot of Father Damien.

Unwillingly I looked at it, with a physician's eye, but I could
see nothing wrong with it.

"Please, Father. Now the leg of the trousers," Doctor Trousseau
said.

The priest, still gazing up at us, began to draw up the black
cloth of his trousers, uncovering the swelling bulge of the calf,
the pelage of curling black hair. There was no surprise here: it
was a normal leg, a comely leg by masculine standards. More
confused than ever, I turned to Doctor Trousseau.

"Doctor Newman, please to look closely at the inner aspect of the leg. Perhaps from this side, you have a better view."

Warned now, I peered closer. Down the lower portion of the inner surface of the leg, under the black hair, a streak of reddened swollen flesh showed. Emerging from the hairy roughness of the leg, it glowed livid and hurtful upon the smooth skin of the instep, before it disappeared under the arch of the foot. Already the tissue fluids were collecting to form a series of blisters. "Why, it's a burn!" I straightened up in relief. "This is not very serious—"

"Precisely, a burn. From hot water, Father Damien tells me. This morning, while he prepares himself to shave, he tips a little bit too soon the kettle of boiling water. Some of the water spills— spills not into the bowl, but upon his leg."

"But what is so alarming about a burn?" I was almost exasperated with his melodrama.

"Only this, cher collègue: that while the boiling water falls upon the foot of Father Damien, while it is burning the flesh of his leg, the good Father—holding the kettle of boiling water still in his right hand, so—sees where the steaming water falls upon the floor, upon his shoe, upon the flesh of his leg, he does not feel the pain of the burning."

"Oh, no!" There was sorrow in my denial, not refusal to believe. There was pity for the man, the human man to whom the foot and the leg were attached, of whom they should have been a pained and paining part, and I did not want to think of him as having fallen prey at last to the insidious foe which now would eat him away, gnaw his bones from his flesh, his body from his spirit, and leave him festering, rotting, stinking, a victim of his sacrifice, like all of the other lepers for whose sake he had offered himself. I looked down upon him with pity—and with a rising rush of anger, for I could not be surprised that his foolish careless behavior should have ended at last in this.

"Doctor, please." He raised his hands in pleading. "Help me— help me to know."

"Father does not trust only me, in my diagnosis. He asks that I send for you—because you know so much about the leprosy. If you say he has the Kalawao sickness, then he will believe the both of us." My colleague was closer to tears than to reproach.

"Then let us examine him," I said, dreading the truth even more than he.

For the next hour we questioned the poor man, prodded,

thumped, and pawed at him, examining him in his body, stripped naked for our search, and in his history, recounted innocently and in all of its innocence for our judging ears. We could see no evidence of the leprosy, or indeed of any other disease, in any part of his body other than his left leg. There were no macules, ulcers, incipient lepromata, to be detected anywhere. We found nothing except for a few swollen nodes in the left groin. However, he did have a history of severe pains in the feet, especially in the left one, since 1881, and of sciatic nerve trouble all along the left leg, since 1882. But, suddenly, all of these afflictions had disappeared, all at once, about three weeks ago, just before he came to Honolulu. He attributed the trouble, as so many Hawaiians attribute all of their ailments, to rheumatism caused by the vaccination for smallpox he received in 1881. "The pains I could bear," he said, "because I understand them. But• when they stopped—this I could not understand."

The most certain evidence for our diagnosis came from our application of the new method of galvanopuncture with the electrical machine Doctor Trousseau had imported from London only a few months before. Using a current of electricity passing through a platinum needle as the detector, I pushed the slender probe deep into the flesh of the left foot. He felt no pain, no sensation, not even the thrust of the needle. Twice more I pressed the charged needle, connected by a fine wire to the galvanic battery, into the muscles of the leg, hoping for some sign of response, some quiver answering the stimulus of the electricity. Each time, as I saw the white flesh of Damien yield beneath the point of the needle, I thought of the brown satin skin of Keanu's arm. But there was no pain, no encouraging response to the current. The only fruit of my probing was a drop of blood, oozing slowly, bright and red, like an inflamed tear, from each of the wounds I inflicted upon him.

We were forced to conclude that the peroneal nerve and its branches were dead.

And, remembering the life he led, and—remembering the pipe shared among his brethren, the common *poi*-bowl, the charity of their fetid breaths, the benison of their foul sores; remembering all these, how could we doubt it?—the inevitability of his contagion, we were forced to tell him at last that he was probably a leper.

Clothed by then, sitting quietly in his chair, he looked up at us standing over him, while gently I told him our verdict.

We saw the look of expectancy give way to one of absolute joy. The softness of wonder changed to the strength of certainty. There was peace where once there was doubt, and before our eyes the victim became the victor, and the spirit emerged triumphant over the dying flesh. With great and unabashed joy he rose from the chair, clasping his hands in that strange gesture of his. "God's will is done. Now I am one of them. O God! O God, I thank thee!"

Now he looked down at us. "I thank you, my good friends. You make me very happy. I am content." The tears, following upon his happiness, began to spill down his cheeks. Removing his spectacles, he put them into one of the pockets of his frock coat. Trying not to weep, expressing over and over again his happiness and his relief, he scarcely knew what he said. Once he started to shake our hands, then withdrew his hand with a sound half sob, half laugh. "But I forget: I must not do this any more, should I?" As though, after our examination of him, his concern now would make any difference to us.

I was relieved, for his sake as well as my own, when he turned to the window. He stood before the great arch of light, wiping his eyes with the backs of his hands, looking out upon the green garden, the shade trees, the potted plants, all of the beauty shut out from the room by the wooden walls and the panes of glass. "I must go home now, where I belong. I must go home to Kalaupapa, to the most beautiful place on earth."

His last words to us came almost as an afterthought. "Please —for my sake, for my people's sake—please do not tell anyone here that I am"—even for him the cruel words came haltingly to his tongue—"that I am a leper. Let me tell them, please, when the time comes. Let me tell my people, in my own way."

And we, men of science, bewildered by this confusion of values, wherein a man rejoiced in being a leper and had no need for our solace—we could only pledge our agreement in silence, and watch him go away, in silence and alone.

14

I caught up with him in front of the Catholic Cathedral on Fort Street. Breathless with my chasing after him for those two busy blocks between Doctor Trousseau's office and the church, I hailed him as he was about to enter the narrow door of his Popish refuge.

"Father. We—Doctor Trousseau and I—we'd like very much to begin your treatment as soon as possible. At Kakaako. There is a chance, perhaps—"

He stopped me with an uplifted hand. "My place is there, with my people. Why should I stay here, apart from them?"

"There are medicines here. And physicians other than ourselves, if you don't want us."

"With what would you treat me? Have you any cure for the leprosy, here in Honolulu?"

I was forced to acknowledge that there was nothing. Not even the chaulmoogra nuts or the gurjun balsam of the distant Indies, not all of the patent medicines of America or the mercurials of Europe.

"It is as I have said. This disease, like all diseases and all the troubles of man, is a gift from God. It is God's way of testing a man, to reward him maybe, or to punish him. I do not fear this disease, Doctor, and I do not fear his will. I put myself in his care, and all will be well with me."

"How can you say this, you who have seen the lepers dying in agony and in terror from their awful disease? How can you be so unaware of the sufferings of others, who do not believe as you do?"

"I am not unaware of them. Surely you must know this? But also, I feel in my heart that their sufferings would be less if their love of God is greater. If they are less angry with him for making lepers of them, and more grateful to him for this chance to show their love for him—do you not see?—then they have no time, no need, to fear his testing."

I could not argue with him in the very street, on the threshold of his fortress-church. Lurking somewhere in the rear of the crouching edifice was the monastery or seminary or whatever it was, the nest in which he stayed with his fellow priests. I half expected a contingent of them to come running out in alarm, to snatch him away from my freethinker's influence. "You're impossible!" I growled. "I have no patience with such arguments."

"No, and this is your trouble. You fight against them too hard. And because you do not wish to understand them, you deny that these things exist. It is a common fault of educated men. In your belief in the strengths of the mind, my son, you forget how there are also strengths of the spirit." He laid his hand on my arm. "I pray for you often, that someday you may know them, these strengths of the spirit. Before it is too late. Perhaps it would be good if you learn to pray, too?"

"Pray!" I flung off his hand. "I have no time to pray! I am busy *doing* things, to improve the world, while you and your kind are on your knees, accepting it the way it is."

Instead of being angry with me, he turned his priestly smile upon me, the sort of infuriating smile in which patience and long-suffering and tolerance for the tantrums of a *Struwwelpeter* were mixed with a parent's hope that someday, perhaps, the difficult child would attain a wisdom agreeable to the parent's own.

He was smart enough to foresee my anger. With a twinkle in his eye (I could not have sworn that he was not teasing me), he lifted his hand in an unhurried blessing. "Then I go now to pray for us both. I know it will be good for me. Whether it is good for you, we see in time."

He left me, disappearing into the darkness of the church. Remote in the gloom, the unwavering flames of many candles upon the altar were like the eyes of cats, spying on us. From the doorway, as the door closed behind him, came the smell of stale incense, of fading flowers, the scent of death.

Only after he was gone did I remember that I wanted to ask him about Keanu.

In mid-January Doctor Pietsch's letter came. Writing in German, he gave me the report on Keanu. "There is no change in the site of the implantation. It remains the same as when you saw it last. But there is a change in Keanu. He acts very strange. I think this segregation is being more than he can bear. Perhaps he misses you? I wish that he has more to do, to occupy himself. If only he could read! I have tried to teach him, but he is not interested to learn. Besides, I am not good as a teacher of this difficult English tongue, needing to learn it for myself . . ."

And so it went, just as I might have predicted it. I laughed at poor dull Pietsch, struggling to light the flame of an intellect in the animal Keanu, just as I had tried to do before him. Only— I checked myself in my comparison, so unfair to myself—at least I had sense enough to stop my efforts long before the second month of my imprisonment with the lout. I drew grim amusement from my picture of the two of them, sitting night after night in their mutes' house, staring at each other, saying nothing because there was nothing more to say—until, finally, torpid with supper imposed upon boredom, they staggered off to sleep in their dank rooms, where the smell of mold was never lost, and the drip of rain was the only sound to break the stillness of the night. "And how well are you sleeping, Herr Doktor Pietsch?" I asked the evocative letter, "with a pet murderer in the house?"

He did give me one further bit of information, however: "Father Damien is returned from his visit to the Bishop in Honolulu. He looks very well, after his change of surroundings, even for so short a time. Sometimes he looks as if he is about to burst with a secret happiness. I wish that he could give some of this happiness to others here, most of all to Keanu."

Tossing the foolish letter upon my workbench, I went back to my research. One of my rabbits was dead, more than four months after I had injected it with blood taken from a leper in the earliest stages of the disease. I was eager to see if I could determine, by examination of the rabbit's viscera, why it should die. Hopefully, happily, I went back to my work, confident that I would find that the leprosy bacilli were the cause of its death.

Three weeks later another note came from Pietsch. It made me sit up in alarm. "Keanu is sick. He keeps to his bed much of the time, he does not eat. There is, however, no sign of leprous involvement, and the site of the inoculation remains unchanged."

Damn the unco-operative beast! I swore. If he's going to get sick, why can't he get sick with the leprosy? But, whether or not it was leprosy, I could not run the risk of his dying on me, without my being there, to study him before his death, and to perform an examination upon his viscera when he died. My dead rabbit had told me nothing, patiently as I had examined him, organ by organ, section by section, slide by slide. In gross and in microscopic examination, he had told me absolutely nothing about leprosy.

But for Keanu I held higher hopes. Or, rather, of Keanu I made greater demands. Because leprosy is a disease of humans, not of animals, I expected the organs and tissues of Keanu to tell me more than did those of my dead rabbit and my thriving guinea pigs. I had too much time and effort invested in Keanu to give him up easily.

Within two days after Pietsch's message alerted me I was back at Kalawao. Unwilling to wait for the *Mokolii*, I went by the *Kilauea*, one of the inter-island vessels reserved for clean passengers. But the landing at Kalawao was made in the same manner, whether one traveled with lepers or without them; and soon after dawn on the second day I found myself once more on that dreadful beach, where the surf rolled and crashed and the rocks groaned in their eternal torment. Wet to my knees, cold and hungry, I was left there alone, with the bags of mail and assorted bundles of freight for the Settlement and my baskets of clothes and boxes of food dumped in a pile at my feet.

No one was on the beach to meet me, because the *Kilauea* was not expected to stop. But I knew what the custom was and, feeling almost like a wanderer come home to his native strand, I sat upon the cargo until the lepers came to carry it away. Within half an hour a string of pack horses, accompanied by a couple of Kalawao's joyless toilers, reached me. This time I rode to the Hospital on a pack horse.

I was cleaning the village mud from my boots on the stone scraper at the Doctor's House. The pounding of heavy feet upon the wooden floors made me feel all the more the voyager being welcomed home. My cheerful *aloha* for Keanu was stifled when, even before he reached the porch, he started to shout. "Go 'way, damn you, go 'way. Nobody come heah! Go 'way!" As I looked up in amazement he burst through the door, features twisted in anger, hand raised to strike, still shouting.

When he saw me he stopped in surprise. The hand fell, he ceased his brutal clamor. "Ah. *You!*" he sneered. His eyes were bloodshot and full of meanness, his clothes were wrinkled and disheveled, as though he had slept in them for days. He staggered toward the veranda rail, bringing with him the smell of liquor and of sweat. He was drunk.

"Why you come back?"

"I—I heard your were sick, Keanu. I came back to take care of you."

He glared down at me with hatred, while I tried to look as if I meant what I said. But even to my ears the explanation seemed false, my voice sounded like a whine.

"Boolsheet!" He spat into the path at my feet. With eyes narrowed, he looked down at me for a long moment, the longest moment I have ever known. Meekly I stood there, suffering his scorn, ready to endure almost anything for the sake of the evidence his body held for me and my work.

"You goddam *haole*. You come look if I get the *ma'i Pake*.— You no care about me, you goddam bloody *haole*. You oney care fo you damn' tes'—"

"Keanu, that's not—"

"Well, I going fool you, you heah? I no going get da *lepera* fo you! I going stay clean—fo two moah mont's, and den—" He raised his head, looking beyond me, beyond the mountains and the sea. "—and den I going get out of heah, out of dis damn' place."

He thrust his arm before my face. "But eef I get da *ma'i Pake*, eef I get 'im from you—Ahh!—" He broke off, raised his arm to strike me. As I shrank before the expected blow he turned and went into the house, slamming the door after him.

Trembling, I sat upon the steps, holding my head on my folded arms. What did he mean? Was it the self-pity of a drunken peasant, expressing himself in the only way in which he could declare his rebellion against a bargain he did not like? Or was it the promise of a murderer?

For a long time I sat there, wondering whether I should go away or dare to enter the morbid house. At last, driven by hunger and by my determination not to let him escape me, I went in.

The parlor, always neat and orderly under my regimen, was a littered mess. The chairs were disarranged, books and newspapers were scattered over the floor, swept there by the furious hand of illiterate Keanu. On the floor, on the table, on the chairs, were empty tins, so bare of food that not even ants could find anything in them to carry away. A scrawny cat lying asleep in a spot of sunlight gave me my clue. I hate cats. Of all animals for the maudlin fool to bring home for a pet, a cat was the worst. Now we would be plagued with fleas.

There was no sound or sign of Pietsch. Nor was there any evidence of Keanu until I looked into his room and found him sprawled upon his bed, fast asleep. "Pig! Drunken pig!" I muttered, trying to ease the shock of finding him there, in that position: he looked too much like a man spread-eagled for punishment, like an animal tied upon a dissection board.

Pietsch's room was empty, even of his clothes. Without much interest, I wondered where in this godforsaken place he could have fled.

My bedroom, at the end of the dark hallway, was as cheerless as ever. Only the smell of mold and of damp dust greeted me home.

In the kitchen I found Keanu's source of liquor. A large wooden barrel, of the kind in which *poi* is shipped to Kalawao, stood on the floor at one end of the counter. Its upper end was covered with a piece of ditry toweling, around which a cloud of fruit flies hovered. Brushing them aside, I lifted the cloth and peered into the barrel, reeking with the results of zymotic activity. A primitive kind of beer, made from Heaven only knew what ingredients.

Taking up a small cooking pot, I bailed out the contents of the barrel, pouring them down the drain. When the barrel was empty, I rolled it to the kitchen door and kicked it down the stairs into the yard. The vegetable garden was a monument to neglect: weeds grew thick in the beds where once beans and maize were sown; and the lacework veins of a few discolored leaves showed where the grasshoppers were devouring the cabbage heads Keanu was so fondly hoping to harvest when I left for Honolulu. The chickens, however, were still in their pen, although its walls sagged in a dozen directions.

I went back into the house and pounced upon the sleeping cat. By the scruff of its neck I carried it, screeching and clawing, to the back door and threw it toward the forest. It landed with a hiss and, in a single leap, disappeared into the brush.

I was just finishing a breakfast of weak tea and sea biscuits when the priest came to the front veranda. His considerate knock did not waken Keanu, but it brought me forth almost as furiously as my arrival had drawn Keanu. A wedge of black against the green shrubbery, he was fresh from Mass, the biretta still upon his head. "I heard you are back," he began quietly. "I am glad. Keanu needs you. He thinks you have abandoned him."

I stared at him, too tired and confused to speak. He had not changed visibly. The unshaven cheeks, with their midweek fuzz, were perhaps a little thinner, otherwise he looked the same.

"How is the boy? I hear he is sick."

"He is drunk. Doesn't Pietsch know the difference between drunkenness and disease?"

"Poor Anton! He knows. He has a terrible time with Keanu. But Keanu was sick, too. This drunkenness—this came more lately, Doctor Pietsch could not stand it any more. There is no place here in Kalawao for him, so now he lives in Kalaupapa."

A whole mile away—about as far away as one can go in this damned prison. But it was far enough to give him his freedom from the violence of Keanu. He was lucky. Already, within an hour of my return, I was asking once again how I was going to stand captivity with my prize beast. Appreciating for the first time the aptness of the imagery, I remembered the ancient mariner and the albatross hung around his neck.

"Good riddance." I gave Damien acid in return for his sugar. Pietsch, damn him, was right about the priest: he was quieter, gentler, than he used to be. I wasn't sure that I was going to like the new man any better than I liked the bumptious old one. "He was even duller than Keanu. I don't blame Keanu for taking to drink."

"In a place like this, it is not good to live alone. I have said this to you before. Keanu is sick in his mind, as in his body. That is why he drinks swipes. Man was not made to live alone, you know!"

The stock phrase, lifted from his supply of ready quotations, irritated me even more. "He'll work, then, by God!" I said, enjoying his distress at my deliberate blasphemy. "He'll work until he's too tired to do anything but eat and sleep. All play and no work makes Keanu a very bored boy. There's another old saw for you. But as long as I am here, watching him, he'll not even speak to anyone in this Settlement except myself. The experiment I've begun upon him has a chance to succeed, and I'm going to give it every chance to do so—even if I have to spend my every waking moment guarding him. Even if I have to chain him to this house."

"You are cruel, Doctor. And there is a terrible price to pay for cruelty."

"I must be cruel because cruelty seems to be the only way. If Keanu were reasonable, as he was when we first came here, then I'd not need to be cruel."

"But Keanu is lonely, and this is a disease not cured by reasonableness. Keanu is—"

"Then I will teach him the uses of reason: I'll wake his mind, unused in that head of his, and show him the comforts of reason."

"He has a mind, and a good one. He is not as stupid as you think. But he has also a soul, and this part of him you do not consider."

"A soul! Such nonsense! It is the same thing as reason, except a sicklier form, a coddled cosseted favored form, indulged by poets and priests, but shaped and disciplined into a *mind* by men of strong will. Reason is the soul sharpened, roused out of its laziness, and put to work."

"I do not understand all of your English words: they are too fancy for me. But I understand the sound of your voice, and it makes my soul sad. There is no charity in it for Keanu, or for any man. Not even for yourself. You frighten me. Do you know why? Because you are the first man I know who tries to kill his own soul."

"I am flattered. This is a distinction I hope to deserve." How easily I laughed off the diagnosis. How readily, in my pride, I ignored the fact that Damien the Priest was a physician to souls, just as I, the Man of Science, was a physician to bodies. In my pride I jeered at him, and I did not lay his words unto my soul because I was confident that, as a man of reason, I had nothing so weak, so unmanageable, so hungry for love, as a soul.

"But do not condemn me," I went on sarcastically, "if I favor reason more than I do the soul, if I prefer to use my mind rather than my heart." But the sarcasm was too sour even for my mouth, and I found it more disturbing to me than to him. It did no justice to my belief, to all the things I wanted to say to him in our meeting in front of the Roman Cathedral in Honolulu. Often enough he made me listen to his philosophy. Now let him listen for a change to mine.

Soberly I gave him the credo by which I ruled my life. "I have learned that a systematic, reasoning mind is the greatest force the world possesses. With it a man can discover things unknown before him, with it a man can devise things undreamed of before his time. With his reason a man can conquer time and space and ignorance, can overcome obstacles in his path that would make unreasoning men sit down by the wayside and weep. I have seen it happen with men I admire." And I told him of my Master, Doktor Koch, of the one great Frenchman, Louis Pasteur, who, by their reason, have brought mankind out of the darkness of superstition into the clear light of knowledge about contagious diseases and their causes. "They did all this in just a few years, and I think their achievements are tremendous. I have patterned myself after them. I am proud to be one of their disciples. To me, as to them, reason is but another name for Science: and in Science, I think, lies the hope of the world."

"Again you use too many words I do not understand. But I wonder if your Doktor Koch, or your M'sieu Pasteur, agrees with you that a man who has only reason for his guide is a happy man. Are they not men who also know the meaning of love? Who have room for love in their lives?"

"I don't know about them. But for me love, as you call it, sentiment, as I call it, is a burden. Love would get in my way."

"Ahh. I have guessed it. There is your trouble. But what does it profit you if you gain the whole world of reason, and yet lose your soul? What good is life, if you have not love?"

"If I have not love? Why, then, I am a free man, a reasoning man, unencumbered by the claims of love." I was happy with my defense. It defined me exactly, as I wanted to be, as I had determined I was going to be.

"If I have not love," he said slowly. "A man wiser than we are said something about this long ago. *Agapē* he called it, the love of a man for his fellow men. Today we call it charity. Such a mean name, for so great a gift as love." Closing his eyes, he crossed himself, and began to intone the ancient amazing words:

"If I speak with the tongues of men, and of angels, and have not charity, I am become as sounding brass, or a tinkling cymbal."

Across the years the words fell upon me, across the years since I first heard their counterpart, as, not understanding them or much else about my child's world, I sat with my father in chapel.

"And if I should have prophecy and should know all mysteries,

and all knowledge, and if I should have all faith, so that I could remove mountains, and have not charity, I am nothing. . . ."

I am nothing. . . . The words fell into my emptiness, cold and hollow. They were meant for me.

"Charity is patient, is kind; charity envieth not. . . ."

I am nothing . . .

"Beareth all things, believeth all things, hopeth all things, endureth all things. Charity never falleth away . . ."

It has fallen away from me, Damien, it has failed me! Where is my meed of love?

". . . whether prophecies shall be made void, or tongues shall cease, or knowledge shall be destroyed."

The words flamed in the air between us, threatening me with destruction. Ominous, they revealed my weakness; terrible, they prophesied my doom, if I were wrong.

"For we know in part, and we prophesy in part. But when that which is perfect is come, that which is in part shall be put away."

But how can I admit that I am wrong? How can I forswear everything I believe, and, recanting, deny my creed and go over to Damien's? In his faith I have no faith. All that he stands for I deny: his tight religion is the antithesis of my broad questioning. Yet he can stand here, durable as the Rock of Peter, content in his faith, and happy. While I—

He opened his eyes, not hiding them from me any more. They were not gentle now: bright and fierce, they sent their message into me:

"When I was a child, I spoke as a child, I understood as a child. But when I became a man, I put away the things of a child. We see now through a glass in a dark manner; but then face to face. Now I know in part; but then I shall know even as I am known."

How much do I know, I who think I know so much? Am I the prophet of a new time, speaking with the tongues of men and angels, breaking through the mold of mysticism and mortmain built up around us by this priest and his Church? Or am I but a fool, a fool of a man, who has not yet put away childish things, peering through a glass darkly, and lost on my way?

The inexorable voice stopped. The eyes behind it watched me, waiting for me to fall upon my knees. But I would not yield. Not to him. Not to any priest.

"Finish it, damn you, finish it!" I shouted. There was one

more thing to come, one more terrible tearing verse, remembered since the terrible time of my childhood. And I demanded to hear it, every hurting destroying inescapable word of it, every canting mealy-mouthed sickening unforgotten syllable of it.

Quietly he finished: *"And now there remain faith, hope, and charity, these three: but the greatest of these is charity."*

And if I have not love? The anguish of my lovelessness was torment, and a cry broke from me that was as the sounding of brass. "Go away! Leave me alone! Go your way, and let me go mine. If I have troubles, they are of my own making. If I have doubts, let me resolve them." In saying this much I said too much. He knew the weakness of my armor.

"Once before I warned you about the power of Jesus. It is he who puts these doubts in your soul. Listen to him, oh listen to his voice."

But I would not listen, to his voice or to any other. With a snarl of helplessness I fled into the house, swearing weakly as I stumbled into the dark parlor and along the darker passageway to my room. The words I summoned up to give me release were weak, futile things, which only made me the angrier with myself. I could not even swear like good resounding brass, I taunted myself, twisting the knife of my self-loathing in the wound which Damien had reopened in me. "Like unto a tinkling cymbal you are," I jeered at myself, "a cymbal signifying nothing—"

For a long time I lay on my bed, cursing, experimenting in cursing, enjoying my experimentation, in a paroxysm of release, cursing the cold nerveless hated man who was my father, cursing the unknown missing woman who died in giving me birth, cursing Damien, cursing Keanu, oh most especially cursing Gibson, the man who had brought all this evil down upon me.

As drunk with self-pity as Keanu was with his beer, I lay on my bed, until at last the crisis waned and, curled up like a child, I found my escape in sleep.

15

ONCE MORE the waiting began. This time it was like a season in purgatory, compared with an idyl long since enjoyed.

For Keanu was changed. Now he was savage and brutal and full of hate. He rarely spoke, and then only in a growl more bestial than his wordlessness. I very quickly gave up any hope of teaching him reasonableness and the uses of the intellect. Nor did I dare to mention the garden, or the sagging fence of the chicken run. He was beyond my reach, withdrawn behind the barrier of his hate for me.

All that he wanted from me was the food I brought for us, and then he prepared only enough of it to feed himself. I was forced to fix my own meals, but I did not protest. I ate little enough anyway. He slept most of the time, or went for long walks upon the cliffs by the edge of the sea. These walks were his only recreation. They kept him lean and strong. Once I tried to follow him, but I lost him among the rocks and the thick-leaved shrubs growing like battlements upon the land where it met its enemy, the sea. When I returned to the house I was exhausted, defeated by the heat of the day, by the fatigue of my body, drained of its strength by the sleepless nights which began again for me. After this single venture beyond the limits of my daily visit to the Infirmary, I did not go again into the village.

In our house of hate, I changed too. Sitting there on the veranda in the long afternoons and evenings, all alone, I found lots of time for thinking. I pondered all that I had learned, and questioned all that I needed to know, not only about the leprosy, but also about people, most of all about myself. The more I thought, the more lonely and frightened I became, until each bright day was like a blazing desert to be crossed, each dark night was a bottomless pit filled with terror, out of which I must be sure to climb by dawn if I wanted to preserve my sanity.

I tried to fix my thought and hope upon Luise. Despairingly I clung to the memory of her, to the promise of her waiting for me in remote Berlin. But she was too far away to be my salvation. When my mind proclaimed that she was my beloved, my heart jeered at the futility of the pretense. What does she know of love, it asked, and what have you had of love from her? And even worse was the knowledge, gained at last, that I felt no love for her.

The words of Damien were coming back to haunt me. "If you have not love?" they asked, whispering in my ear in a dozen different voices, asking their terrible question in such a way that I knew I must soon answer it, or go mad.

But his conquest of me came slowly, and I fought back hard, desperate to keep my pride. I resisted my humbling, and, perversely, even as I became more fearful of the vengeance that Damien and his Jesus were taking of me, I became more determined to resist them with all the force of my reason. My mind became the battlefield of our conflict, and Keanu's body became the prize of our contending.

After a time I did not let those voices go unanswered. When they came at me, out of the air, in the somnolence of the afternoons, in the pressing blackness of the night, I talked back to them, arguing with them, candidly, dispassionately, brilliantly arguing, fighting off their threat and claim upon my mind. Never did I yield to them.

As the weeks went on, my work suffered. I made no more examinations upon the specimens taken from some of the patients who came to the Infirmary. At the end of each morning I threw away the scraps of scabs and snippets of skin, the drops of bloody pus, stolen from them. I was purged even of my hate. The insulting report to Gibson lay ignored upon my desk, as forgotten as was Gibson himself. I was interested in one thing only, I waited for one thing only to happen.

While I waited February gave way to March, and still my prize eluded me.

Sunday was the only day of the week which meant anything to me: on the morning of the Sabbath I would examine Keanu for signs of the leprosy. Despite his hate for me, he never protested the indignity of the examination. He would strip himself of the faded blue shirt and the faded dungarees, and he would stand forth in his nakedness for me to inspect. He was like a sleek stallion, noble of proportion, beautiful to look upon as an example perfect of its kind; and, knowing the degree of his perfection, and being the animal that he was, he had nothing of the modesty of a man who is sensitive about his body's imperfections. I would think of poor Damien, shyly exposing his nerveless foot to our scrutiny, of the embarrassment with which he removed his somber clothing and came naked before his physicians for them to look upon him. I thought of myself, and of how I could compare with Keanu— and hurriedly I would turn my attention to the inspection of my splendid animal.

First I would look at the site of the inoculation. After this I would feel the lymph glands in the axillae, then those in his groin. While he turned beneath my scrutiny, I would peer at his skin, looking for the reddened macules, little craters of inflammation, or the rings of dying tissues, scattered like the coins of Midas, which are the harbingers of leprosy. At the last, because only then would I dare to risk the meeting of my eyes with his, I would look at his face, at the smooth forehead and high cheekbones, at the pink helices of the ears, at the flaring nostrils and the septum of his curved nose. But, always, in answer to my question: "Do you feel this?"—as I pricked certain areas of his skin with a pin—he would answer, "Yes"; or to: "Does this hurt?" —as I pressed upon his firm flesh with a testing finger—he would say, "No," a bold curl of triumph on his lips which told me I was a fool to expect any other answer from a man of his resolve.

But at last there came a day, early in March, when, with the flutter of excitement which comes with hope suddenly aroused, I thought I detected a subtle, a barely perceptible change in the site of the implantation. Innocent still it seemed, well healed in the smooth skin. The mound of the buried leproma still pushed up the flesh from its tomb. The fact that it had not been resorbed showed that the transplant was still alive—an achievement in which I could take considerable pride. Yet when, pressing it, I asked Keanu if it hurt, he answered, "No," not bothering to give it a glance. But I thought that around the margins of the area overlying the implanted tissue I could see an angry flush persisting long after I ceased to touch the place. Time after time, while I continued the inspection of the rest of his body, my eye returned to question that maddeningly uncertain taint of red.

I dismissed him with my usual comment, "Still the same." "*Maikai*," he answered, as he invariably did, picking up his clothes, and, proud and naked, stalked from the room.

Quickly I sped to my notebook, entrusting my secret to it in a hand tremulous and hurried, with a burst of exclamation points and question marks to make conspicuous this first sign of hope after the unchanging entries of all the weeks before.

From this time on, whenever Keanu was near me I could not keep my glance from straying to that tantalizing place on his arm.

About that time, too, I saw Caleb Forrest again, for the first time since the day of the inoculation. From my place in the Infirmary where I attended the patients who presented themselves to my tender care, I looked up to find him watching me. Elegant as ever in his fine clothes, an Englishman's cap set jauntily upon his head, he stood among the ragged folk of the Settlement like a young prince among his vassals. Sour as a green apple he looked, too, baleful as a lizard, with those basilisk eyes sending their disdain for me across half the room. Before I quite knew what I was doing, I lifted my hand in recognition and exchanged my mask of boredom for the most friendly of smiles.

He left the wretches clustered around Damien and came toward me, leading a horrifying creature by the stump of its hand. "Good morning, Doctor." He was as polite as ever, but steely hard beneath the courtesy. "You remember Akala?" With his free hand he indicated the swollen blighted blinded thing at his side. "Akala, you remember Doctor Newman?"

"Akala? Oh, yes, Akala. Good morning." I could hardly bring myself to look at her, and when, in a fit of schoolgirl coyness, the monstrous head began to bobble, the putrescent face endeavored to smirk—oh God! I had to look away.

"She's changed, hasn't she, Doctor?"

I stared down at him helplessly. What did he want of me? Was I to be his whipping boy, the only receiver of his wrath? "Yes," I acknowledged, not seeing her, not asking the question which really mattered. "Yes, she has." And so have you, Caleb, I might have said, so have you. The thickening of the skin upon his forehead, the hardening little accretions in his cheeks, the white scurf of dead skin upon his throat, before it was hidden below the wing collar with its silk tie—Caleb, Caleb! the days of thy beauty are ended, the days of thy life are numbered. In spite of myself I drew back from him.

"We are not pretty, are we, Doctor?" The mocking man would not relent. Beseeching him with my hands, my eyes, to end his

attrition, in Mercy's name to cease his warfare on me, I could find
no words with which to stem that flow of spitefulness.

"Doctor, you must overcome your dislike of lepers, loathsome
as we are." His loathing for me made me seem far more revolting
than all the lepers at Kalawao could ever be. "If you do not look
at us, how will you know if Keanu has become one of us?"

There it was, the cause and source of his hate, the reason why
he stood before me like an accusing archangel. Protest rose up in
me, bursting out in an uncontrollable cry. "Caleb, Caleb! Why do
you hate me so? What I have done to Keanu I have done for your
sake and for the sake of people yet unborn."

He put up his hand to stop me. Upon his fingers I saw for the
first time the open sores, ravening now beyond all healing. "You
mistake me, Doctor. I do not hate you. If I hate anyone, it is
—well, this is my business. But I do not hate you. I pity you."

"Pity? Me?"

"Aye, pity." His tone was kinder now, even his mouth was
softened from its usual cruelty. "Because you are—"

But I did not hear him. "Pity!" I pronounced the word with
disbelief. Pity from the living dead, who have nothing? For me,
who, if I did not have everything, had so much more than they?
It was a frightening revelation. It was as though I stood alone
upon the brink of Kalaupapa's cliffs, thousands of feet above the
Settlement, and looked down upon the lepers, small as ants, living
their appointed lives. They were the ones who lived content, with
no thought for me save compassion for one poised so far above
them that he must be pitied for being denied the comforts of his
kind. The abyss opened fearfully before me, and, dizzy with this
new perspective, I reached out for a saving hand.

"You are right. I am alone. And I am lonely." I was saying at
last what I wanted to say to him months ago, on the beach, the
day we landed. "I have no one to talk to: Keanu is as silent as a
stone. And man is not made to live alone, you know." I tried to
laugh, and my laugh ended in a croak. "But pity is something
new to me. It is much more novel a sentiment, if not much more
flattering a one, than hate. And of that I have plenty."

He frowned at my attempt at humor. "Don't you be offended
now," I said. "I do not want your hate." I was beginning to understand how such a proud fellow could be managed. "Look here. I
would like to talk with you someday, when you can spare the

time. I've a capital idea. Father Damien needs an assistant, to help him in this Infirmary work. I shall be leaving soon, I think, and he can't go on doing all of this work by himself. Why don't you come in and take my place?"

"But I know nothing of medicine."

"I'll teach you what you need to know. It's really very easy."

Uncertain for once, he looked at the roomful of lepers. Some of them were gathering about us, curious to hear our conversation, and I resented their being so near. Not only did I dislike their listening to my private thoughts. I was afraid that Caleb would find in them his excuse for rejecting my plan. But he had a general's mind. "You take me by surprise, Doctor," he said urbanely. "Permit me to think about it for a few days, before I give you my answer."

"But of course. Please do. But please remember, while you think about it, that you could hardly be of greater service to your fellow—to the people of the Settlement than by being a physician to them. This is my own reason for being here, you know."

"I shall remember your example, Doctor." The irony was back in his speech, in the discreet bow, and he was master of himself once more.

"Thank you, Mr. Forrest," I bowed in return, playing his little game. "I shall await your answer with interest. Good morning, sir. Good morning, Miss Akala."

"I bid you good morning, sir." Beside him the girl rasped her duty.

Taking Akala's hand in his, he put his other arm over her shoulder and guided her back to the group near Damien. I watched them leave, with an entirely new sense of expectancy to add to the one Keanu's arm was giving me. Things were improving: they were working out just as I wanted them to.

I found a new and dangerous pleasure, too, in the sleepy afternoons, the troubled nights, I spent in my musty bed. Denied the fact of love, I dreamed about it. Robbed of consummation in the flesh, I resorted to it in fantasy. In my imagination I indulged my starved desire with the thousand exquisite debaucheries I never dared to try in life. Lying wide-eyed in my bed, or sitting quite awake upon the veranda, I would tire of my futile searching of myself for an answer to Damien's question, I would grow angry with the endless argument I carried on with those unseen voices tormenting me from outside myself. Too jaded to read, too bored to move, I lay there, seeking forgetfulness in lascivious sleep.

Sometimes it came, in which event I dreamed my lustful fantasies. Sometimes it was withheld from me, in which case I invented daydreams. However they came to me, those dreams were wonderfully real and marvelously versatile. "If I have not love," I could cackle in answer to my voices, "I have a most excellent likeness of it."

At first I was faithful to Luise. She was my promised one, my waiting one; I was her chaste and faithful suitor. Tender and ardent by turns, I wooed her anew, and won her anew. Tender and ardent, in a climactic dream, in a cloud of bliss, I approached the nuptial bed where her bride's body lay. Full of desire and expectancy, naked I came unto her, as a husband and lover should go unto his beloved. But where I was passion, she was ice; where I was naked and afire, she was clothed and cold; and no plea or threat or oath of mine could divest her of her vestal's gown or lift the virgin's circlet from her brow. Frenzied with love, I beat her, with my fists, with my riding whip, with a monstrous candlestick seized up from beside our marriage bed.

I beat her until the virgin's crown lay broken in the bed and the silken gown fell away from her flesh; and then I ravished her, exulting in her desecration as I arched triumphant over her, claiming her at last for my own. She lay there, cold to my touch, listless to my lust, chattering endlessly in my ear of dances and teas and dinners, of visits to the opera and the latest fashions in gowns, while her icy bloody hands went right on pouring tea, addressing tiny envelopes, painting china, frantically busy with a dozen dutiful deeds to prevent their knowing me . . .

Unbelieving, I looked down upon that talking doll. Defeated by her invincible indifference, I withdrew from her, unfulfilled and unappeased, and crept home to reality. *Pfaugh!* what a delusion she was!

I never wasted another dream upon her. Granted my freedom, I went on to better things.

It was only when I was fully awake again, and aware of my pollution, that I became ashamed of those evil dreams, and full of apprehension because they were happening to me. I would bury my head in my arms, to keep from hearing the accusing voices, from seeing the accusing eyes.

But there was no escaping them. The shrill voices resounded, the laughter of people taunting me in a nightmare scene, while I ran stumbling from them, down an endless flight of collapsing stairs, in an immense room made of glass. Gleeful now, in their hope for victory, the voices closed in on me. *"Pupule!"* they shrieked. "Mad! *Hinfällig! Ungeheuer!"*—dancing around me like demons. "Dirty! *Pilau!* Unclean!" they slavered, reviling me for my impurities, their voices echoing in the blinding brilliant resonant room where there was no place for me to hide.

All of the eyes of all of the people whom I had ever judged came back now to look down in judgment upon me. They peered at me, followed me, wherever I went, whatever I did, bringing their faces with them: eyes that pleaded, eyes that scorned, eyes that accused or pitied or wept. Keanu's eyes, hard with hate, haunted me the most. But the eyes of the Queen, lustrous and cruel; the eyes of the Premier, mocking and cold; those of Caleb, blazing with disgust, were also there in the infuriated air around me. Yet they were not as terrible to me as were the eyes of Damien, soft with pity, grievous with hurt, as though I had wounded him when I wounded Keanu.

Slowly the thought formed in my weary mind that one day one of those pairs of eyes would triumph over the rest, and, with its triumph, would bring me the verdict for which I was being made to wait.

Their torment left me without rest and without peace. The threads of my mind were unraveling, slowly parting, about to break at last.

But even then I could not give up the disease of my fantasies: it was as much a part of me, as ingrown into my flesh and being, as was the leprous seed I had implanted in the arm of Keanu.

Relief came to me from an unexpected quarter.

One morning when I came into the kitchen Keanu greeted me with a sheepish smile, an actual spoken greeting. I'm not mad at you any more, he seemed to want to say. The sight of kindness upon that face startled me, the sound of an unnecessary word almost unstrung me, and I did not know how to respond.

While I prepared my breakfast he began to speak in his tongue-tied way. "Good day fo feeshing. I go catch us some *weke*. Wid luck, maybe I get nice *papio* fo us." Open-mouthed with astonishment, I watched him go. Only after he had left the house did I recognize the vaguely felt wish that I might go along with him. I needed to get away from the brooding silent house, I told myself, away from the voices of my loneliness.

After this beginning our relationship improved steadily, and my own desperate state seemed to mend. But my recovery was slow, and there were many hours of darkness left to me, when I was alone with my demons. When Keanu was at home I was attentive to his wish, hopeful to keep him in good humor. I took to cooking our meals, thinking it only fair that I should be of service to him after his months of help to me. And he, not to be outdone, insisted upon doing his share of the housework.

But he never invited me to go with him on those trips he made to the seashore. And I was still too uncertain of our new accord to ask him if I might go with him. Later, I promised myself, later I will ask him.

One morning, late in March, while I was at the Infirmary, he started to work again in the garden. To help him in clearing away the weeds, he brought out of its resting place the long knife Damien gave him on that strange evening when we went to fetch the chickens home. How angry I had been with the boy then; how little of my anger remained with me now.

The next day was a glorious one, the most beautiful day I'd yet seen in Hawaii. Clear and bright, without a cloud in the sky, it showed every facet of the massive cliffs, every blade of grass upon the land, each dancing wave upon the sparkling sea. The brisk wind was from the north. It brought the cold smell of the northlands in it, tingling in the nostrils, scented with the illusion of pine trees and of snow, the only breath of winter I would find in that southern land: the smell of home. Urgent in me rose the need to escape. I must get away from here, from this treacherous leprous garden of evil.

The house was empty when I returned to it from the Infirmary. In the quiet kitchen I took my lunch. The house itself seemed to be charged with promise, and I received its message that it, too, could not wait much longer for Keanu's answer.

After my light meal was ended, I went to my room to take my

afternoon's rest. For a while I tried to read, with many a wandering glance out of the open window, where it overlooked the bay of Kalawao and the sugar-loaf islands lying in the sea.

I awoke hours later, cold and miserable. The house was dark, illuminated only by the wan light of a day almost dead. Through the window I could see the storm scud driving in from the sea, the ocean dark and vicious: the whitecaps were rows of shark's teeth bared to bite. The beautiful day was gone, betrayed by the north wind. Ill-tempered as the weather, I got up from bed. My head ached, my shoulders were stiff. Everything had gone wrong! Not even the memory of a dream remained to comfort me.

In the kitchen I found Keanu bending over the counter, sharpening his long knife. The room was dark, and only the rasp of the whetstone upon the blade told me what he was doing. "Why don't you light the lamp?" I growled, forgetting in a peevish instant all of my good will of the last weeks.

The whisk of the stone stopped for a moment. "Don' need. Can see." Then it began again, steady, monotonous, grating upon the nerves.

"Nonsense! You'll cut yourself."

The stone was thrown in anger against the counter, the knife was dropped with a clatter. From the shadows his voice came at me, harsh as the sharpening stone. "Wat you care eef I get cut? You went give me one wohse cut."

"I do care. And there are worse ways of dying than from the *lepera*. Have you ever seen a man with the lockjaw?"

He considered this for a moment. Then, quietly, he changed the subject. "Akala went *make* today."

"So soon? I thought she would last for a longer time."

"Aye. An' dey say you went make her *make* more fas'. Because you put da cut in her."

"They're stupid. She was far gone, even then. She would have died very soon, anyway. How can they blame me?"

"Dass wat dey say."

"How do you know? Answer me! Have you been going with the lepers?"

"No. No worry. I heah 'em at da church. I—I went stan' ousside, fo her fun'ral."

His answer astounded me, made me contrite. "I will light the lamp for you," I said gently, feeling the return of my liking for the boy coming back to warm my heart. While I groped for the matchbox, I tried frantically to find some new subject to turn our attention to. All I could think of was his damned knife, and it was no fit topic for conversation.

I struck a lucifer, watching it flare up and subside, like a falling star, in the darkness of the kitchen.

By the light of the match I lifted the fragile glass chimney from the lamp. Leaning over the table I touched the fire to the wick. A flutter of yellow and blue, the flame trembled uncertainly in the drafty kitchen, setting Keanu's gigantic shadow to dancing crazily upon the wall. The knife blade gleamed bright in his open hand, but no brighter than the glint of his eyes, reflecting the light from the unwilling wick.

His voice came to me across a great distance, as I stared at the glittering blade, the glittering eyes. "I nevah tole you befo. Dis my knife," he said slowly, clearly, closing his fingers around its handle, holding it like a dagger. "My knife—from Kohala."

Even then I did not understand what he was meaning to tell me, across the fitful flame of the lamp. Behind him his reeling shadow was enormous, like the djinn released from the Arabian bottle.

"Da one I went keel Charley wid," he said, lifting his right hand slowly, the while he looked with a tender smile upon the evil blade come home to its owner's grasp. In the arm which held the knife I saw the swelling where my knife had wounded him.

Then he looked at me, the smile still on his face.

As I watched him across the table, as slow realization came with awful certainty to me, the flame of the lamp guttered feebly, and went out.

16

As, IN THE DARK, I waited for Keanu's dagger to find me, I heard the frenzy of an approaching mob, the pounding of many feet running up the pathway to our house. Through the windows came the glow of torches, lurid in the night. Recognizing the sound of rescue, I dropped the chimney with a crash upon the table and fled from Keanu standing poised before me, his knife lifted against me. Calling out as I went, I ran to the front door. Behind me Keanu's feet thudded across the floor, as he tried to grab me.

I burst out on the veranda just as the mob reached the stairs. They roared when they saw me. In the flickering light of the *kukui*-nut torches their mouths were black circles of noise, their eyes deep sockets of malice. Lepers all, there must have been fifty of them or more, raising their ravaged faces toward me, shouting, screaming, pressing in toward the veranda in their haste to gain their goal.

I thought they clamored for me, connecting Keanu's mention of Akala with this eruption of violent men. Trapped between pursuing Keanu and the confronting mob, I did not know which was the worse. Crying my innocence of any crime, I picked up one of the veranda chairs and held it before me, as my defense against them, while I backed against the wall, as my protection against Keanu.

In my confusion I was slow to understand what they wanted. But at last I heard them. "Where is he?" they shouted. "Where is Keanu?" And I sobbed with relief. Their faces contorted with hate, the raging light shining on their exuberant flesh, on the red moist ulcerations, they lifted their clawlike hands, demanding Keanu. "Where is he? Where is the killer?" they shrieked. And I wept tears of joy because they did not come for me.

In their forefront, shouting with them, was Caleb. At first I did not recognize him, coatless, hatless, his shirt wet with sweat.

Stunned by their noise, I could do no more than lean against the wall of the house, indicating with my head that Keanu was inside, hiding in the dark.

"Keanu!" they raised their cry like a pack of ghouls. "Come out!" Caleb began to mount the stairs and his henchmen started after him. I made no move to stop them. For all I cared, they could tear Keanu to shreds, with their talons and their teeth. He was evil, and they, no less evil than he, could claim him for their own. I wanted only to be rid of him, forever, to be safe from the threat he offered to my life.

There was a hiss of warning, a sudden hush upon the mob. Keanu stood in the door, his feet set wide apart, his hands upon his hips. Head high, teeth bared, he was an animal at bay. It was he who challenged them: "Wat you want?"

For an instant no one dared to answer. Then Caleb took up the challenge. "You, Keanu!" he yelled, as David might have shouted up at Goliath. "You, you damned murderer!"

Keanu shrugged. The tenseness went out of his shoulders, his hands dropped to his sides. "Wy you get excited? Charley went *make* long time ago."

At this defense the crowd roared in anger. Shouting and cursing, they made such a clamor that Caleb had to screech at them for quiet. When they were stilled he turned back to Keanu. "You think you're smart, talking about that old murder of yours. But that's not the one we mean. The *new* one, the one you did today —*that's* the one we mean!" As he pointed an accuser's finger at Keanu the crowd shouted, again and again, "Get him! Get him!" The light shining down upon Caleb's head touched it with fire. He was an avenging angel, come to rescue me.

Dazed at this fresh evidence of his viciousness, I stared at Keanu. He was not arrogant now: slack with surprise at being found out, he was shaking his head, trying to be heard above the noise. At last they let him speak.

"Wat you talking? Wat you mean, one new murdah?"

"That's right!" yelped Caleb. "Make like you don't know. But *we* know! We found Ah See, just before dark. Stabbed to death in his house. And you were around there this afternoon, by his house. Lots of people saw you."

"Aye!" cried one of Caleb's supporters. "An' errybody know you keel wid one knife!" He was a villainous sight: hideously disfigured, with lips so eaten away that he could hardly mouth the words, he wore a bloody bandage looped around his head, enwrapping it like a turban. Down his neck a thin trickle of blood crept out from under the bandage where it covered his ears.

"Who dis Ah See? I don' know him."

"The last house on the road to Kalaupapa," jeered Caleb. "The last house beyond Siloama, before you get to Kauhako crater. Don't tell us you don't know the place."

Keanu was caught. He lifted his head, seeking a way of escape. I was sick with horror. The knife which already had been plunged into two victims—it was lifted to strike into me.

"I walk plenny places. Nobody call me killah befo!"

"Nobody went *make* here befo," cackled an old man in the front of the crowd. Pleased with his wit, and even more with their advantage over Keanu, they hooted with laughter. Full of malice, it was the mockery of a mob preparing to wreak its justice upon its chosen victim.

"I nevah went neah dis guy Ah See," protested Keanu, lifting his hands in desperation. He was frightened, his face pale even in the bloody light, his brow beaded with sweat.

They roared back at him, beating down his supplication, enjoying their triumph. The taste of blood was in their mouths. Like a pack of hungry hounds they closed in, sensing the time for the kill.

Caleb raised his hands once more for silence. But before he could speak, Keanu turned to me. "*Kauka.* Tell 'em. Tell 'em I nevah keel Ah See."

With amazement I heard this claim upon my charity from a man who had been on the point of killing me. With disgust for his fawning, I stared at him. Humble enough now that he was trapped, he turned those big brown eyes upon me, beseeching me, begging from me a word to save him. But I could not say it, remembering Charley lying dead in Kohala; imagining Ah See now, the blood clotting around the mouths of his newly opened wounds; most of all envisioning myself lying butchered, here in this very house— Shuddering at the toll he had taken, I turned in wrath to the mob, pointing at Keanu. "If you had not come when you did—he would have killed me too! The same knife that killed your friend was lifted against me—in this very house —just a few minutes ago!"

Even as the crowd raised its roar again I heard Keanu's gasp of despair. "*Kauka!* No—no—" he moaned, as I turned away from him.

"Get him! Get him!" the mob chanted. Caleb and his cohorts started up the stairs toward Keanu, their faces ugly with hatred for the monster who towered above them.

But Keanu was not going to be taken easily. Crouching, he put out his great hands, ready to shove the attackers away. "No touch me, you stinking lepahs!" he spat at them. He was the beast once more, preferring to kill and to maim, rather than be captured. "Try an' get me, you *pilau* bastahds!" As Caleb came up the stairs, Keanu suddenly changed his tactics: bringing up his enormous foot, he kicked Caleb in the groin with such a thrust of his powerful leg that Caleb was hurled back upon his followers. Arms outflung, Caleb carried his men back with him to the ground. Writhing with pain, screeching with rage, he lay in the dirt, while his companions lifted themselves up around him. Scowling with hurt dignity and indecision, they took counsel among themselves, while the other lepers bellowed their abuse at Keanu.

Brawlers never know when to shut up, and Keanu was no different from the rest of the tribe. Mingling sailors' oaths with expressions in *kanaka* which I could not begin to understand, he taunted his adversaries while he paced the narrow veranda between the stairs and the door. On the ground fallen Caleb shrieked his counterpoint of execration, foul as a swineherd. The leaderless mob stood helpless and uncertain, baffled into silence. If they had not trapped a murderer on the veranda, next to me, I would have found the situation of combat as ridiculous in effect as it was in fact. But there, three feet away from me, the aroused Keanu circled like a fighting boar, tusked for a fight to the death, and I could not find anything ridiculous in my nearness to him.

In the moment of waiting I heard for the second time that evening the sound of a rescuer. Even as he came storming up to us I marveled that I had not thought of him sooner.

Like a thunderclap from afar his voice came: a call of anger, like the voice of some invisible omnipotent god; or—why should I not say it, since I thought it?—like the terrible voice of Jehovah, falling upon his enemies to smite them. The thunder fell upon us. The mob lost its wildness. Caleb, rolling in the dust, ceased his cursing. Keanu, knowing that his champion was drawing near, stopped his taunting.

He came like a whirlwind among us, thrusting the lepers aside as he ran, chastising them with a vigor and a forthrightness as unexpected in him as it was effective on them. His spectacles flashing, the stole streaming to either side of him like lightning, he carried his wrath up to the veranda stairs.

"What crazy thing do you do here?" he cried, snatching the biretta from his head to shake it angrily at the crowd. "What madness is in you, to make you riot in this way? Are you sharks, hunting the creatures of the sea? Or are you people, with hearts that have mercy in them, with heads that have sense in them?"

The grotesque heads hung in shame, the shadows claimed the tumorous faces, the sunken noses. "Answer me!" he demanded, stamping his foot upon the stair.

Caleb rose slowly to his feet, clutching at the clothes of his inattentive minions. Damien stopped to watch the wounded warrior return to the affray. "And look at you," he said, when Caleb stood at last, dizzy with pain, supported at either side by his gargoyle ministrants. "Look at you, oh man of reason and of intellect. Oh, how the mighty are fallen! And how do you explain this court of law?"

Angrily Caleb thrust his sharp face toward the priest. "We came to get a murderer—to put a stop to him. Before his knife finds its way into the rest of us."

"How do you know that Keanu did this murder?"

How could they tell him of their suspicions, when he held no suspicions of any man? How could they speak of their fear, when the priest felt no fear of anything? Confronted with the test, how could I tell him that I too had been at the point of Keanu's dagger, and make him understand why, without any words at all, I *knew* what Keanu's intentions toward me had been?

Caleb, the man of reason, saw the trap into which the priest had thrust him. Helplessly he shrugged, stammered a weak rejoinder: "How—how do we know?"

"Because we have seen him, that's why!" broke in a big fat man. "Prowling around among us and our houses. He was around there this afternoon. We saw him. He's too stuck up to talk to us, or to join us in our life here—him and his clean body. But he's always snooping around, for what he can steal from us."

"Aye! Aye!" the crowd murmured, nodding their heads, licking their lips.

"He keel befo, he keel again," croaked the one with the bloody bandage around his head. "He alla time carry one knife—da same kine knife he went keel Charley wid."

"Aye, aye," the crowd muttered, a chorus of hideous furies, waiting their time. Among them, in the very front row, was Malie, mouthing her hate as cruelly as the rest.

"But is this proof enough?" asked the priest. "What evidence is this? When all of us walk abroad in the Settlement, is only Keanu to be put under suspicion? When there are hundreds of knives among us, is only Keanu's the one to kill? This is foolishness!" He turned upon the fellow with the bandaged head. "And you, Hanu. How do you know what kind of knife he killed Charley with? Were you there, that time, in Kohala?"

The chorus had no answer. Neither did Hanu. He backed away. But Caleb spoke out, wildly. "I saw the knife. In Honolulu."

"How could you see it in Honolulu?"

"When the police got it, as evidence for Keanu's trial. I saw it in the police station. I saw it in the courthouse. I was there. Now he has it again, or one like it. I have seen it on him."

"A devil!" "An evil thing!" "He makes magic!" the furies moaned.

"He is no devil!" Damien shouted back at them. "He got the knife from me. I gave it to him, here, many weeks ago. I did not know that it was his. But even if I did know this, still would I give it to him."

"You gave it to him?" the fat man asked in astonishment.

"I did. Many things come to me from Honolulu, among them boxes from the police. When I found this knife in one of them, I gave it to Keanu."

"But why?"

"A man needs a knife here—"

"That he may kill again with it?" The fat one's voice was full of poison.

"Alas, Momona!" the priest shook his finger at the fat man. "Your vicious tongues have been at work. They have put this suspicion upon Keanu. Bearing false witness is as great a sin as murder, do you not know it? Where one kills a man's body, the other can kill his good name. This above all others you should know, Caleb Forrest."

Caleb hung his head. Only then did I see that the glow in his hair was not the fire of an angel of the Lord: it was a streak of white hair, white as the dead skin upon his throat.

Pressing his advantage, Damien asked, "And did any of you see Keanu strike down Ah See? And how do you know that Ah See was stabbed?"

"Can tell by the cuts," a tall consumptive leper answered. His white hair had fallen out in great patches, leaving his head ragged and moth-eaten. Holding up two bloody hands, the thin man gave us account of the dead man's wounds. "Seven *pukas*—seven holes," he said mournfully, "through which the life of Ah See flowed away. These hands have counted them."

"Who found Ah See?" asked Damien.

"I was the one," said the thin man. "It is our custom to visit in the evenings."

"When you found him, what did you do?"

"I called in fear upon Momona, his neighbor, upon Caleb, who lives not far away. Soon many people were there, coming from the coffin-feast of Akala."

"That was good, Makaio. You did right." The tall man nodded solemnly, accepting the praise as his due. "But, then, who said this deed was Keanu's?"

They thought back upon the time. Then three different heads were raised, three different voices called out three different names: "Makaio." "Momona." "Kalepa."

"Not me!" cried Hanu of the bandaged head, almost before they were finished.

"I did not say, 'Keanu,'" said Makaio.

Damien turned to Caleb, waiting. "I did not say 'Keanu,'" said Caleb quietly.

"Then who did this shameful thing?" cried Damien, for all to hear. "Who set you running like a pack of dogs chasing after a goat let loose in the fields? Who put the name of Keanu in your ears, and upon your tongues?"

Once again there was no answer, as, of course, the priest knew there could be none. Implacably he forced them to see the error of their frenzy. "You cannot know, because you did not hear it said. In your fear you heard a word here, a name there. Because Keanu was seen walking near to Ah See's house, soon the word was spread that it was Keanu who did the killing. And with a name to fasten your fright upon, soon there was hate to tell you that what you *think* in your fear must also be the truth. Like fire setting grass ablaze, your hate spread until it burned in all of you. And now you are here, eager to shed more precious blood. How noble is your action. How wonderful is your justice."

The weaker spirits in the crowd could not bear his anger. "*Kamiano,*" they whimpered, "*kala,* forgive." "*Auwe! Auwe!*" they wailed in penitence. Many of them on the fringes of the mob slunk away into the night, thankful to escape unnamed. But those who were hemmed in at the front could not escape. To do them credit, some of them did not wish to leave, not being ready to give up so soon their prey. Of these the maenad Malie was one of the most determined. No cry for forgiveness came from her.

"Even so," said Momona stubbornly. "We are guilty of haste, perhaps. But who else would do the deed? Who else is more likely to drink blood, than a shark who already knows the taste of blood?"

"This I do not know," said Damien steadily. "We have here a thousand people. Any one of these could be the killer of Ah See. But there are ways of studying this deed, to find out who did it. Perhaps it was Keanu who did it. Perhaps it was someone who is here, among you. I do not know. But I will be surprised if you find that Keanu did it. I know him. I have great faith in him. I do not think Keanu could do this thing." As I listened to this defense of a convicted murderer, wondering at the incredible blindness of the priest, Keanu lifted his hands to his face and wept.

"But let us not punish Keanu—let us not punish any man—until we learn that he has committed this crime. Let us study this thing, I say, until we learn the truth. Let us do what the law tells us to do. We will send for the police, to Kaunakakai over the mountains, and let them find out who killed Ah See. Is not this the best way?"

"Aye. It is good." Sobered now by the wily priest, many of the people gave their approval of this more lawful course.

"But what of Keanu?" cried Momona, expressing my thought. If he had not asked the question, I would have shouted it myself.

"Keanu can stay here. He will not go away." Lowering his hands, Keanu looked hopefully at the priest.

"No!" I cried out. "No! Not here! Take him away from here!"

Damien turned to me in surprise. "Take him away from here!" I shouted at him, to make sure he heard me. "He tried to kill me tonight too!"

The priest looked from me to Keanu, questioning us both in his glance. For the first time since his arrival he did not know what to do. In the moment of his uncertainty he peered at me once more, judging me. Then he turned to the crowd.

"Then let Keanu come with me. The church will give him sanctuary. You, Caleb, you bring some men to guard him during the night. In the morning we take him to the jailhouse in Kalaupapa. Is this plan a good one to you?"

"It is good," said Caleb. Makaio, Momona, several others nearby, added their approval.

"*Kauka!* You wrong!" Keanu called to me. "I like stay heah."

For the third time I turned my face from him. I would not answer him.

"Keanu?" Damien said gently, holding out his hand. The murderer wiped the tears from his cheeks, dried his hands on his trousers, while the priest waited. Then, ready to entrust himself to the mob and its dangerous care, he drew himself up proudly, like a soldier going to his death.

I groaned aloud when Keanu took Damien's leprous hand.

His bare feet carried him down the stairs, taking him from freedom into imprisonment again. And I groaned once more when Keanu stepped from his isolation into the company of lepers.

The mob opened up around them, yielding them a place upon the trampled path. Like soldiers, torchbearers ranged themselves about the trusting pair. The priest in his black robes seemed disembodied in the dancing light, only his pale head showing above the white line of the stole. Keanu's splendid body, towering above all his guardians, was ringed around by the living dead. I could not see his face. Now it was turned away from me. Immediately behind the murderer, determined not to let him escape, stood Caleb and Makaio and Momona. Before him, behind them, rank upon ragged rank, the disciplined horde stood waiting for the signal to depart.

Alone on the veranda, clinging to the railing, I waited for them to go. Relieved by my escape from Keanu's murdering knife, but sick to my heart under the effect of the evening's violence, I wanted to drop to the floor in exhaustion. Eager to have them go, I yet mourned the end to my hopes, the disastrous loss of my experimental animal, the shattering finish to my experiment. Fighting back bitter tears of relief and heartbreak, I was compelled to watch them go, as they bore away my prize.

All too soon—and yet so slowly that I had time to catalogue a thousand regrets—the signal came, from Caleb's mouth: "Go!"

First the remoter faceless lepers left, a vanguard in the darkness. Then those closer to my view faded softly away into the black night. The light-bearers who preceded the priest and the prisoner went past me, their torches held high, the thick black smoke trailing behind them like funeral pennons. The light, rich and red from the oily *kukui* nuts, cast deep shadows, black as the night, black as their own smoke, among the marchers in that funereal procession.

None of them had thought for me but one. I was expecting the flash of Damien's spectacles, as he raised his head to bid me good night, but he did not look up at me. I expected no sign of remembrance from Keanu, but as he came past he lifted his head to look up at me. Preparing myself for the glance filled with enmity and unforgiving hatred, I looked down at him, unable to turn my eyes away from the expected welcomed needed hate. Beneath the locks of black hair his face was drawn and sorrowful. His eyes were filled with pity, and in their glance they gave me his message of compassion and forgiveness. As he walked by he turned his head to hold me with that overwhelming gaze. I could not break the power of that link between us. Looking back at him until I saw nothing else but those deep pools of pity, I watched him until he and his guards were gone too far into the night for me to see him.

And then I was alone in the dark—alone with the memory of those eyes looking up at me.

Somewhere along their path, disturbed by their progress, awakened by the light of the torches, dogs began to bay, a cock began to crow. In the darkness where I stood, clinging still to the railing, my enlightenment came with a blaze of pain that brought a cry of agony to my lips. Even as, too late, I recognized the enormity of my sin, my informer was kind. I fell to the floor in a faint, and, mercifully, I knew no more.

II. MALIE
(TRANSLATED FROM THE HAWAIIAN)

17

WHEN FIRST I SAW KEANU I turned my face from him. He is a man of evil, I had been told, and I believed those who said this thing of him.

"Keanu"—around me the whispers rose—"the one who killed Charley," or, "the lover of Kamaka." Excited even in their whispering, the people asked, "Why is he here? Why is he not in the jail?"

The question swept over us like a wave crossing the reef, troubling us in its passing. Tall in Mr. Gibson's carriage, Keanu stood before us, his face dark in the shadow of his hair, his hands bound in chains. Because once I was a member of the King's household, and because Keanu was condemned to death by the King's justice, I did not doubt that he was evil. It was not for me to look upon him, and therefore I turned my face from him.

It was not so with the others standing with me in the long shadows of Samuel Wilder's wharf. Eagerly they fastened their gaze upon the man, forgetting their own troubles in the greater troubles of the murderer.

"He goes with Opaekea to Kalawao: this is my thought," said Ioane Paele with firmness.

Opaekea. The white shrimp: this was our name for the small *haole* doctor standing beside Mr. Gibson's carriage, talking with him. Thin and fair, stoop-shouldered as a palm tree curved by the sea wind, he looked to us like the small baby shrimp, white and weak, which is found in inland streams and taro patches. They are not good for anything, neither for eating nor for *opelu* bait, and we natives always speak of them with contempt. For some reason I did not know, the small doctor was not liked by his patients. Some of them called him by names less kind than Opaekea, making fun of his narrow shoulders, of his childish voice, of his clothes, strange even to us who have seen so many kinds of clothing on the *haoles* who rush like hungry chickens along the busy streets of Honolulu. He was not likely to find out the names we gave him, for he did not know our language and he made no effort to learn it. In this he was like most *haoles*, of course, who do not think that we have anything to teach them, and who talk down to us, calling us *kanakas*, as if we had no minds for learning anything from them.

"How is it that Keanu can go to Kalawao?" asked Hamau. "When he is a prisoner, condemned to die."

"*Kie*," retorted Ioane Paele. "Why else would Kipikona bring him here? You watch. Soon they will remove Keanu's chains. Then he will step down from the carriage, and he will come with us."

"Why should he come with us?" several people asked. "Does he too have the separation sickness?" Although I did not say it, this was my question also.

"You remember how, a few weeks ago, this Opaekea was asking about for a man willing to take the *lepera* into his body? You remember how, when we heard of this, we would not pass the word to others how this crazy *haole* was seeking to make a whole man into a sick one?"

"*Auwe*," moaned Kalunu. "Is there not misery enough among us? No, I have not heard this thing." She touched at her cheeks with a colored kerchief, already wet with the tears of parting.

Nor had I heard it. But I was shocked: it was so cruel a thing to do. How can one man treat another man so?

"*Ae, ae*, I remember," said Hamau. "Is Keanu, then, the willing man?"

"I say that it is so," said Ioane Paele bitterly. "To save his neck from the rope, Keanu gives his body to the *haole*. To be his animal, like those others he holds in cages in the hospital."

"Would you not do the same?" asked Mahiai. "Is it not better to live, even as a leper, than to die by the rope?"

"*Ae*," said Puulena soothingly. "It is a hard thing to say, which is the better way."

"Shh!" hissed Ioane Paele. "See: I told you it would be so—"

I could not resist the stillness which came upon the crowd, the force of their looking. Evil as Keanu was, I turned to see him.

In the carriage, swaying beneath him, he was being freed of his chains. White against the black carriage, the small doctor stood motionless on the floor of the wharf. He looked up, it seemed in fright, at the man-killer huge above him. In the silence we heard the clatter of the chains when they fell from Keanu's hands and feet.

Kipikona opened the door of his carriage. It swung wide, and the little folding steps fell open toward the doctor's feet. With the same courtly gesture I have seen him make a hundred times, Kipikona invited Keanu to leave. Swiftly, gracefully as a dancer, Keanu placed one foot upon the stairs and in the next instant stood upon the wharf. Beside him the doctor seemed even more like a sickly shrimp: his head did not reach to the level of Keanu's shoulders.

When Keanu stood free upon the wharf there was a great sigh among us. Some sighed in fear of the man-killer released among them. Others sighed in disbelief that this should be. Some, I think, sighed in yearning for him, with the itch of lust at his beauty. A few sighed, perhaps, out of relief at his being spared a death upon the prison tree. Whatever reasons the others had, I sighed out of pity, for only then did I see the raggedness of his clothes and the nakedness of his feet, the uncombed hair, the prisoner's beard upon his cheeks.

This poor man, I thought, no matter what he has done, he should not be treated like an animal. For the first time I questioned the quality of the King's grace and the temper of his justice. And burning within me grew my horror of Opaekea's plan for Keanu's body—if it was true, what Ioane Paele said.

Yet Keanu held no dislike for the First Minister of the King. Brushing his long hair from his face, he smiled back at Kipikona smiling upon him. Kipikona's face was that of a father, kind and sorrowful, as he touched Keanu on his shoulder and then let him go.

Always, with his white hair and white beard, and the bright blue eyes which look straight into people's hearts, he has made me to think that God in his Heaven must look like Mr. Gibson; and now he looked as God must have looked, when he cast out Lucifer, his fallen son, from Heaven. With a wave of his thin hand, a nod of his noble head, he gave Keanu into the small doctor's keeping.

We opened a way for them to pass among us to the waiting ship. Keanu came first, walking among us as though we were not there. I saw for the first time close to me the strong curve of his mouth, the arch of his nose, the fullness of his brow. At the open neck of the prison shirt I saw the smooth skin of his chest, where it met the column of his throat. I, who in my life had been given no chance at love, I felt the sudden stir in my blood as my eyes sought other evidences of his splendor and his manliness.

Frightened by his effect upon me, I turned away from him, blushing for my evil thoughts. He *is* evil! If he can raise this effect in me, he is something to be shunned. I would not look upon him any more. I turned instead to Opaekea, hurrying after his prize.

An embarrassed grin upon his pale face, his faded blue eyes darting in all directions as though he expected to be the center of all attention, he trotted like a dog behind Keanu. No one else looked at him: their eyes were upon the murderer. Like a dog was the foreigner among us. I felt a dislike being born in me for him, who could do to any man such a thing as he planned to do to Keanu. In anger I turned my back upon him, too, upon the hateful *haole*.

When Keanu and the *kauka* vanished into the ship, we who were going with them to Molokai ended our farewells to those who came to bid us the last good-by. It was like dying, for we shall not see them again, and no more will they look upon us. Tears were not enough to ease our grief. Our hearts must stop their beating, our breath must be stilled, before we can cease to mourn our separation. For those who bade us *aloha* there will be other loves to take our places. But for us who are banished, there is nothing but desolation.

In sorrow we touched for the last time our loved ones, received for the last time their kisses, bent our heads for their blessings, placed upon us with their *leis*. When we turned away from them, the *kanikau* of mourning rose, the ancient terrible wailing. Mingled with their crying were the hymns of the *haole* family, delivering their son into our number. He was their darling, their only son. Fifteen of us who are children of the land, and one of them, who are newly come to the land. Who can say that God is not impartial in his judgments?

My father kissed me upon the forehead. "Go with God," he said, trying to smile, while the tears crept down his cheeks. My mother flung herself upon my breast, hurting the places where the sores are. I did not mind the pain, when I heard her sobbing.

"Forgive, forgive—" She did not say more, but I knew what she meant. We had said all this before. It is I who bring the curse upon you, she meant. The Kahekili blood—it is bad. There is a taint in it, and I have brought it upon you. Wearily I smiled, patient with her superstition. What good is there in blaming the Kahekili blood? Who knows how the *lepera* chooses its victims? We were proud of the Kahekili heritage in the time of our prospering: because my mother was a daughter of this noble family, from whom issued the high chiefs of Maui, I was sent as Lady-in-Waiting to the Queen. Should we disown it now, in the time of my leveling? Should we forget now the days of their glory, and remember only the flaw in their lineage which already has sent two of their men to Kalawao?

"Mama"—for the last time I tried to comfort her—"do not blame yourself." But she was beyond hearing me: she would believe what she wished to believe, as I believed what I wanted to believe.

For me it was the will of God that I should be afflicted. All things proceed according to God's will were the words of my teachers, first in the Royal School, then in the services of the Church of England. And as I was taught so did I believe. He was my Comfort, and his will was my guide. But sometimes, in my loneliness and in my fear of what was to come for me at Kalawao, I grew weak with doubt. I cried out, in my empty heart, "Why, O Lord, why have you chosen this fate for me?"

I did not tell this to anyone, not even to the Bishop at Saint Andrew's Cathedral, when he talked with me and prayed with me that day, before I went into the hospital at Kakaako. "The will of God is unknown and unknowable," he said, lifting his hands above my bowed head, "and it is not for us to question him. We must accept his chastening, as we accept his gifts, with meekness and in faith. Who can say, but that out of this scourge he has sent upon you, there will not come an instrument of grace? All things work together for good, to them that love God." It was easy for me to find comfort in his words then, when the two of us were kneeling in the silence of the beautiful Cathedral, beneath the windows of stained glass, in the very presence of God.

But when, at the wharf, I felt my mother's weeping, I heard the wailing of the people around me calling the last farewell; as, through a veil of tears, I saw my father's tears, how could I be solaced? Weak with sorrow, I loosened my mother's arms from about my neck. "*Aloha ia oe*, Mama. *Aloha*, Papa," I tried to smile at them. And then I slipped away, away from them forever.

Behind me I heard my mother's wail of grief, joining in with the others. When despair comes upon our people, the ancient ways are best. And when great sorrow comes, there is only one voice for crying it out. "*Auwe . . . Auwe . . .*" the voices trembled in the dusk, more terrifying than all weeping, more saddening than tears. Not since the great state funeral for the Princess Ruth, in the month of Kaaona, had the *kanikau* risen from so many throats.

As I pushed my way toward the ship, someone caught me by the arm. "Malie! Malie, wait!" It was little Susana Pahaiwa, one of the chambermaids at the palace. Her pretty face was streaked with tears, her mouth awry with crying. "Malie, please! Take Tutu with you, take care of Tutu. She is so old, help her, please?" She put into my hand the arm of her grandmother, a bewildered old woman, blinded by her sorrow. Looking from the sweet face of the girl, ravaged by her tears, into the marred face of the grandmother, ravaged by her disease, I saw the history of myself. Never before had I looked into such a mirror. Stunned by the discovery, I stood still, in a great silence, as my revelation came upon me. For this I have been born, I saw, gazing into the face of Tutu. Worse than this I shall be, before I die.

"Please?" Susana's voice came to me across a great distance. The tug at my arm was that of the Lord Jesus, asking me to be kind, even to the least, even to the most hideous, of his creatures.

"Of course," I answered him as I answered the little Susana. Was he not kind even to Lazarus? "I will help her. Come, Tutu. Let us go to the big steamer."

"*Mahalo, mahalo*," the old one said. "You are kind."

"*Mahalo*, Malie, *mahalo*," Susana said. "We will not forget your goodness." Around us Tutu's large family called their thanks to me, their farewells to her.

Once more I turned toward the ship. Slipping my arm around her waist, drawing her old body close against mine, I said, "Come, Tutu, let us go."

Come, Tutu, let us go together, to the island of the dead.

In the night I could not sleep. While the swift ship moved across the smooth water, I stood at the rail, taking my leave of Oahu. In our cabin Tutu lay in her bed, not ready to sleep but not well enough to watch with me. I was alone in the dark, straining my eyes to see the beloved mountains of the island of my childhood. But the night lay heavy on the land. The clouds were low, brought up by the warm *kona* winds from the south, and I could not see the high peaks of my mountains. The lights of Honolulu fell away behind us, and for all the stretch of shore until we were abreast of Waikiki there was darkness. Waikiki I found by the torches of the people fishing for squid on the reef. Warm and soft, the orange light of the *kukui*-nut torches winked above the water, like sparks fallen from a fire. Then we passed beyond the point of Leahi, which the *haoles* for some reason call Diamond Head, and one by one the torches were blotted out. I could not see the proud mountain, black in the black night, but I could feel it there, crouching like a great animal, its head held high, its feet washed by the sea. There were no more lights, no more torches for me to gaze upon. There was no more Oahu for me to yearn toward. The last tie was cut. Farewell to you. To you, my land, farewell.

I lay my head upon the cool rail, and wept until I had no more tears. Futile were the tears falling into the salt sea. Even as I wept I vowed that henceforth I should weep no more. What is there left to weep for, in one who is going to the other side of death?

I went to my bed to rest. Tutu slept, but her whimpering told me that her dreams were not kind. In the dim cabin I covered her with her shawl before I climbed into the upper berth. But still I could not sleep. I was awake when the hush of the engines told me we were come to the bay of Kalawao.

When I looked out of my window it seemed that the torches of Waikiki had journeyed to Molokai to greet me. They were there, in the distance, glowing warm and cheerful. They were a promise that I should find my people upon the land of Molokai, as I had found them upon the land of Oahu. Almost happily I went to awaken Tutu.

We prepared for the landing by exchanging our *haole* clothes, with their silly bustles and heavy skirts, for the more sensible *holoku* of our people. Chattering like schoolgirls we broke our fast on hard-boiled eggs from her *puolo* of food, and sour Chinese oranges from mine. "Save the seeds," Tutu commanded. "We shall plant them in our garden. Palupalu—he is my middle son— has heard how there are few food trees in this new place." Heeding her, I wrapped the eight seeds in a piece of old newspaper, and tucked them away in my valise. I did not ask if either of us would be present to gather the first fruits from the trees which would grow out of those soft white seeds.

When we went out on the deck into the dawn most of our fellow passengers were already there, standing at the rail, gazing across the sea to the waiting island.

"*Auwe! Molokai ahina,*" sighed Tutu. Gray Molokai. The grim island lay low in the gray sea. Upon the cliffs the clouds pressed heavy and thick, weighing them down with an unshakable immense weight. All of the graveclothes in the world were there, gathered in one dreadful pall, heavy enough to crush the cliffs down to their knees.

Unspeaking, as though already dead, the other patients made room for us at the rail. As despairing as they, we stood beside them. For Tutu and me our short time of pretense, of taking part in ordinary human joys and pleasures, of gaiety in the sharing of an egg and of hope in the saving of an orange seed, was ended. In the desolation from which the sun was forever shut out, the pitiful torches upon the shore were paled into nothingness. O *Molokai ahina,* the sun can never shine on thee.

From an old man standing near me, from Ulukou of Hana, there came a groan, a long drawn-out groan of defeat. He needed no words to tell us of his breaking. With his groan his spirit issued through his mouth to run away. He fell to his knees upon the deck—we thought because he could stand no more upon his feet. But even as he sank to his knees, he slid his body between the pipes of the rail and he dove into the cold gray sea. Quietly he went, almost without a splash, as a man of the sea would go. We had no time to reach for him, to cry out to him to wait: he was gone beneath the water, and he did not come up again.

Stiff as corpses we stood, staring in horror at the circle of bubbles and froth, green and white in the yielding sea, each one of us alone with his thoughts. From horror to admiration to envy: this was the progress of my thoughts. For Ulukou his trying was ended, and who could say that he had not made the braver move, the wiser choice? Each of us, alone with his *manao*, did not dare to look at the others. Not one of us raised a sound to let the Captain know, or his crew, how Ulukou was taking a quicker way to God than any of us would take.

Above our heads, from the bridge, Captain MacDougal shouted his orders to the crew. "O.K. O.K! Get ready, you guys! First boat, get ready for shore." I looked up in surprise. So soon? We were still far out from the land.

"O.K. O.K! First boat away!" cried a sailor from the stern of the ship. It was then that I saw Keanu moving to the rail, to stand by the side of the longboat being prepared for lowering. In the early light the faded prison clothes seemed molded upon his body, like skin: at first I thought he stood forth naked for his entry into Molokai. The curls of black hair upon his head rose full above him like the *mahiole*, the feather helmet worn by the warriors of old. After him, moving clumsily over the things scattered upon the deck, crawled Opaekea. His white suit hung loose and crooked upon him. He was like a shrimp about to shed its skin.

Keanu stepped as easily into the boat as he had stepped out of Kipikona's carriage. Turning, he reached down and lifted the little doctor in after him. The *kauka* sat down at once, clutching the side of the boat with both hands. When he was settled, Keanu sat next to him, turning his face toward the land. The rowers took their places and, with a cry from the sailors at the ropes, the boat was freed to swoop like a seabird to the water.

"E, you!" the bosun called. "You nex'! Two *wahine* firs'—t'ree, foah *kane* too. Come on, come on! *Wikiwiki!*" He was not bullying us, with his good-natured grin: he was trying to rouse us from our sadness. Not knowing what to do, we moved toward him.

"E, *Tutu! Mahea* you *puolo?* An' you *papale? Eia mai!* You going get sunstroke, you no weah you *papale.*"

"Still in our cabin," I called back to him, trying to put a lightness into my answer, for his sake. "May we go and get them?"

"O.K., lady," he dismissed us with a wave of his hands. "You go get da *papale.* I send Keoki fo da bags." Whistling furiously, he called Keoki to our assistance, shouting his orders as the boy came running. The cheerful youth did not stop before us, but hurried on to our cabin. Tutu and I followed after him, to don our hats.

When we returned to the deck all of the patients were gathered together. The *haole* boy's blond head glowed like a little sun among my dark people. And the bosun was discovering that one of us was missing. "*E!* One no moah, S'posed to be seexteen. Were da udda one?"

No one wished to be the first to tell him.

"He still *moemoe?*"

"*Ae,*" said Ioane Paele slowly. "He sleeps." He pointed to the water beyond the ship's side. "In the sea, a man at peace."

The bosun was quick to understand. "*Auwe,* da pooh buggah . . ." He stole a glance at the sea. In Hawaiian he pronounced Ulukou's funeral sermon: "Perhaps he chose the right way. It has been done before: it will be done again." Then he turned to us. "Which one was he? I will report this to the Captain, when you are gone from the ship."

"Ulukou, the fisherman of Hana," said Ioane Paele. "That was his name. We know little more of him."

"He leaves a wife, in Hana. Who will tell her of his end?" spoke a young man at the far end of our group. I saw him then, for the first time, as one of us: it was Caleb Forrest. I looked upon him with astonishment, and with an aching heart. Poor Caleb! He, too?

This Caleb of the elegant person, the sharp tongue, the brilliant mind: I knew him well in Honolulu. We went to the same dances, to outings at the King's beach cottage at Waikiki, to teas at the Princess Ruth's, before she died. The Princess was his foster mother, and she was so fond of him that she treated him as a son—as, indeed, it was said he might be, by those people who knew of her collection of lovers, in the days when Caleb was sired. Others said that Caleb was but the last of those lovers, but I, seeing her vast ugliness, her great age, could not believe their vicious tongues.

Sometimes he would ask me to dance with him, during those wonderful glittering balls at the palace, at Mr. Gibson's, at the Princess Miriam's. I was in awe of him, in the beginning, made timid by his shrewd talk and frightened by his reputation; and at first I feared that he danced with me only out of lechery, or out of politeness when he could find no other partners—until I learned how he chose me to annoy the Queen. She did not like him. "Beware of a man with such a sassy tongue and such cold eyes," she warned me once, tapping my arm with a hard finger, after she watched me romp through a schottische with him. But in spite of her suspicion of him I liked Caleb, even though, as he made his malicious comments about people and things he disliked, I became as silent as one of the palace's statues he considered so ridiculous.

"Look at this thing," he jeered once, pointing at a bronze Diana (I think that was her name, or was it Daphne?), standing on the toes of one foot, while, with an outstretched and dimpled arm, she held an electrical lamp above her head. "Look at it and tell me what, in Heaven's name, a foolish thing like this is doing here in Iolani Palace? Why can't we have a statue of a naked Hawaiian warrior holding a *kukui* torch? Or"—and here he ogled me most embarrassingly—"a statue of you, in a *pa'u*." When he said things like this I blushed, and hid in modesty behind my fan, shocked at the thought that my grandmother, as well as his, had worn a style of skirt which covered her only to the waist. "Oh, Caleb!" I would cry, hoping to quiet him. But I never could, he was so outspoken.

"The Board of Health will tell the wife of Ulukou," the bosun answered Caleb. "That's what they are for."

"Will they also send his things to her?"

It was like Caleb to be concerned for the unfortunate. In spite of his great wealth, the misfortunes of the poor made him bitter, and he always sprang to their defense. Rescuing them from improvidence and hunger, from charges of theft and harlotry and furious riding: this was his chief concern when he was a young lawyer, learning his profession with Mr. Judd, to whom the Princess Ruth put him apprentice. But for the wealthier natives, or for *haoles*, he never made an effort. These he preferred to mock, even to insult, whenever he could. He mocked the Queen through me, for he liked her royal arrogance as little as she liked his fearless quarreling with the authority of the Nobles. Her cruel opinion of him became quickly known when he first appeared at Court: "*Opala*. Trash. Trash with green eyes," she sniffed, condemning him without bothering to know him, not for his self but for his heritage. In dismissing him she condemned his whole family, all the way back to the remote ancestress who, in the time of Captain Cook, played the whore with one of that evil dirty man's dirty diseased sailors.

Risking the Queen's displeasure, I continued to speak with Caleb when I could, and to dance with him whenever he asked me. When I came to understand that he was not interested in me as a partner for his bed, I enjoyed his company the more. I was so tired of slapping at men's hands, of holding them off, of defending my virtue! I became easier in Caleb's presence, more the enjoyer of his wit than the cause of his mockery; and I think that he came to like me as the simple listener to the expressions of his quick and complex mind.

All was going well between us when suddenly, about the time I was taken with the sickness, he disappeared from Honolulu. His going was a mystery: no one knew where he went, or why he dropped from sight. But now I knew. Alas for poor Caleb. Crueler than the arrogance of Kapiolani, more brutal than the bite of quick death, I knew, would be this rotting away for Caleb, this slow end to his proud ambitions.

The bosun made his promises to Caleb that the belongings of Ulukou would be safe. Caleb's scowl of suspicion faded away as he spoke his thanks. How thin he was. The lines of his face were those of a man whose soul is being eaten away within him. Yet his body, like mine, showed almost no outward sign of the disease. His back was as straight as it always was, his clothes were as elegant, his narrow feet as finely shod, as if they were come fresh from London. Even the English hat was perched upon his narrow head as if he strolled along Fort Street in Honolulu, on his way to the Courthouse. Only the raw sores on his ears set him apart from other men. But this was more than I showed, and I was here, a leper.

I went to speak to him, making my way behind our stolid group, waiting like cattle for the next longboat to be loaded. "Aloha, Kalepa," I said softly, when I reached his side. This is the Hawaiian form of his missionary name. It means "the trader, the seller," and he liked it because he wanted, he said, to be a trader of thoughts, a seller of new ideas to his people. But that morning, on the Mokolii, as, unthinking, I said it, it filled the air between us with a new and horrid sound.

He whirled upon me, snarling. "So? The princess speaks at last to her servant." I drew back from him in alarm. Never had I seen a face so harsh, or eyes so bright with anger. "Does Your Highness need my hand to step into her carriage?" he rushed on, sweeping an arm toward the longboat, making a footman's bow.

He knew that I do not merit titles, that between us there is no need for bows. While I looked at him in dismay, too surprised to stop him, he finished his hurtful charge: "Majesty or trash. Now they ride in the same boat."

"Caleb," I tried to ease his hurt. "Caleb, please—" I put out a hand to him, but he would take no comfort from me. And he would give me none. Furiously he pulled his arm away from me, angrily he turned to go.

"O.K. O.K.!" cried the bosun. "Secon' load aboard. Two *wahine*, foah *kane*." Helplessly I stood between his order and Caleb's malice. Of the two the bosun's command was the stronger. "*Hele!*" he insisted. "Come on!" Stepping forward, he took Tutu by her arm; reaching out, he seized me by the wrist. His glance picked out the four men who were nearest: Caleb, Ioane Paele, Hamau, were among them, and one other whose name I did not know.

My cavalier was the skinny wrinkled old bosun. He handed me into the boat, unafraid of my touch. When I sat down, upon the boxes of freight, he put Tutu beside me. The four men climbed in as best they could. Caleb, perforce, found himself sitting with his back against mine. Two pieces of trash, riding in the same boat.

I was sick with misery, that he should think I thought so highly of myself, so lowly of him.

This is the one blessing which lepers enjoy: only once do they need to cross the beach at Kalawao.

Perhaps it is best, in God's Providence, that the ordeal of the beach must come first. After it has been suffered, the trial of living and dying at Kalawao is lessened.

Somehow Tutu and I managed to stumble and crawl the length of that terrible beach. I cannot remember much more than the cold wind, the slippery rocks covered with green *limu*, the black crabs hurrying to get out of our way. Like a monstrous crab ourselves, Tutu and I, tied to each other by our need, slipped and tottered and fell along the way, and rose again to try once more. The rumble of the sea was not louder in my ears than the sound of Tutu, gasping for her breath.

When we came to the top of the cliff the people of Kalawao

were there to greet us. I was not prepared for them. I stopped in dismay at their number, at the swelling sounds of their greeting. So many of them! So many of my people, to be victims of this foreigners' disease. Never until then had I known how terrible is this affliction upon the people. But now, in the presence of the dwellers of Kalawao, I saw the price we were made to pay for our entering into the world of nations. My body was as a pebble upon the shore of Kalawao, compared with the number of bodies gathered there upon the plain. I was but one among many, and in the instant of seeing the many, I was made one with them.

Out from under the trees, into the great field of grass, we walked. So did I imagine would come a group of pilgrims, approaching Zion. The grass was the greenest and loveliest of grass. Thick and full, it stretched like a carpet between the lines of people, inviting us into the village of Kalawao. Above the heads of the people a church steeple rose, slender and tapered, pointing to the cross of promise. Zion could not be more fair.

As we walked between their rows the people smiled upon us and called out their *alohas*. Then they began to sing. Lovely and clear, the voices rose, bringing us the comfort of the message of our King, written by him for those of his people who live at Kalaupapa:

> The Almighty's chastening hand
> A sore affliction sends;
> But trusting still we feel
> His wrath with mercy blends.
>
> The Christ: His blessed Son
> The lepers' woe did feel:
> He touched the unclean sores,
> The incurable did heal.
>
> Your King and Queens and Chiefs,
> Hawaiians everywhere,
> Unite with loving hearts
> In this our hope and prayer.

Who could deny this hymn its claim upon the heart? Who could resist the comfort of those beautiful words?

I could not. Happy in my tears, I heard the voices of my people, singing as they welcomed me home.

18

IT IS THE CUSTOM of Kalawao, since Father Damien's time, to receive newcomers into the hospital and to give them shelter there until they recover from their weariness. This is a kind thing to do, because almost everyone arrives half dead at Kalawao, after the passage of the beach. In the old days, before Kamiano came, the new arrivals were left to themselves. They sought shelter under trees, or in the open fields, and many of them were dead of their exhaustion before they had time to live at Kalawao.

At the hospital, Tutu and I went to the side for the women, Caleb and his companions went to the side of the men.

A *wahine kokua* met us at the door, and took us from the hands of Father Damien. "Good morning to you, Loke," he called up to her from the foot of the stairs. "Here are two new friends for us. I leave them with you now. You make them feel at home."

"*Aloha oulua,*" she greeted us cheerfully. "Come into the house." It was like coming to the home of a friend. She was a large woman, with great arms filling her sleeves, and great breasts swelling the bosom of her *holoku,* and cheeks as round and full as mountain apples from Maunawili. Yet, when she came smiling toward us, she moved as lightly as a cloud drifting across the face of heaven.

"*Mahalo,*" sighed Tutu, going stiffly up the stairs, one step at a time. "*Mahalo,*" she said with each upward step, having no strength to say more.

Loke fed us bread and tea in the small parlor. Then, when we were rested, she took us to the cool wash-house, to be undressed and bathed by two young girls who were her helpers. The water, clear and cold, came from the mountains, flowing through a long pipe into huge wooden tubs set upon a stone floor. I shivered when I stepped into my bath. The water at the palace is always warm from the sun. But Tutu lay gratefully in her tub, clucking with pleasure at the coolness. "It is like the pool of the spring at Kuliouou. There we bathe every day, my children and their chil-

dren and I. Until the policeman came, to take me away . . ." Her
voice broke off at the memory.

The girls would not let her grieve. With the quick wisdom of
the young they talked to her. "Then must you go swimming with
us, in the forest pools of Waileia," said one. "There the water
is cold, colder than this, under the shadow of the mountains, and
the ferns are thick upon the cliffs," said the other.

"Where is this Waileia you talk of?" Tutu asked, tossing her
head indignantly. "Who, indeed, has heard of this place?"

"Where is this Hulikoukou you talk of?" one of the girls mimicked her. She was the one with the smooth face, and the braids
of dark hair looped over her ears, like bird's wings.

"Sassy thing! At least you can tease me by its right name,"
laughed Tutu. "But you are right. 'What matters the source, if
only the water washes clean? It is the water of life.' I shall go to
swim with you, my dears, in the pool of Waileia, in the waters
of my new home. And I shall not speak of that other place again."
She flicked the cold water at the girls until they ran squealing to
me for protection. I was sitting in my bath, pinning my hair back
into place.

"How pretty your hair is," said Akala, kneeling down beside me.
"Is that the new style in Honolulu?" She was the one with the
face I tried not to see. I looked instead at the top of her head, at
the partings in her hair where the braids were begun.

"Alas, it is. Now the ladies must wear it this way, or be ashamed.
No more do they wear it in braids, or held low on the neck. Now
it is all piled up on the top, with a little fringe on the forehead,
like the lock on the head of a cow."

"Who tells them to change? Is it the King?"

I laughed at the thought of His Majesty telling the Queen how
to dress her hair. He is afraid of her, not only because of her great
rank, which is nobler than his own, but also because of her age
and her sharp tongue. She is older than he, and, because she has
learned many times over that he married her for her rank and
not for love, she treats him with harshness whenever she can. So
often have I seen it. Yet he is always gentle with her, patient
with her hardness, as if in his courtesy he would make amends
for the coldness of his heart.

"Well? Does he?"

"Oh, no. It is some people in Palani, where Paris is, I think. Or perhaps in Beretania. I do not know. They change their minds so often! I cannot keep up with them."

"Do you have a dress with a bustle?" Kapule wanted to know.

Before I could answer her a church bell rang, merrily and clear, almost over our heads. "*Auwe, auwe!*" Akala shrieked. "Time for Mass." Pulling off her apron, she ran from the room, splashing through the puddles of water on the floor.

"Do you not go too?" I asked Kapule.

"Oh, no. Today is her turn for Mass, and my turn for Vespers. Tomorrow I go to Mass." With the briskness of a busy housewife she ordered me to get on with my bathing while she went to scrub Tutu.

After two days of rest in the hospital, we had a visitor come to see us in our beds. Ambrose Hutchinson, he who is the Board of Health's Superintendent of the whole Settlement at Kalaupapa, came to call upon me. He lived in Honolulu, before he caught the separation sickness, and he kept the books of the Settlement telling where the people stayed, who of them was close to death, and who of them died. He appeared so quietly beside my bed that only when I turned my head from looking at the light of the sun sparkling upon the distant sea did I know he was there.

"You are Malie, the daughter of Kekoa? The daughter of Kekoa-wahine, who is of the Kahekili family of Maui?"

Who is this man who knows of my family, I wondered. And how does he know so much of me? I did not know of his importance then, and I could only nod my head to tell him that I was indeed the Malie of whom he spoke.

"Her Majesty, the Queen, has sent me a letter to tell me of your coming. She has sent me these words: 'Do you take care of Malie the daughter of Kekoa. See to it that she comes to no harm. See to it that she has every comfort. She is as a daughter to me, and to the King.'" As my heart grew big with love for the Queen, who stretched out her hand to me even though we were forever parted, the quiet man told me who he was and why he came to my bedside.

"There is a house, near to Kalaupapa, where you can live in comfort. It is the house of the brother of your mother—"

"The house of Uncle Pita? Does it stand empty?"

"Empty to this day it is: the *kapu* is on it, for these four years

since he died. Empty it stands, awaiting another. It is a fine
house."

A fine house. But I did not want to live in it. I could remember Uncle Pita, from the time before he went to Kalaupapa, the
first of the sick *alii* to wish to live out his days in exile. In those
times—Was it ten years before? Was it eleven?—he was a great
joyous giant of a man, full of laughter and music, who could
feast the whole night through and then spend the next day working like a slave for the people, in the House of Nobles. His love
for the people, and his fear for their fate if the Kalawao disease
should spread among them, told him, when he caught the sickness, how he must show them the only way to stop its spread.

Well did I remember the day of lamentation in our household
when he limped in to bid us farewell. His swollen toes bulged out
of a felt slipper, slit at the sides to hold the misshapen foot. His
face was sad, as it was never sad in the days of his health, and his
eyes were full of fear. He was a broken man: there was no joy
in him. And I, who used to climb into his lap and hang upon his
neck when he was well, delighting in his moist kisses and enormous hugs, I ran crying from him when it came my turn to say
good-by. I ran to hide in the mango tree growing at the back of
our house. I could not kiss him upon the cheek, in the kiss of
farewell, and even as, with arms outstretched, he waited for me
to come to him, I ran away from him.

"No! I cannot live there." How could I tell Ambrose Hutchinson
that I feared the sad eyes of Uncle Pita, gazing at me in sorrow,
across the years, because I fled him when he needed me most?
"No, I cannot live there," I said again, to talk down his astonishment. "Is there not some other place?" Desperately I tried to find
a reason why I should not go to Uncle Pita's empty haunted
house. "Is there no place close by to this hospital? I—I have it in
mind to help Loke here, after I have become settled." Out of
my terror of Uncle Pita's ghost I fashioned for myself a reason
why I should stay in Kalawao.

Ambrose was puzzled. "*Alii* do not need to work."

"Here there are no *alii*," I said sharply, finding the taunt of
Caleb in Ambrose's humble statement. "Here there are only the
sick and the well." The blood of chiefs might run in my body,
but it was the blood of *alii* who cared for their people. Uncle Peter
proved his concern to the nation, as well as to me. And in his
way, by proving my concern for my people, by following in his

footsteps, perhaps I could please his grieving spirit, close those accusing eyes.

I, the meek one who always will do the bidding of others, whose very name means gentle and mild: I was seized by a devil. Sitting up in my bed, I said boldly, trying to capture the manner of the Queen when she sends someone to do her bidding: "I wish to stay here in Kalawao." I was clever enough not to shout.

"Let it be so," he bowed, smiling wearily. Immediately I felt sorry for him, and full of contrition for my stubbornness. Did he have to please every new arrival in Kalawao as I was forcing him to please me? Behind his brown mask of politeness was he calling me names, and sneering at me, as Caleb did, calling me "Your Highness" with a hatred in his thoughts such as he dared not show in his voice?

"Here there is no empty house for you. Will you live with others?" He gave no sign of impatience.

"Would that not be better for me?" I was soft now when my argument seemed won. "Where do you put Tutu?" I called her to his notice with a wave of my hand. "Mrs. Pahaiwa?" Sitting alert in the bed next to mine, she was not missing a word of our talk.

He looked across to her, bowed slightly. Unhurried, he studied the bent and wrinkled body, the thick gray hair falling below her shoulders, the signs of her sickness. He had the glance of a doctor, judging, reckoning the days or the months or the years of life left in her.

"The doctors in Honolulu say one year," she snapped. "But I do not intend to oblige them so easily. I say it will be two years."

"Good for you," he laughed, showing a humor I did not think he owned. "Good for you, Tutu. A tough old thing like you: I'll bet you will last longer."

Regally she wrapped her shawl around her. Never has the Queen done it better. "Might even outlive you," she sniffed. But there was a wink of teasing for him, which he did not miss.

"I know where I will put you. How would you like to keep house for a *Pake* gambler?"

"Not me," she huffed. "I have some self-respect left."

"Then how about a handsome Hawaiian man—about your age."

"Now you talk sense."

I was shocked. "But is this permitted?"

Ambrose looked down at me, sober again. He had the commoner's respect for the *alii*, and I wished he would forget it when he spoke with me. "I do not know any man more respectable than Makaio. He is a pillar of the church. He is the wisest man in the Settlement—after Father Damien—and the most trusted. And now he lives his days in grief: Kenahu, his wife, died a day or so ago. Her dying makes room for you in his house. It is the only way—"

"How old is he?" interrupted Tutu with a leer.

"Too old for what you're thinking."

"*Cha!* Is there a man too old for that?"

"Tutu, hush!" I called to her, protesting her immodesty.

"We will go to the house of Makaio," decided Tutu, settling back into her pillow. "I think perhaps we will be good for him."

The next morning we walked to the house of Makaio. Kewalo showed us the way, taking our baggage in a small cart drawn by a bullock which was bigger than the wagon. The heavy wheels squeaked like a sky full of sea birds circling above a school of fish.

Kewalo pointed out to us the important places of Kalawao. At first he was not much more talkative than the ox, but with Tutu to goad him into speech we learned something about the new place which was going to be our whole world.

Between walls of loose rocks the dusty road stretched to the west, toward Kalaupapa—and, beyond it, toward Oahu. Upon our backs the morning sun shone warm. For the first time we saw the majestic cliffs unveiled: the clouds and the mist were blown away, and the great green *pali* lifted their heads proudly above the land. Beautiful were they: covered with verdure from foot to crown, they looked as soft and cool as does the moss in the shaded clefts of Nuuanu. Gone, lost with the clouds, was the grayness of the morning of our arrival. Who could speak of *Molokai ahina* on a day as brilliant as this?

"Up there is the *kauka's* house," said Kewalo, pointing to a big house at the edge of the cleared space above the hospital. Shabby and weather-beaten it was, sad and alone. "It is *kapu*. Patients may not go near it." Beyond the house the thick forest ran up the hill to the foot of the cliffs. A little-used path, winding across the grass, connected the cottage with the hospital.

"Which *kauka* lives there?" I asked.

"There is only one *kauka*, at any time," growled Kewalo, "when there is a doctor here. Now it is the small *haole* who came with you. The one who brought the man-killer among us." He spat into the dust. "They say he is sick."

"Keanu is sick?" By this I meant, has the doctor done his evil deed so soon?

"Nah, nah, the small *haole*. He is sick in his bed—but not with the *lepera*, like the rest of us—and Kamiano takes food to them. Keanu does not come out of the house. The people wonder why." His spitting confused me. Among commoners it is usually a sign of contempt for the thing being talked about. But Kewalo spat so often, breaking into his speech to spit as other people pause for breath, and I could not tell for whom he was showing his scorn. Keanu or Opaekea or me: which of us did he dislike?

"Here is the house of Iokepa the bell ringer. And here is the house of Palolo." The cottages were half hidden behind stone walls and trees. All of them, as far as we could see, were on our left hand, on the mountain side of the road. Except for the Catholic church, and another small white church farther along the road, nothing stood upon the right of the way. Between us and the sea, lying far away, stretched only the broad green plain of Kalaupapa.

The houses of Iokepa and of Palolo and of most of the people Kewalo named for us were freshly whitewashed and neatly kept. Only a few of those we passed were unpainted and disordered. "Why do some look so clean, while others are so old?" I asked our guide.

He looked down at me with weary patience. He was such a peevish man! His dark skin, pitted with the scars of smallpox, seemed almost purple in the sunlight. The hair upon his head was at the stage of turning to white where the mixture of black and white is itself a silvery blue. But the huge mustache curling beneath his broad nose was glossy and black still, as if he anointed it each day with stove polish. A bull of a man was this Kewalo, and about as clever with words as was the beast he led.

The mustache wriggled, the lips rolled: I expected him to spit upon me. "The sick ones," he rumbled, finding the words at last, "as they come closer to death, they have not the strength for painting houses." Once more we were left without conversation, with only the creaking of the cart wheels to fill our ears.

We came to a house almost hidden behind a thicket of bushes and trees. Tangled *hau*, tall *ohia* and *kukui*, hedges of cotton, broad-leaved *wauke*—all of them grew wild as a jungle, all mixed up. And over them a mantle of morning-glories was flung, their lavender blossoms long since opened to the sun. "And who lives here, who is so close to death?" asked Tutu, peering curiously at the forlorn place.

Kewalo chewed the ends of his mustache, did not bother to look at the house or at us, waiting for his answer. "It is my house," he said at last, very unwillingly. "I—I have no time for cutting down trees."

Mercilessly did Tutu laugh at him. "Lazy buggah," she scolded him in English. "Such lies you tell us." Mocking him, she directed her spit upon his rock wall. She was like a grandmother dog, showing her teeth at him. "Big talk, small work."

"Woman: with so sharp a tongue, you will need no knife to clear your patch of earth." After that he would say no more.

We came to the other church. This one was white and pure, unlike Father Damien's, colorful as the *ohia lehua* in blossom. But where Father Damien's church was open, this one was closed. The doors, even the shutters on the windows, were folded shut. Above the gate through the stone wall was a sign: Siloama, the Church of the Healing Spring.

"*Kie,*" snorted Tutu. "A spring that flows only on Sabbath days."

Kewalo looked at her as if he would take joy in beating her with his heavy hands. "Tutu," I pleaded, "*kulikuli*. Hush."

Sweetly she smiled back at me. "This place needs the tongue of a scolding woman." To the big man walking beside us she said, her voice as small as a choirgirl's: "Tell me. Do you have a wife?"

A groan, a turning away: this was the only protest Kewalo dared to make.

Beyond the church of Siloama the houses were more scattered, the spaces between them more filled with trees and underbrush. Tutu quickly tired of the walking. "Where is this palace of the high chief Makaio?" she grumbled. "Is it in Kalaupapa? Or is it perhaps in Honolulu, that we must walk so far?"

At the last house, where the village of Kalawao came to an end, Kewalo turned into the yard. "The house of Makaio," he informed us, pulling the bullock to a halt.

There was no laziness in Makaio. His yard was kept like a garden, the cottage was clean and in good order. The house was small: a central parlor, with a bedroom at either side, were fitted under the high peaked roof. A narrow veranda was built across the front of the parlor. Tutu and I saw the house with relief, even to the sturdy posts holding up the roof of the *lanai*, even to the green plants growing in the borders around the house itself. *Ti* plants and mountain ginger and ferns were there, and the great crinkled leaves of dry-land taro.

There is room here, the thought came to my mind, there is room here for my orange trees. Already I could imagine them, growing against the far wall of the yard, their leaves shining in the sun, their branches heavy with the green and yellow fruit.

Rising from his chair in the shelter of the *lanai* was Makaio. Tall and thin, his white hair soft as mist, he came down the low stairs to greet us. His smile was small, but it was kind. His grief was still upon him: we could not expect much show of joy from him. In his shadow came a boy, nine or ten years old. The boy was far gone with the sickness, but the old man's sores were healed. Only the faint brown scars upon his cheeks, around his mouth, showed why he lived at Kalawao.

Slowly he walked to us, stately as a chief in the presence of the nation. He was a handsome old man. Wide-eyed with admiration, Tutu stared up at him, forgetting her manners as she forgot also her saucy reason for coming to his house.

"*Aloha*," he said, bowing slightly, a man of dignity, who did not stand humble before anyone. "*Aloha* to you, daughter of Kekoa. *Aloha* to you, widow of Pahaiwa. Welcome to this house. May you know happiness here." It is the ancient greeting, and it fell like a blessing upon us who had come to him in our need.

"*Mahalo*," I answered for both of us. "We are grateful that you permit us to share your house with you."

"If we do not help others, then we ourselves are not worthy of help. We are the ones to be grateful, because of the help you bring to us. Not only for myself do I speak. The boy, too, is in need of your company." He brought the lad forward. "Here is Moki, my foster son." Fondly he looked down upon the boy. "He has not seen the world beyond these cliffs or beyond the edge of the sea. He was born here, and—and here he stays. He has a thousand questions he saves for you, to ask about the wonders of Honolulu, the mysteries of the places across the sea."

Filled as he might be with questions, Moki was tied of tongue that day. He looked to be a bright child, from what little I could see of him beneath the top of his bowed head, with the stiff black hair as short as the bristles in a brush. Tutu was smitten with him even more than with his *hanai* father. Her face was soft with love for the boy: he was a *hanai* son for her, too, one who would help to take the place of those left behind at Kuliouou. But Moki was afraid of her strangeness, and he did not come forward when she held out her hand to him. Perhaps it was because he did not see it, his cheeks being so puffed up.

"Come inside, come inside," the old man urged. "Moki will show you the way."

Like a family come home we crossed the grass of the yard to the humble house.

Makaio's cottage was well suited to our needs. He and Moki slept in one small bedroom on the left side of the house. Tutu and I slept in the larger bedroom on the right. In the parlor between we lived and visited and took our meals. On the nights when we were at home, we sat around the large table, reading by the light of oil lamps or writing letters or—if it was not the Sabbath night—playing the card games which Tutu and Moki enjoyed so much. Moki soon forgot our newness, and when he and Tutu and I were become friends, there was peace in Makaio's household.

In the separate cookhouse at the back Tutu and I helped Emma, she who was Papakolea's daughter, to prepare the meals. In time I learned Emma's story. A buxom girl, she had been wed to four husbands, one after the other. Each of them died of the Kalawao sickness. But she was clean still, not a leper. She had come to the Settlement as a *kokua* with her first husband, the companion of her heart. When he died, she could not die. Nor could she leave. She stayed at Kalawao, to be the consoler of men.

"Sometimes one of them will think he must marry me," she laughed, shrugging her comely shoulders. "If he is a good man, I let him marry me, for his comfort. But he does not last very long," she sighed, "and soon I am a widow once more." Out of pity she was a perch for birds to light upon. But Emma was sad in her heart, since her first man died, and selfless in her bedding. And because she took no money for her kindness to men, she was poor and she had to work for us.

At first I was embarrassed by her presence and scandalized by her history, which Tutu was not slow to pry out of her. Her readiness to talk of it shocked me even more: these were things, I thought, which people did not talk about with frankness and with laughter. But if Makaio hired her and Tutu liked her—more than once I heard her say of Emma "she is a good girl," with a certainty which left me confused about the meaning of goodness —who was I to hold myself apart from her? Surely the Lord Jesus would forgive her and honor her, as he had honored the fallen Magdalene. But Tutu knew Emma's worth, not only to us but also to the many men in Kalaupapa who lived without women. She said it to my face one day: "Because there are a few like her in the Settlement, virgins like you and old women like me can dwell here in safety." So quickly had I learned to accept Tutu's knowledge of the world that I did not shrink from her plain-speaking. But not until later did I learn how right she was in her understanding of Emma's part in the life of the Settlement.

As neighbors in the houses around us lived people who came often to call upon Makaio and who came early to meet us.

Closest by was Ah See the Chinaman, who lived alone in a small house of his own, because he wished to live alone. "One peepul, no *pilikia,*" he explained to us one evening, addressing us in his singsong speech, his long yellow fingers counting with him, "two peepul, oney tlouble. Mus' give love, mus' give hate. Too muchee tlouble! Me no likee *pilikia.*" With his narrow eyes, his wispy beard, the skullcap and the braided queue dangling down his back, and with this kind of talk from him, I thought him a very sinister old man.

But Tutu felt otherwise. She had the country Hawaiian's sus-picion of foreigners. "If you ask me," she said in English hardly better than his own, "I bet you smoke the *opiuma,* and make love in your dreams."

"Moah bettah," answered Ah See, far from silenced. "Dleam-kine *wahine,* he no come back, he no makee tlouble. Get new one erry time!" His laughter rose high and shrill above Tutu's snort of disapproval. She was ill-humored, knowing how he was besting her. Slyly he looked at her, his narrow eyes closed to mere slits in the yellow face. "You likee dleam, I give you *opiuma* . . ."

Now was her time to cackle in triumph. They were well-matched, those two, and they enjoyed their contests of earthy humor. *"Cha,* you sassy ol' *Pake,* you! When I am so old I have to dream, *then* I come to you for the *opiuma.* But not yet."

Ah See was always a gentlemanly loser. His yellow face would crinkle, his polite laughter would rise from his half-closed mouth for two short shrieks, and then he would fall silent again, to let the conversation take another turn. It was a long while before I realized how much the gentleman Ah See was, and how he managed always to let Tutu have the final word.

A neighbor I did not like was Momona, with the fat body and the dirty mind. His tongue oozed poison, as they say the snakes of foreign lands have in their tongues. He would say one thing with a smile, and mean another. If a newcomer to Kalawao would ask him, "Where is the trail to the mountains?" Momona would say, "Go that way," pointing to a path which led to the sea. As the *malihini* would take the downward path, Momona the Fat would sit wreathed in smiles, enjoying the success of his lie. He would maintain that mountain apples came into fruit in January, when everyone else knew they were eaten in July; and yet so skillfully did he talk that when he was done most of us would be ready to swear how the blossoms came in July and the fruits were ripe in January.

He told lies for the pleasure of lying, this fat Momona, and no one could be sure when he spoke the truth, when he uttered lies. But he was clever: he told the truth just often enough to let it be known that he could speak straight if he had a mind to do so. This could give him great power over simple people.

I could not understand why Makaio made him welcome at our house, and I would turn my back upon him, or pretend an interest in my crochet work, when, in the twilight, he would come to us, waddling like a capon across the thick grass. I would feel his eyes upon me, studying me as he talked. His was not the look of lust, for in his swollen sick body the fires of desire were long since perished. Only his mind was unsmothered in fat; and his eyes, peering out from behind the rolls of flesh, were shrewd and cold and piercing. I did not dislike him for his lies as much as for the evil I saw lurking in those spiteful eyes.

Ah See and Momona: these were our nearest neighbors. Beyond them, in the direction of Kalawao, lived Miele, she who was the grandmother to Akala. In the same house with them lived Puupuu and Kekalohi, who were wife and husband to each other. And near to them, in a house of men, lived Caleb. This I learned from Akala, when on the fifth day after our arrival, she came to see Tutu and me.

"O na maka wale no keia i hele mai nei," she said when she appeared at our door. "Only the eyes have come." By this she meant that she brought no gift for us, as was customary in the old days, but brought only herself. We were to learn in time how she took her quaint speech and her old-fashioned manners from Miele. Tutu and I were won immediately by her sweetness and by her need for the company of women other than the two who lived in her house. We could tell by the way she stared at us, examining every detail of our dress and of our home, that she came from a poor household, where clothes were little more than rags and food was very scarce.

Tutu knew at once how most to please her. "Susana gave me some kookoolau from home. I will make tea from them, and we will have bread, still warm from the oven." While Akala, speechless with expectation, went to help Tutu in the cookhouse, I hurried to my room and looked through my clothes for a dress to give her. Mine were all too long for her, or too full, but in a box of Kenahu's things, she who was the dead wife of Makaio, I found two of her dresses. Cut in the older mode of Kenahu's time, they were more suitable for Akala. Drawing them out of their resting place, I took them with me to the parlor. Akala's joy upon receiving them was almost more than Tutu and I could bear.

"The pink one," she breathed, holding it up to her. "It is beautiful—"

"It fits your name, too," said Tutu, trying not to weep. The dress, made of faded pink cambric, heavily decked with pink lace and coarse needlework, was not beautiful any more, in our eyes; and nothing, any more, could make Akala beautiful. But it was a better dress than the tatters she was wearing, and it would serve to cover her nakedness as she grew into it. We made her put it on, and we spent the rest of the afternoon sipping tea and cutting and sewing the dress to fit her.

"Don't make it too small, you know," warned Tutu. "Give her room to grow in. She's getting to be a young lady now."

While we were fitting the shabby thing to her she, flitting giddily from one topic to another, told me about Caleb. "He is asking about you, and about where you live. I have told him. Is that good?"

"That sassy thing!" cried Tutu. "After the way he talked to you on the boat, he should be horsewhipped!"

"Tutu! Shame on you! There is no reason why Caleb Forrest and I should not be friends. Yes, Akala, you did right. But if he asks about me, why does he not come to see me, as you have?"

"He is sick, I think. He does not leave the house."

"What of the small *haole* boy who came with us?" asked Tutu, changing the subject sooner than I wished.

"He lives with the *haole* men, near to Siloama. I have seen him, crying under the big *kamani* tree. He does not play with any of us, even when we ask him to."

"The poor boy," said Tutu. "We must go to see him. Perhaps we can bring him some comfort. Moki and he are of the same age. Why should they not play together?"

"Are there many children here?" I asked.

"Plenty. Some sick, some well: all mixed up. We have much fun. I think the *haole* boy will play with us, when he is tired of his weeping."

"When do you go to school?"

Akala looked up at me as though I were the stupid one, to ask such a question. "No school here." Why should we go to school? What can we learn that will do us any good? These were the questions she did not need to ask.

That same evening, before the darkness came, we heard the story of the *haole* doctor's visit to the store at Kalaupapa and of how angry he became with the storekeeper for refusing to sell him anything. Kewalo brought us the news, heard from one of the men of Kalawao who went to the store for the occasion.

"Opaekea raged like the Devil-Wind from Pelekunu," Kewalo told us. "He ran up and down, up and down, he pounded his fist upon the table, he shrieked like a woman taken with jealousy, but still Kuoo told his lie, how he could only sell goods to patients."

Makaio shook his head in disapproval. "Why does he say this? Certainly a doctor can buy from the store."

"Because of what he would do with Keanu," Kewalo all but shouted, swinging his arms wide in his excitement.

"Who is this Keanu? And what is it the doctor would do with him?"

"You do not know?" Kewalo's mouth hung open, his thick shoulders were hunched in amazement. "You are sheltered here, I see, from the news. For this I am surprised." He could not help but see Tutu sitting in her rocking chair, innocently waiting for him to go on.

Proud at being the bearer of such tidings, Kewalo told Makaio and Ah See, and Momona, who sat entranced, who this Keanu was. He was wrong in so many of the details of Keanu's story, as even I could tell, and as Tutu's growing sneer and rolling eyes convinced me while he strung out his story. Every woman in Hawaii knows the thrilling story of Keanu's crime for love, down to the finest point. But what male has bothered to fix in his mind the tale of our country Romeo and the murder he committed for his Kohala Juliet? Not one, to judge from Kewalo's excited recounting of a gruesome murder, full of stabbings and bloodshed and brutality, with none of the softnesses of the love for the beautiful Kamaka which forced Keanu to slay her ugly unwanted husband. Kewalo was much more interested in describing the knife with which Keanu did the killing than he was in telling why it was that Keanu killed the mean little Japanese. Kewalo was much more precise in counting the number of wounds Keanu dealt than the Sheriff of Hawaii had been, or Chief Justice Judd. Hacking and stabbing furiously enough to kill a dozen Charleys, Kewalo waved his arms and shouted on, his voice becoming hoarse and his words tumbling over each other, until he was as silly as a scarecrow flapping his rags over a rice field already harvested. Momona watched him with admiration, perhaps seeing in Kewalo a bigger liar than he was himself.

But when Kewalo began upon the story of Keanu's trial in Honolulu, Tutu pulled the reins on him. "Never mind that now. We all know how Keanu was judged guilty. What happened this afternoon? What of Kuoo?"

Poor Kewalo. While Tutu toyed with her earrings, he floundered in a tumult of sounds, a shark thrashing in shallow water. Willingly would he have taken his dagger to the sassy woman sitting within reach of him. But there was only one weapon he could use, and even this he dared not loose upon Tutu. He diverted his spit of disapproval into the shrubbery twenty feet away. Fighting to control himself, he started slowly, in a mere bellow. "Kuoo says, 'Why should he make life easy for a doctor who wishes to make life so hard for Keanu?'"

"In Heaven's name, Kewalo, what does he mean by these words?" asked Makaio. "Not yet have you told us what this doctor is to do with Keanu."

"Oh. Oh yeah. That. They say he wants to give the *lepera* to Keanu."

"*Auwe!* A cruel thing to do! Is this the truth?"

"How would I know? I know only what is being said."

Tutu broke in. "This is the story we have heard at Kakaako: Opaekea asked for a man—a clean man, mark you—to offer himself, to help the *kauka* in his studies of the *lepera*. No one would step forward. Then, at the last minute, just before Opaekea is to sail with us for Kalawao, lo!—Keanu is delivered up to him, straight from the jailhouse. By no less a man than Kipikona, the First Minister of the King. What do you make of this, brother?"

Makaio's white head was sunk on his breast, while he gave thought to her account. "I think it is a terrible thing," he said at last, "to wish to give a clean man this disease. Suffering enough there is at Kalawao, without adding one more sick body, one more broken spirit, to our number. But surely," he looked up hopefully, "there can be other reasons why Keanu is here?"

"Why is he kept apart from us? Why does he not come out of the doctor's house?" asked Kewalo.

"Perhaps he is sick? With another sickness which keeps him at home?"

"Perhaps he is a prisoner still, chained in the house?" suggested Momona, taking pleasure in the thought. His was the kind of smile evil boys show, as they pull legs from centipedes, watching them wriggle.

"Why does Opaekea forbid Kamiano—even Kamiano—to go to the doctor's house?" Kewalo wanted to know.

"Does he indeed forbid his house to Kamiano?" Makaio was unbelieving. "Does he dare to close his door to this good man?"

Kewalo nodded grimly. "He tells me so himself, does Kamiano."

"If this is so," said Makaio, seeing the doctor now in the way we saw him, "then I say that Kuoo did a good thing. I will stand with him, in holding my hand from this—this Opaekea." His mouth was twisted, as one always twists his mouth at the sight of a white shrimp, lying ugly in the mud.

"*Ae.* And this was the feeling of Kuoo, and of all who went to stand with him in the store today," said Kewalo.

"Does Kamiano know of this?"

Kewalo shrugged. "Sometimes I think yes, he knows. Sometimes I think no, he does not."

"Of course he knows," Momona said. "All these *haoles* help each other. Why else would Kamiano carry food each day, with his own hands, to the doctor's house? E? I have heard it from the mouth of Iokepa the bell ringer, who is also cook in the hospital kitchen. And why else would Damien go with the doctor to Kalaupapa, to buy things for him in the store? Does he take anyone else to Kalaupapa in his wagon? No. Kamiano knows."

"*Ae,*" remembered Kewalo. "They say that Kamiano *ordered* Kuoo to sell Opaekea things from the store."

"See?" said Momona, spreading his hands before him.

"And in this way Opaekea got all he wanted, although Kuoo charged him double for everything, without his knowing it." Kewalo waited for our laughter, but it did not come. We were too hurt by this latest proof of the *haoles'* strengths, and of our weaknesses. They won every battle; we could cheat them only in small ways.

"I would not think this of Kamiano," said Makaio, giving up his loyalty slowly. "The priest: he is a good man."

"Each man has his price," murmured Momona, "and Kamiano has his. I will wager you that his price is escape from this prison for helping the *kauka*. You will see. He will be taken away from here, he will be sent to some better place."

"But why?" asked Kewalo. "Why does one of our people sell himself to the *haoles?* Why does Keanu offer himself to be this doctor's animal?"

Next to me Tutu hissed in annoyance, preparing to give her verdict. But the sly Momona spoke first. "Why?" he giggled, his great body shaking with something that was not a laugh, yet was not a sob. "Why? Because, as even you must know, life is bright and death is dark. To live a leper is better than to be hanged a clean man."

This was one of the times, I felt, when Momona spoke the truth.

If on the evening of the fifth day we wondered why the doctor brought Keanu to Kalawao, on the evening of the seventh day there remained no doubt in our minds about his reason. The

word of his operation upon Keanu in the morning was spread
all through the Settlement by noon of that day. And by sunset
people everywhere were meeting to talk over the terrible event.

In my own heart I was sick with pity for the murderer. The
waiting, the long time of wondering, of not knowing, of hoping
against hope that he would escape the claim Opaekea's cruel
operation laid upon him: this was dreadful enough an ordeal for
the poor man to have to bear. But what if—my pity throbbed in
my throat with the horror of the thought—what if, at the end of
his time of waiting, Keanu should find that he was indeed a
leper? The torment of his waiting would be as nothing to the
despair which would come upon him with its ending. I sorrowed
for Keanu as though I knew him well, as though he were my
brother.

"So, ellybody *huhu* today," Ah See began his evening's visit.
Usually he sat silent, impassive as an idol in a joss house, resting
upon the stair where it joined the *lanai*, because he did not like
chairs. Often he dozed in the slow evenings, when talk was as
unhurried as the drone of honeybees in a *kiawe* tree. But the
smoke of his tiny pipe was welcome, because it kept the mosquitoes away. When I first saw it, narrow as a reed, with a small
metal bowl perched at one end, I thought that it must surely be
his opium pipe. But the smoke coming from it bore the scent of
tobacco, and I was almost disappointed that Ah See should
smoke tobacco as did ordinary men.

"Ae, it is done," sighed Makaio, heavy with disappointment.
"A crueler deed I have never heard of. There have been many
cruel deeds in this world of people. I have seen some. I have
done some. But this one—*Kie!*"

Momona came to join us. With his heavy legs, his heavy belly,
the rolls of fat upon his chest, he moved like a sow swollen with
carrion. Puffing for breath, he mounted the stairs, which sagged
beneath his weight, stepped upon the boards of the *lanai*, which
trembled under him. Politely we waited for him to lower himself
into his sturdy chair.

"Now we know," he said, fanning himself with his plump
hand. "Now we have seen an evil done, from which there will
come more evil." He was pleased with his prophecy. A little pout
of satisfaction hung upon his moist lips.

Ah See lifted his head, shining where the hair was shaven away.
It was the head of a scholar, and like a scholar he raised his waxen

hand to stop Momona's talk. "How you know, oney tlouble come? Maybe doctah moah smaht dan you?"

"What you mean, *Pake?*" The fat one put his question scornfully.

"Maybe diskine doctah he likee look-see-*nana* somat'ing insi' *kanaka* boy. Somat'ing fo help ellybody."

"Like what?"

"*Haole* smaht, not *Pake*. I no *sabe*. You go look-see-*nana kauka* bimeby. He talk you. I t'ink so, maybe he likee fin' one new medicine—" Before he could finish Momona interrupted him.

"*Cha!* Another one of those! Every *haole* who comes here has a new medicine. How often we have seen it."

"*Ae,*" said Makaio. "Each one brings a cure, he says, but no one is cured. How many medicines have we tried? Medicines from America, medicines from Europe, we have tried. Oils from China, powders from India, ointments from the Holy Land, made by the priests in Bethany. But they have done no good: our flesh still rots away, our lives are still cut short."

"The medicine of Peter Kahekili: that is the best," said Momona, giggling as he watched me, to see my response. But he would not go on until I asked him to say what I yearned to hear.

"It was—nothing," he said, unfolding his empty hands before him, displaying their burden of nothingness. "In the beginning he tried everything, he was so afraid to die. He tried bathing in the sea, he tried bathing in the sweet waters of Waileia. They were no good. He put alcohol on his foot, he put *popolo* juice on his hand. They were no good. He ran to the priest, he ran to the *kahuna*. No good. He sent to his cousin, the old Queen"—here Momona hardened his voice, and I saw with a shock the hatred in his eyes when he spoke of my vanished uncle—"to the Queen Emma, if you please, for 'Kenedy's Discovery,' because someone told him it was a good cure for the leprosy. Alas, even from the hands of a Queen it was no good. He smeared his sores with the red earth of Waimea, he washed them with the urine of babies." His womanish voice broke in a fit of giggling.

Stop, I wanted to cry out to him, Stop! His cruel listing of poor Uncle Pita's useless remedies was not hurtful. It was the picture of my poor uncle, frantic with his despair, running like a hungry dog from one house to another, seeking the magic which would stay his dying—it was this that tore at my heart.

Mercilessly the fat man continued his tale. "Everything our

proud prince tried, everything. Hee, hee. It was so funny! And all
the while his sores became worse. They spread, they burned, they
bled. His ears: they became swollen, until they were as big as
bananas. His legs: they were so sore, he could not walk. At last,
when he could move no more, he ceased his frenzy. Moaning in
his princely bed he lay, attended by his servants. Hee, hee."

"But this is not so!" protested Makaio, upright in his chair.
"The *Kalani* Peter was never like that—"

Momona hissed him silent. "Would you know? Were you there,
one of that proud man's servants?"

"No. No, I was not there."

"Then listen while I speak, for I was one of the *Kalani's* servants. A *kokua* to him I came, bound to him from childhood by
the loyalty of my family. Clean I was, too, when I came, and
young, and handsome to look upon—" To our horror a woman's
tears were rolling down his fat cheeks. But ever the high voice
continued its tale, determined to reach its end. He was like a
woman come to full term, and the monstrous child of his mind
could not be denied its birth. Helpless to prevent it, we listened
to the fulfillment of Momona's long travail.

"In his house he lay, lamenting his dying. 'Nothing does any
good, nothing,' he moaned. 'This disease: it comes from Iehovah.
What is man, then, to think he can cure it?' And from that time
on he would take no medicine. No longer did he seek out patent
medicines, or recipes from *kahunas* in faraway lands. 'Nothing
does any good,' he wept, spurning even the medicines the Board
of Health sent up to him from Honolulu.

"And lo! He was right, the *Kalani* was. The sores upon his
body: they were healed. The marks of the sores: they faded."

We listened, bound as by a spell, to his tale of a miracle.

"The swelling in his ears: it went down."

Waiting for the end of his story, I ceased to breathe.

"Hee, hee! Instead of wasting away, his flesh was restored."

"And then?" Tutu's harsh voice rose above his. "And then?
What happened to this *Kalani?* Did he go away? Was he taken
up into Heaven, that we do not see his presence here today?"

Sorrowfully Momona shook his head at her doubting. The tears
upon his cheeks told us how he felt one thing, the smile upon
his mouth said he meant another. But his answer left us most
uncertain of all.

"And then? And then he died. What else was there for him to do?"

No more could I bear the cruelty of his mind. With tears rushing down my own cheeks, not only for Uncle Pita's sake now, but also for Tutu's, and Moki's, and for my own, I stood up and I fled into the darkness of the house.

The closeness of death was upon us all that night.

19

As is the way with people who know sorrow by night, the next day's sun brought us a return to the measure of happiness which was permitted to each of us. Because we were not yet too sick to do the work of living, we found forgetfulness in our tasks. And in this forgetfulness we thought and acted as if we were well and all was well with us. We looked out upon our little world—the green bosom of Kalaupapa, the splendid cliffs, the overarching heaven above us, the embracing sea—and we found it fair. This fairness, we saw, is home. And in the new home we thought we had found our peace.

With Moki and Makaio to guide us, Tutu and I entered into the ways of Kalawao.

We went to call upon friends in the village. We sat in their little houses, not much different from ours, drinking Chinese tea or, if we were fortunate, *kookoolau* tea from Oahu. Often, if the day was warm, we sipped a glass of punch, made with limes grown in the gardens of Kalawao and with the cool water brought in the pipes from Waileia.

In this way I saw Caleb again, when we went to call upon Miele, the grandmother of Akala. We were walking along the grassy lane, between the rock walls which border each household, to keep the horses out and the cows and pigs wandering across the fertile plain. We were almost come to the house of Miele when I saw Caleb, standing in his yard, gazing out to sea. He held a book, his finger marking the place where he was reading before he allowed his thoughts to roam. He was bareheaded, and the afternoon sun, slanting in over the mountains from his left side, lighted up the slender body, the lean face, the lines of suffering which ran beside his nose and turned down the corners of his mouth. They said to me that Caleb had not yet found his peace.

I wanted to greet him, to wish him well, to let him know how even in Kalawao it is possible to know contentment. But, remembering the anger with which he had thrust me from him, I hesitated. Nor could I call out to him, as a commoner woman might have done. There was no choice but to lower my gaze and to walk past him. But Makaio, not knowing my intention, lifted his voice in greeting: "*Ke aloha no, aloha,*" he called, to a man he did not know.

Caleb looked up in surprise, the old response falling from his lips: "*Aloha ia oe.*" Seeing how his greeter was accompanied, he broadened the salutation to include us all: "*Aloha oukou.*" He was blinded, perhaps, by the sun. Until he put his hand to his forehead he did not recognize me.

"Malie!" he exclaimed, and hurried to the gate. "Malie. I am glad to see you." Reaching me, he looked steadily at me. "How are you? I've been wondering how you were getting along." He spoke in English, stammering in his haste. "Do you live nearby?"

I was struck dumb by the change in his appearance. I had not really looked at him, on the morning of our arrival. Perhaps even if I had looked at him I would not have seen, under the hat he wore, the blaze which marked him, as if a bolt of lightning had been hurled out of Heaven to brand him.

But now, in the afternoon sunlight, the mark was there upon him for all to see. A slash of white cut boldly through the jet-black hair of his head, from back to front. And, looking closely, I could see where the streak of white continued down the front of his face, under the fading color of his skin. Two fingers or more in width, the line of dead flesh worked its way down his forehead, through the thinning eyebrow and the curling lashes, down the cheek, down the side of his throat, until it was lost to sight beneath the open collar of his linen shirt. I could not doubt but that the strip of whiteness continued for the length of his body, running like a brand made with fire down the flesh of his side, until it left his body at the toes of the foot and disappeared into the ground, as they say lightning does after it has struck. The sores on

his ears were as nothing, compared with the strake which was
laid upon him.

"Caleb, *aloha*," I said, pretending I did not notice the mark.
As I looked into his face I could see where, with a vanity that
made me want to weep, he had tried to hide with a woman's
dyestuff the whiteness of his eyelashes and his eyebrow. "*Pehea oe?*
How are you?" I wanted to show my concern for him in more
than one of our languages.

"I asked you first, remember?" he laughed. "But I am well, I
thank you. Getting along fine—except for a guilty conscience."
As I waited for an explanation of this unexpected twist to his
conversation, his face took on its usual harried expression. The
bright green eyes, which a moment before were alight with merriment, were now dark and hooded. "Malie. Will you ever forgive
me for my rudeness to you on the *Mokolii?* I was—"

"Of course, Caleb, of course. I felt no hurt from it. To tell the
truth, I quite understood why you needed someone to shout at."
I, too, could have used someone to shout at, in my moment of
anguish, when a scream would have been as cleansing as a flood
of tears. But I could not say so to Caleb, for it might have upset
him to know how well I understood him. He tried to be so different from everyone else.

"Then I am relieved. I hope that I shall learn here how to
become a good man." He looked around him at the serene mountains, at the golden air with its unhurried clouds, at the unmarred
lovely peacefulness of Kalaupapa. "A good man . . . I have not
done so well in this respect. Not nearly so well as others I have
met here."

It was time for me to remember my companions, waiting near
us. Tutu did not even pretend to be disinterested in our talk:
she clung to me as an *opihi* to its rock. But Makaio and Moki, being
better mannered, were searching for sea birds in a sky much too
bright for sea birds. I presented Caleb to my family. I called them
so, and I was mildly surprised by the scowl which darkened his
face when he heard the word. But, knowing how unpredictable he
was, I did not let it worry me.

With great dignity Makaio acknowledged the introduction.
Tutu, of course, could not resist a few suggestive winks and eye-
rollings as she invited Caleb to come to call upon us. She was
fascinated by the handsome young man with the Hawaiians' skin,

the *haoles'* eyes, and the unbelievable streak of death upon his body. Forgotten was her dislike of him. I suspected the marriage-maker's instinct at work, and I rebelled at it when I heard her adding detailed directions to her invitation: "the last house on the road to Kalaupapa—you can't miss it." This busyness I would have to combat, not at home, but at once. Taking her by the arm, I turned her firmly toward Miele's house; and even while she was still naming the good things we would serve him with our tea, I bade him a proper farewell and started my family once more on its way. We left Caleb, dazed speechless by Tutu's spate of words, standing in his gateway, the book still closed over his long finger. She was still chattering about him when we reached the turn in the lane, beyond the place where the mountain apple trees grow, and could see him no more.

We joined a singing society. We were invited to join a funeral society also, one of the many rival groups which tries to find in the pleasures of funerals an escape from their sorrows. But to this we said, "No, not yet," not being ready so soon to prepare ourselves for death by preparing those who die for their burying.

We found in the Hui Iiwi, the Club of the Singing Birds, the people we liked and the singing we liked. On two evenings of each week we would meet, each time in a different household. There were sixteen households numbered among our singers, so it was no great hardship on any one house when, at the end of the evening, the tea was brought in, and the small cakes, with which we rewarded ourselves for the song-making.

In our group there was a man, Kumakani was his name, who played a bass viol. Several of us could play the Spanish guitar or the mandolin. I was one of these, who learned this maidenly accomplishment in the hours of boredom at the palace, while we waited for Their Majesties to go to some ceremony or to return from one. Momona played a violin, with lightness and beauty. And, to my astonishment, he had a voice, high as a woman's, pure as a child's, which showed no trace of evil and told no lies when he sang.

There was one among us, a clownish fellow called Hanu, who owned one of the new "baby guitars" recently brought to our country by the Portuguese. We natives call it the *ukulele*, from the way the fingers hop upon the strings, like jumping fleas. But we would not let Hanu play upon this silly instrument except in his joking. Its sounds are too thin, too tinkling, to please our ears, and we cannot understand how the Portuguese, having made the first *ukulele*, could ever want to make a second one. It is useful only for causing us to laugh, as when Hanu pretends to be an *Hispaniolo* serenading his lady love. In a ridiculous mixture of pidgin-English and Hawaiian, in which almost every word he sings holds a double meaning, Hanu can bring shrieks of delight from the women, roars of laughter from the men.

"*Eia!*" Tutu would call from her place among the singers. Often enough she spoke with the squawk of an *alae* bird, a mud hen, but when she sang her throaty soprano blended well with the voices of the others. "*Eia mai.* Make with a *hula!*"

By this time we would be ready for gaiety, and a little bit of restrained fun. Hanu, his mouth open from ear to ear, his fingers really as nimble as fleas upon the frets and strings of his chattering instrument, would oblige us with a version of a *hula*. He would play "*Alekoki,*" written by the King himself in his younger days. Gay and impudent, the music would lift us at once to a different mood. And if there does not breathe a Hawaiian who cannot sing, is there a Hawaiian who cannot dance?

One after the other, we would spring to the center of the floor, to take our turn at dancing. Sometimes the *hulas* would be fast and, as Hanu put it in a word, "sexy." Sometimes they would be slow, almost imprisoned in a dream, as when we sang "*Makalapua,*" the lovely name-song the High Chiefess Konia composed for the Princess Liliuokalani, when the little one came to her as an adopted child. Then would they entreat me to dance for them. Slipping off my shoes, I would dance in my stocking feet, as slowly, sweetly, they all sang Konia's tribute to her *hanai* daughter:

> O Makalapua ulu mahiehie,
> O ka lei o Kamakaeha,
> No Kamakaeha ka lei na Lia-wahine,
> Na ka wahine kihene pua . . .

For relief from this tenderness they would swing to the wildness of "*Meleana E,*" which tells of a lover's chase "down by the old spring." The shouts of enjoyment, the clapping of hands and stamping of feet would shake the house, as, voices and instruments blending, we watched Hanu and some old dame—often enough it was Tutu—enact in the *hula* the passionate search by the lover of his haughty and uncaptured beloved. Even at her age Tutu was an untiring dancer, if no longer a beautiful one, and she was as proud of her accomplishment as I was.

Promptly at the hour of nine our merriment would end, our innocent indecencies would be put away until the next time. We would have a light refreshment, chatting primly about the latest news of the Settlement or the most recent word from "outside," as though we sat in the Reverend Lowell Smith's own parlor at the Kaumakapili Church in Honolulu. At ten o'clock Makaio would lead us in a short prayer, in which we thanked the Lord God for his great gifts to us of friends and songs and things to eat, of shelter and of peace, and implored his blessing upon us for the days and nights to follow. Then, with soft thank you's, and the kiss of friendship upon our cheeks, we lighted our lanterns or the torches of *kukui* nuts, and stepped out into the night. Quietly, guided by the stars, lighted by our torches or perhaps by the bright moon, we found our way home.

On Sabbath days we went to church, out of habit as well as need. Makaio and Moki belonged to the Catholic faith, and they went early in the morning to Father Damien's church. Because there was no Anglican chapel in the Settlement, I went to the Congregationalists at Siloama. Tutu, almost a heathen from the country, went with me, "to keep me company." She liked the singing and the dressing up and, I think, the pastor. A fine figure of a man he was, with pure white hair like Makaio's, a deep voice, and a comforting simplicity in his preaching. A true Christian he was, and it was easy for his congregation to believe that he practiced what he preached, for he was not a patient in our midst, set down at Kalawao like the most of us by the laws of the land. He entered willingly, a few years before, as *kokua* to his wife, sick with the *lepera*; and when she died he asked if he might stay on, to minister to his people. A good man he was, devoted to his flock.

Kalawao was my home for about a fortnight when I discovered the children. I did not forget my plan, told to Ambrose Hutchinson, about wanting to help Loke in the hospital. But neither did I do anything about going there to help her. In Kalawao there is no need for hurry. And besides, what sensible person rushes to do a thing the instant the thought enters into his mind? If there is anything the *haoles* have shown us, it is the foolishness of haste. See all of the troubles they fall into, because they rush into doing things they have not thought enough about.

But there came a day so fine that Tutu and I could not sit at home, letting it go to waste. Because most of our food was used up, Emma needed no help from us in the cookhouse. Makaio and Moki were at the seashore, where, with many of the other men, they sought the fish, the eels, the crabs, and the seaweed God's Providence puts in the sea for us to live upon, until the *Mokolii* comes again from Honolulu.

"Let us go for a walk," I said to Tutu in the middle of the morning. My body complained at sitting at home, my *mana* was outside the house, walking along green paths I did not yet know, in its eagerness to see the beauty of the day. "Then let us go," said Tutu, rising quickly from her chair. "I was having the same *manao*."

We put on our wide-brimmed hats, to protect our faces from the sunburn, we kicked off our house slippers to free our feet for walking, and we began our adventure. "One good thing about this place," said Tutu, who every day found new reasons for being pleased with Kalawao, "we don't need to wear those damn' *haole* shoes."

When we came to the main road there was only one way to turn. We faced toward the east, toward the high peaks of Molokai, where they rise at the end of the island which is across the waters from Maui. Into the distance the mountains marched, blue and purple and green in the sunlight. At their feet, where the bay of Kalawao bites round into the land, the two islands floated, Mokapu and Olala, like two swollen green flower buds of the mountain ginger resting in the sea. The valley of Waikolu opened inland from them, far away and haunted, beyond the reaching of those of us who would walk only once upon the rocky beach.

We strolled toward the heart of Kalawao, to where the hospital was, and the church of Saint Philomena. The road was empty. "And where is everyone?" was the question we put to each other.

Past shuttered Siloama we walked, kicking up the warm dust from the hollows and ruts in the road. For several days no rain had fallen upon Kalaupapa, and the water casks set beneath the eaves of the houses were almost empty of water. Makaio was worrying about how to fill the barrels at our house, if the rain did not come soon.

At Kewalo's yard we saw an astonishing change. The jungle was gone, hacked away, cleared to the very stubble of the grass: bare as an empty calabash was his enclosure. The house was freshly whitewashed, shining in the sunlight, clean as a shark's tooth. "Ha!" exclaimed Tutu. "This old tongue is better than he thought. A whip it is, as well as a knife. Who dares to say that I have no power left in me?" Leaning upon her arm, to show my love for her, I laughed with her at Kewalo's defeat. "You know what?" she said, stopping in the middle of the road, "I am coming to like this place. It is not so bad as I was afraid it would be."

"I have been thinking the same thing. Already I am beginning to forget my longing for the mountains of Oahu, in the presence of these."

"If the truth is told, this place is better than Kuliouou. And Makaio's house: it is much better than was my house at home. If only the children were here: ah, then I would gladly forget Oahu. Let the *haoles* keep it."

When we came near to the Infirmary, we saw the people standing in the small house, heard the sound of their gathering, many voices all at once. We went up the steps to the *lanai*, to learn what brought so many people together. At the door the great smell of their sores made us wish to turn away. Inside, everyone was talking at once, paying no attention to his neighbors. Tutu pulled at the sleeve of a young woman. "What happens here?"

The young one looked on us in pretended disgust. "Where have you been, that you do not know? Kamiano dresses the sores of the sick here each day." Then she turned back to her talking.

We could not see the priest: he was hidden by a throng of patients. But at the far end of the room, sitting high on a stool near the open window, perched the *haole* doctor. With great impatience he was telling a poor *Pake* how to dress his own sores, pointing with a stick at the things he would need. No other patients awaited Opaekea's attention. I thought it was because he was faster at his work than Father Damien was, until I saw the black looks turned upon him by some of those who waited for the priest's care. "*Sonakapiki*," they swore, and I understood how their dislike of him was growing, not fading away.

"Sassy buggah," muttered Tutu. "He sits there like a chief, he looks like a monkey, he acts like a knave. Let's go." Eager for the sweet air, grateful that it was not yet our time to stand in the foul room, we returned to our walking.

"My! Such a pretty church," she sniffed, squinting as though she were blinded by Kamiano's painted box across the street. "*Cha!* These *haoles*. They must think us savages. Putting such crazy colors on our churches, sending us such crazy gaudy stuff for our clothes. Great big ugly flowers scattered all over it—flowers that cannot grow anywhere under heaven. Great big splashes of too many colors thrown all over it, all mixed up, like rubbish in a street."

"I suppose it is the *haoles*' idea of a pretty thing—"

"Then why don't they keep such stuff for themselves? Why must we be the ones to wear their rubbish? When I put my clothes on, I don't want to look like the behind of a peacock. One color at a time, not all of them at once: that's good enough for me."

It was my thought to stop at the hospital, to see Loke, but we could not give up the beautiful day so soon. Tutu agreed with me that we should walk past the cemetery to the green field beyond. There we found many of the people of the Settlement. And there we found the children.

The women strolled about, or sat by the side of the field, in the shade of the trees. They were gossiping, sewing, weaving with fine strips of *lauhala* the baskets or mats they would use in their homes. Some of them carried babies in their arms, or sat nursing the infants. Amiable among them idled the few men who were too sick or too lazy to go to the sea for food. Running loose upon the grass were the children, playing tag, racing, filling the air with their happy noises. It was like a holiday in Queen Emma's Square, when the people of Honolulu gathered to hear Captain Berger lead the King's Band in a public concert. The only thing missing was the Band—

In the beat of a heart a great longing swept through me, a longing for Honolulu, for the Royal Hawaiian Band, for the pleasures and delights of the wonderful life I knew so briefly. The music I longed to hear: would I never hear a band again? Would I never whirl in a waltz again, upon a polished floor, under the sparkling chandeliers, before the gilded mirrors? Would I ever sip sweet ices again, from a crystal cup, flirting over its rim with a handsome gentleman playing at flirting with me? Would I—? But then my yearning was brought to a halt as, with a stab of grief, I realized that these fancies I chased were the most foolish of dreams.

Open yours eyes, Malie, my mind screamed at me. *Look about you!* In those faces, eaten away, I saw myself for what I was. In one of those graves, beyond the gossipping women and the lounging men, I saw the only bed I would ever share, the only lover ever to hold me in his embrace.

In an instant I learned anew the leper's lesson of his long dying, the most terrible lesson he can learn: until he is dead, he is never able to give up his claim upon life. Each time he thinks he has made his peace with the knowledge that he is a leper, he but fools himself into thinking he has found his peace. Until he has no future he clings still to his past. The hold upon him of the past is too great, and it sinks a thousand hooks into his memory with which to pull him back. This is the greatest cruelty of all: he can never forget that once he was well; he can never remember that now he is but a living corpse, cut off forever from the company of the living.

In an instant my joy in the day was gone out of me. Ugly it was, stark and blazing and hideous with the truth. Gone was my peace, lost was my contentment. I thought I had died on the evening of my departure from Oahu, but now I knew that I was not to be let off so easily.

My legs grew weak, and with a cry of hopelessness I fell to the ground. Tears dropped from my eyes as I beat at the earth with my fists, seeking to hurt it in return for its vast indifference to me.

"Malie, Malie, what is the matter? Tell Tutu, tell Tutu." On her knees beside me, she took me into her arms. "Tell me. What is this trouble which comes upon you so suddenly?"

How could I tell her my sorrow, when she had her own to bear? I would not let the words come. I am proud that even in my grief I thought also of her. Yet how could she be my companion in misery and not know the cause of my distress? Quietly she gathered me in her arms and held me against her breast. Holding me, as once I had held her, she let me weep, saying not a word until I could weep no more. Then, wiping away my tears with the sleeve of her *holoku*, she spoke.

"Hear me, Malie, in the wisdom of my years." Her voice was harsh, almost cruel. "You are filled with a pity for yourself. This is a disease worse than the Kalawao sickness. With it you have two afflictions to bear, instead of only one. The one kills only the

body, the other kills the heart." She shook me. "Who is to say
that a woman here cannot know happiness, even though her body
be sick, as long as she has love in her heart?"

"Love?" I turned my head away from her. "Who would love
me?"

"Must you be loved? Can you not be the one to love?"

"Who is there for me to love?"

"Malie! Look about you. Look upon these women. Do they
weep because they are bound to Kalaupapa? Do they die in their
hearts, because their bodies are sick? Look at that one: she has a
baby at her breast. Her face is scarred, but her milk is good. Look
at the others: they sew, they talk, they weave. Are they any
different from the women of Kuliouou, from the women of
Honolulu? Do they not have homes to care for, even here, and
husbands to love, and—and babes to love?" Her voice broke at
this, even her voice.

But I would not hear her wisdom. Stubborn in my self-love, I
shook my head again, denying all because I thought I was denied
all. Forgetting all that had gone before, all of my long thoughts
and noble resolves, I thought only of myself, the center of the
world. "No," I moaned, "love is not for me. I do not want to be
hurt any more. To love is to fear—"

"Ae, it is so," she said softly. "There is fear in love, it is true.
But fear is only a portion—a small portion—of the fruit of love.
Like the seeds in a Kona orange. There are other things in it,
too, in this mixed-up thing called love. To receive them, you
must take sorrow, too, and hurt, and the bitter rind of death.
But the sweetness of love: ahh, this is worth all the rest. Hear an
old woman's word, my dear: open your heart to love."

I had thought this all out for myself, in the time when I lay
waiting at home. I saw then what I must do: I must close up my
body to love, so that there would be no issue from me, to be weak
and leprous like me, and to suffer hurt as I was being hurt. "The
bad blood of the Kahekili," my mother called it. If it were so,
then must I seal it off at the font. And with my body closed, I
must also close up my heart to love. Then I would know peace,
and—if God were good—I would die in peace. Alone I would be,
yes, but I would be untroubled.

"No," I told her my resolve, but not the reasons why I made it.
"Love is not for me."

"Kie! You are as stubborn as the surf upon the shore, you.

You *wahine* mule, you! Get up, get up! I will not spoil you any longer." She spilled me out of her lap, upon the grass. Swearing like a sailor at me, sighing with her aches and pains, grunting with the labor of getting to her feet, all at the same time, she stood up at last, while I lay sprawled upon the ground, astonished by her anger. "I am going home," she announced, starting back along the road, straightening her hat as she went.

I did not hold her back. But I sulked because of her sharp talk. What right did she have to speak like this to me? So I let her go alone, and as I watched her go, I closed my heart against her too, leaving it empty, at last, and ready for death.

Long did I lie there, not knowing where to go, not caring what might befall me. Like a drunken harlot I lay there, my eyes closed, resting my head upon one outstretched arm. The hat, tumbled from my head when I sank to the ground, lay by my side, as debauched as I.

The sun beat down upon me, burning through the thin fabric of my dress, heating the side of my face. Upon my breasts the warmth of the sun fell. Those small young breasts, which had never known the touch of a lover, were fondled now by the sun. Those breasts: never would they know the touch of a lover. I thought of them with loathing: the sores were upon them, as if God had put his fingers' touch upon them, to deny them their use in the delights of love, in the suckling of a babe. Blighted they were, like buds diseased before their flowering: dry and withered and devoured they would become. Even now the patches of red and white, like the scars of burns, like the marks of mildew, upon the smoothness of my flesh, even now they were spreading. Eating away the flesh of my bosom, they claimed for themselves those parts of me a lover's kisses would never know, a babe's lips would never touch. And, hungry in their despoiling, ravenous as sharks in a school of fish, they were leaping now upon other parts of me: upon the smooth skin of my belly, upon the tender places of my thighs, their red mouths were opening now to feed—

Out of the depths of my grief I groaned aloud, crying out in my despair. I was forsaken, abandoned: and I writhed upon the ground in my hopelessness.

"Why does she cry? Is she sick?" Even as I heard the child's question, I heard other voices hissing at him to be still. Startled,

I opened my eyes. Blinded by the sun, I raised myself to my knees, shading my face with one hand until I could see again. Slowly, through the shifting tears, I made them out: a swarm of children, squatting in a half circle before me. In my shame I did not know what to say to them. But their faces told me that they brought me the one thing I needed most: the gift of their concern.

Their eyes were big with sympathy, their voices stilled out of pity. Without uttering a word they silenced the clamor of the cries of my soul. They were like dark angels, come to announce to me a gift from God. So hungry was I for love, so quickly was I appeased.

Scarcely knowing what I thought, only knowing that I was grateful for their being there, I tried to smile my thanks. Upon my knees before them, I said, "*Aloha oukou.*"

"*Aloha ia oe,*" they said in a cheerful chorus. Their smiles made them urchins again; the sound of their voices set them to chattering. The younger ones among them began to squirm and wriggle. Their sympathy was put away, under the cover of noise and pushing and evasive glances. I knew why, having seen it. It is too precious to be worn openly and uncovered: it must be shielded, wrapped in pretense and laughter and the thousand little dissemblances of each day's living, because in itself it is too consuming to be endured. It is like the light of the sun.

"Feeling better?" one of them asked. He was the biggest of the group, the leader of the gang. A fine-looking lad he was, with a scattering of freckles upon his brown cheeks, close-cropped black hair gleaming in the sunlight, and steady eyes looking out unsurprised upon the world. His only flaw was his teeth. They were *haole* teeth: crooked and wide-spaced, not like the fine teeth of the natives. But his engaging grin made me overlook the crooked teeth.

"Better, thank you." With his knowing eyes upon me, I put up my hands to straighten my dress, to fix my hair. He was not more than thirteen or fourteen years old, but he looked at me as if to buy me. Without knowing why, I hurried to make myself pleasing to his sight.

"Akala has gone to get you some water."

"That will be good." As close as we were, I could see the fine fuzz upon his cheeks, the coarsening hair upon his naked arms and legs, among the scratches and the flea bites. He was a boy becoming a man, and the awareness of it embarrassed me. Hastily I looked away from him, to the others. They were younger than the boy-man, and their interest in me was waning. All of them were boys: they were like a basketful of worms, wriggling and tumbling and pushing at each other, laughing and giggling nonsense like children just escaped from school.

I fastened upon the thought, to have something to say to the disturbing youth. "You are finished with school for today?"

"School?" He shrugged, he sneered, both at the same time. "There is no school here." Too late did I remember how, with Akala, I was caught in this same trap. "Who would teach us? Who would make us study?"

"Forgive me. I did not think. But then: what do you do with all your time?"

"We play, we fight, we steal. We run wild, like goats in the mountains."

"But do you not tire of this? Do you not want to learn about other things? I mean, about the world—"

He looked at me, an old man's sourness about his mouth. "Of what use is it, to know about the world?"

Akala's return saved me. She came running up, bearing one of the long green bottles full of cool water. Shyly she gave it to the boy-man, then stood back, wiping her wet hands upon her ragged dress. In the presence of the boys, she was a servant girl. Upon her swollen cheek I saw the fresh-made wound given to her by Opaekea. More fiery it was than the dull redness of the many lumps of flesh of which her face was made.

Gravely the boy handed the bottle to me. "Thank you," I said. "And thank you, Akala." I was fascinated by the sight of the scar. From there came the seed which Opaekea planted in the arm of Keanu. Seeing her, hideous with the disease, remembering the murderer, sleek in his health, I felt a pity spring up in me for Keanu that was like a storm of raging wind compared with the breath of regret I knew upon the day I learned what the *haole* had done to him. O Heavenly Father, don't let him look like her, I found myself praying, as I lifted the slender bottle to my lips.

"Ahh, this is good. It is what I need." I returned the bottle to the boy. Then, remembering a saying of Tutu's which she used often, I said it to add weight to my simple words: "It is the water of life, the water of Kane." I meant nothing more than a kindness.

But the strange boy took it up. "This water of life, this water of Kane: I have heard these words before. What do they mean?"

His mind hungered for learning, as the people of Kalaupapa hunger for food. In the moment I thought of this fancy, I knew how I could answer the youth's question and his need. Greater than the hunger of his body for food was the yearning of his mind for knowledge. "It is a thought from the olden days. From the time before the *haoles* came. Do you not know of those days?"

He shook his head, most unlike a boy.

"Then did Hawaii Nei have three great gods, and many lesser ones. The names of the three were Kane, Ku, and Lono. Did you not know this?"

"No. I have heard of one God only."

Akala sat down beside him, leaning upon the water bottle. Around us the other children continued their play. Only Akala and the boy listened to me.

"Now do we know there is only one God, yes. But in those days of ignorance, when our ancestors lived in darkness, they believed in many gods. One for each thing in nature, one for each person, almost." I was not certain of this myself, but like many teachers, I suspect, I let my manner persuade my listeners that I knew whereof I spoke. "And in those days, the water of Kane was the rain, which brought life to all things on the earth. Lono's were the clouds, but the water falling from them as rain was Kane's. Today we know that the water of life is Iehovah's gift to us. As is the gift of his mercy, which falleth upon us as a gentle rain from Heaven." Long ago I heard the Anglican Bishop say this beautiful thought in a sermon, and I remembered it. Now I gave it to my listener, for his mind to marvel at.

"How do you know all these things?" The student who questions his teacher sharpens the minds of both, I have heard, but this one was too direct for me.

"Why, from my teachers at school, from my parents, from the books I can read," I answered unwillingly, naming all of the things he did not have. But I was not ready to tell him that I had not read a book for many months. The reading of books is not a pleasure for me, alas, and I have shunned them ever since I left the Royal School for my service to the Queen.

"I wish to learn to read. And to write. Can you teach me to do these things?"

"*Ae,* that I can do," I said, thinking how easily I had sensed his need and how cleverly I stirred his interest.

"O, Eleu!" squealed Akala. "Wouldn't that be good?" Never was a Hawaiian's name more misgiven. He was the most sober, the least lively, boy I had ever met. I wondered what his missionary name would be. But I did not ask it, knowing I would learn it in time.

"It is good," agreed Eleu, not bothering to look at Akala.

"Then shall we start some day soon? Next Monday, perhaps?" I would go to the store at Kalaupapa, to buy letter paper, and copybooks, and pencils for my pupils, to give them a proper schooling. How better could I spend my money than on school things, how better could I use my time than in being their teacher?

But I did not know the mind of Eleu. "Monday!" he snorted. "Too late. We start now. I have no more time to waste."

"*Eia mai!* And how can I teach you to read without books? How can you learn to write without paper?"

"You too *haole,*" he said in pidgin-English. "Wassamatta wid right heah, like dis?" Leaning over the road, he smoothed the dust with his hand, making a writing tablet of it. With his finger he scratched a mark in the dust. "See?" Quickly he wiped it away, made another mark. "See!"

"Then let it be so, Eleu. But let us at least move to the shade of a tree. This sun is too bright for me."

"O.K. You da boss." Springing to his feet, he shouted at the other boys. "We going have school now, da lady an' me. You fallas go play. V*amoose!*"

"No faih!" they yelled. "We like have school too." From the ground at his feet Akala shrilled her claim. "Me, too, Eleu! Me, too!"

Hands on hips, he laughed at them. "You don' know wat is school, an' you like some?"

"Sure! Wy not? Eef you have 'um, we have 'um too."

"O.K., O.K.! Le's go, den. But eef you no min' da teachah, I going bus' you head."

We moved to the shade of a *kukui* tree, where the light fell in green and gold upon the ground. At Eleu's direction they kicked the fallen leaves away, baring the dark earth beneath, where the insects scurried in terror at the destruction of their homes. The earth was damp, smelling of mold, of death. Each of us had a patch of dirt on which to make his writing, and sticks and stones for pencils.

After much excitement and shifting of places, they were standing before me, stilled at last by Eleu's sharp commands. I looked with pride upon my eight pupils, attentive and eager to begin upon their learning. These were my people, even though they were young, even though they were sick; and I saw them with the eyes of a teacher on her first day at school, before she has learned what demons her charges can be. Smiling sweetly, as I had seen Miss Beckwith smile upon her class at the Royal School, I looked from one to the other of the children. "Will you learn Hawaiian?" I asked, thinking of the two languages which are taught in the Government schools, "or English?"

They blinked at each other in the solemn shadows of the school tree, until Eleu ended their uncertainty. "American!" he cried. "American."

It was my turn to be uncertain. Smiling patiently upon him, although with a bit of stiffness in the smile, I was about to explain to him, in my best schoolteacher manner, how there is indeed no American language, when I saw the fierce scowl with which he glared at his companions, ready to shout down any other suggestions they dared to make. Wisely I submitted to his will. What difference did it make? They are almost the same.

"Then let it be so. Come close, now, and watch me. See how I make the letter A . . ."

20

WHEN I RETURNED HOME I found Tutu waiting for me at the gate. Tears in her eyes, hot words in her mouth, she could not decide which to use upon me.

"Malie! And where have you been? Why didn't you come home?" Hands waving in the air, eyes imploring the patience of Heaven, she came toward me in the road. But when we met, her worry found its release in weeping. Throwing her arms about me, she cried, "Forgive me, forgive. I am a crabby old woman. Do not mind what I said." The scent of her fresh dress was clean and sweet in my nostrils, the hold of her arms as heavy as a mother's. Poor Tutu: she, too, was jealous for her love.

Once again I learned something new of the part which each of us plays in life. What is life but the seeking of happiness, the running away from sorrow? If we do someone hurt, are we not then sorry for our action? If we feel hurt, do we not seek ease from its pain? It is so. How, then, could I deny my love to others, or deny that I had any need of it in myself?

In the hot sun-brightened road of Kalawao I received my gift of enlightenment. And, being enlightened, I knew how easy it is to bring comfort when one loves. Holding Tutu in my arms, old and bent and near to death, I lifted my face and my heart unto Heaven, thanking God for his message to me. If I have not love, I acknowledged, how can I say that I live?

"Tutu, hear me," I said, as we walked arm in arm back to the house of Makaio. "Wise were your words to me this morning. I have heard their meaning."

She stopped, held me away from her to look at me. "Praise God," she said softly, "praise the Lord. Then indeed is your happiness won."

When we reached the shade of the *lanai* and sat in its coolness, fanning ourselves with the broad leaves of the *loulu* palm, I told her the story of my morning's work as a schoolteacher. She laughed at my tale, and, as I knew she would be, she was enchanted with my talk of Eleu. "A rascal," she chuckled, "a sassy one. He will do well for himself." This was not quite the opinion I held of him, but her conclusion took me even more by surprise. With a wink and a toss of her head she let me see how much of myself I revealed in my telling about him. "And he will be good for you, too. He is just what you need: someone to care for."

Not for long did we keep our school under the *kukui* tree. Father Damien soon heard of it and invited us to use the Infirmary in the afternoons. On the first day it held two pupils: Akala and Eleu. By the fifth day it held nine. When the second week was ended, twenty-one boys and girls sat in the schoolroom, learning to read and write and to do sums. Among them were

Moki, and Joel, the *haole* boy who came to Kalawao when Tutu and I came. Because these two already could read and write a little, they became my helpers. But it was Eleu who was the monitor, who took care of the books and the papers and the pencils, who handed me the guava switch when I was in need of it.

I learned, alas, that I was as all other schoolteachers must be: sparing of freedom, jealous in my demands for the attention of my pupils, liberal in my use of the supple switch Eleu brought to me the second week of school. "Here," he said with a straight face, thrusting it into my hand, "a stick for teaching with." Given this permission from him, I did not shrink from using the stinging rod. How else was I to keep the discipline? "*E, hoopono loa he kumuao*"—I heard my pupils say one day when school was done —"Strict is the teacher." But not for a long time did I learn how, away from the schoolhouse, they called me "Miss Switch."

Inside the school there was good order. But it was not so outside the schoolhouse. When the men of Kalawao learned of it, they gathered around to see this new thing and to laugh at it. And when the school day was ended and my pupils dashed away to their play, and the men saw how I went alone along the road to my home, some of them tried to molest me.

This was one of the evil things in Kalawao. The other evils were drunkenness and gambling. But the lusts of the flesh were the most difficult to satisfy. For it is a part of the sickness, in certain of its stages, for the diseased flesh to burn with a rage for love. When this time comes upon a sufferer, it is said, there is no denying him his need, and no sating of it.

But I did not know of these things when I walked alone through the village to the school. Not even Tutu's plain-speaking, not even Emma's service to the Settlement, prepared me for them, or for the men who whistled at me, when I stepped forth from the schoolhouse, who called their evil thoughts to me, thinking to excite me, who offered me money to lie with them, thinking to buy me.

At first I was angered by their indecencies. With my head lowered, I hurried away from them, where they lounged against the stone walls on either side of the road, just as they do on some of the street corners in Honolulu. Dressed in their tight trousers and *palaka* shirts, with bright kerchiefs knotted at their throats, and brazen smiles fixed upon their faces, they sang their dirty songs or played at cards and dice, to while away the time. In Honolulu there are policemen to keep such loafers from molesting decent women, but in Kalawao there was no one to guard me from their intentions.

When, on the third day, they took to following me along the way, serenading me with their suggestive music, beseeching me with their calling, I grew frightened. When, on the day after that, one of them, bolder than the rest, called to me from a lane, entreating me to go to his house, I was terrified. Breathless from running, I asked Tutu for her counsel when I reached home.

"Filthy dogs!" she cried, "*pilau* bums!" and much more. I sat upon her bed, open-mouthed at her language. "Wassamatta?" she laughed, "you think I do not know about life? Those loafers need horsewhipping. Let us talk with Makaio about this."

"No, Tutu, no! I—I don't want him to know about it."

"Malie, you *aku*-head. Do you think Makaio does not know about these things? Do you think his white hair makes him innocent? Come, we go now, for his advice."

Makaio listened to my plight, told more by Tutu's mouth than by my own. When we were finished he said sadly, "This is not a new thing to Kalawao. Sometimes, too, it is the other way, when a man is endangered by a woman. This sickness: it does strange things to the appetite of people. Perhaps I should have told you of these dangers, before you learned of them in the street. But it is better now than it used to be. The priest has made it so."

"Should we tell Kamiano?" asked Tutu.

"No, there is no need. To hear of it would make him unhappy. He thinks that since his coming the people of Kalawao have learned decency, if they have not learned goodness. He does not know how, when his back is turned, some of them still show their evil ways. Let us spare him this disappointment."

"Well, then, will you be her bodyguard? Her policeman?" Tutu's voice was sour, like the taste of *poi* four days old.

Nothing disturbed Makaio, not even the impatience of Tutu. "No. No, there is a better way. I will speak to Ambrose about this. It is his business. He will take care of it."

The next morning Makaio walked to Kalaupapa to speak to the Superintendent. In the afternoon, at four o'clock, when school was ended and the hoodlums were gathered again outside the schoolhouse, as the men of Sodom were gathered outside the house of Lot, big Kewalo came into their midst. They knew him, they paid him no heed. From the window of the schoolroom, where I hid, I watched Kewalo take his stand on the schoolhouse steps. Still they did not think anything of his being there. Laughing among themselves, strumming their guitars, they waited lazily for me to come out. Fifteen or twenty of them, of all ages, from old to young, they were the wastrels of Kalawao.

From the pocket of his dirty work pants Kewalo drew a piece of crumpled paper. In a loud voice he called to the men: "Hear you the words of the King! Hear you: these are the words of the King!"

Startled by his summons, the men ceased their chatter. Mouths open, hands stopped upon the strings of their guitars, they looked up to Kewalo, where he glared down at them.

"These are the words of the King," he said, shaking the paper to smooth it for his reading. Profound was the silence when he began.

> "There is a *kapu* placed upon this schoolhouse, and upon all it holds. Books, papers, pencils, chairs, they are mine, the King's. Let them be preserved.

> "There is a *kapu* placed upon the pupils of this schoolhouse. They are as my children. Let them be protected and fostered, for the good of the land.

> "There is a *kapu* placed upon the teacher of this schoolhouse. She is as a daughter to me and to the Queen. Let her be honored and protected, for the good of the land.

> "Hearken to these words: they are the words of my mouth, the words of my heart. Surely, the life of the land is preserved in righteousness.

> KALAKAUA, THE KING."

Quickly did the men steal away. Without a sound, without a backward glance, they vanished.

No longer did they foregather at the schoolhouse door. No longer did they molest me. With the King's hand outstretched over me, I was safe. And thereafter I walked without fear in the paths of Kalawao and across the face of Kalaupapa's plain.

One rainy evening, when we went to sing in the house of Deborah Makanani, Caleb Forrest came in to sing with us. He was invited by Kumakani, the man who played the bass viol. "I have heard him play his flute," said Kumakani, when he introduced Caleb to the group, "and I said to myself, this is a bird to sing with the *iiwi*."

Deborah could not contain herself, so pleased was she to have such a handsome young man in her house. Tittering with excitement, she charged around the little parlor like a cow in a kitchen, bumping into people, toppling chairs, upsetting a vase full of leaves, in her eagerness to rearrange the furniture that she might seat her stylish guest. In all the turmoil Caleb stood to one side, surveying the upheaval with his most lordly air. Smartly dressed, in a dark-green coat of heavy stuff, with fawn-colored trousers and shining yellow boots to match, he was enough to turn any woman's head.

"*Auwe, nohoi e!*" Tutu nudged me. "What has brought him to join us at last?" We had asked him to join the Hui Iiwi long before, through the mouth of Momona, who knew him well, thinking it would give him pleasure to spend some of his evenings with the hui. But no: we were snubbed. Politely, but in a manner which told Momona that the very idea of it bored him, he said, "No."

But there was Caleb, in Deborah Makanani's parlor, making her gallant compliments, rolling his eyes at her, showing his white teeth, like an eel about to bite. Could it be Deborah who lured him to join the group? Looking at them, the citified Caleb, with his princely airs, the fat and giggling Deborah, soft as overripe fruit, who had never been out of the country, I could not imagine a more ridiculous match. I was piqued. Tutu sniffed. "Some men like 'em fat," she announced in a voice that I was sure could be heard throughout the Settlement. But only skinny Tuesday Lokahi, who sat next to me, laughed, and I found hope in the thought that Caleb had not heard her judgment of his tastes.

Caleb blew very well, indeed, upon his flute, a pretty thing of polished dark wood with an ivory mouthpiece. It was a joy to hear him play his merry trills for some of the *haole* airs, to hear him add the light and gentle line of its melody to the throbbing beat of the guitars and the bass viol and to the sweet violin of Momona.

Just as a soaring bird will rise and fall upon the breath of the wind, so did Caleb's flute sounds rise and fall with the breath of the music. He gave our music a poetry it had never owned, which we did not know it needed until we heard him add it. He made us play and sing so beautifully that, hearing it, we were cleansed for a while of our meanness and our sorrows. We sat in Deborah's parlor in quiet happiness. For once we did not break the spell of magic with any calls for *hulas*. "*Nani ka maikai*," we exclaimed. "How lovely is this music we have made."

While Deborah bounced around in the cookhouse, heating the water for the tea, Caleb came to speak with us. He looked well: unlike most of the men we saw each day, he was freshly shaven, and his skin was dark from being in the sun. The emerald eyes were darker, too, than usual, in the shadow of his brow. The white streak in his hair blazed like the new moon in the night.

"Caleb," I said, "we are so glad to have you come to join our group. You play beautifully. Our music is going to be much improved."

"*Ae, ae*"—Tutu must have her say. " 'Like the love call of the *iiwi* in the mountain forest' it is: 'beautiful and beyond reaching.' " The quotation was fulsome enough, but she felt she must cap it with an invention of her own. "And every bird in the forest hears its call, and gives answer." With her mud hen's cackle and the poke she aimed at his ribs, how could Caleb miss her meaning?

Putting his hand over his heart, he assumed a look of grieving. "Forlorn is this *iiwi* in his mountain forest; empty is his nest of love . . ."

"*Kie!*" she replied. "He should have no trouble, this pretty bird, in filling his nest with love."

I left them to their ribaldry. This Tutu! Sometimes she could be so vulgar. I was talking with Sophia Kahumu and Hanu, straining at nothings with them, when the thought came over me: This Caleb! He is no different from those men in front of the schoolhouse. My heart grew small and hard within me for him. This bird from an empty nest: let him take his fat Deborah into it. She will keep him warm.

Seeking out Tutu, I tugged at her arm. "Come. We must go. I cannot remain here any longer." Never have I been so unmannerly.

"*Auwe!* And what is the matter?"

"I—I have a headache. Let us go home."

"Of course, my dear. Let me get our wraps."

Caleb was at the door with my cloak, waiting to put it on me. Grinning as they say the ancient idols grinned, with their sharp teeth and their red mouths, he draped the cloak upon me with slow and exaggerated concern. "Take care of yourself," he said. Putting my umbrella into one hand, my lighted lantern into the other, he said with an emphasis so thick that it was sickening, "Don't catch cold. We must not have our schoolmistress taken ill." With a flourish he opened the door, letting us out into the windy night. "Forgive me if I do not walk you home. I have my duties as a guest."

Tutu was completely taken in. "Of course you cannot leave. We are all right. Don't you worry about us."

"A *hui hou aku*," said the *iiwi* in search of love. "Until we meet again."

"Isn't that Caleb a nice boy!" exclaimed Tutu, as we walked out of Deborah's yard, the two of us huddled under one umbrella.

I said nothing, not knowing any more what to make of him. Until then it was so easy for me to think of him as a friend. But after this evening, when he proved to be so false—I did not know.

Not knowing what to say, I said nothing.

21

So PASSED THE TIME for us, with our little joys and our little sorrows to help us to forget the one great joy we were denied, the one great sorrow which hung over us, as the clouds hung over Molokai in the mornings. The clouds: those were the signs of our burden. But we lived under them, as plants will do even when they are denied the sun. We found new friends to take the places of those from whom we were banished, we found new pleasures to make up for those we had left behind. And with steadfastness we pretended that everything was well with us. After a time we did not see any longer the signs of our sickness:

grown familiar, as are the things in a house which are in daily use, they were as if they did not exist.

The days were filled with my pupils, especially with Eleu. He was my pride: no other in the school could match him. For a time my evenings were taken up with the attentions of the men of Kalawao, vying for my body in marriage. One by one the unmarried men came to call, to inspect me, "to give me the eye," as Tutu said—and to drop out of sight again, after a few foolish evenings during which they were given little chance even to say a word to me. Makaio and Tutu and I, we were my guardians, and I sat protected in a corner, like the betrothed of a high chief. But always there would be more men to take the places of the discouraged ones, and often our *lanai* was so filled with people as to be in danger of falling down. Sometimes, among the callers, I would recognize one of the men who besieged me in my school-house, before the *kapu* was laid upon me, and I would be amused by the difference between his present manners and his former wantonness.

"Like hounds after a bitch in heat," Caleb said of them one evening, little caring who heard him in his judgment. He had deigned to come at last to visit us in the house of Makaio. It was not with Tutu or with me that he would converse, but with Makaio and Momona and the other argumentative men who would gather there. Tutu and I, we sat wordless and unnoticed, like gray moths upon a gray wall, while the men talked about the affairs of the Settlement and about the politics of the nation.

Caleb was not liked by the men of Kalawao, even before he spoke that thought, but they liked him the less after he uttered it. Too proud, he was, too smart, too "sassy" for their comfort. I could only agree with them, because once again he was frightening me with his sourness. Not like the carefree red *iiwi* flitting from nest to empty nest was he now: he was the sour green *amakihi*, with no nest at all to lie in.

But still he continued to come to our house. I was glad when he came, for his presence did me a service. By his arguing and his sarcasm he kept the company so stirred up that they had little time to pay any attention to me. Each got in the way of the other, he got in the way of all; and I was left unbothered, as was the Greek woman of olden times in the years while she waited for her husband to return from his roaming. For his part, Caleb did little but glare at me from a distance, as though it were my fault that men should seek me out. He made it plain that he thought me a bitch, and for this plainness, I, too, liked him less.

Those were busy days and quiet nights, and I thought of them as setting the pattern of our lives. I was foolish enough to think that in their passing they were bringing me the happiness I hoped to find in Kalawao.

The sixteenth day of November is the birthday of the King. Because, in 1884, it fell upon the Sabbath, the celebrations in his honor were held on the Saturday before. Throughout Hawaii Nei, from Hawaii to Niihau, wherever his loyal subjects were found, there was holiday. Those who did not like him, being loyal still to the dead Kamehamehas, kept away or jeered from afar. But after eleven years upon the throne Kalakaua was undoubted King to most of his nation, and the voices of the die-hards were very weak.

At Kalawao there were many festivities.

In the morning of the great day, at ten o'clock, the bell of Saint Philomena was joined by the bell of Siloama, summoning the Settlement to a parade. Already we heard the voices of the people passing by our house from Kalaupapa's side, and the thudding of horses' hoofs racing along the road. Excitement was in the air when at last we stepped from the house.

The morning was fresh and cool, just as Makaio said it would be on his return from Mass. The sun withheld some of his heat behind scattered patches of cloud blowing in from the northeast. But there was no rain in those clouds, and the land was dry. "A perfect day," everyone pronounced it, feeling its goodness.

In the road between our house and Siloama the parade was assembling. Most of the people in the Settlement were in the procession. Only a few—the very sick, those unable to ride or walk, the aloof supporters of the Kamehamehas—would sit by the side of the road to watch the parade pass. "Who," I asked, "will be left to watch us march?" And Makaio said, "Wait, you will see it."

Amid shouts of excitement from the children, running about playing tag, the grown people were collecting according to their singing clubs or their burial societies. At the head of each burial society rose its colored banner, high upon a polished pole: The

Comfort in Death Society, the Water of Life Society, the Help Your Friends Benevolent Association, and many others were there.

"Isn't that a lovely one," said Tutu, pointing to the banner of the Rest in Peace *Hui* a cheerful red and green, merry as Father Damien's church, with its letters spelled in orange. Knowing her taste, I did not have to approve her example. I called her attention to the gray and pink one of the Mormons, with its letters done in black. It seemed more fitting. The other banners were colorful enough: each society seemed to be trying to invent the combination which would remind them the least of death, putting it together out of the most brilliant silks and satins the *haoles* could make for them.

Death was not in the minds of the people that day. Dressed in their best clothes, with *leis* upon their shoulders or around their hats, they were as many-colored as the coat of Joseph, as shifting in their hues as are the feathers in the neck of a pheasant.

At the head of the line, prancing on their restive horses, were the *pa'u* riders, about fifty of them. Even Honolulu does not often see so many in its parades. Their long, colored skirts, of gleaming silks and velvets in purest colors, or of costly patterned stuffs in a score of shades, flowed down from their bodies over the flanks of their steeds, until the swirls and folds of material almost touched the ground. Much as Tutu and I might object to those garish colors upon ourselves, we were forced to admit how wonderful they were to see upon the *pa'u* riders and their mounts. A few of the women rode sidesaddle, but most of them sat their horses like men. All of them wore *leis*, some of feathers, some of flowers. The most favored of all wore strands of the fragrant *maile*, brought down early in the morning from the wet valleys of Waileia and Waihanau.

Compared with the gorgeous women, the men were clothed almost soberly in white duck trousers, stiff with the *pia* starch, and in red fireman's shirts, open at the neck. This had been the King's riding habit when he was a youth, and now, everywhere in Hawaii, men wore it in compliment to him. Around their shoulders they, too, wore *leis*. The long leafy vines of the *maile* were cool and dark upon the crimson shirts: like the flowers of the *ohia lehua* upon the tree, like the scarlet *iiwi* alighting upon a bough, did they look, those men.

"*Eia hoi!*" exclaimed Tutu. "Is such beauty possible?" Coming as she did from country Kuliouou, at the end of Oahu's pointed toe, never before had she seen a parade. "I did not dream such things could be."

"Ambrose," said Makaio. Nothing could shake him from his dignity. He did not point to Ambrose: he was content to inform us that the Superintendent was near. I found him, guiding his jet-black mare back and forth along the edge of the crowd. Shouting at them, again and again, he was urging them to fall into place. But they were too busy: gossiping, renewing acquaintances which could not have lapsed by more than twelve hours, few of them paid any heed to him. Across his chest, slanting from the right shoulder to his waist, Ambrose wore a broad yellow ribbon, the color of the *ilima* flower, the color of a King's Officer. He was the Grand Marshal of the parade.

We were only half an hour late in starting, but everyone was having a good time and no one complained of the delay. At last the harried Ambrose gave the signal. The bells rang, the children shrieked, the grownups raised their hurrahs, and we started on our march. We did not have a band, but we had guitars and drums to play our music. The soft guitars we could not hear, where we marched with the Hui Iiwi, but the boom of the drums gave us the beat and we followed them. In a great ragged centipede of a procession we went, taking our laughter and our chatter with us.

Our jubilee mood found expression in noisy salutes to the few people along the way who were there to see us, in teasing comments tossed among ourselves. "E, Hanu! You out of step," someone cried, this to Hanu who was hopping as excitedly as his fingers did upon the *ukulele*. "E, Caleb! Why you nevah bring your flute?" Caleb scowled at everyone, as unhappy as though he had eaten of the red *panini* and got his mouth full of the tiny cactus prickles.

Along the road past the Catholic church and the hospital, past the wistful graves, we walked, until we came to the grassy field above the bay of Kalawao. With our banners streaming in the wind, with our *pa'u* riders and our *leis*, we made a brave show. And when the head of the procession made its grand swing at the end of the field, beginning the return march to the village, and we who were still going met those who were coming toward us—lo! it was a noble sight, to see the broad chests of the horses coming at us, their legs prancing and dancing, their riders sitting proudly upon them, the skirts of the *pa'u* riders flowing gracefully, like pieces of rainbows falling to the ground. It was a sight to make one glad, and whistles and shouts of pleasure, hand-clappings and merry wavings, passed from one part of the procession to the other.

In front of the hospital the riders stopped their horses and, turning, made a wall across the road. On the hospital steps stood Father Damien in his long womanish dress and his funny pompom hat, the Reverend Hanaloa, who was the pastor of Siloama, and Iokepa Napela, who was the Elder among the Mormons in the Settlement. On the birthday of the King there was no barrier between the churches: all joined as one, to pay homage to the Highest Chief.

When the end of the procession came to a stop, and we were all crowded into the space before the hospital, Ambrose Hutchinson swung from his horse and went up to stand by the men of God. Raising his hand, Ambrose commanded silence. It was not long in coming. Much as we like parades, we like also the pleasure of speeches .

"Life to the King!" cried Ambrose.

"Life to the King!" responded the people.

"Let the speeches begin and end in prayer. Kamiano will say the blessing."

Father Damien's invocation was short. In Hawaiian, which held little of the *haole* in it, he called the Lord's blessing upon the King and his nation, and upon us, his people, who were gathered there. Making the sign of the cross over us, he stepped back to his place.

Then it was Ambrose's turn, as the King's Officer, to make his speech. He talked long, but he talked well, in the fine poetic phrases which our orators use, which we love to hear. We watched his gestures, the grace with which he lifted his hand, with which he turned to point. When he said something especially pleasing to us, putting it in words which were old but in thoughts which were new, we murmured *"Maikai,"* looking from one to the other to express our approval of his style. He was a good speaker, this man who in himself was so shy, and he made us proud of our heritage as he spoke to us. We liked best the noble message with which he finished:

"The King: he is the father of our nation, and the guardian of its people. Great is his love for us, deep is his concern. Long does he labor for us, that our nation might flourish."

Raising his hand to point to the mountains standing high above us, Ambrose bade us look up to them.

"As long as these mountains do endure, so long will there be a Hawaii Nei. As long as there will be a Hawaii Nei, so long will there be a Hawaiian nation to dwell in it, and a King to sit upon its throne, to guide his people and to watch over them."

These words made our hearts to swell, our eyes to fill with tears.

"Life to the people: may its numbers increase," prayed Ambrose. "Life to the King: may his years be long." He was finished.

"Amene," prayed the people, sending their breath up to Heaven.

Then stepped forth the Elder Napela. "Now is the time for the hookupu." He was a big man, and his voice was deep and measured. "Bring gifts to the King, so he may know we have love for him in our hearts."

Forward to the steps went the leaders of the clubs, the deacons of the churches, the people who were appointed to bear our gifts to the King. In the olden days each of us would have crawled on his knees before the King, or knelt before his deputy, to lay our small gifts at his feet. Then we would have taken pigs and chickens and dogs, taros and sweet potatoes, and fish from the sea, that the Great Chief and his Court might eat; or bundles of kapa and tufts of yellow feathers from the mamo and the oo, that he might be clad in the glory of his land. But now, in the new times, things were different: the Christians have brought us dignity and release from fear. Where before our people gave because they must, now they gave because they wished to give. Our emissaries walked upright, carrying the gifts of our making: mats, purses, bags, covers for books, woven of hala or of the fine ferns from the mountains; bowls shaped from the wood of the milo and of the kou; leis made of polished seeds or of matched sea shells; fish nets in the old style, made from fibers of the olona. In other places in the kingdom gifts of greater value might be presented, but no one could match us in the love with which we placed our offerings at the feet of Ambrose, the konohiki of the King.

When the hookupu was ended, Ambrose gave us the King's thanks, and promised that our gifts would be sent to him in

Honolulu, "to bring him joy, and the knowledge that his children at Kalaupapa are grateful for the care he has always given to them."

The Reverend Hanaloa said the prayer of leave-taking. When he was done there was a moment of deep silence, while we waited for him to lead us in the national anthem. When all eyes were upon him, all voices were ready to sing, then did he raise his hand, and we sang the song written by Kalakaua himself, when first he was made King. He wrote it to honor the Great Kamehameha, but now we sang it to honor him, thrilling to hear its splendid chords:

> "You who are Hawaii's folk,
> Be loyal to your King,
> Do honor to your Chief,
> The Highest Chief:
> The Father of us all,
> *Kamehameha E,*
> Who guarded us in war
> With his great spear."

The rest of the day was given over to games, horse racing, visiting, until it was time for the feasting, in the late afternoon. Only the cooks labored, preparing for the grand *paina*.

At half-past four o'clock those of the people who would share in the *luau* gathered in the wide yard in front of Father Damien's church. There, upon the grass, *hala* mats were spread, and over these *ki* leaves and fern fronds brought from the mountains. More than four hundred of us sat upon the mats to eat.

In the lee of the young trees planted between us and the sea, we were sheltered somewhat from the cool wind. Monkeypods and flame trees, they were new to Hawaii, as they were new to Kalaupapa. I looked upon them with interest, because Makaio had told me their history. "Your Uncle Peter brought them here, seedlings from Honolulu. His cousin, the Queen Emma: she sent them to him." They were planted throughout the Settlement, and they struggled now to grow in its foreign soil. "His own house, in Kalaupapa, is almost hidden by their foliage," Makaio had said.

I looked upon them, but not with sadness for Uncle Peter. Were they not a good memorial to leave behind him? They were happier things, those graceful trees with their fine green leaves and their long branches tossing in the breeze, than was his abandoned house in Kalaupapa, which I did not want ever to see.

And who, there in the churchyard, found time for sadness? A *luau* is a time for fun, and, as we streamed into the decorated yard, we were in our happiest mood. Dressed in our fine clothes, ready to eat our favorite foods, we put our sadness away for a while, until the day was done. Already there was laughter and joking, the shrieks of women in merriment rising above the deeper rumble of talk from the men. On the church steps the musicians were singing popular tunes and favorite songs, accompanying themselves with guitars and fiddles. The children got in the way, as usual; the wonderful aroma of *kalua* pig was wafted over us from the newly uncovered *imu*. Everything was as it should be. The King's own birthday *luau* in Honolulu would not be different from ours.

We sat together, we of the Hui Iiwi. I was not surprised to see Caleb next to Deborah Makanani, several places away from me. He gave no thought to me, busy as he was with entertaining his adoring Deborah and timid Sophia and others who were within hearing of his jests. They were all laughing at the things he was saying, and Deborah, every time she rolled with her laughter, would rest her hand heavily upon Caleb's knee, where it lay next to her fat haunch.

"Make way for the food! The *kaukau* comes!" the servers cried. Ambrose said the grace, and soon the steaming pig was brought to us, with baked bananas and sweet potatoes, *lawalu* fish in their wrappings of *ki* leaves, and pieces of sweet *ki* root for the dessert. The *poi* was already before us, in calabashes and bowls, scattered along the mats; the *inamona*, made of red salt, seaweed, and pounded *kukui* nuts, was there, too, for savor, and the onions and the chile peppers, for those who would want such hot things. How good it all was and how we did eat! Tomorrow we would be hungering again, for half a week's supply of *poi* and a whole week's measure of pork were gone into the *luau*, but such feasting was worth a week of watery stew. No one pretended that we feasted to honor the King: this feast was for ourselves.

After the food was consumed, down to the last bit of pork fat, the last shred of onion skin—there were some among us who behaved as the starvelings of desert Kau are said to eat when they visit in Puna: they even licked the juices from the *ki*-leaf wrappings in which the food was served—after the eating was done and the stomachs were full, then the singing contest began.

"The voice is smoother if first it is greased with pork," our people say. And, again: "What tongue can sing of gladness, when the belly is empty?" But I think that our people of the Hui Iiwi lost their voices with their appetites. We won no prize for our singing, either of *haole* songs or of Hawaiian. The judges were more impressed by Caleb's fluting than by our singing, and they congratulated us on our fortune in having him in the Hui. But Caleb alone could not win us a prize. We could only agree with the judges when we heard some of the other clubs take their turn.

We did not mind our defeat. As mischievous Hanu said, while we were returning to our places, "Nemmine, errybody. We oney seeng fo fun, yeh?" But Caleb was black with mortification at our disgracing. Before the other groups finished their singing, he got up and left us, without saying good-by. The eyes of Deborah followed him with longing, while the rest of us tried not to see how unsporting he was in going away.

When the singing contest was over and the prizes were given out, the night had come. Cold it was, and clear: the clouds had vanished from the mountaintops and the stars were shining forth, bright and blue as lamps seen in the distance. Then was it time for the fireworks.

Like a river of lava pouring down the wall of the mountain did they come, like a fall of Pele's blood coursing down the face of the *pali*. High up, on the very edge of the cliff, burning embers were emptied from great caldrons, one after the other, and the fiery coals and the smoldering sticks burst into flames as they fell those thousands of feet toward the plain on which we sat. Like waterfalls afire they descended, grandly and slowly, loath to plunge into the darkness of the little valley into which they disappeared.

With the cascades of embers came sticks of *papala* wood, flaming brilliantly as they fell, like falling angels. So light is the wood, so much like the foam of the sea, that, before the burning sticks had fallen far, the sweep of rising air caught them up and carried them, upwards, sidewards, in all directions, like shooting stars. Rising and sinking upon the breast of the air, they flared and glowed, lighting up the face of the cliff as though ghost-people danced upon its steep sides, until, burned out at last, they were suddenly extinguished, and left only the remembrance of them, traced like ghost pictures, upon the blackness which swallowed them up.

With cries of pleasure we greeted each new toss of the *papala* sticks, each fresh fall of fire tumbled over the edge of the cliff by the people of the highlands. This was their gift to us, their *aloha* to us who lived in the enclosed kingdom below. Mingled with our pleasure was our gratitude for their kindness to us.

In one last burst of flame a whole enormous blazing tree was sent sliding over the edge of the cliff. Roots first it fell, the fire streaming upward over its long trunk into the outspread and twisted branches, to which the leaves still clung. As the fire reached them they, too, burst into flame. It looked like a woman falling, her hair ablaze as she came, feet first, down into the darkness.

"Pele! It is Pele!" cried a hundred voices, some in pride, some in fear. Indeed, it did seem as if the Fire Goddess were come to visit us. When the blazing tree crashed upon the ground at the foot of the cliff, there was a great eruption of fire and smoke, lighting up the cleft of the gorge for a moment, as though Pele were bursting out of her underground home. But in another moment the ravine was black again, the mountain was dark again, and only the distant stars glittered in the heavens.

A long sigh went up from us who sat upon the ground. A day so happy, so full of excitement and of forgetting, is a day difficult to part with. After so much joy, can the return to the reality of each ordinary day be borne? Feeling this, if not thinking it, we sighed for the ended day.

Yet I was content, even in my sighing, for in the sharing of the great day I was happy among my people. And, in finding this happiness, I thought that I had found my peace. Quietly did I sit there, content with this reward.

Then boys came running among us, with torches of *kukui* nuts and tapers for lighting our lanterns. In their warm glow we made ourselves ready to go home.

"Malie." The voice was close to my ear, the touch was upon my arm. Unthinking, moving still in the world of my content, I turned to see who called me.

"Caleb. I thought you had gone?"

"Malie. I—I must see you. May I walk home with you?"

"Of course. But what is the matter? Are you ill?" All at once I was concerned for this man, with whom I had not felt anything but unease for so long. All my friendship for him came back, in the recognition of his plea, at the sight of the lines upon his face.

"No. Yes. Oh, I don't know. Come, let us go." Taking me by the hand, he started to draw me away.

"Wait. I cannot go without Tutu, without Makaio. Can we not walk together?"

He glared around him at the crowd, as an animal does when it is caged. There were so many people about us, waiting to pass through the narrow gates: how could he expect to walk with me alone? He said nothing, but he did not release his hold upon my hand.

"What is the matter, Caleb?" How frightening this strange man could be. With him near, where was my peace of heart?

"Later, later," he said impatiently. I became unhappily aware of fat Deborah, standing across the mat from us, watching us with burning eyes. I felt no joy at taking her hope from her.

"Should you not walk with her?"

"*Cha*, why should I walk with a cow? I owe her nothing. Come, let us get away from here."

We pushed Makaio and Tutu ahead of us, into the crowd. Soon other people came between us and Deborah. When we reached the road the walking was easier. To the east, to the west, the torches and lanterns lighted the way, shining upon the heads of the people, upon their backs, their moving legs. It was a beautiful scene, but I dared not speak of it.

One by one the groups of people turned from the road. With cheerful calls they sent their farewells each to the other and to us. This pleasure Caleb could not take from me. After a while there were only the people who lived near us, at the edge of the village; and at the last there was only the household of Makaio upon the road.

At the gateway to our yard Makaio turned to us, the hissing torch shining upon us from one side. "Come into the house, you two," Tutu spoke her duty. "We will have some tea."

"No, not yet," said Caleb. "Please. I would speak with Malie. There is something I would say to her. Do you go in. We will come soon. In five minutes."

"This is not good," said Makaio. "It is not fitting."

"Come, Makaio." She put her hand upon his arm, as a wife would do in persuading a husband. "Let us put the kettle on the fire. They will come to no harm." How sweetly she said it, how readily she betrayed me to her designs for me. It mattered not to her how already I trembled in fear of being left alone with Caleb, how my heart cried out to her not to leave me in the dark with him. My mouth was dry, my stomach sick with foreboding. "No, Tutu," I began.

But Makaio's strong voice overwhelmed the small sound of my own. "I will leave the torch here." Thrusting it between the rocks of the wall, he made it to stand upright. He turned to Caleb. "Five minutes. Then I will come back." Stern as a father he was, and I was glad to hear his concern for me.

"Thank you," Caleb said humbly. His body was trembling with his eagerness to have them go, but his tongue was as steady as a fish in the water beneath a wave.

When they were gone, he pulled me into the darkness, beyond the reach of the light. My limbs were numb, my feet were as stone. I did not know how I moved.

"Malie," he whispered. Now did his voice tremble. "There is something I must tell you."

My eyes fixed upon the torch, I wanted to cry out, to stop him, to keep my ears from hearing what he had to say. Blinded by the light, I could not see him. I could feel him, close to me, I could smell the sweetness of his breath.

"Malie, hear me. Open your heart to me. I—I burn with love for you."

It was as I feared. O Caleb, Caleb, what am I to say to you?

"Malie, do you hear?" He put his hands upon my shoulders, gently he shook me. "Do you hear my words? They are words of love, Malie. For you." He moved closer to me, coming between me and the light. Sweet was his breath, sweet were his words, the words a woman should rejoice to hear. There was a time—I knew it now—there was a time, in Honolulu, when I would have rejoiced to hear them come from him. But he had not said them then, nor had any man said them, those words which every woman waits to hear.

Now they were as all words he said: a mockery, a sour joke upon me, upon him, upon the whole world at which he sneered. For now they came too late. Too late—

He shook me again. "Do you not hear? I love you, I say. I wish to marry you. These are words I never thought to say to any woman. But you, my sweet, you have conquered me."

"—Too late!" The cry broke from me at last, rising up out of me as water wells up from a spring.

"Too late?" His pride was stung: he pulled his hands from me as if I were a burning brand. "What do you mean? Have you given your love to another?"

"No, Caleb, no. It is not so. It is just that—" My voice choked on my pity for him, and for me. Sobbing, but without tears, I tried to tell him. "Love is not for me. What right have I to love, with the Kalawao sickness in me?"

Harshly did he laugh. "Is love to be denied, then? What of me? Do I not live, do I not ask for love, even though I am eaten with the same disease? Look at all of these others here, who have found their love here, even in this place."

"Ae, Caleb, I have seen them, and I have envied them. But in me—in me there is no heart for love. In me there is only emptiness, and coldness, and a longing for death."

"Do not say it! This is a falseness, a pity for yourself, eating you away worse than the *mai Pake* does." Once more he put his hands upon me, drawing me close to him. "Let me show you, let me show you how easy it is to love. Let me awaken you. I will teach you how to forget your fear of love . . ." His arms went around my waist, his lips sought my cheek.

Behind him the torch flared in its last burst of light, preparing to go out. In an instant there would be only the darkness.

"No, Caleb, please." Cold was my body to his touch, rigid to his claim upon me. As I held myself back from him, his passion burst forth. "Malie! Let me show you the manner of love!" Eager to touch me with his lips, he kissed me upon my brow, upon my closed eyelids, upon my cheeks, my nose, my mouth. Hungry for the taste of me, he put his tongue upon my ears, upon the curve of my cheeks, upon the hollow of my throat.

Unmoved by his kisses I stood there, cold as a stone, and as unyielding. My gaze was fixed upon the torch: now only the embers of the stump burned, with a faint flame, feeding upon the last drops of oil from the seeds long since consumed. My mind thought only of the hurt that would be Caleb's when he had measured the depths of my coldness. I was as a lamp without oil: neither light nor warmth would I give. Poor Caleb. Wounded in his pride, he would hate himself now, as well as me.

The torch went out. There was only the darkness.

He raised his head, loosed his arms from around my body. His voice, when it came, was low and hard. "Do you hate me so much? Am I so disgusting that you cannot—"

"It is not you," I started to say. It is not you alone: it is any man, every man, whom I fear. It is love which I fear: it is love of this kind which I do not want.

But he did not let me explain. Coldly, formally, he stopped me. "I am sorry I have bothered you. I shall not bother you again. Good night." I could imagine his quick bow, his parting sneer. Quickly he went away, quietly was he lost in the night.

When Makaio came for me, bringing with him the lantern, I was leaning against the gatepost, looking up at the stars. Cold and aloof and out of reach, they were no more remote from me than I had been from Caleb.

"And where is Caleb?" he asked, holding the lantern high.

"He went home. He did not wish to have tea."

"I see," said Makaio, shaking his head, not understanding anything.

Together we went into the house. I watched him shut and bolt the door against the night, against the stars, against lovers who lay that night beneath the stars, held in each other's arms. I knew, as I watched him, that he was shutting the door upon life, closing me up in the tomb of his house.

22

SLOWLY I PUT my disordered life into balance again. I was like a mender of broken china, hoping that the glue I used would not come unstuck, and yet never being quite certain that the mended ware of my life would not fall apart again one day, as I was in the act of using it.

One afternoon I was playing with the children in the street in front of the schoolhouse. It was the birthday of Agnes Hoopili, the youngest of my pupils. To please her we made a party; and, because the woman in whose house she lived was sick, we moved the celebration to the schoolhouse. There we ate the small cakes Emma baked for us, and some of the Kona oranges sent to me by my mother on the last *Mokolii*. When we were done with eating, and while our hands and faces were still sticky with cake, still fragrant with oranges, small Ilio snatched the beanbag from Agnes' lap. It was the gift of Akala, sewn with her own hands from a scrap of red calico, and filled with Job's Tears gathered in the valley of Waileia. It was Agnes' only treasure, and she was the envy of her schoolmates, who owned nothing like it.

"Ilio," she wailed, "you bring that back." She did not know whether to chase him or to cry. "Come and get it," the mischievous boy teased, dangling it just out of reach.

Half of a schoolteacher's life is spent, I think, in preventing fights among her pupils. "Let us play tag," I hastened to say. "The one who gets the beanbag is Master."

With whoops of glee from the boys and squeals of worry from the girls we began our game. Forgotten was Agnes' alarm over her beanbag while we chased each other up and down the road. We played, with much noise and no unhappiness, until it was almost dark. Never could I catch the holder of the bag, and I did not touch it until small Hema himself, gasping for breath and almost ready to drop, brought it to me and thrust it into my hands. Immediately the others were after me, shouting and trying to seize the bag from my uplifted arm. Eleu, the tallest among the boys, almost took it from me. He was not shy in the game, as he was in the classroom. "*Pau*," I called, laughing even as I cried out to them. "*Pau*. No more." It was time for us to end our sport, I could see by the heated faces and sweating bodies swirling around me, raising such a noise.

For a moment they continued their struggle, paying me no heed. And then, as if my voice had been slow to reach them, they stopped and drew back from me, as a wave falls away from the shore. In my mind I was complimenting them on their obedience when I saw how they stared beyond me, like young animals surprised by a hunter. Even as they turned and fled from the intruder I whirled to see who was behind me.

I did not expect to see them who stood there: the white doctor and the dark murderer. I had forgotten about them. But now, as they appeared before me, I realized with a shock that they had been in Kalawao all the time I had been there.

The little doctor was in the front, his white suit clean but wrinkled, gleaming bright in the twilight. He stared at me, as astonished by the meeting as I was. With his boyish face, his smooth pink cheeks and the weak wisp of a mustache, with his long blond hair carefully combed, he looked like a very young angel come to earth.

Behind him, tall above him, stood Keanu. Broad were his shoulders, stretching the faded blue shirt, dark was his face, with the short black beard upon it, the long black hair hanging in tangles about his ears. His mouth, too, was open, but not with surprise. His teeth showed, large and white, like those of a dog at seeing a bone he covets. I had seen faces like his, coveting women, coveting me. His was the crooked smile of the men who stood in the street outside the schoolhouse—

With a gasp of fear I fled from them, running for home.

After that time Keanu was seen often in the open places of Kalaupapa. Always he was alone, and always did he shun the company of the patients. If ever he met someone from the Settlement upon the plain, he would depart from the path, striking off across the grass or the barren rock to make a way of his own. If he met with someone on a narrow path, he would step to the side of the trail, turning his back upon the patient, answering his greetings in a faint voice.

At first, when they saw how he shunned them, the people of the Settlement were angry. "Who is this Keanu?" they asked, "Does he think himself better than we?" Or, "Is he so good, this murderer, this stealer of other men's wives, and are we scum to his feet, an offense to his eyes?" Forgotten was their concern for him at the time of Opaekea's operation upon him.

Remembering how he appeared to me, in the path by the schoolhouse, I thought, Ae, he is proud. Then, when I met him walking along the road, I saw the straightness of his body, the way he walked, tireless and with an animal's grace, his head held high, looking upon the mountains and the sky as his equals, surveying the land of Kalaupapa as his domain. Remembering what he had done with his hands, for the sake of his lust, I trembled. And he is a man to be feared.

The same thought came to others. "Guard yourself," said Makaio to me. "Do not go out alone."

"*Paoa ka waha o ka mano i ke kino*. The mouth of a shark loves the taste of a body," said sly Momona, pleased with the expectation. "Nothing good will come of this shark, swimming free among us." Wickedly did he linger over the word *mano*. To us it means not only a shark but also a man who pursues women, a man who is a passionate and insatiable lover. Momona wanted none of us to miss his meaning.

The women whispered, the men scowled; and for a few days there was alarm among the people of Kalawao. When they saw him walking, even the children ran the other way.

Only Emma thought of him with charity. "Lonely is he, this poor man. The company of people: this is what he needs." She did not say more, but I knew what she was thinking: if he comes to me for comforting, I will give him comforting. Studying her, big and strong, wearing her compassion in her empty heart as generously as she wore her solid flesh upon her bones, I marveled again at the differences with which people are made.

But after a few days the word spread among us, from one cluster of gossips to another, how it was not pride which kept Keanu from us. "It is Opaekea: these are his orders, so his test upon Keanu will not go wrong." Because this message was sent among us from Father Damien, through Kewalo, we accepted it. We liked it better this way, with Opaekea to blame, because we did not like to think that one of our own people would shun us of his own will.

We liked it better, too, because as we became accustomed to seeing Keanu we began to lose our fear of him. Soon some of the people began to renew their pity for him. "We are all here together in this place. Why cannot we be friends?" As is the way with us, we shifted our dislike again to the doctor. "Who is this Opaekea, that he can come among us and tell us what to do, what not to do?" More vicious than our enmity toward Keanu was our hatred for the *kauka*. We began to see Keanu as a man cast alone upon a desert isle, more alone than we could ever be. In our talk, first in jest and then in seriousness, we spoke of him as "*Ka Meha-meha*," the Lonely One. And we began to think of ways how we might bring some ease to his loneliness. But we did not know how we could do it, with Opaekea there, sitting like a watchful squid in his house upon the hill.

Then one day a new *haole* doctor came to stay in Kalawao, and soon after Opaekea was taken away.

"There you are," said Momona. "He is in trouble, for what he did to Keanu. Hearken to my words: he will not come back. The King is angry with him."

We were sitting on our *lanai*, in the usual evening's visiting. Beyond the end of Molokai, over against Oahu, the sunset was decking the sky in pink and green, all at once, in a gentle end to a quiet day.

"You make noises like an empty gut," snarled Caleb. "What do you know of the King's thoughts? And why should he punish Opaekea now, when four months ago he gave Keanu into the *haole's* hands?"

Momona was never without an answer, even if he must make one up for the use of the moment. "I am told that the King is exceedingly wrathful with Opaekea for the test he makes on Keanu," he said smoothly, his fat face as innocent as a sleeping pig's.

"You are told! Then why is it that the King's Privy Council has banished Keanu forever to Kalaupapa? This in exchange for not hanging him, as he was sentenced to be hanged? Is this the usual manner in which man-killers are treated?"

"Oh you lawyers," chuckled Momona, "always making things more complicated than they are. Always so close with your noses to the papers that you cannot see the great ones who shape the laws to their uses. *Kie!* Why else but to cheat those damned *haole* judges and those damned *haole* laws out of a victim for their rope?"

"Well I'll be damned!" Caleb swore in English, striking his forehead with his fists. He was stunned into silence—but whether by Momona's logic or by his stupidity he did not say.

Momona clapped a hand to his broad knee. "This would be only right. What Hawaiian would hang a man in cold punishment? What Hawaiian will waste another life for one already lost? Especially because of a deed committed for love? *Eia!* A smart one is Kalakaua: he knows how to fool the *haoles*." Kewalo, Hanu, Makaio, Kepule, each of them nodded approvingly.

"*Ae.* Pretty soon he'll have them all sent home, to wherever they come from. From their Americas, their Germanies, their Old Englands and their New Englands, from their Saint Francis towns and all those faraway places." Here was Momona speaking the hope of our race, the hope felt by all supporters of the King when they heard of his efforts to rule our nation without interference from the *haoles*. Good *haoles* or bad, they are all dangerous, and they must be sent away before too many of them are settled in our land. "Then will we have the olden times again, then will Hawaii be saved for Hawaii's people."

"Hah, do you think the *haoles* are as stupid as you?" This was polite and agreeable Caleb, making friends for himself. "Do you think they are sitting idly—talking nonsense as you talk nonsense —while the King and Kipikona plot to hold the power from them? *Kie!* You are crazy if you think so." He was so scornful that I thought Momona would take offense.

But no. "It will be as I say," he said smugly, lifting his heavy shoulders. Addressing the rest of us, he explained his certainty. "The signs say it will be so."

"What signs?" Caleb put the question harshly. Beyond him the sky was turning red, as though in response to his ire.

"There are signs. To those who will believe in them. And Kaupea has dreamed a dream—"

"Who is this Kaupea?"

Momona looked uneasily around him, feeling that already he had said too much. Mercilessly Caleb pressed him: "A *kahuna?*"

"*Ae.*" The answer was given grudgingly. "A seeress. She lives here, a very old woman now, but learned in the ways of ancient times."

Thus did I hear for the first time of Kaupea. Indeed, it was the first time I heard of a *kahuna* among the people of the Settlement. So ignorant was I, that I thought the *kahunas* were gone with the wooden idols and the ancient gods, overthrown when the missionaries brought the One True God to Hawaii Nei. A thrill ran through me, of unbelief that some of my people still clung to the old ways in spite of the new ways which have been brought to them. Superstitious they might be, and evil, those old ways, compared with the power of Iehovah. But how exciting it was, to learn that the ancient past survived still in an old woman who was one of my neighbors. I leaned forward to hear more of this Kaupea.

"And what was Kaupea's dream?" Sharp as the fin of a surgeonfish was Caleb's voice, cutting through Momona's unwillingness.

"It was this: a great wind came up, a devil wind, and blew down all of the temples of the Christian God. Broken were their steeples, roofless were their houses, and their tongues were silenced in the sea."

"And what does this mean, this crooked talk?"

"Even you can see, country boy, what it means. It means that the *haoles* and their invisible God will be blown away into the sea. Then will the land, cleansed and purified, be restored unto the children of Hawaii-loa, and to their waiting gods."

"And this will be a good for the nation?"

"It will be a good for the nation," avowed Momona, himself sitting like an idol in the light from the blood-red sky, the red sky of evening, a foreteller of death.

"If only it could be so," said Caleb, hitting his hands upon the railing where he perched. "But I cannot be as sure of this as you."

Enwrapped in his dreams, each of us kept silent, not breaking the spell.

Then Makaio spoke, starting slowly. "*Ae.* In many ways the ancient times were good. Before the *haoles* came, with their strange gifts, their guns, their greed for money and for land. And with their terrible sicknesses. Without them, we cannot forget, there would be no need for Kalaupapa, there would be no need for us to sit here in exile, for all the days of our years. There would be no desolation in the land, with its empty villages, its forlorn valleys, empty now of people. *Ae.* We have cause to hate the *haoles.*"

Hearing the old man's thoughts, uttered in the flaming sunset, I grew frightened. If he can speak like this, out of the serenity of his age, what comfort is left for the others of us, who have not his years or his wisdom? Where is the peace the wise do attain in time?

With a smile of triumph Momona looked upon us, while Makaio spoke his bitter thoughts.

"But," stern Makaio said firmly, "there is one good thing the *haoles* have brought to us, which makes all of our uncomforts as nothing. Without this thing all else is false: without this thing the olden days were vile. This is the love of God. Without it we are as beasts. With it, we are the children of God."

"*Amene, amene,*" said Tutu quickly. And I was restored again to my comfort, by the wisdom of Makaio.

On Momona's face the smile of victory changed into a sneer. Ah See, an image carved in ivory, sat with his little pipe held in his lap, the smoke from it curling up before him like incense. Hanu peered up at us from his place beside Ah See upon the stairs, to see how this strange conversation would end.

It was Caleb who brought it to a close. With a wild and savage impatience he rose from the railing and hurried away from us, hiding his face, and his thoughts, in the darkening night.

When they were accustomed to the sight of Keanu, the people of the Settlement saw him not at all: he became a part of the land to them, as a tree growing upon the hill, as a house standing aloof behind its wall of rock. He became a kind of ghost of the place, a ghost with flesh.

But I could not easily keep him from my mind. When I saw him, it was not as a ghost that I saw him, but as a man, a man shut out from the company of his people. It was not good, I thought, that there should be such a division between us: to me he was a haunting of the conscience, a reminder that something was wrong with those of us who suffered him to live apart and lonely.

There were times when I would meet him close by, as I went with some of my pupils upon the plain of Kalaupapa, to explore the underground caves and the black stretches of the lava tubes boring like worm holes beneath certain parts of the land. Moving to one side of the path, he would bid us *aloha*, smiling pleasantly upon the children, upon me, as we went past him. At our first meeting I was faint with fear. By the time of our fifth meeting I looked upon him as directly as I would look upon Caleb or Momona. But even at the first meeting I saw that he was no ghost, no insubstantial thing like a conscience. A man of flesh and bone he was, a man who yearned for words of greeting, for acts of kindness, which would make him a man again. There was nothing evil in his face, and nothing frightening in his behavior. Standing tall and pleasing by the side of the path, his body was too real to my vision to be that of a ghost. His smile was too frank and open to belong to a fearsome man, his eyes were too hungry for kindness to be the eyes of a man who would act unkindly. Why should I fear him? I asked myself, as, smiling back at him, I went past him with the children. A man so nice-looking?

I spoke of him to Father Damien one afternoon when the old man stopped to talk with me on my way home from the schoolhouse. It was proper to talk of Keanu then: we could see him on the trail going down to the sea cliffs, a bundle of fishnets slung over his shoulder. "What of him, Father?"—I pointed to the forlorn man upon the deserted path. "Can nothing be done to ease his loneliness?"

"Ae, Malia, you have said it. That poor boy is the greatest of my worries here." This was the first time I heard him call me by this name, the name of Mary, the Mother of Jesus."

"He is a man shut out. Cannot something be done, to bring him among us?" I put my question as properly and as primly as a schoolteacher would, speaking to a priest.

He groaned. "I have tried, believe me, I have tried. First when Dr. Newman was here, then since he has gone away. 'It is not good for a man to live alone,' I told them, the both of them. The doctor, God help him, he is unyielding. Keanu is not to come close to anyone in the Settlement, he says, for at least half a year." He pointed his finger angrily in the direction of the doctor's house. "Not even to me!" This was a new side to the priest: I did not know he could be angry as are other men.

"But what of Keanu?" I asked softly, seeking to turn his mind from its wrath with Opaekea, the hateful *haole* who looked like an angel and who carried death in his touch.

"Yes, it is Keanu we must help. He is the one to save. The other: alas!—he is too proud to do anything with. But Keanu: he is a good boy, he is not beyond helping." It was sweet to hear my opinion of Keanu confirmed. I did not think it strange that, in our concern for Keanu's future, each of us forgot Keanu's past. But my satisfaction was taken from me by Kamiano's helplessness.

"But how to do this? How? I do not know." He waved his hands excitedly, he glared at me through his smudged and dirty spectacles.

"Poor Malia. Why do I grow angry with you? I talk as if it is your fault, when really no one is at fault. Who can say that the doctor is to blame? He does what he thinks is right. He does what he does to Keanu for the sake of all men. It is I who am confused."

But what of Keanu? I wanted to know. Oh, this old man, forever getting lost in words, confusing not only himself but me as well with his talk. Impatiently I stood there, a model of maidenly patience, waiting for him to remember why I waited.

"Yet what can we do to help Keanu, when Keanu himself is unwilling?"

"He is not willing?" This was a new thought to me. How can a man be unwilling to take his place among his people?

"It is so. I have asked him to church, to help me make coffins, to walk with me to Waikolu, where he can help me with the new pipe line. 'No one will touch you,' I promised him; 'you need touch no one. Just to be with other people will be good for you.' I invite him to my house, to talk with me if he will talk with no one else. I even tempt him with *kanaka* pudding"—he smiled, while I wondered how he could think that anyone could like that horrid dish—"but no, he will not yield to my tempting. A priest plays the part of the tempter, and is not successful at it."

"What does Keanu say?" How could I hold myself back? If I did not learn soon, I would explode, like a Chinese firecracker at *Pake* New Year's time.

"He says, 'No. I have given my word to the doctor. I will keep my word to him, so then he will keep his word to me.' Thus speaks a man of honor, and I must admire him for it. How can I go on, priest that I am, urging him to break his word? No. I am trapped, he is trapped, we are all caught, we who are people of good will, in this net of good and evil which has been woven for us.

"Has Dr. Newman woven it, I ask, or the Devil? I do not know. The more I think upon it, the less I know. But oftener do I think, now of late, that perhaps it is neither of these. Then who else is there?" He tapped his fingers upon my hand, begging me to answer.

Helplessly I stood beside him, drowning in a flood of words which held no meaning for me. His face was drawn and pale. His distress embarrassed me. I could not understand why he should be so worried over a question which has no answer. It is the kind of question that missionaries might argue, that men like Caleb and Momona could chew upon for hours of delicious contention. But for me it was a foolishness, a waste of time. I held my tongue, with the wisdom of a woman who knows when the foolishness of men must be permitted to run its course.

"There is only one other. It is God," he said humbly. "And perhaps this net is not a thing of evil. Perhaps it is a way of doing good, out of which will come God's own grace?"

It was only one more answerless question. Wearily I wondered how I might escape the talkative old man, wondered why I had ever stopped to ask him for advice. He was like all *haoles*: full of words, but not of help. "For help, go to a native; for talk, go to a *haole*," as we say to each other. Next time, I promised myself, I will think twice before I seek him out.

But escaping him was easier than I expected. He left me, forgetting I was there. Limping, his left foot dragging, so that it raised a little cloud of powdery dust with each step he took, he hurried toward his church. But his head was lifted, as though he heard messages from afar, his eyes were turned inward upon some unseeable goal, upon a vision of his heaven, perhaps, as he went away from me, leaving me standing in the empty road.

In the time of Maka-lii, in the month the *haoles* call December, after a long period of fine weather the cold winds and the chill rains came down from the north upon Kalaupapa. Many of the people in the Settlement took to their beds with sore throats and colds, and with the lung fever. Some of the ones who were sick with the *mai Pake* died of the lung fever instead. The new doctor was kept busy writing the death certificates telling Ambrose Hutchinson the reasons why the people died. Father Damien was kept busy making coffins, and with burying those who belonged to his faith.

In the house of Makaio I was the first to catch the sore throat. But it was quickly finished in me, and in three days I was well again. Then it was Tutu's turn, but she was not so lucky. She had to take to her bed. In the same week small Moki was afflicted with boils, great painful swellings upon his right arm and his back, coming one after another at intervals of a few days, to make the poor child groan with their aching and almost unwilling to move. Slow with the fear of being hurt, he sidled about the house, his arm held in a sling made of one of Makaio's red kerchiefs, his mouth open with suffering.

"Malie," croaked Tutu one morning from her bed, where she lay in double misery. "Do you go out and pick some *laukahi*. We must make a poultice for poor Moki's boils. And if you can find some of the *uhaloa* for me . . ." She needed to say no more: the bitter red tea of the *uhaloa* is good for soothing the burning throat and for stilling the ache of a throbbing head when one has a cold. And the leaf of the *laukahi*, as everyone knows, is God's gift to the sufferer from boils. If a poultice is applied with the lower surface of the leaves upon the boil, the poison will be drawn out of the flesh and the matter will come to a head. If the upper surface of the leaves is laid upon the boil, the poison will be forced inward, and the matter will be drained away. Great indeed is the power of the *laukahi*.

I put on my oldest *holoku*, I gathered up my gray shawl, should the rain fall while I was out upon the plain. With a *lauhala* basket to hold my harvest, I went in search of the herbs.

The long slender leaves of the *laukahi* were not hard to find, growing in their flat clusters in the close-cropped grass just beyond the edge of our own yard. Soon I gathered more than enough for our day's need. Fresh and rain-washed, they lay crisp in the bottom of my basket.

But the hairy heart-shaped leaves of the *uhaloa* were not to be found. They like the dry and sunny places, such as abound in Honolulu, but where was I to find them on the wet prow of Molokai which is Kalaupapa? Far from home I wandered, from the main road down to the sea cliffs and back again, in a path as unplanned as the one the butterfly takes; and when the sun stood halfway between the horizon and noon I had not yet found what I wanted. The tender green leaves and the juicy black berries of the *popolo* I found, to make a health tonic for us all; and some strawflowers of varied colors, to make a nice bouquet for our parlor. But nowhere could I find the *uhaloa*.

Almost at the foot of Kauhako's gentle crater, which is the mother of all of Kalaupapa's black substance, I decided to return home. As I crossed the plain again, using as my guides the two steeples in Kalawao, I thought of the underground caverns and the lava tubes lying hidden in the earth. Perhaps in one of those, in a place where the light is strong enough but the rain does not fall, a chance seed of the *uhaloa* might have lodged. Changing my direction, I went toward the caverns.

While I walked I let my mind play again with the dangerous delight of Keanu, even as I had thought about him for most of the morning's search, and for most of the days before. More and more was I thinking of him, in ways that a maiden should not think of a man. Grown far beyond my concern for him as an outcast were my thoughts of him as a man. Thus had my pity entrapped me.

Is he not the handsomest man the world has ever seen? I inquired of the winds, teasing them to answer me. What is the half-sized Caleb, sour and cruel, compared with the fullness of the splendid Keanu? I asked of the mountains and the sea. Caleb and his kisses: the memory of them did not bother me any more. How ill-favored Caleb is, compared with the man I would choose, if I could . . .

If I could! Then the reality would sting me with its hurt, and I would waken from my daydreams for a while. You silly thing, you! I would scold myself. With my eyes opened, I would look upon the imprisoning mountains, the encircling sea, the stretch of Kalawao's jail yard. "Love is not for you, you leper," I would tell myself aloud, trying to keep my reason about me, as close as my shadow.

But not for long. Before I went ten paces farther along my dallier's path, my thoughts leaped from Kalawao's lepers to Kalawao's one clean man. It was his body I saw, not Caleb's, or Kumakani's, or any of those others of my spotted suitors'. His smile it was that lured me, not theirs. His hand it was that I reached for, to be the companion of my walking, while I wandered, happy and witless, upon the plain of Kalaupapa.

In the mouth of the first cave did I find some small seedlings of the *uhaloa*, but no plants big enough to warrant my uprooting them. Climbing out of the first cave, I crossed the level ground to the mouth of the second one. And there, just as I hoped, I found a noble crop of Tutu's medicine. Lighthearted, I went down into the sunken mouth of the pit, working my way slowly down the slope of loose earth and broken rocks and tangled weeds until I stood upon the floor of the cavern.

Singing at my task, I went about the work of pulling up several of the largest plants, enough to last Tutu for a week. The song was a sweet one, telling of my desire:

> My heart yearns for thee,
> *Hinahina* flower,
> Wreath of adornment,
> To be worn by me.
> Ever returning
> To this heart of mine,

Pangs of love that tell of thee,
Loving one of mine.

The fourth plant lay uprooted at my feet when, behind me, I heard a loose rock slide down the slope of earth. A little sound it was, not much more than a grasshopper's call, but it told me that I was not alone. My heart was beating wildly as I stood up to face him.

It was Keanu.

At sight of him I screamed. He was not more than his body's length away from me, come more than halfway down the slope. Shoulders hunched, head thrust forward, arm outstretched to balance himself, he came toward me, a beast stalking his prey. He looked down at me, while his bare feet felt their way down the treacherous slide.

At the sight of his face I screamed again. He was not smiling. The eyes were narrow, the mouth was hard. This was not the handsome companion of my dreaming. Gone was the dream, gone the stupid schoolgirl's trusting innocence. Forgetting the yearning, I felt now only fear, and I screamed again, and once again.

But who was near to hear me? Only the echo of my screams, resounding in the shallow cave behind me, answered my cries, a mocking of my helplessness.

Staggering to the side of the cavern, I placed my back against the lava wall. "What do you want?" I cried, as if I did not know what he wanted of me, as if with words I could tame him to my terror and conjure him away from me. But still he moved closer, on those quiet and certain feet, until he stood before me, an arm's length away. The frayed edges to the shirt, the soft curl of the beard, the flare of his nostrils when he licked his lips to moisten them: I saw these things with a dreadful fascination. I saw the tips of his white teeth as his lips parted in a hopeful smile.

"Don't you touch me," I growled, as a cat in season growls at a tom she is not willing to accept. "Keep your hands off me," I snarled, showing him my sharp teeth. "I am *kapu!*"

Waiting, knowing he had me in his power; like a tomcat, well content with himself and willing to wait his prize, he purred: "Are you a *kokua?*" he asked, as though we were in polite conversation at a church social.

"I? I a *kokua?*" His question amazed me with its stupidity. But it showed me a way of escape. "No, I am not a *kokua*. No one who has looked upon me would make that mistake. I am not a *kokua*. *I am a leper!*" I spat the terrible name at him, filling it with all the poison of my loathing for myself.

"You do not look it," he said, his voice thick with hoping. "I cannot believe you."

"Then why else would I be here? Here in Kalawao?"

"*Kokuas* have come here before, with their families. You could be one of them. You look too clean."

"But I am a leper! Believe me—I do not lie to you!" Crouching against the black wall of the cave, driven by an instinct I could not betray, I shrieked at him, desperate to keep him away from me.

But he would not hear. He put out his right hand. I watched in dread the arm extend toward me. The torn shirt sleeve fell away, hanging limp toward the ground, and I saw the warm flesh of his hand, of his arm, making their journey toward me. On the inner surface of the arm was a lump of flesh, an ugly blemish upon the smooth skin. Even as I recognized the swelling for what it was, his hand ripped the shawl from my shoulders. I did not see where it fell.

"I cannot believe you," he said once more. Now, at arm's length from me, I could see the beads of sweat upon his brow, the rainbow flash of sunlight in the oil of his hair. I could smell the scent of his body. His eyes were narrowed, gazing down into mine, sure of himself, of his claim upon me.

With the strength of terror I thrust him away. As he fell back I lifted both of my hands to the yoke of my *holoku*, and with all my might I tore open the faded weakened cloth.

"See for yourself, then!" I cried, as I tore open the fragile lace of my chemise, revealing my nakedness and the taint of my disease.

"See for yourself, then!" I cried, inviting him to feast his eyes upon the sores which made of my body a thing of hideousness.

"Look! Look! Look your fill!" I shrieked at him, rending the fabric of my clothing down to my waist, inviting him to see where the sores had spread, where they were making their havoc upon the flesh of my belly.

Even as I shrieked at him to frighten him away with my loathsomeness, I felt a terrible joy in revealing to him my nakedness.

No man had yet seen what he looked upon, and what no other man would ever see I delighted now in showing to him.

It was his turn to cry out. With hands outflung, to ward me off, with face turned aside, he backed away from me. "No! No more! No more!"

"See! See! Will you believe me now? Would you lie with this? Would you clasp this body to your body? Would you press your lips to these speckled breasts?" In an ecstasy of fury I screeched at him, and even as I lifted my voice to scream at him in my victory and in my pain, knowing I had won my fight to preserve my virtue, I knew also how in that instant I had lost my innocence.

Putting his hands to his face, moaning as a man does for the dead, he turned and ran away from me. Stumbling over the loose rocks, slipping as he tried to climb, he went like a blind man, up the steep slope and beyond its edge.

And I below, at the bottom of my pit of despair, gazing up to the place where the grass grew like green lace against the white clouds drifting overhead, at the place where he had gone out of my life—I sank to my knees among the rocks, shuddering with a grief too great for tears. For now at last I knew that, by a terrible trick of Heaven, I had succeeded in denying my body forever to the one man who could awaken in my body the ardor of love. In the act of sending him away I discovered that it was Keanu whom I loved, and that even as I quenched his lust for me he had set ablaze the fire of my love for him.

Upon the barren ground of the cave I rolled, pressing my naked bosom upon the sharp black gravel until it bled from a thousand new wounds. But all my grief and all my cries, all my wanton desecration of my own flesh with the cold rocks of the cave, could not ease my desire for Keanu, nor could they bring my beloved back to me.

23

Now was the time of my sorrow, the season of my despair. As mist upon the mountains under the morning sun was the unhappiness of my earlier sorrow in Kalawao, compared with the misery that fell upon me with the discovery of my love for Keanu. By day and by night I yearned for him, longing for the sight of him, for the knowledge of him. With the fire that is unquenchable I burned for him, and I cried out in my heart because I could not have him.

And the more I longed for his love, with the wild untamed desire of the leper's burning, the more I loathed myself, thinking that I sinned so grievously that surely I must be denied the respect of myself as well as the respect of my people. Of God in his judgment seat I was sore afraid. Where is the Malie gone, who was so chaste? I asked myself, as I dreamed of Keanu's body pressed against mine. Where is the Malie who screamed for her virtue's sake? I wondered, seeking the Malie who left her virtue with her blood, upon the stones of the cavern's floor.

Monster of foulness, or fool of the *haoles*: what am I? I asked myself, seeking to know myself, that I might find my fever's cure. What is this virginity, which the *haoles* prize? A scrap of flesh, a daub of blood, no more: my savage body urged this answer upon my questioning mind. But wait! shrieked my Christian soul, making such screams as I had made when Keanu moved toward me in his lust. Stay! It is a Christian maiden's greatest treasure, her gift of purity for her chosen groom. Once again I would be shaken with doubt, wounded with a grief more tearing than a man's ravishing of me could ever be. And the knowledge that, by listening to my soul's shrieking I lost forever my body's joy, my bridegroom and my delight: alas, then did I grow sick with longing for the beauty of Keanu, and eager to die if by dying I could escape the memory of him lost.

Driven almost to madness, I thought to throw myself into the raging sea, to drive Makaio's long kitchen knife into my throat.

Watching Emma slip away into the dark, one evening, I thought how I should follow in her footsteps, and seek in the arms of many men an end to the emptiness that could never be filled by one. To Caleb I would give myself, to those lustful men who had beseeched me in those afternoons outside the schoolhouse. To Eleu, yes, even to Eleu my pupil, would I give myself, to ease his need and mine—

When this thought came to me, dirtying me with its ugliness, I ran in terror to my room. Seizing up my prayer book, I fell upon my knees to ask for guidance. But no voice spoke to me. Taking up my Bible, I opened it for a sign:

> By night on my bed I sought him whom my soul loveth, I sought him but I found him not.
> I will rise now, and go about the city in the streets, and in the broad ways I will seek him whom my soul loveth.

Heeding the sign, I looked for him, going in search of him upon the plain, in the caverns, in the lava tubes, even to the edge of the distant mound of Kauhako, the womb of Kalaupapa. Had I found him I would have thrown myself upon him, hungrier for him than he was for me. So strong would I have been, that I would have leaped upon him, tearing the ragged clothes from his body in my eagerness to possess him.

> I sought him, but I found him not.

He was gone from my sight, disappeared from the earth.

Thus did the weeks pass, and thus, somehow, did I live. Because Tutu, in her sickness, needed me; because my pupils in the schoolhouse needed me, I went on as before. No one saw the sickness of my soul. All they saw was the same Malie who always moved among them, soundless as a spider weaving her web, and their blindness to my despair was my only comfort. If they cannot see it, I said, then I will go on. Until they learn of my disgrace, I will suffer for my duty's sake. Fear of death, or hope of happiness: which was it that kept me alive? Scarcely knowing why I bothered to live, I lived.

Christmas was a joyless time for me. I took no interest in it, in the parties of the singing clubs, in the church services. Tutu's cough, lasting long after she got out of her bed; Moki's lingering boils, resisting the power of the *laukahi*: these were my reasons for saying I was too busy to join in the festivities of the season. I stayed at home with my family, when I was not at school or out upon the plain of Kalaupapa, looking for medicines and for Keanu.

Soon after Christmas Father Damien went down to Honolulu. Kewalo brought us the news. He was often a visitor at our house now, where Tutu and he would quarrel with each other, as often as they could.

"*Eia mai!* He is courting me," Tutu would announce to the whole group after he said something especially insulting to her. "If he is not careful, I will marry him for his goodness to me." From the way he glared back at her I was certain that marriage with the saucy old woman was the last of his wishes. "Don't be so sure," she said to me once, when we were alone in our bedroom. "He has a wagging tongue and a weak mind, but a good heart. He has the look of love in his eyes, when he thinks I do not see him." I was shocked at the thought of love passing between those two old people, already beyond their fortieth year. When the realization came to me that here were two who might be granted in their age what I was being denied, I almost choked upon my envy.

"An' wy he stay go?" asked Hanu on the evening when Kewalo told us about the priest. Hanu's eye was cocked in questioning, his mouth half open with stupidity. In him only his fingers worked quickly. His mind moved as slowly as a starfish crawling upon the ocean floor; and often, it seemed, his mind had as much difficulty knowing in which direction to move as the five-footed starfish does.

"Oh, he goes there every few years," answered fat Momona, settled like a huge woman in his chair. This evening he chose to speak in English, being vain of his ability in it. At other times he would speak in Hawaiian. We never knew the reasons which prompted him to favor one or the other, but usually, for the sake of peace, we would follow his inclination. "To escape from this prison, as I have told to you once before. When he cannot stand us here any longer, he goes to Honolulu for the good time." Giggling, he played with a beautiful red hibiscus, plucked from a shrub along the way.

"Lucky buggah," said Hanu, rocking his body in envy. "I do da same eef I can." Poor Hanu! Over his right ear, swollen and rotten of late, hanging upon his head like an overripe guava, he wore a huge wad of cloth, torn from an old cotton dress, tied in place with strips of the same material. The soft colors of the print made the bandage look like a *lei* of tiny pink and blue flowers in his greasy hair. But the wad of cloth holding his ear in place was soaked with blood and pus, and the flowers seemed to grow in a field of dark brown earth.

"All the food, all the whisky, all the women he wants . . ." As he mentioned each of the delights for which men yearn, Momona carefully tore a petal from the red hibiscus. They fell like great drops of blood upon his white shirt, where it was stretched over the swollen belly.

We looked at him in disgust. Half rising in his place, his bull's body hunched forward in anger, Kewalo shook a heavy hand at the lewd Momona. "*E*, wy you say dese t'ings? Dis pries': he's a good man. He leeve wid hahdly any food, wid no weeskey, an' no *wahine*."

"Heh," shrugged Momona, tearing yet another petal from the despoiled flower. "And who says this?"

"By Iehovah! Errybody say dis!" roared Kewalo, getting to his feet. "Never have we seen him take a woman to his bed, never," he rushed on in our native tongue. "Is this not so, Makaio? Tell him."

"*Ae*, it is so. When first he came here, the priest, a young man good to look upon, we thought how he would be as other men. The women, they yearned for him, they put themselves in his way. But he did not see them. They were defeated. And they went away, ashamed."

"He did not know what women are for," said Kewalo, wondering still at his ancient surprise. "Indeed, not even yet does he know what they are for. He is a pure man, of this I am sure. It is a strange thing, this, but it is true." Heavily he sat down, the chair creaking under his weight.

Calmly did Momona pull the last petal from the broken flower. "What of the women who go to his house, even by the broad light of day?"

"*Cha*, Momona, you have the mouth of a pig!" said Kewalo. "A pig that eats anything for food, even the excrement of dirty minds. The women who go into his house: they go to clean it for him. They clean it because he is too busy to do it. They clean it because it is one of the ways they can thank him for his help to us here. But they have little to do there," he turned to the rest of us. "Would you believe it? A bed is there, but they do not have to fix it. He sleeps on the floor, on the bare boards of the floor—"

"Then what does he do in Honolulu?" asked Hanu once again.

"He goes to see the Bishop of his church," said Caleb impatiently. "He reports to the Bishop, as the chiefs report to the King. I have seen them there, those black priests, as thick as sea birds soaring over the cliffs at sunset, returning to their nests. They live, these priests, in a church on Fort Street, locked up like prisoners in a jail. No, they do not have a pleasant life."

"Speaking of prisoners," said Momona smoothly, gliding from one subject to another, leaving the first in which he had been defeated for another which he could toy with for a while. "What has happened to our own favored one? Our own Keanu, I mean. I have not seen him for many a day."

My heart all but stopped at the sound of my beloved's name. The blood drained from my face into the aching emptiness, while I waited for someone to tell me of Keanu. But no one came to my aid. They were indifferent to the Lonely One, to the remote one upon whom my heart and hope were hung.

"Perhaps he is sick?" said Makaio at last, to fill the silence.

I almost swooned in my chair. Could he be sick? Is it the *lepera* which keeps him at home, the effects of Opaekea's testing of him? Or did he catch it from me, the time he reached out to touch me? Mingled now with my yearning was my worry over him.

"*Ae*, this is so," said Hanu. "Not for a long time have I seen him."

Could he have gone with the priest? I wanted to ask, could he have gone to Honolulu, to Opaekea? I did not dare to speak, for fear my voice would give my secret away.

"Nah, nah, he is not sick," Kewalo waved the suggestion away. "Only this morning did I see him, feeding the chickens in his back yard."

"He has chickens?" Momona asked. "He has chickens, but the rest of us do not? Well," he sniffed, "and why is he so favored?"

"Oh Momona, you hissing old woman, you!" Kewalo was aroused once more. "You, too, could keep chickens in your yard, if you had a mind to care for them. Kamiano, he gave Keanu some of the birds to raise. The poor man: he has little enough to do in this new prison. We who are patients here are more favored than he is. We at least have company in our misery. But he: he is alone, alone in this big jail yard. My liver groans for him. His punishment is far worse than ours."

"Ae, you are right," said Tutu in a soft voice, agreeing for almost the first time with Kewalo. "For us, this place is like the garden of Eve and Adam. For that one, it is like a desert island."

"Such sentimental slop you utter, you two," growled Caleb. "You can have your damned Garden of Eden! I'd rather have his desert island, and my health, too. Remember," he pounded the rail with his fist, "even Robinson Crusoe was rescued from his desert island in time to enjoy a long life at home again."

"Dis guy Robinsona Karuso," asked Hanu. "Is he from Honolulu?"

Caleb did not even hear him. "Besides, your pitied prisoner has company up there, in his palace on the hill. Doesn't he have the new doctor to speak with?"

"Oh yes, the new doctor." Kewalo agreed, much as one might say, "Oh yes, the new wave" in a sea full of waves.

Sensing something hidden in Kewalo's manner, Momona pounced at once. "What is *wrong* with the new doctor?" he asked, in a delicious expectation of scandal.

"Nothing is wrong with him," replied Kewalo. "He is all right, I guess. Indeed, he is a very good man, much nicer than that sassy little one who was here before him. The one who brought Keanu. What was his name?"

"Opaekea."

"Opaekea, yeah, yeah. Much better than that one. This one will go among the patients to help them, whereas that small bastard sat as prickly as a cactus upon his stool, and would not lift a finger to help the sick ones. No, this one—his name is Beach, or Bitch, something funny like that—this one is O.K. But—"

"But, but, but," pushed Momona. "In the name of Kane, tell us!"

"But who can get companionship out of a *haole?*" Kewalo gave us the reason with so much of Hanu's bewilderment that we could not help but laugh at his explanation.

"By God! you are right," chuckled Caleb. "I see your point."

"That's what I mean. Either they talk too much, always about things us *kanakas* don't know anything about, or don't want to know anything about. Or they are so busy working that they do not have time for the important things."

"Dese poah *haoles*," clucked Hanu. "Somebuddy bettah teach 'um how to ree-lax . . ." He picked up his *ukulele* and strummed on it a wild and unrelaxed version of one of the Protestant hymns we have always thought so laughable. "*Something to do in Heaven*," he sang, bending his bandaged head over the ridiculous instrument, "*something to fill our hands . . .*"

Soon after the New Year Father Damien returned to Kalawao. "Something happened to please him in Honolulu," Kewalo told us. "He walks on the foam of the wave."

A few days later, the new doctor moved to Kalaupapa. Nobody knew why he left the doctor's house.

A few days more and Opaekea returned. "He was on the beach, when I went to carry the mail," said Kewalo with some surprise. "He did not tell me why he came back."

"Such a great running to and fro," Momona scoffed. "Soon we shall be as busy here as is Honolulu."

Two evenings later we heard that Keanu roamed the land again. "Thin he is, and pale," declared Hanu, "like a man who has been sick for a long time. Or drunk. But how can anyone here be drunk for so long. A glass of rum, a taste of whisky: *cha*, that's all we ever get in this lousy place . . ."

"I saw him a couple of nights ago," Caleb said.

"A couple of nights ago? In all that rain? In all that thunder and lightning?" Momona's sharp memory caught hold of Caleb. "And did you go walking in it with Keanu? To keep him company, in his loneliness?"

Caleb looked unhappy at having to answer. "No," he said at last. "No, I did not go walking in it. I—I am not a *haole* poet"— he tried to laugh, without mirth—"one of those nature-lovers who walks in the rain."

"Then how is it that you saw him?"

"In the lane in front of my house. A flash of lightning came, showing him to me. Soaking wet, he was—and running. Running as if the Marchers of the Night were chasing him."

"Poor man," sighed Makaio. "He is like a dog, sniffing for the scent of people."

"And you followed him?" asked Momona.

"No, I did not. Why should I follow him? I told you, I do not like to get wet. I have told you all I know." But there was something in his manner which said he had not told us the whole story of Keanu running in the stormy night.

"This is not good." Momona shook his big head. "Why does he come among us in the dark of night, when he shuns us by day? What does he seek among us? I do not like these news."

"And why should he not walk where he pleases?" snapped Tutu. "Does he do any harm by walking? E?" Setting her jaw, clenching her teeth, she glared at the fat one.

Disdainful as an ox of a terrier, Momona plodded on. "There are things among us he could steal." He turned for agreement to Kewalo, to Makaio, to Hanu. Each of them nodded in turn, sober as chiefs in council.

"But has anything been stolen?" I asked, not able to sit quiet while Keanu was placed under suspicion.

"There are women he could seek"—Momona looked straight at me—"there are flowers he could pluck." Stabbed by his meaning, I fell back, not knowing which was the worse hurt: the fear that he had guessed the secret of my passion for Keanu, or the fear that Keanu might find in the arms of some other woman the comfort which once he sought from me. Biting my lips, I sat back in my place, having nothing more to say.

"Yes, it is possible," Caleb said reasonably. "But I do not think he comes among us to steal. As Malie has said, we have not heard that anything has been taken. I think he goes through our lanes only because they are the shorter path to the sea."

"*Paha*," said Momona, "perhaps."

"Whafo you falla wolly now, so late?" asked Ah See. "Long time alleady dis falla, he walk, up, down, up, down, ousside you falla house, ousside my house, ousside ellybody house. He no makee tlouble: he oney look-see-*nana*."

"You have seen him?" Momona wanted to know. "Here? Before last night?"

"Sure, sure. Befo plenny time he come, befo Kalissimass time. Evelly night he come. Den, maybe t'lee-foah week, he no come. Las' night he come one moah time, allsame like befo."

"How you know, *Pake?*"

"Plenny t'ings I look-see-*nana* my house. I see, I lemembah, I no makee talk-talk. Too muchee talk-talk, oney makee tlouble . . ."

The smooth yellow face, the wise tired eyes, were turned upon the bloated Momona, upon him with the poisonous tongue.

"*Paha*," said the fat one. "But I think we should keep a watch over this man of shadows. Who is to say that he does not but wait his time, that he does not plan to make some crime among us? Is he not a murderer? 'Once the shark has tasted of a man, he hungers thereafter for the taste of a man.' "

"I do not like these news," said Makaio mournfully. "That he should walk among us by day is one thing. That he roams among us by night is another." He was talking to the others, but he was looking at me. "Let us not forget how this man has done a murder. Over a woman." Like a knife cutting in the bowels were the words of Makaio to me. He spoke of the man I yearned for, and his words were the truth.

"I guess you're right," Caleb said. "You never can tell about a man like Keanu. He's completely unprincipled."

"Wat you mean?" The big word was lost upon Hanu.

"He does what he wants to do, takes what he wants to take. He recognizes no law, neither the new ones of the *haoles*, nor the old ones of the chiefs. He thinks he is above the law."

"Why?" asked Momona. "Is he a high chief, that he should look down upon the law? Is he, perhaps, a son of the Kamehamehas, to make and break the law as he wills?"

Caleb laughed. "No, he is not of the *alii*, although he does come from the Kohala of the Kamehamehas. No, he is just a *kuaaina* like me, a boy from the country. But even if he learned of the law, I do not think he would heed it. As I say, he is a child of his passions, he does just as he wishes."

"That poem," said Momona, "the poem you read to me the other day. How does it go? I am reminded of it now, when I think of the man-killer."

"*Ae*," said Caleb. "It fits him. I was thinking the same thing, when I read it to you. Let me see if I can remember the words." Putting his head back, he looked up at the ceiling as he brought the poem back from his memory:

> "The world is made for the bold impious man,
> Who stops at nothing, seizes all he can.
> Justice to merit does weak aid afford;
> She trusts her balance, and ignores her sword.
> Virtue is slow to take what's not her own,
> And, while she long consults, the prize is gone."

"Whooo, ka fancy words, boy!" exclaimed poor Hanu, lost before Caleb finished the first line. While the rest of us laughed at Hanu's bewilderment, seeking in it a way to hide our own, Caleb said, "Well, even if it is a bit fancy, it describes a fellow like Keanu pretty well."

Ae, in my corner I brooded, and does it not describe myself as well? Slow Virtue, who lost her prize: is this not another name for stupid shrieking Malie?

"And how do you know so much about him?" Momona wanted to know. "Are you a kinsman of his? Have you talked with him here?"

"Far from it. Neither one nor the other," Caleb raised his neat hands to ward off Momona's suspicions. "No. I was—well, let us say I attended his trial in Honolulu, and made a study of him there. As a matter of fact—you might as well know it—I helped the King's Court to prepare the case for the Crown against Keanu. I was practicing the law at the time."

This was not news to me, but to the others it came like the word of Pele's blood flowing out of Puna's earth. Excited by the prospect of hearing at firsthand the story of Keanu's trial, they put question after question to Caleb. And he, not unwilling to enjoy their attention, talked for the rest of the evening upon the scandalous, sordid, delicious story of Keanu and his crime for love. Momona was in delight, forgetting even to slap at mosquitoes in his concern not to miss a word.

And I—filled with love and fear and pity for Keanu, torn with hatred and jealousy for his paramour, the fortunate Kamaka who had enjoyed him—I was too weak to leave, and I stayed and listened with the rest, until the night was old and the voice of Caleb was thin with weariness, until the chime of Makaio's great clock, sounding the hour of ten, sent us all to our lonely beds.

In vain did I look for Keanu upon the plain, in the valleys of Waileia and Waihanau. But Hanu, who found pleasure in hunting him down, saw him twice within the week.

"He carries a knife!" Hanu reported to us after the second meeting. "Like the one he killed the Japanee with." But his dramatic description of the knife Keanu wore at his side was cut short by Tutu.

"*E*, you *lolo* buggah, you! You fool, you! Do you not carry a knife? Does not every man carry a knife? Is it not a man's privilege to carry a knife, for when he works? You big mouth, you: shut up. You only make trouble with your silly talk."

"*Auwe*, Tutu. I oney telling you . . ."

Momona came to his rescue. "Tutu is right," he said sweetly. "Only when the knife of Keanu is used in another crime can we think ill of Keanu. Until then"—he spread his hands in his womanish way—"until then we must think only that he uses it for scaling fish. Or perhaps for cleaning his nails."

"You son of a bitch, you," said Tutu in as sweet a voice as his own. "If your age had not done it already, I would ask Keanu to use his knife to cut off your *laho*—"

"Tutu!" From Makaio and from me the shocked cry went up, too late to remind her that she was supposed to be a lady.

But Momona was enchanted with the old woman's retort. It was just the kind of suggestive talk he liked to make, and we could be sure that he would not delay to tell it to his other gossips in Kalawao. "Hee, hee"—he pretended to clap in applause—"hee, hee, that's a good one. You sharp, Mama, you sharp."

Her thin lips tightened when he used the familiar term, which more than once she had forbidden him and which he continued to use in spite of her. Caleb hurried to change the subject. "Where is Ah See tonight? Is he not well?"

"He is well," answered Makaio. "He plays fan-tan with some of his countrymen tonight. They will have a good time, I think, talking of their homeland."

"And dreaming of it, afterwards," said Momona. "A new smuggling came yesterday." Lest any of us escape his meaning, he made the motions of loading an opium pipe and raising it to his puckered lips. If he could have crossed his heavy legs, he would have completed the picture of Ah See enjoying his quiet bliss.

"Momona!" shouted Makaio, rising from his seat. "You stop this kind of talk!" His voice quivered with rage, his body trembled, as he lifted his lean hand to point to the stairs. "If your thoughts must be unkind ones always, then do not say them here. Tired I am, sick unto weariness, of your dirty mind, of your unkind words, of your troublemaking tongue." We heard with relief the rebuke which brought Momona low.

"I ask you to go from this house if you cannot be a decent man when you are with us. For too long I have been quiet, while you have fouled us. Now I will take no more. I did not like the way you talked about Keanu, a man unknown to us. But because we do not know Keanu, because we will never know him, I kept my peace. I did not like the way you talked of Kamiano. Yet for his sake, who likes the peace, I have kept my peace. . . . But when you turn your ugliness upon a man dear to me, as Ah See is, then I must speak out. . . . Do you hear me?"

Unmoving, a sickly grin upon his face, the fat one heard Makaio until the end. With his false smile he tried to disclaim the anger of Makaio, as though it were not meant for him. But his hands were white with their pressing upon the rails of his chair. The glitter in his eyes, small in the pig's face, showed how stung was his vanity, how ugly would be his revenge when it came.

"I hear you, Makaio. And I ask you to forgive me. I do not wish to leave this pleasant company." His voice was small as he looked from one to the other of us, embarrassed because of his shaming. "I will try to put a new tongue in my head, and kinder thoughts in my head, for my tongue to speak." It was made with dignity, his apology, and with a humility we never thought to hear from the vain Momona. We were robbed by it of our anger.

Makaio was weak with remorse. "Good, then let it be so," he said, the belated tears filling his eyes. "And I ask you to forgive me my evil temper. A better man would have found a better way to keep the peace between us."

Sighing, he sank back into his chair. "I will tell you something. I will tell you about Ah See. And of the reason why I bear such a love for him."

"Makaio. There is no need," said Kewalo, leaning forward to touch the old man's arm. "There is no need."

"Kewalo knows, because he is a friend from long ago. But no one else knows. Yet it is a story that all should know, because it is the story of a good man. And of another, who was not so good."

But we were not to hear the story of Ah See that night. Even as we waited to hear this tale from Makaio's heart, Hanu hissed a warning. "Shh! He comes!"

Not in the main road was he walking, but in the lane which, turning off from the road, connects the houses lying between us and the mountains. The rock wall marking the edge of our yard hid his body below the waist. But even in the last light of day there was no mistaking him. Swiftly he went past, not noticing us in the shadows of the *lanai*. Over one shoulder, hanging halfway down his back, was the fishing net. The head, once so proudly borne, as he took his walks upon the plain, was bent forward, as though in the dim light he searched the ground for the path upon which to put his feet. As though the weight of his loneliness was too great for his *mana* to bear.

We watched him go past, until the corner of our house hid him from view. Hungrily did my lips part at the sight of him, wildly did my heart beat within my breast.

"Let's go," whispered Hanu, "let's go after him." Crouching in his place upon the stairs he made ready to run into the lane.

"Leave him alone!" cried Caleb, grasping Hanu's arm. "He's all right. He's just going fishing. Does he do any harm?"

Then did they fall to wrangling again about Keanu's right to walk in the lanes of Kalawao. In the heat of their talking, they forgot Makaio and his story of Ah See.

But I paid them little heed, with their noise and their contention. My thoughts were fixed upon the morrow.

Not in search of the *laukahi*, not in search of the *popolo* or of the precious *uhaloa*, would I go forth upon the plain tomorrow.

24

BUT ON THE MORROW I did not find him. Even though I stayed all the morning upon the plain, picking *laukahi* until my fingers were stained green with their sour juices, searching for him until my eyes ached, I did not find him.

In despair I returned to the house when the sun stood at its highest. With heavy heart and dragging feet I went in the afternoon to the schoolhouse. I do not know what I taught my pupils. But they were aware of my distress. They bent over their work, afraid of me. At length Eleu could bear no longer my fits of anger, the times when I forgot them sitting in the same room with me. He came up to where I sat upon the stool by the window, looking out upon a small part of the village. Not a creature moved in the empty space of green trees and black rocks and drab houses. Ugly was the world, and empty, empty . . .

"You are not well today?" Eleu's low voice woke me from my wandering through the desolate byways. My first thought was to scream at him to mind his own business, to leave me alone, to go back to his work. But even then I could not shriek such abuse at my favorite pupil, standing trustingly before me. Alas for Eleu! How little I had thought of him since my rage for Keanu came upon me. How little of the love and affection I promised myself to give him had I given, in my running after another. "Auwe, Eleu. I am not a very good teacher for you," I said, ready to weep with contrition and despair.

"Do not say it. It is not so. But it is not good for you to keep the school when you are sick."

"I must say yes to this. I am sick today, in body and in heart."

"Then why do we not send away the school, until you are well again?"

"Perhaps it is better so. Perhaps a holiday will be good for all of us."

In a few minutes he cleared the schoolhouse. Without the usual shouting and bustle, the students disappeared. Only Eleu remained with me in the ordered schoolroom. "Shall I walk home with you?"

"No, thank you, Eleu. I am not that sick. You go and play with the others. You deserve a holiday, too, after all your hard work."

"Study is not work. But I like to play, too."

"You are a good pupil. And a good boy. Tell me: there is a question I have been meaning to ask you, since the first day of our school, there under the *kukui* tree. Do you remember?"

"The day I remember well. Of the question, I am not sure."

"Why is it that you chose the American to learn, and not the English, or the Hawaiian?"

The expectant face lost its half smile, as he turned his gaze from me toward the open window. Into the eyes, replacing their usual glint of brightness, crept a softness as Eleu lost his hold upon himself. "Because," he said after a long time, "because I wish to find my father."

"Your father?" Had I thought for a moment more, I would have kept the prying question to myself.

He lowered his head, in sorrow and in shame. "He is a sailor. I have never seen him. But I wish to find him. To ask him to give me a name," he finished softly, in the hush of the schoolroom.

Then he turned and went quickly from the ugly house, bearing his own burden of sorrow, even as I bore mine.

O, ugliness, ugliness! Grief and despair, horror and heartache! Is there nothing else in this world, beneath the arch of heaven? In the foul and filthy room, stinking of lepers and their sores, its furniture scabbed and scarred and discolored, as the body of a leper is when he is rotted close to death, I saw the world as it was. And with Eleu's grief added now to mine, I found new depths of hopelessness to drown in.

On my way home I went in agony to Siloama, to the House of God, to call upon him for his help. The church was locked. Hushed and abandoned, white and cold, heedless of my need, it stood empty in its little yard. God was not at home, and he did not answer my call. Throwing myself upon the steps before the locked door, I wept. I beat my fists upon the door, half hoping that the noise I made, echoing through the empty church, would summon God to me from his Heaven. But no. Not even an angel came to stand by my side, to dry my tears upon his robes, to bring peace to my dying heart. Perhaps it was because my heart was filled with evil, because my cries were not for forgiveness. How can God or his angels countenance such an evil thing as was my yearning for Keanu?

Heavy with my burden of sin, I crept home. I could not eat. I could not face the glance of Tutu, the trusting grace of Makaio, who had made his peace with God. Saying that my head ached, my throat was sore, I went to bed. In saying this I did not lie; but my throat was sore from weeping, not from the chill I allowed Tutu to think I had caught from the draft in the schoolroom.

In the evening I did not go with them to sing in the house of Miele. Akala was sick, taken to her bed, and it was said that the singing of the Hui Iiwi would cheer her. In my bed I lay in a fever of desire and a torment of bitterness, praying to God in one moment, cursing him in the next. What goodness is in him, what justice, who allows such misery to be, as this which afflicts me? How can he endure the sight of my agony, and of Akala's, and of Eleu's, of everyone else who lies in bondage to his cruelty in Kalawao? No better than the demon gods of old is he, no different from those ancient ones who ruled with fear and who killed for pleasure.

At last, when my hate was spent and my body was exhausted, I saw another way to hope. This new faith is no good: what peace does it bring me, this *haoles'* talk, of God the Father, of God the Son, of God is Love? Good for the *haoles* this jealous Iehovah might be, but is he good for me? The old faith, the faith of my people: why should I not try it? In the dark of the room, the memory of Momona's soft voice came to me, whispering of Kaupea, as outside in the night the dogs of Kalawao sat howling at the moon.

In the morning I went in search of Kaupea, she who was the *kahuna*. She lived at the far edge of the village, near to the Bay of Kalawao, in one of the oldest houses in the Settlement. Remote from neighbors was the house, as though they shunned her and her ways. But the path to her door was well walked, and I had no trouble learning where she lived, from the patients who sat along the side of the road.

The *naupaka* grew in great clumps around the sides of the house which faced the sea. Almost as high as trees, shaped by the wind, the bushes with their thick fleshy leaves formed a windbreak against the ocean breeze. The *naupaka*: how like to the *naupaka* flower am I, cut in half, shorn in two, forever incomplete, as was the broken love of the constant maid and her warrior, slain in the day of battle.

In the shade of the bushes and upon the narrow *lanai* of the house the people waited for Kaupea. I was astonished to see how many of them were there. Three sat upon the *lanai*, in stiff chairs made of beautiful old *koa* wood, burnished by use to a deep red. Four more visitors sat cross-legged upon the long grass, in the cavern of green and yellow light sifting down through the canopy of leaves. I went to take my place a little apart from them, because I did not wish to speak with anyone.

But theirs was a different thought. They called *aloha* to me, and invited me to sit with them. Three were women, middle-aged and fat, the fourth was a sickly youth, thin and cold, shivering under layers of clothing hung in loose folds around his fleshless bones.

"Come and sit with us, and pass the time," one of the women said cheerfully. "The waiting then is easier." The thin youth said nothing. As I settled into the grass near the women, he dabbed at his mouth with a rag sodden with his blood.

"What brings you to see Kaupea?" the genial woman asked. All smiles and winkings, she did not look to be sick; but the two with whom she sat were, beyond a doubt, patients. They were sisters, those three, but the two who were patients were blind. Their eyes were dull with rust-colored scars. They looked, those two, as though they were made incomplete, with eyes sightless from birth.

The seeing one put her hand upon the knee of one of the blind women. With great gentleness she said, "These are my sisters: Kake and Kakea are their names. And I am Kakela. We are the daughters of Kalaheo of Hanapepe." It was the name of one of the chiefly families of Kauai, a great name in the history of that island, as mine was a great name in the history of Maui. But theirs was a name vanished from the mouths of the living. I had thought all of the Kalaheos were dead. All the men of their clan were gone, one after the other, dead of the new diseases. Some weakness there was in them, as there was in the Kahekilis, which did not allow them to survive the new times of the *haoles*. The smallpox, the measles, the whooping cough, and many more: one after the other these sicknesses were visited upon the nation, making the people to fall like rotten *kukui* branches broken by the wind. And with their coming the Kalaheos were departing, one after the other, until of them all there remained only these three.

Where is the justice of Iehovah, that this ruin can be pleasing to him? With hate in my heart for the cruel Iehovah, I tried to talk with Kakela. The old days were best, I told myself, as I told them who I was.

"Ah, yes, the daughter of Kekoa," said one of the blind sisters. "We have heard how you are here." She spoke with difficulty: the inside of her mouth was eaten away. "*Ei nei!* Remember how we used to say, he is the best-looking man in Honolulu?" The other two, the one blind, the one keen-eyed as a mother hen, nodded happily. "Ah, those were the good times," they agreed, thinking of the distant past, paying no tribute to the ghastly present.

"And what brings you to see Kaupea," asked the beaming Kakela again. "A new medicine? A telling of your fortune? A medicine for love? Aha, I will guess. It is the third: for a *hana aloha*." The other two laughed gleefully with her, patting each other, falling over each other in merriment. I could not help but join in their laughter, even while the blushes warmed my cheeks, my ears.

"I did not think of a love potion. But if one would help me in my troubles, then indeed I shall ask for it."

"A pretty girl like you should have no troubles," said Kakela, examining me frankly. "Nor any need for potions." Her straight-forwardness pleased me more than her compliments did.

Out from Kaupea's parlor stepped a visitor. As he hurried down the stairs, his white shirt gleaming in the morning light, one of the men on the *lanai* moved into the parlor. "Only two more, then it is your turn," Kakela said.

"Do you not wish to see her?"

Again their laughter rose, slightly drunken, slightly mad, yet friendly as the twittering of birds. "Oh, no. We do not come to see her. We live here, with Kaupea. She is our auntie. When she has callers, we come outside here, to sit in the shade, to give her the room she needs in the house." Gurgling and tittering, they pushed and prodded each other, while I wondered if anything could ever make them sad.

"And he?" I nodded toward the young man beyond them. His eyes were closed, a thin froth of blood bubbled upon his lips.

"Not Umalu, either," said Kakela softly. "No more does he have need for Kaupea." Turning her head, she called gently to him. "Umalu— How is it with you?"

Slowly Umalu opened his eyes, seeking her in the bright immensity of light and shadow in which we sat. His great eyes were innocent with wonder, as if his spirit had come back into his body from a far distance, in response to her summons, and could not find her who called to him. His eyelids fluttered, as he tried to see her beyond the mists which were closing in around him. But he could not find her, and the weary lids closed shut again, and his spirit was enclosed again. Not yet was it ready to escape, through the *lua uhane*, the soul-pits, the corners of the eyes where tears are made, where the spirit enters and leaves the body as it must.

"No," said Kakela, "he does not stand in your way. Umalu comes here today to die. 'I wish to die outside, in the light of the sun, beneath the sky,' he has said. 'Not in a bed, not in a house. —I wish to die as a *kamaaina* should, a child of the land, who has loved it, this land which bore him.' And who is to say that he is not right in this?"

I looked upon the young man, not knowing whether to cry out against their heartlessness or to envy him the simplicity of his dying. Should he not be in bed? Should not the doctor be called? Could not some one of us do something to make him more comfortable? But to each question my mind asked another: Why? why should it be otherwise? And at last I was forced to agree with them that Umalu had chosen a noble way to die.

Kakela knew what passed through my mind. "You see?" she asked, her broad face no longer smiling. Her sisters, by some magic of communion between them, wore the same expression of compassion. They were like the three Fates, infinitely wise, infinitely patient, infinitely merciful. Almost with awe I looked to their hands, to see where the thread of Umalu's life was even now about to be cut. But in the hands of Kakela there was only her needlework, scraps of cloth to make a quilt. By the side of Kake and of Kakea were only the strips of *hala*, for plaiting into mats. There was no thread to the life of Umalu in their hands.

An awakening of my spirit it was, and I was in need of it. Too much of the *haole* had I become, out of touch with my people. In the palace I had dressed in foreign clothes and followed foreign ways. But was I happy there? In the schools, in the churches of the *haoles*, I learned strange things and foreign speech, I learned of their cruel God and his cruelly sacrificed Son. But did those things comfort me, did they sustain me now in the time of desolation and despair? No. The English words: Where are they now, when I sit among my people, speaking with them in our native tongue? The *haole* God: where is he now, when I need him? Absent is he, gone from his house, deaf to my cries: a remote, an unfeeling God.

But here are the three sisters of Kauai: I sit among my people, not among strangers from another land. These three: they have found happiness, even in their sickness and their exile. With them I am at ease, here in the thick grass in the shade of the *naupaka*. And here is Umalu, dying as he wishes to die, beneath the cover of heaven, faithful unto the end to his gods, attended by them to the end. Kane of the glowing sun is here, warming him. Lono of the long cloud, he of the green grass and of the sheltering *naupaka*, of bird calls and sea spray: Lono is here, to solace him.

And tonight, whether he still lives or whether he lies dead and cold beneath her gentle eye, Mahina of the moon will be here, to shed her light on him. As they are here with him, so are they here with me.

O Kane! O Lono! Forgive me, forgive. I have been blind, and I have gone so far from thee. But lo! now have I returned, now have I found my way back to thee—

Deep in my joy I plunged, exulting in my discovery of the ancient gods: like birds swooping in the air, like butterfly fish dancing in the sea, like leaves trembling upon the boughs of the *koa* tree, was I in the delight of my awakening. Soaring, trembling, glowing with bliss was I, as the weight of my despair fell away from me, as the heavy hand of Iehovah was lifted from my head.

The touch of Kakela was upon my knee. "Now is your time, daughter of Kekoa." I opened my eyes. Her face, more familiar now to me than my mother's, wore no smile. Old and wise it was, full of understanding and of quiet promise. I felt the truth of her words, without knowing what she meant. *Ae,* now is my time, my heart sang. Smiling, drunk with joy, I looked at her, thinking how wise she is, how good.

"Kaupea waits," said Kakela, nodding toward the quiet house.

Did my legs lift my body from the ground? Did they carry me across the yard to the house of Kaupea? Or did the breath of Kane waft me there, seated in a carriage of cloud? I do not know. In one moment I smiled at kind Kakela. In the next I stood in awe before Kaupea.

Old was Kaupea, old as a mountain, and wrinkled as the waters of the sea when they are ruffled by the wind. Huddled in a great chair she sat, with a cloak of soft gray *kapa* upon her shoulders. Her eyes were bright and shrewd, black as the polished pebbles scattered upon a little table beside her chair. Her face: this was the strangest thing. It was the same face as the three sisters wore, but old, so old that all the generations of earth seemed to be summed up in it, while theirs were as young as those of babes. And yet her hair was not an old woman's hair: parted in the middle and falling in wide loops to either side of her head, covering her ears in the style of twenty years before, it was as smooth and as black as my own.

"And what do you seek of Kaupea?" It was a voice of weariness, of patience worn thin. How many times have I asked this question, it said, and how many times have I heard the same thoughts? Vanity, all is vanity, says the man in the Bible, and Kaupea but repeated his lesson gained from life.

Before this great weariness, what could I say? My joy in the discovery of my people and their ancient ways fell from me as water does when one steps from the sea. I was alone with her, unsustained. My question, the one for which I sought her out, seemed foolish now, and selfish. Meekly I stood before her, a little girl with bowed head, not knowing what to say.

"People come to me for one of three things," she said, sweeping the black pebbles from the table into her hands. The rattle of the stones was sharp and cruel. "For medicines to cure their illnesses. For medicines to help them to die—or to make others die." She threw the stones upon the table, making them to clatter upon the smooth wood like teeth upon the bones of skeletons.

"Or for ways to gain love." It was as I feared: she jeered at the thought of love. But her scoffing made me rebellious: I thought it important enough.

"I am no different from the rest," I said, as humbly as I could, while my anger grew within me.

"*Kie!* I did not think you were. At your age love is all that matters." Once more the pebbles were swept up into the bony hands.

"And should it not be so? What is more important, when one is young and hungers for love?"

"So, you have spirit after all. You are not so meek as you look." The stones fell again, a cascade of violence to match the harshness of her laugh. The long yellow teeth showed briefly before the thin lips closed over them again. "I have no potions for you, girl. Potions are for fools, who believe in them."

"Then what do you have for me?" I demanded. If she could be curt with me, I could be bold with her. Perhaps it was my months with Tutu which made me so ill-mannered with the old. Perhaps I felt that it was necessary to fight her for my love.

"Only this," she snapped. "If you wish for love, take it. Don't just sit at home in your parlor, like some damn-fool *haole* virgin, waiting for love to come to you."

Nothing she might have said could have angered me more. Did I need such advice, after all the times I had gone in search of Keanu? Was my last hope to be buried under this old woman's spitefulness? Speechless with rage I stared down at her.

"One more thing will I tell to you. It is as a Kahekili that you will find happiness. A Kahekili: this you must be, free and alone. Not a servant of the fat Kalakaua." She uttered the name of the King with hate, reaching beyond me to make her thrust at him. A whole new vision of her and her past was revealed to me.

"You know me then?" I asked foolishly.

A burst of hard laughter came from her. "Do you think that Kaupea is an idiot? Why do you come to see me, then?" Cackling evilly, without bothering to say anything more, she dismissed me with a wave of her clawlike hand. Brushing me away, as if I were trash, she leaned back in her chair, closing her eyes that she need not see me any more.

I turned and rushed from the house, poisoned by her hate. The exaltation with which I entered her abode of evil was gone.

Gone, too, were Kake, Kakea, and Kakela, from their place under the grass beneath the tall *naupaka* bushes. Gone, too, was the dying Umalu. Disappeared, they were, as if they had never been there. Fearing for my mind, I ran to the place where we were sitting, all of us, just a few minutes before.

I found the place where I had sat, the grass still pressed flat upon the ground from the weight of my body. Where my thighs had rested, where my legs had been curled under me, even where my skirts had lain: these places I could read in the tangles and whirls of grass not yet sprung back to their full height after my rising.

But of the three women, sitting cross-legged in the grass, of Umalu, dying in the embrace of Kane, I could find no sign. Nothing was there to show that the same green cushion of grass in which I sat had received them, too. Nothing.

Thus did I learn of the strength of Kaupea, of the power of her *mana*. My heart was small with fear of her as I stole away from the silent house, over the path by which I went to her.

"Be a Kahekili," Kaupea said. But what did she mean? Sorely puzzled, I cast about in my mind for the *manao* she meant for me.

Many were the meanings I could read into her words, by twisting the meaning of that one word. Was it only as the name of my family that I should heed it? Then it meant "thunder," and what did "thunder" have to do with me? Was it the hidden poetic meaning of the word she meant for me to discover? But every lover knows how this "thunder" is the sound of passion, roaring in the ears of one who lusts. I did not need her to acquaint me with this meaning: it was to help me quiet the sound of this fury in my ears that I sought her out. If I broke the word into fragments, and studied the meaning of each of its parts, then even fouler were my choices, even wilder grew my confusion— The old witch had tricked me, and I was no better off than I was before I went to see her.

Angered with her, and with myself, I went out upon the broad green plain of Kalaupapa, to calm myself after the distress of the morning. Forgotten was my delight in the discovery of my people and the kindness of the ancient gods. Now, too late, did I remember the other gods, the cruel ones with the bloody mouths and the tearing teeth, like Ku the Killer, Ku the Devourer of Men. Ku and Iehovah: they were the same. And all men were their victims.

The sunshine, which earlier was warming and kind, now was hot and blinding. The growing plants, gifts of Lono, they clutched now at my dragging skirts, to make my way labored and slow. The clouds, which were others of his manifestations: they were withdrawn from the mountains, and the tall peaks were revealed, sharp as the teeth of Ku, hard as the stones of Kaupea's prophesying.

Upon all the desolate waste, I was the only thing to move, I was the only thing to beat my breast and, weeping, curse the gods.

And then a new thought came to me. Does she mean for me to live as a Kahekili lives, in the house of a Kahekili? Is it in Uncle Pita's house where I am to find my happiness? Taken with this new idea, I went to see.

Although I had not yet seen it I knew, from Ambrose, from Momona and Makaio and others, where the house of Peter Kahekili stood. On the road between Kalawao and Kalaupapa, just beyond the hill of Kauhako, it was built, those long years ago, when Uncle Pita came to the Settlement. "On the curve of the road," he wrote to us at home, "with a view of both the mountains and the sea. From here, on a clear day, I can see Oahu, where my heart is. And I stand on my *lanai*, singing, 'Home, Sweet Home,' across the sea for you."

There did I find it. But it was a dead house. Forlorn as a forgotten grave, it lay hidden behind a tangle of trees and vines and weeds. The trees he planted with such love—the flame trees, the monkeypods, the Australian ironwoods—they were tall and wild, their branches grown thick together. They were intruders, and among them the ghosts of native plants grew weak and oppressed. Over them all the purple bougainvillaea and the white moonflowers hung their vines like funeral palls. The flowers were like sores, great clusters of sores, like the purple and red and white sores scattered upon my body.

Dead it was, the house, and empty, dead as my hope was when I saw it. No, there was nothing there for me. Uncle Fita had now his revenge: he failed me, in the end, as long ago I had failed him. And for my punishment, I saw, I was condemned to the same frenzied running to and fro as he had known, the same frantic search for a balm to soothe my fear. Now at last I learned the full measure of horror in Momona's dreadful story of Uncle Peter's search for a cure.

And now at last I saw myself as pitiless Momona would one day describe me, when he talked of me to his friends: a creature mad for love, running endlessly in search of love, and never finding it.

Sickened to my soul, I stopped. Defeated, I would go no farther upon the path. As Uncle Pita did, so could I. I gave up, I ceased my frenzy.

I turned back.

Slowly I wandered along the narrow road to Kalawao. The sun, fierce and unhelping, warned me that I must go soon to the schoolhouse, to be with my pupils. But I shook off their claim upon me: let them do without me, let them have another holiday. This day was for me, to live in, to die in. I was weary unto death, and I yearned for death: as it had come for Uncle Pita, so could it come now for me.

Not knowing how I came to it, I found myself upon the trail to Kauhako's summit. It was not steep, I did not have far to go. Soon I stood upon its height. Around me was the green breast of Kalaupapa. Behind me soared the great cliffs, before me lay the flat sea. I looked out upon my whole world. There was nothing more, nothing but emptiness. And in all the emptiness nothing stirred save the breath of the wind blowing in from the sea.

But at my feet lay Paradise: I looked down into the crater of Kauhako, into Eden. The lips of Kauhako were open to the light of Kane, as a woman's womb is open to her lover's seed. In the depths of the crater, at its center, a lake of water gleamed, green and clear, receiving the golden seed of Kane. Upon the steep sides of the crater's throat, beginning at its lips and falling away in ripples of verdant loveliness, were all manner of native trees and grasses, things which did not grow upon the windy plain. Thriving there, they made of Kauhako a bower of beauty: the breadfruit, the mountain apple, the red-flowered *ohia* grew there, the *koa*, the *kukui*, the *milo*. Beneath them, in their cool shade, the *honohono* grass ran thick, the mountain *awapuhi* raised its broad leaves, the *mamaki*, the *olona* shaded in their turn the lacy ferns, the tender mosses. From the trees came the calls of birds unseen: only half remembered, their singing came to me across the still air; and, as I gazed in wonder into the leafy arbors, streaks of burning red, of flashing yellow, showed where the *iiwi*, and the *mamo*, and the *apapane* played.

"O loveliness!" I cried, forgetting my cracked heart in the discovery of this new wonder. "Beautiful is Kauhako."

Crossing over the brink, eager to see more of the sacred place, I began my descent into the depths of the crater. In the hushed stillness the bird calls came clear and unworried. In the moist warmth of the forest I threw off my hat, opened the yoke of my *holoku*. Like a pagan did I feel, like one of those creatures whose home is the forest, whose abode is a tree. I wanted to shed my clothes, to walk innocent and naked in the unspoiled world of another time, as my people did in the days before the *haole* came. Halfway down the slope I took the pins from my hair, letting it fall down my back, exulting in my freedom. Giddy with joy and despair combined, smiling yet weeping, as full of unwanted love as a mother's breast is with milk when her child is dead, I wandered in search of a makeshift lover, as the mother must search for a *hanai* child.

Life is good, I tried to tell myself, despite my loneliness. The gods are kind, I tried to feel, despite my sorrowing, as farther and farther I walked, as closer and closer I came to the font of Kane, which is the lake of Kauhako. I will swim in those cool waters, I promised myself, I will bathe in the water of Kane, in the healing spring. I will go down into their dark depths, and there will I find my peace.

Like Papa in the beginning of the world, like Eve in her garden, did I walk through the glory of Kauhako.

When I reached the narrow shore of the little lake, the far side was already in shadow. I leaned over to touch with my hands the cool water, I knelt to drink of the undefiled spring. While I bent low, watching my image rising through the water to greet me, I heard the rustle of leaves as a branch, pushed aside by some unknown hand, fell back into its place.

In the instant my Paradise lost its perfection. In the instant I was no longer an Eve in Eden, a nymph in some sacred grove. With the rustling of those warning leaves the madness went out of me: I was made a woman again, alone and far from home. Too late did I remember how even Eden held its serpent, and how I was a woman trapped.

I sprang to my feet, ready for flight. I turned to face my danger.

Close upon my footsteps he stood, still in the shadow of the trees. I did not need to see his face. I knew that body, the fall of those hands by his sides.

He stepped from the shadows upon the shelf of the shore. As in a dream I watched him come toward me. The voice of my fear cried at me to scream at him, to shriek for help, to run, to run away. The voice of my virtue cried at me to seize up a stone, to take up a stick, to beat him off. But the voice of my love called him to me, and, unmoving I stood, knowing that this was the moment I had been yearning for.

Slowly he came to me, as once before he had come to me. A look of pleading softened his face. This time there was need in it, not lust.

An answering look was in my face. I needed him, I wanted him. Keanu, my Keanu, at last, at last we meet . . .

But I would not say it. Greater than my need for him was my love for him. I knew it then, the moment my eyes beheld him. How can I, in loving him, sully his body with the touch of my own?

As before, he reached out his hand, to take me by the shoulder. "We meet again," he said, his voice low, his eyes soft with longing.

The touch of his hand awoke me from my spell. "No, Keanu, no," I said, trying to shrink away. "Do not touch me. For your sake, please, for your sake."

But he would not let me go. He drew me to him, gently, until I stood in the compass of his arms. Dizzy with joy for myself, wild with concern for him, I cried out, "I am unclean! Oh, can you not see what you do to yourself?"

Shaking his head, he smiled down at me. "Does it matter? There are things more important than the *lepera*."

Turning my face from him, that I might not befoul him with my breath, I tried for the third time to send him away. "Go, go now. Go, before it is too late."

With one of his big hands he took me by my face, forcing me to look up to him. In his grasp I was like a doll. He made me to see him while he spoke. "I come to you in love. Not as before."

These were the words I longed to hear. They pierced my soul. But my love for him was great. Once more I tried to save him. "Love," I sneered. "Can you love a leper?" All the loathing, all the ugliness I could summon up, I put into this ugliest of all words.

He did not answer me with words. Gently he loosened the dress from about my shoulders. Where once I tore the clothes from my body to show him the blight my body bore, now did he loose them, pulling them down from me, until I stood bound by my own sleeves and the hold of his hands upon my arms. Naked to the waist I stood before him, watching with dread for the least sign of his flinching before the signs of my corruption.

But he did not flinch. "It is you I love," he said quietly. "Not myself." And bending over me he kissed the sores upon my breasts, upon the soft places of my belly. With his kisses upon my loathsomeness did he prove to me his love.

Weak with love, I felt the warmth of his lips upon my throat, upon my cheeks, my forehead, at last, at last, upon my mouth. Conquered at last, a most willing conquest, I turned to life in his arms, hungering to return his kisses.

Burning with our need for each other, we pulled the clothes from my body, letting them fall at my feet. An instant more, and he stood forth, urgent and naked before me. Beautiful was his body, delicious was the sight and the scent of him.

Like glorious Adam and unhindered Eve we faced each other. Like Wakea and Papa, the parent gods, we lay upon the unspoiled earth, taking our delight of each other. The gift of his pain was a joy to me. The weight of his body was a joy to me. The yielding of my love was a joy to him.

Beside the waters of Kauhako's spring did we find our healing. We two, who were divided and set apart, were now made whole by our love.

25

THEN WAS THE SEASON of our joy, and in it all the world was fair, as if no withering winds had ever blown across it, as if no long hunger had been endured. It was the gift of Heaven, this joy we knew, and we delighted in it, not asking whether it came by the power of Kane or whether it was Iehovah who was kind.

But in my prayers I thanked them both, rather than risk the offending of either. And Keanu, when I told him of the strange counsel of Kaupea, he took her offerings of fish from the sea, and crabs and seaweeds, that she might be pleased, and so too the ancient gods whose messages she spoke. "It was her *mana* guiding your feet upon the path to me," he said, "even though you did not know her meaning. How else would you have come to Kauhako, the place of my refuge?"

The mornings were ours. Going by different ways, we met in the crater of Kauhako, eager to behold each other again in our nakedness, insatiable in the sharing of our love. The storms of passion long denied, the burning of a leper's lust—these I knew, as we found the ways of love. But we also knew the tendernesses of a love gained at last, as harbor is gained after a dangerous journey upon a violent sea. And, afterward, as we lay in each other's arms, or swam in the glowing lake, the wondrousness of our love made us gentle in our touching, in our speech, we were gentle, in the caress of our glances as we went apart and drew together again, in the softness of our sorrow as we resigned ourselves to separate at the hour of noon, when the sun blazed like a guardian spirit directly over the wellspring of the world in which we lay. Oh, beautiful was our love, and glorious was the time of our loving.

Jealous were we of each moment stolen from us by the claims of my family, by the need for me to go each afternoon to the schoolhouse. Impatiently I would sit through the supper around our family table, wanting to scream at their slowness, at the very sounds of their chewing. Storming within I would listen to the dull conversations on our *lanai*, when the men gathered for their talk. Their talk, the music club, the school—these kept me from the arms of my lover, and I fretted under the demands they made of me.

But at last, when the darkness was fully come, and it was safe for Keanu to walk through the lanes to the house of Makaio, I would excuse myself from the company sitting in the yellow lamplight of our *lanai*. Saying that I must do some reading for tomorrow's school, or that I had my pupils' papers to correct, I would retire. Except for a wave of dismissal from Tutu, a scowl from Caleb, annoyed that I should interrupt his talk with my excuses, the company would hardly notice my leaving. Swiftly I would go to my room and light the candle, to let them think I sat beside it at my work. Then noiselessly I would glide out the back door of the house, closing it softly behind me. My blood racing, my body eager, I would hasten past the cookhouse across the grass to the low stone wall at the edge of the yard. And there, waiting for me, his arms ready to receive me, would be Keanu.

Naked he would be when I arrived, waiting for me, ready to lift me over the wall, eager, eager, to strip me of my clothes. And there, upon a blanket he brought from the doctor's house and spread upon the ground, with the stars this time for guardians, we would hasten to calm the fever of our bodies. In a sweet ecstasy of danger and desire combined, we said our lovers' good nights.

Alas, we did not have much time for them: in half an hour, or forty-five minutes at the most, the talkative company on our *lanai* would break up, and Tutu would be going to our room. Sooner or later I would be caught, I knew, found out in the game I played. But, such is the wildness of love, I did not care if I should be caught. It was Keanu I protected from them, not myself.

I worried more about the weather. "What if the rain should fall, to deny us a couch for our lying?" I whispered one night, when he received me into his arms.

"Then will we go to the Puka of Pele." This was his name for the cave where first he touched me. "I have thought of this. It is ready for us."

"Can we find the way, in the night?"

"I will know the way, even in the dark of night."

Then was I content, having no other worries about my love.

In the mornings there was time for talk, as we lay in peace, like Wakea and Papa, beside the water of life.

This was not the first question I asked him, but it was the one which cried out the most for answering: "*Kuu ipo*, what if, in our loving, you should catch the *Pake* sickness from me?" I lay beside him, with my head in the hollow of his shoulder, watching the rise and fall of his chest, hearing the beat of his heart. It did not falter.

"A man needs love without love, the rest of life is nothing." He pressed his mouth against the top of my head, his hands caressed the curve of my back. "It is you I need: without you, my life is nothing. What is the *mai Pake*, compared with this love we share? It is nothing." Thus did he make me clean again, in my sight as in his.

Another morning I asked him, "What of Opaekea? Why is he so cruel to you?" We were sitting among the ferns, at the edge of the forest, he cross-legged, I leaning against him, looking close at his perfection. Never did I cease to delight in the sight of him: at the dark depths in his eyes, at the way his silky beard curled around his strong mouth, yet stopped short of the red lips, at the hard smoothness of the flesh upon his lean body, except where the black hair swirled about his loins. Beautiful was he, as Lohiau the lover of Pele, sitting in his *holua* sled. And grateful was I for his beauty, in the manner of my smooth-skinned people. I do not think I could love a man whose body is covered with hair, as a dog is covered with fur. The *haoles* are like this, I have seen, shuddering as I have observed them: upon their chests and arms they have so much hair. It is to keep them warm, I suppose, in the cold lands from which they come.

"Cruel to me?" he turned in surprise. "No: it is not so. He is not cruel. He is good to me."

"But this," I put my fingers upon the lump of Akala's flesh where it lay in his strong arm. "This planting of the *lepera* seed in you: is this not a cruelty?"

"We have made a bargain. He keeps his part of the bargain." He stopped for a moment, staring at the ground beyond his knees. "It is I who have betrayed him." Then he fell silent once more, before he went on, speaking slowly, as though ashamed of what he must say.

"And this is not all. For my part, I have been cruel to him.

There was a time when I hated him, the poor little man, and when I could not keep my hate from showing. This was when," he reached over to take my hands, "I was wanting you and I could not have you. I was afraid of everything, then: of the *mai Pake*, of the test the *kauka* makes upon me, of you, of him, because I thought he went away from me, leaving me here to be forgotten. So full of hate was I that it made me sick. And when he came back from Honolulu I lifted my hand against him in anger. I am ashamed of this. I was sick, then, with my need for you. And more drunk with anger than with the swipes I made in an old *poi* barrel.

"But after he came back from Honolulu—this is a funny thing, I cannot explain it—he was changed. He was more gentle with me, more interested in me. Where once he was silent with me, forgetting I was there, now he watched me, and seemed always about to say something lying on the very front of his tongue. But the words did not come. Something held them back. I think that he is afraid of me, because I lifted my hand and my voice against him. I am sorry for this, for I do not hate him any more. Not since the first day when he came back.

"When I saw how he was in fear of me, when I saw how my hate and my fear were making me unhappy, and everyone else around me—do you know that I drove the other *haole* doctor out of the house, with my hate and my drunkenness?—then did I begin to see how wrong was my fear. In our silent house on the hill there was much time to think.

"My fear of the *lepera*, I thought: it is a fool's fear. When I learned this, I lost my fear of it. When I lost that, I saw my love for you. And when I came to you in love, then everything was put aright. Now I have no more hate in me, for anyone."

I pressed close to him, to let him know how he had lifted my fear and my hate from me.

"Now we are easy again, in the doctor's house. We are talking again, where once there was nothing to say. But I am still weak in one thing, there is still one thing I cannot speak with my mouth. I have betrayed him, in my bargain with him, and I do not know how to tell him I have cheated him. It preys upon my liver, this trickery."

"What is this bargain you have made with him?"

"To stay away from the patients here, until the time of my testing is ended."

"How long is it, this time of the testing?" Dreading to hear his answer, I waited. In the trees above us the birds sang, the sunlight danced. Over the surface of the little lake the dragonflies skimmed. Never was the world so fair as in the moment when I waited to hear of the time in it which would be Keanu's gift to me.

"Six months," said my beloved, not looking at me when he spoke the sentence of my own death. Six months: this is all. Half a year, of which almost nothing is left to me.

"What happens then?" Faint was my voice, but how could I endure to live, without knowing the answer?

"He will ask the King to let me go free. If I am still clean."

Easier was it for me to turn my bitterness upon the doctor, than to bear the hurt of my dread. "And you believe him?"

"I must. If I do not believe him, I have no hope." Still he did not look at me. His gaze was upon the farther wall of the crater, where the ferns and the gingers and the trees were as a mirror to the side where we sat.

"What if he lies, this cruel man? What if he but fools you?"

"Then will I go away from here, without the King's pardon, without the doctor's help. One wall only has this prison. And I do not fear the sea." Turning to me at last, he looked down at me. "I will swim away in the sea, to Maui, or to Lanai. If I should reach the other side, then I will be free. If I do not reach the far side, then will I be free also." His lips parted in a sad smile. "It is better for you to know this, now. I was not born to live my life in a jail."

"Ae, this I know," I whispered, pressing my mouth against his shoulder. "But do not go too soon."

Putting his hand upon the back of my head, he brought my face close to his. Touching his nose to mine, in the ancient manner of kissing, he said, "I will not go too soon. This love we have: it is a good thing, for the two of us. Let us not spoil it with worry over its ending. Let us remember only how it is at its beginning." He drew me close to him, to comfort me.

"Besides," he said with a laugh, in one of his quick changes of mood, "if it were not for the kauka, would I be here with you now?—I would be rotting in the dirt of Oahu, dead of a broken neck. Would you wish that this lump of Akala's flesh was still in her cheek?"

For answer I needed no words. Bending my head to his arm,

I kissed the place where Opaekea, by putting death into him, gave life not only to Keanu but also to me. So great was my love for Keanu that I would have licked the dirt from his feet, and cleaned his body with my tongue.

On another morning we spoke once more of the doctor, when I told Keanu of Akala's last sickness, and of how the people in the Settlement were saying that her wasting away was the fault of the *kauka*.

"Perhaps so"—Keanu frowned over the problem—"perhaps not. Who can say? I am sorry for Akala, though, that she must die. But how can they blame the *kauka* for this? He is a learned man, and he did with Akala and with me what he thought was best. I do not question him in this. If his test in me will help our people to get well, then I am content to be his animal. Why do the people complain of something when it is done to help them?"

"They are sorry for Akala. And for you."

"*Ae*, and even sorrier for themselves. But it is the *kauka* they should be sorry for, not me, not Akala. The patients have their friends, their families. I have my love, in you. But he: he has nothing. Malie, would you believe it? He has nothing, no friends, no love, nothing. He is hungry for love, and he does not know it."

"Yes, I have seen it. Those eyes of his, they tell it. I know that look well."

"He seeks to kill his loneliness in work. He works hard, all the time. Always he reads in a book, or thinks, staring off into the far places, seeking to fit the pieces of the puzzle of this sickness into their places. At night he cannot sleep for thinking, his mind is so busy. I hear him stirring, talking to himself, even crying out in the middle of the night. I am sorry for him. And yet I do not know how to help him."

"Do you talk with him? To find out what makes him worry so?"

"I have tried. But it is hard to talk with him in a language I do not know. I do not speak the English very well, you know. And when he talks to me, *auwe!* I do not understand him. He uses such big words, he talks about things I never heard of." He traced the line of a vein upon my arm laid next to his. "And when he tells me about his homeland— What is snow? What is ice? What kind of a dance do they do in his *haole* world? It is not a *hula*. I cannot even remember its name. And where is this

island he calls Germany? I never heard of it, before his talking
about it."

"My sweet sweeting, how could you know of these things? Who
from Hawaii can know of them, who has not been to those
foreign lands? I do not know them either."

"It is as you say. But when I tried to speak of things of
importance here, in Hawaii Nei, did he listen? No. He did not
care to hear of swimming, of fishing, of working the land. He
looked away from me, yawning, or took up his knife, to cut
his fingernails." Remembering something else, Keanu turned to
me in wonderment. "Would you believe it? He knows nothing
of love! He was as ashamed as a missionary when I talked to him
about the women I have had."

He did not see the frown of jealousy wrinkling my face. This
was a subject of which I did not wish to hear.

"I believe that he is a virgin," said my lover. "Tell me, how is
it possible for a man of his age to be—"

"Well," I said, drawing away from him, "not all men have the
advantage you enjoy. He comes from a Christian land, where there
is a high price placed upon such virtue, in both women and men."
My back was toward him, my voice was very polite. "But you
come from a land where the men seem to learn very early—"

"*Auwe nohoi e!*" he broke in with a shout of laughter. "And
isn't it a good thing, too! Else what would our hot-blooded women
do, in a land which held only virgin men?" Taking me in his
arms he drove my frown away with kisses, banished my jealousy
with the magic his body knew so well how to call up in mine.

This was the morning when, after we bathed in the lake and
we stood drying ourselves in the sun, he seized me in a kind of
madness and drew me close to him. Holding me in his embrace
until I could not breathe, he covered my face with kisses, uttering
no word. When the two of us were dizzy with breathlessness he
set me free and flung himself away, to run wild along the shore,
back and forth, like a noble stallion galloping in a field of grass. I
watched him, enjoying his happiness, understanding his inability
to give it words.

When he returned to me he held a sharp clean stone. The
drops of water on his body sparkled like diamonds, each jewel full
of rainbows of promise. Dropping on his knees before me, he
scratched his mark with the stone into the skin of my belly, a

jagged streak like the writing of lightning. It was the old rite of the lover claiming possession of his beloved.

"This is my sign," he said with great seriousness. "Now you are mine."

This was the morning of my greatest happiness.

There was yet a third question I must put to him, before I was done with asking. But this one I feared to ask, for I remembered the fate of the wife of the God of Love, and I did not want her doom to fall upon me. Yet there was a ghost in Keanu's past to haunt me, eating at my liver; and until it was driven out of me I could not be at ease. Such is the foolishness of women who love: they can never let the happiness of the moment be enough for them.

On the seventh morning of our meeting in Kauhako's solitude I dared to ask the question.

"What of Kamaka?" I said, trying to make my voice light, as though it were someone's pet pig I asked about, or the health of some remote relative whose well-being does not much matter. No one could know, from the way I said it, how small was my heart with jealousy of Kamaka. It was not jealousy of her part in Keanu's early life that worried me. It was her place in his heart now, even now, that I wanted to probe. Kamaka and Malie: the two of us fought for Keanu, in my mind, and I must learn where she stood, and where I stood, in the great heart of my beloved.

"Kamaka? Why do you speak of her?" We were lying on a cool bed of ginger leaves, in the shade of the *kukui* trees. The sharp spice of the crushed ginger was strong in the air. Above us creamy clusters of *kukui* flowers weighted the tips of the branches, bending them low. There were horsemen on the plain of Kalaupapa that morning, rounding up the cattle for the weekly slaughter of beef; and we did not dare to lie out in the open for fear that a rider might see us if he came to the brink of Kauhako in search of a lost calf.

Gazing out upon the open place in the throat of Kauhako, I did not say my question to him directly. "Did you love her?" I said softly. I meant by this, did you love her more than you love me? Do you love her now, even though I am here? Always, I suppose, when a woman puts such a question she is seeking a comparison, a pairing in which she hopes to hear, of course, that she is nothing less than first best in the thoughts of her lover.

And men being what they are, they will always say, I suppose, what is expected of them. At least it seemed to me to be so, from the tales of her downfall many a tearful girl recounted to us at school, when she believed a lover's whispered words at a cost she later found was too great. But it was not so with Keanu. There was no flattery in him. "I had love for her. She was my woman then—as you are my woman now."

Seeing the side of my face, he said gently, "But she was different from you. She was a whore, a bitch to lie with. She was what I needed then, to relieve my body's need." After a moment he found the words I wanted. "You are what I need now: you are my bitch when I need a bitch." He tugged at my ear, to make me look at him. "But you are something more. Malie, you are well-named. You bring a peace to my heart I did not know with her. Malie, you are the love of my heart, as well as the love of my body."

Beautiful were these words in my ear. But I needed to hear more before I could lock the ghost of Kamaka in its grave, forever. "But how is it that you can put her behind you so readily? Is it always the way with men, that they can forget an old love in the arms of a new?" Looking at this man beside me, I thought: What woman would not be overjoyed to give herself to him? And: How could he have time to remember a past love, when there would always be a present one to relieve his body's need?

. He sat up, snatching a fern frond from the growth at his side. "It is not I who chose to forget her," he said harshly, as he tore the fern to pieces. "No. She it was who forgot me. She betrayed me, when I was put into the jail. Thinking that I was to be hanged with the rope, she turned away from me. Such was her love for me." He threw the naked rib of the fern away from him. "Such was her great love for me."

"Even after—after what you did for her?"

"*Ae.* It would seem that the life of Charley was ill-spent."

"Did you really kill him?" Never did I think that I loved a murderer, never did I believe that the man with whom I found my joy was a man who had slain another. Not even now could I believe it. Surely there was some other explanation to the death of Charley, one which only Keanu knew? One which, if he would only say it, would lift the guilt from off his head and wash the blood from off his hands?

"I killed him, just as it has been said." He reached over to the *mamaki* bush upon which his clothes were hung, and pulled his knife from its sheath. Its blade lay cold and dark in the shadows beneath the trees. "With this knife I stabbed him, and with this hand. There was no other way by which he died."

At the sight of the knife I shuddered, but at the sight of his face I was frightened. Full of scowling it was, and of an ugliness I did not think it could ever show. There are so many faces to a man. A woman can never know what kind of a creature it is, to whom she gives her life.

"I would have killed others, too, if they were there."

"But why, my love, why did you do that terrible thing?"

"They tried to take my woman away from me. Kamaka. She and I: we found each other, in the part of Kohala where we lived, and we were content with each other. She lived in my house. She was my wife, in the olden style. We were willing for this to be." He began to prick the sharp point of the knife into a ginger leaf on the ground between us, making a design in the smooth green surface as, in the old days, the *kahunas* made tattoos in the skin of a man.

"But her family, *Cha!* They lived in the new style, like *haoles.* Potato Christians they were, and they did not like me, or the way Kamaka and I lived, in my house in Makapala. 'You live in sin,' they said to us, barking at us like angry dogs. But yet they would not give me Kamaka to marry in the *haole* way when I asked for her. 'Go 'way you,' they called at me, 'she is meant for a better husband than you, you taro-patch farmer smelling of mud.' Many times they made Kamaka leave my house to go home to theirs, but always I went and brought her back. They did not like it, but they were afraid of me.

"Then this Japanese came, this Charley. A peddler he was, with a pair of mules, and he went from village to village, selling things. He wanted a woman. In his country it seems they do not have many women, for none have come here, to be with the men in Hawaii Nei. And when he saw Kamaka, she was the one he said he must have. He asked for her, giving her mother and father presents from his bags. Kamaka says he gave them money for her, also: twenty-five American gold dollars. But of this I do not know with certainty. Kamaka did not always speak the truth.

"While I was plowing in my field at Waiapuka one day, they came to my house with a policeman for Kamaka. When I came home, there was no Kamaka, there was no supper. Only an empty house.

"Once more I went to get her, but this time she could not come. 'She is married now, by the judge, to the Japanee,' her father said. 'Chase him away from here!' screamed her mother, telling the policeman to point his gun at me. So I went home, alone. And I waited." A slow smile came into his face. "I knew Kamaka. After three days she was back in my house. Then it was Charley's time to come for her." Now he laughed aloud.

"From my house to his she went, only because the policeman was there. But soon she was with me again. After two or three weeks of this traffic back and forth, even Charley had to give up. He was a smart one, that Japanee. He said to Kamaka: 'Let us live together in the house of Keanu, the three of us. When I am away from home, on the road, you will be Keanu's wife. When I am at home, you will be my wife.' I was well content. 'Good,' I said, 'let it be so.' And this is how we lived for many weeks. When they moved together to my house, I killed all of my chickens and my suckling pig, and we had a big party for us and for Kahiamoe and his family, who lived near to us. But the family of Kamaka did not come. 'Trouble will come of this sinful living,' they said. Kahiamoe told us of their feelings."

He looked up from his marking of the ginger leaf. "But what is sin? What was sinful about our manner of living? Charley and I: we were good friends. Never was he jealous of his place as Kamaka's husband. If he came home tired, at the end of his journey, he would tell us 'Charley no stop tonight,' or, 'Tonight free *pani-pani* for you,' things like that. And I: when Charley wished to take her to his bed, I could wait until he was gone again. If I could not wait, there were other women I could lie with.

"We lived together in peace. Until Kamaka was with child. Then did Charley become different. All at once he was jealous. I did not know why. Perhaps it was because he wanted the child to be his? He would not let me touch Kamaka. He could not bear to go away with his mules and his bags. One day he came home early, in the middle of the week. To her he said, 'Charley get new job. Work fo Sam Pahkah, at Kamuela. Tomorrow we go. You get ready.'

"The next morning they left, each of them upon a horse borrowed from Kamaka's father. This time I knew she would not come back. Sam Parker's ranch was too far away." His hands stopped their torture of the leaf. His head was lifted, his memory far away, turned upon the morning when his whole life was changed.

"When they were gone, I sat in my empty house. Then did my anger grow big in me. Looking around at the emptiness, at my house without its woman, without its baby—who perhaps was my baby—I grew mad with rage. She was my woman, I told myself: she was my woman before Charley bought her. To hell with Charley: let him go to Kamuela. But Kamaka: she is mine.

"I saddled my horse, and I went after them, to bring Kamaka back. I came upon them at a lonely place in the road, where waterfalls, from the green mountains above, made noise enough to cover the sound of my horse. There great *kukui* trees lean over the road, making a deep shade. It is a winding road, along the side of a gulch, and the turns did not let them see me coming. No. They did not see me coming . . .

"They were in the middle of the road. Kamaka was rolling in the mud, screaming with fear and pain. Charley was beating her with his whip, and kicking her, kicking her in the belly, to get rid of the child lying inside her.

"Shouting at him, I threw myself from my horse upon him. Before I knew what I did, he was dead at my feet, bleeding from the wounds of my knife." With a groan he thrust the knife into the soft ground between us. It sank into the skin of ginger leaves, into the flesh of mud, as easily as it must have sunk into the body of Charley.

Wanting to comfort him, I searched for words to say. Putting my hand upon his hand, clasped still about the hold of the knife, I said, "It is hard to say—"

"I am not sorry for the deed," he said slowly. "I would kill again if—"

"No, no! You must not think this!"

"If someone tries to take you from me, I will kill him."

"Keanu, please—"

"If someone tries to cheat me again of what I want, of what is mine, I will kill him."

"You must not do that! It is—"

"Why should I not? How else is a man to keep what is his?"

"There is the law."

"*Cha*, the law! It shelters the strong and the rich. I have seen it working. Did the policeman in Kohala work for me, the mate of Kamaka? Or did he work for the father of Kamaka, who paid him with money? Did the judge in Honolulu ask me why it was that Charley was killed? No. Only who did the killing, and how it was done. The law: it does not guard the poor or the weak. I am not rich, but neither am I weak. Now I know what I must do: I will fight for what I want. And I will take what I want."

"But this is wrong Keanu."

"Is this not how I got you? Is this not how I saved my neck from the hanging? What would I have gained, by sitting and waiting for something to happen, there in the jailhouse? What?"

Unhappily I waited beside him, while he worked out his anger. "And when my time is ended here, and my bargain is fulfilled, I will go from this place, if they like it or if they do not." The crack of his fist as he hit it upon the palm of his other hand was the sound of my hope falling around me into ruins.

"Nothing can keep me here, in this given grave. I will *not* get the *lepera*. I will go, even if I have to swim away from here—"

Unable to sit any longer with me he rose from our forest bed and pushed off through the gingers and the ferns, like an animal eager to escape from its caging. Watching him go I knew how for Keanu there could be no caging, how, despite the crying of my heart, there must be a time when he would go from me. And I knew that when the time came I must not hold him back.

While he walked that morning like Adam in his forest, I lay like Eve in her bower, grieving, grieving . . .

26

EARLY ONE MORNING Caleb knocked at our door, while we sat at breakfast. "It is about Akala," he said quietly. "Miele asked me to tell you. She is dead."

"*Auwe!* The poor thing," exclaimed Tutu, rising from the table. "I will go to Miele. But first: come in and take a cup of tea."

Caleb would not stay, having other errands to perform. With a strange lingering glance at me he bowed to us and left. His shoes made patches of wet grass where he trampled upon the dew. Such is the imprint of death upon the people. And short as the stay of dew was the life of Akala.

I could not make love with Keanu in the garden of Kauhako that morning. It was not only Akala's death sitting heavy in me: it was the remnant of grieving, the foreshadowing of my loss when he would be gone from me. Like the piece of Akala's flesh in Keanu's arm was the worm of sorrow in my bosom: whether Akala's little germs took him from me, or his own longing for the world beyond our green prison, I knew that when he left me I would be broken and emptied. Like unto the vanished dew would be the happiness of my time with him.

Nothing of this could I tell Keanu. A man dislikes weeping, dislikes the show of grieving. Clinging to him, when he met me just inside the lip of Kauhako, I told him only of Akala's death, letting him think that I was sad only for her.

"Alas for Akala," he said. "So her spirit has left her eyes for the last time. But why are you so full of sorrow? Is Death an enemy? Is it not better this way, for Akala, with the sickness so strong in her?" I could not answer him, neither could I agree with him. Death was no friend to me: he was my great enemy still.

"I cannot stay," I told him when he turned to lead me down to our couch of leaves. "I must go back, to help with the funeral."

For a moment he studied me, his face lighted up by the morning sun. "*Ae.* It is right. I shall not keep you." He pulled me to him for a gentle kiss before he let me go. "I will make a *lei* for Akala. When do they put her in the ground?"

"Caleb said this afternoon, at four o'clock."

"Caleb said? You have seen him this morning?"

"Yes. It was he who brought us the word of Akala's dying. He is a friend to Akala's family—"

"Yes, I know. This is not what I am thinking. I am thinking how he saw me last night, when I was walking home, after I put you back across the wall. Did he speak of this to you in your house?"

"No, he said nothing to us. But he did give me a funny look. What of last night? Did he speak to you?"

"*Ae,* as one who talks to an unwelcome dog. 'Who's that?' he called out, when he met me in the darkness. 'Stop, you!' What could I do? Never had he walked that way before, and I did not expect him to come out of your gate. I stopped. When he came up to me, he lit a match in my face. He was surprised to find me. Perhaps he was frightened. He dropped the match." A grim pleasure made my lover's face cruel.

" 'You! What are you doing here?' he asked, like a policeman of someone he has caught in a crime. I did not like the sound of his voice.

" 'Just walking,' I said. 'Is this a wrong?' *Kie*, the little stick! With my hands I could break him in two. The sassy little pup! With my foot I could kick him into the sea. But there he was, hopping up and down in front of me, waving his hands at me. It was not so dark, in the light of the stars, that I could not see his white shirt and the blackness where his hands were, and his hard head, made of bone."

"Oh, Keanu, tell me! What did you do to each other, you two?"

"Nothing but peck at each other, like two *kolea* cocks after the same hen." I had not told Keanu of Caleb's proposal to me, delivered upon almost the very spot where he challenged Keanu, but I could not help smiling at Keanu's name for those two who sought the same hen. The lustful plovers, those wanderers who alight upon our shores to feed and to breed: their name was usually applied to the *haoles*, but I could not deny that Keanu and I deserved it too. But Caleb? Could that cold man know the pleasures we enjoyed?

"He said to me, 'You have no business around here and you'd better stay away from this place. Do you hear me? Stay away, or there will be trouble. His words made me burn. So easily could I have punched his face for him, broken his head against the stone wall."

"Oh, you men, always ready to fight. Must you always be so violent?" I thought of Caleb's body lying in the road of Kalawao, as once Charley's corpse lay in the road of Kohala. Why had I taken a brute to be my love, when I might have had a gentleman like Caleb? But one look at Keanu told me why I chose him, one look melting the bones in my body and making me soft with love. He was not a brute, a beast who knew only the ways of violence. He was a man, proud, indeed, and easily inflamed to violence, but a man lost in the foreign world of people whom he did not understand, among whom he walked as an innocent walks among the wicked.

"Do not worry, my fragrant one. Your man has learned some

lessons along the way. What was to be gained by breaking his head? By slicing him up with my knife? Nothing. Besides, I rather admired the little fellow, snapping at me like a cock pecking at the feet of a horse passing by.

"And what do you do with such a cock? You put him in a place where he cannot be hurt." Keanu put his great hands under my arms and lifted me from the ground. "This is how I raised him up." He swung me up above the edge of the crater's lip. "This is how I set him upon the top of the wall." He deposited me with a thump upon the brink of Kauhako. " 'There,' I said to him, 'if you wish to be the cock of this place, it is better for you to have a roost to crow from.' And I left him there, swearing his head off, knocking the loose rocks down from the wall in his hurry to reach the ground again. While I walked off in the dark, feeling very much pleased with myself."

"Poor Caleb," I laughed. "How it must have hurt his pride. He is so mad at God for having made him small. And he hates people who are taller than he is. Now he will be mean for a week." I put out my arms for Keanu to lift me down. "But you served him right: he was much too sassy to you."

While his arms were still around me, I hugged him. "You did the right thing then, with him. And for this I am glad."

"It is easy to do the right thing, when a man is happy." Then he put me down. "A *hui hou aku*."

"Until we meet again, beloved. Until tonight."

Death is common at Kalawao, and few of us can remain long in fear of it. When it comes, it comes as a grace to most of us, putting an end to our sorrows. Most of the patients are well content to go, when their time comes; and I hope that when it is my turn to die I too shall be of this mind. But when I mounted the steps to Father Damien's church, in the afternoon of Akala's funeral, the fear of death was strong in me. I wished to cling yet awhile to life and to Keanu.

Early in the morning the members of Akala's funeral society bore her body to the House of the Dead. There, from the little stream wandering down from the mountain, they took some of the water of life to wash her with, and they dressed her in the pink frock which was her best dress, and they laid her in one of the plain wooden coffins made by Father Damien. When we gathered in the little church the closed box was in its place before the altar, and the church was full of the friends of Akala and of Miele. Dressed in their black *holokus*, and their black hats, the women sat on the left side. On the right hand sat the men, unnatural in their dark suits, with their white shirts and tight collars holding them as as stiff as were the women in their stays. We sat in respectful silence, in tribute to the presence of God, in awe of the presence of Death. I sat with Tutu and Deborah, the two of us with her almost filling one of the tiny pews. Among the men were Makaio and Moki; and Caleb sat in the front row, with Kumakani, Kekachi, and Tuesday Lokahi, who were chosen with him to carry the coffin to its grave. In vain did I look for Eleu, who was Akala's special friend.

At the right of the church, hanging limp from its crosspiece, rose the orange-and-blue banner of Miele's funeral *hui:* The Comfort in Death Society. High upon the altar a shroud of purple cloth covered an image from our view; and against the front wall, at either side of the altar, other purple sacks hid two more statues. At first I thought the Catholics protected their sacred idols from the gaze of those of us who were not of their church. But then I remembered the purple altar cloths and the purple vestments were brought out at Saint Andrew's Cathedral, too, during Passion Week, and my suspicions of the Catholics were quieted.

Upon the coffin lay a beautiful thick *lei*, woven in the olden style, made of the yellow-green leaves of the *kukui* tree and the thick clusters of its small white flowers. I knew at once that it was the gift of Keanu.

We were not long in our places when the bell of Saint Philomena began its slow tolling. It did not sound like the same bell which rang out so joyously on the morning of our arrival, when Tutu and I met Akala in the hospital bathhouse. Only six months ago, I counted back, and she did not seem very sick then. Would my time be as short? I wondered, feeling my dread flutter within me. Or was there some truth in the charge, that it was Opaekea's meddling which aroused the disease in her from its slumbering?

When the bell ceased its mourning Father Damien came to take his place at the head of the coffin. This was the first time I saw him dressed in his priest's robes. They were black and grim, as befitted a ceremony for the dead. The service I could not understand, it being said in Latin, with much moving about and waving of his hands, much sprinkling with holy water and burning of incense, and with a strange kind of singing from him and from a choir of small boys who joined him when he directed them. They all sang off-key, in a kind of chanting which fell harshly upon my ears. It was not at all like the splendid music we used to hear in the Anglican cathedral in Honolulu, or the loud hymning in the Congregationalists' churches.

Only toward the end of the service did I hear something I could understand: "*Requiem aeternam dona ei, Domine*," the priest sang in his shaky voice, and I knew then that he was asking for Akala the long rest which death is supposed to bring to all of us.

But not yet, O Lord, not yet for me. Permit me, O Father in Heaven, grant me a longer time—

Within the tiny church I forgot Akala, newly dead; I forgot the kind old priest, mumbling his ritual; I forgot all those others of Akala's people and of mine, who were there to conduct her body to its grave while they prayed for the passage of her soul to Heaven. As if I had never known the time of my despair and of my treason to Iehovah, I forgot my outcries against him, my seeking of Kaupea, my desperate running to Kane and to Lono. I thought only of myself and of my love, and of how necessary it was that the God whom I had abandoned should not abandon me in my begging for yet a little while longer with my love.

As I thought of us I saw him. Close by the church he stood, at the window nearest the altar on the side of the men, his noble head bowed while he listened to the service for Akala. My heart leaped within me, exulting: he is here, he is near! But in the next breath there was pain: he is the one shut out, he is the lonely one . . .

"*Kyrie eleison, Christe eleison, Kyrie eleison,*" chanted the priest.

"Lord have mercy, Christ have mercy, Lord have mercy . . ." I slid to the floor, upon my knees, to pray not for the dead but for the living, for the life of Keanu. As I rested my head upon the pew in front of me I saw the round holes bored in the planks of the floor. Like the dark empty eyes of death they stared up at me, cruel reminders of the fate waiting for me.

When the services in the church were ended, the march to the graveyard began. The altar boys, in their lacy cassocks, walked before the priest. One of them led the way, holding a golden cross high above the procession. Only when Eleu went by, eyes downcast, swinging the heavy vessel holding the smoking incense, did I recognize him, performing this last kindness for his friend.

After Father Damien came the four men, bearing the weight of Akala's bier upon their shoulders. And after them walked the rest of us, emerging slowly into the shadowed churchyard. I searched for Keanu, but I could not find him.

"Did you see him?" people were asking. "The Lonely One: he has a kind heart," said others approvingly. Momona tried to jest: "A soft spot in him, he has, a soft spot for Akala." But Tutu glared him down. "I think it was very nice of him to come," she announced, as though her decree would forthwith settle the gossip according to her will. No one heeded her, they were so busy searching for the Lonely One. And no one thought to ask how the Lonely One could know that it was Akala who was being buried.

Excited shouting went up from the boys at the head of the procession. The air was loud with tumult, and the swift thudding of horses' hoofs shook the ground. We looked up to see the golden cross held awry, to see Akala's coffin rearing and swaying, like a boat tossed by waves. The *lei* slid from the coffin into the path, under the trampling feet of the mourners.

"What is happening?" we cried, even as the cause of the disturbance went rushing by: a mob of riders, racing for the meadowland beyond the cemetery. Shouting and whooping, unaware of the funeral procession they were vexing, they dashed past in a cloud of dust and a riot of noise. In the silence they left behind them, the curses and exclamations from the people in the churchyard sounded thin and weak.

"Bad luck for somebody," said Deborah Makanani, licking her thick lips. Even after my rebuff of Caleb I was not recovered from my dislike of her; and her quickness at imagining misfortune even at a funeral annoyed me.

"How cold it has become," I complained to Tutu. Low clouds were moving in from the sea, a cold wind was blowing from the north. Over beyond the edge of the land the whitecaps were thick upon the ocean and the waves sent spray high upon the steep sides of Mokapu and Olala, across the bay.

"A stormy night," said Makaio, lifting his head to smell the wind.

"*Auwe* for Akala," sighed Tutu. "Cold will be the earth in which she lies, dark will be the night."

Shivering, I drew close to her. More than the north wind pierced through the thin stuff of my dress. "I do not want to go to the grave, Tutu. Let us go home."

"It is not proper, child. We must be with Miele, when she needs us."

Makaio nodded in agreement. "It is our duty."

"Then let me go home, I beg you. I do not feel well enough."

He was the first to soften. "Then we will make your excuses. Go home and lie down. You do indeed look tired. There is time to rest before the funeral feast."

"We will come home for you," Tutu promised.

With a parting kiss for each of them, I turned away and hurried home. But I did not rest. Upon the way a thought sent warmth into my blood to chase away the cold. Snatching up a shawl from my room, I hurried into the cookhouse, where lay the food we had prepared for our part of the funeral feast. From the bowls and plates, set in flat dishes of water to keep the hungry ants out of the food, I chose some of the better morsels for Keanu and wrapped them in a clean kerchief. Never did I have the chance to bring him food, and now I wanted to feed him out of my own bounty, to watch him eat things prepared by my own hands.

I hurried to the rock wall at the back of the yard, expecting to find him waiting for me. Surely he must know my thought, surely he will be there.

But there was no sign of him by the wall. It was foolish of me to expect him there, while the light of day was still upon the plain. Yet I was disappointed. Where, then, was he?

I could not go to distant Kauhako, he would know that. The cave, then, the Puka of Pele? Hoping against hope, I hastened to the cave. Even as Akala was being lowered into her grave, I hurried to the hole of Pele, yearning for my lover and for the comfort of his love. So depraved was I, so selfish was my passion.

But there was no sign of him in the cave.

Throwing the food upon the plain, for the birds to peck at, for the dogs and the foraging pigs to devour, I ran home in anger. I did not know which angered me the more: my disappointment in Keanu's thoughtlessness, or my shame at my own wantonness.

The funeral feast was a dismal one, as such things always are, and we of Makaio's household left it as soon as we could. When we came out of Miele's house, the sky was already black with night to the north and to the east. But to the west, upon Oahu, the light still showed in a wide yellow band. The jagged peaks of Oahu stood up like a blue wall raised against the golden curtain of the sunset.

Surprisingly, the wind had died away almost to nothing on the ground, although above us the clouds still swarmed in thick and fast. In the strange clear light we could see every blade of grass, every hummock of rock in our path—and every piece of shadow lying on the earth. "Ahh, this is a lovely ending to a hard day," sighed Tutu, as we were walking home.

It was an evening for sitting quietly upon our *lanai*, for looking at the looming cliffs, their heads lost in the soft mist, itself golden in the light from the west. It was an evening for thinking deep thoughts, and for saying nothing. We were alone, for a change. In peace we sat, the three of us, not needing speech, enjoying the serene time, until the light faded away, and, in the west, too, the darkness began to creep in.

Then did Makaio remember something left undone. "Ah See. Was he there? At Miele's?"

"I did not see him" answered Tutu. "I do not think he has a mind for such things."

"He has gone to others. I will go to see him. Perhaps he is not well."

"But why do you worry about Ah See? Others were not there: Kewalo, Hanu, even your son Moki. Do you go to ask after them?"

Makaio did not bother to answer her. With a shrug of tolerance for her small-mindedness, he went calmly on his way. I called after him, "Invite him to come for tea on this cold night." I did not want this evening to end in other than its usual fashion. My disappointment in Keanu was faded with the day. Now I felt only my need for him.

"You are a good girl. I will do that," the old man said, and I was pleased because I succeeded so easily in my plan.

Straight of back, stiff in the knees, he walked away from us. We watched him until he was gone from our sight, beyond the hedge separating our yard from the yard of Ah See. "*Cha*," said Tutu, "those two old men: how they love each other! I cannot see why," she pouted, stretching her legs before her in a manner Makaio would never approve. In her black silk *holoku*, with its high collar, with her gray hair pulled into a high full crown upon the top of her head, she looked beautiful in the soft light, and young again.

Knowing how she was taken with Makaio since first she saw him, I felt a rush of pity for her. In my concern for myself I had given her little thought of late. But what could I say to comfort her? It could not be denied: Makaio was not interested in her as a wife. Kind and polite to her he was, as to a guest in his house. But there was nothing more to his speech, or to the way he regarded her. A woman can tell these things. "What of Kewalo?" it was in my mind to ask.

Then did we hear the cry from Makaio: like the roar of a bull in frenzy it came across the space from Ah See's house.

Tutu and I stood up in alarm. "Makaio!" I called. "What is the trouble?"

He stumbled through the bushes, staggered toward us as though he were blind. When he was close to us he began to sob. "Dead—dead. Ah See is dead."

When we reached him, taking hold of his hands to guide him, we found them covered with blood. The blood was thick, too, upon his coat, dark and wet upon the black cloth. "Makaio!" shrieked Tutu, drawing back in horror. "This blood: from where does it come?"

Dully he looked from her to me and back again to her. Then her screams, and mine, woke him. He stared at his hands, stained black in the last light of day. "The blood of Ah See is this," he said calmly, "the blood of my friend. Stabbed is he. Here—and here—and here . . ." Slowly he pointed out the places where Ah See's wounds had shed his life. "Who would stab this old man? Who would—" He stopped, aware at last that murder had been done. "The curse of Iehovah upon him!" he cried, lifting his fists in the air. "I will find him, I will find him, this murderer. I swear it, Ah See, I swear it!" In an instant he was quickened into vengeance.

"Hear me, you two. Light lanterns! I go for help." Without another word he went hurrying up the lane, in the direction of Miele's house. Tutu and I, trembling with terror, ran into the house.

"Who would do such a thing? Who could be so cruel?" wailed

Tutu, over and over again, as we stumbled through the dark house
to the place by the back door, where the lanterns were hung.
"Murder—it is murder," she cried, scarcely knowing what she said,
while we fumbled for the matches. I struck the first one and, as it
flared into flame, bringing the weak comfort of its small light into
the darkness, while the ugly word rasped in my mind for the
sixth time, for the seventh time, the thought came to me at last
that my lover might be the one who had done the evil deed.
"Murder," Tutu was crying, and who else did I know of whom
the word was used? And the prediction of Momona came back
to me: "Once the shark has tasted of blood, it yearns to taste of
blood again."

"No, God. No!" I said aloud, dropping the match with horror,
as with it I dropped the terrible accusation.

"What's the matter with you, girl? This is no time for you to
burn yourself. Try again now, try!"

The wick of the first lantern was slow to take fire. The faint
blue flame clinging to its side was feeble, like the spirit of a babe
unwilling to be born, like the breath of a man about to die. A
fluttering flame, say the kahunas: it is a sign of death to come.

"Oh, light up, light up," implored Tutu, horrified as I was by
the omen. Unable to do more than moan, I stared down at the
thing, waiting for it to fulfill its destiny. But still it would not die,
nor would it spring into life.

"Damn you!" she shouted. "Damn you!" Seizing an unlighted
match from the table, she thrust it into the blue fire. "No more
dying, you hear? No more dying!" The heated match burst into
flame, setting the wick to burning. "That's better," she said
grimly, clamping the chimney into place. "That's better. Now let
us light the other one."

We were waiting at the gate in the lane when Makaio came
back with his friends. They came running down to us, the lane
echoing with excited talk and the rush of many feet. They carried
no lanterns, they came in such a hurry from the funeral feast.

"Here, give it to me," cried Caleb, seizing the lantern from my
hand. I did not see who took Tutu's. Left blinded in the darkness, she and I could only feel our way in their wake, supported
by the backs of nameless people whose eyes were accustomed to
the dark. Pushing through the hedge, they guided us to the light
shining out from Ah See's house.

Over the shoulders of people huddled in the doorway, we

looked into the parlor of the murdered man. Behind us other people gathered, to peer over our shoulders.

Ah See lay on his face on the floor, the clotted blood thick and dark upon the woven mat and already crusted upon the blue cloth of his plantation shirt. Kneeling around him were Caleb and Makaio and fat Momona, puffing still from his running, his face glistening with sweat. Leaning over them, holding a lantern in each hand, was Hanu. His head was wrapped in clean rags, as though he wore a Hindu's turban. With the light shining up from below, his mouth open to show his rotten teeth, he looked like a lascar. The lanterns shook as they hung from his hands.

"He's dead. No doubt of it," said Caleb briskly, turning the body on its side. I was glad that Ah See's face was not shown to us. "Stabbed. Three—four—seven times. With a dagger, or a long knife. He put up quite a fight, the old man did." When he took his hands from Ah See's body it did not roll back upon its face.

"*Auwe, auwe.* Terrible, terrible," wheezed Momona, shaking his head until his jowls quivered.

"Terrible, terrible," echoed the crowd outside the door.

"*Auwe!*" came the awful sound from Makaio, as he touched his head to the head of his dead friend. "*Auwe . . .*" came the dreadful wrenching wail of grief, the *kanikau* of mourning. Forgotten was his Christian faith, abandoned was his dignity, as in the presence of death he cried the ancient parting over the friend of his heart: "Dead is my friend, dead the companion of my years. My friend in the time of storm, my friend in the calm. Gone is my friend, alas! Gone is he, and no more will he return . . ."

In the darkness outside, many of the people joined him in the eerie *kanikau.* Others crossed themselves, or clasped hands in prayer. And all of us wept to see such grief.

When his lament was ended, Makaio raised his head. "Who would do such a thing?" he asked, the tears running down his face.

The three men looked from one to the other, not knowing what to say. But I, remembering the evenings on our *lanai*, I looked with a horrible suspicion upon Momona.

"Why should such a thing be done?" asked Makaio.

Caleb shrugged, always the reasoning one. "It's hard to say. Robbery, perhaps. Did he have money? Hate, perhaps. Did he have enemies?"

Once more Momona showed his dislike of the dead Chinaman.

"*Opiuma?*" he asked in his high voice, clearing his throat after he said the word, giving us to feel that it stuck in his throat and that he spat it out only to keep from choking on it. I marveled at his coolness, while he knelt beside the corpse of the man he hated. Oh, what an evil thing he was! If Caleb, or Makaio, or Hanu did not share my suspicion of him, they were deaf as well as blind.

"Perhaps," said Caleb. "This we can find out later. But first we must find the man who did the deed."

"Alas," sobbed Makaio, "who is the murderer among us?"

As lightning flashes through the heavens, so did a shock of awakening flash among them. As a spark touched to a pool of oil sets the oil to flaming, so did those three take fire. I saw it, in the sudden tightening of their jaws, in the quick turn of their heads, in the sharp intake of their breaths. Before it was uttered, I knew what their thought would be.

Seeming to come from on high, as a revelation from heaven falling from the mouth of an angel, the name fell among them, softly, as a leaf drifts down from a tree. "Keanu," it said. And who could tell from whose mouth the name fell?

"Keanu," said one man to his neighbor: Momona to Caleb, Caleb to Makaio, Makaio to Momona, each to the others as he spoke the name to himself.

"Keanu!" they shouted, all three, as they leaped to their feet, sending Hanu staggering aside with the lanterns. Their shadows danced like devils upon the walls.

"The murderer has struck again!" "The shark has bitten again!" Cruel were their faces, eager for their prey. Wide were their mouths, showing their teeth, hungry for Keanu's blood. Narrow were their eyes, as they planned their hunt for him.

"Call the people! Bring torches!" Caleb ordered. "We'll catch the killer tonight—before he kills again."

"Bring a rope," Momona said. "We'll hang him now. We will do what was not done in Honolulu."

"No!" I shouted, pushing past Kumakani into the room. "No!" I faced them. "How can you say it was Keanu?" While they looked at me in surprise I hurried on. "What proof do you have that he was the one?"

Caleb turned upon me in anger. "How do you know it was not Keanu?"

"I am sure that he could not do this thing!"

"Since when do you know that he could not do this thing?" Caleb's mouth was crooked, but his eyes blazed with righteousness.

"Has he not done such a thing already?" came the shrill voice of Momona. "Remember the Japanee?"

And Hanu, dipping one lantern toward the corpse upon the floor, cried, "Remember the knife?"

"No, wait," I begged. "We have said this before. Do not other people carry knives? Do not—" But Caleb interrupted me, sweeping me aside with his arm.

"This woman talks, while the murderer runs away. Let us catch him first. We can ask our questions later."

In desperation I made my charge. "Why should Keanu kill Ah See? A man he did not know? I say that the man who killed Ah See was a man who knew him, who hated him. I say this man is Momona!" Shrieking my suspicion, I pointed at the fat one. "He did it! He did it!"

In their amazement they stood as if they were statues, staring from one to the other while each tried to see Momona as the murderer. Then the fat one laughed, a smooth unshaken laugh. "The girl is crazy. How could I have done this thing? I have been with Miele the whole afternoon. You who were there, too: you saw me."

It was true. Too late did I remember. Realizing my defeat, and my shaming, I put my hands to my face and cried.

"Call the people!" Caleb shouted to the men crowded into the doorway. "We meet in ten minutes—in front of Siloama."

The men scattered. Even before they were in the lane we could hear them shouting. Inside the house there remained only the five of us: I who loved Keanu, and the four men who hated him. I made one more effort to save him.

"Caleb, please," I lifted my hands to him. "Do not do this terrible thing. Send for the police, to find out the truth. Remember the law—"

"The law! 'In this place there is no law!' "

"Where was the law tonight," tittered Momona, "when Ah See was slain?"

"Woman!" roared Makaio. "Take this girl home. She is in our way."

From the doorway Tutu called to me. "Malie, come. Come away from this evil place."

"Go home, Malie," said Caleb roughly, "and keep out of this business. You have no place in it."

Then they left, the four of them, pushing past Tutu at the door. They took the lanterns with them, running across the trampled grass and through the broken hedge into the lane.

In the darkness, in the dead man's parlor, Tutu and I were left alone. I did not fear Ah See or his ghost: they could not hurt me as much as could the living, who ran now, like hunting dogs, in pursuit of my beloved.

Faint with terror, weak with helplessness, I would have sunk to the floor, content to lie in Ah See's blood, willing to add my own to his, if only I might die before my lover did.

Tutu's voice called me back from my despair. "Malie, hurry! Get the priest: run for Kamiano! Only he can stop them now."

27

As I RAN THROUGH THE NIGHT, along the familiar road of the village, I saw the doors open in the little houses, the warm light streaming out of them upon the clusters of people summoned by the messengers. I did not need to hear what they were saying: too well did I know the burden of their talk.

In my mind I heard the voice of Tutu, speeding me on my way. Her wisdom astonished me still, even as it sent me to do her bidding.

"It is Keanu, then, whom you love?" she said, when she drew me from the house of Ah See.

"It is he," I answered, relieved to acknowledge it at last. "But how did you know?" Even in my fear for Keanu I could still be surprised at being discovered in my secret.

"Am I a woman for nothing?" she said bitterly. "Do you think that because I am old I have no eyes, no nose? I knew that you lay with someone, but I did not know with whom. Until tonight."

Passing through the hedge, we came into the lane. She turned us toward the sea, toward the main road. The clouds hid the stars, and the night was dark and cold.

"You knew? And you said nothing?"

"Why should I speak out? You are in need of love. I was happy that you have found it. For me that was enough. With whom, it did not matter." We were clinging to each other while we felt our way along the lane. "The name of the man: I would know it in time. But you and I: we did not know it would come like this—"

"Tutu, I cannot believe that Keanu killed Ah See."

She stopped in the path, and took my hands in hers. "Are you certain of this?"

"I am certain. He is a good man, not an evil one. This I have seen. I know it!"

"I believe you, if he has won your love."

"How can I make them see what I feel?"

"You cannot. They are mad with the scent of blood. They are like dogs, when a pig has been wounded in the hunt. Even Makaio: grief has crazed him."

"And Caleb. How could he be so cruel?"

"That one, ahh. He thinks he is so smart. He does not know that it is envy, not justice, which moves his tongue."

We came at last to the main road. Dimly I could see the rock wall at our side. And my feet felt the slope of the ground where the path led down into the road.

"Envy? For Keanu?"

"Envy of any man he suspects of taking you away from him. Have you not seen how he watches you?"

"Auwe! I thought this was all done with. I have told him so— almost in this very place have I told him 'No.' "

"Is this enough to stop a man? But now, go. You must stop all of them from this wildness. Run to Kamiano, and ask his help. God be with you."

"Thank you, Tutu," I embraced her. "You are the only one here with a heart in you."

She put her arms around me. "A woman must guard her love, and fight for it." Then she pushed me away. "Now run!"

The Church of Siloama was dark, but in the lanes between it and the mountains the glow of torches was lighting up the night. Soon the mob would be there. Thank God I was ahead of them. But where would I find Kamiano? And what if I could not find him? The worry that he might be away from home, attending someone in the sprawling village, brought a sob of protest from me.

Past the low crouching schoolhouse I ran, past the Catholic church, dimly lighted, and down the lane to the priest's house. But the house was dark. Gasping for breath, I took pause to look beyond his house, to the House of the Dead. He was not there. Praying that he would be in his church, I ran again, across the churchyard, to the front of the little building. So long ago, it was, since I entered it, since I bowed my head in prayer. Not for Akala, but for Keanu—

The door to the church was open. Upon the altar, at the feet of the shrouded statue, a few candles burned. A lone figure knelt in one of the pews. It was not the priest.

"Oh," I cried in disappointment. "Where is Father Damien?" In the empty room my question startled the old woman who prayed.

"Shh!" She raised a finger to her lips. "He hears confession now," she whispered, when I slipped into the bench beside her. The stink of a leper's sores was strong upon her, but I did not move away. Beneath the black shawl over her head the cheeks were round and puffed, with swellings of the kind which had filled Akala's face.

"*Mahalo*," I whispered also, "but where?" She pointed to a closet against the wall at the back of the church.

What a sinner he must have been, on his knees before the priest! For what seemed an entire lifetime I waited, before the rings of the curtain rattled on their pole and the confessed sinner slipped out. Hands clasped before him, he tiptoed to the door, knelt in obeisance to the altar, crossed himself. As he backed from the church into the night, he had time to wink at me and to flash a toothful smile.

While I was watching him take his leave, expecting the priest to come out of the closet after him, the old woman left my side and sped to the confessional. The rattling curtain, closing upon her, sounded like Kaupea's prophecy stones, like the rattling of bones.

Only a few minutes did she need before her whispering was done. But in those few minutes I paced the length of the church a dozen times. While I waited I heard the roaring of the mob on its way to the doctor's house. Through the open windows I saw the glare of their torches, lighting up the night with the color of their rage. Even through the holes in the floor the light came in. For a moment they came alive, those holes, like the shining eyes of beasts hunting their prey. Biting my lips to keep from shrieking my fear, I watched them glow, full of evil, before they closed again. Like the light of a lamp dying out . . .

The old woman left the confessional, her hands put out before her to part the heavy curtains. I pushed past her into the black box, calling out as I went. "Kamiano! Please. Come quickly. There is trouble. We need your help." The closet was shallow: I bumped my face upon its inner wall, stubbed my toes against the bench on the floor. I felt as though I were in a coffin, and in terror I pounded my fists upon the wall.

From beside me came his voice. "Who is this?" The smell of tobacco filled the black shroud in which I stood.

"It is Malie. Oh, please, please—where are you?"

"Malie? Yes? Yes? What is it?"

"There is trouble for Keanu. He needs your help."

"I come at once." Strong and confident, his voice calmed me. I will take your burden, it said.

When I pushed my way through the curtain he was waiting for me, his hands outstretched to take mine. He was in his womanish black dress, with the many buttons down its front; and upon his head he wore the small black hat with peaks and valleys in it and the fuzzy pompom at its top. Around his neck hung a narrow purple scarf, embroidered at each end with a cross worked in gold.

He drew me to the nearest pew. "Now tell me, slowly. Now don't be excited."

"Something terrible has happened." I dared not look at the floor. "Ah See, he who is the friend of Makaio: Ah See is killed. Stabbed to death."

"Auwe for poor Ah See. God rest his soul." He crossed himself. "A terrible thing. Who could have done such a thing to a harmless old man?"

"They say it was Keanu who did it."

"Keanu? They blame Keanu for it?" Surprise, unbelief, shock showed themselves in swift succession before he shook his head. "I do not believe Keanu would do such a deed: it is not like him."

"This is my feeling, also." Torn between joy at his faith in Keanu and my eagerness to start him running to Keanu's rescue, I began to weep. "But still they say it was Keanu."

"Who says this?"

"Caleb, Momona, Hanu, Makaio." With each name his frown grew deeper, his face more haggard.

"These are good men. They do not speak lightly, when they speak." His faith in Keanu was slipping away.

"But they have no proof! How can they know it was Keanu's knife? And yet they have called for help, and they have gone to get him, to kill him. Even now they are at the doctor's house—"

"The shouting, a few minutes ago: it was their noise?"

"*Ae.* They are like dogs, hunting—"

"Then we must stop this hunt!" Springing to his feet, freeing my hands, he was on his way. "Even if Keanu is the guilty one, they cannot judge him in anger." There was no uncertainty in him now: fierce as a guardian soldier he was. "Come, let us go after them. One wrong does not permit another."

At the open door of the church he paused to cross himself and to kneel, as did the sinner earlier.

And then there were two of us, running through the dark night to help Keanu.

Dreadful was the scene at the doctor's house, frightening were the sounds coming to our ears. The smoking torches made it seem as if we labored through Hell, and the shouts and jeers of the mob were as the cries of Beelzebub and his demons torturing the souls of the damned.

Upon the *lanai* stood my lover, tall and proud, his head held high, shoulders back, keeping the howling pack at bay. "Thank God! He is still safe," I cried. Now there are three of us to fight for him. But where is the fourth? Where is Opaekea? Why is he not in front of Keanu, defending him?

And then I saw the little *haole.* In the farthest corner of the *lanai,* as far from Keanu and the mob as he could move, the craven little man hid, hugging the post of the porch. His face was a mask of fear.

Roaring like a warrior in battle, Father Damien pushed through the crowd. I followed close after him, until I stood at the front of the people, fallen suddenly silent. He mounted the steps of the *lanai* and turned upon them in anger. "What is this madness?" he cried for all of them to hear.

I did not hear what else he said, I did not see what he did. I saw only Keanu, rejoicing that he was safe, yet knowing he must still be rescued from the hunters. The quick smile he sent me, across the emptiness between us, was like the touch of lips. It brought me peace, and a great stillness, in which only he and I faced each other, as in the womb of Kauhako.

Into Damien's hands I delivered us, and he did not fail us. How he imposed his will upon the mob I do not know, but soon I saw him reach out to take Keanu's hand in his. I shared the trust with which Keanu gave him his hand as he stepped from the doctor's house to the ground. Forth from the house of misery did he descend, and when he took his place beside the priest I felt that he was saved not only from the hunters but also from the *haole*, throwing him like a scapegoat to the mob.

Gone was my fear. Now I knew what I must do. When they left the doctor's house, Keanu and Kamiano, ringed around by torchbearers and guards and retainers, as in olden times the great chiefs were, in their moving from one place to another, I ran before them in the night, an outrunner to prepare the way.

But like jailers, grim and silent all around him, they brought Keanu as a prisoner to the church. The tread of their feet upon the ground, the hissing of their torches, these were the only sounds made under heaven when they delivered Keanu to his jail. They closed in around Father Damien and my lover, pushing them up to the church steps as a wave in the sea will push floating leaves upon a shore.

As Keanu and the priest came up the stairs I stepped forth from the church door. Without a word I went unto my lover, and rested my head upon his breast.

"Malie"—he held me close to him. "It is you, it is you."

"Keanu, my love, my beloved," I whispered up to him. And that there would be no doubt in the minds of any, I kissed him upon the mouth, for all to see.

Then did the fury of the mob rise once more. Like the waves of the stormy sea crashing upon the shore did their surprise and their anger surge upon us, threatening to draw us back, we three, who were the leaves upon the shore.

"*Eia mai!*" they cried. "What is this? What is this cheat?" "Bitch!" "Whore!" they bellowed, and other shouts of rudeness. At the front of the crowd Caleb, too, howled at me the abuse which relieved his pride. It was as Tutu said: he had not given up his hope for me.

And Makaio, the one I most feared to face, he cried: "You have played the whore with this murderer?" Then did I think that perhaps I had chosen to do the wrong thing, in proclaiming my love for Keanu in such a bold way.

Once again Father Damien did not fail me. He was as surprised as any of them, to see me as Keanu's paramour, but he also guessed what I sought to do by the revelation. Turning to the crowd he called upon them to be still. At last they were quieted, even Caleb, looking up at us with a twisted mouth.

"Let us hear them fairly," said Father Damien.

I loosed myself from Keanu's arms to face them. Pride was in me, not shame, when I spoke: "Keanu and I: we are lovers. When he went among the houses of the village, he went to see me."

"*Ae*, this is the truth," said Keanu steadily, his arm about me. "I did not go to steal. Or to kill."

"But steal he did: a flower," someone screeched. "*Haka kau a ka manu*," bawled another. "A perch for birds to light upon." He meant me, a promiscuous woman. Another took up his thought: "And yet many fine birds were denied that perch!" Their lewd laughter made me hope that their violence would give way to good humor, and that in good humor they would let Keanu go.

"Gouger of eyes!" "Bait-eater!" "Woman-stealer!" yelled others, turning their viciousness upon Keanu. "A man who steals food from another man's table," screamed Hanu. "How can such a man be trusted?"

"*Ae, ae,*" they shouted. "Who can trust a shark?"

Their mood was ugly again, and the priest saw the danger. "Enough! *Pau! Lawa!* There is nothing to be gained by this foul talk. We must wait for the policeman, as I have said. Tomorrow will we see things in a better light."

Makaio spoke. "It is best so. Do you lock Keanu up in the church. I will take this—this sinning woman home, and lock her up. Perhaps I will beat her, I do not know. Tomorrow we will speak more of all these things."

"Caleb," said Father Damien sharply, "I put you in charge here. Yours is the burden: let nothing happen to Keanu."

Hard as iron was the voice of Caleb. "I will guard him well."

The priest put his hand upon Keanu's arm. "Keanu, my son. Please go into the church. You will be safe here, in God's House."

Keanu freed me from his embrace. "Until tomorrow," he smiled, in a way to make my heart ache. "Until we meet again."

"Tomorrow will bring us peace," I answered him, trying to smile back.

"This I know: I feel it. A *hui hou aku.*"

He went into the church, looking around him at the unfamiliar place. The candles still burned upon the altar; and slowly, slowly, as if drawn to their light and their unwavering life, Keanu entered into their presence. In all the months of his staying at Kalawao this was the first time he stepped under a roof that was not the one of the doctor's house.

The priest watched him go in. Then quietly, not disturbing the sacred stillness, he closed the door of his church.

"Now is the first time this door is closed," he said to us when it was done. "It is closed by hate. When it is opened again, I hope for one of you to open it—in love."

Their silence doomed his hope, even at its beginning.

"Come," he reached for my hand. "I will take you home."

"There is no need, Father. I will go with Makaio. I do not fear him. And if he beats me, it will be what I deserve."

He shook his head sadly. He was very tired. In the shadows of the torches the lines in his face seemed drawn with soot, they were so deep. "It is not Makaio's hand I fear for you. It is these —these birds, who seek a perch to light upon." He finished his accusation with disgust: disgust for me, I knew, as well as for them, who flitted from perch to perch.

Meekly did I bow my head.

"I will go with you," Father Damien insisted.

Feeling like the woman caught in adultery, I descended the stairs with him.

Caleb turned his back upon me when I reached the level of the ground. "Hanu, Kalia, Iokepa. You stay with me, to guard this place," he shouted. "Three others come back at midnight."

Makaio caught me roughly by the arm, shaking me as a man in anger shakes a naughty child. He said not a word. Nor did I cry out with the pain. I rejoiced in it for Keanu's sake, and for mine: for now I knew that I must be punished for my sinfulness. The hand of Iehovah was laid heavy upon my head once more. But pain I would endure, contempt and disapproval and banishment would I bear, and any penance demanded by God or by men, if by bearing it I could save the life of Keanu.

As on the night of the King's birthday, many torches were around us to light the road, but one by one they fell away, and when we came to our lane only three torches accompanied us.

As we turned into our yard, Makaio gave a great groan. "Kamiano. My friend. Ah See. How can I let him lie there, in his blood?" His voice was strained. It was ready to break into pieces, each piece a sob.

"Shall we go now to care for him?"

"I—I wish to do so."

"And Malia?"

"Let me go with you. I, too, can help." Never had I washed a dead body, never before tonight had I been so close to awful death, but I did not wish to leave Makaio in the time of his sorrow.

His hold upon my arm softened. "Then let it be so."

With our neighbors to light the way, we went once more through the hedge of Ah See's yard and across the flattened grass to his door. In the dark house everything was as we left it: no one had dared to come back to disturb the spirit of the murdered man, haunting his house until he was avenged.

Stepping carefully around the disordered room, we lighted Ah See's lamps, the ones upon the tables, the ones hung from standards on the walls. When the room was bright with their steady glow, the flickering torches were stamped out, and were left smoldering outside in the green grass. Our curious escorts would not leave. They peered through the open doorway, watching to see what we did.

Ah See's body still lay on its side, his face turned toward the floor, as though he slept upon one outflung arm. Around him swirled the clotted blood, in great pools of smooth darkness, like the coils of *pahoehoe* lava issued from Kauhako's belly upon the green fields of Kalaupapa.

Father Damien made the sign of the cross above the body. "Poor man. May his soul rest in peace." Then he knelt beside Ah See.

"*Amene, amene,*" said those of us who knelt with him, in the room and in the doorway.

"*Auwe,*" moaned Makaio. "That he should die in this way."

"He was a good man, I know—even though he was a heathen. Never did I hear of trouble from Ah See."

"*Ae*," said Makaio. "No better friend could a man have than this man. There was no hate in him, only goodness."

"You do right to sorrow for a good man," said Father Damien, trying to end the flow of words from Makaio. But the old man would not stop.

"Even when I did him a wrong—a great wrong—he did not hate me. Even when I stole his wife from him, he did not hate me."

The priest, I, the others—we all looked up in astonishment. Father Damien put up a hand to halt the old man, but still there was no stopping him, just as there was no stanching the flow of Ah See's blood, once the wounds were made.

"Let me tell of it now. Hear me say it at last, in payment to my friend. 'A nest of fragrance is a friend,' and I will not let Ah See go to his grave without this sign of my love for him.

"In the lust of my youth did I take his wife from him. Young were we then, Kenahu and Ah See and I, and clean, living in the village of Hilo. When our lust drove us to lie with each other, while Ah See labored in the fields, Kenahu and I, we laughed at him. But when our lust grew into love, we feared him, and we ran away from him, to Honolulu. There, it was our thought, we would be safe from him. And for a time were we safe, indeed, from his revenge. For seven years were we there, enjoying our stolen life.

"The husband, he did not seek us. But God, he found us. He touched us with the Kalawao sickness, the two of us, almost at the same time—" The tears dropping upon the blue cloth of Ah See's shirt gave it now another dark stain, to add to the seven already there.

"When we arrived in Kalawao, Kenahu and I, who was here to greet us, stepping out from the crowd with the hand of friendship? It was Ah See. Who took us to his house—to this very house—and fed us, and made us to live with him? It was Ah See. In mistrust and fear of him did we spend our days and our nights, thinking that he meant to take his vengeance upon us. In my fear I thought to throw off his hand from us. I plotted to kill him."

"Makaio, no more, no more!" cried Father Damien. "Tell me these things in the confessional. There is the place for them. But not here."

"No, Kamiano, no. Too long have I kept this in my heart. Too long, in my pride, have I hidden this from you, and from the others. Now, over the body of Ah See, will I finish the tale I should have told long ago."

Forced to hear the end of his story, we listened. In spite of me the seed of suspicion grew into an ugly thought. The story of Keanu and his Kamaka was too fresh in my mind for me to have forgotten it.

"Feeling my hate for him, Ah See helped me to build a house for Kenahu and me. Far away from here it was, near to the house where Kewalo lives. When it was done and we were moved into it, my fear was weakened, my hate grew quiet. Each day away from Ah See helped my fear to die a little, and after a long time I thought it was gone forever.

"But all the while I tried to study him, to learn how he could be so good to us, he who was so wronged by us. He would not speak of it, this evil deed of ours. Instead, he would bring us gifts, of meat, of *poi*, of tobacco, when he would come to see us.

" 'How can this *Pake* be so good to us?' asked Kenahu. 'How can this heathen teach us the ways of Jesus?' After a long time we dared to speak of this to him. He laughed, and he said: 'Who is so foolish as to place love of the flesh above love of a friend? Love of the flesh is like a fire. It burns hot for a while, and is then consumed. What is left is ashes. But friendship: it is like the sun in heaven, compared to an ember. It endures, it gives comfort in all seasons. Not until life ends does it end.' "

Choking upon his sobs, Makaio could scarcely speak. Yet he must go on. The story was not yet at its terrible end. "But still were we poisoned with our guilt, still were we unsure of him. Until the time came when Kenahu's sickness began to eat her away from within as well as from the outside. In great pain she was, a pain too great to be borne, and she sank groaning into her bed. Then did Ah See bring her the greatest of his gifts: the opium, which soothed her pain and eased her long dying. For two years, until the day of her death, he brought her the opium, buying it from his countrymen, with his money. To be near him, we moved into the house across the lane, where now I live. This was not long ago." The old man paused for breath, bending low to ease his tired lungs. When he spoke again his voice was so quiet that the words were almost not heard.

"When she died, she died in his arms, not in mine. Saying her thanks to him, not to me." His head was bowed, and the tears flowed down his cheeks, to fall upon the mat, upon the dead man's blood. His hands upon the floor—they were still stained with Ah See's blood.

Loathing for the old man's hypocrisy mingled with my pity for his humbling. Here, indeed, was the first made last; here, indeed, was the great one brought low. "A pillar of the church," Ambrose Hutchinson called him, "the wisest man in the Settlement." And yet this wise man, this good man, was a worse sinner than any of the rest of us. Where was his goodness when he cast upon my lover the blame for the murder of Ah See? I could stand no more of him.

"And yet you killed him," I forced the words between my teeth. "After all his goodness to you, you killed him."

With a cry of dismay Makaio raised his head, searching for me through his false tears. "What is this you say? Auwe!" Struck by my charge, he groped for answers with which to save himself. "Malie. How can you say this thing? I—I did not strike down my friend." He was a good actor. Almost I could believe him.

Hard of mouth, harder of heart, I looked back at him, fighting his craftiness for my lover's sake. "With your own tongue you have said it."

From the people at the door came the cries and the shouts, telling me they believed what I believed.

"I?" the sly old one whined. "But that was for long ago! Not for now." Turning to the priest, he bleated, "Kamiano. Can you believe me, in what I say?"

But there was no help for him from Father Damien. His face gray as cold ashes, his hands clasped tight, the priest's eyes were raised in prayer to Heaven.

Makaio struggled to his knees. "No! No! I did not do it! I swear it, upon the body of my friend, I swear it." He laid his hands upon the dead man, shaking him, as if to waken him from sleep. "Ah See! I did not do it. Tell them I did not do it!"

Even as we watched, Ah See answered his summons. Slowly, slowly, as though he stirred from his sleep, he rolled over on his back, showing us the waxen sunken face, the accusing open eyes, the long yellow teeth bared in a grin from which the lips were already shrinking away, the tip of the tongue caught in the clenched teeth—

As, slowly, he settled upon his back, a long low groan issued from him, causing the skin to crawl on us who watched in horror this response of Ah See to the call of his friend.

"He lives! He lives " screamed someone in the doorway, while others wailed in terror.

"Ah See?" Makaio called, his bloody hands still held out toward his friend. "Ah See?"

But it was the behavior of Father Damien which terrified us even more. With a fierce shout he threw himself at Ah See's head, prying with his hands at the mouth, shut so firmly in its hideous smile. In horror I watched the grim wrestling, trying to keep from shrieking at the sight of the priest forcing the evil spirit of the dead man out of its haunt. Makaio and the others were babbling as if the Devil himself would issue from Ah See's body if Kamiano had his way with it.

As, unbelieving, we watched the weird contest, the priest pushed his fingers between Ah See's slowly opening teeth and pulled something from his mouth. With a cry of triumph he held it up for us to see.

"Thanks be to God! He has heard us! He has given us a sign!"

It was an ear: a ravaged rotten leper's ear, with the blood still wet upon the ragged stump where Ah See's teeth had bitten it from the head of his murderer.

28

AT MIDNIGHT was my lover restored to me: at the end of that day of death was he given back to life and to me.

It was Kewalo who brought him, accompanied by two others who carried lanterns to light their way. The wind was raging again, in wild gusts from the sea, shaking the house of Makaio in their passing. With all the windows shut against the storm, we huddled in silence around a single lamp, waiting for the message from Father Damien. Tutu and Makaio and I, we had no more words to say, we were so spent. But we could not sleep.

Ever since Father Damien left us at the house of Ah See, to

hurry back to his church, we had been waiting. Too wearied to follow him, Makaio and I dragged ourselves home. Briefly we told Tutu of what had happened to Keanu at the doctor's house, of what we discovered in the house of Ah See. And then we sat down to wait, while Tutu brought basins of warm water and washed our hands and faces.

Only once more did we break the long silence. This was when Makaio and I stood at the table in the parlor, about to take our seats near the lamp. My head bowed in penitence, I went to him. "Forgive me. I said a terrible thing. I am ashamed." I put up my hands to my face, to hide my shame. I could not cry, having no more tears.

He put his hands upon mine, to make me look up to him. "Much hurt has been done to all of us today. And I—I am more guilty than all others for what has happened to Keanu. I should have been strong, when the others were weak. I ask you to forgive me." Tutu watched us in wonderment. We had not told her about my crime against Makaio. Never, I knew, would she hear of it from him. And it would be a long time, I felt, before I could bring myself to tell her of it, and of my shaming.

When we had exchanged the kiss of peace Makaio said, "Now we must take up again, all of us, with more love for each other than we have shown this day. And as our wounds are healed, I pray the good God will make us better people than we have been." Turning away from me, he sat down with a sigh in his rocking chair. With fumbling fingers he reached for his reading glasses, for his Bible, lying near the base of the lamp. But he did not read. With his glasses in his hands he sat staring into the past.

And Tutu and I, we sat with him, waiting, each of us with her thoughts.

At last they came, bending against the wind. In the blackness of the night their lanterns brought the light of a new day into our yard. I was at the door to greet them when they reached the *lanai*. I saw only Keanu, his arms opened to receive me, his face happy with smiles. I needed no other message: I clung to him, sobbing with joy. Without a word he lifted me to his breast and carried me into the parlor. After him came Kewalo and the lantern bearers. Then Makaio closed the door upon the violent night.

"He is free," boomed Kewalo. "Kamiano sends him to you." The pleased grin with which he looked down upon me was repeated in the faces of Kumakani and Hinano.

"Thanks be to God," said Makaio.

"*Amene, amene*," cried Tutu. "Come in, come in, sit down and rest awhile."

"Tell us," urged Makaio. "We have been waiting. But first: there is something I must do before you begin." Coming up to Keanu, still holding me close to him, the old man said humbly, "Welcome to this house. Now is it yours, and you must be one of us." Holding out his hand he finished quietly, "Tonight, perhaps, your heart will be hard against us. I hope it will soften in time, and that you will come to feel for us the love which, alas, we did not show to you. I ask you to forgive us."

Keanu gave his hand to Makaio. "The heart is not hard. Only now does it begin to beat, now when it comes home." I was so happy that I could not look upon them, the two men whom I loved.

"Now tell us," said Makaio.

"The ear," began Kewalo, making a dreadful face. "It was Hanu's."

"Is it so!" gasped Makaio.

"Hanu?" I asked, unwilling to believe. "Did he do it?"

"*Ae*, he was the one. The ear: it belonged to him. He ran to hide, when Kamiano came back to the church with the telltale ear. But there are not many patients in the village with covered ears. One by one, we thought of them, and went to see them. But even then we did not think to look for Hanu." Searching around him for a place to spit, he was forced to stop talking. Rolling his eyes, twitching his fierce mustachios, he finally went to the door for his relieving.

Eagerly did Kumakani take up the tale. "It was Eleu who thought at last of Hanu. The rest of us: we were so used to seeing him. But that Eleu—he's a smart lad, I must say—he remembered."

Kewalo returned to take the story away from Kumakani. "And when we found him—*Aia la!* There it was, the head from which the ear was bitten off. We needed to look no more."

"But we made a long search before we could find him," interrupted Kumakani. "Can you guess where he was?"

"How could they know?" said Kewalo impatiently. "They could guess all night, and never think of it."

"For heaven's sake, tell us!" commanded Tutu. "Get on with the story, you jackasses!"

This time Kewalo swallowed his spittle, rather than risk having Kumakani steal the stage from him. "In the Church of Siloama was he hiding. If Keanu was safe in Kamiano's church, he thought, then would he be safe in Hanaloa's."

"*Auwe* for poor Hanu," mourned Makaio.

"But why?" asked Tutu. "Why did he do it."

" 'For money,' he says. 'All *Pakes* have money. I need money.' "

"And did he find any?"

"Nothing—" began Kumakani.

"He found nothing," rumbled Kewalo. "Even in murder he was a fool. While he looked through the house, he said, Ah See came home. 'I did not mean to kill him,' says Hanu, shedding many tears."

Makaio groaned. "Enough, enough."

"What will be done to Hanu?" asked Tutu.

"Hah," said Kewalo. "This is the best part of all. He is much beaten, already, for the trouble he has caused. He will be sore for many days, not only in the place where his ear was. And there will be no more chirping from that crazy *ukulele:* it is broken."

"We did these things to him before we took him to Kamiano," said Hinano gleefully.

"When we got him to the church," Kewalo continued, "some were for hanging him right there, as they were for hanging the—" He broke off, sending an embarrassed glance at Keanu. "But Kamiano would not let them do it, of course. After a while we thought of a better punishment. Even the priest could not tell them no to it."

Enjoying his moment, he made us wait. "We condemn him to live," he said, laughing with hideous delight. " 'To die now is too easy a way out,' we decided. 'Let him live to suffer.' *Kie!* Is there a worse punishment for a leper than this?"

As Kumakani and Hinano joined him in loud laughter, and Tutu chuckled with an evil pleasure to match theirs, I felt Keanu draw away from me, loosen his hold about my waist. I turned to him in questioning. But already he was going away from me, walking unsteadily toward the back door of the house.

When I caught up with him, hardly daring to ask myself why I felt such a terror in my heart, he was fumbling with the latch. His face was pale, his hands were cold, when I tried to pull them away. "No, I must go," he said faintly. "This air—I cannot breathe it—"

He opened the door, and plunged into the dark. He was gone, swallowed up in the furious night.

During the night the storm that raged in my spirit was matched by the Devil-Wind blowing down upon us from the northern seas. Wild as a madwoman, it swept down upon us for the rest of the night. Cold and searing, it was the *Inu-wai*, the water-drinking wind, and it left the land parched, the trees stripped of their leaves, the verdure upon the mountains burned brown by its breath. Great was the havoc. Many houses were blown down, crushed flat by the push of the wind; others were shifted on their foundations. Among these was the house of Makaio. Even as we lay in our beds, too frightened to sleep, listening to the screaming wind and the ghostly clanging of the church bells being taunted by the Devil-Wind we could feel the house being lifted by the gusts and dropped with a thud upon the foundation stones. After an hour of this some of the posts slipped from the stones. Then the house lay tilted, and we in our beds could feel the cant of it as we heard the glass and the chinaware and the lamps crashing to the floor. Mercifully, the position into which the house fell kept it from rolling over and being blown like a hollow box before the wind, and after this the storm paid little attention to us, finding other victims for its anger.

Among these were the Church of Siloama, which also was blown from its foundations, and the Church of New Canaan, in Kalaupapa: there the belfry was blown down, and the great bell, the voice of its church, was rolled by the wind over the edge of the land into the deep water off the shore. At the Church of Saint Philomena all of the windows facing the ocean were shattered.

By morning, when the sun rose bright over a stormy sea, the Devil-Wind ended its punishing of us and went away. Slowly, in fear and trembling, we crawled out of our homes. We did not dare to ask how many people were killed in the crushed houses, how many were wounded by the falling trees, the flying boards. When we looked about us at the signs of his passage, we could guess that Death was even more greedy during the night than he was during the day before.

Some, like Momona, remembered the prophecy of Kaupea. They smiled to themselves, saying: "Lo, this is the might of Kane, foretelling the pushing of the *haoles* from out of the land." Or, "Just as the bell of Kanaana Hou has been rolled into the sea, so will the *haoles* be rolled away. Then will the land be ours again, from Hawaii to Niihau."

I did not listen to their talk. It was Keanu only for whom I listened, Keanu only for whom my eyes searched. Hollow with misery, I stood with the others outside of our leaning house, searching the road for sight of him, searching the lane for as far as I could see. But there was no sign of him upon the harried land.

Sick with wondering, I turned to view with the others the enormous waves rolling in upon the shore from the angry sea. As I watched them crashing against the ocean cliffs, sending their spray high into the air, the answer to my question came to me.

He was gone, gone from me into the sea.

III. CALEB

29

Raging at heaven and at Hell, and at all Earth between, I stood by the rail of the *Mokolii*, seeing gray Molokai lying in wait for me in the sea, lying in wait like Death.

The Island of the Dead—an immense corpse, floating in the sea, as Ulukou floats, shrouded in water, as he is. It is worse than I thought it could ever be—

Like a dying distrustful dog I bared my teeth. Wanting to cry out in fury, to howl my helplessness into the face of Heaven, I stood silent, bent-backed and dog-tailed, pretending that I peered over the water to *Molokai Ahina* and but showed my teeth in a careless smile. No one who looked at me could have known how I was filled with hate. Hate for life, which had betrayed me; hate for people, who had banished me; hate for myself, who had earned for me my passport to this hell. Far more than with fear of death was I filled with hate.

Hate for myself—this was the worst. When you discovered life's treachery, why did you survive the day? Remember that lazy lovely morning, when you thought the world so fair, and already it had played you false? Why did you not kill yourself then? Many a scathed maid has killed herself for less of an outrage than you have suffered. You coward! Why didn't you do it then? Why do you live now, when like the trash you are, you are being thrown away, unclean and forsworn?

I listened to my spirit, raging at my body, until I could endure the goading no more. In a passion of loathing I decided to end the ordeal as I ended my life. Ulukou of Hana showed me the way, when he dived into the water. But I could not follow him into the cold sea.

Subtly, lest the others see my intention and make some move to prevent me, I drew the little package of poison from the pocket of my waistcoat. Hurriedly, before they could stop me, I lifted it to my mouth, tearing the paper with my teeth to get at the bitter white powder. No one saw what I did. Added now to my despair was this further proof that no one cared what happened to me. With perverse joy I felt the thick dry powder stick to my tongue, cleave to the roof of my mouth. I swallowed it, flake by flake, searching the last ones out with my greedy tongue in the corners of my mouth, where the helpful spittle aided me to make my escape. Smugly I congratulated myself on my foresight. Scornfully I looked at my fellow passengers, certain that not one of them had had the courage to approach the druggist in Honolulu as I did. They would cling to life until the last putrid gasp was torn from them. But I would not: I was done with it.

That damned *haole* druggist! He cheated me. In exchange for my American five-dollar gold piece he gave me five cents' worth of an emetic, not the poison I asked for. The shrewd mercenary son of a bitch! But what else could I have expected from a Yankee? He was clever enough to know why I wanted the little packet. And he knew very well that I would never be able to come back to accuse him of his fraud.

"I need it to kill rats with," I mumbled to him in the stillness of his empty shop. And how often has he heard this excuse from other lepers seeking this boon of him?

"Ah, yes," he nodded. "Then you will need flowers of arsenic. Rats are such a problem, these days." With a great show of precision he prepared the packet, warning me to be "very careful with this: it is very *poisonous*, and a little bit of it will take you a long way." I can see his smirk now, wrinkling the lean face. Fool that I was, I smiled back, thinking he shared a double meaning with me rather than a double-cross. The crooked snaggle-toothed bastard! For me he is the model of Jehovah the Cheater, weighing out poisons and pestilences in the pans of his scales, while trusting men and hopeful women render unto him the coins of their faith.

He was very careful not to touch me while I stood humble before the counter, while he ushered me toward the door. "*Ka kou wa le no,*" he muttered as he let me out into the street, keep it between ourselves. But the color of my gold was too much for him to resist, and he did not refuse to accept that, sullied as it might be by my diseased hands. More cunning than I credited him with being, he made me put the coin upon the edge of the counter. It lay there all during our transaction, a tarnished accessory to our complicity in crime, while each of us pretended to ignore it. When I was put out into the night he hastened to it as a homing canoe rides the wave to shore. I saw him: enjoying my chance to sneer at *haole* avarice, I watched him through the dirty glass of the shop window, beyond the hanging globes of colored fluids, the litter of crocks and vials, which were his advertisement. Deftly he scooped up the gold piece with a sheet of foolscap, crumpled the paper around it. He held the wad over the chimney of the lamp, until the paper caught fire. As it blazed up he tossed the ball of fire into a metal dish, leaning over it carefully until the flames died out. When I turned away from the window he was scrabbling through the ashes, looking for the gold.

Well, I have my comfort: he is a slave to money, as I am a slave to despair. Yet I cannot forgive his cheating me. I hope he burned his scalled fingers on the hot coin. I hope he catches the Kalawao sickness. Nothing would please me more than to meet him here at Kalawao, and to extend my festering fingerless hand to him in a frangible greeting, to encircle him in my graveolent embrace . . .

Yet he who believed in germs, that learned honorable chemist who did not want them for himself, he was not willing to help me cheat them out of their nibbling victory over me. By cheating me out of a quick death, he did me the unkindest service of all: in giving me life, he robbed me of my self-respect. For when I had swallowed his acrid powder, and I was quite assured that there was nothing more to be done but to wait for a quick if painful death, how did my bitter scorning haughty self react to the imminence of death?

It hurts me to confess that in this crisis I was no different from other men. I discovered that I did not loathe myself quite as much as I thought I did, and that I did not want to die quite as soon as I had arranged to die. I am embarrassed even now to remember how *commonplace* was my revulsion, how swiftly second thoughts and counterarguments began to sober me. Have I acted in haste? I wondered, as I waited for the pains to begin. And shall I repent at leisure? I inquired, only to have to growl: What leisure? at my quailing dying self. The alternation of arguments in my remorseful self was a marvel of impassioned inconsistencies piled upon irremediable fact; and quickly I came to regret my haste as, in the same breath, I also vowed that I'd rather die than admit my regret to anyone.

Wanting to put off death, I saw again the good things in life. And only then did I permit myself to remember that if today the clouds were heavy upon Molokai, certainly the sun would shine upon it in some other day. From a shut-off cavern of my memory came the sound of lepers, singing and laughing and having a carefree time, even among the horrors of the lazar house at Kakaako: "We going have wan good time, *e*, wen we get to Kalawao. Plenny food, plenny time for play—an' *no work!* Jus' like in Heaven, yeh?" When it was too late, their jaunty philosophy appealed to me, making them sound like wise ones, making Ulukou and me seem like fools. Here was another lesson for a proud man; but I was reluctant to accept it, as I waited for the poison to bite at my belly, to eat its way in fire and agony into my bowels.

It is characteristic of me that I vented my rage not upon myself but upon every one around me.

I snarled at poor stupid Malie, shocked at finding me there with her. "Kalepa," she called out, pronouncing the nickname I liked to hear in happier times but could no longer abide when it took on a newer and ghastlier meaning. Her witlessness stirred me to a storm of irritation, when I should have been kind to her, forlorn and frightened as she was. Her hand-wringing infuriated me even more, when she sensed her error, and I took out upon her innocence the rancor I have nursed for so long against my adversary, the Queen. "Majesty and trash," I jeered, "riding in the same boat." I judged myself more damningly than ever the Queen did, when I spewed those words upon hapless Malie.

I flung Damien's hand away when, on the dismal beach, he came up to welcome me, and to brush the sea wrack from my clothes. I wanted no truck with a priest, when I was about to die as arrogantly as I had lived, and as priestless. A cheat, a hypocrite, he was, I was convinced, as I was convinced all men of the cloth must be, by definition. Who can trust them? I demanded to know, when no trust can be placed in their cheating malevolent God. *Quod erat demonstrandum.*

I shouted at the inoffensive *haole* doctor, bawling at him to do something for the exhausted old woman who staggered with Malie across the rocky beach. "You are a doctor, aren't you?" I yelped, knowing very well how the priest and the girl were doing all that needed to be done to help old Tutu, and yet wanting terribly to bring some of my unhappiness down upon him, who sat so aloof and so white and so *clean* upon his rock, apart from us who were lepers.

I hated the sight of the lepers, reminders of myself, and yet continuing to live, in spite of their disease.

Above all, I hated Keanu: long of limb, broad of shoulder, virile as a stud-slave, the picture of health—Damn him! What the hell is he doing here? I wanted to know, all of my ancient dislike of him exhumed in a stink of meanness. A brute, a country lout, a boar to run after the sows, I had called him, when I saw him in Honolulu; and nothing about him, when I saw him on the beach of Kalawao, led me to change my opinion of him. The only thing we had in common was murder: he had killed a man, I was killing myself. Here is justice for you, I reminded my sage juridical self: he, the murderer of another man, will pay no penalty for his crime; while you, the innocent victim of a foul disease, you must die by your own hand.

Full of love for myself, I hated them all as my nausea began, as the sick sweat broke out upon my brow and the green swirls of vomit began to churn in my belly. And I loathed myself, as it came my turn to die, for not having the courage to die willingly. I was dying regretfully, lingering over my departure as a guest does who does not want to go home from a party. But the time was close when I must go, whether I wanted to go or not; and I was proud enough still to want to be left alone when the time did come. Half blinded with tears of mourning for my moribund self, I slipped from the rock on which I sat, and I lay me down to die in its cold shadow.

I was confounded when Ioane Paele and Hamau came to me among the wet stones. "Come, brother," they said softly. "We will help you." Together, one at either side, they lifted me up and set me on my feet. The beauty of their words made me weep: to discover brotherhood so late, from men I did not know . . .

"No. Let me lie, let me lie. I—I am finished." I did not shout at them.

"It is not far. Lean on us." Supporting me, encouraging me with country expressions, they helped me up the steep path leading from the beach to the land of Kalawao.

At the top of the trail the druggist's medicine made its exaction of me. Moaning, I fell to my knees. My companions let me go. Like a sick dog I crawled away into the bushes, vomiting as I went, waiting for the darkness of death to close in upon me.

The druggist's cheat was not very strong: even with this he was a niggard. I was not sick for long. *Ea!* Perhaps I do him an injustice: perhaps he did not cheat me. Perhaps he knew me better than I knew myself, and, foreseeing my regret, gave me back my life to use again. The thought did not occur to me then, but it has come to trouble me many a time since that dismal day.

Patiently my companions waited for me, sitting in the shade of the trees, until I was emptied of the packet's poison and of the poison of my disdain for life. Until I was reborn. When I was done, I knew that I was glad I had been saved from death by arsenic, even if I must yet suffer the long dying of a leper. I shall not try this road again, I promised myself, when my new friends helped me to rise and go with them the rest of the way upon the old road.

Once again the knowing druggist proved more friend to me than foe. Thanks to him, I was too sick to see the horror of the multitudes who greeted us, too weak to hear the dreadful sentimentality of their singing, as we walked among them into the charnel house of Kalawao.

This futile attempt at running away is for me the symbol and allegory of my life. Impetuous action followed by crawling failure, boldness succeeded by weakness; liking succumbing to hate, hate melting into the semblance of love: this is the pattern of my life, an alternation of antipodes. In my better moments I wonder if this is not the portrait of any man as, like an inchworm, he thrusts and falls and crawls his blind way in the progress of his life. On other days, when I am more savage with myself, I think that it must be the portrait of my singular self: the hopeful seeker, aping the happy in search of happiness, hobbling after the faithful in quest of faith.

Only gradually have I discovered this pattern, I must submit in my defense. And only reluctantly have I discovered that I must be something ridiculous not only to myself but also to the people who know me. There was a time when I could sneer at those others and not give a damn about what they thought of me, the while, of course, I thought myself entitled to laugh at them unmercifully. I had no humor, then, about my sacrosanct self, and I could not have joined them in their ridicule of me.

That was the time when I could not laugh, that was when I consorted with Caliban, and from him learned how to curse.

30

MALIE TAUGHT ME how ridiculous I could be.

I never dreamed, when we were in Honolulu, how one day I should want to marry her. She was so young, so virginal, so simple and so dull; and at first I could scarcely bear the sight of her. She was a product typical of the missionaries, with their catch phrases stuffed into her for thoughts, and their horror of any of the enjoyments of life well worked into her flesh. When she spoke, the goodness of preachers fairly oozed from her; when she walked, even in the halls of the King's crowded palace, she walked as preachers' daughters do, fearfully and skittishly, certain in their preoccupied souls that every man exists solely to offer them the threat of rape. I was amazed to find her in such a frivolous setting, until I learned from personal experience how inviolable she was, armed by her insuperable innocence and guarded by the eye of that old beldame, the virago Queen.

But Malie was safe from me: she was not to my taste. I preferred the company of bolder women, more forward in their converse, more free in their giving; and in the days of my health and handsomeness I did not lack for their company. "A woman is like an easily opened calabash," as we say, and I had my pick of them, much as a man has his choice of watermelons in a market stall. Such companionable women are numbered among the charms of Honolulu by all males who are not smothered in the churches' cloth.

Yet I could not escape the attentions of Malie. For some reason she conceived a great liking for me, and I could not go to a ball at the palace or to an occasion at one of the other great houses in town without finding her at my side before the evening was far

advanced. After the first such exposure to her and to her appalling naïveté I vowed that thereafter I would avoid her at sight.

But how can one be deliberately cruel to anything so young
as she was, and so unprotected by the armor of experience? To
turn away from her was like kicking a friendly kitten. This was
how I argued with myself as, decked with false smiles and assumed
charm, I braced myself when I saw her moving toward me from
the corners where she lurked. I could not turn my back upon the
timid smile, nor harden myself to the thought that she would be
hurt if I did not speak with her. Such an excellent cynic I was, such
a model for the hard of heart. So gradually, unavoidably, I was
drawn into the trap of her trust; and before I knew what was
happening Malie was considering us to be the greatest of friends.

"Oh, Caleb," she would laugh, "you are so clever! You say the
most awful things!" But, because she laughed as a woman should,
with delight at my frankness, and did not squeal or giggle like the
usual trial of a girl, I began to see some possibilities of spirit in her
and, after a time, I did not dread to meet her.

Besides, let me come out with it, she had one attribute to which
a man is always susceptible: she was beautiful, beautiful beyond
denying, worthy to be a princess in the court of a king. Young as
she was—she could not have been more than seventeen when I
met her, very soon after she came to Court—she had the freshness
of youth in her skin, in the luster of the dark hair piled in its soft
masses above her brow, in the slimness of her body, no heavier
than the rustle of satin and the scent of a flower in my arms, as we
danced beneath the dazzling chandeliers. The "Presbyterian dancing," as I called the virtuous calisthenics she had been required
to perform at school (shocking her as I did so, of course), had not
robbed her of her natural grace; and she and I made a fine pair
when I allowed her to dance with me in the glittering ballrooms of
Honolulu. She was lovely, even I could see, forced against my will
by her beautiful body to overlook the childishness of her mind.
And what man can resist the flattery of the attention paid to him
by a young and beautiful woman?

She did not need to speak: I could provide the talk, and I did,
filling the emptinesses of her intellect and of our conversations
with chatter about any subject I felt like sharpening my tongue
upon. All she needed to do was to observe me with those calm
heavy-lidded eyes, to curl those full lips in an encouraging smile,

and I was sent into prodigies of witty wordplay and shameless showing off. Only when she spoke was I disenchanted: "Oh, Caleb! You say the most terrible things . . ." Then I would groan, inwardly, of course, being a polite young cynic; and I would wonder how the hell I had got involved with such a stick as this Malie is.

I was sustained by malice. I teased Malie, I danced with her, I deluded her, more to annoy the watchdog Queen than to please Malie or myself. Her proud Majesty did not like me, and of this I was well aware. It was easy to understand why: I am an upstart, of tainted birth, the latest bastard in a long line of bastards in a family noted for its irresponsibility toward its blood as well as its possessions. How could the Queen, the most noble *alii* in the land, how could she approve of me, a man who does not know who his father was? A man who had nothing of his own, except his body and his hungry, ambitious mind?

She would not have known, nor would she have cared, that we had nothing but our bodies and our wits to make our way with, at home in Napoopoo, where I came from.

Not even a bright wit and the sleek supple body of a youth lengthening into a man were enough for me, nor was Napoopoo, by the time I reached my fifteenth year.

My great-great-grandfather, they say, was the by-blow of one of Captain Cook's men, a sailor with red hair and green eyes, who, before he sailed carelessly away, presented my remote ancestress with the makings of a son who bore his colors and his capacity for dalliance into succeeding generations of our lusty family.

No other souvenirs than our green-eyed selves marked Sailor Forrest's sojourn in our land. But across the bay of Kealakekua from Napoopoo, at Kaawaloa, near the spot where Captain Cook was killed, the white shaft of his monument rose above the dark deep waters, like a missionary's reproving finger. It was Beretania's chaste memorial to her fallen explorer, and, I suppose, a reminder to us of our native ancestors' lack of hospitality. But three fourths of us who lived and played in the little world of Kealakekua held British blood in our veins, infused into our ancestors at one and the same febrile fertile Lupercal; and we knew no history of the Englishmen's visit that was chaste: to us the gleaming shaft was not so much a reminder of Hawaiian savagery and of death as it was an erection to British venery and to life. We children called it *ka ule o Kuke,* delighting in the concrete obscenity; and in our laughter we paid our tribute to those ancestral lusts which were so much the same as the ones we were discovering among our explorative selves.

A true son of my forebears, I was in a fair way to starting a few bastards of my own throughout Kona when, at the age of fifteen, I was plucked from the amiable pleasures of Napoopoo and was sent away to make my fortune. It was high time, for I was the last of my line.

My mother was carried off in the epidemic of '59, when uncounted thousands of the people of Hawaii Nei died of the scarlet fever. Perhaps it was her sinning which made her weak, perhaps it was the shock of my uninvited arrival which made her wish to die. In any event she slept the long sleep of Niolopua when I was six weeks old, and when she herself was not much older than a girl needs to be in order to bear a child. I never knew who my father was, if only because his name was never mentioned in the home of my grandparents, in whose care I was left. It might have been because they, too, did not know who he was; but it was just as likely that they thought him unimportant, once he had served his generative purpose and gone on his way. Whoever he was, he bothered himself as little about me as I did about him. We did not need his name, when we had a usable one of our own. They wrote me down as Caleb Forrest in the family Bible, and let our history explain away my lack of a father.

"Go see the Princess Ruth, at Kailua. She will help you," my grandmother said to me on the quiet morning when the decision was made. Her wrinkled face, marked with a lifetime's worry, was soft with grief. In his broken chair my grandfather sat stiff and wordless, the gnarled hands resting on his thighs, his faded eyes gazing out upon the somnolent bay. He was not so much withdrawn from the family council as holding back his display of sorrow. Their house would be empty when I was gone, their wellspring would be dried up: I was the last gourd to hold the water of life issued from their loins. Yet neither of them spoke a word to hold me back.

Nor did I say it, for I was ready to go: I was bored with the smallness of Napoopoo. With the cruelty of the young I was eager to make my escape, not only from my grandparents and their poverty but also from the impoverishment of the entire village. It was dying, with nothing to live for, and the minds of its people were dying, faster than their bodies were. In the whole district, for miles around, there was not a person who could tell me of the world beyond, who read a book for pleasure. Although I did not know it, my mind was hungering for knowledge and my soul was thirsting for change. I accepted the decision without doubt or worry. The same morning I left, my legacy from my *kupuna* a parting kiss from each of them upon my cheek. When I bade them good-by I expected to return, someday, when my fortune was made. But I did not see them again. Somehow, I never got around to remembering them in time.

Barefoot, for in Kona no one my age owned shoes, wearing the same tattered clothes in which I played and went to school, I walked the few miles into Kailua. I chose the cool mountain road along the shoulder of Hualalai, rather than the hot trail along the shore, because I was tired of the sea.

Knowing nothing of manners, I did not present myself as a petitioner at the door of Hulihee Palace when I reached it late in the afternoon. I simply walked into the great house, the most magnificent structure on the whole island of Hawaii. When I saw it, rearing its high *haole* head two whole stories above the dusty street, with its alien gables and mullioned windows and the carved woodwork of its eaves, I thought it must be the most splendid house in the whole world. What else would be proper as home for the Royal Governess of Hawaii?

When I stepped through the open doorway into the entrance hall, there was no sign of anyone in the vast rooms. Beyond the hall in which I stood, dwarfed by the furniture of giants, I could hear the waves of the familiar sea falling upon the beach. Through the high windows and the farther doors I could see the coconut palms leaning over the water and, beyond them, the blue ocean itself, a furrowed plain stretching to the very rim of the world. The sea, the palms: these were the only things I knew, in the realm of the *alii* into which I entered.

For the first time I began to question if I could make my way in the great world, with my confidence in myself my only protection and my hunger for new knowledge my only spur. The enormity of my brashness I was not to realize until much later, but the smallness of my self in that awesome setting was immediately apparent. In the high-ceilinged hall—with the great staircase leading to some remote heaven above me, with the gorgeous feather *kahilis* of rank towering above me, with the immense tables and massive chairs, the soft, colored rugs upon the floor, the expanses of gilt mirrors upon the walls—I stood in wonderment in the splendid room, overwhelmed by it, and feeling the first waves of uncertainty beginning to wash over me. How did I dare to enter here?

"*E,* boy! What you doing here?"

Swift as a cat, I turned to face my challenger. He was an old man, standing in the entrance to one of the adjoining rooms. A huge silver tray, laden with a silver tea service, scented with fresh bread and rich sweet jam, rested upon his hands and against his lean belly. I had no idea what the display of treasure meant—at home we drank water out of coconut shells, and we could never have so much as seen such a thing as a silver teapot—and the glitter of the tray both dazzled and baffled me. In search of explanation I looked up from the burden to the bearer.

He was just as puzzled by me, as he might well have been: dusty and sweaty, with my long black hair uncombed about my ears, and the wary suspicion of a half-tamed animal in my every motion, I was hardly the sort of visitor to make a footman comfortable. Yet the puzzlement did not drive from his countenance the signs of a natural kindness. He was just another gray-haired grandfather to talk with, and I lost my instinct's fear of him.

"I come to see the *Kalani* Keelikolani," I answered him in Hawaiian, because I had little acquaintance with English. The *haoles*' tongue was not taught in the Common School at Napoopoo, although I, like most country Hawaiians, owned a smattering of the "missionaries' gabble." They were everywhere, those humorless folk, with their prying eyes and their praying mouths; and they left their strange words behind them wherever they went, as birds leave their droppings.

"*Auwe nohoi e!* And do you think you can just come in to her house, then, to see the *Kalani?* As if she were any old *tutu* in any little fishing village along the coast?"

This is exactly how I did think of her, and the old man's skill at reading my thoughts both amused and instructed me.

"Is there another way?" The question was made to reveal my innocence, but it was also intended to appeal to his sympathy for an ignorant country lad.

Coming into the hall, he placed the heavy tray upon one of the shining tables. "*Ae, there* is another way. There are many other ways than the one you choose. You have chosen the wrong way. The best way," he paused to chase off a perceptive fly, "is to come here in the morning time, and to ask for a minute to see her, when she is not too busy."

"In the morning!" The food on the tray reminded me how hungry I was. My hunger reminded me how poor I was. "And what am I to do until then?"

"Go home." He waved me away, as he had chased away the fly.

"To Napoopoo? To Kealakekua? Only to come back in the morning?"

"You come from Kealakekua?" To him Kealakekua was a place hidden away in the smallest corner of earth. No one ever came from Kealakekua: to him, and to most of the nation, it was a place of the dead, remembered with shiverings because of the First *Haole*, who had died there, and whose bones were thrown into the bay to rot. It was his curse upon the place, the people said, which made it die after him.

"It is so: I have been walking all this hot day."

"You walked?" The city man's horror of exercise showed in his open mouth, his wide-opened eyes.

From above our heads came the sound of heavy footsteps, of doors opening and closing. The floorboards creaked and groaned, the house trembled. I looked up to the ceiling, wondering what ambulant gods made such a great house quake.

"*Auwe, auwe!* She comes! Run, now, boy, run! Come back tomorrow." Grasping the curved handles of the tray, he struggled to lift it.

But I refused to be so easily shut out. I was not going to wait for tomorrow, when today would do as well. I did not dash out through the open front door. Instead I took a position at the foot of the stairs, where she could not help but see me. By the time he lifted the tray and turned to discover me in my new place, it was too late for either of us. "Gonfoun' it, boy!" he muttered through his teeth, thinking perhaps to make me vanish with his exotic curse. But already she had begun her heavy progress down the stairs. While he groaned at my rashness, she came into view on the landing, where the stairway made its turn toward the hall.

Slowly, massively, like a flowing of lava, she came down the stairs, one step at a time. She was the most enormous woman, the most ugly person, I had ever seen. Tall in stature, broad of body, she looked like a man in woman's dress. But beneath the black silk *holoku* an old woman's heavy breasts hung to her thick waist; and the dry gray hair of an old woman hung about the hulking shoulders. One plump hand pressing upon the balustrade helped her to make each labored step. Beneath the outspread hem of the skirt her swollen bare feet felt their way from tread to carpeted tread. All this I noticed in the moment before my astonished gaze was caught up and held captive by the imperious strength with which she looked down upon me.

From far away came the old man's warning: "Bow, boy, *bow!*" But I was held immobile by my awe of the great woman: I could not bow, I could not run, I could not think. Slim as a reed, I held my place at the foot of the stairs, rooted to the floor, a blade of grass confronting a mountain that walked.

She stopped on the lowest step, looming above me as the cliff looms above the bay at Kealakekua. Even at rest her face showed the cruelty of generations of tyrants: she was the last of the proud Kamehamehas, and she could not forget it. In the bloated visage her flattened broken nose pushed the thick lips into a pout. Her eyes were dull, disinterested. They did not see me as a person: I was no more than an ant in her path to be crushed, a blade of grass to be trampled upon.

Behind her, like ghosts upon the staircase, three elderly attendants hovered, each of them wearing a *holoku* made of the same soft gray muslin.

"What is this boy?" The voice was as indifferent as her inspection was.

The footman ran forward, bending low. The tea tray was abandoned. "A country boy, Your Highness," he whined. "He came in while I was in the pantry, fixing the—"

"What does he want?"

"He says, to speak with Your—"

"Tell him to come back tomorrow, when the others come." She lifted her heavy arm to wave me aside. A bracelet made from a boar's curved tusk slipped along the black sleeve, clicking against buttons of yellowed bone. It was an ill-omened sound: the chatter of dead men's teeth gnawing upon each others' jaws.

The hardness of her heart aroused me: tight and small it was, like the buttons of bone. Heedless of her rank, I thought only of my pride. "No! I will not come back. If I do not see you now, I will not crawl before you tomorrow, like a slave." Between us the cringing old man moaned at my churlishness; beyond her the shadows upon the staircase bit their lips in dismay, rolled their eyes in warnings sent too late.

For the first time she looked at me, seeing me as a person should be seen, as an individual in himself, with features of his own, with a pride of his own. There was almost the suggestion of a grudging smile upon the thick lips. "This country boy: he has spirit. Well, boy, what is it you want of me?"

"The help a great chief owes a loyal retainer." These were the words my grandfather told me to say, when she would put the question to me.

"Then you are no different from all the others: this is the claim they all make upon me, because I am rich. Help from me they want. But which one of them thinks to bring help to me? Go away, boy. Come back tomorrow. Now is my time to be alone." Once more she waved me aside. The smile was dead, before it could be born.

"No." This time I did not shout. "If I go now, I do not come back." I was as cold and disciplined as she was. I had divined her weakness: she was a bully, conscious of her power. With the sure reason of the intellect I knew that her haughtiness would yield only in respect to a superior force. I commanded only one force superior to her own. At my age I had hardly begun to use it, but in the moment I knew that mine was a far better mind than her own. I determined to test it on her.

"Great chiefs are born to their great estate: their strength is not denied. But commoners must make their way by the work of their bodies, or by the work of their minds." Listening to me, in spite of herself, she did not stop me. "A good chief helps a worthy commoner to rise. A righteous chief knows how in this way the life of the land is preserved."

The life of the land is established in righteousness: every school-boy in Hawaii Nei knows this pious motto. It is the utterance of her kinsman, the third Kamehameha, and she could not deny it without denying the burdens of her lineage.

"You spill words like a talking chief. Many words, but no meaning." She pointed an indolent little finger at me, the most disdainful insult in her armory. "Waste no more of them. What is it that you wish from me?"

"I wish to be a man who rises high. It is my thought that I can rise higher with your help than without it."

I had guessed aright: a snort of amusement escaped from her.

"This is not a commoner's speech. Nor does it issue from a common mind. Tell me, boy: have I not seen you before this day? There is something about you which tells me this is not the first time I have looked upon you."

"No, we two have not looked upon each other before this time."

"How can I trust you, who use words so glibly? Tell me, little rooster, what is your name?"

"It is Caleb. Caleb Forrest. From Keala—"

A shout of laughter, a bellow of delight, drowned me out. "Of course! I should have known it! Your hair: it is not that *ehu* red. But those eyes: *aia la!* How could I forget them? A pair like them was close to me once, very close." Over her shoulder she spoke to the wraiths: " 'The Forrests of Kealakekua: they are easily felled.' Remember?"

A chorus of giggles and titters assured us how well they remembered my family's one distinction.

How much difference a smile made in her! It was possible to forget her ugliness. "Tell me. The one who was named Eben: Would he be your father?"

"No, ma'am." I could permit myself, now, to be polite. "He would be my grandfather."

"*Auwe, auwe.* Was it so long ago?" A flash of pain, of regret over lost youth and forgotten lovers, made her sorrowful again. "He was a handsome man. A fine man. I was quite in love with him once."

"This he did not tell to me."

"Then do you follow in his way, and keep your secrets just as well, when your time for talking comes."

"I shall remember your words," I began soberly enough. "As well as my memories," I finished with a grin.

I knew what she was thinking, with her speculative eye upon me. With as ingenuous a countenance as I could manage, I took another risk. "The cockerel can chase the hens just as well as the old rooster could."

A shriek of laughter from Her Highness set them all to cackling, even old Paliku, the footman. Vastly relieved at the Princess's change in humor, he laughed louder than the rest, and longer.

Stepping down at last to the floor of the hall, Princess Ruth clapped a heavy hand upon my shoulder. "Little Rooster," she said, running the appraising hand over my back, my arms, my head, while I tried to stand still beneath its vigor, "your pretty feathers will serve you well enough."

Taking my thin neck in her big hand, she shook me gently. "Boy, I like you. You make me laugh. You make me to feel better than I have felt for a long time. This gloomy house is filled with old women: it needs a young cockerel like you. Do you stay here with me, and I will help you on your path to righteousness."

Chuckling over her joke, she moved her hand to my shoulder. "Come, let us go and drink some tea. You have not been overfed, in your house." Leaning upon me as we walked, she guided me past the grinning Paliku, through the open doors to the *lanai* facing upon the sea. Behind us, like sea birds in the wake of a barge, came the ladies in gray, twittering in their excitement.

She kept her word to me: she helped me on my way. In the beginning she treated me as she might have treated a pet dog or a new toy; but, as the weeks passed and she became accustomed to having me near, it was inevitable that she should grant me the role of an adopted son. Two sons of her own had she borne, and both had died young, years before I walked into her house. When I entered there the heavy habits of grief were lightened: with me to tease her, to entertain her, to pay her the attentions of a solicitous male, there was laughter and gaiety in her house again. She grew to love me, I think, reviving for me the thoughts and the considerations which she had believed to be buried forever with her sons. I was fond of her, I was good to her; and if I did not love her as much as a son would, or even a *hanai* child grateful for his keep, at least I did not misbehave myself in ways to make her unhappy.

She sent me to the missionary school in Kailua. There I discovered the world in books, and I learned with an insatiable hunger the English language which opened up to me the wisdom of the whole world. I was born to be a scholar: I needed learning as the coconut tree needs the salt of the sea.

When Keelikolani returned to Honolulu she took me with her,

as one of her family. Under her care I finished my schooling, under her doting eye I grew into manhood. "What a fine rooster our little cockerel is becoming," she exclaimed more than once. "Ah, if only I were forty years younger," she sighed, thinking again of her vanished husbands and lovers, even, perhaps, of the one who broke her nose for love.

It was her rank and her wealth which opened doors for me, but I like to think that it was myself who made the fullest use of the opportunities she presented me with. Of what value would have been her money and her power, if I had not had the mind to put them to use? They would have been wasted, poured into the earth as the vanishing waters of Kona's springs sink into the porous ground. But with her power and my mind there were no limits to my ambition: the future beckoned, and I was content to study the law in preparation for the time of achievement.

The impurity of my birth was my only flaw. Because of it I learned the ways of dissembling, of modesty, of charm. False they were, as false as the shifting sands of Waikiki, where nothing enduring can be built; but they were the cover for my pride until I should reach the pinnacle where my attainments would be all that mattered and people would forget the dirt which was in my blood. "The Forrests of Kealakekua: they grow tall," I would make them say of me and my sons. Meanwhile, the envy and the spite of others were as gnats to be waved aside, as grains of sand to be stepped upon.

Not even the ill will of the Queen could daunt me. The arrogant old autocrat! She was made of the same stuff as Princess Ruth, and I knew very well the need she felt to rule, to dominate everyone who came within range of her taut voice, her haughty glare. If I but bent my back and crawled before her like the rest, she would accept me the better, no doubt, but she would respect me the less. I would not give her the satisfaction, and to spite her I danced with her favorite, Malie. Gleeful at Kapiolani's rage, I pretended not to see her, up there on the dais, while Malie and I danced lightly past the twin thrones where she and her husband sat in state. He, poor man, tied to her by her jealousy, would wink at us, when he was sure she was not looking.

For ten years I enjoyed the life Princess Ruth gave to me. And then the finger of death reached out to touch me: within four months I lost everything. First she died, old and sick and full of years. Then it was my turn to suffer.

The leprosy changed everything. Proud ambitions, vaunting self-esteem, the arrogance of my opinion of myself: all of these fell, crumbling into ruins, before the gnawing of the conqueror germ. A myriad of little creatures, one thousand times smaller than the eye of a louse: these were the enemy which brought me down, the learned doctors said. Not men, not women, not beasts of the field or of the ocean water, but minuscule ruthless things which I could not even see.

The banishment to Kalawao brought changes not only to my body but also to the fastnesses of the spirit which theretofore I had been pleased to call my immutable self.

About a week after our arrival I saw Malie again. One lazy afternoon I was sitting in a chair propped against the shady side of our shabby house, where I could look out to the sea, to the conical islands across the bay of Kalawao and to the stretch of desolate coast beyond. Once again I was reading *The Tempest*, renewing my acquaintance with Prospero and with Caliban, wondering again with which one I would stand against the other.

The finely made book, in its soft leather binding, was part of a costly set of the plays of Shakespeare sent to me by the Queen. Ambrose Hutchinson delivered the heavy box to me on the second day of my stay, while I lay miserable in my ugly room. The gift was accompanied by her capitulation. On a sheet of heavy paper she had written, in her own hand and in our native language: "My heart grieves at your affliction, my eyes weep at your going away. But my *mana* tells me that you will be a chief among our people in Kalawao, as you would have been a chief among us in Honolulu. Farewell to thee. Kapiolani." I was touched by her generosity, I rejoiced in the richness of her gift. And I was forced to acknowledge that it was a gesture I would not have thought of making, had I been in her place and she in mine.

It was the time of day when I could not help but be struck by the brutal grimness of my own island. The sun, already low beyond the mountains in the west, was sending long shafts of cruel light upon the sea, upon the tip of Kalaupapa, where the black rocks met the leaping surf. I gave up reading of Prospero's isle, to give myself up to the examination of my own. It was easy for me to think myself Prospero, surveying my stark domain.

Kie! How vulnerable is the mind of the proud man. Prospero, indeed! Caleb the Dog, who was in need of a sop for his comforting, used *poi* for brains that day. How else can he explain the ridiculous pride with which he matched himself with the magician King? How else can he explain the ludicrous ease with which, having but recently read of love, he decided how he must himself have a try at this game of love?

For just then, just at the fleeting moment, when I was not my scheming guarded self, Malie came walking by. She came, "so perfect and so peerless," and I was smitten.

Dressed all in white, with a white parasol to shade herself from the sun, she walked in the narrow lane as though she were taking a promenade with the Court in Queen Emma's Square, during a concert by the King's Royal Band. Enchanted by her beauty, perfect as the gardenia's unfolding untouched loveliness, I went over to the gate to greet her.

With sweet simplicity she presented her "family" to me. I resented their nearness to her as she smiled upon them, robbing me of her attention to waste it upon them. The old man and the boy were not so difficult for me to accept. But the vulgar old Widow Pahaiwa, drab as a molting hen, clinging to Malie's arm, rolling her bloodshot eyes at me, chattering incessantly, when I wanted only to talk with Malie, to tell her how glad I was to see her, to tell her how beautiful she was: I could hardly be civil to the old harridan.

Controlling my resentment of the crone, I managed to mumble an apology to Malie for my conduct aboard the *Mokolii.* Even as I was saying it I congratulated myself for having thought of it in time; for, indeed, it had not crossed my mind (as Malie had scarcely entered my mind) ever since we'd left the dirty little vessel.

"My feelings were not hurt," she assured me. "Well did I understand your need to shout at someone." Her perception brought me more surprise than did the remorse of the distant Queen.

I looked closer at this new Malie, who had something to say and who said it well. She was changed: the girlishness was gone, she was a woman at last. The face was thinner, as was the figure beneath the tight bodice. The dark eyes, doubly dark under the halo of her white bonnet, were no longer the sparkling eyes of an adolescent, playing the flirt over a fan. Now she looked

upon the world with the sadness of a woman who has been hurt
by life and who is not yet recovered from the wounding. She had
reason to feel hurt—how well I knew it—but I sensed danger
in the tight lines of her lips, drawn thin and bloodless even when
she tried to smile. I felt sorry for her, and in this moment, no
doubt, my unguarded self confused compassion with love.

"And you, Malie? What of you?"

"I'm afraid we must be on our way. We are going to Mrs.
Mahoa's to call." To speak of herself was a commitment to living
she was not willing to grant. She was withdrawing from the world
even before she could know it; and just as I was being forced to
choose mine she was choosing her way to end a short and blighted
life.

I could not make her stay. All too soon she was gone, departing
in a frenzy of shoutings and cacklings from the old lady who, it
was obvious, had never learned either manners or sensibility. Her
invitations to "come and see us" could not be missed, even when
she was halfway down the lane.

Strangely excited, terribly alone, I watched Malie make her
way, a dark Venus borne upon a froth of white lace and ruffles,
until, at the turn of the lane, beyond the cluster of mountain
apple trees, she disappeared.

I had no heart to finish reading the tale of proud Prospero.
I tried, instead, to think myself Ferdinand:

> Might I but through my prison once a day
> Behold this maid: all corners else o' th' earth
> Let liberty make use of; space enough
> Have I in such a prison.

But my prison walls, black in the growing dusk, reared their
ramparts above me like the walls of a grave. More terrifying than
Prospero's magick'd isle could ever be, they denied me the consolations of make-believe love. I did not know the joy of Ferdinand
in love, nor the power of Prospero, reaping his revenge. Only the
futile glowering helplessness of the deformed Caliban did I know;
and I lifted up my fists against the mountains and the moat of the
sea, reviling them.

Such is the fickle heart: during the long night of wakefulness
the memory of Malie's present self was dimmed, the remembrance
of her as she had been in Honolulu returned to sober me. How

can you love a doll? I asked myself, a lawyer confronting a foolish plaintiff. How can you love a woman with a beautiful body and a vacancy for a mind? Leave her alone, Caleb: she is not for you. Her future is plain, in the primness of her walk, in the haste of her smile. Leave her alone, Caleb: you prefer lustier company for your rutting. All the night long I harangued myself as prosecutor, argued back as defendant. By morning I dismissed her once again from my thoughts, and I did not go to seek her out, as in the afternoon before I decided that I must.

It was not easy, moreover, to recover from the wounds which had been dealt to my own spirit. A man can tell himself, when he has fallen, that he must rise and walk again. Yet his body will resist the rising, his legs will be reluctant to carry him away. There was a perverse pleasure in enjoying my hurt, and for many days I lay in my house, sulking at my fate.

To have been so full of hope, to have been so close to the goal! And then to have the rules changed in the middle of the game, to find myself plucked from the contest and barred from reaching for the treasure displayed before me. Ahhh, this is the foulest unfairness a man can know. Writhing anew in my vain regrets, I sank again to the bottom of my despond, suffering again the torment of the leper's long travail. Raging at Heaven, I cursed it for its unfairness. Raging at God, even though I did not believe in him, I cursed him for his cheating me. Who else was there to blame? The name of God is shaped for prayers and for cursing, and I did not know how to pray.

In my house they thought I was sick, and they left me to myself. I read until I was dull with reading. I wrote—letters, poems, fables, stories, lawyer's briefs, diatribes against stupid man and his evil gods—until my hand was numb and my mind was as dry as my inkwell. Each morning the papers I covered the day before with those beautiful words I have learned to love and to use so lovingly: each morning my papers made the fire to warm the water with which I shaved. Such is the value of words, when they are written by a leper.

Then one day I found my flute. It had lain unused for so many months among my possessions in Honolulu that I had forgotten it. Paliku must have slipped it into my sea chest when he was packing it in his last service to me. While I was rummaging through the chest in an aimless search for something new to do, I came upon it, at the very bottom of the box.

I stared in astonishment at the slender wooden case, with the German silver medallion set in its cover. On the darkened tarnished surface the engraved inscription was scarcely legible: "For Caleb, on his seventeenth birthday, from Luka Keelikolani." Even after death her great love reached out to comfort me.

Across the years I heard her again, both tender and admonishing, as she put the flute into my hands on the morning of my birthday. "You must learn to make music, Caleb," she pronounced. "It is a great pleasure, for those who make it, for those who hear it. And it is a great comforter, in times of sorrow. I know this. It settles the liver, as nothing else can."

I saw her again, seated in her huge chair in the enormous sitting room of her immense house. In honor of the occasion, and most unusually for her, she was wearing a morning dress of rich dark green and black brocade, cut in the *haole* style. Her ladies were arranged around her, attired as usual in their pallid smiles and dresses of gray. Upon her fingers massive rings of dark-green jade and of dark emeralds mounted in gold elegantly repeated the accent of her dress. But in her ears clusters of flaming cinnabar added the flourish of savagery which was a part of her every action, as though to proclaim that she had not yet fallen a victim to conformity. Pride in the past: this was the demon which made her turn her back on *haole* diplomats; which incited her to kick off her shoes at royal receptions; which, in the last year of her life, made her order for herself a palace bigger and better than any structure in the kingdom, save only Kalakaua's.

The valiant old heathen! She would never accept the *haoles'* teaching, that the heart is the seat of the emotions and the brain is the citadel of thought. For her the belief of the olden times was the only truth: the liver is the proper site and origin both of emotions and of ideas. To humor her liver, she built her palace; to keep it well, she slept on mats spread on the floor, beside the high foreign beds; to solace it, she called for music.

Forthwith, at my birthday ceremony, she beckoned Mrs. Alapai to emerge from her shadowy place among the Ladies-in-Waiting. "Teach him," the *Kalani* commanded, lifting a languid hand, and my instruction was begun. No one thought to ask me if I wanted to learn, and neither did I ask the question of myself.

Mrs. Alapai was one of the timorous widows who flitted among shadows and hid behind chairs, slowly waving the hand *kahilis* which were the sign of Keelikolani's rank. Sometimes Mrs. Alapai performed alone, for the soothing of the Princess's tyrannical liver; sometimes she was accompanied by Mrs. Kekumanu, who played the Spanish guitar. On such occasions, they would forget their dreary widowhood, their dependence upon the terrifying Princess, their own sorrows of the liver, and they would play with a virtuosity which never ceased to impress me.

Mrs. Kekumanu wore a smile of rapture as she plucked at the strings of her guitar, not deigning to look at them. Mrs. Alapai nodded so vigorously in time with the music that her soft hair came undone while she played, falling wispily and gradually from its decorous bun until it hung about her in a dark haze which made her seem excitingly dissolute. I saw her then as though I were looking at a graying daguerreotype of herself taken out of her past: so must she have looked when she was newly a bride, full of the tender wantonnesses of the young, before the fact of widowhood was dreamed of, and the cold chastity of a widow's servitude robbed her flesh of its meaning.

When they made music, those two, they seemed slightly mad, they seemed to be maenads out of some ancient feminine mystery, possessed by an intense power which was absent from them at all other times in their ineffectual lives. With those two Calliopes to persuade me, I could not doubt Princess Ruth's word about the strength of music. I proved to be an apt pupil of both Mrs. Alapai and Mrs. Kekumanu.

The discovery of my flute, that day in my room at Kalawao, was my salvation. Drawing it from the case, I put it almost fearfully to my lips, dreading the sadness that would come with the first notes I would draw from it. My spirit was in turmoil as, with soft breath and trembling fingers, I blew the sweet fluent sounds from the little piece of old wood and yellowing ivory. The memories came crowding in; and once again I saw Mrs. Alapai and Mrs. Kekumanu in their mystic affinity, and the vast bulk of the Princess Ruth, with a gratified liver, filling her archiepiscopal chair . . .

She was right in her judgment upon music, as she was right in every pronouncement she made: it was my comforter in sorrow, the solace of my diseased liver. I had known this truth before I came to Kalawao, in times of lesser troubles and lighter sorrows, but, as with so many lessons, I had forgotten it. This day I learned it again as I took up the power she had given me those eight years before.

I played for almost an hour, beginning with runs and trills and fanciful bird calls which made me feel like a boy again. From these I progressed to some of the simple pieces learned from Mrs. Alapai, things like "Flow Gently, Sweet Afton" and the melody of one of Purcell's "Aires," which now at Kalawao seemed written especially to apply to me:

> Music for a while shall all your cares beguile
> Wond'ring how your pains were eas'd and disdaining to be pleas'd
> Till Alecto free the dead from their eternal bands,
> Till the snakes crop from her head and the whip from out her
>   hands.

Having thus regained much of my former skill at fingering, along with the semblance of an embouchure, I was about to end my practicing when I chanced to look out my window into the open yard beyond. I had an audience: six children, two dogs, and a very fat man.

The children were sitting cross-legged in the grass. The dogs were asleep, their noses resting upon their paws. The fat man, too swollen to be able to sit upon the ground, leaned against the stone wall at the side of the yard. His eyes were closed, his face was lifted to the sky.

I stopped playing. The children looked up at the window. Eleu and Akala I recognized from an earlier meeting. The others I did not know.

The fat one stirred, opening his eyes. "*Keia he nani la.* That is beautiful," he called in a high voice. "Please. Do not stop." The children shared his eagerness for more, expressing themselves with whistles and hand-clappings and shouts of the kind which encourage *hula* dancers to continue their art. The dogs, wakening, added to the frolic with their barking.

I am not one to be embarrassed by attention, and with an audience of their quality I was stimulated rather than disturbed. Standing at the window, a performer upon a narrow stage, I raised the flute to my lips. Scarcely thinking of what I chose to perform, wanting only to please them with the most beautiful music I know, I played for them the long slow sustained melody of the lost souls in Hades which Orpheus heard, that time he went in search of his Eurydice. Clear and soft rose the voice of the flute, like a prayer, like a breath of smoke from the altar where Orpheus laid his sacrifice. The children sat with heads bowed. The fat man wept: the tears stole down his cheeks, glittering in the light. Music, the gift of Orpheus, helped us to forget for a while, in beauty, the ugliness of our fate.

When it was done, they were quiet for a long time. Then the man lifted his bulk from the wall. "*Lawa, lawa,*" he sighed. "Enough, enough. There is too much of beauty in this song. We must thank you for it by hearing no more." He waddled away through the thick grass, wiping his cheeks with his plump hands.

"Eleu," I called. "Come. Come here." The lad ran at once to the window.

"Who is that man?" A man who could be moved so readily by music was a man I wished to know.

"Him? Dass Momona."

"Where does he live?"

"Not fah. Two, t'ree houses up da lane, I tink."

"Thank you, Eleu." Forgetting him, I turned away, to the emptiness of my room.

"You going make music again sometime fo us?"

"If you wish it. Did you like what I played?"

His disembodied head, propped upon the window sill, split open in a wide smile. "Yeah. Good music, dat. He make me feel like one bird, flying up and down. I dunno wy Momona cry." Quick as a bird he was gone. The other members of his shrill covey took flight from the grass, striving noisily to catch up with him.

When Kumakani and Hinano, my housemates, heard me play upon the flute they urged me to join their singing club. "The Hui Iiwi will sing the sweeter with a bird like you in their midst." Their flattery did not win me, nor was it the promise of tea and cakes. It was my hunger for the company of people which drew me from my room.

I was annoyed with myself for submitting to this vulgar need. They will be as dull as Kumakani and Hinano are, I was certain, remembering how impatient I can be with most folk. Very few people can interest me for more than five minutes at a time: in this exposure I can pick their brains of all they know, and I am ready to throw them away, as crab shells and limpets are, when they have been picked of their meat. To consort with such people for long is to learn their sorrows, their troubles, their stupidities; and I was weary of adding their burdens to my own.

But Kalawao was doing strange things to me, and the loneliness enforced upon me in the Settlement was not the same thing as the aloneness I desired for myself in Honolulu. "I will try it, *once*," I assented graciously, "to see if I like it. Unless I like it I will not go again."

They should have clubbed me for my offensiveness. But they smiled good-naturedly. "*Maikai*. We can ask no more."

To my surprise I enjoyed myself thoroughly at Deborah Makanani's. The process of dressing up to go out was in itself pleasurable, but the entry into the warmth and light of her parlor, filled with new people whom I did not know, was exciting. I who had existed in a palace found myself enchanted with a cottage; I who had turned my back on princesses took delight now in the company of commoners.

I do not know what influence worked this change in me. Was it the glow of candles, was it the scent of flowers, great clusters of late-blooming mountain gingers overflowing from the vases into which they had been stuffed? Was it simply the sight of so many people laughing and chatting like civilized folk, in the crowded parlor of the civilized little house? Or was it the glimpse I had of Malie, the instant I stepped through the door? I do not know what agency it was that made me feel like the bewitched prince in the fable who has been turned back from a beast into a man: all I know is that I was unaccountably lighthearted when I stepped into Deborah's parlor, released at last from my morbid spell.

Deborah herself helped to transform me. She is the kind of woman whom men delight in teasing. Fat and giggly and good-hearted, this type of woman expresses herself in gasps and burbles and in little screams and half-uttered sentences which she can never finish because she is breathless with laughter at what you are saying, or at what she is thinking you are saying, or are about to say, or said the last time you pressed her arm. She never quite hears what is said to her because she is never quiet long enough to comprehend it. This is the kind of woman for whom a roll of the eyes is the equivalent of a kiss, for whom a touch of the hand is most piquant seduction—and for whom, sadly enough, a toss in bed is never attained. Everyone's friend, and no one's wife: this is the fate of women like Deborah.

Before I knew it I held Deborah's moist hand in mine, I was rolling my eyes at her, out of habit, as I had rolled them at half a dozen others of her bovine kind. And I had fallen into my old habit of saying nonsense, because I knew she would be expecting it from me.

But in pleasing Deborah I succeeded in irking Malie. All during the music-making she ignored me, looking the other way when I tried to catch her eye, puzzling me by her odd behavior. In the soft light of Deborah's candles Malie looked lovelier than I remembered her. But there were moments when those perfect lips shaped themselves into something very much like a pout. Never dreaming that I was to blame, I turned my attention to the enjoyment of the music.

It was surprisingly good, made better by the unaffected purity of Momona's violin. He could not read a note, and he played everything by ear, as most of us do; but in those melodies which both of us knew, his violin and my flute were perfectly mated. Across the room we shared smiles of approval for our new-formed partnership, and I looked forward to spending many an hour with him, not only in making music but also in conversation, for in the intervals between tunes I could hear that he owned a graceful wit.

When the music was ended I forced myself upon Malie's notice, bowing before her and the old gorgon who was her duenna. She made a dutiful speech about my playing, but there was a coolness about her which robbed it of sincerity. Not so with Tutu: she is a woman who keeps her mind on the essential facts of life. With a surprising aptness, she quoted an old chant, in which she made a charming reference to the *iiwi*, likening my flute to its love call in the mountain forest. As I grinned in pleasure at the compliment, looking upon her with a dawning respect, she gave an unmistakably earthy cast to her allusion: "And every bird in the forest has heard the call, and gives answer."

The line was carefully invented, apparently to bring every female in the room into the uproar of jungle sounds she suggested, but the way she wrinkled her nose and pointed her chin at Malie, staring pensively off into the far side of the parlor, left me in no doubt about her private meaning. She saw where my fancy yearned and she was encouraging me to express it. Really, I thought, I have misjudged this old woman, and I hurried to take advantage of her lead: "Lonely is the *iiwi* in the distant tree: empty is his nest of love." Even as I spoke my clever little speech, devised for her wooing, Malie turned away, deserting us to seek the company of others.

"Well," I vented my chagrin. "Not every bird is willing to heed this call. Some, it seems, would perch in other branches."

"Don't give up so soon," said the woman of experience. "Go after her. She is unhappy. Why should you not be the one to make her happy?" Tutu was very serious: gone was the high-flown language of poetry. "There is no better one for her than you. Is there a better one for you than she? Go, go!" She pushed me toward Malie.

I went in pursuit of the elusive female. But she was almost rudely inattentive to my chatter. If I had snarled at her, or beat her, or left her there to sulk alone, her contrition might have brought her round to tug at my arm. But no: I was being gentle, in the new *haole* style; I thought I was falling in love. And the gentle man, the poets had told me, is patient with the humors of his beloved. Hell! I should have boxed her ears, and bashed in her nose, as our sensible ancestors did.

With a great ruffling of feathers, a shrill feminine chirping, the explanation came out of her at last: "Our hostess is much taken with you," the maiden lady bird pecked at me, with a viciousness that would have made her missionary teachers fall in a faint.

I could not conceal my delight: I laughed aloud. "I didn't know you cared," I crowed, trying to explain both my happiness and my laughter.

Perhaps this brought too soon into the open the unsuspected depths to her feeling for me. Or perhaps it was merely her female's instinct to put the presumptuous male back into his place. I do not know: women are creatures I never could understand, and of them all this *haolefied* Malie was the one most incomprehensible. Whatever the reason, she left me with a flick of her *holoku's* train, a toss of her lovely head, making me all the more captive to her beauty.

But I knew when to desist. Women have no sense of humor, I explained to the attentive walls; and I went to find Momona to talk with, in sweet reason, and with a man's sensibility.

From that time on I had no more doubts about my need for Malie or of her suitability for me. Her show of temper made me realize how much I had underestimated her. But more alluring to me than her aroused spirit was her body: I wanted it for my own. And I was certain I would get it. No woman has ever withheld herself from me.

Convinced of my need for her body, I told myself I loved her entire. It was the thought of love which I fell in love with, of course; and, as happens to many a poor fool of a man, I was caught in the trap of my delusions, baited with my own lurid fantasies during the long nights while I lay in my cheerless bed.

Quickly the need for her grew into an obsession: like many of the men in the Settlement I lusted after her, and dreamed my dreams about how I would get her. When I heard of their siege of the schoolhouse, I scorned them for their stupidity: dullards and fools they were, gathering like flies around the juice of ripe sugar cane. I would show them how the conquest of Malie would be achieved. Patience and planning: these would be my weapons, I avowed to the night air, as I waited for the proper time.

"How is it that you do not burn, like the rest of us?" asked Kumakani one evening when we three sat around the supper table. His long narrow head was shaped like a canoe, on which the beaked nose was stuck like a foreigner's keel. His stiff black hair, parted in the middle, fell out from the conical pate like the half of a halo. Oh, he is a veritable beau, is our Kumakani, straight from the farthest taro patch on the farthermost point of outermost Kauai.

He was going, it was obvious, to enjoy the comforting of one of the women of the village. "Why do you not come also?" he asked me. "Emma is generous. She does not even have a calabash by the bed, for to leave some money in." He is a man who knows the value of a *kala:* his cotton shirt was of the broadest stripe, rich in green and black; and the armbands holding up the full sleeves were done in a beguiling pink. I shuddered to think what his necktie would be when, after the talk was done, he locked himself into the gleaming celluloid collar which is his greatest treasure.

"A woman is like money: fun to feel, but hard to keep," intoned Hinano, letting me know with a wink that he, too, was aware of Kumakani's two interests.

I ended my admiring inspection of the gallant swain. "I burn,

I burn. Am I not a man?" In truth, the needs of my body, too long pent up, were becoming urgent. "But I do not lie with whores." I tried not to sound too puritanical. I was as familiar as a visiting sailor with the bawdy houses of Honolulu. But my pure and transcendent heart was fixed upon Malie, and no one else in Kala-wao could take her place. Kumakani would not have understood this kind of delicacy.

Thinking I disapproved of his looseness, he tried to shift the responsibility for his behavior. "It is terrible, what this disease does to us." One would have thought him a Christian martyr about to climb upon the rack, he made such a sad face.

"Aha, aha! It is not the *mai Pake* which makes you burn." How well I knew the old excuse! It is the leper's favorite device for explaining almost every action of his irresponsible life. "Why do you blame the sickness for faults which are your own?"

"My faults? And what are you meaning by this?"

"Only this: the fire is in your loins because you think of nothing else but how to put it out. Is this not so? Search your *manao*, and tell me!"

He took inventory of his thoughts while I concluded my argument. "If you would work in a taro patch all the day, as you did at home, or if you went fishing, or used your body for some better purpose than lying around this house here, all the day, the fire would not burn so high." I did not condemn Kumakani for his burning. I only wanted to explain to him its origin.

This is another of the diseases the *haoles* have given us, a sickness of the mind such as we did not know before they came among us. As it is with them, so it has become with us: the concern of the mind with the forbidden pleasures of the flesh leaves a victim with thought for little else. The signs of this infection are well known. Frankness gives way to lewdness. Honesty of speech and deed is corrupted: innuendoes, obscene gestures, words with double meanings displace the natural forthright phrases in our talk, even in our songs. And the *holoku*, this voluminous creation of hypocrisy, drops like a funeral pall upon the golden bodies, making the meeting of lover with beloved more arduous than the reefing of a clipper ship's sail.

"Is it so?" The immensity of the idea left Kumakani as agape as a fish when it is taken out of the water.

"It is so, of this I am sure. The patients here who work: I will bet you they are not in perpetual heat. The patients who do not labor: I will bet they are the ones who feel this fire."

While Kumakani's slow mind searched for an answer Hinano came to his rescue. "Pity the poor people who must work. Me, I hope to feel the heat of this fire for as long as I do live."

Well, I suppose he was right: a leper has little enough to enjoy. The two of them went off, the one to his Emma, the other to his Kumu. The women of Kalaupapa are as lascivious as are the men, and just as virtuous in blaming their itching upon the leprosy.

It was my turn to wash and dry the supper dishes, an onerous task which I despised. This is the aspect of bachelorhood which I dislike the most, and the first one I proposed to sacrifice upon the altar of marriage. Let them go off to their shopworn calabashes, I grumbled. I wait for the one not yet opened.

When I was done with my woman's work, I took my evening's walk to the house of Makaio.

The first time I went to call upon Malie I learned that it was about as easy to see her alone as it was to call upon Kalakaua in his palace. Makaio held a veritable court of his own, in which Malie was the chiefest ornament if not the actual Queen. But in his keeping she was little more than a decoration, a portrait in pastels: she sat in a corner of the *lanai*, flanked by the grizzled Tutu and the watchful Makaio, suspicious of any man. Around them, some in chairs, others on the floor or on the steps, sat half a dozen men. The fat Momona I knew, and the giant Kewalo, but the rest were strangers. Cursing my luck, I took my place among them. She is besieged by men, I groaned, as a ripe fruit is set upon by hungry birds: I might as well try to seduce her in the midst of a church supper. At nine o'clock, after an evening of muddled conversation and weighted pauses, Makaio turned us out, with a civil enough good night. I had not said a word to Malie.

Fortunately for my temper, most of the callers were older staider folk, who visited Makaio regularly because they were friends of long standing. This discovery, and Tutu's very evident pleasure at seeing me there, kept my hopes up. The old lady wasn't a bad sort, really: a litle loud, perhaps, a little too raucous in her arguments, she more than made up for her deficiencies in manners by possessing one great attribute in style: she was marvelously earthy. Such natural honesty was needed in the house of Makaio, the mealy-mouthed one.

Makaio was a professional Christian, "an Irish-potato Hawaiian," as we natives call those of us who fawn upon the *haoles* for the sake of a meal, a job, a place in their Heaven. When he spoke he bleated like a goat, his voice cracking with earnestness. The most narrow-minded man in the world was he: only his way of doing things was right. And he never tired of mentioning his friendship with God

The sharp and subtle mind of Momona provided the relief I needed from the sanctimoniousness of Makaio. If Momona had not been there, I doubt if I could have endured many of those evenings, even with a dozen alluring Malies sitting near. Momona was a man with an original mind, and with a wonderfully subtle way of exposing the weaknesses of people. He loved to tease, to set arguments in motion, to stir the minds of people grown too small with their isolation or their laziness. When he had aroused them, he would sit back in his chair, enjoying the battle he had started. He was not malicious—what fat man is ever a trouble-maker?—but he was an accomplished manipulator of people. What a politician he would have made!

He was the kind of man who found interest in everything under heaven. Like his mind, his hands were never still: they were always shaping strips of paper, or studying the parts of flowers, or prying into the nests of birds fallen from the trees.

But this is my memory of Momona. One day when the two of us were out walking, we came upon a new leak in the rusty pipe line bringing water down from Waileia stream. The water trickled from the hole in a cheerful wasteful burble, as it had done in a score of other places along the line before they were bound up with rags and pieces of rope. At sight of the newest leak I reached by habit for my handkerchief, thinking to bandage this most recent wound in the single arteriole through which we claimed the blood of Kane.

"Wait," said Momona, holding me back. "Let us show our power: let us change one god into another."

Enjoying my bewilderment, he inspected the jungle growth at either side of the trail "*Eia*, here is what we need." He plucked a dry stalk of the jointed *ohe* grass from its parent clump.

"Stand back," he warned, as he squatted beside the leak. With a quick thrust he forced the grass stem into the hole, as far as it would go, and then he stepped away.

From the stoppered hole came a spray of finest mist, and in its insubstantial rain glowed a beautiful, a perfect rainbow.

But he showed a fat man's sentimentality, too, this Momona. He told us, one evening, of Prince Peter Kahekili, who had been a patient here a few years ago. The story started out to be one of the drollest tales I ever heard, showing up the silly *alii's* frenzied search for a medicine to cure his disease. Momona's picture of plump Peter, running from *kauka* to *kahuna*, from seashore to mountain, in search of treatment, was devastatingly funny. But, as he continued with the telling of it, something went amiss: almost before our eyes, Peter became the futile frightened fool of fate, running in terror from the inevitable reckoning: he became the figure of Everyman, of our listening selves, running, forever running, from his doom.

Yet, in telling the scarifying story, Momona revealed his own weakness as well: before he ended it, he was weeping vain tears of sorrow, and his tale degenerated into a sentimental parable of such mystic intent as to be meaningless. All of the splendid irony went out of it, when he lost his control over himself. Why he did this I could not say; why he wept I could only guess. He was too much the realist to weep over his own plight, I thought; so I was left with the suspicion that he was deeply attached to the Prince Peter in the years during which he served him, and that his affection for the miserable man still lived within him.

If this was so, his was love wasted, for Peter was no great chief. The quiver of anger in Keelikolani's voice told me as much, when she rendered judgment upon her profligate cousin: "*Auwe!* This Peter! A good-for-nothing, all the time playing and fooling around, a disgrace to his family. Now he has gone and caught the *mai Pake. Kaii!* It comes from drinking too much of this *haole* whisky, I know it, this damn' *haole* booze . . ." At the time I knew neither booze nor Peter, so, with the carelessness of the unconcerned, I accepted her verdict for the truth.

Righteous Makaio saw that neither I nor any man would have the chance to speak with Malie alone, either in his house or in the houses of others, where the Hui Iiwi went to sing. Even when we gathered in the churchyard, on fine evenings, to practice or to compete in the singing matches with the other clubs, he would sit between Malie and the circling hunting males.

She did nothing to free herself from his domination. Placid, with folded hands, she sat in her corner. She was beyond reach, a *wana* guarded by an eel; and like an eel, with beady eyes and sharp teeth, Makaio watched over her. After a time I suspected that he wanted her for himself.

Frequently, as the shadows lengthened and the darkness thickened under the roof of the *lanai*, and Malie's thin form was drawn into the night, I had the feeling that she was not sitting there at all. Then I would wonder if I were not wasting my time in pursuit of a wraith, if I should not take my need for love to free Emma, as Kumakani did, or buy my easing from the whores in Kalawao. As, in the dark, I slapped at mosquitoes, stung less by them than by some of the stupidities expressed by my companions, I wondered what the hell I was doing there, in the limbo of Makaio's *lanai*, listening to the chitter of fools.

But always the answer was the same: What else is there to do, in the perpetual boredom of Kalawao?

And then, almost as an afterthought, I would remember: Malie is here, I would remind myself, the diligent suitor, the man in love.

At last there came a time when Makaio could not prevent my speaking to her. This was the eve of the King's birthday, when half the Settlement attended the feast in the yard of the Catholic church. The whole day was given over to tributes of devotion to Kalakaua, and it saw an almost endless succession of pitiful testimonials to our ineptitude and our stupidity. While the plump sybarite lolled in his palace, unaware of our ceremonies, we stumbled and straggled around in a tragic tattered parade which brought joy to no one marching in it and not one nod of acknowledgment from him. While he gambled away the kingdom's treasure, in poker sessions with his *haole* cronies, we held a *hookupu* for him, robbing ourselves of our meager possessions to lay them at his unheeding feet. While he gave our nation away to the sugar barons, insatiable in their demand for land, for water, for laborers of any color and any breed to slave for them, we listened to brave speeches from idiots.

They must have been touched by the sun, those speakers, when they spouted their fine phrases about the King's great love for his people, when they gave us their assurances that our nation would endure forever. Fools they were, or charlatans, who could speak so smoothly of the life of the land and the increase of the people, when a thousand of us who were dying of the most loathsome of the white man's importations stood before them, arrayed in the glories of our hideous rotting flesh. How could they be so blind, those speechmakers?

Furious with them, I turned to share with my companions the scorn I felt. But they were not snickering, my fellows of the herd, nor did they question what the speakers said. Like cattle they stood in their patient masses; like cattle they lifted their heads to hear the lies sent down from above. Their faces rapt, smiles of ecstasy upon their ravaged lips, they drank in the delusion that they still lived, that they belonged still to the nation. How could they be so blind, those listeners?

My mind, my liver—O savage splendid sanguine gift of my savage foster mother! O savage magnificent Keelikolani! If only you were here now, to shake this deluded rabble into wakefulness, to sweep these soft-mouthed preachermen from their pulpit, to rouse the nation from its apathy!—my liver tightened in anger, squeezing the bitter potion of violence into my blood. I could taste it in my mouth, the taste of rusted iron. More bitter than the taste of defeat is the taste of helpless rage, when one wishes to wage war and the enemy is beyond reaching . . .

Crowded together in the hot sun, stinking like a bunch of goats, they were singing "*Hawaii Ponoi*," bleating out their exaltation, when I left them to run home to hide. This foul little, this stinking little Caliban: trotting in the dust, he cursed all the way home.

And yet, at the end of the day I was back among them, milling around in the churchyard, waiting for the *luau*. My week's ration of pork and half my portion of *poi* were going into this feast for the damned, and I did not intend to be robbed of them. Less important, but worrisome enough to rout me out of my hovel, was my duty to the Hui Iiwi: I was to play my flute with them in the contest of singing clubs which would bring the *aha aina* to an end.

A singing contest, I snorted, a songfest, by Heaven, full of dole-

ful hymns and aching references to "Home, Sweet Home," a
sickening flow of drivel, when what we need most is an exhibition
of wild and sexual *hulas*, culminating in a grand orgy, a joyous
public release of our inhibited lusts. These damned *pialu* preachers, with their eunuchs' constraints upon us: why don't they leave
us alone? And Kalakaua, the Merry Monarch: *Cha!* he wouldn't
be caught dead at a singing contest. If we really wanted to honor
him, now, a match of lewd and lecherous *hulas* is the way to do
it. But no: we must sing, yowling like a bunch of spayed cats,
virtuous as seraphim, when, really, in our unspayed bodies, we
burn to be devils—

These were the devotional thoughts with which I entertained
myself when I entered the hallowed ground of Saint Philomena's
Church. The reason I did not give was the most important one
of all: the hope of seeing Malie, and of talking with her alone.
All the edifices of philosophy fell before the battering ram of my
need.

From the very beginning my luck was against me. Cow-thighed
Deborah attached herself to me the minute she saw me. "E,
Caleb," she mooed, sending the tidings of my arrival throughout
the whole assembly. "See how handsome he is," she bawled to
everyone who had ears. "Come and talk with us," she tittered,
seizing me by the arm. With her on one side and sour Sarah
Kunia on the other, I was trapped between ramparts of rancid
flesh. Soon we were surrounded by others of the Hui Iiwi—Hanu
the Clown, and Kumakani the Bore, Momona the Glutton, and
phthisic Tuesday Lokahi—all seeking the comfort of the same
familiar phizzes and the same repetitious banter with which we
lived every day in the week. Ringed around by them, I did not
see Malie arrive. When we took our seats she was already in her
place, nested like an egg between Makaio and Tutu.

Momona's suggestion that "we of the Hui sit together on the
same mat," gave me the chance to be near her. She scarcely
noticed me. Aloof as ever, she picked at her food, hardly soiling
her fingers, eating almost nothing. My humor, delicately poised
as it was, was pushed again over the edge. Damn her eyes! Didn't
the girl find anything in life enjoyable? Couldn't she unbend a
little, even at a *luau*?

My temper was not improved when we of the Hui Iiwi lost our
chance to win the singing contest. I do not like to lose. But the

Hui sang shrilly and off-key, and our selections were as insipid as fresh *poi*. When we were finished, I was in my state of high fury again. No longer able to bear the sight of such flatulent pigs, too full of garbage to sing, I stalked away from them as they wandered back to their disordered mat.

Among the tombstones in the graveyard I went, and there, as the dust of evening settled out of the darkening sky, I cooled my brow against the iron crosses, growing like rusty flowers from the mounded earth. Yearning for the solace of Death's cool hand, and yet not willing to reach out once more to take it, I walked in her eerie garden, kicking at graves to insult her, to call down her wrath upon my head.

I was there, in my recurrent agony, when the *oahi* began upon the mountain top. They took me by surprise; and when the first shower of embers came falling down the face of the distant cliff, and all the people in the churchyard squealed their delight, I thought the end of the world was come, in answer to my sacrilege, and that the people shrieked in terror. Lifting my head to the mountains, I felt the pain of fright pulling at my heart—and in the same instant knew the relief of recognition.

With the next breath came something else to complain about. "The *haoles*: they are right," I growled into the night. "They are right, Keelikolani, in their anatomy as in their poetry. The heart it is which tightens, not the liver. We *kanakas*: we are wrong, Keelikolani, when we say it is the liver." In this descent to the ridiculous, as I stood among the gravestones talking with the ghost of Princess Ruth, I could not help but laugh at my crazy morbid self. And with this self-mockery my humor was helped to mend again.

The fireworks also helped. Against the dark wall of night they were a syllabary of beauty: they were the writing of some light-bearing god, painting upon the canvas of darkness with a brush dipped in flame. They were like pure music heard at a little distance, when only the sounds come to the ear and the performers cannot be seen: the listener is not distracted, and beauty comes undiminished to the attentive ear. So it was with the fireworks: they plunged, they whirled, they hovered, they flew, like notes afire, like flames torn from the living robe of Pele, like the glad gambolings of bright Lucifer when he played in the mornings of his grace, that time before he fell.

The *oahi* came to an end in the spectacular descent of a blazing tree: swiftly it fell, like a falling angel cast out from the threshold of Heaven. It was Lucifer, son of the morning, plunging to his hell. I saw him fall. I saw the gates open up, in the bowels of the earth, to take him in. I heard the screaming of the damned.

Leaving the place of my vigil, I went to find Malie. Well, Philosopher, I gave me my charge, go in search of your love. Philosophers do not have to live alone. Go, lay your heart at her feet. Get the foolish ritual over with. Tickling my mind was the thought that perhaps the *haoles* had decided wisely after all, in their choice of the seat of emotion. How can a man hope to win the hand of a fair lady, if he lays his *liver* at her feet?

With the help of the lanterns and the flaring torches I managed to join her at last. But I could not make off with her as easily as I wanted to. How could I forget her family? she demurred. So we had to collect the pillows, the wraps, the stiff-kneed old man, the garrulous old woman; and we had to wait patiently for one of the linkboys to bring a torch of our own before we could take our leave.

At the entrance to their yard Makaio, the perfect host, was all for dismissing me, but Tutu, my only ally, intervened. "Come inside, Makaio. Go put the kettle on the fire. How can they come to harm?"

A fine loser was Makaio, a most trusting man. Sticking the torch into the rock wall beside Malie, he grumbled, "Five minutes. Then I will come back for her."

Then at last we were alone, Malie and I. All my weeks of waiting, of dreaming, of hoping were converged upon the one moment. Trembling with nervousness, I scarcely knew how to begin. And, of course, all my pretty speeches, planned for this time, were forgotten.

I needn't have worried: they would have been of little use to me. In a foolish fumbling scene which I cannot endure to think about, she spurned me

31

KEANU TAUGHT ME the enormity of my pride: through him I learned the meaning of humility.

It was not because he had killed a man that I disliked Keanu. As an attorney I knew enough of crimes of passion, and of the people who commit them, to be sparing in my judgment of him. There are always reasons for murder which explain to some degree the murderer and his violence. As a matter of fact, the accounts of Keanu's crime led me to sympathize more with him than with his victim: I suspected the Japanese of having done Keanu the first wrong.

My dislike of Keanu was instinctive: it began on sight, even before I knew who he was.

Mr. Judd had asked me to interview one of our clients, detained in the King's Prison for some minor offense. My mind was not on Keanu—or on our client—when I made the hot ride to the western edge of Honolulu, and crossed the long causeway spanning the malodorous mud flats at the mouth of Nuuanu's stream. On the raised reef at the end of the road lay Kawa Prison, a fortress squatting on a coral hillock, a barrier between the virtuous folk of Honolulu and the habitués of the brothels in Iwilei. The coral roadway, built years ago by the labor of prisoners—most of whom were convicted of infringements upon the seventh commandment —served virtue and vice alike. As my lazy horse ambled along the way, I took a wry pleasure in contemplating the paradox.

In the open courtyard of the prison the guests of the King took their ease in the shade of the great *kamani* tree. It was a nice way to live: room and board were provided by the generous state, the few chores of housekeeping the prisoners were required to perform were not oppressive, they were not fettered by day. Most of the prisoners had not been acquainted with such luxury when they were free men; and many of them were made very unhappy when, their sentences having ended, they were expelled into the world of work and worry outside the sheltering walls. Hawaiian justice is seldom carried to the white man's logical legal conclusion, even in the judgment of murderers, and very rarely does the sturdiest limb of the *kamani* tree bear the long gaunt fruit of a hanging.

While I sat on a bench in the shade of the jailer's veranda, listening to our client's rambling answers to my questions, I had ample time to observe the other residents as they paid the terrible price for their crimes. Two of them lay on the hard-packed earth, sleeping. Half a dozen others sat cross-legged upon the ground, playing a noisy game, slapping filthy cards upon the trampled earth. No money was in sight, but obviously they were gambling.

My man was exceedingly slow of mind, and I scarcely heard him as he maundered on about his innocence and the malice of his neighbor. "The water of my stream: he steals it. The boundaries of my land: he moves them." How often I have heard these same complaints. The consequences of them I already knew. "Why, then, should I not put my cow to graze, in the grass he calls his own? And why should I not hit him, when he comes to take my cow?" The damned imbecile: that's exactly how he managed to get himself into the jailhouse. I was half asleep, lulled by the shifting light among the *kamani* leaves and by the drone of my persecuted client, when another prisoner entered the yard.

Thick-lipped, sleepy-eyed, he was a good-looking fellow, in a brutish way, even with the unkempt beard and uncut hair which showed he had been in prison for a long time. From the way he walked, head high, shoulders back, hands clenched at his sides, I could safely presume that his was a crime of violence. The hard cast to the face, with its high cheekbones and the cruel curve to the nose, confirmed me in my guess: a street bum, I said, or perhaps a stevedore, when he works. But a man of temper, beyond any doubt. Good-natured enough when he has his way, but a devil when he's crossed. Probably guilty of beating his *wahine* . . .

"E, *Keanu! E hele mai.*" The cardplayers raised their greeting. Before he acknowledged it he looked at me, insolently taking my measure, from head to foot. He did not bother to disguise his disdain of my *haole* attire, and he laughed outright when he saw the narrow French shoes on my feet.

So this is Keanu, this is the murderer from Kohala . . . Whatever sympathy I may have felt for Keanu unseen slipped away as I saw the arrogant swagger, the toss of the head, with which he joined the gamblers. A man of violence, cheered by his henchmen.

A lustful boar, with a killer's tusks. Poor Charley, poor Japanee: he didn't have a chance.

When the story of the Kohala Murder Case aroused the nation, I was almost certain that Keanu was one more example of the *kuaaina,* the simple rustic, who lived according to the ancient customs but who was being judged according to the new laws. How else could I interpret the behavior of the woman Kamaka, who cohabited with Keanu as his paramour whenever her Japanese husband was away, who, as the newspapers said so clearly, "did not want to go to live with her husband, because she wanted to stay with Keanu"? For a time I played with the idea of offering myself to be Keanu's counsel for the defense. I was not unaware that most of the natives were outspokenly on his side: their soft hearts are always captivated by romance, no matter how illicit by *haole* standards. If I could gain an acquittal for Keanu, my name as the champion of the natives would be secure. After that there would be nothing I could not get from them.

But when I saw him in the prison yard I changed my mind: such a troublemaker was not worth saving. I was touched with enough of *haole* hypocrisy to know that my career must be built upon worthier causes, and Keanu's was not a cause which would impress the people I needed most to impress. I turned instead to helping the Crown develop its case against Keanu.

It was I who drew up the bill of arraignment for the Attorney General to sign. It was I who chose the witnesses to be imported from Kohala to Honolulu, to tell the Court of Keanu's actions before and upon the day of the murder. It was I who supervised the policemen when they took from the box the bloodstained clothes Charley was wearing when he died, the vicious knife with which Keanu was alleged to have taken Charley's life. The spots of rust upon the two-edged blade seemed like remnants of Charley's blood.

Keanu's behavior at the trial did not win him much sympathy. Stolid, unaffected by the gravity of the Court, he refused to admit to any knowledge of the crime. "I was plowing at Waiapuka," he mumbled. "Only when the Sheriff came to arrest me at my house, did I know about Charley." His lying did not save him.

His paramour betrayed him. And it was I who made her tell the truth by filling her with fear of the laws of man and of Jehovah against people who give false witness. During the trial she changed her story, maintained since the day of the killing, which had been the prime evidence in Keanu's defense, that two strange *haole* men had set upon Charley and killed him for his money.

"No," she said, her head low, hands twisting in her lap. "There were no *haole* men. There was only Keanu. It was Keanu who did it . . ." In the thrill of surprise which ran through the crowded courtroom the rest of her statement was lost. Only a few of us, sitting near her, heard the sobbing finish: ". . . for love of me." It was Keanu's epitaph It was Kamaka's farewell to her stupid lover, who thought he could flout the law for the indulgence of his passions.

He was found guilty of murder, by a jury of his peers. He showed no emotion when the verdict was read.

Two weeks later he stood again in the same Court, before Chief Justice Judd, to receive his sentence. Mr. Judd, usually so gentle and kind, was stern. Tall and lean, pale above the dark robes, he represented the power of the Kingdom and the conscience of its Law, looking coldly down upon Keanu. He spoke in Hawaiian, for the prisoner's sake, making no concession to the many foreigners present in the courtroom.

"Keanu: You have been convicted by a jury of your countrymen of the crime of murder. You were defended by able counsel of your own selection, and every effort has been made by them in your behalf; but the proofs of your guilt are so convincing that the Court can find no just reason for granting you a new trial."

Dull Keanu did not understand much of this language. The sentencing in itself was a mockery, held to fulfill the letter of the law, not its spirit. The populace, crowding the courtroom for their public titillation, heard more of it than did Keanu.

"It is indicated by the evidence that you planned to take the life of the murdered Japanese in order that you might have his wife; and that you rode on that fatal morning by an unfrequented road to where you met your victim, and with *aloha* on your lips you smote him down with savage strength, and with repeated blows took his life, and left his body on the highway. The only other living witness of your crime has detailed minutely each step in your terrible crime.'

Beneath the Justice's words, falling upon Keanu like Manoa's pelting rain, we could hear the whispering of the translators seated

among the *haoles*, hissing in their haste to relay the dreadful
judgment, frothing at the mouth, as do raindrops when they
touch the muddy earth.

"The murdered man was your friend. There is no evidence that
he had injured you in any way, and no facts are known to the
Court which would tend to extenuate your guilt."

For the moment of terrible silence he paused: this is the moment of awe, which makes prisoners blanch, which makes even me
weak before the power of justice. The audience held its breath.
Keanu lifted his head, confronting his judge, as a beast in a pen
confronts its slayer.

"The law of the land demands your life as the penalty of this
crime. It is the judgment of this Court that you be hanged by the
neck—"

Only then did Keanu understand. The handsome body
wilted, the proud head bent forward, as though his neck were
already broken, and had no power left in it to raise his head
again.

"—until you are dead, the sentence to be carried out between
the hours of eight o'clock and noon, in the morning of the last
Tuesday of October, in this year of our Lord, 1884."

Amid whispers of horror and little cries of dismay from the
softhearted ones, and suppressed cheers of gratification from the
righteous, the Chief Justice left the bench. Keanu stood dazed in
the prisoner's stall. He did not move until the guards came to take
him back to the prison in Iwilei.

Satisfied with the course of justice, at ease with the world in
the lawful way it was managed, I strolled out of the Courthouse
to join the people gathered in little groups beneath the shading
milo trees. A strutting cock I was, making my progress in a filthy
barnyard. Like a cock pecking at hens, I reproved some of the
impressionable ladies mourning this sad end to such a splendid
fellow as Keanu. "It serves him right. No man is above the law,
no man can take the law into his hands—and go unpunished."
I sauntered on to the next clutch, clucking their distress. "What
else can you expect, for a fellow as bold, as impious, as Keanu is?
My dear ladies: he is dangerous. He should not be brought into
a community as unguarded as ours is—and as full of susceptible
women." Whether they agreed with me or not I did not care: it
was enough for me that I should put a check to their misdirected

sentimentality, and remind them, if only for a while, of the paths of virtue and the price to crime.

In this way I added another little portion of gratification to the subtle pleasure I found in the humbling of Keanu.

That same evening a great ball was held in one of the fine *haole* houses in town. The Royal Household were just emerging from a period of mourning after the death of the Princess Victoria Kekaulike, one of the Queen's sisters, and from a semblance of mourning for my foster mother, the Princess Ruth Keelikolani. Because the Queen's grief for her sister was not quickly stilled, it was made known that the Royal Couple would not attend the ball. But almost everyone else from the Court was expected to go, eager to enjoy a party after the months of austerity in the palace.

I felt no qualms about going. My foster mother's ghost would have scolded at me if I stayed at home out of grieving for her. "Do not mourn for me, like those missionaries do for their dead," she commanded me more than once while she lay on her death-bed. "Enjoy yourself while you are young. Sorrows, and grief, and mourning: later they will come in plenty." She was kind, but she was also shrewd: she knew I was not a man to grieve for anyone.

I missed her, of course, but I was not inconsolable over her death. She would agree with me, that with her sick liver and her dropsical body she was better dead. The need for me to move from her palace into an establishment of my own helped me to forget her. Within the month I was living my own life, taking up my pleasures again where they were interrupted by her death. Her legacy to me was generous, in lands, in money, in furniture: I was left a wealthy man. By the exercise of his wit, the country boy had made his fortune.

But now he was more than ever alone. It was time, I instructed myself, to look about me for a wife. This was the chief reason why I thought I should go to the Chathams' ball.

But when the hour came near I was feeling strangely out of sorts: I was tired, my body ached, my eyes hurt. I was not entirely ill, but I was not well. I wanted to stay at home, yet I felt I must go to the party. It was one of those times when nothing is right with the world.

In the quiet dusk I took my Saturday bath, not bothering to light the lamp in the dark bathroom. But then, just as I was about to don the evening clothes Paliku had laid out for my use, weariness overcame me. Gratefully I went to bed, forgetting the party, forgetting supper, in my need for sleep. Must be catching a cold, I grumbled, the last thought I had before I fell asleep.

I awoke the next morning feeling much refreshed. It was not a cold after all. I was relieved, for I dislike to be kept from my work—or my play—by sickness.

When I opened my eyes, still heavy with sleep, the sunshine, filtering through the lace curtains, filled the room with a gentle light and fell upon my naked body in flecks of gold. Half asleep, I lay in my broad bed, enjoying the peace of the morning. A fine day for riding, I was thinking—whom shall I invite to go with me?—when I heard the church bells ringing. First the bells of Saint Andrew's rang, just around the corner, then the bells of the Catholic cathedral, three blocks away. In the distance the great bell of Kawaiahao Church added its deep voice, calling people to the last service on the mellow Sunday morning. Almost eleven o'clock, I yawned. Later than I thought: the sun is already high overhead—

But then, if this is so—if this is so—it should not be casting its light upon me—

I sat up. The flecks of light upon my chest and belly moved with me, holding their places upon my skin, clinging to me as limpets to a rock. Looking down upon them in unbelief, I saw that they were not the gift of the sun.

Springing from the bed, I stood erect: the accursed spots were on me still. On the tight curves of my chest, upon the flat belly, down the inner surfaces of my taut thighs, the hideous blotches showed. And they were not golden, like coins cast by the sun. My eyes had played the sleeper's tricks on me: they were dull gray and dead white, those spots, and only the untouched skin around them retained its golden hue.

Moaning in horror I staggered toward the mirror. I did not need a mirror to tell me how the ugly splotches had crawled upon my back and down my legs: I could *feel* them there, itching, spreading, growing with each pulse of my blood. Across the room I stumbled, until I stood before the long pier glass hung upon the wall, the long elegant French mirror at which I adonized before I went out into the world.

There, for me to see, as soon the world would see, was the

weird motley which marked me out a leper. I cried in agony when
I saw it. My face was a mask of horror: it stared back at me from
the mirror, and only the moving mouth, moving as mine moaned,
only the tormented eyes, widening as mine widened in disbelief,
told me that the terrible face was mine.

Upon my image in the glass I sought out each one of those dap-
plings which had been scattered so carelessly over me. It was as
though the fiery hand of God had reached out to prod me, to
turn me around and about for his casual inspection: wherever his
burning fingers had touched me, my body was blighted with the
ashes of dead flesh.

"No! No!" I wailed, raising my face to Heaven. "This is not I
—This is a dream, a nightmare. This is a mistake—" Hopefully
I turned back to the mirror.

There was no mistake. The mirror was pitiless, as Heaven was.
This was my body, my cock's strutting body, with the fine perfection of its parts, the beauty of its golden skin, of its strong
bones, its black hair and white teeth, its eager vital flesh. There
was no mistake: the hand of Death had been laid upon me.
Prodding me in the tender places of my body, turning me with
a disdainful flick, it had marked me for its own. There was no
mistake: and the body to which I had paid such little heed when
it was mine alone I found I loved immeasurably when it was no
longer mine to own.

To the clangorous sound of church bells, rocking the room
with their brazen glee, the world of my proud hopes went crashing down into ruins. The towers of ambition, the palaces of
achievement, the monuments to fame: one by one, with roarings
of noise and clouds of dust, they fell inward, collapsing one upon
the other, and upon the dreamer of my dream. Above them all
the church bells rang, a tocsin of alarm, a clamor of mad joy, ringing, wildly ringing, to tell me how Heaven mocked me, how God
rocked with laughter at his grisly jest.

"What have I done? What have I done, that I should be
treated in this way?" It was my high voice, screaming up at God,
storming the bar of Heaven.

But there was no answer. Only the sound of the church bells
filled my ears, and the sobs of my rage, calling upon a God in
whom I did not believe.

I could bear no more. With a cry of fury, braying with all of the wild unleashed anger of a man helpless and betrayed, I seized a heavy bronze candlestick and hurled it at the mirror. The shards of glass, as they fell crashing to the floor, could not drown out the sound of my raging, as I cursed a malicious God for doing this thing to me.

Hours later, when the day was ending, I called Paliku to my room.

"Bring light," I ordered, when he appeared. In the darkness he could not see the shattered mirror, the littered room, my blighted self.

"It was my thought that you were away. You were so quiet," he said cheerfully when he returned, bearing the oil lamp before him. "I have only now returned from my holiday. *Auwe, auwe!* And what has happened here? How is it that the big looking glass is broken?"

"I broke it. Do you not think I have cause?" I moved into the circle of light. Naked still, I stood before him, wanting to enjoy the sight of his horror. A thing to frighten people: this was all I could be. And because they were well, and I was doomed, I hated them, I wanted to frighten them. Because Paliku was nearest to me, the only one I had, I wanted to hurt him. The sight of his fear would hurt me deepest of all.

He stared at me, examining me from my head to my feet. The smile was quickly frightened away, I noticed with grim satisfaction. Without a word he put the lamp upon a table. It pleased me to see how his hand trembled, how his mouth quivered. I waited for him to turn and run from me. I would have rejoiced, because this is what I wanted him to do. But he disappointed me.

"Caleb, Caleb," he said, coming toward me with arms outstretched. The tears were heavy in his eyes, his cheeks were sunken in. "My heart grieves for thee: it grieves as for a son."

"Beware!" I snarled. "Come no closer! It is the *lepera*." For the first time I said the dreadful name. It issued from me like a cry of despair.

"And do I not know it? How many times have I seen it. It is a terrible thing. But does it mean that I should run away from you?"

The foolish old man came up to me and took me in his arms. "No, it is not right, that I should run away." Enclosing me in his embrace, scented with tobacco and the sweat of his clean body, he put my head upon his shoulder, held me tight against his breast. And I, who never knew the comforting of a father or of a mother, who never had a shoulder to lean upon, a bosom to unburden myself upon, what did I do? I, the hate-full Caleb, who expected to keep him from me with a curse, I found myself weeping in his arms. The grief came pouring out of me, as rain from the clouds when they are torn by the peaks of the mountains, and I wept as I had never wept before, as men are not supposed to weep. The old man wept with me: his tears fell warm upon my diseased flesh. But they could not wash my uncleanness away.

When I was done with weeping, Paliku put me gently from him. "Your clothes   I will bring them. You will catch cold, this way."

He did not know why I laughed so brokenly. "Does it matter?" I had to explain to him. "Why should I fear a cold? I want to die."

Now indeed was he shaken: now did the horror come into his face. "Do not say it   These are not good thoughts."

"Why should I live? Why?" In the long afternoon there was much time to think. A quick death: this was the way I would choose. The long years of waiting, of rotting away, of hiding or of exile upon Molokai: no, I would not submit to them.

"Caleb. Do not be angry with God."

"Should I love him, for what he has done to me?"

"Can you know what is in his mind? Can we tell that what he sends to you is not what he thinks is best for you?"

"What could be worse than this?" Once more I began to rage, shouting at him in my hatred for his God, before whom he bowed so unquestioningly. "Look at this—and this—and this! Are these marks signs of the favor of God?"

Calmly he waited for me to stop, softly he answered me. "Can you say they are not? Who knows the ways of God? Do you?"

How could I argue against such stupidity, against such faith? He gave me the one answer to which I had no answer.

"There are worse things than the *lepera*. Have you seen a man who is blind? Have you seen old Kahana, who lies helpless in his bed because of a stroke? And those people who must be chained to trees in their yards, because they are mad? Have you seen them?"

"No."

"No, you have not, because it is not the way of the young to see these things, which are the cares of the old. There are indeed many things worse than the *lepera*, my son."

Valiantly he struggled with me, to turn my mind away from its thoughts of death. He was a wise old man, and a loving one, and he succeeded in blunting the edge of my despair.

"And who can say that you will not get well in time? It has happened. The *mai Pake* does not always kill. There are people—I have seen them—who come back from Kalaupapa. After five years, after ten years, something happens in them: the signs of their sickness vanish, they are well again."

"This I did not know." I seized upon the hope. "Is this the truth you tell me?"

"It is the truth. I swear it, before God."

I did not give Paliku the comfort of knowing he had won his contest for my life. I merely ceased to argue with him over it. This was how ungrateful I was with the good man.

With my anger went my strength. Suddenly I was worn out. Feebly I turned toward my bed.

Paliku helped me into it, he smoothed the disordered sheets and arranged the crumpled pillows to support my head. "I will fix for you a sleeping potion, of the kind I made for the *Kalani,* when her pain was great and she could not sleep."

In a short time he was back, with a glass upon a silver tray. The liquid in the glass was thick and red, the color of blood. It was bitter, with the juices of a dozen herbs. Keelikolani had put no trust in *haole* medicines. As I fell asleep I was thankful to the *kahuna lapaau laau* who had made that philter for her comforting, and mine.

When I awoke the next morning the faithful old man was still with me, sitting asleep in a chair which he had placed at the side of my bed.

That day Paliku went to ask Dr. Trousseau to come and examine me. He knew almost as much about the leprosy as the visiting physician from Germany, who had come to Hawaii to study the disease. I wanted to have the best. I would have called in the German, if I had known where to find him. Deep in my mind lay the hope that perhaps it was not the leprosy after all which appeared in me, but some other one of the foreigners' diseases which, in my ignorance, I was mistaking for the *mai Pake*.

The Frenchman did not keep me long in doubt. Protecting his hands with gloves made of thin red rubber, he turned me about, stuck a pin into my flesh in a dozen different places. He did not see me as a person I was an arrangement of whorls and splotches, held together by stretches of healthy skin.

"I am mos' afraid, M'sieu," he began, carefully stripping off the gloves, folding them delicately in a piece of heavy linen, "that it is indeed what you fear: the leprosy orientale . . ." He had the thin face, the hooked nose, the piercing dark eyes of a fanatic, and the full lips of a sensualist, surrounded by the beard of Mephistopheles. He spoke with the lisp of a child, full of sibilant zisses and zoses, and yet with the quick rush of words of a man impatient to get on with his work. I respected him at once, even with all his contradictions of features and of speech, and I knew there was no questioning his verdict.

"Thank you for your frankness, Doctor." The calmness in my manner disguised the dread lying coiled in my liver. But if a man cannot be brave in the presence of his physician, when can he be brave? "I wished to know the truth."

"It is a truth I am telling too many times, these days. The number of cases of the leprosy among the people in this country, sir: it is unbelievable. There is no end to them, and I am much worried. Soon, if they continue to sicken in this way, there will be no 'awaiians to live in these beautiful islands of ours."

"I thought most of the cases were already found—were already on Molokai."

"*Hélas!* It will be many generations yet, before all of the leperous are found, and put in Molokai."

"Have you doctors found no medicines to treat them?"

"*Tiens!* Is there one simple disease which can be treated with the certainty of success? Do we have medicines to cure a cold in the 'ead? Can we stop a pimple from becoming a boil, a boil from becoming an ingrowing abscess—and this from becoming the poisoning of the blood? No, no, you ask for the impossible, when you ask for a treatment for the leprosy. This will come at the last, if it comes at all. First we must learn how to treat the smallest of pimples."

"Then what of me? What is in store for me?"

He looked down at me, stroking his Imperial, a worried devil appraising a sinner's spotted body. "You are in the good Lord's hand, M'sieu. This is all I can say to you, all that any physician can say." The advice seemed most incongruous, coming from him.

"This is no comfort to me."

"Then I am indeed sorree for you. There is no other comfort with this disease."

"I suppose I must go to Kalaupapa?"

"I do not know." He lifted his hands, as though weighing in them the evidences of my station and wealth. "The rich, they 'ave their privileges. Yet I must report to the Board of Health the existence of your malady. It is the law. The rest: it is for you to say."

I could imagine the wave of gossip which would sweep through the Board of Health when they saw my name in Dr. Trousseau's report. I could see Mr. Gibson's white eyebrows rearing in excitement when he saw my familiar name upon the list of unknown others. What chance does a man have for privacy, when his affairs become the property of bureaucrats? Soon it would be all over town that Caleb Forrest is a leper. Natives would come knocking at my door, to wail their woe and ask for my money. The *haoles*, the few who would bother, would send aloof notes, protecting their bodies as well as their sensibilities with brittle phrases of regret. I hated the thought of the unwelcome attention I would be getting, from all the busybodies in town.

"Would it be better for me if I should go to Kalaupapa?"

"Not for you, no. It is a terrible place. But for your people, yes, it would be better. It is always better for the common folk when the *alii* show them what is the right thing to do."

It pleased me that he should think I was a member of the nobility. But it annoyed me, too, how the *alii* must always pay a price, especially in this matter of the segregation of the lepers from the well. Now I knew how Peter Kahekili must have felt, when he was confronted with the choice. And why the Princess Ruth should praise him for his decision to go to Molokai. "Pita has done the right things," she pronounced, nodding her heavy head until the earrings jangled. "It is a strange thing, how only in sickness can he show the way. In the days of his health he was *not* the best example."

"Well, what Peter Kahekili did Caleb Forrest can do as well." (But who will praise me now, Keelikolani, now when you are gone?)

"Pardon?"

"I will go to Molokai."

"You are a man of courage."

"If you will do these things for me—"

Warily he waited for me to state my terms. He was a shrewd one, this Frenchman.

"First, you must tell the President of the Board of Health to suppress the news about my sickness until I am gone from Honolulu. I want no talk about me, no visitors, no pity."

"I understand. Perfectly. I will ask for his assistance in this matter. And the second?"

"Permit me to stay here, in my own house, until the time comes for me to go to Molokai. I promise you that I—I shall not be a danger to my people." I was about to say that I would not leave the house when a returning thought warned me to change my promise.

"I do not see why this, too, cannot be arranged with Mr. Gibson. When I 'ave 'is answer, I will let you know."

"Thank you, Doctor. I am grateful for your help."

"It is to my sorrow, M'sieu, that there is so little I—or any other man—can do to help you in the time of your distress. But I think you have a strength of your own, coming from within. I pray it will not be lost to you."

Bowing stiffly, he hastened from the room. Paliku escorted him to the front door, leaving me alone with my emptiness.

It was arranged, just as I wished. The next day a letter came for me, written in Mr. Gibson's own hand:

MY DEAR MR. FORREST:

Permit me to express to you my sorrow and my sympathy over the affliction which God in his Wisdom has visited upon you. My words at this time, I know, can bring you little comfort now, but I do not refrain from sending them, in the hope that they will bring you sustenance in the future. It is often the way with sorrows laid upon us, by both God and men, that they are followed by blessings we cannot foresee; and I pray that this experience, which I have known in my own life, will come to you, in time, to lighten yours.

Last evening I told Their Majesties of your sickness, knowing of their interest in you, and knowing that you would forgive me this breach of your confidence. The Queen wept. His Majesty shared her grieving. "The nation loses a good man and a brilliant mind," he said. "We can ill afford the loss." His sentiments will be shared by the rest of our people when, very soon, your absence will be marked.

I cannot commend too highly your nobility of purpose in resolving to go to Kalaupapa. The King is grateful for the good example you are setting the people, and I, his responsible Minister, join him in this gratitude.

When you are ready to go, please send to let me know. I will make the arrangements for your passage to Molokai.

Believe me, sir, when I say that I am

Your most humble servant,
WALTER MURRAY GIBSON

"The Queen wept. The King grieved." There was little comfort for me in their distant artifices, or in the Premier's artful consolation. It seems that even trash can serve a purpose, I sneered, as slowly I tore up Mr. Gibson's letter into little pieces, making useless rubbish out of it.

For the whole month of my waiting I did not leave the house. "If people ask for me, tell them I have gone away," I instructed Paliku to say. He was more faithful a liar than the Prime Minister was: after the first few days there were no inquiries for me at either the back door or the front one.

During the month the leper's spots upon my body were joined by a mark even more monstrous. Faintly at first, but gradually growing more intense, a streak of white, half my hand in width, began to show in my hair, and a jagged strip of whitened skin led from it down the right side of my face and neck. Far worse than the blotches upon my body, this mark burned upon my head like a white flame in a bed of coals. The hand of God was crueler than I thought it could be, for with this straking it marked me out from all other men.

I watched in wonder as the blazon appeared and grew, much as a man might watch the burgeoning of a naked loathsome grub. Why? Why should it be me? I asked over and over again, trying to understand why I was chosen for this trying.

But nowhere could I find an answer to my question.

In the evening before I was to board the *Mokolii* I slipped out of the house. An English cap hid the streak in my hair, and the mark on my face was covered up with the woman's powder I had asked Paliku to buy for me. Before this last resort I had tried the juices of the banana stalk, but they were no good: they did not stain the dead skin evenly, and left only a thick dirty scum on my cheek. Nor was the juice of the *kukui* nut's thick rind of use: it was too dark for my light complexion.

Two errands sent me forth that night, errands which I could not entrust to Paliku, or to any other one.

The first was easily done. I waited in the street until the drug store was empty, and then I went in and purchased my packet of poison. Paliku's superstitious fear at my talk of suicide had not changed my mind: I merely put off the time, for his sake, until he would not be able to see me dead.

The second errand was done with difficulty: I walked through the shadows of the city, saying farewell to Honolulu. This was my most sorrowful parting. Far more than anyone who lived in it did I love the fair haven from which I was being cast out.

A dying moon lighted my way, a solitary tear in the sky: shed for me, it was the emblem of my waning. In its eerie light I wandered as a ghost must wander, haunting the places of its former joys, of its lifetime's triumphs and defeats. From the druggist's grimy shop I walked down Fort Street to the Old Courthouse, where I had made my studies as an apprentice lawyer. A whited tomb it was now, holding the bones of my dead hopes.

Eastward I turned, led by the malevolent moon, white as a skull, riding high above the serene mountains. In the great Square I halted, hurt to my heart by the beauty of Kalakaua's Palace. Many a time have I scoffed at it, when others were listening, pretending to laugh at its alien form and parvenu's pretensions. But this night, glowing with the warmth of a thousand soft lights, it was lovely beyond all imagining: a faery castle, fashioned out of crystal and of ivory, it rose, tier upon tier, its towers and battlements crested with silver, its rooms suffused with the color of life. Standing on the outside, looking in, I was sick with envy for those who lived in the realm of its enchantment. How fortunate they were! And how little did they appreciate their good fortune. The girls I knew: Julia and Abbie and proud Pililua: they wished only to escape it, into the house of a husband. Malie: she existed in it, as a plant does in a conservatory, breathing in its air, filling her corner of it with a touch of impermanent beauty, but drawing nothing more from it than her sustenance, giving nothing more to it than her presence. The gentle King, the amazon Queen: for them it was the setting for their high estate, but they did not love it, as I did; and, overwhelmed by it, they could scarcely bear to live in it: they fled whenever they could to the more prosaic comforts of The Cottage, tucked away in a corner of the palace yard. In all the kingdom, there were only two of us who could make fullest use of this enchanted castle: Mr. Gibson, who had evoked it, conjuring it up out of the nation's gold and masons' hardened hands; and I, who loved it, who wanted it for my own. And now, when Mr. Gibson would be gone, I would not be here to take his place.

At my back the massive pile of the Government Building was dark: the Prime Minister was managing the kingdom from some more pleasant setting. All of the King's men were at home, that night, enjoying the rewards of their littleness. Only the motionless statue of the Great Kamehameha stood watch, his right hand uplifted in the ancient greeting, the long spear held in his left hand, ready to ward off the spears of the enemies of his people.

"Where is your *mana* gone, O Lonely One?" I called up to him, thinking of the death of his seed. Of them all there was only one weak woman left. "Where is the might of your spear?" I cried, thinking of how wasted was the nation, of how fast it was dwindling away under the attack of invisible enemies his spear could not parry. Hopelessly I turned away from the mute effigy, as powerless as I. To call upon him was to *hanehane* with spirits, a twittering in the dark.

I had one more visit to make. Before the monumental heap of colonnades and stairs and soaring turrets which was Keelikolani's Palace I stopped for the last time. I could acknowledge it now: it was partly for my pushing sake that she determined to build this new palace. But it was entirely to please herself that she made it such a splendid one. Alas for our pride! We did not enjoy it long: three months after we moved into Keoua Hale she was dead. True to herself, she died not in the palace but in a grass hut in Kona, near to where she was born. And I was not with her when she died.

In the darkness, as I looked for the last time upon the enormous edifice, the grief welled up in me beyond damming. I do not know for whom I wept the more: for the lost Keelikolani, no longer here to save me, or for my lost self. The taste of a woman's powder, washed from my blighted face by my tears, was bitter: it was the taste of dying.

On the day of departure I went aboard the *Mokolii* early in the afternoon, to avoid the stares of the curious.

Only Paliku accompanied me to Sam Wilder's wharf. "Let me go with you to Kalawao, to be your *kokua*," he begged me again, as we drove away from the house. But I forbade him this greatest service to me. "You have given enough of your life to others. Now you must live for yourself." I did not tell him how I was giving him the house in which we two had lived, and a generous pension. He would read of it in the letter I left for him, on the silver tray in the hall. There was no better use for my money: when I was dead, there would be no one to use my wealth.

We parted without words. Our *aloha* needed no saying. I went alone into the shadows of the wharf, while he drove off in the hired hack. I did not look back.

By this last exercise of privilege I escaped the maudlin excesses of farewell which I knew my fellow passengers would draw upon them. But because I hid in my hot and dirty cabin I did not learn that Malie was aboard the *Mokolii* with me, and the German doctor with Keanu.

32

WHEN I SAW KEANU on the *Mokolii*, I was astonished. What! Is he, too, taken with the leprosy? I wondered, knowing a leper's flush of pity for the ill-fated fellow. But on the beach the talk of Ioane Paele and Hamau gave me the information I lacked. With this my attitude toward Keanu swung again to its old dislike, intensified by the reversal in our positions. Is this the reward of crime? I muttered, clasping envy to my bosom as I began to feel the poison gnawing at my bowels. I was waiting to die, and the sight of Keanu free, ready to gamble once again with life, was more than my small store of charity could abide.

And yet, a few days later, when Dr. Newman wanted to perform his test upon Keanu, I tried to save him from the *haole's* devilish experiment. "Don't let him do it, Keanu!" I called out to him, forgetting my dislike of the person in my eagerness to save the man from the possibility of a leper's end. But neither my concern nor Father Damien's wrath could deny the German his victim: at first a child whining for a toy, then a hunter wresting his prize from the hounds, at last a madman thrusting aside all restraints we laid upon him, the doctor would not hear our pleas for Keanu's sake, and he had his way with him. When Damien stormed away from the vile scene, unwilling to be a witness to the deed, I should have gone with him. But, held in my place by a fatal indecisiveness, I stayed. Sickened as I was, as a flinching human being, by Newman's cruelty, I could not deny the justification which his plan called forth in my reason: he was right, the test must be performed, if ever a cure is to be found. And, more eager for a cure, for my sake, than I was willing to fight for Keanu's sake, I stood silently by, while Newman performed the brutal marriage between Akala's separate flesh and Keanu's.

After the terrible act, I held, in common with most of the people of the Settlement, a certain sympathy for the abused convict. But in the slow weeks of our lives in Kalawao it was easy enough to forget both the murderer and his keeper, immured in their prison on the hill. I had other things to worry about, most notably my very precious self: just as in some diseases there are relapses and remissions, after long periods of quiescence, so it was with my sickness of the soul. In Kalawao's idle days and useless nights, there was too much time for me to indulge my self-pity; and in this way I kept the fever of my soul's sickness strong.

Malie's rebuff of me did not help my recovery. When I left her, after offering her my heart, my liver, my whole vulnerable self, I was sick with aggravation. Ahh, that evening of my shaming!

How have other men lived with chagrin? How have they mended their heart's receptacle, and their pride, when their most precious gift has been rejected? Books are useless on the subject of the rejected suitor: they prattle on and on about the raptures of the lover who has been accepted. But what of the man rebuffed? Because I was such a one, I could not think that the man who is turned away is something to be thrown aside.

Leaving Malie standing alone in the road, I hurried away to hide, feeling that the whole Settlement was lined up along the lane to jeer at my defeat.

"Bitch!" I swore. "Bitch!" with each fleeing step, timing my progress with the deliciousness of abuse. I had no humor in me to see how wrong was my choice of the epithet.

I could not go home; sleep was out of the question. I walked for hours among the stony lanes and winding pathways of Kalawao, plunging headlong where my feet had never carried me, heedless of danger. Why should I care what happens to me? I asked the cold and pitiless stars. Does anyone care? I am the man rejected.

I found myself at last upon the path following the line of the sea cliffs. Standing at the edge of the land, I thought to throw myself into the sea. *Then* she'll be sorry, I promised myself with my tongue, knowing in my mind that she would not give a damn about my broken body, lying in the wash of the waves upon the cruel sharp rocks below. Hating her, who had been the instrument of my shaming, I stood upon the brink of the cliff, watching the froth of the waves come hissing and churning in, listening to the moaning groaning sobbing sounds the water made in the caverns and clefts which riddled the rotten earth beneath my feet. They are the voices of my desolation, I sobbed, echoing through the rottenness of my body The great breakers thundered and crashed, shaking the land with their might. So am I shaken by the cruel hand of Fate . . .

Gradually, irresistibly, their violence quelled the little violence which was my own. In the face of that immense monster the sea, my troubles were awed into nothingness. Not for the first time, nor for the last, the sea showed me how puny I am, and it quieted me. Wet with wave spray, chilled to my disgruntled liver, I crept home to bed at last, and fell asleep without another thought of Malie.

After that night I returned often to the sea cliffs, to learn anew my lesson in smallness. By day the insidious germs of my self-pity did their work, filling me anew with their poison. By night I purged myself of it, standing at the edge of the sea.

But there were times when even the cleansing ocean could not free me of my anguish. Those were the rare nights when, only a little beyond the reach of my hand, but forever out of reach, a glittering ship went by, glowing like a floating city moving upon the blackness of the sea. Across the water the mournful cry of the ship's siren would come, in salute to the people of the Settlement.

Upon the sea cliffs some of us would be gathered, each huddled in his lonely niche in the rocks, to watch the world pass us by. Our separate silence was more terrible than tears. And when the ship was gone out of sight, its beauty washed away by the dashing spray, or drowned in the lapping water, then, ah then, would despair roll in upon us like an engulfing wave.

O Caliban, brother Caliban! I would cry above the heedless waters, let us together curse the world and all the vile people in it. Let us rage and swell our souls with hate! Let us shriek and raven and rend and destroy! Let us pull them all down to our bestial hating depth—

Poor Caliban. He had a right to curse, diseased and dispossessed as he was by Prospero's haughty meanness. I always did feel a sympathy for Caliban, even before the red plague seized upon me and made my body as monstrous as his, and bent my soul until it became as misshapen as his. But when I became a leper the nearness of my state to his was almost more than I could bear, and the ease with which I could think myself Caliban racked me with cramps to the very guts of my aching rage-roaring soul. The anguish was unsupportable, and it burst from me at times in fits of howling and wild weeping, as I walked the desolate shore of my prison-island. Then did I curse, and shake my fist in Heaven's face, raging at it and at all beneath it. Then did I curse, as cheated Caliban might have cursed, cursing mankind, cursing the *haoles* for what they have done to me and my people, most especially cursing God, that invisible Prospero who hid himself from me, but who made me feel his malice and the hurt of his burning hand.

O, I knew how to curse, and to hate, and to scream my fury at the Ariel winds, until, spent at last, I found the one comfort of exhaustion. And, as I learned my ritual of profanation, there beside the indifferent sea, I learned also that while I could curse in half a dozen languages I knew how to love in none.

Perhaps this was an effect of the leprosy, opposite to the one which most others of the lepers feel; perhaps it was the effect of my preoccupation with other things. Who can say, when so little is known of the resources of the heart, and of its emptinesses? But when those seizures of misery were done and I was quieted again, I had time to study myself, and in the study I discovered how little I knew of love. Lust I had known, in its brute's measure, the rampant lust of the animal seeking the release of his desire. But of the delirious raptures of love, the sweet torments and blissful needs of Ferdinand's true love, the delectable disease of the heart which seeks its cure in the pleasing of the beloved, I saw that I knew nothing. My heart was as a stone, dead, unacquainted with joy, not much different from Malie's stony unmoved body. I was as much a stranger to love as she was.

This hardness of the heart is the lesion which aches the most, in this rotting tormented body of mine compounded all of aches and pains. For if there is hurt in the thought that there is no one who would love this hideous Caliban, how much greater is the hurt of knowing that there is no heart in Caliban for loving? There is only a wound of a mouth for sneering, and a voice, harsh as the rasp of files upon stones, for cursing.

And a mind, bright and sharp and flashing, delighting in the pleasures of thought, eager to be used, eager to use—and unused, cast off, useless, except to remind me a thousand times a day, a million times in a minute, that I am doomed, that soon I shall die, alone. Stinking, befouled, frightened—and alone.

Because suffering is what I expected of me, I tried to make myself suffer by staying away from the house of Makaio. After a week of denying myself the pleasure of the company there, I went back to them.

It was not Malie I went to see, I persuaded myself, not unaware that I might be deluding myself with the argument. But the sight of her did not disturb me at all. The fact that I had actually hated her for a while I found merely silly, but not quite as ridiculous as the idea of wanting to marry her. Thus easily does the rejected suitor mend his heart, and take up once more the business of living. No wonder he is ignored by books.

Tutu did not know it, but she held the finest salon in the Settlement. Even then there were times when the gossip and the small-mindedness of the group exasperated me. One such evening we fell into an argument over Damien. Momona made some of his usual prickling statements about the priest's deportment. He did not believe for a moment the truth of what he said, wanting only to stir up Makaio, who cherished an adulation for the priest which was almost sickening.

Perhaps it was the sultriness of the weather which affected our tempers so. In any event, all at once, fretted by Makaio's stupidity and Kewalo's bellowing, I could bear no more of them. I left the group abruptly, I went out into the glowering night. With the inconsistency of the hopeless, I wanted to be alone again. I walked down to the sea cliffs, to find my quieting there.

A *kona* storm was coming up from the south: the flashes of lightning over the bulwark of the mountains, the rolls of distant thunder, warned me that one of our rare electrical storms was sweeping over the islands. It was a "time when Heaven leans back in pain, is in travail, a time when violence is about to be born."

On the headlands around me frightened fishermen prepared to run for home, their torches moving in excited patterns as they gathered up their scattered gear and raced across the plain toward the villages. Soon there were no lights left upon the cliffs, and I was alone. I kept telling myself to go home, too, before the storm broke. I am not such a poetical fellow that I like to get wet when I am out cleansing the black bile from my spirit.

Despite everything, I sat too long in my seat upon Kalaupapa's prow. It was as though the tension in me could not release itself, because of the heavy and ominous power in the air. Even the sea was oppressed by the weight of the clouds above us: flattened almost smooth, heaving and sighing as with a fear of its own, it rose and ebbed, wanting to escape and having nowhere to hide.

The first warm drops of rain fell upon me. I listened to the patter of the raindrops as they fell upon the skin of the water, upon the dry breast of the land. Never had the sea been so still: it ceased even to sigh.

Helplessly I waited for the wildness of the storm to come. It came, inexorable and mighty, after a forerunner of warm moist wind. It came, a roar of rain falling from the freighted clouds, a central fiery heart of lightning making the earth blanch, a cracking of thunder, splitting the dome of night.

Tremendous it came, like the footfalls of God striding across his darkened universe. For me, huddled in my seat of stone, upon the very edge of this infinitesimal piece of earth beside the cowering sea, the thought was inescapable. Mightily did he advance, hurling his bolts of wrath, bellowing his power and arrogance, indifferent to the earth whereon he trod, disdainful of the people, vermin in his path. How like unto a god he came!

Furious with such cruelty, violent in my rebellion against such ruthlessness, I sprang to my feet. Seized with madness, I shook my fist in his face. "Monster!" I shouted, spitting my venom at him. Like a scorpion I sought to sting the heel of the foot which was about to crush me. "Demon! Devil!" I shrieked, pitting my tiny voice against his trumpeting one.

For answer, he smote me with lightning, rocked me with thunder, pissed on me. Gasping for breath, spluttering in the deluge of rain, I was drenched in the space of a heartbeat.

"Shark! Man-eater! Lying cheating killer of men!" Raising my fists, baring my teeth, I jumped up and down in my tiny arena, chanting ugly epithets in my litany of hate, dredging my mind for all the filth I could remember or invent. A miserable sodden Caliban, I danced my dance of desecration upon the threshold of hell, cursing God. "Kill me! Kill me now! I dare you!"

Did he hear me? Did he feel the pinprick of my poisoned mind, as I stood forth to do battle with him? Were the blasts of thunder, the cracklings of fire, his acknowledgment of my challenge? Or were they the brazen tongue of his mockery?

For a minute of terror I thought he heard me. A blaze of fire lighted up the pit in which I howled, revealed a naked giant standing above me, only a few feet away. Rain sheathed his huge body in molten steel. Lightning glowed from the corselet round his chest, suffusing it with blue fire. Standing upon his rock, he looked down upon me. And then the darkness closed in again.

My voice died away in dread, but my heart leaped with joy. He is here! He exists: he has sent me a sign! And in this sign of grace I would have found meaning for a lifetime of sorrows.

The next flash of lightning showed him stepping down from his rock, coming toward me.

Paralyzed with fear, expecting the touch of death, I waited for a blaze of wrath from his hand to consume me.

When the fire came, he was standing an arm's length from me. "You!" I snarled. "You! What the hell are you doing here?"

It was Keanu, looking sorrowfully down upon me. The long

black hair, the black beard, hung limp about his face. The faded
blue prison clothes were stuck to his body, a second skin.

In the darkness I turned my hate for God upon Keanu, and my
shame at being seen in my wretchedness. All of the oaths I had
been hurling into unhearing Heaven I now cast upon Keanu. The
hissing of the rain upon the sea was as joyful laughter compared
with the hissing of my serpent's tongue.

He heard me until, breathless, I was forced to stop. Then, strong
and low, his voice came to me out of the darkness. "Are you
the only one who suffers?"

I fell back from him. Stunned, I found no words to say to him.
When the next flash of lightning came, he was already gone away.

Spent, unable even to groan, I sank to my knees upon the rocks,
streaming with the rain. Falling upon my side I lay there, cold
and worn, sick with misery, until the tempest was gone far out to
sea.

The sorrowing countenance, the shattering words: they burned
in my mind, haunted me in my sleep and in my waking. By making me aware how others, too, had grievances with Heaven, and
sorrows which they did not share with other men, Keanu took
away from me the solace of my self-pity. I felt ashamed of myself, and I hid from the sight of men.

It was easy for me to withdraw into myself, to live alone, paying
no attention to anything or anyone other than my all-important
self. I asked little from the world, wanting only that my comfort
and convenience should not be disarranged.

My need for a woman no longer existed: where others burned,
I was a torch burned out. Six months before I would have thought
this old man's affliction worse than death, but when it came upon
me I did not even notice it because the part of my life which it
affected had become so unimportant to me.

In those six months I discovered that all other afflictions of the
flesh are as mosquito bites upon the skin, compared with the
ravening leprosy of the mind which is the fear of Death. I learned
what all mortals dread to learn: there is nothing worse than
Death.

One day in January Eleu rapped on my window sill. We were
rather good friends: I liked his inquiring mind, he liked my an-

swering one. We talked of many things, and I helped him with his lessons when Malie was too busy in their school to teach him, or when—as happened all too frequently, I am afraid—she did not know the answers to his questions. I was never at a loss for answers, even if I had to invent them, and in this way we two got along very well.

"We going sweeming," he announced, poking his head through the open window. "You like come wid us?" Bad as his English was, he usually insisted on speaking it with me.

His ragged hair was all matted and glossy. From the mere sight of him, before the spicy scent was wafted across the room to me, I could tell that he and his gang had been playing in the forest, swatting each other over the head with the soft flower buds of the mountain *awapuhi*, the one the kids call the "shampoo ginger." I could not hold back my smiles: he is a boy who knows how to enjoy life. I looked with approval upon his good features, the fine shoulders.

"E, how come? No moah school today?" I was seated at my table, writing an order to San Francisco for books, and I did not want to leave my refuge for a swim in the cold mountain pool we usually went to when we wanted to bathe.

"Nah, nah. Miss Kekoa seeck again. She alla time getting seeck now. We going da islan'. We going 'flying.'"

"*Eia iho!* Wait a moment! You want me to walk all the way across that beach? And then you want me to swim all the way out to that steep mountain in the sea?"

"Sure. Wy not? You not too ol'." Even the irregular blackened teeth, where the decay had been at work since the teeth were sprouted, could not spoil the pleasing effect he made. With something of an older brother's amusement, and perhaps a little of his pride, I noticed for the first time the signs that Eleu was close to being a man. When he is full grown, I could predict, he will be something to set the women afire: *ke kane mamane*, they will call him, a man who is not necessarily the handsomest man to walk before them, but a man who will excite them with the gifts he has.

"No. I cannot go. I am too old: I would drown in the ocean. Or, if I am not dead of tiredness before I get there, I am certainly *make* when I get back. Nah, you fallas go."

"But you say you like go 'fly' nex' time we go." Flying: this was their name for their dangerous sport. They would swim across the deep channel to Olala, the nearer of the two sugar-loaf islands. They would cut the big fan-shaped leaves from the *loulu* palms growing on the islet, and they would carry those leaves to the top of the sheer cliffs overhanging the sea. There, a hundred feet or more above the water, the experts among them would tie the stem of one leaf to each arm. Then they would jump and, using the broad leaves like birds' wings, they would glide on the currents of air down to the sea. The less daring would weave umbrellas from several of the leaves and would use this device, like a balloonist's parachute, to break the speed of their fall. It sounded like a game of fun—for them. I had sense enough to know it was not a game for me to try. Harder than Icarus would I fall, if not so far, and I did not have a mind to be drowned in the sea.

"I said I like watch, not fly." I had made some kind of a commitment long ago, and, as with so many promises glibly made to children, I had forgotten it. But Eleu's disappointment made me look for a compromise. "Oh, all right, all right. I tell you what. You fallas go. I give you a head start: two hours. Then I come to the head of the trail. You know, where it goes down to the beach. There I will stand and watch, while you fly."

"O.K. We go. I wait for you, unteel you dere."

"So long. And look out for the sharks."

"Nevah worry," he winked, one bright eye enfolded by the blackest of lashes. "Dey no like dahk meat." With a flick of the hand he went off to his perilous game.

Two and a half hours later I was in my place, under the wind-bent trees at the edge of Kalawao. Not since the day of my arrival had I returned there, and I did not like my memories of the ugly time. It was an illusion, of course, but I fancied I could still smell the evidence of my sickness among the bushes. "Damned druggist!" I cursed him again, finding it more pleasing to blame him for making a fool of me than to scorn myself for being so easily made a fool.

I was cold, under the trees, so I moved into the open space about ten yards seaward of the trail. I sat on a rock, sunning myself like a lizard. Eleu would have no trouble finding me: my white shirt and Panama hat would draw his attention, even across the stretch of water.

The boys were right: it was a day for swimming. It was the kind of golden day which, if I had been living in Honolulu, would have made me forsake my lawyer's desk for a drive to the Pali of Nuuanu, or to the beach of Waikiki, provided with a basket lunch and an agreeable young lady as ready for holiday as I. It was the sort of day when one says, out of instinct, how glad one is to be alive.

But in Kalawao I was not so grateful. I admitted that it was beautiful, in its way, but I tried to find flaws in it, as a man tries to find flaws in the beauty of a woman who has deceived him. The deep-blue waters of the bay, with the green islands and the curving green shoulder of the mountain at the far side of the beach: they were not likely to be matched for beauty in any place in the world. And the long miles of the tremendous escarpment carrying the green wall of Molokai to its mysterious end far in the east: they could not be surpassed for grandeur anywhere else in the world. But I would not admit it. The greens of the forest trees and of the thick grasses upon the *palis* were too yellow, too garish, I argued. The streak of raw red earth breaking into the expanse of grass, where the mouth of Waikolu's stream was eating away at the mountain, was like a scar on a woman's chin. Or worse: like the reddened sores about a leper's mouth.

Not even the sight of the magnificent waterfall far down the coast, toward Pelekunu, a torrent plunging for more than a thousand feet down the perpendicular *pali*, could make me admit I was in the presence of almost ineffable beauty and that, out of sheerest gratitude to a fate which had put me down to live with it, I ought to confess that I was glad to be alive.

No: the distant slash of white, marking the face of the cliff, was too much like the blaze slashing across my face. No: the parapet of mountains was too much the prison wall, denying me the whole wondrous earth—

It was not my day for rejoicing at anything. I sat upon my rock, less alive than a lizard, squinting across the dazzling bay to imagine Eleu and his company at their sport, picking fretfully at the scabs upon my ears until they bled, wondering what the hell I was doing there in the heat of noon, when I should have been at home, eating my lunch.

The swimmers, at least, were having their fun, swooping like sea birds from the cliff into the sea. The wings were not much help, and sometimes the flyers plummeted like crippled birds, losing their wings as they fell. The woven parachutes served better: they slowed the fall of the jumpers, and their bodies, suspended from the arching umbrellas, swayed in the air during the long descent from the black cliff to the blue sea. Every now and then, when the wind was right, shouts of pleasure came faintly across the water. They were too far away for me to know which one was Eleu, so I watched them all, occasionally waving my hat in the event that Eleu happened to be looking toward me. Fifteen minutes of this fraternal attention, I promised myself, and then I shall go home, my duty done.

Although I was not in any danger of enjoying myself, I was intent upon the swimmers when someone came up behind me, calling his *aloha*. Thinking it was one of my fellow patients, I turned to give him my response. I was not pleased to discover the priest limping toward me. Oh, it's that one, I groaned, not very quietly. *Wahaohi!* The old chatterer! What does he want of me? Troubling me, beneath my bother, was a reaction to his limp. He favored his left foot, as a leper would with a leg in pain.

He had aged, since last I'd seen him. When was it? I couldn't remember when it was. The hair was grayer, the face thinner, with creases and wrinkles scored deeper into it. Yet he did not seem ill, certainly he was not sick with the *lepera*. No man can be a leper, with a leg sore enough to make him limp, and not bear the proof of it in every line of his body, in his every gasp for breath. Sharp-eyed infallible physician that I was, I dismissed the suspicion of leprosy. He showed, I concluded, always the expert in diagnosis, the leanness which comes with hunger, or with the consumption, when a man is eaten up by something from within.

He stood beside me, where I sat cross-legged on my rock. "They are having a good time, those *malolo*." He meant the flying fish across the bay, but he was studying me as I had been studying him. It was his privilege, yet I felt uncomfortable. I had the feeling that he looked for something in me which I did not possess, and that he sorrowed over its absence. This sense of deficiency in a virtue known only to him irked me all the more. I did not answer him. The hunch of my shoulders, my frown, showed all too openly how I considered his arrival an intrusion.

"They enjoy this place, as their elders do not."

Damn the man and his preaching! "Would you have us all

out there, thrashing in the sea as bait for sharks? Why don't you go with them, then, flapping your angels' wings?"

"Such a pretty picture it would make," he chuckled. "But I cannot swim, I am such a landsman. I must stay close to the shore, hanging on to the rocks, like a crab. No, Mr. Forrest, I do not mean for everyone to go swimming. I mean only that this would be a happier place if the people in it but lifted up their eyes to the mountains, and saw how beautiful they are."

"They are the walls of a prison."

"A city can be a prison, also. A palace can be a jailhouse. So can a church be, or a seminary. I, for instance, I know this. I did not know happiness until I came here, to this place."

"Then why do you leave it, whenever you can?"

"For one reason only," he answered quietly. "There is no priest, in Molokai, to hear my confession. I go to Honolulu to be absolved of my sins. And when I am there I cannot wait to get back, as soon as I can. Now I think I shall not leave this place again." He was not speaking to me: he was addressing the mountains, the waters of the bay. His spectacles, reflecting the brightness from the sea, seemed to be glowing with a light coming from within.

"You like this place? This hellhole, this sink of pestilence, this little heap of lava rubble and leprous rubbish?"

"Yes, I like it. Look at it! See it! Is it not beautiful?"

"Yes, it is beautiful. This I will grant you. But the people who live here: they are not beautiful. They spoil the landscape for me."

He was as untouched by my sarcasm as by my hostility. "I tell you something," he said solemnly. "When I came here, at first I was like you in this matter. I saw their—their unsightliness, and I shuddered. But after a while I did not see it any more. I saw only people: men, women, children. I did not see their suffering bodies. Only their hungering souls."

"Hungering for what?" I know my people well. I know of their hungering bellies, of their unappeased lusts, but I have seen no evidence of their hungering souls.

"For the solace of God. All of God's creatures need him."

"Damn it! You can say this, in this place, where every mutilated body is a sign that God does not exist, where every putrid stinking sore is a mockery upon the name of God? You talk nonsense, damned hypocrisy!"

He fastened his innocent stare upon me. "I say it because I

know it. I have seen how the love of God can bring joy even to a
leper. I have seen how his love can soften even the hardest heart,
and make well even the sickest of souls."

"Ahh, you and your God. You have so much faith in him."

"I do."

"To me it's a lot of nonsense. I don't believe this stuff about
God." I spoke as vulgarly as a city barfly, hoping to chase him
away with my scoffing. "I'm a realist: I have my feet upon the
ground. None of your mystic's tricks for me."

"He is never far away." With all my jeering, I might just as
well have abused the wind.

"Then how is it the rest of us are not so fortunate as to see
him?"

"Perhaps it is because you do not wish to see him? There are
people who do not look for him, you know. And there are others
who do not wish to look. If God himself were to appear before
them, stretching out his hand to them, they would talk back to
him, arguing that he does not exist. There have been many such
men, and I think they are with us still."

Damn! I couldn't help but acknowledge his point: he certainly
was describing me, down to the last hairsplitting disputatious fleck
of spittle. "You win," I conceded, laughing, forced to admire his
perseverance, his level head, even under the fire of my rancor. "I
admit to the identification. And I admit to the hope that I shall
have the pleasure of meeting him someday. I have a few things
I'd like to say to him, to let him know what I think of him and
of the way he runs this world." I laughed again, to let the old
man know I was teasing him, and rather enjoying the game.

But now when I was ready for humor he lost all sign of his.
"Do not jest with God, Caleb. He has a way of challenging such
pride. A man up there on the hill is making war with God, and I
live in worry for its outcome." He did not say who the man was,
nor did I care to know. Men are always warring with God, and
my sympathies are always with mankind. I was more interested
in me.

"I will be content to wait and see," I said, shrugging him off,
and his God with him.

"This is better," he replied, almost with relief. "God is closer
to us here than you think." Once more he lifted his arm, to put
the little world of Kalaupapa into the province of his God. "Here

you will not be able to escape him. Why is it, do you think, that he has sent you here? Why is it that you bear this mark upon you? Have you thought of these things, Caleb?"

With this he went away, limping off toward the path going down to the beach. I sat upon my rock, too overwhelmed by his cruel reminder of my blight even to swear at him as he went.

Not until he was out of sight did the oaths come to my tongue, and only when he could not hear them did my futile jeers spill out of me at him and his imagined God.

33

My awakening came one quiet evening, when all the world seemed at peace. Nature had called a truce among boisterous wind and nagging sea, resisting land and thieving rain. For once they ceased their wrangling, and in their armistice Kalaupapa lay in tranquillity.

The evening was too fine to waste at home, or in sitting at Makaio's house. I went for a walk, to enjoy the end of the day.

Many of the people of Kalawao held the same opinion. Some were out strolling in the lanes, or stood gossiping in little groups. Others sat upon the stairs of the houses, or on the cool grass, singing sad songs to the soft music of mandolins and muted guitars. It was a time when peoples' thoughts are turned inward, in quiet pondering upon their needs, in the bittersweet enjoyment of a mood which is not without its tinge of hurt and yet is not entirely painful. It was the kind of evening when peoples' senses turn to the perception of beauty, in the color of a cloud, in the shape of a tree, or of a leaf upon the tree; and when, having seen how ephemeral is this beauty, they understand, perhaps without wanting to understand, how ephemeral is man. As a leaf upon a tree is man, they see: no one knows when it is made, no one notices when it falls.

While I was passing their house Mahiai and Ioane Paele hailed me. "E, Caleb. Pehea oe?" They were sitting on the front steps, dressed only in their underdrawers. I turned in at the gate to exchange a few words with them.

"And what is it you two are doing?" Between them a solitary candle lifted its unwavering flame. Foul in my nose was the stink of scorched flesh and burned hair.

"Burning *uku*," said Ioane.

"Are you so fortunate that you do not have pets as we do?" asked Mahiai.

"Lice? Are they here, with you?"

"And where are they not? Lice, fleas, cockroaches, mosquitoes, bugs of every kind: we have them. Help yourself to some."

"No thanks." Already I was beginning to itch, with the imagined crawling of their vermin over my body. "You keep 'em."

"You will get them very soon, never worry," Ioane promised cheerfully.

"We have found a new way to get rid of them," said the other one proudly. "Watch." He took a thin branch of hard guava wood and held the tip of it in the candle flame. When it was alight he removed it from the flame and blew out the fire on the twig itself. Then deftly he applied the glowing end to the nape of Ioane's neck, where the hair was short. "*Aia!* Got him," he crowed. The stench of burned louse, burned flesh, burned hair, rose to sicken me. All around the line of Ioane's hair, scattered about the graying head, were blisters of burns, where other lice had been incinerated.

I stepped back. "*Auwe nohoi e!* Does it not hurt?"

"Sometimes," answered Ioane. "It depends where my playmates hide. In some places there is no pain. I am lucky, I guess. Mahiai: he hurts all over."

"Better to burn 'em than to scratch 'em," said Mahiai. "Their crawling around: it is something I cannot bear. It is like the singing of mosquitoes. I would not mind if they would only just bite me, and be content to suck my blood." Gnawing at his lip, he peered closely at Ioane's blue-black skin. "But no: they must sing, they must crawl, they must—*Aha!* Got him!"

"This disease," began Ioane, in a speculative tone, "it is a funny thing. Can you tell me, you who are a learned man, why it is that I, and many others who have the *mai Kalawao*, have lost the feeling in our arms or our legs or in others of our bodies' parts? Why is it that I do not feel the burns Mahiai makes upon my skin, whereas Mahiai feels not only the fire of this little flame, but also knows most intensely the fire of the pain which is always hurting him from within?"

"No. I do not know."

Ioane held up a swollen foot, a ghastly gnarled thing, looking like the root of a tree but recently dug from the ground. "How is it that I do not feel the loss of my small toe? It came off today— I think. Somewhere, I do not know where. But I did not know that we two were no longer together until we sat down here, a small while ago, to rid ourselves of our little friends. Only then did I say, 'Auwe, auwe! And what has happened to my little toe?"

"I do not know, I tell you! Am I a doctor? Does anyone know? Is it not just the manner of this disease?"

"Cha! Then of what use is your learning, and your reading in many books, if you cannot tell us of these simple things?"

"Hold still," warned Mahiai. "Here comes another one from the bush of your hair, to look out upon the world. Hah! His view of it was short."

Before the nauseating smell could reach me I left them, hurrying for the gate. "E, da high-class buggah!" Mahiai sent his farewell after me. "He no like ouah kine fun."

"His stomach: it is still weak," roared the other one.

Half sick with the experience, wholly impressed with their hero's method, I went down the lane and out upon the field of Kalaupapa. After such entertainment, I needed to be alone.

There was no wind from off the sea: the evening was warm and still. Smoke from the afternoon's cooking fires filled the space beneath the canopy of cloud, tinting the air with a blue haze which softened the faces of the cliffs and blurred the stretches of coast unfolding from either side of Kalaupapa. Mountains and the ghosts of mountains, they stood, one after the other, silent and mysterious, their feet in the sea, their heads lost in the clouds. Peace was upon the land, and upon the sea, a watchful brooding peace.

I walked upon the grassy plain, among the black rocks and the treacherous lava tubes, until I came to the end of my world. Beneath me the sea was singing its splendid threnody for the dying day, and in the gathering dusk I stood and listened to its mourning. Far to the west the last fires burned upon the altars of heaven, three sullen spots of red. But where I stood upon the cliff there was no light. It was night. I was alone.

Pleasantly melancholy, for the darkness upon the land was the counterpart of the darkness in myself, I gave myself up to my enjoyment of the night, steeping myself in it as they say the dead are steeped in the river of Styx, before they enter Hades.

I had not rested there for long when, in the west, near the village of Kalaupapa, I saw lights moving upon the land: three points of red, they were, a reflection of the torches burning in the western skies. Fishermen going to the sea, I thought, turning to watch them. The night will be fine for fishing, without wind, without rain.

But they were not going to the sea: they were coming in my direction, moving along the edge of the land, near where it was bordered by the ocean. My curiosity was aroused. I walked a few steps inland, until I came to the path which is the seaward road for those who journey the longer way from Kalaupapa to Kalawao. My eyes were well adjusted to the darkness. The grass was less black than the stones and the holes in the ground. I saw well enough where I was walking, I knew what I was doing.

I stood there waiting, interested to see those who liked the evening as much as I did, still thinking that it would be the fishermen who came.

Then, across the quiet air, from them to me, floated the sounds of their progress. I was slow of mind, and I did not come easily to accept their meaning. At first I would not believe my ears: who could be going fishing to the sound of drums, attended by the cries of forerunners and the chanting of many voices? Sneering, I asked the night if the lordly Ambrose traveled in such a splendid manner, as would a chief in state.

In the next drumbeat I knew who it was. It was not Ambrose. The drums told me who it would be. My blood turned to sea water, my bones to the slime of jellyfish. *Ka Huakai o ka Po* they were—the Marchers of the Night! Unable to move, I chattered my foolish protest: No! No! They cannot be—

Swiftly they came toward me. There was no denying them: they were there. Deeper beat the sharkskin *pahu*, shriller rose the warning cries. The points of light became clusters of flaring torches, one at the head, one at the middle, one at the end of the procession.

Excited with their message came the forerunners, clearing the way. "*Nauane!*" they cried. "Moving along! On the way!" Their eyes bulged, their chests heaved, their bellies were drawn in tight, but still they ran, with arms outspread, the ends of their white *malos* tucked in at the waist to free their loins for running. "Make way!" they cried, their lips wet with foam. "Make way! The Gods come!" Their mouths were twisted in fear: fear went before them in their cries: I felt it pass from them to me. "The powerful Gods, the awesome Gods, the Great Gods come! Lie down! Lie down in the prostrating, the abasing, the burning *kapu!*" Like a whirling wind they went by me, and I trembled in the turmoil of their passing.

Fearsome in the wild light the tall warriors marched, their long spears upraised, their long naked legs moving in cadence with the thunder of the drums. The flames of the torches gleamed upon their helmets, upon their broad chests. Beyond the stalwart warriors the white capes of priests glowed, like the edges of clouds behind which the moon hides.

Four abreast they marched, seven feet tall they were. The earth beneath me shook with the heaviness of their tread; the dust swirled around their naked feet. Yet their feet did not touch upon the green grass of Kalaupapa. And their bodies were white, powdered with dust from the realm of the dead.

The warrior wave was almost upon me. "Strike him! Kill him!" they shouted, shifting their spears to pierce me. Their faces were terrible with wrath, the dark *kauwila* spears shone red with blood.

"*Kapu a moe!*" chanted the priests. "Lie down, lie down, in the prostrating *kapu!* It is for the Gods: the Great Gods come!"

Helpless I stood, unable to move, helpless to fall upon my face, to spare myself the thrust of those spears, the fatal sight of the Gods. Louder than fright, more insistent than wonder, was the protest of my divided reason: *This cannot be . . .*

"Kill him!" roared the warriors. "A proud man is he." Beyond the ranks of the savage soldiers, beyond the priests, I could see the high curves of the feather helmets and the golden feather capes of great chiefs, the lofty *kahilis* which were the standards of greatest chiefs, bright in the light of the blazing torches following them. "Kill him!" roared the chiefs. "The sight of the Gods is not for him."

From the line of the priests one came running toward me, his

arms held wide. Before his advance I stepped back, fearing that
he came for me. As I moved backward I tripped and fell heavily
to the ground. Above me, as I lay upon my side, I saw the priest
turn, his arms still outflung, his body standing over me. "No! He
is mine!" he cried in a mighty voice, "he is mine!" I saw the over-
lapping fibers in his *kapa* cape as it moved with his turning, I saw
the straining muscles in his powerful legs. But his feet did not
touch the earth on which I lay: they stood upon another plane
in another world. "He is mine," he called out again. "Son to
Kailiki is he, son to Puou, son to fifty generations of priests who
have served the Gods."

"Then is he saved," shouted the warriors, lifting their spears
in the instant before they passed the place where I shrank in terror. "Then let him live," said the priests, "because he is one of
ours." Lying upon the grass, my head upon a pillow of stone, I
heard the sound of their sparing.

The great chiefs were not so kind. "Shame! Shame upon him!"
they jeered. "See how he lies, stiff with fear. See how he lies,
clothed, in the presence of the Gods. Sick fruit is this, of a once-
mighty tree." The voices of high chiefesses rose, shrill and taunting. "Rubbish is he, trash: a thing to be thrown away. But let him
live. Let him live for yet awhile."

Above me my protector stood, his arms outspread, his hands
opened to fend off any of the savage company who might still
want my life. But his head was bowed in shame, he had no answer to their taunts.

Great images of the Gods went by, held high on poles. Fierce
they were, of vicious mien, with baleful glaring eyes, with sharks'
teeth lusting for the taste of blood, with red feathers and red
kapa and human bones and poisonous woods, sacred to themselves. Evil they were, and cruel: their great lips curled wide in
scorn, their mouths opened to devour.

Then, for a moment, there was a space in the procession, an
emptiness filled with an immense silence. After this utter hallowed
stillness the central sacred fires came: three glowing leaping flowing whirling vortices of red light they were, violent and alive,
purest spirit. The eyes of men could not gaze full upon them
without being blinded: I was forced to look away. Even my guardian *aumakua* dared not look upon them: throwing off the *kapa*
cape, he bared his body; falling to the ground beside me, he

shielded me from their awesome power. Before I closed my eyes I saw his noble face, inexpressibly familiar to me in the curve of the forehead, in the line of the nose, the shape of his soft beard. Yet it was the visage of a man I had never seen.

The air crackled and hissed as the Great Gods went by, the earth heaved and groaned, rising as a wave rises to follow them upon their way. Twigs and leaves and branches were broken from unseen trees and tossed upon the trampled path. Whirlwinds of dust, pillars of fire, rose in their wake, following after them, roaring as they went. Then again there was a silence, a void of nothingness, which sucked the breath out of me as it passed.

Only when the earth and the air were quieted again did the end of the procession come. My protector rose to his feet as they drew near. I opened my eyes to see them, and him. A horde of commoners, they carried the treasures of the chiefs. Large gourds filled with tufts of feathers and fine *kapas* were borne by women dressed in short skirts, their breasts bare, their shorn hair bleached and mottled with burnt lime. Muscular men, clad in the ancient loincloth, bent under the weight of carrying-poles, from which swung heavy gourds caught up in nets of sennit. Quietly they went by, paying me no heed.

Last of all, illumined by the third cluster of torches, came the lesser chiefs and their women, and the women of the warriors and of the priests. Some of them looked from my protector to me, pointing me out to the others, as though I were a thing to be laughed at. Some averted their gaze, to avoid the sight of me and of my guardian's shame.

At the very end of the procession, separated from it by a few paces, walked a young woman, alone and forlorn, her shoulders weighted down by sadness. When she came near to my protector she gave a low cry and directed her steps to him. Sorrowfully she looked down upon me, as sometimes the distant beautiful moon looks sadly down upon the smallness of men. In her face was the grief of a longing unrequited, mixed with a growing awareness that something lost had been found. Unbearable was her sorrow: my heart cried out with the heaviness of her pain.

"He is ours," said the priest gravely, pointing down at me. There was the look of my grandfather in him, stern and judging, but softened by love. Now I knew why he seemed so well known to me.

"His face," she asked, half in wonder, half in loathing. "What is this mark upon his face?"

"I do not know this mark. It is something of his time, not of ours." He picked up the cape from the plain at his feet. "Come, it is late. We must leave him." Taking her by the hand, he led her away, in the path of the Night Marchers. Already in the distance the beat of the drums was waning, the light of the threefold Gods was fading away.

Wait! Wait! I wanted to cry after them, yearning to ask who they were, what they meant to me. But, as in a dream, the tongue stuck in my mouth, the words refused to issue from my throat. Unable to call them back, I rose upon my hands to watch them go, wanting to go with them. Even as this new need came to me, I knew I could not go with them.

Gazing back at me over their shoulders, they seemed unwilling to leave me, yet forced to go by a fear more compelling than love.

"O my father," I heard her say, "will he find the way?" The low murmur of his answering reached me, but not the meaning of his words.

Then even the pale trace of them upon the dark screen of night was lost. I was alone again upon the plain, the man rejected, the man left behind. In the village of Kalawao the dogs were barking and howling, sensing the approach of the terror which had left me broken by its passing.

Ghosts, Night Marchers, Gods: they did not exist, according to my belief. But now I myself had seen them, had heard them. I had been close enough to one of them to see the dust upon his feet, the texture of the hair upon his legs. Peering from between his legs I had seen manifestations of that other world which once I denied. From his loins, it seemed, I was born again into another world, a world insubstantial and uncertain, as shifting as shadows, yet full of awful might. Never would I forget the magnificence of those warriors, the haughtiness of the chiefs, the strength of my guardian, noble in the presence of his danger and my own. Never would I forget those flaming incorporeal Gods and the majesty of their violence. Never could I forget that it was I, the unbeliever, the man of reason, who was left behind, when they went on.

For the hundredth time I put my fingers to my head, to feel for the lump which would tell me that I had fallen upon the plain and, in injuring myself, had imagined the visitation of the Gods. But no: the outside of my head was sound. There were no wounds upon it to explain my vision.

Then was I mad? Were the insides of my head so addled that they could conjure up, out of night's eeriness and dark's illusions, whole armies of roaming ghosts and spheres of swirling fire? With a grim honesty I was forced to admit that I could not be sure my mind was untouched by madness: if it were only as slightly diseased as my body was, what aberrations might it not invent, what foolish imaginings might it not evoke?

And what was the meaning of my vision? To forget it was beyond my capacity to do; to laugh it away, as I have laughed away the tales of other men, was to ignore the most overwhelming evidence of the spirit I had ever known. To disown it meant that I must deny my sanity. Yet to acknowledge it was to invite disaster, for once I admitted immortal guardians and primordial Gods into my cosmology, then the door was opened to other deities— even to the baleful punitive Jehovah.

He was the one I feared, of all the Gods, for he was the con- quering one, before whom all other Gods were dying. I had fought him, resisted him, with every weapon my reason could command. I had vowed that I was not going to submit to him, to become a gelded bleating thing like Makaio, a slave to him like Damien, a dour and dried up bone-servant like every one of the missionaries from New England.

When dawn came I was nearly exhausted from my wrestling with the messengers of Heaven, but I had not yet submitted to them. Unconquered still, clad still in the fragments of the armor of my reason, I went out into the morning to take counsel of another man of reason.

Momona was still in bed when I knocked at his door. He loved the soft comfort of his mattress, and he hated to leave it, his "wife and mother," as he called it.

Often enough had I sat with him on the *lanai* of his house, but this was the first time I went into his private room. When I entered it I stared around me, incredulous.

Under the great cloud of the mosquito net he lay like a moun- tain shrouded in mist. Under the white sheet his huge body lay, rounded and massive, like the bulk of Mauna Loa. Upon the pillow his head rested like Mauna Kea, a peaked appendage to Mauna Loa. He was not asleep, but he was enjoying the disinclination to get up. I scarcely heard his exclamations of surprise over the earliness of my call, I was so amazed by the room in which he lived.

Around the bed, on tables, on shelves, upon the floor, within reach of the bed, were great piles of old newspapers: in English, in Hawaiian, in Norwegian, Portuguese, Chinese, in all the languages of earth he collected them. Hanging by spidery threads from the exposed rafters of the house were scores of paper birds, whole flights of them in all sizes and shapes, stirring gently in the soft breeze. Fashioned from papers of every possible color and texture, they were as beautiful as the birds of the forest, as unreal as the figments of a dream. Hats, bells, boats, cups, plates, flowers, fish, animals—all made of paper—were strewn upon the furniture, upon the piles of newspapers. The high tinkling notes of an aeolian harp filled the wizard's cell with a luminous shimmering music, as though the paper birds were singing an *aubade* for him upon the start of the new day.

"Pull up the net," he commanded, a king at his levee. While I gathered its limp folds in my arms, he struggled to sit up. "And what rouses you out of your bed at this dismal hour?" Grunting and puffing, he heaved himself up, leaning at last against the ornate headpiece of the great brass bed. He wore the strange clear gaze of a child newly waked from sleep: innocent and unaffected, he looked up at me while I tied the net in a loop and hung it from a nail in the wall. From him, I thought, will I hear the truth.

"I have not slept."

"What? You have lost a whole night's sleep? *Ki-e*, there is nothing so important that it will not have a different look for sleeping on it. Sit down, sit down."

"This cannot wait," I said, moving a pleated paper duck from a chair beside the bed. The weird beauty of my first impression had held off for a while the service of my other senses. Not until I sat down did my nose tell me how the room smelled of molds and mice and of Momona's chamber pot, half full beneath the bed. The dust lay thick upon the yellowing newspapers and the unswept floor. Alas for this wizard: he is not a very good housekeeper.

"*Ea*, a woman perhaps . . ."

"No. Would I lose sleep over a woman? Tell me: what do you know of the Marchers of the Night?"

"Ahh. So this is the reason the dogs were baying. I thought perhaps it was someone dying. You saw them, then?"

"I did."

"Fortunate one! I would give this hog's flesh of mine for a sight of the Marchers of the Night."

"You have not seen them?"

"Never. But I have known of people who met them. I could not believe that the stories they told were true. Yet always did I envy them, because always I wanted to believe them, in what they saw. Even those who were found dead beside the road I envied. They saw things, before they died, which I yearn to see, things out of the ancient past."

"It is not pleasant, to look into the past."

"Is the present any better to look at? But you have seen it, the past, and you have lived. Tell me of it."

Briefly I told him, even to the quality of my fear. If I wanted truth from him, I must give him only truth. When I had begun upon my account he reached for a pair of scissors and a newspaper. While I talked he cut the paper into strips, two columns wide. Then he cut each strip evenly into precise squares. It irked me, at first, when he did not give me his full attention, but as he cut and snipped I saw how he missed nothing of my story. The finished squares he placed in a pasteboard box at his side, already nearly full with other pieces of the same exact dimensions.

When I was done with my tale he put his mind at once upon the crux of it. "Those names: Kailiki, Puou. What do they mean to you?"

"I know them not."

"This is a pity. A pity. Upon them all else is hung. If they are the names of men who are numbered among your ancestors, then indeed have your *aumakua* brought you a message. If they are not— then perhaps it was a dream . . ."

"Can a man dream with his eyes wide open? Can a man dream of things of which he has no knowledge? Those idols: I have not seen them before. Chiefs in state, priests from the temples, women skirted only from waist to knee: how could I have seen these in my lifetime?"

He took up a square of the cut paper before he answered me.

"A man will dream anything which pleases him. In this the thoughts of his waking are not different from the dreams of his sleep."

"This jeering does not help—"

"Is it jeering? Or is it the advice of a man wearier than you in his searching? I do not think it is jeering. But here, in Kalawao, a man has much time for thinking, and even more time for dreaming." While he talked, his nimble fingers were crumpling and opening, crushing and softening, the squares of stiff newspaper.

"But why does a man have thoughts like these? Why does a man dream, if not to—"

"Ahh, Caleb, my friend. What is man but a louse on the body of God, scurrying for refuge, in terror of being scratched? *Cha!* He will dream any dream, this louse, think any thought, to forget for a while his terror, to tell himself that the finger of God does not yet search for him." The piece of paper in his hands was worried soft as cloth. He laid it down, and picked up a fresh square.

"Do you, then, believe in God?"

Those eyes from which I expected only the truth: they could not look at me. He watched his fingers crumpling the paper, while a little smile of embarrassment tried to lose itself in the corners of his mouth. "No. I cannot say that I believe in God. But I will tell you this: I am filled with envy of those who can believe in him. And one more thing I will tell to you, because you are my friend. I am in search of him." Softly he concluded. "Am I different from you in this?" He lifted his head to look upon me. Now there was no innocence in those deep eyes. There was only the haunted loneliness of a man who has nothing to which he can pin the meaning of his life. I have seen those same eyes staring back at me, from out of my own mirror.

I sat open-mouthed before him. This wizard: he has seen into my emptiness.

"I cannot help you in this matter, for I too am lost on the way. Only one who has faith can be of help to those who have it not. I am not such a one. Go to see Hanaloa, at Siloama. Ask him. Go to see Kaupea, she who remembers the Gods of old. Ask her. Or this priest of the new God, Kamiano. He is a holy man. Ask him. They will have answers for you. Perhaps one of them will have the answer you seek."

"No! This is for me to decide. This is my search. Must I parade my need before the whole Settlement?"

"Sometimes those who have gone before can help to show the way."

"In this matter they have only their prejudices to tell me. How good are these? In this matter each man must find his own way. I am a man of reason: I must have reason, not faith."

"Is it so? And does a man of reason know everything? Does a man of reason always use his reason, to answer all of his many needs?"

"I do!" The old pride flared up in me still. With such pride to contend with, he had the right to anger. But he was kind.

"Tell me, then. When you go upon your visits to the little house, and when you are done, there, with your need, what do you use?"

The shift in subject, the delicate indirection of the question, confused me: for a long second I did not understand what he was getting at. "Why," I spluttered, catching his meaning at last, "leaves, grass, old rags, like everyone else. Pieces of paper snatched up on the way— What the hell are you trying to say?"

He tossed me a packet of softened newspaper squares, neatly held together by a loop of string sewn through one corner. "Then take these, a gift—" I held them in my hand, watching the tide of laughter work down from his lips to the soft womanish bosom to the huge swollen belly—"from one who has traveled oftener along that familiar path than you have, and farther."

The meaning of his lesson was all too clear. With a chastened grin I accepted it. "I will do as you say, my friend. I will go now, to ask those who know."

As I turned to leave I saw a small metal canister lying on the floor near the door. Without thinking, impelled to do so only by my passion for neatness, I picked it up, to restore it to its proper place. The fading death's-head label came into view: FLOWERS OF ARSENIC. POISON! LAAU MAKE! Beneath the skull-and-crossbones warning, in smaller letters, the name of my druggist leaped up to taunt me.

"Where did you get this?"

"From Honolulu. And where else? I wrote a letter for it, a long time ago, to—ah, what's his name? I forget it now. You know, the *haole* who has a medicine store on King Street, near to Fort Street. I saw about it in a newspaper, and I thought it would be a good thing to have. I asked him to let me try half-a-dollar's worth."

"Half a dollar? For this much?"

"*Ae.* It is not very costly."

"And for what did you want it?" Time stood still, the morning song of the birds and the glass harp faded into nothingness, while I waited for Momona to answer my need. If he had been tempted by death, and if he had been saved from it by the intervention of some restraining hand— Eagerly I waited, to hear from him that my story was also his story, and that there is a pattern to miracles which will reveal the kindness of God. If I could see this pattern, I knew without knowing how I came to the knowledge, then I knew that I could see the way to God.

"I thought to use it for killing the mice, who came in here to live with me. But I did not have the cruelty to use it. These mice: they are too soft, too pretty, to kill. So I let them live with me. Now we are friends. No, we are more than friends: they are like my children—"

Groaning with disappointment, ready to break under the burden of my confusions, I could not help but laugh, too, at the foolishness of my hope and at the weakness of Momona's sentiment. I threw the can of useless poison upon the bed and, while it was still rolling down the sagging mattress to lose itself in the folds of his sheets, I rushed from Momona's room to begin upon my pilgrimage.

Now behold the heroic Caleb: mouth open, a fish, willing to bite, routing out the Fisherman from his haven; clipped of wing, a bird, wanting to be caught, challenging the Thrower of the Net to issue from his lair. Fierce and clamorous was this vocative Caleb: a dog, raising hell with Heaven for not honoring his question on demand. Such a fuss and frenzy did he make, as he ran about, such an uproar to crack open the indifference of the Inscrutable and to force a smile of comfort out of the Immovable. *Cha!* This thin and scrawny Caleb, who once did laugh at fat and puffing Peter: he was wiser now, and a sadder man. He saw nothing funny, now, in his running, running down the empty spaces of his world, crying for someone to show him the way.

I stopped at the Congregationalists' church, at Siloama, to see the Reverend Hanaloa. I found him sitting in a little musty cell underneath the church house. The whitewashed rocks of the walls were damp and moldy with old men's beards. The single oil lamp hung from its standard in the timbered ceiling, casting a waxen glow over a ledger upon the table before him. He was writing in it, slowly, in a large awkward hand.

When he saw who visited him he rose stiffly to his feet, a weary old man even at the start of the day. "Good morning," he said in his politest tones. "And what brings you to the Lord's House?"

"A question, to which I seek an answer." I was more direct with him than I was with Momona. Surely here was a man from whom I would receive the truth.

He peered at me from under his shaggy eyebrows. "And the question is?"

"The Marchers of the Night: can a man see them?"

"Cha! A superstition, an imagining." He wiped them out of the realm of possibility with a wave of his soft hand. "They do not exist, except in the minds of foolish ones, who listen to the tales of the olden days, when fear ruled the people, and ghosts were thought to roam in the land."

"You are sure of this?"

"I am certain. They are the worries of the ignorant, given meaning only in words. How can they be? Would Iehovah permit them to exist? Who has seen them? Many people talk of them, but has anyone seen them? Talk is cheap, but only fools talk about things of which they know nothing."

"Thank you. You have told me what I wanted to know."

"Come again," he beamed. "Any time I can help—" He was still buzzing like a bumblebee as I went up out of his whited sepulcher into the fresh air of the morning.

I left the Church of the Healing Spring and walked eastward, into the yellow light. Outside the Infirmary a solitary figure sat, warming himself in the gift of the sun. He was a beautiful old man, with pure white hair and a pure white beard, carefully trimmed and combed. Against this angelic whiteness the dark skin looked like wonderfully seasoned old *kou* wood, lovingly preserved with rubbings of oil by some attentive hand.

"*Aloha ia oe,*—" I said to him. "Can you tell me, please—" Only then did I see how the fingers were gone from the hands lying in his lap, how the toes were gone from the feet resting in the dust.

He turned his head toward me, where I came between him and the sun, seeking me with the limpid eyes of an idiot. His head wobbled upon the weak neck. From his mouth a thin trickle of spittle slipped down into the snowy beard. But not even the leper's stench of his dying body was more dreadful than the silence in which he lived. It was a world where I could not reach him, where I did not exist. Aghast, I fled from him.

Upon the green meadow beyond the graveyard I saw three boys playing. Their heads held high, their arms entwined, they tumbled and rose again and bumped each other down, with song and laughter on their lips. They made a charming scene, all the more so after my encounter with the old man.

So encouraged I walked behind—until I saw that they were blind. What I had thought was fond embrace was misery's enforced company; what I took for happiness was only a leer on an empty face. And the sound I thought was singing was deaf-mutes' crazy babbling.

I fled from them. What is a man to believe in? I moaned, slipping upon the treacherous grass in my haste to escape the wounds of their crying.

In the shade of a *kukui* tree by the side of the road I came upon an old woman. Her body was bent as though it had been broken at the waist, after a lifetime of laboring in the fields. The weight of its upper half rested upon her swollen hands, buttressed against her knees. She held her head to one side, the better to see me. "They are all right," she croaked from a lipless mouth. "I am watching them." Piercing the lobes of her ears were little buttons of gold. Even in the shadows of the tree they were like glowing suns.

"I feared for them."

"They cannot go far. And the playing is good for them. They must learn to make their own way, poor things."

"You take care of them?"

"Ae. They are my family: they are my joy. I have begged for them."

Her joy! I wanted to weep, and I could mumble only foolishness. "You are good to them—"

"Is there another way to live?"

"Tell me, *tutu*," I barked, desperate to escape from her. "Where is the house of Kaupea?"

Grinning like a resting dog, she shifted her position with little shufflings of her feet. The litter of dead leaves rustled beneath the trailing skirt: it was the sound that centipedes make, with their hundred hurrying feet, as they scamper across my pillow at night. "Up there," she pointed to a winding path. "There is the way. The house beyond the *naupaka*—" She was still talking when I ran away from her.

Old and weather-beaten, without a trace of whitewash, the house was as gray as a mullet's belly. It looked as though it had sat forever in that aloof place, with its back turned to the village; and the hooded eyes of its windows seemed to peer inward, into the mysteries of itself, rather than out upon the encircling sea, where nothingness was.

But the worn stairs to the porch were freshly swept, the floor of the *lanai* was still damp from a morning sprinkling. When I reached the porch I heard someone singing within:

"Yearning, longing in love,
Is the woman,
Swaying, swaying by the sea,
A loveliness in my sight . . ."

In answer to my knock a merry creature came to the door. Singing still, she opened the door almost violently, throwing it back with a flourish, finishing the last phrase of the song.

"Ah, good morning!" Hands on hips, she laughed cheerfully. "Early is the morning bird, but earlier still is the catcher." She was a motherly person, big of body, dressed in a faded-blue gingham *holoku*, with a red kerchief bound about her neck. In the plump good-natured face I could find no sign of the leprosy.

"You are Kaupea?"

"Oh my goodness no!" For some reason of her own, she chose to answer me in English. "She is eating breakfast. Are you the first one?" Seeing my bewilderment, she looked beyond me to the empty yard, the deserted *lanai*. "Yes, you are the first one. Come in. Sit down." Backing into the house she drew me with her, waved me into a high-backed chair. "She will be here in a long minute." Singing her love song, she floated out of the parlor into an adjoining room. "Auntie. A gentleman to see you." In a torrent of Hawaiian she conversed with Auntie, clattering dishes upon a tray all the while she talked.

The parlor was fitted with heavy *haole* furniture, pots of maiden-hair fern, and a profusion of fading photographs and daguerreo-types in tarnished silver frames. In a Chinese jar a furled umbrella tried to keep its composure in the company of three hand-*kahilis*. The *kahilis* told me of Kaupea's chiefly rank. The umbrella's coat of cobwebs and dust told me she rarely left the house—and that her niece was not much better a housekeeper than Momona was.

Before I could finish my appraisal of the old-fashioned room the jolly messenger was back, helping with a firm hand the bent and shrunken version of herself who was Auntie. The family resemblance would have been more striking if the old woman's flagrantly false wig had been settled a little more decorously upon her head. As it was, it hung rather rakishly over one eye, obviously flung upon her by the same vigorous hand which swooped to pick up the tea things before it fell upon the old woman's bony arm. I had the feeling that I was back in Iwilei, in the presence of two rather ribald madames come to strike a bargain with me.

"Here is Kaupea," the younger one announced in our native tongue, leading the ancient dame to an armchair opposite the one at which I stood. "Auntie, this is Mr. Forrest."

"How did you know?"

"From Kealakekua."

"How did you know?"

"Oh, we know everything in this house. It is our business to know."

Deftly she settled Kaupea into the chair, and threw a cape of soft gray *kapa* over the old woman's thin shoulders. I did not see her do it, but with the same motion she succeeded in straight-ening the wig: when she turned away the jet-black hair sat properly, if incongruously, upon the old lady's head. I was forced to deplore the wig: its color and smoothness did not suit Auntie's obvious age, although the antique sweep of its wings did belong to the past of which she was a part.

"Leave us," the old woman snapped.

"I go, I go," sang the irrepressible niece. But before she left she placed a large round wooden bowl upon the table next to Kaupea, shaking it, as she set it down, to jingle the few pieces of silver lying in its polished bottom.

These two: they were no different from the whores of Iwilei. Kumakani's Emma is not as greedy as they. Reaching into my pocket, I brought forth one of the King's new half dollars, shining even with Kalakaua Rex's puffy dundrearied profile on it, and I tossed it with an uninhibited clatter into the calabash. What Momona spent on poison, I guess I can spend on my folly.

Only then did the diligent treasurer obey the old lady's command. Large as she was, she did not seem to walk: she drifted among the chairs and the tables, like a blue cloud, humming the air of another love song until she was gone from the room.

"Sit down," the old one commanded. I complied instantly.

Deliberately, while she glared at me as though I were the one to be blamed for all the faults of the world, she put her thin hands to the wig and adjusted it to her liking. It was an act of rebellion against the tyranny of her niece: it had no other purpose. I expected her to mumble complaints, or to snarl at me, for the relief of her temper, but she who knew no pity for her petitioners had none to waste upon herself.

"What is it that you seek of Kaupea?" she asked, gazing beyond me to the ferns and the photographs ranged at my back. She spoke in the dialect of the people of Kauai, using the old-style *ts* for *ks*, and *rs* for *ls*. It is a speech which I have always felt to be harsh and primitive.

What did I want of this old witch? I was not certain. Comfort? Advice? "Knowledge," I said, stumbling upon the right word. "Out of your learning of the ancient ways." I did not hope to learn the truth from her.

The sharp face did not soften, the grim reserve was not broken. Dark liver spots gave her flesh the color of a decaying corpse. At her throat, upon her arms, the wrinkled skin hung soft as crepe.

"It is of the Marchers of the Night that I would ask."

"You saw them, then, last night."

"*Ae.* Upon the plain of Kalaupapa. I have come to ask: What does it mean, my seeing them?"

Mocking me, she drew up her lips in a death's-head grimace. Long were her teeth, and yellow, yellow as buried bones. "Death. It means death."

"Death?" I croaked. It was as I feared. "Death? For me?"

"Is death so much to be feared?" The narrowed eyes opened wide in scorn, glowing yellow in the dim light, before they closed again in weariness. "No, it is not for you, if you live to tell of it. Not yet. But death for someone who is close to you, for someone who does not have an *aumakua* to protect him."

It was a reprieve. I could breathe again, I could think again.

"The *aumakua* who stood over me: is he of my line?"

"It is even so. Only such a one would bother to keep the others from striking down the living, of whom the dead are envious."

"The names I heard him say: they mean nothing to me."

"And what are these names?"

" 'Son to Kailiki is he, son to Puou, son to fifty generations of priests who have served the gods.' "

"*Ae*. And across five generations have you forgotten him who came to your aid. It is the way with the young, that they forget so easily the past. And the dead."

"Do you know them?"

"*Ae*. I know them well. The lines of all the old families of Hawaii Nei are known to Kaupea." She took a deep breath, squared her shoulders for the accounting. "In the time of Kalaniopuu did they live, those two, before the time of the upstart Kamehameha, in the years when the first white man came to Hawaii Nei. Then was Puou High Priest to the god Lono, and Kailiki was his son and Second Priest. When the foul man who was Captain Cook came, they were fools enough, those two, to think he was Lono returned from his wandering, and they worshipped him, saying, "Lo! This is the return of Lono." For this offense against the gods the pretender was slain, there upon the shore of Kaawaloa, in the bay of Kealakekua. And for their sacrilege it seems that the ghosts of Puou and of Kailiki are made to wander with the Marchers of the Night. *Luai po* are they, night vomit, spirits of the dead who cannot die yet, who cannot go down to the Land of Milu, to sleep the sleep of forgetfulness."

She raised two wrinkled hands, claws to call down terror upon my head. "Until the last fruit of their sinful line is dead must they wander, in search of peace."

"There was a woman with them: daughter to my *aumakua*."

"*Ae*, she would be there also. Hinahina was she, the daughter of Kailiki. She is the one who will suffer the most, for she it was who lay with a sailor, playing the whore with him, defiling her body and her father's blood. Who can know what was his name, this dirty sailor? Perhaps it was Forrest?"

Her malice was revealing. It gave tongue to all the pent-up hatred of Hawaiians for the disasters which have fallen upon them since the *haoles* came. Here was the source of the scorn which had slighted me and my family. "*Opala*," I said it aloud, remembering the Queen's gibe at me. Trash with green eyes, she called me, and I was stung with its poison every time I thought of it: I could admit it now, after years of pretending that I did not care what they called me, those proud ones, as long as they feared me.

"He may well have been so," cackled Kaupea. "Men who roam the sea, they are the trash of the sea."

One more question. I needed to ask: my lawyer's logic insisted upon it. Calming my fear of the unknown was the memory of my *aumakua's* body standing guard over me, of the compassion in his face, as he looked down upon me, lying at his feet. He, who could have spat death upon me, who could have killed me with a glance: why did he look down upon me in pity? "I am the last of their line," I said to waiting Kaupea. "Why is it that they did not let me be struck down, in the night, and thereby find their peace?"

"*Ti-e!* Who can say with certainty that he is the last of his line?" she scoffed. She was enjoying my discrediting, rolling her eyes over the disgrace of my whoreson family. "When the last *ohelo* is picked, search can always find one more berry upon the bush. This is one reason."

"*Auwe nohoi e!* It is a reason I did not think of."

"The other," she said softly, looking beyond me to the photographs of her remembered dead, "the other is more wonderful, more pleasing. Even the dead can show their love. Knowing the fullness of death, they will sometimes spare the living for yet a while, before they return for the last time. In this they are often more kind than the living." She closed her eyes, leaning back in the chair. Weary was she, weary unto death, and soon it would be her time to sleep the long sleep.

Quietly, trying not to disturb her, I stood up, knowing it was time for me to leave her. Just as I reached the door she called after me: "The Way: it is not easily found. Yet there are signs that will lead you to it."

Then she waved me off, as though regretting that she had revealed so much of the future, into which only she could see.

Puzzled still, I pushed my way past the men on the *lanai*, waiting to consult the ancient oracle. In the yard, beneath the *naupaka* bushes, some women sat upon the grass. Not until I was almost at their side did I see Malie among them. She was strangely bedraggled, as though she, too, had been up all the night, running from ghosts. She did not notice me, so intent was she upon the conversation of the woman who sat before her, knees to her knees. Eager to avoid being seen, I hurried past them.

It was the niece of Kaupea who sat with Malie. Her voice, low and urgent, was full of dark power and forceful persuasion. The lightness of laughter was not in it, nor the joy of the woman who sang of love. And the hand she pressed upon Malie's knee: six fingers were on it, the sign of a most powerful *mana*.

Shuddering, I ran from the fearful place.

Feeling a fool, I called at Father Damien's house. I did not want to speak with him, but because I was still under the sway of Momona I forced myself to seek the priest.

The little bird's nest of a house was empty, the unkempt yard was littered with boards and wood shavings and tools, left where he dropped them. A most untidy creature, I clucked in disapproval, having little patience with a man who does not put his tools away, who goes dashing about, from this end of the Settlement to the other, like a wayward butterfly, without staying fixed in one place. This gadabout priest: he is like a bee who flits from flower to flower, but never twice to the same kind of flower. Of what use is such a bee?

Annoyed and relieved at the same time, I was walking away from the neglected place when someone called to me. "He is taking food to the chickens." It was Eleu, coming slowly toward me from the back of Damien's garish church.

"The chickens? And where does he keep those?"

"Down there, near the cliffs. I will show you, if you like."

After he'd pointed it out to me the chicken-run was easy enough to see, beyond the small wind-bent trees. I could have got there without him, but he was so listless that I did not have the will to turn him away. Poor Eleu: he knows trouble too . . .

"How have you been?" I asked instead.

"I am well, I thank you. But Akala: she is sick now." He spoke in Hawaiian, in an almost unprecedented departure from his usual insistence upon what he called "American." Because he used the soft native tongue, his sadness was all the more disturbing.

At Kalawao one must be cautious: sickness may mean a headache, or the last agony upon a deathbed. "I am sorry to hear this. Will she be sick for long?"

"*Auwe* for poor Akala. I think she will not play with us again."

"*Auwe* for poor Akala. —So it has come to this?" My breath caught on the hope that hers was the death of Kaupea's prophesy. But how can this be so? I asked, starting to breathe again. Akala is not close to me. I would not have known her, if it were not for the doctor's test upon Keanu.

The slow pace, the bent head of Eleu told me that he would mourn her, if I would not. "What is this shelter?" I asked, hoping to divert him to happier thoughts. It seemed like a fine place for a picnic.

"It—it is the House of the Dead—"

Neither of us looked at the place where soon Akala would be lying, where only a little later each of us would be. Neither of us dared to speak. Only when it was safely behind us did Eleu return to his worry. 'Her grandmother: she says it is because the *haole* doctor cut her face, that time."

"What do you think?"

"I think the doctor cannot be blamed. Whether he cut her or whether he did not, Akala would be coming now to her time, I think."

"I believe you are right. A little cut like that, in a body already so sick: how could it cause her dying?"

"Even if it did, I say the doctor did the right thing. I would give my body for him to test like that."

"Even now?"

"Yes!" He stopped in the path, putting his muscular body in my way. A youth's soft beard was darkening his chin and cheeks. He was not much younger than I had been when I left Kealakekua to make my fortune. Poor Eleu! I winced before the blaze of hope lighting up his face, as he cried out. "Yes! I would do anything to help him to find a cure for the leprosy." The tears he had suppressed for Akala clung to his lashes, making them dark and thick against the widened eyes.

I looked down in sadness upon this boy, so desperate for his rescue. But then: am I so different from him? I looked down in pity at the two of us, standing in the lonely field, at the door of the House of the Dead, desperate for our saving.

"I fear that it will not come in time, Eleu," I said gently, looking beyond the thin eager face to the weeping sores upon his ears, to the fat and drowsy lice basking in the margin of his hair.

"Not only for me," he cried, "not only for me! Who am I, one among so many? No: I would do it for your sake, for Papio's and Kaleo's, for Miss Kekoa's sake, for everyone who lives in Kalawao."

I would have scorned a man for mouthing such heroics, but I put a tender hand upon Eleu's shoulder. "Yours is a noble thought, my friend. But what can we do, who are only men, to check a disease which has been killing men for as long as they have walked the earth?"

"Are we to lie down, then, and do nothing? Are we to be like ants, seeing only the one track they must follow, and no other? No, I do not believe it."

"Eleu, do you remember what Kamiano said, about God's will?"

"I remember. It is God's will, he said, that men should be sick. But I do not believe this. Kamiano does not believe this, in his heart. He tries to change the will of God. 'God is love,' he says in the church. He believes this, not that God is cruel. Kamiano nurses the sick, he feeds the poor, he brings water to us from the faraway valleys. By loving us, he shows us how God can love us. If this is so, can he believe that God will not want us to find ways to drive out the leprosy from us?"

"Yes, but—"

"Do you remember what the doctor said, that morning? I wish to do this for the sake of my fellow men, he said, to learn something about the *lepera*. Then perhaps other men will find a cure for it. They were good words to me. I believe them."

"Then, my friend, you must follow your belief. I am of this opinion, also, although perhaps I am not so certain about it as you are." By this I meant that I was not so sure Dr. Newman was the man for us to place our trust in. I could not forget the impression gained on the terrible morning of the inoculation. "A madman," Damien called him, hurling the word at him in a curse; and Newman's wild speeches and incoherent arguings made me fear that the priest was close to the truth. But when the doctor performed the operation, with a mastery of his instruments which showed that he knew very well what he was doing, I was able to hope that perhaps there would be some value in the test after all.

"Yeah. Sometimes I get excited. When I think how much there is to do, and how nobody is doing anything, except the doctor and Kamiano . . ."

"Has he made any tests on you?"

"Yes, in the House for the Sick, with the others who go to him there. He has taken a piece of my ear, some drops of my blood, and put them in little glass tubes. Now, he says, we must wait. But most of all, we must wait to see what happens in Keanu. And I think that as he waits he grows worried. I do not think he knew me, when he took the blood from me."

"I do not wonder. So much depends upon the results of the test. And I would worry, too, if I had to live for such a long time, in the company of a man like Keanu."

"The waiting is hard for Keanu, too, I think."

"Yes, I suppose so. I—we are not the only ones who suffer."

"*Ea mai!*" He pulled me to a stop. "Look!"

Beyond the low fence of the chicken yard Father Damien was calling to his birds. Not only chickens were there, but shy sparrows and wild doves and rare forest birds, their flashes of red and yellow, of brown and green and white, making the air bright with darting color. Hovering over him were the little birds, a nimbus of whirring wings and soft feathers. Upon his shoulders and outstretched arms the doves were gathered, eager to show their trust in him, their soft gray feathers melting into the soft gray of the distant sky. Around his feet clustered the chickens, making their obeisance to him. The air was filled with bird songs, canticles of pure joy, blending with the crooning of the priest.

In the midst of the wingèd conventicle he stood, raising his arms with a beautiful grace, turning his head with a slow wonder, as of a man seeing the freshness of the world for the first time, or for the last. Upon his bare head the sunlight shone, making the tonsure to glow.

We could not see his face. For this I was glad. I could not have endured the radiance shining there: it would have been brighter than the sun s. The sweet love of a Saint Francis for his brothers is more than sinful men can bear.

I tugged at Eleu's shirt, to tell him that we must go, to leave the holy man in peace. The moment of joy was his. The little portions of it which came to us were enough, as crumbs from a table are enough to please sparrows.

Unthinking, Eleu put his hand in mine. Trusting me, as the birds trusted in Father Damien, he went away with me.

At the church, as though we waked from a trance, we parted. "*Aloha*," he said softly, as he turned toward the open door. "*Aloha ia oe*," I called after him, as I turned toward the empty road.

34

ONCE AGAIN it was Akala who drew me into trouble, this time into the trouble of her dying.

I was sitting on my *lanai* one morning when, chancing to look up from my reading, I saw her feeling her way along the stone wall bordering the lane. Her cheeks were so swollen that she could scarcely see, and she stumbled frequently upon the rocks lying in her path.

"Akala," I called, not thinking of what I did. "Where are you going?" I asked, hastening down the stairs.

Her answering grimace was sickening to see. Her explanation, when it issued from between the bloated lips, meant nothing to me. At last I was able to understand: "To the House for the Sick."

"But why do you go so far from home?"

"To put clean bandages upon my sores. They smell . . ."

"Do you go alone? Cannot Miele take you?"

"She is sick. Everybody is sick, even Eleu. With the bowel fever."

"Then I will take you." The promise was made before I knew it was coming to my tongue. "Wait for me."

I changed into better clothes for the walk into the village. Then, with my arm around Akala's stinking body, and my face turned away from it, I began to guide her upon the long walk to the Infirmary. Before we went a tenth of the way we were forced to stop. "*Auwe, auwe*," she gasped, "I must sit down."

For the rest of the way I carried her upon my back. She was not heavy. But the rage growing within me was enormous: heavier and more violent it grew with each step I took, until it almost choked me. Quarreling again with God and man, I plodded down the dusty road with my burden upon my back. Never more was I to be freed of it.

The morning was brilliant and clear. The green *palis* soared up from the azure sea, the peaked islands played in the waves like *mahimahi*. But I did not see them as I trudged through the dust, with Akala on my back.

. . . *You devil, you. You cheat, you monstrous torturer. Sitting in your faraway Heaven, a fountain of mercy. And yet you let such things as this happen, upon earth here below. Why? Why?*

Aloof he was, beyond reaching. I was a gnat, lost in the depths below his high Heaven.

It was more satisfying to turn my rage upon someone easier to reach. This priest! What the hell is he doing? Why doesn't he help? And those doctors, sitting around in their big houses, doing nothing—

Blinder than the blind boys was Caleb, weaker in his fury than was Akala in her dying. Caleb, with his chatter about the evidence of the senses, the nobility of thought, the freedom of reason. *Cha!*

Not even the evidence of my senses, when we entered the Infirmary, could purge me of my pride.

Never had my nose been assailed with such an abundance of scents and stenches, of unguents and sores, of foul breath and jasmine blossoms and tobacco smoke, all compounded into one thick miasma of corruption. I could taste it: and the stink of it made me sick.

Never had I seen such delights to the eye, such variations upon the human theme, as were assembled here, in a witches' Sabbath of perversions of the limpid eye, the shapely nose, the shell-like ear, the kissable lips. I could touch them, as I passed among them, one by one, and the feel of them made my own rotting flesh creep with horror.

Never had I heard such pure sounds as were uttered here, such choirs of angelic music, as the noisome patients shouted and gurgled and wheezed and babbled in their elegant promenade. Before my sun-dazzled vision the liquid language clotted into festoons of bloody bandages, into bags of vowels filled with pus which, swelling as bubbles do, broke with the sound of shattering glass, drenching us all in vileness.

At the center of this delirium, a black wedge of silence in the kaleidoscope of bedlam, sat the priest. Swiftly, lovingly, he dressed the loathsome wounds, washing them first with wetted rags held in his naked fingers, applying the ointment with his thumbs, pressing the bandages upon the gaping sores with the palms of his hands, until, moistened by the weepings from the ulcers, they were held in place while he tied them on with strips of cloth and pieces of string. He was the one whole and healthy man in the roomful of lepers, and I watched in unbelief not the skill with which he ministered to the patients but the gladness with which he exposed himself to the disgusts of their mortifying flesh. Not once did he shrink from touching a lesion which made many of us turn away in nausea, not once, in the long hours of his service, did he pause to rest. He leaned over the lepers as though he would kiss their wounds with his lips and clean them with his tongue.

I was slow to discover Dr. Newman at the far end of the room. When at last I saw him I could scarcely believe that the man I looked upon was indeed the *haole* doctor.

The ridiculous uniform he affected was mussed and dirty: he had lived in it, slept in it, for many days and nights. But I was most shocked by his face, wan and unshaven and soft. The blue eyes were enormous: they seemed to be full of hot tears, waiting to spill down the pale cheeks of a frightened child.

He was brandishing a guava branch at a cringing Chinaman. "Now the ointment," he shrieked, "the yellow ointment. Put it on the bandage." The *Pake's* hand moved uncertainly toward the several jars on the table. "No, no! The *yellow* one. What's the matter with you? Can't you understand?"

The Chinaman began to hop from one foot to the other, shouting "Me no *sabe*, me no *sabe!*" while the doctor screamed his instructions always a tone louder than the patient. As an example of the comity of peoples it could hardly be improved upon.

The *haole* brought his exercise in tact to a gracious end. He banged the stick upon the edge of the table with a crack that made the poor *Pake* jump. "Here! Here! This one!" He thrust the stick into the jar of medicine, spooned up some of the buttery salve. "See? *See?*"

Nodding furiously, the pigtail writhing down his back, the Chinaman hurried to take some of the ointment from the jar. Hastily the doctor withdrew his stick from the contaminating touch. "Now put it on the bandge. *On the bandage!*" He shouted at a man who could not understand, just as people always shout at men who are deaf.

Shouting is done for the sake of the shouter: this I know. I recognized the voice of terror, because I have heard its cry.

While he directed the miserable patient in dressing his sores, I noted the signs of the doctor's disintegration. They are familiar enough. How often have we seen the proud *haole* come among us, with his white skin and his clean linen, his weekly baths and Saturday shaves, and, above all, with his arrogant airs. And how often have we seen him give up one by one each of these attributes of his lordliness, except for the arrogance: first it is the bathing, then the linen, then the shaving. Gradually the cleanliness is overwhelmed by the dirt, and soon he is a filthy smelly ragged derelict, an offense to everyone around him. "Going native," the *haoles* call it, indifferent to the insult they heap upon the clean natives, who view the metamorphosis with disgust. "Becoming a pig," the natives call it, knowing how they degrade the pig by saying this.

For some, drink is the cause of their undoing, for others it is women, or boredom, or loneliness, when they are removed from the company of other *haoles*. Watching the ruin which was once a learned man, I could guess the reason for his breaking: he was frightened, frightened almost out of his wits. His very posture, as he crouched upon the stool, revealed a terror so close to the surface of his mind that, like the tears lurking in him, it waited to burst out at any instant.

A man who has everything: a man of sensibility, with a respected profession, a healthy body, a white man's unspotted skin —what could possibly reduce him to such a state? One by one I discounted the usual forces which broke a *haole's* will and robbed him of his self-respect.

And then it came to me. Of course! I myself had said it to Eleu: in his lonely house upon the hill, how could the *haole* live with a murderer for company and not be afraid? Especially after what he had done to the man of violence? I myself would live in terror of Keanu, if I were forced to share the same house with him week after day, month after week.

Dismissing the *Pake*, now finished with his treatment, Newman straightened up with a sigh. Turning to the open window, he leaned far out over the sill, breathing deep of the fresh air. I could not blame him for this need: the stench of the room was more than any man, even a leper, should be made to breathe.

That same afternoon, after I was rested from the walk home, I went out and bought me a horse. The tired old mare, and a Spanish saddle, cost me fifty of Kalakaua's dollars, but I considered my money well spent.

On the second day thereafter, when it was time for her bandages to be changed, Akala rode in comfort to the Infirmary. She was delighted with the arrangement: "Like a *pa'u* rider: this is how I feel," she croaked. But she was frightened, too, because she was unaccustomed to sitting upon a horse, and she made me lead her spiritless palfrey, while she played the princess in the Spanish saddle.

As we plodded along we met two young women, standing at the entrance to one of the lanes. Dressed in *muumuus* of bright colors and exuberant design, with red hibiscus tucked in their hair, they looked like a patch of huge and restive flowers growing by the road. They were pretty to find, in this wasteland, and I was preparing myself to greet them, giggling already at me, when one said to the other: "Behold! See the grand lady, riding on her steed. How is it that she is so fortunate?"

"And see the groom who leads the way," replied the other, nudging her friend in the ribs. "If I had him to lead me, I would leave the horse at home."

Whereupon they both ogled me until I grew uncomfortable at their indecency. They must have seen my embarrassment because, in the manner of native girls, they began to laugh in high shrill peals of delight, pushing and slapping at each other as they shrieked. It is an unseemly laugh, full of artificiality and double meaning, and I hate to have such merriment directed at me. I felt as unsafe as though I were a small boy again, being teased by the nubile girls of Napoopoo; and I wished that I were far away from those two noisy creatures waiting like rude sirens to waylay me.

"E, bruddah," one of them called. "You like come church wid us?"

I turned to glare her down, knowing very well she did not have church in mind, when I saw that they, too, were only teasing me: the wild rolling of the eyes, the ludicrously rapid rise and fall of the eyebrows, the careless affectation of their stance, with hands on hips and rumps outthrust, all told me how they were treating themselves and me to a good-natured parody of the professional approach, and I broke out into laughter as happy as their own over their vulgar show, while Akala and Lehua and I ambled slowly past them.

"Not today," I joined in their game. "Some other day, perhaps?"

"Ah, too bad," they pretended to pout. "Bettah luck nex' time, yeh?" Leaning back against the rock wall, they lapsed into a decorum which would have earned the approval of the strictest missionary.

They put me into a good humor, and I approached the Infirmary with kinder thoughts than I had known for many weeks. By the time we arrived I was thinking again of the doctor. But when I entered the foul room I had not yet worked out a plan by which I could be of service to him. I was forced to leave to irresponsible chance the means of bringing myself to his attention.

He himself found me when he looked up from his work. I had been watching him for several minutes, while he screeched instructions at his one patient, a dark and hairy Portuguese. I was sorrier for the physician than for the leper. My pity made me unafraid to be seen: in certain fact, I wanted him to look out upon the crowd and to find me there, I wanted to be drawn into the realm of his thought and need. My newly aroused interest in my fellow sufferers, whetted by my service to Akala, grew reckless: out of compassion, this most dangerous and meddlesome of emotions, I knew that the doctor needed help. Of all who were corralled in Kalaupapa, I told my modest self, I was the only one who could offer him help. Silly Caleb was about to essay a new role: tired of being hateful Caliban, now he would an Ariel be.

I was not prepared for the joy which lighted his face when he saw me. The querulous lips parted in a boyish smile. The brow lost its frown. "Hello," he said, coming toward me. The message was beyond mistaking, and I was touched by it to a degree I had not intended to permit.

Taking Akala's hand, I went to meet him. The Portuguese made his escape. "Good morning, Doctor," I said, careful not to show my own pleasure at the meeting. Now when the bridge had been crossed, I was ill at ease: what was there for us to talk about,

who had never really talked together before? Where do two
strangers find a common meeting place for their friendship to
begin? Almost, it seemed, I had forgotten the graces of society,
in the months since I had become a leper. The touch of Akala's
hand in mine reminded me that we had in common our adventure
with her. "You remember Akala?" I began.

"Yes," he said quickly, not even looking at her. But he looked
at me closely enough, searching for the changes the disease had
wrought in me. In spite of my good intentions, I was hurt. As a
sensitive plant folds its leaves when they are touched, I closed up
the unprotected places of my shyness. A sensitive plant has its
little thorns, and I let him feel the prickle of mine.

Of course he misunderstood me, and I can't say that I blame
him. I was so busy guarding my thin skin that I forgot how
vulnerable he was. "Caleb! Caleb!" he cried. "Why do you hate
me so? What I have done to Keanu I have done for your sake,
for the sake of people yet unborn—"

"I do not hate you, Doctor," I tried to assure him. "If I hate
anyone, it is—" It is myself I hate and loathe, for the foulness of
my body and the trusting stupidity of its wasted youth, for the
weakness of the spirit which sets me craving now to find my peace.
But why should I confess this to any man? This is my business,
my secret. I thought it best to be direct with him: there was no
time to waste on polite civilities. "On the contrary, I pity you
sometimes—"

"Pity me? *Pity?* But why?"

"Because you are so alone," I said gently, trying to convey to
him my esteem of him and the new-found kindness with which I
thought of him. Around us the other patients were listening to
our conversation, some of them nodding in approval of what I
was saying. "Because you are one, and we are many. Because you
are shut out, and we are together. We have nothing more to fear,
but you seem to be afraid." And we want to help you, I was going
to say, if you need protection from Keanu.

But he was beyond listening. His *haole's* arrogance was aroused.
"Pity!" He lifted his thin nose, curled his pale lips to swear at me.

His answer surprised me with its meekness. "You are right. I am
alone. I have no one to talk to. Keanu is as silent as a tomb." He
babbled on, saying things which had been pent up in him for so
long that now they rushed out as wind hurries through the mountain pass at Nuuanu. I tried to make sense out of them, frowning

with the effort of keeping up with him, but most of what he said was meaningless.

All at once he interrupted himself. "Look here!"—he snapped his fingers—"I've a capital idea." Almost dancing with excitement, punctuating his speech with lunges of haste and erratic shiftings of point of view, he told me of an absurd plan to make a physician out of me, for helping Damien in the Infirmary. Despite my protests that I knew nothing at all of medicine, and my unspoken dislike of the whole business, he persisted in pushing his proposal far beyond the limits of my willingness to hear it.

I was forced to cut him short. "This is so unexpected, Doctor. Permit me to think about it for a few days." He was sensible enough to yield, and bade me a cheerful enough farewell when Akala and I took our leave.

It had not gone well, this meeting, I concluded gloomily, as Akala and I waited for Damien's ministration. We had talked at cross-purposes, in almost everything we said: the words I had used, with meanings so clear to myself, were transmuted by him into thoughts which held different meanings for himself.

And yet a beginning had been made, from which I hoped good effect would come. I felt, too, the hunger stirring in me which had been sleeping for so long: the hunger for learning which would come with the chance to talk with a learned man, the eagerness to think again, and to study again, from the learned man's books and from his learned mind. Only from his mind, in Kalawao, could I gain the tutelage I wanted.

I promised myself that I would speak again with the doctor very soon, for my sake as well as his own.

35

BUT THE TIME NEVER CAME. With the foolishness of all men, who think that there will always be time for doing the things they promise themselves to do "someday," I put off for too long my visit with the doctor. I did not know how near to its end was the time of our trying.

Akala's dying marked the beginning of the end to our somber

mystery. She went swiftly: the day after her royal ride to the Infirmary she took to her bed, too weak to rise from it again. In three more days she was dead. There were many of us to accompany her to her grave, but few among us to weep for her.

In the mournful evening after the burial I was about to make my escape from the funeral feast in Miele's house, where I sat with the dutiful others for Akala's grandmother's sake. With them I lingered, stiff and miserable, in the crowded parlor where Miele's friends came and wept their dry tears with her. We tried to sustain the halting conversation, caught halfway between deference to the remembered dead and the chatter of pressing forgetfulness. The familiar faces, seen so often on kinder occasions, made it difficult for us to cherish Miele's grief, and yet, for her comfort, we tried to pretend it. But, in truth, most of Miele's callers came more for the food than to console the bereaved. A funeral feast is a time of plenty in Kalawao, where there is never enough to eat.

"Crissake, let's go! It's late," I muttered to Momona, sitting next to me. I wanted to go spying on Keanu. I was smarting still under the insult he had offered me the night before, when I was going home from Makaio's house. In the lane near Ah See's house I met the huge man-killer and, taking him by surprise, I challenged him to tell me why he was there. Instead of telling me what I had a right to know, he bullied me. "If you would be a rooster, crowing in alarm," he jeered, "then you must have a perch to crow from." While I struggled and swore, helpless in his grasp, he lifted me up and tossed me upon the top of the rock wall. Before I could scramble down he was gone, laughing at me as he fled.

My suspicions were aroused by such behavior and, whereas before the incident I had defended his right to walk freely throughout the village, now I intended to keep a watch over him. Momona shared my secret and promised to watch with me until we saw where Keanu went and what he did.

"Why should we rush away so soon?" replied Momona to my impatience. "It is only now the sunset." In his spidery fingers he twirled the flower he had fashioned from strips of newspaper while we sat in Miele's parlor. Black and white, it was a lily of mourning, which he would toss upon the table, among the crumbs and the dirty plates, when he made his departure. "I am waiting for another cup of this tea," he informed me where I needed no instruction, "and for another piece of this good bread. Should I go home to cook, when there is supper here?"

I stood up, annoyed with his laziness, his gluttony. "Then I am going," I was saying, when outside we heard the shouting of Makaio, crying out the news of Ah See's murder.

The paper flower falling from Momona's hand to the floor, the lily of death trampled under rushing feet: this is the last clean thing I remember, before I was caught up in the whirlwind of evil in that night of our measuring.

Howling for Keanu's blood, we swept up to the doctor's house, a tidal wave of bloodlust, not a company of men. In the bloody light of our torches we flung ourselves upon the doctor's house, summoning Keanu to our justice. "Get him!" we screeched, "kill him, before he kills again!"

The madness, the unexplainable madness, which made me join the others: how can I remember it and still keep my sanity? I cannot admit to myself that I, with all my learning of the law, with all my humane thoughts and stern judgments, as stern toward myself as toward other men, could still be seized with an insane hunger for Keanu's life—No, no! It was not I who was the hunter.

It was some other creature, a monstrous thing which inhabits me, a creature beyond control, which cherishes hatred and remembered insult, which lives on sour envy and the sustaining hope of vengeance, which scoffs at charity and stores up imagined wrongs, until they burst from him in a destructive flood. Ahh, but let me have this comfort: it was not Caleb who ran that night, hunting Keanu in hate. It was not Caleb: it was his black misshapen twin. It was Caliban—

Salvation comes to men in different ways. Some find it in flashes of blinding light, or in the melee of the battlefield; others find it in the quiet of their monkish cells, while they pray upon their knees. Mine came through the agency of Keanu's mighty foot. When I rushed upon him he kicked me with a most unbelievably powerful kick, right in the belly. It was his only defense, but it damned near killed me.

Someone caught me as I fell back and laid me upon the ground. Gasping with fury and pain, I could only lie there and curse,

easing my wretchedness with noise when I should have been sending hosannas of thanksgiving to Heaven for my preservation.
Above me other men took up the battle for Keanu, while I rolled
in the dirt.

Then did my salvation begin. As the hurt in my belly eased,
and the breath came back into my lungs; as I ceased to deafen
myself with swearing, there was time for me to think. What the
hell am I doing here? I asked, not able to remember how I had
got myself so stupidly involved in a murderous affair like this.

Over the heads of the mob I heard a harsh voice. "Are you
sharks, hunting the creatures of the sea?" I did not recognize the
speaker. Only when he went on to ask, "Or are you people, with
hearts that have charity in them, with heads that have sense in
them?" did I know it was the priest who was calling us to account.

Faint still with my hurt, but weaker still with shame, I pulled
myself to my feet. Before I could stand upright Father Damien
saw me. "Oh how the mighty are fallen!" he jeered. "Look at
you, O man of reason! And how do you, a lawyer, explain this
court of law?"

No man likes to be mocked in public, and there was enough
false pride in me still to be aroused. "We came to get a murderer,"
I yelped, "before his knife finds its way into the rest of us."

"How do you know that Keanu did this murder?"

Ae, this was the question which Reason had been trying to ask
me, while I lay upon the ground. I could not answer him, as I
could not answer Reason.

Nor could anyone else answer him. For all the opinions they
put up to him he found counterarguments. His logic was unshakable. Skillfully he beat them down, showing me, if not
them, how our case against Keanu was built upon a pool of blood,
upon the shifting sands of envy. He would have made a fine lawyer, this priest.

"And then who said the deed was Keanu's?" The probing finger
pulled the corrupt flesh away from the very heart of our rottenness. I groaned. This was the moment of my chastening.

"Not me!" Hanu was the first to shout, drawing back, the ragged
turban trembling upon his bloody head.

"Momona?" the priest asked sternly.

"I did not say it."

"Makaio?"

"I did not say 'Keanu,'" whined that one, turning away from Damien's gaze.

He did not speak my name: it was a thing too foul. When at last it came out of me, my voice was small. "I did not say 'Keanu.'" To my shame, it resounded in my ears like the whine of Makaio. But I was not so weak as to turn away. Awaiting his judgment, I dared to look up to the priest, standing tall above me in judgment.

But I was not to be let off so easily. My punishment was not to come from his mouth.

Facing the mob, he scolded all of us. He did not ask Keanu to turn the other cheek. He did not implore his Father in Heaven to forgive us because we knew not what we did. Roundly and soundly did he scold us, as a very human father will chastise his children who misbehave.

"Kala," they whimpered. "Forgive," they moaned. But I did not: I was still too proud to bend my neck to him. I wanted only to go home, to hide myself from the priest, and from Keanu. Let Keanu go free, let us go home: this was my only thought.

But we had forgotten the doctor, clinging to the rail of the lanai. "No!" he screamed, shaking the rail until it chattered with his fright. "Take him away from here! Don't leave me alone with him!"

"Let Keanu come with me, then," the priest decided. "The church will give him sanctuary." It was found this easily, the solution of a man who spent his life in settling the problems of others. "Let it be so," the murmurs went through the crowd.

We moved back, to make a place among us for Keanu and the priest. Four abreast we ranged ourselves, before and behind them. In the ordering of our stations I put myself behind Damien. I could see the side of Keanu's head, where the orange light fell upon him from the uplifted torches.

With a thrill of recognition I saw the past and the present meet as one: before us, behind us, the procession was forming, the torches borne aloft in the dark night. Upon the shoulders of the men who had come to kill Keanu their sticks and clubs rested, the polished hafts gleaming like spears. In the distance dogs were baying; within me drums were sounding, in unison with the pulse of my blood.

The broad back of Keanu, the sweep of his brow, the curve of his nose, took now their inevitable shape: I had seen them before, in the vision of my ancestor-spirit standing over me, guarding me from harm. "He is mine!" he had cried out, when the cruel warriors clamored for my life, and he had saved me from their striking. But where was I when our cruel horde stormed up the path to take Keanu ?

Now at last the meaning of the Marchers of the Night was made clear. From out of eternity the past had reached out to warn me, but I had kept no thought of the warning when I needed it.

Somewhere a cock began to crow, a reminder of betrayal, a portent of death.

"No!" I cried out, shouting to deny my guilt.

At a signal from some unknown leader, the grim procession began to move. Four abreast, with torches flaring and the heavy cadence of many feet, we went down the path into the darkness below, where the unknown future lay in wait among the tombstones of the past.

In that night of surprises the rest was confusion gone mad. When we reached the church there was Malie, stepping forth to claim her lover. I was astounded. In my conceit it had not occurred to me that she might give to another man what she denied me. This is how marvelously intelligent I was, how well endowed to be a spy.

"Behold her, this cheat!" bawled the men, "this harlot who prefers the hanging tree for her perching," righteous in their wrath because they envied Keanu his success where they had failed. "Bitch! Whore!" screamed the women, denying her the pleasures of the game they liked so much to play for themselves.

But I was stilled, even I, who had wanted her for myself. I did not wish to stand in judgment of her. Mingled with my astonishment was admiration, for the transformation wrought in her by love. She was a woman of passion and of pride, as she kissed Keanu upon the mouth. Gone was the timid virgin, who stood cold and unmoved at my touch, who wept that love was not for her.

Standing at their feet, I could only force a twisted smile, in which I tried to convey my good will at her happiness, while I fought back the bitterness of the discovery that my imagined love for her was a poor thing compared with the power of Keanu's love.

Angrily the priest brought an end to the lewdness of the crowd. "Not even now do you heed the word of Jesus," he cried. "Who are you, to throw stones upon these two?" Turning his back upon us, he put Keanu into the little church and shut the door upon the lonely one.

He looked down upon us once more. "This door: it is closed now, for the first time," he said solemnly, leaning against the barrier which kept us out of the sanctuary. "It is closed by hate. When it is opened again, I pray that it is opened in love."

I was glad when he chose me to head the guard for Keanu. "I will watch him well," I promised, not knowing what I promised, only knowing that I must say something to tell him I was not entirely evil, that I repented of my part in the evil which had been done.

The telltale ear Kamiano brought with him in his hand told us how we could find the murderer of Ah See.

Poor stupid Hanu. Beaten and in terror, his clothes in shreds, the rags torn from his head, Hanu was led before us in Saint Philomena's graveyard. Damien wept. In the trees, the wind joined him in moaning over Hanu's crime. "It is you," the priest said, between his tears. "Never did I think you would do such a thing. How long has it been, that you have made music in the House of the Lord?"

"Forgive, Kamiano, forgive," blubbered Hanu, kneeling before the priest, his hands covering his face. "It was a mistake. I did not mean to do it." The bloody stump of his ear seemed to dance in the light of the torches.

"For six years have you sung in the House of God, on Sundays and on feast days. And yet, during all this time, when God was listening to you, you did not hear his voice calling to you? Alas for poor Hanu, deaf to the call of God."

"*Kala*," wailed Hanu, groveling in the dust. Few of us could hear him, above the rush of the wind sweeping through the graveyard, above the roar of the torches responding to the rage of the wind.

"Ask forgiveness not of me, Hanu, but of the Lord God above, and of his Blessed Mother. It is he who sits in judgment on you, not I. It is she who will intercede for you. Ask her."

He raised his voice, for all of us to hear. "What do you think his judgment will be, of a man who kills another man?"

While Hanu wailed in desperation, Kewalo stepped forward. "Kamiano," he said meekly, "hear us. Hear our thoughts on this foolish man."

The priest raised his hand. "Have you thought well, Kewalo? Have you remembered the example of the Lord Jesus?"

"*Ae*, this we have done, Kamiano. And this is our *manao*, come out of ourselves, by the Lord's bidding: no man has the right to take the life of another man. Not in anger, not in thievery, not in vengeance, nor yet in justice. A man's life is a precious thing, with many uses for it. And because God has given it, only God can take it away. This have we learned tonight, when we were in danger of not learning it in time."

"Let him live, Kamiano," said Hinano. "Let him live, to think of his crime in the time that is left to him, and to repent of it. Can there be a more just punishment for a man than this?"

"*Ae*," said Kewalo. "This is our *manao* for Hanu: let him live."

"I do not know, Hinano, Kewalo, you others, about punishment," replied Father Damien. "Perhaps it is as you say. But your thought is a good one, because it has mercy in it. I think the Lord Jesus will like it, for this reason. If this is indeed the will of you who guide the people, we will together tell this *manao* to Ambrose Hutchinson tomorrow, and to the Sheriff's man from Kaunakakai, when he comes."

"It is good, Kamiano. We will do this together."

"Let it be so. Then for tonight where shall he be?"

"Let him go home. He will not run away. Where can he run?"

Leaning forward, the priest lifted the culprit to his feet. "Hanu, do you hear this?" Speechless with relief, Hanu nodded his bloody head.

Gently Damien took him by the chin and turned that battered head. "This—this sore: it needs a bandage put upon it. Do you come with me to the Infirmary."

"Thank you, Father. I will go with you."

"I will take you soon. But first must we tell Keanu that he is free."

This was the moment I waited for. "Let me do it, Father. Please. Let me do it." I spoke softly, so the others could not hear me.

"You, Caleb?" He was stern. He did not look at me, letting me see only his sunken cheek, the grim line of his jaw.

After his kindness to Hanu I did not expect harshness for myself. In my need I said more than I wanted to say. "I will open it in *aloha*, Father. I, too, have learned my lesson."

My first reward was the softening of the mouth which he had hardened against me. "This night is not misspent, if it has brought you to this door. Then open it, my son: open it, and go in." This was my second reward.

At the threshold, in the presence of mystery, I opened the door. It turned unwillingly until the wind flung it back against the wall. Upon the altar the candles trembled, lighting up the sanctuary with their weak glow.

Fearfully I stepped into the darkness. Only a few hours before had I sat in the front pew, an ungrieving coffin-bearer at Akala's requiem. Sneering at the tawdry church and at the mummery of its ceremony for the dead, I had been an alien in a foreign world. Now, at midnight, I entered in, a pilgrim, a wanderer in search of peace. In the darkness the tiny church was a firmament without bounds, the fires upon the altar were distant stars. Slowly I began my journey to them.

"I am here." The deep voice came out of the night.

I halted, not certain whose voice I heard.

"Do you come for me?" Taking shape out of the darkness, he stood before me. The eyes were luminous in the dark face, the beard was blackest shadow. "Do you come to kill me?"

"You are free, Keanu. The killer of Ah See: he has been found."

"It is good. But I am sorry for him."

"Keanu—" I had to say it, there was no time for waiting, for eating up my shame. "Can you forgive me for what I did to you this night? Can you forgive us? We were worse than dogs, we who should have been your guardians."

His hand fell upon my shoulder, gave it a gentle tug. It was a sign of friendliness such as I had not felt in many years, not since I left the country boys in the village of my childhood.

"Are you the only one who suffers? Once before did I ask this question of you, but you did not heed me. Now I ask it again. Do I not know the wildness of anger? Do I not know the meaning of regret?"

"How blind I have been! Thinking only of myself . . ."

"This is a lesson I have learned well. When a man lives alone, who else is there to think about but himself?"

"You are right. But I will change from that way, beginning with this night." Now it was not so hard for me to find the words. "You have taught me much."

Again there was the friendly push at my shoulder. "Do not say it. We have been shaped, the two of us, by better men than I. And by—and by Malie."

Once again had I forgotten her. "You are right: and by Malie. And now you must go to her. She will be waiting. Go and tell her that all is well for you two."

"I thank you. I will go. And I will tell her it is you who send me."

Softly he went away. For an instant he was framed in the open doorway, golden in the light of the torches, before he disappeared.

Then I was alone, alone in the House of God.

36

ALL THROUGH THE NIGHT I waited in the church, waiting for God to send me a sign. I bargained with him: send me a sign, I called up to him, and I will believe.

Outside a great wind blew in from the north, shaking the little building in fury, thrusting against the windows until they broke with a splintering of wood and a shattering of glass. Leaves were stripped from the trees, branches were broken and scattered all over the churchyard. Sweeping through the open door and the broken windows, the cold blast blew out the candles upon the altar. Only the small flame in the sanctuary lamp did not go out: swaying in the distraught air, sheltered by its red glass cover, it hung like a bodiless heart above the dark altar.

At my feet the dying leaves rattled and rasped across the floor. Above my head the church bell rocked, pealing its crazed alarum, mocking me again, as once before bells had mocked me. Ghosts ran, fleeing from the tumult in the sky; and devils hid in the lanes and among the tombstones.

But God did not come. He did not choose to walk that night in Kalawao. He did not choose to send me a sign.

All the rest of the night did the wild wind blow, until Iao, the morning star, brought the new day. Then the storm sped away, running down the slope of the sky to the west, in fear of the sun. The shadows of the night were thrown off by the dawning, and it was day.

When the sun rose above the boisterous sea I was still sitting in the church. Stiff with waiting, I watched through the holes in the floor the molten light flowing beneath the church. I was too spent to see the sunlight streaming through the broken windows, to notice the flame still burning in the sanctuary lamp.

The bell rang, clear as the newborn morn, calling the faithful to Mass. When I lifted myself up to go, the church was full with people. Some were kneeling in prayer, others were sitting patiently, with rosaries in their fingers. Among them were many who ran with the hunters of Keanu. In the corner at the back of the room, Iokepa was pulling upon the bell rope, gathering the people in.

Like a man caught in a dream, I sank back into my seat. Like a soul newly released from its body was I, waiting with others outside the sphere of earth for the morning's flight to Heaven or to Hell. Poised in a strange state of awareness, wherein I saw every detail of the little world from which my soul had departed, I knew very well that I sat helpless in the ugly world from which I seemed to have escaped.

With painful concentration, with the eye of a dying man striving to remember forever the time of his dying, I looked upon the pitiful church. Between the windows a dozen or more crude paintings hung crooked upon the walls. Full of posturing weeping people and of massive brutal crosses, with their faded colors, their excesses of anguish, they portrayed the triumph of death.

Beneath one of the pictures an old woman was kneeling in prayer. Gaunt of body and of face, she was the personification of faith. A madwoman she was, for only the mad can know the comfort of her kind of faith. She wore a mass of gray hair piled high upon her head and falling far down her back in thick loose braids. Among these she, or someone equally mad, had entwined colored ribbons of purple and gold and black. A little bow of the same colors, perched upon the very crest of the mountain of hair, performed the duty of a hat. In contrast to the fantastic coiffure, her *holoku* was of severest black: it hung from her lean frame like a shroud, and I could guess that at night she slept in a coffin filled with moldering leaves.

She prayed with a heathenish fervor, addressing Jehovah as her mother must have invoked paramount Kane: the swaying body, the graceful arms and hands, supple as a *hula* dancer's, the scarred lips, all were put into the service of her petition. Yet, with all this feverish commotion, as of a whole orchestra of devices to gain the ear of God, she did not make a single sound.

I wondered if her approach was any more effective than was mine in winning his attention. Almost overcome with a fit of laughter at the picture I was drawing for my instruction, I dismissed the thought: I could not imagine grave, omnipotent Jehovah leaning out from Heaven to listen to the summons of such a mad thing as she was. Indeed, I could not imagine him responding to the call of a thing as poor and ugly and rotten as any human being is. He is a tyrant, this Jehovah, indifferent to the weak and to the poor and to the diseased. Worse: he is a fraud, invented by the weak and the poor to be their grandest delusion.

His shoes squeaking as noisily as his oxcart, Kewalo came to the front bench. He sank heavily to his knees, crossing himself as he went down. Soon Makaio and Moki joined us. Too embarrassed to leave, I stayed with them. I felt less conspicuous when Kewalo heaved himself up into the seat, wedging me against the corner of the pew.

An altar boy came in, from the right side of the church, a dark angel in the black cassock with its flowing surplice of purple. Only when he finished his obeisance before the altar and rose to begin his duty did I discover that he was Eleu. He was so clean, his hair was so neatly combed, he bore himself with such restraint: he was a different person from the ragged lad I knew.

Swiftly he straightened the purple cloths lying twisted upon the altar table, and the purple veil covering the object of mystery upon the center of the altar. With detached and critical interest I watched each step in the churchly housekeeping, approving Eleu's brisk efficiency at his task, deploring the poverty of taste and decoration upon the holy table. The least they can do, I grumbled, is to put some flowers up there, or some leaves. And the question which bothered me at Akala's funeral returned now in full-fledged irritation: what the hell have they got covered up so carefully under those purple veils?

Another acolyte came with a smoking taper, to light the six tall candles in the golden candlesticks. Upon their unshod feet the two virginal servers moved in their solemn dance, as silently as shadows. I envied them their faith when, their duties done, they bent the knee unto the shrine and bowed their heads in reverence, before they returned to the room beyond the door. Perhaps the Church is wise, I was sneering, to teach them its ways while they are so young, when Iokepa ceased his tugging at the bell. The hush made my heart to leap: it was the hush of expectancy, the waiting for a moment to arrive which is to be a moment of perfection.

In the stillness the tinkling of little bells sounded beyond the open door. What? Is God to come in to the music of cowbells? I was scoffing, when Father Damien stepped through the door into the sanctuary, followed by Eleu and his twin. At the sight of the great crowd rising to greet him the priest stopped. In his vestments of lace and stiff brocades, heavy with gold and royal purple, he was like a painted puppet. His features were waxen, like a doll's, but marked with pain and weariness as no doll's face is ever shown. When he moved again toward the altar he limped, dragging his left foot through the dead leaves upon the floor.

Attended by the two servers, he began the ceremony of the Mass. It held little meaning for me, and, because I did not know when to rise and when to kneel, I remained seated, stubborn even when Kewalo signaled for me to follow his example. Yet in spite of myself I was impressed with the beautiful grace of the priest's gestures, as he raised his hands, as he clasped them before him, as he crossed himself. Unhurried he was, performing with devotion, as though he brought his faith in those strong hands to lay upon the shabby altar, and found his faith enriched by the proffering of it. Then I understood the meaning of the time when Eleu and I found him with his birds: this is a man completely good, I saw, and even the birds know of it. Only men are slow to learn this fact. Only his God ignores him, as he disdains the summons of the dancing madwoman.

He leaned forward to kiss the altar, but Eleu had to support him when he bent his knee. The boy was quick to help, his worried frown showing his sympathy for the man who suffered even as he worshipped his unheeding unhelping master.

Lost in the meaningless service, I was growing bored when Father Damien turned away from the altar. He limped to a lectern placed at the left side of the church, next to the fluted pillar supporting the wooden canopy above the altar. Resting his hand upon a great book, he looked for a long minute upon the congregation.

"*Dominus vobiscum,*" he said in a loud voice, opening the book to an appointed place.

"*Et cum spiritu tuo,*" said Eleu, as the people rose to their feet. I was impelled to stand by the grasp of Kewalo about my arm.

"The beginning of the Holy Gospel according to Saint Matthew," announced the priest, making the sign of the cross.

"*Gloria tibi, Domine,*" said Eleu, crossing himself, as the people signed themselves on forehead, lips, and breast.

" 'Then Jesus came with them into a country place which is called Gethsemani; and he said to his disciples: Sit you here, till I go yonder and pray.' " Thus simply did Damien begin for us the long and appalling story of the betrayal and death of crucified Jesus. For almost twenty minutes he read the account of the Passion, while we stood in our places, aching in every muscle, shifting from one foot to the other, coughing, sighing, waiting for it to end. Although I had not escaped hearing the essential facts of the story of Christ—what man, woman, or child in Hawaii can escape the teachings of the Christian missionaries who have claimed our nation and our souls for Christ's benevolent Father?— this was the first time I heard the whole gruesome business of his betrayal. His betrayal by his people, even by his disciples, I could understand, for they were human; but as I heard his pitiful tale I was repelled again by the cruelty of the despot Father and amazed at the acquiescence of the submissive Son. I could not understand the savage demands of the One, who was King of Kings and Lord Omnipotent, who, if he wished, could shatter mountains and blow out the light of stars. If he is this powerful, why did he demand the life of his only begotten son? Nor could I understand the humility of the Son: why did that meek weak one submit so limply to the ordeal of his sacrifice? Why did he not fight back? Was his life not worth fighting for, even as mine is?

I could not accept it: this was not a religion to comfort me. A fable it was, to soothe madwomen and weaklings with, but it was not a faith for quieting my quarrel with God. A church is nothing more than an elaborate cheat, for gulling poor widows out of their mites, and rich men out of their property. How can a man like Damien believe in this? Furious with the trickery of men, I was thinking of ways to contend with them when the priest finished his reading of pallid Jesus's useless sacrifice.

"By the words of the Gospel may our sins be taken away. *In nomine Patris, et Filii, et Spiritus Sancti, Amen.*"

"Praise be to Thee, O Christ," sang believing Eleu, and the reading was done.

Like a field of grass under the press of the wind the people sat down, rippling back from the front row to the rear. From his place Damien studied us. He saw that I was there, that Kewalo and Makaio and Kumakani were there, and all those others who had tried to kill Keanu. In absolute stillness, heavy with guilt, we waited for him to speak. I could not deny him his victory: it is why we were there, to be punished for our crime.

In the soft light the lines and furrows in his face were smoothed away. In the structure of bones, in the palimpsest of flesh, I saw how he must have appeared as a young man, before the cares of Kalawao were laid upon him. Clean and smooth and soft he was, once again, full of loving-kindness and youthful purity; pale and fair, the color of milk scented with the freshness of his northern spring. Beneath the heavy chasuble the shoulders were straight, the body was slim, not knowing yet the weight of the ugly world which was to be his burden.

"Today is Palm Sunday," he began, in a voice high and strained, as though dust were caught in it, or anger. "This is the day when we remember the time our Savior entered into the Holy City of Jerusalem, to claim his Kingdom. The words of the Gospel for today tell of the words he spoke on that day of days." He took a step forward, toward the congregation. The change in his position was small, but it was enough to put the lines back into his body, the grayness of age into his hair. In the palms of the lifted hands I saw the calluses and the scars, the stigmata of his labors.

"That day long ago it should have been a day of great rejoicing. But it was not. Today, in this his House, it should be a day of rejoicing. But it is not. More than a den of thieves do we have here in Kalawao, and in Kalawao there is no peace. Not men of peace, but men of violence do we have in Kalawao—*ae*, and women, too—men who murder, and others who would commit murder.

"The Lord Jesus would not walk among us today. He would be *ashamed*—"

Down his cheeks the tears began to flow. "O, if thou hadst known the things which belong unto thy peace! But now," he groaned, "but now they are hid from thine eyes."

From the congregation came moans of penitence, the sniffling of women, the uneasy stirring of men. I lowered my head, wishing for a place to hide.

"Why is this so?" he went on more calmly. "Why have we lost our peace, and fallen upon evil ways? Why is it that among us are men who steal what is not theirs, who waste their days in idleness? And women who will cast their purity upon the ground, and men who will despoil it? And why are there among us men and women who are so lost in sinfulness that they will rise in violence, shouting to take the life of another man?" Demanding an answer, he leaned over the lectern, searching among us for a defender of our ways. But no one stood up to be our champion.

"I will tell you why I think this is so. The very stones would cry out if I held my tongue and did not speak. It is because we have forgotten the words of Jesus: 'Love ye one another,' he said. 'Love thy neighbor,' he said, but we have forgotten what he said. 'Do unto others as ye would have others do unto you.' We say these words with our mouths, but in our hearts we do not know their meaning. We are deaf and blind to them, we are fond of our sinful ways, we cling to these ways because they are full of pleasure to us, because they are easy."

Now we're going to catch it, I assured my attentive self, remembering my lessons in rhetoric, remembering the lawyers in Honolulu, as they wound themselves up for the peroration. Now listen to the anathemas roll.

"It is difficult to love, as Jesus bade us love. It is the hardest thing in the world, to love. This I know." Resist as I might, I could not shut him out. Squirm as I might, I could not escape the pointing finger: with his finger he was touching the hard stone which is my heart.

"But love is the only salvation, the only way. It is the rescue of the one from the terrors of loneliness. It is the shield of the many against disaster. Can you not see this? And can you not see how Jesus, our Savior, has shown us the way?

"See what happens when we forget his message. A defenseless man is slain, taken by surprise in his own house. An innocent man is hunted down, by a mob of unthinking maddened men, and he, too, is almost murdered. He, too, is a man of violence. And he is already the victim of another kind of unloving man, a man who, in his pride, thinks nothing of risking the life of his fellow man in his quest for fame. Where does it end, this chain of pride, of lawlessness, of lovelessness? You have seen its end, you have seen it: it ends in death."

From the people a groan went up, to stop him.

"O, listen, listen to the words of Jesus Christ! 'Love ye one another,' in the way of the spirit. In the way of the spirit, I say, not in the way of the flesh. The way of this love of the spirit is not an easy way. But it is the way of life." There was no anger in him, only pleading.

"Often have I said these words to you, but you have heeded them not. Hear me say them again to you, for your sakes." Gently he began, and softly: "Love is patient and is kind; love envies not, it is not puffed up." The pleading was left behind. He gave us only the wonderful words, the soft and fluent Hawaiian phrases with their rounded rhythms, letting them speak their own message.

As I heard them I looked up in amazement, forgetting my shame, in my thirst to take the beautiful words into me.

"*He mea pau ole ke aloha.*" Love never fails. I listened as though he were a *kahuna anaana*, binding me with a *hana aloha*, a charm for love. Out of what God's mouth have these words come? If this is the message of Jesus, then do I feel the power of the Son.

"And if I should have prophecy"—he looked down at me—"and should know all mysteries, and all knowledge, and if I should have all faith, so that I could remove mountains, and have not love, I am nothing."

Ae, the words were meant for me: I am nothing, a hollow empty misery of a man, without love, without hope, without purpose. Now at last I knew the depths of my emptiness. Unable to endure the pity in Damien's eyes, I turned my own away from him, sinking my head upon my breast.

"Now, on this holy day, in the holiest season, let us learn our lesson from the happenings of yesterday. Let us heed the words our Savior spoke so long ago, upon the eve of his sacrifice for our sakes. And let us remember the words of Saint Paul in explanation of our Lord's message. Let us try to follow in their footsteps, remembering the power of love, not only of their love, but also of our love. I know this is not an easy thing to do, especially for those of us who live in Kalawao. We who are lepers bear a double burden. Not only are we afflicted with a sickness of the flesh. We also have a sickness of the spirit, consuming us with a pity for ourselves."

At first, in the reasoning reasonable sound of his urging, I did not hear its full meaning. But the gasps of wonder from the people behind me, the slow stiffening of Kewalo next to me, made me suddenly aware of the all-inclusive "we" entering into his speech. With a last flaring up of suspicion I looked sharply at him. Is this a trick of showmanship, a cheating with words and emotions already worn dangerously thin?

Unconscious of the effect he was having upon us, he went steadily on, giving us, in utter simplicity, the warning he wished to convey. "We think that because we are lepers, we must have special treatment from the world. We think we have special license to do as we please, to do terrible things. In this we are wrong. We must not fall into this trap of self- —"

"Kamiano! Kamiano!" they interrupted him. Those who were seated sprang to their feet, those who were standing surged forward. "*Kala!*" they cried, while they wept tears of amaze and unbelief, of grief and joy and sorrow, brought together in one unbearable discovery.

As they moved toward him, Damien backed away in dismay. Turning to flee, he started to limp toward the vestry door.

The sanctuary was too small for him, and Eleu was too quick. Weeping unashamedly, his mouth wide open, Eleu ran forward and flung himself upon Kamiano, hugging him around the waist, pressing his face into the stiff fabric of the robes. Throwing themselves upon their knees, Makaio and Kewalo seized the roughened hands, covering them with kisses. Others crowded close, falling to their knees, reaching for his chasuble, kissing the hem of his alb, the fringes of his stole. The church was filled with crying and hysterical laughter, and, rising above all, with the ancient heathen wailing, the *kanikau* of grief.

And I? What of me, the man with the hard heart and the doubting mind? I found myself kneeling at his feet with the rest of them, crying *"Kala!"* and beating my breast as I wept.

In our midst, one with us, Father Damien stood, his face, pale with suffering, raised toward Heaven. One with us, he was the completest sacrifice we would ever know.

37

LATER, MUCH LATER, the people ended their tribute to Kamiano, and they permitted him to finish saying the Mass. When it was done they dispersed quickly to their homes, eager to spread the news, while Iokepa's jubilant ringing of the bell sent them on their way. Only I stayed behind in the church, waiting to speak with Father Damien.

It was not long before he came out of the vestry. Dressed in the black cassock, he was the familiar man again, the laborer in the vineyard. "Father, please." I stood before him. "I—What can I do to make amends?"

He came up to me, taking my hands. "Caleb, I am glad to hear you say this. There is much you can do. Dr. Newman: he is very sick. Will you go up there, to his house, and take Keanu's place?"

"Keanu is there? I thought he was with Malie."

"He is a good boy, Keanu. Last night, in the storm, he went back to make his peace with the doctor." Swinging away from me, he limped to one of the broken windows. Supporting himself against the open frame, he hung there by his elbows in such a manner that his weight was shifted to the right leg. It is a trick every leper must learn, for relieving his legs of some of their pain.

"He found the doctor lying on the porch. Senseless, half dead. He was covered with blood, but we could find no wound. We think perhaps he had a nosebleed. Perhaps it was a stroke. But Keanu says he has bled from the nose before. Whatever it was, we think he fell down when we left that sad house, to bring Keanu to this sanctuary. Keanu put him to bed, trying all the time to wake him. But he will not wake up, even now. All the night long Keanu sat with him, and I, whenever I could go up there from the houses blown down in the wind. I am worried for him. So is Keanu. And he should not be there: he should be with Malie."

"I will go and take his place with the doctor. I thank you for telling me, Father."

"You will help us very much. I thank you. I will go up as soon as I can, with Dr. Pietsch. But first I must go to see Henry Opunui. He is dying, and his need is greater. Although maybe the doctor needs me more than I think, more than Henry does. I do not know. I do not know."

"All right, Father. I will give your message to Keanu." I turned away from him, eager to begin upon my mission.

"Caleb," he called after me. I stopped, looking back at him across half the length of the light-filled church. " 'The world of God is full of wonderful things,' " he said slowly, " 'and of these the most wonderful is man.' Somewhere, long ago, I read this, or I heard it, I do not remember how or where. Yet I have never forgotten it, because I know it to be true. I would like you to think upon this."

I who have thought that a man is a louse: what could I do with his new message, so kindly given? I could only send him a sober nod, and then I hurried away.

How different was my approach that morning to the doctor's house from the savage assault of the night before. The devastation of the storm lay everywhere, in broken branches, drifts of twigs and leaves and paper, pieces of shingles and shiplap, in sagging houses, in all of the scattered debris of the Devil-Wind. It was as if the Marchers of the Night had come again, this time walking upon the Land of Pain, loosing their fierceness upon the evil place.

But now, when the storm was over, Kalawao lay in peace, and so did I walk in peace among the ruins of my life. Of the doubts and madnesses of yesterday, nothing remained to me but shards and fragments. And with these I must fashion my life anew, just as Kalawao must rebuild itself from the sticks and boards strewn among its bushes and in its narrow lanes.

How I would build, what I would build of myself, I could not say. Of one thing only was I sure: I walked upright, as a man does. I did not crawl, blind and furtive, as a louse does. Caliban, the ugly creature with the soul of a louse, was dead. And out of

Caleb, I vowed, a new and better man would emerge, a man worthy of Damien's accolade.

At the doctor's house a brooding quiet lay upon the place. It was easy to feel that Death waited within. Almost fearfully I walked around the house to the back, unwilling to enter it until I heard the sounds of life.

It was more sturdily built than most of the houses in Kalawao, and it did not appear to have been hurt by the storm. At the back door Keanu was sitting upon the steps, shaving off his beard. A bowl of soapy water lay beside him, a small round mirror hung on a nail driven into the edge of the door. On the stairs, on the ground, were the soft strands of the beard which he had shorn away with scissors before he put the razor to his face.

He did not see me. Unwilling to disturb him, I went away, to stand in his garden until he was finished. The bean plants were almost eaten up by the grasshoppers, and the young cabbages lay rotting in their grave-like beds. They were as diseased as are the people of Kalawao. Not even chickens could thrive there: beyond the fence of sticks, sagging with rot and the push of the wind, there was not a cluck or a cackle. Poor Keanu: all his work, all his hope were gone into nothing.

The futility of trying to do anything worth while in this dismal land! Keanu and I: we were as helpless as the little flies which breed among the stones in a river bed. One flood, and they are washed away. I was on the brink of falling back into my old habit of despair. It was so easy to forget my new resolve, to slip back into the old ways of sneering at every effort of a man to help himself. Firmly I took myself in hand, almost angrily I ordered myself to turn back, to follow the other road I had promised myself to take.

As I retraced my steps to the kitchen door I met the chickens coming out from the forest: a rooster, two hens, six or eight half-grown cockerels and pullets, in a greedy pecking parade. They were not gone away: Keanu was theirs, and they were his. And when I came to the house, high on its stilts, I saw a shining white egg lying on the bare earth beneath it. This sign of a new life was all I needed: seeing it, I was safely started on my new path.

Whistling softly, to warn Keanu of my approach, I rounded the corner of the house. Clean and beardless, he looked down in surprise from the door.

"Ah, it is you. And what brings you here?" He was friendly, not suspicious. The loss of his beard made him seem a different person, very young and very handsome. With the beard went the resemblance to Kailiki and to my grandfather. And yet I knew that I must ask him about his lineage. I would not be content until I learned whether or not he was another berry upon the dying bush of my family's stunted tree.

"Kamiano sent me. To help you with the sick doctor."

"You are kind. The doctor is very sick. I am full of worry."

"I will watch by him. Do you not wish to be with Malie?"

"This is my great wish. But how could I leave him here alone, when he needs help?"

My dislike of Keanu, begotten in Honolulu and nurtured in Kalawao, was gone. I did not even remember it, as we spoke together in the morning of our changing. I saw only a man whom I scarcely knew, but a man who, with every word he said and everything he did, filled me with the wish to know him better.

"I will watch by him. Kamiano and others will come later to help me. You have been his prisoner for long enough. Do you go now, and share your freedom with Malie."

"Caleb, I thank you. But there is one thing I must ask before I go away. Who says that I was the doctor's prisoner?"

"Is it not so? We have thought it, all of us here."

"Then you have thought wrong. It was not as a prisoner that I came here. When I made my bargain with him, to serve the doctor in his test. Mr. Gibson set me free. Not as a prisoner did I stay in this house. Do you think I could not climb those mountains, if I wanted to run away? Or swim the little space between Molokai and Maui? No: I stayed in this house because of my promise to the doctor. This was our understanding, and he did not go against it. I was the one who betrayed him, because of Malie. What will he think of me, when he wakes?"

"This is a new thought to me, and I am glad to hear it. But let us talk of it later, when he wakes, and only then. For now, you must go. Show me what I must do."

Taking me in, he guided me through the house. I was amazed at its poverty. We in Kalawao talked of it as a palace, but in reality it was bare and gloomy and uncomfortable. A few stiff chairs, a few crooked tables, three beds: this was all it held of furniture. My home was more comfortably furnished, even Miele's shack had better claim to being called a dwelling place. The only luxury I could find in it was the kitchen, put into a room inside the building, to which water was delivered through a pipe. In all other respects, even to the bathhouse and the privy in the back yard, it was like the houses of the patients.

Keanu led me down a long dark hallway, to the doctor's bedroom. It smelled of mold, of dank earth, of death. Small and flat in the narrow cot lay the doctor, covered up to his shoulders by a sheet. He was so pale, so still, that I thought he must be dead. "*Auwe!*" the involuntary cry escaped me.

"He lives. But by a thin thread does his life hang." Taking one of Newman's limp arms, Keanu felt his pulse. "Very weak." Putting one of his warm brown hands upon Newman's waxen cheek, he reported to me over his shoulder: "No fever." Leaning close to the doctor's ear, he called tenderly: "*Kauka . . . Kauka?* You can hear?" The cold figure did not stir; under the eyelids there was no flutter of awareness.

I did not know which moved me the more, Keanu's loyalty to the weakling who had delivered him into the keeping of death, or the little doctor's nearness to death. Staring down at him, I wondered what had brought him here, to this narrow bed. For one of my nature the question was inescapable, the answer something I must know.

"Kamiano has sent for the other doctor, the one in Kalaupapa. He is called Beach, I think. Until he comes, there is nothing to do but wait."

"I will wait here with him," I said again. "Now you must go."

"First I will show you where the things are. Then I will go."

In a few minutes he disclosed to me the secrets of the house. He was very efficient: what little there was, in their poor abode, was neatly put away in the proper places. With a few deft motions he cleaned up the shaving things. "The doctor's razor: I borrowed it. I do not have one of my own." He was impressed by the faucet which brought water into the house. "These *haoles*: they are smart. So many fine things they do, to make a man's life easier. They are good for us countryfolk, do you not think so?"

He made a quick survey of the ordered kitchen. "I can think of nothing more. It is all here. If he asks for me when he wakes, send for me." He was a young adventurer, about to start upon a new course into an unknown world. The smooth jaw, the rounded chin, where the beard had been, were paler than the rest of his skin. The clean scent of shaving soap was still upon him.

Now was the time for me to ask who his family was, to learn if there was a connection between his line and mine. The question was in my mouth, ready to be asked, when, between one breath and the next, I realized that I did not need to know its answer. What difference did it make, whether or not he shared with me the heritage of Kailiki's blood? A man is what he is in himself, a creation of himself and of his time, as I am. A person to be treated with care for his own sake, not for the sake of his ancestors, of his beliefs, or the color of his skin, as so many of the *haoles* think, and so many of my people. In the moment of understanding I learned the lesson that Cain would not accept, the same lesson Damien gave to us in his sermon: all men are my brothers, as I am brother to all mankind. And in the next breath I saw what Damien wanted us to see: if we are not fierce in our concern to be each the guardian of the other, then who will be left to see that all of us together come to no harm?

I tried to hide my shame. I who had betrayed Keanu three times: I did not deserve a place in the same world with him. "Good luck, Keanu. I wish you happiness."

He wiped his right hand upon his threadbare trousers, to clean it—O my God! to clean his unblemished hand—and reached it out to me. "Thank you my friend," he smiled, as he gripped my leper's hand. "And I do wish you the same. Now I will go. *Aloha.*"

Ducking through the door, he cleared the stairs in a single bound. In two long steps he reached the corner of the house and disappeared, striding down the green path to his waiting love.

In the middle of the morning Father Damien came, with the new doctor from Kalaupapa. He was a small plump young man with a hesitant manner and thick foreign accent. "Vere iss Keanu?" he asked, as soon as we were introduced. The heroic mustache he wore did not seem to have found the right man to grow upon. "*Ach, gut, gut,*" he sighed when I told him Keanu was gone.

In single file we tiptoed down the corridor to see the sick physician. Dr. Pietsch pulled back the sheet, exposing the slender body. It had the yellowness of a corpse in it, the smoothness of marble. Expertly he examined the pathetic decumbent thing, lifting its arms, its legs, feeling its pulse, pricking it with a pin in almost as many places as Dr. Trousseau had poked me. He leaned over the thin chest, to listen to the distant heart. "Almost I cannot hear it, it is so veak. And yet it beats . . ." Kamiano and I hovered beside them, waiting for his opinion. How helpless I was, before the mystery of the little doctor's sickness. Yet only a few days ago the dying man was offering to make a physician of me, he who could not be a physician to himself.

Dr. Pietsch straightened up, shaking his head. "I cannot say vat it is. It is not a stroke. Perhaps it is his heart? He has received some great fright, perhaps?"

Father Damien and I looked at each other. "Yes," said the priest. "Yes. Last right there was some trouble here. Perhaps it was enough to make this poor frightened boy fall into this state."

"Trouble? From Keanu?" Pietsch was as determined as once I was to make Keanu the cause of all of Kalawao's troubles. I began to be impatient with him, and with his small-mindedness about natives. He is the kind of *haole*, I was willing to bet, who refers to us as *kanckas*.

"No. It came from outside this house," answered the priest, "not from Keanu. From outside this house—and, I think, from inside this man."

"Please? I do not understand."

"In the hospitals of your homeland, Doctor, and in the madhouses of Europe, have you not seen men—and women, also—lying in such a condition? They are not dead, but neither are they alive. And there is no explanation for their sickness. Their souls have fled from their bodies: they have gone somewhere to hide. Sometimes they come back to the waiting bodies, sometimes they do not."

"*Ja, ja,* I remember hearing of such things. Hysterias they are called, not so? But so little do I know of them. In such maladies of the soul is medicine helpless."

"Aye. This is God's realm, not man's. If God is kind, the doctor's soul will come back into his body. If not—" He left the rest of us to imagine: if not, his soul, naked and unarmed, as now his body is, will stand before his God, to be judged.

"*Ja,* he is in God's hands. Ve can do nothing." The meek physician drew the sheet over the unconscious man. "There is a blanket here? He must be kept varm." I hurried to fetch a blanket from the closet where Keanu stored them. Worn and grass-stained, it was a castoff of the Royal Household Guard.

We returned to the parlor, Pietsch looking nervously about as though he expected whole coveys of witches and errant souls to leap upon him from the dark corners. "Is there brandy here? Or visky, perhaps? In this house I did not think I vill someday ask for spirits. He must have something to keep him alife."

"I know of none. Keanu showed me what food there is. But no spirits."

"Such a change," he tittered, stroking his mustache, staring in suspicion at the empty chairs. He was so frightened of the great big wide world into which he had been thrust, and I wondered how he had ever managed to leave the nest of home. I was toying with the idea of whispering a dirty word at him, to see if he would collapse, when Damien saved him.

"I send some wine from the church. The Bishop does not mind this use of it, I think."

The impressive physician furrowed his brow, consulted his remembrance of church law. "If it helps to save a life, no, I do not think he minds. And soup? Vat you call bross?"

"From the hospital kitchen. It will be no trouble. Umekahana is easier to talk to than the Bishop"—Damien winked at me—"I send Kewalo with it."

"So, then it is arranged. Ve vill leaf you, then, Mr. Vood, to take care of him. If he vakes, keep him in his bed, please. He is too veak for getting out. And send for me. If he goes on shleeping, then feed him some of the vine, or some of the bross. A shpoon or two, vonce in an hour . . ."

Father Damien took me by the elbow. "Caleb, you must get some rest, too. You are all tired out. I don't want for you to get sick, too."

"I'm all right, Father. Don't worry about me." He was as exhausted as I was, with even more need for rest than I. But I could not tell him why I was so confident for myself. For the first time in my life someone needed me, needed me desperately. Across the gulf of time, across the abyss of loneliness which separates one man from another, I remembered the sick doctor's smile of pleasure at seeing me in the Infirmary, I heard again his cry for help. Now I knew what I must do.

Then they went away, leaving me alone. I was afraid. Where is the wandering spirit, where does it lurk? Is it in this house with me, watching me in every move I make, disdaining the corpselike body for the pleasure of haunting me? Or has it gone away, to some distant place I have never known and which only Newman knows, some scene which pleased him in his childhood, or to some dearer place out of his youth, where happiness came to him once upon a time, and where he seeks it now, that he might live in it forever after?

Or—the fear of it made me shudder—will it fight me, snarling and screaming and moaning, and come at me to drink my blood? I knew nothing of medicine, I knew less of souls, and I was very much afraid.

And if, as Father Damien said, God is to have a part in the healing, how can I be certain that God will be kind to him? And to me?

I did not know how I would do it, but I knew that I must unite the divided spirit again with the waiting body. Nurse, physician, *kahuna* I must be, even intercessor with God, exerting every effort of my own body and my own will to call his spirit back into its home again. I must do it, as much for my sake as for its own.

About half an hour after Damien and the doctor went away Kewalo came to the kitchen door. "Here is the Blood of Christ," he greeted me, thrusting the long green bottle into my hand. "And here is the soup from the kitchen," he deposited the small iron pot upon the cookstove. "It smells good." With the more ordinary things of life he was himself, huge, earth-bound, and kind.

"You look half dead yourself," he decreed. "Better get some sleep."

"I am all right for now. Sleep will come later. Tell me: how did my house fare, in the Devil-Wind?"

"Not so bad. You people in your house: you were lucky. The trees around you: they took away the force of the wind. A glass window broken, a rain barrel blown away: that is all, I think. Already Kumakani and Hinano have fixed it."

"Ah, this is a relief to me. And your house?"

"It is well, I am happy to say. Makaio's house was pushed from its posts and lay crooked upon the ground, with all of the things in it made crooked inside. But there is not much damage. It was lifted back into place, with the help of Keanu and the others in the lane. That was a joyous time. Now they are preparing a feast, to celebrate the coming of happiness to Malie and Keanu. Too bad, you cannot come to it."

"No matter. I will feast with them some other time. But I am glad Keanu is made to feel welcome among us."

"*Ae.* Of our friends it is Momona who has fared the worst." The benevolence with which he announced Malie's feasting died away, while he studied me to see what face he should put on for the story of Momona's fate. I gave him no help, waiting as patiently as a palace footman.

"The roof was blown off from his house," he began mournfully. "Then the walls were blown flat. Only the floor stood up. Perhaps because fat Momona, lying in his great bed of brass, was holding it down."

The picture was too fantastic to be resisted: both he and I began to grin. "And the birds?" I asked. "And the many papers?"

"*Eia ala!* Such a sight has never been seen before in all of Hawaii Nei, I think. I wish I could have been there when it happened! The birds: they flew away on the wind, all of them, vanishing like *kolea* when the winter is done. Not one is left. And all of those newspapers: oh my goodness! They went fluttering about, thick as ashes in a fire-pit, until the wind caught them up and blew them away. Now there are pieces of paper all over Kalawao, caught in the bushes, caught in the trees, like bits of cloud. *Auwe!*"— he wheezed, wiping the tears from his eyes—"it will be many months before all these pieces of Momona's rubbish are picked up."

"Such a housecleaning!" I gasped, between laughs. "But he can fill his treasury again. There are always more newspapers. But what of him?"

"This is the funniest part of all. When the dawn came, and I went out from my house to see what the storm did, I found him sitting in his big bed, the sheets tucked in all around him, to keep them, too, from blowing away. It was still gusty, you know, although the strength of the wind was already dying down. The floor of his room: it was as bare as the beak of a hen. Never have I seen it so clean. Even his chamber pot was blown off the edge of his stage. Lonely as a high chief was he, sitting there, the wind blowing the hair about his head, a great unhappiness pulling down the corners of his mouth. But no harm had come to him. As, indeed, little harm came to anyone else in the village."

"He was lucky."

"He does not think so. Do you know what he said, when I came up to him?"

"That Kaupea's gods have played him false?"

"No."

"That soon the *haoles* will be dispersed, as his papers were?"

"No."

"I can think of nothing more. What did they say?"

" 'My mice,' he said, his lips quivering, a tear rolling down each cheek, shining like a piece of glass, in the first light of the sun. 'My mice: they have gone away from me . . .' "

"Alas, for poor Momona." I could not laugh at his bereavement. "What will he do now?"

"Oh, he will be all right. He goes to stay with Hinano and Kumakani, until his house can be built up again."

"In our house? Where will they put him?"

"Where else but in your room? You will not be needing it for yet a while, from what I hear."

"Then why did you not tell me this in the beginning?" From the shrug, the tongue roving around inside his cheek, I could see that I could do nothing to prevent Momona from using my room. I hated the idea of anyone else but myself lying in my bed, sitting in my chair, reading my books. Yet I could not begrudge Momona his shelter, the poor homeless mouseless Momona whom I called a friend. "Oh, hell! You win, you win," I conceded him his victory in wharf rat's English before I joined him again in our native speech. "Tell him he is welcome to stay in my room, but to keep his mice out of it, for my sake. *And* his damned chamber pot!"

The old rogue chuckled. "This I have done, knowing how sensitive is your nose. Do not worry, my friend. He will be gone out of your house in two or three days. It will not take us long to put the pieces of his house together again."

"For this I am relieved. I do not wish to stay here any longer than I must. One more thing, if you will do it for me: in my room, upon the shelf by the window, there is a set of shaving things, in a brown leather case. Bring it to me, please, for my use here."

"*Hiki no*. All right, I will do it."

"In my sea chest, beside the bed, is another set, a new one, in a

black metal box. Take that one to Keanu, please, and give it to him
from me. He has no razor of his own. Say to him, it is a marriage
gift, from me."

"Gladly will I do it. I, too, feel how there is much that we must
do to make amends to the Lonely One. I will take him the gift of a
shirt, perhaps of a pair of trousers as well. White ones, which I
wore long ago, before this belly of mine began to blow up. It has
some use in it yet—the shirt, I mean."

Waving farewell at me, he lumbered off, spitting generously into
Keanu's vegetable garden as he went around the corner of the
house.

All through the long day I tended the inert body lying in the far
room. Forcing wine and broth into the soft mouth was not easy:
he gave me no help in swallowing it. For every five spoonfuls I
gave him, perhaps one trickled down the throat to reach his stomach.
Patiently I kept at it, not once did I become weary of trying. I was
like a father feeding his infant son.

Twice during the day, when I found that he had wet his bed, I
changed the sheets, washed his body, made him clean again. This
was when I learned the meaning of humanity.

Poor pitiful *haole*: he was weak, and he was human, like all the
rest of us. His skin, when I looked closely at it, was not much
whiter than my own, nor was it made of a different more precious
stuff. And the pitiful insignia of his being a man: he was made no
different from other men. With an unexpected tenderness I covered
him again with a fresh sheet. "All men are the same," I informed
the quiet room. "Even *haoles*. 'Hath not a *haole* hands, organs,
dimensions, senses, affections, passions?' " I asked, echoing the
bitter Jew, not in vengeance but in compassion. I wanted to hear
my own voice, guarding me against the sick man's demon.

God hath made of one blood all nations of men: thus begins the
first Constitution of our Kingdom, written for us by the missionaries from New England. *Above all nations is humanity*: this is
another of our mottoes, invoked by orators at political meetings
and by students at their exercises in elocution. For many years
had I laughed at the noble phrases, calling them the moralizing
of people who preached fine things, but who did not practice as
they preached. Now, in the quiet room, with Newman's limp body
lying like the crucified Jesus across my lap, one more of my prejudices was stripped away. And even as I washed away his defilement

I washed away my own; and there was no more hate for the *haoles* in me when I was done.

With the examples of the missionaries before me, of the Binghams, the Richardses, the Judds, and all of those others of their company who by their labors have saved my people from extinction, how could I have hated them?

With the example of Father Damien before me, daily and in a multitude of ways making the perpetual offerings of his flesh and of his spirit, how could I have persisted for so long in this hatred?

And this little *haole* doctor: how could I have hated him? He has come halfway around the world to help my people, to try to save us from our most dread disease. And what have we done to help him, my amiable grateful people and I?

Cha! We have been fools, the worst kind of fools: stupid ones who are proud of their ignorance, and who fight to preserve their ignorance, unchanged.

Alas! There is no worse fool than the one who blames others for his own shortcomings.

When night fell the doctor's condition was not changed. Late in the afternoon Father Damien came to the house for my report and went away again, shaking his head. "I will say more prayers for him," he said, as he left me alone again with my burden.

Aye, only prayers will save him now. In the last glimmer of dusk I untied the mosquito net and tucked it in around him. Then, stumbling with exhaustion, I went into Keanu's room and threw myself upon his bed. Painfully I pulled the mosquito net down around me. I did not have the strength to tuck it in around myself. Content with having it protect my head and arms, I let it fall where it would. My last thought, before I fell asleep, was that I must wake up after an hour of rest. I left the lamp burning beside the bed, in readiness for my awakening.

But my flesh was weak, it was terribly weak. All night long I slept, and I did not awaken until the ringing of Saint Philomena's bell was calling the people to Mass. The lamp was burned out; the cloudy heaven of the net was spotted with sleeping mosquitoes, swollen with my blood. Outside the house the trees and shrubs were heavy with raindrops, and the gushing torrent of the nearby stream told me much rain had fallen during the night. The air in my room, inside the net with me, was cool and damp.

Furious with myself, I fought my way out of the net and ran

into the sickroom. All I could think of was the mildew, thriving in weather like the morning's, and of how they would have flourished upon him, during the long night when I was not on guard against Death and them.

I ripped the net aside. "Thank Heaven!" He was not green and black and covered over with the mossy pile of a shroud grown out of his own skin. Thin and wasted, smaller than he was the day before, he lay like an effigy upon a tomb. A quick touch of my hand to his throat told me he still lived.

Sitting on the edge of the bed, I lifted him against my shoulder. I poured a few drops of wine into the spoon. "The Blood of Christ," I murmured. No: "The Blood of Christ," I prayed. "Let it work its miracle now."

Beneath the ragged mustache the bloodless lips opened at the touch of the spoon. As a babe sucks at its mother's breast, blindly, hungrily, so did he suck at the spoon. He swallowed the wine, and opened his mouth for more. Hurriedly I filled the spoon and gave him more. Six spoonfuls I gave him, before I thought it best to stop, but the greedy mouth would have taken as much as I offered it. Grateful with this sign of his return to life, I laid him back upon the pillow. "*Kauka*," I called. "Do you hear me? How do you feel?" He did not answer. But I was relieved, knowing that his spirit was gone back again into his body.

Through most of the rest of the day it was the same with him. He was like a newborn child: he ate of the warm soup and drank of the dark wine, but he did not know who gave them to him.

He did not hear Father Damien or Dr. Pietsch when they came to see him. "I think now he recovers, maybe," said Pietsch with false cheerfulness. "He is stronger: his heart beats better now."

During the rainy afternoon, while I was sitting in the parlor reading in the old Bible I found there, I heard my charge cry out. "Go away!" I thought he said.

When I ran into his room he was tossing about in the bed, babbling eruptive words, meaningless phrases, in English, in German, strange bubbling ugly sounds I could not understand. They were the splatterings of thoughts, flung up out of the depths of his mind, as flecks of molten lava are tossed by Pele's violence out of the volcano where she lives. Soon their profusion choked them off, as falling cinders will choke off even Pele's burning flood; and he settled back into his sleep. When he was quieted, I returned to my reading.

But soon he started to talk again, and this time he did not stop, even when I bent over him to soothe his brow, to press him back into the bed. Now the words came forth, in an unending flow, spilling over themselves in their haste to leave his mouth.

I could make no sense out of them, at first. Mixed as the rubbish is in a dirty stream, they came out of him, chaotic and useless: there was no clue in them, I thought, to his sickness. But after a while, in the rush of the torrent, there came phrases which repeated themselves, names of people—even my name, even Malie's—who drew cries of hate from him or moans of love, fragments out of his life which revealed the secrets of the poor creature who uttered them. I listened with interest, unashamed of my listening, thinking how in this unguarded converse I might find the reason for his madness. For by then I could not deny that he was mad.

"The rocks! The rocks!" he shrieked. "They are going to crush me!" Scarlet beanbags, filled with clicking crystalline staring eyes, were thrown at him by a woman's cold unerring hands. When he tried to catch them, the beanbags broke and the accusing eyes shed tears the size of pigeons' eggs. "The waves, the waves," he moaned, "they are trying to drown me." Seizing him in their sucking grasp, they pulled him down into tubes of glass filled with lepers' blood. Immense envelopes, white as bridal veils, were wafted through the air to him, bearing invitations to debauchery written on tea leaves which crumbled into clouds of lepers' germs as, frantically, sobbing with eagerness, he tried to pick them up before they fell apart. He frolicked with whores and consorted with pimps; and, with an imaginativeness which annoyed me, he pulled even Malie down into his passionate bed.

I listened in dismay, and then in horror, as he babbled on and on, giving me the portrait of himself in the displaying of his desires. The picture was not a pretty one.

His hates and his fears and his loves: they were all mixed up in him, until he was so confused that he did not know which way to turn in his search for the meaning to his life. This man, who in his life was given everything a man would seem to need for happiness, he had nothing. This *haole*, with his fair white skin, owned the blackest mind a man can have. This physician, who came to minister to us, had a sickness of the spirit which he could not treat. No longer could I wonder why his spirit should flee from a body so sundered by its conflicts.

I listened aghast, as gradually, with fury and tears and moans, the tale of his need unfolded. And when at last I learned the meaning to the most terrible wound of all which had been sent down to hurt him, I was soft with pity. Unable to endure any more of the awful confession, I fled from his side.

Wherever I went in the house the hoarse unstoppable voice followed me. I could not hide from it, I could not shut it away. Nor did the patter of the rain drown it out. I was beginning to fear that I, too, would go mad when, at last, the rain ended.

I found my refuge in the garden, among the damp weeds and the clucking chickens. I was there, squatting on a rock among the barren beanpoles, watching the dozens of waterfalls flowing down the great cliffs, wondering at the mystery of the distant rainbow, far to the east, when Kewalo found me.

"Here is your shaving case. You need it: you look like a peeled coconut. And here is your supper. I hope your appetite is better than is mine tonight."

"Why? What have you to complain about?" It was a relief to hear his deep grumble, to exchange insults with a man who kept no secrets in his heart.

"A terrible thing: the other night the wind, last night the rain. *Auwe, auwe.*"

"What's the matter, you henless old cock? Did the rain wet your roost?"

"Ha! If this were all, I would not lose my taste for food. No. The rain last night: you know how heavy it was?"

"Yes, yes, I heard the stream."

"It was very heavy, indeed. And the water, after it flowed down the hill, the water sank into the ground, down there."

"And so? Get on with it, man. Does not rain always sink into the ground. Where else is it to go? And is Welo not the month when dark storms arise? 'When sea roars, when wind roars, and the black clouds break under the weight of their rain'?"

"Patience, my friend, patience. I am telling you. Why are you so fretful? Do I not know about the water-drinking wind and the water-bringing wind? Well, this water last night: it filled the new grave, the one we put Akala in, the other day. The coffin came floating up."

"And is her canoe of death so heavy that it cannot be put into the ground again?"

"This is not the trouble. The trouble is that there is little left to bury. The dogs and the pigs: they got at her. Before she was found, they ate most of her—"

"O my God! Stop, stop! Tell me no more! I cannot bear it."

I fled from him and his ghoul's tale. There was no place for me to go except into the house.

The sick man was still begging. Maddened, I ran into his room. "Quiet!" I shouted, "Stop it!" But he did not stop. "Enough!" I yelled, shaking him, slapping his face. "Enough! I cannot bear it!" He was unreachable: while I shook him and beat him the words were jarred into formless noises, but when I flung him back on his pillow they were there again, precise and revealing, as revealing as were the red marks of my fingers upon his cheeks.

Only with the night did the hoarse wheedling cease. Mercifully, he slept. I did not dare to feed him. Gratefully I left him to his sleep, hoping it would heal him or kill him. The thought of food sickened me, and, almost as weary as I was the night before, I sought my bed to find in sleep my escape from the memory of his croaking, more haunting than his wandering silent spirit had been, more haunting even than was the specter of Akala's flesh being rooted up by the pigs.

He was awake when I went in to see him the next morning. The blue eyes were deep spots of worry, beyond the veil of the mosquito net.

"You?" he said weakly, as I lifted up the net and folded it away.

"Yes," I smiled cheerfully. "I am here to take care of you. You have been ill." I reached for his hand, to let him know I came to him in friendship. But, then, remembering his fear of lepers, I withdrew it.

"Where is he? Keanu?" His voice, so insistent yesterday, was so faint that I could scarcely hear it.

"Keanu?" I found the lie quite easily. "Oh, he is with Father Damien."

"Thank God. You did not—?"

For a moment I did not know what he meant. The night of the mob was so far away. Then I remembered. Looking away from him I said, "No. Father Damien saved us from doing that terrible thing."

"Thank God . . ." He closed his eyes, and did not open them again. I stood by him for a long time, until I was sure that he slept.

After this his body made steady improvement. But I was not so certain about his spirit. Obediently he took the broth and the wine when I brought them to him. But he did not speak, in spite of my determined cheerfulness; and when Father Damien and Dr. Pietsch came to see him, he did not say a word to them. Uncomfortable under his cold stare, they left as quickly as they could.

There were times, during the long day, when I wondered if he knew where he was.

The next morning, when I gave him greeting, he pushed himself up on one elbow with unexpected strength. "How long have I been here?" he asked quietly. "What day is this?"

"Let me see. This is Wednesday morning, I think. Yes, it is Wednesday. You were taken sick—you've been here since the night of Saturday."

"I want to get up."

"Fine, fine. I will help you." I knew that neither Dr. Pietsch nor I should delay his release from the prison of his bed.

He chose to say nothing more on Wednesday, except for the necessary expressions of thanks when I helped him to a chair in the parlor, or brought him his food at noontime and in the evening. Milky pale, thin as a stickfish, he sat huddled in the chair, wrapped in a blanket. He appeared to be sleeping much of the time, but I could never be sure when he was not just brooding. Not once did the cruel curl of his mouth soften, even if he slept. He had the look of a man full of hate. I was very uncomfortable, and I spent my time sitting in the kitchen, like a servant, or standing out in the garden, like a beast.

I was sunning myself on a rock, listening to the spiders weave their webs and the worms bore through the mud, when Kewalo brought up the evening's supply of food.

"And are you so in love with the mountains that you must watch them all the day?" he growled as he set the heavy basket at my feet. We ate better now when my patient no longer subsisted on broth. "Have you not a splendid house to live in?"

"*Kulikuli!* Shut up!" Almost in a whisper I explained why I liked the quiet of the garden.

"Gonfoun' it!" He spat with elaborate contempt upon the *kauka's* house. "This sassy *haole*. He doesn't change. His sickness does not make him a better man."

"How can you say this?"

"He was this way before, too. How often was Keanu driven out of the house by that one's silences."

"He was this way with Keanu?" It had not occurred to me that anyone else could have been subjected to the same ordeal by silence.

"Of course. Many a time have I come to talk with Keanu here, in this very place, while he worked in this garden. I would stand here, he would stand there, keeping his distance from me, as the doctor wished. 'The *kauka* is thinking,' he would say to me, just as you have said it. *Cha!* So do the squid think, when they lie sleeping in their holes in the reef."

"Well, an eel am I, then, blinded by the ink of the squid. Now I am even more sorry for Keanu. It is not easy, living in this house with him. But he does think, the *kauka* does." Slow to come to my fraternal mind, but arriving there, none the less, was the wish to defend the doctor against the dislike of my fellow patients. "He has much to think about."

"So does every man. But this is the first man I have known who needs a whole house to keep his thoughts in. Most of us need only a single head." Slowly, with all the massive state of a Kalakaua, he settled himself upon a nearby rock. Groaning like a bass viol at a wake, he took the big *lauhala* hat from his head and fanned himself. "Hot today," he tried to change the subject.

"I, too, have been thinking. And this is my *manao*. We of the Settlement have done a great wrong to this doctor. We have been cruel to him, as we had no right to be. And in part it is because of us that he sits here, sick and alone."

"Perhaps. I do not know. What I have seen of him I do not like. Why should I be kind to a man who is not kind to me?"

"It was our place to make him welcome among us. Were we ever kind to him, did we ever show him what kindness is?"

"You are right, I suppose. Ours is the land, and he is the stranger among us. We know this, in our hearts; we do not need to be told this truth. But we know, also, how just as each man must have someone to look down upon, that he might feel well off, so must each nation have another nation to look down upon, that it might feel the better. For us of Hawaii Nei these crazy *haoles* are such inferior ones: with their unending busyness, with their running fro and to, they are as useless as rock crabs. Why should we not dislike them, for not knowing how to behave as sensible people do? Why should we not thank them to stay at home, in their own lands, to live in their houses of frozen water, to wear the skins of hairy animals?"

"*Auwe*, Kewalo! You are as sassy a man, in your own way, as this poor *haole* you slap with your tongue. In your hard head you, too, have no wish to change. But be warned: these *haoles* are smart. They are not rock crabs. They are the industrious ants."

Scratching his neck, Kewalo grinned complacently, making his big mustachios to wriggle. "Why should I change? I like myself the way I am." He paused for a moment, a suspect pause. "So do other people, I might add."

"And what is meant by this?" I know when to follow a hint.

"Me and Pahaiwa-wahine." He stroked the glossy mustachios, as vain as a youth. "We are going to marry."

"You and Tutu?" I checked my roar of laughter just in time. This big bull and that little mud hen? Why, she'd have a ring through his nose before the marriage bed was rumpled.

"And why not?" he huffed. "I like a woman with spirit."

"*Ae*, there will be no long silences in your home, my friend. There will be no escape for you from the noise of a clacking tongue. Well, when you need a place to think in, you are welcome in my house. There you can talk in peace—or sit in peace, for that matter. I will treat you to quiet, instead of to chatter."

While I laughed gleefully at my picture of his future, he said quietly, "Everyone tells this to me. But I do not believe them. I think she talks much now out of her fear of loneliness. When she no longer fears to be lonely, she will no longer talk like this foreign bird with the curved beak, this—what do you call it?"

"Parrot?"

"You have said it. Then will she be a gentle woman. I wish to be the one to make her gentle. You will see: a singing *elepaio* will she be, happy in her nest, not a noisy parrot."

I stopped my laughing. "Then I hope it will be as you say, my friend. I wish you nothing but happiness."

"I thank you. You will come to the wedding, I promise you. It will be soon, now that Malie is gone."

"Malie is gone? Where did she go?"

"Have you not heard? But yes, I forget. You have been here, all the time, listening to learned silences."

"Stop this crawling like a sea slug! Tell me! What has happened to her?"

"Why, everything—or nothing, however it is you look at it. She has gone with Keanu to live in the house of her Uncle Peter, over there in Kalaupapa, beyond the birth-hole of Kauhako."

"What is this you say? Is Malie the niece of that one?"

"Of a certainty. Did you not know it?"

"No. I did not make the connection. I do not know all these stupid genealogies."

"*Kie!* With all your learning, you still do not know the important things. Then do you listen, while I tell you some of them. The Prince Peter and Kekoa-wahine, the mother of Malie: they were brother and sister. Malie knows this much, and has spoken with pride of her Uncle Pita. What she does not know," he went on slowly, observing me closely, "is that she is niece of a sort to Momona as well."

"How do you mean this?"

"Peter Kahekili and Momona: they were as good as wed, each to the other, when they came here. It was kept a secret, of course, because the *haoles* do not approve of such things. Kamiano, for one: he does not know even yet how Momona was bed-friend to the Prince Peter. And Momona has begged us to keep this knowledge from Malie. 'She will not understand,' he has told us, and I think he is right. But in the old days we of Hawaii Nei were more broad-minded. I do not know how it is with you, who do not care much for the old days."

"Is this indeed the truth you tell me? You do not jest?"

"Why should I jest about so important a thing? *Pau Pele, pau mano:* may I be consumed by Pele, may I be consumed by a shark, if I have not spoken the truth."

"But—how could it be? With Momona so fat—"

"Do not forget: in those days Momona was young, he was not fat as he is now. Slender he was, and good to look upon, although perhaps he was too much of a *mahu* for those who like to be sure a boy grows into a man and a girl grows into a woman. Nor was he called the fat one then. His real name is Jared, but few of the people here know this missionary name. Nor do they know that he does not have the separation sickness, or that he came here

willingly with the Prince Peter, out of love for him. They see only
a fat man, with a sorrowful liver and a sharp tongue. But we
who remember, we have grown a respect for Momona. And most
of the time, as you have seen, we are long-suffering with him when
his tongue becomes sharper than we would like it to be. He, too,
has his grief and his loneliness."

"Fortunate is he to have such a friend as you, Kewalo. I
am glad you have told this to me. His secret is safe. Why should
I not keep it for his sake? And why should I be offended by it?
Many are the ways of showing love. And I am as broad-minded as
you, who are closer to the olden days. But tell me more of Malie:
what of her move to the house of Peter Kahekili?"

"Oh, yes: Malie. She is a better thing to talk about, because
happiness is better than sorrow. It was her wish to go to her
Uncle Pita's house, which has been empty since he died. She
wanted to leave the house of Makaio, become too full of people
after Keanu went to join them."

"They are married, then?"

"Nah, nah. Not under this new style. In the old way."

"And how does Makaio look upon this?" I could not give up
my suspicion of the old man.

"He gives his blessing. And why should he not?"

"No matter, no matter. And Momona: does he not feel wronged
at being left out of the Kahekili's house?"

"Not Momona. Willingly did he leave it, five years ago, when
Kahekili died. It is too full of ghosts for him, that house. He
moved here, to Kalawao, to have a change of view."

"A good thing for everyone, it turns out. But is the old house
fit for Malie to live in?"

"Here, my young friend, any house which stands is fit to live
in. Only the Kahekilis' strong *kapu* held this one empty for so long.
Waiting it was, we knew, for another Kahekili to come and live
in it. Ambrose tried to put Malie there, when first she came, but
she would not go to it. Now she goes willingly, on Keanu's arm.
The day before yesterday some of our burial society went over
and cleaned the house, cut down the bushes in the yard, pulled
up the weeds. We even planted the young *kona* orange trees Malie
said she must have with her in her own yard." He lifted his big
hands. "Do not ask me why. Now the place is like it was new
again, as in Peter Kahekili's time. They went to live there yes-

terday, the two of them. A good-looking couple, with a fine home: they have everything they need to be happy."

Everything they need! O you sacred gods in Heaven! The man is an idiot! Everything they need except Malie's good health, except the uncertainty of Keanu's life, except for the misery of being imprisoned forever in Kalaupapa. I was about to shriek him down, arguing with him point by point, when, suddenly, in the beat of a bird's wing, everything was made beautifully clear and beautifully simple. Kewalo was right. What more do they need than each other? They know what they want from life, and they have reached out to take it, without asking permission from anyone. With their love they have happiness. But lonely Newman, huddled in his chair; I, sitting alone in this wasteland: what do we have, because we do not have love? Oh, it was a bitterness to admit it: we have our great imaginations, our vast learning taken from out of books, our cracked minds, and our empty hearts. We have nothing. Nothing. Not even the seedling of an orange tree, to hold out its promise of a future.

Unaware of my sorrowing, Kewalo continued with his report.

"Yesterday, when she walked into her new home, Malie said a strange thing. As in a dream did she walk, a little smile upon her lips. 'Now will Uncle Pita be at peace,' she said, and no one could tell what she meant. Do you know why she said it?"

"No, I do not know what she meant. She is a strange girl, a quiet girl with deep thoughts. It has meaning for her, and this is enough. I hope she, too, will find her peace there."

"Keanu is the man for her, this is certain. She has eyes for no one else, when he is near. Never have I seen a girl change so much, she who was so seemly. But what I will never understand is this: how did those two manage to meet? When we kept our watch on the both of them?"

Alas for trusting Kewalo! May he never be father to a girl. I let him ramble on. There are things about each of us it is best for other people not to know. Let Keanu and Malie keep their secrets, as I wished my own to be kept, as I knew of others which must be kept. Only those who have no secrets of their own wish to learn the secrets of others.

"*Kie.*" He got up, dusting the broad expanse of bottom. "It seems that the disease of silence in this house is catching. Before it attacks me, I will go home, to my intended, where I am wanted."

"*Aloha*, Kewalo. *Oia mau no ke aloha.*" Affection still abides. Full of fondness for him, for Tutu, for everyone in the sprawling Settlement, I regretted to let him go. "I will see you tomorrow. You are better than any newspaper."

The next morning the doctor and I ate our breakfast at the table in the kitchen. Ruefully I listened to the noises of our chewing, wondering where all of those fine conversations were gone, which once I looked forward to holding with him.

I was clearing the dishes from the table, grateful for the task, when he spoke. "While I was lying in there, did I say anything? Did I talk?"

Carefully I set the load of dishes upon the table. The hard glitter in his eyes, the harshness in his voice: they demanded the truth from me.

"I have a remembrance that I spoke about—about many things."

"Yes," I answered reluctantly. "You talked. You talked for a long time." But could he endure the truth?

"I thought so." He looked away from me. "It is common enough, at such times." He started to put his hand to his face, to hide behind it, then put it back upon the table. The slender fingers were pressed hard against the worn wood. Fiercely he confronted me: "What did I say?"

"You spoke of many things." I wanted to stop there, but his quiet forced me to go on. "Of things out of your childhood, I suppose, and of your years in another country. Germany, I guessed. I did not understand them all." Hoping this answer would appease him, I reached for the dishes.

"What else did I say?"

"It was all mixed up. How could I tell? None of it made sense. In one breath you talked about somebody named Louise, in the next breath you argued with a doctor named Coke. You cursed Mr. Gibson." I tried to make a joke of it. "Something we all do, at some time or other."

"That old charlatan! He hates me, because I've found out what a fraud he is. I saw through him the first time I met him. He's hounded me ever since, trying to get my discoveries for himself. But I'll not let him have them!" The violence, bared so suddenly, increased my alarm. "Go on: what else did I say?"

"Your work here, in Kalawao."

His face was as white as the hands gripping the edge of the table. But he was ruthless, with himself more than with me. "I talked of Keanu?"

Weakly I looked down upon the table top, as though I were the guilty one. "Yes, you talked of Keanu."

"You know, then."

"Yes. I know."

"And you despise me for it."

"No." I looked straight at him. "No, I do not despise you. Why should I do that?"

A cruel curl to the thin lips: this was his only answer.

"Why am I to judge?" I cried, striving to convince him. "Does it matter, what I think?"

"You *kanakas*. You're all alike. Immoral, sinful, rotten. Anything, anything goes with you. No wonder you are a dying race. It is the punishment for your sins."

Before this vicious sting I fell back. I did not know whether to hit him for his insult to me and my people, or to try to comfort him for his misery. In my confusion he rose to his feet, leaning upon the table. "No. I cannot accept your relaxed standards." He squared his shoulders, lifted his head to look me full in the eyes. "I have sinned. I must pay for my sins." Loathing was in his voice, hate for himself and for his sin. "I am damned. Forever damned." Almost I could not hear him finish. "The power of Jesus—is very great . . ."

As a blind man would walk he left the kitchen and went to the *lanai*, supporting himself with his hands against the sides of the door, the wall of the parlor, the table by the front door where his instrument case lay. He sat there the whole morning, sunk in his chair, deep in thought.

In my part of the house I wondered what I could say to him, what I could do, to break down the barrier he had put up between us.

Kewalo came to the garden in the afternoon, bearing a great worry.

"*Pehea kou piko?* How is your navel?" I asked him cheerfully, in the familiar address of a friend. But he would not answer me. Navel, liver: they were both despondent.

He sat on his private rock, fanning himself with the hat. He did not even name for me the things he brought for us to eat. Never had I seen him so gloomy. But there was no hurrying him. While I waited for him to find his tongue, I entertained myself by thinking of the likely reasons for his complaint. My favorite one was Tutu: undoubtedly she was jilting him.

"It is a terrible thing," he began, shaking his shaggy head.

"What is a terrible thing?" I was trying not to laugh, sure as I was that he mourned the loss of his ancient bride-to-be. *Ke a nui, ke a iki:* big jaw, little jaw. The old adage was made for the likes of him—yesterday's bragger is today's weeper.

"This thing about Eleu."

My laughter died within me. "What has happened to Eleu?"

"You know what a lively fellow he was? Always running around, always helping the other fingerlings here? He was their leader, their elder brother—"

"Yes, yes, I know all this. Tell me: did the sharks get him?"

"This morning they were playing in the grass field, as they often play. There is no school, because Malie has given them a week of rest. 'For the vacation of Easter,' she says, but we all know how this is not the reason. Well, anyway, it was a bright morning— you know what a sunny day it has been—when in the middle of their playing Eleu tells them, 'E! We better run for the trees. Getting dark. Rain is coming.' This is the story as Kaleo, his friend, tells it to me."

" 'Wat you talking?' they yell at him. 'No rain coming. No more clouds in the sky.' Then Eleu stops his playing, a funny look upon his face." Shaking his big head from side to side, his jaw slack, Kewalo groaned. His big eyes, as bulging as those of an ox being led to slaughter, stared in bewilderment from me to sky to sea to mountains, as though in search of the slayer who would strike him down. But I could have told him that the slaughterer was a coward, who never let himself be seen, who always struck from behind.

"Saying nothing, Eleu left them in the field. He walked to the Infirmary, where Kamiano was dressing the sores. He waited until all the sick were gone. Then he went up to Kamiano."

Knowing already the ugly truth, yet not wanting to hear it, I waited for Kewalo's story to come to its inexorable end. "Kamiano told me this afternoon. *Auwe!* In a few more days, he says, the boy will be blind. Blind as this rock." He slapped the black stone with his huge hand. Against its wrinkled darkness the hard yellow fingernails were five blinded eyes staring up at me, accusing me for being able to see.

Alas for poor Eleu! Where, in this realm of grief, is there room to crowd in one more grief? Where, under Heaven, is there space for one more wail of lamentation, one more curse upon the name of God?

"*Auwe* for poor Eleu," I said softly. I had no power left in me for anger. And I was done with raging at Heaven: what good does it do, to rail at God, when he does not hear? Instead I asked Kewalo: "And how does he take Kamiano's words, that he will be blind?"

"Quietly. He is never one to make trouble, as you know. Only this did he say, Kamiano tells me: 'Now I will not be able to read books.' Then he went home, alone."

Yes, he would go alone. He was never one to make trouble. And I could see him in a few more days, when he was blind, stumbling about the house, stumbling along the lanes, falling to his knees upon the stony ground, because even in his blindness he would not want to give trouble to anyone.

"No. This fate is not for Eleu." Now I knew what I must do, in the time that remains to me.

"And how will you stop it?"

To discover the fullness of life, in the ordinary everyday little-nesses of life: this is what I must do, and this is what I must help Eleu to do. I saw them now, at last: the sweetnesses of life, not the bitternesses of dying. Seeing life, I found it wonderful. Look-ing into myself, I found myself wearied of my despair, eager to reach out to take the blessings of each minute, as they are given to me, for as long as the minutes shall last.

I have been slow to learn, but I have learned in time, what Damien has been trying to tell me since the day I arrived. What the two laughing teasing girls in the sunshine could have told me, what every other leper here has learned long ago; what Keanu and Malie seized for themselves, and oxlike Kewalo and his wrinkled bride do not need books to learn, I, the man of intellect, have been the very last to discover.

"Kewalo," I said, a general commanding his courier. "Give this message to Eleu for me. Tell him: I will be his eyes, as long as I have eyes of my own. Tell him: he will come and live with me. I will read to him, I will talk with him and care for him. I will show him how to make music on the flute. I will show him how there is good in life still, how even here in Kalawao life is not entirely a thing accursed."

Kewalo stared up at me, his head cocked in astonishment. "You will do this for him? You will take upon your shoulders this heavy burden?"

The three blind boys upon the green meadow, crying in their darkness, and the bent old woman who cared for them, out of love: I remembered them.

The unhappy doctor, alone in his empty house, brooding over his loneliness and his hunger for love: I thought of him.

Father Damien, and the heavy burdens he bears in this desert of despair: I remembered him.

"I will do it for him, Kewalo. And for others who are blind." I who have been so blind: now the blind would help me to see.

Kewalo heaved himself up. "*Amene, amene!* Gladly will I be your messenger. And gladly will I be your helper."

"Tell him, for me—tell him I will do it"—I faltered—"out of friendship for him." Tell him that I will do it out of love: those were the words I wanted to say. But I was afraid of this great word *love:* not yet was I ready to use it, and it would not come into my mouth.

"I go at once. Your gift will bring new life to Eleu." He hastened down the path with perilous speed.

"And to me, old friend, and to me," I said, into the quiet of the evening.

Never had I felt so virtuous, so lifted up.

I remained in the garden while the lovely day died away, taking with it an uncounted number of those precious minutes I had just resolved to spend so efficiently. Not content with achieving a comfortable warming of my *kanaka's* liver, I must needs rush on to exercise my entire missionary's soul, until it was as fevered as a babe with the croup. Greedy for the rewards of belonging, and wanting the rewards before the labor, I sucked every drop of gratification out of the decision I had talked myself into. And, drunk on the ferment of my own honeyed persuasion, I soared in my fantasies to the very cloudland of my woolgatherer's sheepy heaven.

With tears in my eyes I saw myself, the Leper Apostle, adjuring multitudes of the clean to 'love ye one another, even as do we who are the unclean.' With hymns of praise from the massed choirs of the nation singing in my ears, I watched myself dedicating sumptuous hospitals for lepers, endowed by myself, of course. Amid the cheers of thousands of my countrymen and the thunder of saluting cannon, I saw the King advancing toward me, with the Ribbon and Star in one hand and a Patent of Nobility in the other, while in the background the Queen wept, and a dozen princesses, in tribute to the largeness of my soul.

With the goose flesh of pride running deliciously up and down my back, put there by the stirring of angels' wings, I saw myself opening a copy of the book I would write, addressed to the snorting unbelievers of the world: *How I Found Happiness at Kalawao,* I would call it, calculating that the contradiction would dazzle the skeptical and rout the infidel. But is *Happiness* enough? I questioned. Or is something stronger needed, something more nearly the impossible, to win the praise of parsons, to draw alleluias from the young men and the young women who, on Friday evenings, are so full, so strenuously full, of earnest Christian endeavor?

A moment's thought and I had it fixed: with a catch of delight it came to me, the hackneyed quintessence of the Risible Impossible, certain to attract every eye, to appeal to every taste: *Blessed Are the Living Dead;* Or, *Love Among the Lepers.* My nom de plume was beyond resisting: Kalepa the Leper Helper.

When I saw the ridiculous title flash before me, all splendorous in sunset's gold and ecclesiastical red, the silly dream broke in a howl of laughter, and suddenly I was saved for my natural doubting self. In one instant I was as flatulent with virtue as a belch is with sour gas, lifted up by my vaporous conceit above the gross and polluted world. In the next instant the ballooning bubble was pricked, and I was back on earth again, with my feet in the muck of dead leaves, of dead worms, of dead and dying men.

It was like being turned inside out. It was like the flash of awareness in which one discovers the secret to an optical illusion: at first one is staring at a representation of a ladder ascending into Heaven, unable to discern any other meaning to it than the one Jacob saw. And then, in the wink of an eyelid, the lines shift, the planes change, and one is looking down the stairway plunging into Hell.

This was a perspective more familiar to me: I was safe upon the ground again, upon Earth, the Threshold of Hell. The most snorting, the most determined unbeliever of all in this stinking lazar house where God is not and can never be, I brayed into the evening: "Welcome back, Brother Jackass. Welcome, you *kanaka* Lazarus, to Makanalua, the Given Grave."

Sliding down from my rock, I came back again to Molokai's unclean mire, where the down of angels' wings will never fall. "All this talk about God, all this worry over nothing," I growled, kicking at the immovable rock. "To hell with God! You've wasted enough time on him."

Without another glance at the fetch of my tomb, I went into the darkening kitchen, to contend with the realities of pots and pans and a smoking cookstove, with the dreariness of a meager supper for the *pupule* doctor, arguing with his God, and for my mad mocking self, freed of the tyrant by my laughter.

As I slapped the potful of inevitable beef stew on the stove to heat and put the rice on to steam, I sang my favorite tribute to the churchly hypocrisy from which I'd just been delivered:

> O God, the cleanest offering
> Of tainted earth below,
> Unblushing to Thy feet we bring
> A leper, white as snow.

"O Gawd!" I scoffed. "It's too much, really too much to bear." I went to the kitchen sink, to fill the teakettle with water. The six-inch centipede I found there, sleeping in the mouth of the pipe, did not startle me in the least. Not interrupting my singing, I washed him down the drain into the cesspit below, where he belonged, along with almost everything else the foreigners have brought into Hawaii Nei. There he could swim or drown, taking his chances of life or death, as the rest of us do in the cesspit which is the world.

"O God," I cackled, setting myself to improvising a parody as I put the teakettle on the roaring stove. Running my voice up and down the scale, in a burlesque of all the crack-toned Sunday School hellions who ever steal a penny from the Mission Fund while they sing this cheerfully lying ditty for lepers, in an angry antiphon against all the virtuous young maidens of either gender who shed a hypocritical tear while they warble this ridic-

ulous invocation to ignorance, this insult to all decent lepers,
I bellowed my variation upon the simpletons' theme:

> O God, of all the foolish things
> On damnèd earth below,
> The worst is the one who stupidly sings
> Of things he doesn't know.

Well, it wasn't much of a verse, I guess, even for an improvisation, but that evening, in that house of madness, it brought a cracked and crazy pleasure to me.

I suppose I made such a show because I wanted my *pupule* patient to hear me and to conclude from it either that I was as mad as he was, in which case he did not need to shun me, or that I was not mad at him, in which case he did not need to fear me.

It was effort wasted: all my fine talents as cook, poet, singer, nurse, and general dispenser of cheer, all came to naught against the wall of his sulking. When I went to call him to supper he was already in bed. "I am not hungry," he said, in a way that cut off all further talk. He was like an animal crawled into a cave, licking its wounds.

Once again I ate alone, and in silence. But for once in Kalawao I had aplenty: while he punished himself for his sinning, it was I who got the benefit of his fasting.

38

THE NEXT MORNING he swallowed a few bits of hardtack and a cup of tea for breakfast, before he deigned to speak. "I heard no church bells this morning. The quiet is worse than their noise. Is something wrong down there?"

"Not that I know of."

"What day is this? I have lost count of time."

"Friday. Day after tomorrow will be Easter."

"Easter? Already? Well, that explains it, then. This is Good Friday. The Day of the Sacrifice. On Black Friday Holy Church mourns. No bells are rung, no flowers are placed on her altars, even the candles are put out, while she pretends to weep in darkness. A fine show of sentiment. But superficial, meaningless." Impatiently he pushed aside his plate. "Meaningless because— When does the next boat stop here? I must get away from this place."

"On Wednesday the *Mokolii* will come again."

"Good! I will be on it when it goes."

I was relieved to hear him say it. I was tired of him and of his morbidness. I wanted to go home, to my own house, to live my own life the way I would plan it, as master of myself and as servant to no one. Already, in my reaction to the giddy exaltation of the afternoon before, I was withdrawing much of my large promise to Eleu.

"Your studies here are done, then?" I thought it a reasonable question.

"Yes, they are done." The lips were thin and bloodless, the face was stony. "They have shown me nothing. I have wasted my time in your hospitable country. Everything I put my hand to has failed in this miserable place. Everything. Meaningless. I can do no decent work here."

Thrown off my guard, I blundered into another question. "You have not found a cure?"

"A cure? Impossible. You might as well ask for the philosophers' stone, and hope to turn lead into gold. I haven't even proved the cause of leprosy. How can I find a cure for it, then, when I'm not even sure of its cause?" It was the same impatience with the yearning of men and with the secrets of nature which Dr. Trousseau had expressed. Nothing he might have said could irritate me as much as this brutal dismissal of my hope. No: of our hope, for I was not thinking only of myself. I was thinking of Eleu, and of Father Damien, and of others in the Settlement, even of those not yet born who would be born in jeopardy when I no longer lived.

"For this I am sorry," he said softly, looking away from me toward the forest beyond the kitchen door. "It would be a wonderful thing, if a cure could be found. I—I would like it for your sake. You are a man worth saving."

I said, "I was not thinking only of myself," but I was pleased by his opinion of me, and touched by his unease over saying it. This poor tight *haole*: he is afraid even to be kind.

"The name of Newman," he said bitterly, "will join a long list of failures."

"For this I am sorry." Earlier in our talk I would not have meant it, but now I did. He shrugged off my mite of sympathy, just as I had pushed off his. He and I were so much alike in our pride: I could understand him only too well.

"The one thing in which I thought I was making some progress: it, too, has come to nothing. The inoculation of Keanu: that, too, is wasted."

"How did it end?"

"I do not know. That's just it: I do not know!"

I was astounded: I echoed his cry of defeat.

"No. There was not enough time. I thought—last week, a couple of weeks ago, whenever it was—that perhaps the time was close. But now all my work has been undone, all those months of waiting have been wasted."

"Can't you tell by looking at him now?"

"I cannot see him again." He shook his head, as though the memory of Keanu filled him with moans he would not let himself express. Pounding his fists upon the table, he cried: "It is this place, this accursed place! I should never have brought him here. I should have put him in a cage, in Honolulu, and locked him in it until the test was done. Now, even if he should yet become a leper, the experiment must be discounted."

"But why? Isn't this what you want to happen?"

"No! Not any more! But that's not true, either: Yes! In a way, I do. But what I want no longer matters. Don't you see? The success of the experiment depended upon keeping him apart from all contact with lepers. But now, since he has gone to stay with that dirty leper-priest, I can never be sure."

"You knew about Father Damien?"

"About his leprosy? Of course I knew: I made the diagnosis. Months ago, when he was in Honolulu."

"In January? And he kept silent about it all this time!"

"Didn't he tell you people here, when he came back? He was in such a hurry to return, to spread the glad tidings."

"No. Not until last Sunday did we hear of it." Excitedly I began to tell him how we learned that Kamiano was a sharer of our affliction. But Newman interrupted me before I had scarcely started upon my account.

"The old cheat! Making a melodrama out of it. All to strengthen his hold on you. This place, already gruesome with lepers, is now about to be hallowed with a saint. I can hear the fuss and the furore now: 'Greater love hath no man, than that he should give up his life for—' "

"No! He is no cheat! He is a good man, a—"

"So, he's got you, too, into his fold, has he? With his talk of love, and devotion, and sacrifice. With his platitudes about the goodness of people and the perfectibility of man. Such drivel! I— I know better. And you? How can you believe his nonsense? There was a time, I seem to recall, when you were not so easily taken in."

"Damn you!" I jumped to my feet, flinging the chair behind me. "Damn you and your sarcastic doubting mind! You have no right to say such things about Damien." Oh, how I enjoyed the pleasure of unleashing my anger upon him, the wild pleasure of seeing him draw back from my violence.

"The trouble with you," I rushed on, "is that there is too much selfishness in you, and not enough charity. Too much greed to take what you want, and not enough of the wish to give. Too much head, and not enough heart. You would be a happier man if you could learn a little of Damien's kindness. Yes, of his saintliness, at which you sneer!"

While I shouted at him, pounding on the table to give emphasis to my arguments, he sat pale and still, the prisoner of my noise.

"I know what I'm talking about," I bawled, the preacher proclaiming the one true salvation from his tree-stump pulpit, "because once I was like you. But I have learned—and I am glad to admit it—I have learned from Damien what it means to forget myself a little, and to give of myself to others. But you, you smug little bastard! Christ! You never learn. You are too proud to learn from a 'dirty priest.' You are too much the lordly white man to learn anything from kanakas like me. Damn it! I don't know why we waste our time on you! What do you care about compassion? What do you know about sacrifice? About love? . . ."

He winced under this cruelest thrust of all. When he lifted his face to me and I saw those eyes, full of pain, I knew that I had said too much. Even as I regretted my viciousness he stood up and left the room, running away from me to his refuge beyond the front door.

Quivering with the effects of my anger, I stormed out the back door, to find my solace in the garden.

When I returned to the house half an hour later I was thoroughly ashamed of myself, and prepared to make the most abject of apologies. Oh, that was a fine fair speech I had made. A tirade of arrogance and anger, lacking in every single one of the virtues I was so busily commending to him: it was fuller of vaunting I's than a hive is with bees. It was a perfect description of myself, and I stood revealed by it, and damned, not he.

The moment I stepped into the kitchen I sensed that something was wrong. The whole house was filled with an evil heavy menace, swelling the rooms to bursting. Not stopping to think, I dashed into the parlor in search of him. The first thing I saw was his instrument case, lying open on the table beside the front door. Flashes of bright metal littered the table and the floor beneath it.

Then I heard him. The kind of crying that people make as their wounds are being probed, when the pain is too great for them to withstand and yet they know they must not cry out; a whimpering, a gasping for breath, a choking back of tears, a gritting of teeth: all this in one inarticulate sound, together with an animal's hopeless awareness that the pain must be endured: all of this I heard from him.

I could not see him until I reached the *lanai*.

And there—O Christ! I cried out in horror.

He had arranged the chairs in the way they were placed on the morning of Keanu's inoculation. He was seated in Keanu's chair. With one of the sharp knives he was cutting into the flesh of his right forearm, in the exact spot where he had cut into the flesh of Keanu's arm. Spurting from the incision, the dark red blood was flowing down his white skin, splashing upon the floor. In the bubbling wound he was twisting the knife, twisting it, twisting it, bending over his task with a fanatical delight, unaware of the dreadful sounds his body was making.

Yelling with all my might, to wake him from his madness, I pounced upon the armed left hand and pulled the knife from its grasp. He looked up at me with a little smile of triumph.

"A sacrifice—for Keanu," he said weakly, before he fainted away in the chair.

Somehow, with rags torn from my shirt, I stanched the flow of blood and bound the wound. Fright made me a better physician than ever I thought I could be. With the strength of fright, too, I was able to carry him to his bed.

When I was done with washing him I was too weak to leave the room. I sat upon the floor beside him, leaning against the bed for support. It was a long time before I could bring myself to clean up the clotted blood on the *lanai* floor, to wash the spattered chair, the wicked bloody knife.

When I went to the kitchen sink for water the centipede was there, basking in the wet curve of the basin where it meets the Charybdis of the drain. Once again I flushed the repulsive creature down into its underground realm.

Last of all I washed the blood from my hands. But no matter how much I washed them, I could not escape the responsibility for the doctor's action. The Lady Macbeth and I: we would wash our hands in vain. Not water, not tears, could take away the stain of our guilt, just as the flowing of the doctor's blood could not wash away the stain of his guilt for what he had done to Keanu. An eye for an eye, a tooth for a tooth: this is the old law. But what is the punishment for a man who has done violence to another man's spirit?

A lawyer's books do not touch upon this point, but I have learned the answer. A lifetime of remorse: this is the only expiation for a crime against the sanctity of another man's soul.

Not until the middle of the day was I strong enough to walk down the hill to the Infirmary. Father Damien was alone in the empty shack, washing bandages. Peering at me over the rims of his glasses, he asked: "You are sick? You look pale."

"Indeed, I do not feel well. Please, may I sit down?"

"Of course. Here." He brought me the stool upon which he sat when he dressed the patients' sores. "Now, tell me. Where do you feel sick? In the lungs? In the bowels, perhaps?"

Haltingly I told him about the doctor, not sparing myself as the cause of his act. But I did not tell him that he was the reason for our argument. He listened carefully until I was finished.

"This poor boy. He is very sick. He must go away from here."

"Yes, he wants this, too. He said his work here is ended."

"*Ae*, it is ended. It is work he should never have started. This business with Keanu, especially. This is the man I told you about. Do you remember? The man who challenges God."

"I have guessed it." I did not need to tell him I was another such man, squeaking my challenge into the face of nothingness.

"And now God is beginning to smite him down."

Is it God who smites him, or himself? Someday, perhaps, I thought wearily, I can discuss this question of philosophy with you, Father, but not now, not now.

"Now he knows it, too. The knowledge of his guilt: this is what makes him sick in his soul. For in his soul the guilty man is afraid to face God."

Here was my answer, ready made and readily delivered by the priest who knew all about souls, all about the nature of God. Who can say? I wondered. Perhaps they are the same, God and the suffering sinner, a part of God because he suffers. Would God exist, if the sinner did not need him? Does God exist for the man who does not think of him? Would I be so worried about God if, in my secret heart, I did not yearn for him? Ahh, I checked myself impatiently, these are questions for Damien to ponder, not for me. But even in my weakened state I would not accept Damien's answer on faith: I needed stronger proof than his pronouncement that it was so.

"Perhaps. Perhaps you are right, Father. Whatever it is, he is breaking under his burden." I did not tell how the doctor's burden had put him in triple jeopardy.

"On Sunday the *Kilauea* comes by, from Kahului to Honolulu. We can burn a signal fire, to stop her for the doctor. Or do you think perhaps he should wait, until the *Mokolii* comes again? How do you feel about this?"

"The sooner he goes, the better. For him, and for me. But should he go alone?"

"You are right. I will ask Dr. Pietsch to go with him to Honolulu. When the sick man goes away from here we hope he is safe from himself. Here he is in danger. This is not a place for men who are at war with themselves, or with Heaven. Also, I will write to Mr. Gibson, asking him to take care of the boy."

"He does not like Mr. Gibson. He thinks Mr. Gibson—well, picks on him, persecutes him."

"He is so wrong. Mr. Gibson has a high regard for him. He tells this to me himself, in Honolulu. He has great hope for the knowledge about the leprosy that will come out of the doctor's work. Surely the doctor knows how Mr. Gibson has done all that can be done to help him in his work?"

"How confused everything is! How confused the doctor is! He

thinks that the King, Mr. Gibson, the Board of Health, even you, even I, all work against him. You tell me they help him. What is the poor man to believe? What am I to believe?"

"He mistakes Mr. Gibson's interest in his work for persecution of himself. Mr. Gibson wants only for Dr. Newman to tell the Board of Health what he has learned from his studies here. He has a right to know this, does he not? After all, the Board of Health brings the doctor here, it pays his salary. But, do you know? Not one single report has the doctor made since he is in Hawaii. During more than a whole year, not even one report. Now, what do you think? Is this right?"

"No, I suppose not. A contract is a contract, and it must be honored. But the doctor does not have this understanding."

"And you know why? Because he is a very proud man. You know how it is with proud people. How they will see only one side of a thing, only the side which they want to see. Will they turn this thing about, to see it from all sides, before they give their opinion of it? No, they will not. Will they ask to learn more about a thing, so they are well informed about it, before they talk as learnedly as schoolmasters about it? No, they will not. How many of them bother to be even half informed, before they pronounce judgment upon it? Alas, this is the curse of people: they will not use the senses which God gives them, to be sensible people."

Uneasily I looked away from him. I needed no more preaching upon this text.

"Always there are at least two sides to a matter, usually there are more. You who are a man of learning, a man of the law, you know this. But how many people see more than the one side they want to see? In the testing of Keanu, right here, we have a good example. How many tales are told of it now, among the people in the Settlement, how many will be told of it in the future? Who will see it whole, from all of its many sides? Who can see the truth?"

"Ae. The truth: it is hard to find." Tired with the effort to follow his long argument, I wanted only for him to stop talking, to let me go.

"This is why I say God must be the guide, not man. Man searches, perhaps, and stumbles on his way. But God *knows* the way. Therefore, I say, let God show us the way, in his own good time. When he is ready for us to know, then will he send to let us know. And when we do not know what to do, if we ask him, he will help us to find the way."

I could not argue with him about his devious God. Only last night I thought my contest with him was ended, with me the victor by default. Laughing, then, I thought I had saved myself by laughter. But now, after the morning's horror, I knew that last evening he was but teasing me when he let me think I had routed him. This morning he was come back again, come out of Newman's wound and out of Damien's mouth. And now I was mortally afraid of him, for now I saw how he was assailing not only me but also the poor wreck of a man whose body I was nursing and whose broken spirit I was trying to mend. He spared no one, he denied himself no advantage, in the ruthless war he waged.

He was like my specter, the centipede, coming at me with a hundred wriggling arms and legs, for to grip me, hip and thigh, possessing a hundred Plutonian lives with which to harry my ephemeral one. He was a centipede God, bearing the fatal sting to kill me with, when he was bored with his sport.

"Why doesn't he leave us alone?" In my weariness, scarcely knowing what I did I cried it aloud, my plaint and my rebellion.

Damien's spectacles flashed as his head went up, a champion rushing to serve his Lord. Instead of a lance he carried a forefinger, couched and tilted against me. "Leave us alone, Caleb?" The champion's voice was very gentle. "But this is not possible. How can he do this? He does not leave anyone alone."

"Not even to rot away, in this hellhole? *Not even to die?*" I shouted at him, the good man in whose footsteps, once upon a time, I had resolved to follow. Tears of anger were gathering in the folds of my eyelids, stinging them into making more unwanted tears.

Damien reached out, through the veil of my tears, through the wall of my anger, and took my hands. "Caleb, Caleb, my son. Do not be so afraid of Death. Look upon Death, so you may know what Life is. When you have done this, then you will no longer be afraid. What is there to fear? Death is but another form of the mercy of God. It is the last and the greatest of his gifts. Have you not seen this? Death is not to be feared: it is to be welcomed, when it comes, for it is the messenger of God. And life for us here on earth is but the season of waiting, until God is ready to invite us to the great feast he prepares for us in Heaven."

In my throat, almost strangling me, were the noises of outrage at his simple philosophy. How could he expect me to believe such nonsense? Show me Heaven first, and I will believe in its banquets. Show me God first, and I will believe in Heaven.

Folding my cold hands between his rough ones, he strove to quiet me. The smell of tobacco, the reek of stale sweat, came to me, and the stink of lepers' sores, forever sunk into the fabric of his clothes. Those feasters in Heaven: will they smell like you? I wanted to jeer. Is this the odor of sanctity? Will Heaven stink like the rush of air from the grave of Lazarus? And I, when I join the banquet there, how will I be? *Will I look like this?*

"Do you see?" he asked me as if I were a child. "I tell you what I believe, what is in my heart. This is the promise Christ Jesus makes for his Father, to each of us. It is his promise I tell to you. Do not be afraid, for God is love. When your times comes, you will not be alone. He will be here with you, by your side, to bring you his comfort, his peace, which passeth all understanding."

I could not hear any more of his false comfort. With an animal's snarl I broke away from him. His hands were still reached out to me as I ran from the ugly room into the street, into the hot brilliance of noon, almost stumbling down the stairs in my haste to get away from him, who talked so easily of my dying.

As I was returning to the doctor's house I was struck by the fear that Newman would have killed himself while I was gone. The thought had not occurred to me earlier, but now it made me run up the hill in terror. I expected the worst, but I found him as I had left him, unconscious in his bed. Just as I had found him, six long days before, when first I went up the hill.

While he slept I hid his instruments, our razors, all the knives in the house. The ropes in the kitchen, the clotheslines in the back yard, I took down and concealed in the jungle. I would have hidden his clothes and taken the sheets from the beds, if I could have found harmless substitutes for them, with which to cover his nakedness.

But he was not brave enough to commit suicide. Or perhaps I underestimate him: perhaps it would be more honest to say that he was not weak enough to kill himself. I should know, if anyone should, that the man who thinks with longing of death, and is always promising himself the escape it offers, is rarely the man who kills himself. But the man who gives himself and his companions no warning of his intentions, he is most courageous in accepting Death's invitation: he is the brave man, who leaps from a boat into the sea, or who hangs himself quietly, in a solitary fig tree.

When Newman awoke he was very weak, and his arm was swollen and painful. Despite my warning, he insisted on getting up. After one attempt he fell back, groaning. With that he was willing to lie there, his arm propped up beside him, his face turned to the wall. He would not speak to me when I came to put a poultice of *laukahi* leaves upon the wound, to shut the mortification out of it.

During the afternoon of our Black Friday came my turn to feel the nearness of the *makukoae* hovering over me, the phantom of the tropic bird, which is the spirit of Death. There was a time, a few days before, even on the day before, when I was forgetting Death in my discovery of Life. But on this grim day Death returned to remind me that she was waiting for me, and that her waiting would not be long. This is the last irony, in my lifetime which is a collection of ironies: capricious Death, when I courted her, would have nothing to do with me; yet when I spurned her, in my turn to life, she came for me, ardent as a woman mad with love.

Perhaps it was my fright of the morning which weakened my *mana* and sent some signal to Death, for her to come near. Perhaps it was only the next stage in the progress of my disease. I do not know. It is enough to know that this was the day when pain came to live in me, the burning fire, the aching which will remain in me until my tormented nerves are consumed and nothing is left of them to tell me the meaning of pain. Not for me will there be the deadening of skin and flesh and limb, and the unnoticed parting with fingers and toes, such as Ioane Paele shares with his lice; and the sinking in of the nose and palate, such as Tutu shows, and her well-matched mate, Kewalo. I shall burn, suffused with a flame which does not go out, afire with the heat which does not bring pleasure. This one is the heat of Hell. Perhaps Newman is right, and I burn because of my sins.

O Paliku, Paliku! What of your promise to me? Why did I
listen to you so trustingly?

I was standing in the little yard at the front of the house
when it began. I was looking out upon a Krakatao sunset, flaming
in the heavens above the mountains, filling the whole sky with
its furious reds and oranges and purples, as if the enraged volcano
were exploding again, just beyond the barrier of the dark cliffs.
Black against the lurid sky, like priests in frock coats, the fork-
tailed sea birds were coming home to nest.

How gorgeous it is, I was thinking, looking up into the burning
firmament, when a fire began to burn in my right leg. One moment
it was an ordinary leg, that is to say a leg ignored. The next
instant it was full of shooting pain, as though lightning was set
free in it, or some of the fire leaped down out of the flaming sky
to make its home in me. The coming of the pain was so sudden
that my leg gave way under me, and I fell to the ground, crying
out in agony.

As I went down, dizzy with hurt, the sky became a thing of
ugliness: it held the color of clotted blood, and crusted pus, and
the spreading gaudy sores upon a leper's body. And, slinking in
from the east, were the harbingers of Death, the black bands of
eternal night.

Then did I hear the cry of the tropic bird calling to me, a
mocking of my own cry of pain.

O Paliku, Paliku—

But my new affliction could not keep me from my duties.
Limping, as I have seen dozens of lepers limping, biting my lips,
as they do, to hold back the little gaspings and hissings which
are the only antidote to such pain, I prepared our supper from
the leftovers Kewalo brought to us in the afternoon.

I took the doctor his meal, setting the plates on a piece of
board for a tray. Once again I fed him, patiently and wordlessly, a
spoonful at a time. My leg ached so much that I wanted to weep
over it, and use my two hands to rub it, to ease the pain away.
Yet I would not let him know I was in distress. Pride for myself
and concern for him made me force myself to look as if nothing
was more important to me than the passage of a spoonful of
overcooked beef stew from the plate to his mouth, and the return
to the plate of the empty spoon.

All the while I fed him he watched me, studying me with

those hooded blue eyes, until I could scarcely keep my mind upon my task. Never have I been so conscious of eyes: with his gaze upon me I felt that the room was full of invisible spies, seeing everything I did, keeping record of everything I thought.

He did not eat much. Soon he said, "No more, thank you. I am not hungry." Not a word had I said to him, not even the words of apology which I knew I must say in time, when it would be safer for me to speak them. Obediently I stood up to go back to my place in the kitchen.

"You see what happens," he said quietly, "when you let yourself be drawn into other peoples' lives? The only reward is trouble. The reward of the good Samaritan. In exchange for one's concern, one gets back grief. In exchange for one's freedom, one is forced into bondage."

I recognized it as his answer to my harangue of the morning. It was a well-reasoned rebuttal, such a one as I might have made not long before. There was nothing of the madman either in it or in him.

I sensed the time of crisis in him: it was the turning point, beyond which he would go down into madness and to death, or from which he would return to reason and to life. He, too, knew this: in the dark blue eyes, looking up at me from the wasted face, was the same beseeching which had shown itself in the unguarded moment in the Infirmary. I had failed him once, by not going to his side. I could not fail him again, for there would not be another chance.

Standing above him, looking down upon the broken thing which was the remnant of a man, I did not know what to do. I was of two minds: and both spoke at once, each at war with the other.

The long-suffering *kanaka* in me, sick of the insults heaped upon me and my race by this arrogant *haole*, rejoiced to see him fallen. Is this, then, the man of the new times, the greatest gift from across the sea? I gloated, studying the sunken cheeks, the drooping mustache, the thin fingers upon the strengthless hand. Around the narrow fingernails his dried blood showed how imperfectly I had ministered to that hand. The swollen arm lying across his flat chest showed how imperfect was his sacrifice, how unacceptable it was to his demanding God. No mere *kanaka* would ever lie so flat and so weak, so broken down by worrying

about his soul. The things which broke Hawaiians down were
diseases of the flesh, not of their unconquered spirit. Look at
them, even here, in this open tomb: living and laughing and
loving, as they always do, and caring not a grain of sand about the
fate of their souls. The thought of them made me proud to be
one of them: they are mine, I said, lifting my head high.

But the new man in me: ah, it looked down in pity upon my
fellow man. He was so weak, this youth who was not yet grown
into a man. And so lost, so far from the path which he must yet
find. How could I stand by, while he stumbled on, and withhold
my help? He, too, was one of mine, and how could I not give
him my help to find his way?

I knew, as I looked down upon him, that I must speak out,
as much for my sake as for his own. In the angel's fallen body,
hidden somewhere behind the haunted eyes, there must be an
angel's soul.

But what could I say that would have any more meaning for
him than it had for me? I was enough of a man of his world to be
caught in the same maze he was in. I was not enough of a man of
Hawaii's olden times to have escaped the sickness of the spirit
which shattered him asunder. Perhaps this was the gift of my
haole ancestors, both known and unknown: with their blood came
also fragments of their souls, but there was never enough of a
portion, in the parental lottery, to give me a soul complete.

Yet I must tell him something, I must lead him somewhere.
Fighting for time, I set the tray down upon a chair, the while I
searched for an answer.

What does he want to hear? What is this man? I asked myself,
seeking in the answer to this riddle to find the words for comforting him. What is a man? I asked, veering from the sick
and mystifying one to the known and unfrightening mass of men.
A thing of deceits and deceptions is man, I answered, thinking
of my wholesome self, the measure of all mankind. Grasping at
straws and shadows, diddling himself with words and delusions.
Believing anything he can imagine, anything anyone will tell
him, to fool himself into thinking that he is important, that
he has meaning, even on the other side of death. Momona had
said it before me: dreaming any dream, to ease his vanity and to
hide his fears. A dog, seeking to be a lion. A shrimp, wanting to
be a man. A crab louse, lost upon the infinite ass of God.

My helplessness made me turn my annoyance upon him. These anxious *haoles!* Always worrying about their souls, and their souls' respect to God. How can I tell him what he wants to hear? I cried, feeling the panic rising in me. He is starved for want of love, and what do I know about love? Why the hell isn't Damien here, the Preacher of Love, to answer this sick man's need?

With the vision of earnest Damien came the answer to my dilemma. I determined to undertake an act of calculating will: with the utmost cynicism I began an exercise of the intellect, using the power of words to bring the sick man back from the brink of his perdition.

"What you say is true," I conceded. "Where there is concern for another, there is also the risk of hurt. It is the same with love: to love, I suppose, is to fear. The two, I think, are inseparable, as are the left side and the right side of the heart. But this hurt, when it comes, can be as nothing compared with the greater hurt of being alone. When one is alone," I went on slowly, carefully feeling my way into my thesis, because I did not want to reveal too much of myself, "life has no meaning. When one has found his place among the people who need him, he finds that he needs them. Without them, he is nothing. With them, he is—" I stopped, seeming to grope for a word, but in reality testing him, to see if he was listening to me.

"He is what?"

"He is fulfilled: he is a man. Have you not seen it?"

He was slow to answer me. I was afraid that he had drawn away from my leading, when he said: "Is it any better to love many, rather than none? I can see no difference. A man can be alone, whether he is among ten people or is closeted in his room. The love of many is the refuge of priests."

With a thrill I realized that he, too, was thinking of Father Damien. The priest was a third man in that room.

"And it is well known that priests are men who run away from love."

Now it was my turn to think, and to think clearly. I had gone into my game of persuasion lightly, feeling that I would need to utter only platitudes, of the sort Damien preached and which most men were content to hear. I had not known the mettle of my pupil.

"This may be so," I said, more calmly than I felt. "I will admit that with me it touches very close to home, for once upon a time I, too, thought little of priests and pastors and others of their kind. Whether your opinion fits all priests I cannot say. I really do not know any other priests than Father Damien. But I do not think it fits him."

"I wish I could say I knew him."

"But let us look at this matter from another way. Is it not possible that this thing we are calling love is a thing with many sides, and that there are many different ways of seeing it?" Fresh in my memory were the opinions of Damien about truth; it was easy for me to adapt them to my need. They rolled out of me as pontifically as if I were bleating Makaio come straight from his communion with God. "You see one side of it, Damien sees another, I see yet a third. Who is to say that my way is the right way, and Damien's is the wrong way?"

"But mine?" he groaned, turning his face to the wall. "What of mine? I have sinned—and I am damned!" The cry came back from the wall, hollow with despair.

These stupid *haoles*, I swore, always screaming about their sins. And just when I thought things were going along so well. I wanted to shake him, to make him give up his childishness. But I dared not: a soul was my prize, and I was arguing my case before its most inexorable judge, itself. I must show him that he was possessed by a devil of his own devising.

"Is it a sin?" I asked instead, moving slowly and carefully toward his private demon to lay hold upon it, before it could hide itself again in the caverns of his mind. So is a hooked eel pulled from its watery grotto. Just so have I seen the immigrant Portuguese slowly draw from a nostril the long white worm which has been coughed up from a child's sick lungs, neatly coiling it around a stick to coax the possessive thing forth from the inhabited body.

"Is it a sin?" I repeated. "What is a sin? And who calls it a sin?" Perhaps it is my disdain of churches which made me ask those questions so lightly; perhaps because I am not a prisoner of his alien code I could find such freedom to examine it. I will not agree that it is because I am only an immoral *kanaka* that I found it so easy to shake off from me his burden of guilt.

For what do I, a heathen, know of sin? To me, it is a privilege of the Chosen People, the Hebrews and the Christians, and none of the rest of us, who are the Unchosen, has any claim at all upon it. As far as I am concerned, they are welcome to it: this is one *haole* commodity for which I have no use.

Perhaps because it was so new a thought to him, my patient could not answer me. Enjoying the prospect of enlightening him, I began upon his instruction. "To me sin is nothing more than the penalty for a man's being caught in his attempt to take something which somebody else does not want him to have. And who catches him? Not God: it is never God who catches him. Always it is other men who find him out, who impose a penalty for his crime and exact of him a forfeit. Do we not see this every day in our lives? If he makes off with his theft, he is a success. If he fails, he is a sinner. Is this not so?"

Only the certainty that he would not understand why I laughed kept me from enjoying my sarcasm: he had no sense of the ridiculous, and therefore no capacity for laughter. But my awareness of the irony which arranges our lives, and of the humor in its whims, is the only reward I find in living. Why not enjoy it, then? I shrugged, and thereupon continued to entertain myself.

"My people are more sensible: before the missionaries came, we did not have a word for sin. Did you know this? Right and wrong they recognized, and the different degrees of theft. These covered the same infringements as do all of the Christians' deadly sins, and almost none of the venial. And theft is so much more manageable a word than is sin. Sin has such a sinister sound! No one ever died of a 'sense of theft' among my naive people. No one wasted away under the punitive glare of Kane, Ku, or Lono. If a Hawaiian died for his crime, he died of plain old-fashioned understandable violence, inflicted upon his person as punishment for his theft of someone's pig, someone's wife, someone's netful of fish. He did not take to his mat to languish away just because he coveted his neighbor's wife, or his maidservant, or his manservant, or his pig, or his *poi*. *Cha!* What a lot of trouble *haoles* have imagined for themselves. When they started their Jehovah's disease they started a blight of the spirit which makes it as rotten as a leper's body."

Such lies, such artful deceits I told him, for his sake, as often I have lied to Eleu for his instruction, as always I have lied to Malie for her deceiving. As I have lied to almost every person I have known, including myself, stretching a thought here, dropping a fact there, speaking with the persuasive tones of one who knows all the answers to all of the world's mysteries. And for what purpose? All for the sake of having my little victories over them. I knew very well that the Christians' Heaven, if it exists, is a nobler place than the dolorous Land Beneath the Sea to which dead Hawaiians go; and I knew that Jehovah's justice, if he exists, is fairer than the tyrannical whims of the savage pantheon which ruled my people in the olden days. Even after I had seen the ancient gods in their visitation I could ignore their cruel violence for the sake of my rhetoric, in my role as physician to a physician. And blandly, as he accepted my every smooth and oily word, I could overlook among my people the black power of the *kahuna anaana*, the witch priest, who could terrorize a man to death. But I did it all for my patient's sake, I assured myself, as I talked and argued and lied, faithful to my picture of him.

He did not answer, nor did he turn his face to me. Unwilling to lose my slight hold upon his slippery devil, I hurried on: "Therefore, I ask you: what is this sin which worries you? Is it something real, or is it something imagined? Is love a sin? I do not think so. The sin, if sin there be, is to suppress love, to run away from it."

Aia ka! I had him there. The devil-worm was intrigued by my arguments: its pale white head was brought out far enough now for me to begin coiling it around the slender weapon of my logic. "There are many ways of showing love. The love of a man for a woman is one, the love of them both for the child of their flesh is another. The friendship of a man for his comrade: is this not a great thing in your country, as it is in mine? The love of a man for another man: is this so much different? If it should happen, should love be changed then from a virtue into a vice? The love of one man for mankind, Damien's way: is this not considered the highest way of all? Many, indeed, are the guises of love."

Slowly, slowly, I turned the spindle of my words. The sick man was gazing up at me, intent upon my reasoning, yielding to my suasion: the demon was almost drawn out of him.

"What is there to be afraid of in love? What are you Christians so afraid of, in this thing called love? I have been reading lately in your Bible, and I notice how even there, where you preachers of love are supposed to speak most praisefully of love, you fear to use the word. You call it charity there, not love. 'Charity never faileth,' you mumble. You do not sing, as we Hawaiians do, 'Love never faileth.' And again: 'Faith, Hope, and Charity,' you name them, in a limping shaméd anticlimax, not 'Faith, Hope, and Love.' Now why is this?"

Somewhat to my discomfort, my argument was getting out of control. The words spilling from my mouth were not the ones which in cold reason I would have chosen. But they came forth, and I could not stop them. Nor did I know where they were taking me.

"Why is this, when love is the thing which ennobles a man, which sets him apart from the beasts? Without love he is—" I hesitated, hating to say it, yet forced to go on, "—he is less than a dog: he is a monster, a Caliban. Love is the way that lifts man up. If he has not love, his soul must wither away in him, and perish."

I was almost run out of strength, and of words. Not much longer could I contend with the resisting demon. My leg's pain, almost forgotten in the excitement of my game, returned now with terrible intensity. My head ached, my very teeth throbbed, but still I could not give up. My adversary said nothing: he stared up at me, as though he saw in me a dark devil sent to add to his torment.

"I am afraid I do not make myself clear," I tried to laugh, unwilling to admit that I might yet be defeated, but not knowing how to go on. In my ears the laugh sounded like a dog's yelp. In my mouth the tongue was dry, and bitter with the dust of words. "But I will say this: if Damien runs from love, then I wish to learn his way of running. 'The narrow path of priests': this is a good way for a man to take." It was the only conclusion I could think of to the argument over which I had labored. But when it was uttered I knew that it was reaching into myself, too, and that some part of me was responding to it, a part not yet known to me, as in music unseen parts of an instrument will vibrate to make the overtones and the undertones which add fullness to the sound of the plucked string.

"He has a great hold upon you, this priest," he said bleakly.

"He is a good man." This much I could admit. It was his religion I fought against, not himself. "The finest man I know."

"I wish I could believe you. I wish I might learn what you have learned from him."

"Then stop running away from him, and from his message. Stop fighting him, and the life he shows us how to lead." Now was the time for boldness. Just as, near the end of its unwinding, the Portugee worm must be pulled out swiftly, lest it shrink back into its refuge, so must this *haole* demon be exorcised by daring. "With all of its griefs and sorrows, the life of a leper is a happier one than yours is. Why is this so?"

Once more he turned to the wall, hiding from me and from his truth. I could almost see the leering devil mocking me, before it glided back into its hiding place.

"Why is this so?" I shook him by the shoulder, forcing him to answer. He must choose, and I must be the one to make him choose. Even if I have to slap his face again, and beat him, to make him choose. "Why? Why?" Fiercely I shook him until he lay upon his back, looking up at me.

"I know the answer," he said slowly. "I think I have known it ever since the day in the Infirmary, when you said—when you said you pitied me. But I would not admit it."

"Then admit it now. Say it: it must be said. It must be said, so that it will never be forgotten!" The power of words: it is very great. Words bind, and words make free. But their *mana* is greatest when they are spoken, because once they are uttered they can never be unsaid, and I was summoning them forth, in all their power, to aid me in my combat.

"Because—because they place a value upon life which I have never given it. Because what I hold cheap, even in myself, they hold dear."

"Yes, this is so. But is this all?" The white demon was on the run now: I could feel it, writhing and tugging, thrashing wildly, to make its escape from the host it had possessed for so long.

"No, it is not all. Because even here—God help me!—even as lepers—they are not afraid of love."

"You have said it!" It was a cry of triumph, proclaiming the departure of his tormentor.

"You have said it." My hand was still upon his shoulder. Because there was no further need for it, I lifted my hand away. "This is the lesson which I, too, have learned since I came here. It is not so dreadful a truth, but oh, how we two have fought against learning it."

"I have been so slow to learn it. I was so afraid of them, and of their foul disease. I could not see them for what they are. . . . I am ashamed."

"But you have learned, my friend, and you do not learn the lesson too late. Is this something to be ashamed of?"

My work was done: I had set his feet upon the path. The rest of the way he must go alone.

In the darkening room he did not see me wince when I stood up, he did not observe the limp or the twisted mouth which helped me to bear my pain. Picking up the makeshift tray, I turned to go.

"Now you must sleep," I said with false heartiness. "We will talk some more in the morning. Good night."

"Caleb, wait." He put out his left hand to me. "I want to— I thank you for your help."

"Is there another way to live?" I asked, as I took his hand in mine.

When I limped back to the kitchen I could not help grinning over my powers as a *kahuna*. What a fine lawyer you still make, friend Caleb: even the demon believed you.

But underneath the grin, as pain lay underneath my skin, I recognized the sadness of regret, because I could not believe my arguments half as much as he did.

When Father Damien came to see him on Saturday, Newman made no objection to leaving by the *Kilauea* on Sunday. He was less interested in going to Honolulu than in going to Mass at Damien's church on Easter morning. I was surprised when he made his request. But then, I thought, why should he not? It might be his way of saying farewell to us and to the Settlement. Let him go. Other men have found it a good way to begin a new life.

"But yes, of course," Father Damien was saying, not pretending to hide his amazement. "I am delighted that you wish to come. I save a place for you and Caleb, and one for Dr. Pietsch."

"Never mind me," I said. I didn't want to go again into his box of a church, where a man is squeezed by emotions until he loses all control over himself.

The priest did not hear me, in the pleasure of planning. "And after Mass, if you three will be my guests for Easter breakfast, I am most happy."

Breakfast? Well, this was another matter. I was bored stiff with kitchen work, and a meal which I did not have to prepare was a lure I could not resist. Breakfast is worth a Mass.

"Thank you," said the doctor. "It will be a nice way to say good-by. Shall we have *kanaka* pudding?"

"You know about *kanaka* pudding?" asked Damien, expressing my own astonishment. Where under Heaven did he make acquaintance with this revolting dish? "Oh, but yes, I forget: we talked about it with Keanu. Yes, we can have *kanaka* pudding, if you like. By all means. It is within my ability as cook."

"Oh, not for me, not for me," Newman smiled. "The fare you provided on the morning of our arrival was most satisfying. I shall need nothing more. But, of course, if you want to provide it for Keanu . . ."

The priest blinked at him. "For Keanu?" I was all but unstrung, hearing the two of them talking at cross-purposes, with neither one knowing how I had lied for the doctor's sake. To divert them from the dangerous subject, I broke in: "What time is the *Kilauea* supposed to come past tomorrow?" just as if I didn't know.

"Usually about twelve o'clock noon she goes by," said Damien, hoisting out his dented watch. "It is now three o'clock. This will give us plenty of time to care for both soul and body." It was a moment of craziness in which I feared that he was as mad as the rest of us. "I must go now, to baptize a baby. I promised to be there at three, but they know I am always late. A fine boy, born to Sophia Kahumu. Poor child! If only he could know who his father is."

"How will you name him, if he has no father?" Newman inquired, very politely. But I, who know well enough how bastard brats are named, I wanted to hear no more of the miserable child. Born in a grave, of a leprous mother: what chance does he have for happiness?

"I give him a Father in Heaven. This is the most important thing. As the child grows, and his life unfolds, he will know how his heavenly Father is watching over him. His life, then, is what he makes it, under the care of God. The name, this is not so important. What is there in a name but the sounds by which we remember a person?

"But on second thought, perhaps I am a little bit hasty when I say this. We do have some strange names here. Some the mothers have thought of, in the olden style, when they choose a child's name to remember an event at the time of his birth. Thus we have Fireworks Kainoa, who was born in the night of the King's birthday celebration, last year. And Devil-Wind Paki, who was born last week. But some of the names are in the new style. The saints, for example, have given us quite a few. So, I regret to say, we have Hildegarde Kalima and Athanasius Aa. These names I do not like, I fear, as much as I should, or as much as the Johns and Anthonys and Annas and Marias which are kinder to the ear. Still the mothers are fond of them. A few, even, are named Joseph, after me."

Seeing our expressions of pretended scandal, he hastened to shake a finger at us. "Not that I am responsible for them, you understand. But I confess I do like a little these small Josephs and Iokepas who are beginning now to run around. I feel toward them as a man with his own sons must feel: there will be someone left behind to think of me, a little, when I am dead. It is a very nice thought." He retrieved his hat from the floor beside his chair and struggled to get up. I watched him with a newly discovered sympathy.

"Well, I must be going. I am too late, already, and here I sit talking. It is a long time since I have the chance to talk with someone from so close to home." With both hands he set the strange hat squarely upon his head. "It is something to be wondered at," he went on quietly, to neither of us as much as to himself. "No matter how long I am away from home, never can I cure myself of homesickness. Caleb, I fear, will find this a contradiction in a man who expressed so loudly his love for Kalaupapa. Perhaps you, Doctor, can explain to him how it is possible?"

Waving gaily at us, he rushed out. "Now I go, for sure. Until, then, tomorrow: *aloha*." While we called our farewells after him, he pushed through the door and disappeared.

"What did he mean, his name is Joseph?" I asked. "Is he not called Damien?"

"That's his priest's name, I guess, chosen when he took his vows. His real name is Joseph, all right. Joseph de Veuster. I had to put it in my report to the Board of Health. Belgian, I assume, from the name, and from his accent."

One question led to another, and soon he was telling me about the marvels of Europe, of all the things I have wanted to see and taste and hear which now I am to be forever denied. Somehow

I did not mind any more the losing of them: my yearning for them was quieted, as are almost all the desires of my flesh.

We talked until lamplighting time, thoroughly enjoying our conversation, forgetting ourselves and our troubles in our interest in the greater world which lies beyond the ocean moat.

"*Himmel!* How I'd like to take you with me," he exclaimed. "You'd be the ideal companion. How you'd love the operas of Wagner at Bayreuth. You know, there's something of Parsifal in you, the Holy Innocent." Not knowing who this Parsifal is, or what a Holy Innocent means, I could only hope that he meant to compliment me. "And the wonderful music we could hear in Berlin, in Leipzig, in Vienna."

My silence called him back to reality. "Ah, forgive me, Caleb, forgive me. You see what you've done for me: already you've made me forget where I am."

To ease him of his embarrassment I stood up to light the evening lamp. As I fumbled in the darkness for the matches, his voice came to me, affectionate and consoling: "Caleb, I will never forget what you have done for me. Never."

I was right, I congratulated myself, no longer hesitating to give myself my due. There *was* a man worth saving, in that sassy *haole*.

39

BEAUTIFUL WAS KALAUPAPA on the morning of Easter. The island, the sea, the sky: they rejoiced and were at peace, bringing their loveliness in tribute to the reborn earth. The light of the sun descended upon the land like a blessing, and I saw that the land was fair. Space enough have I in such a prison, I thought, when I came out of the house into the yard. And then I saw that it was no prison.

It was a cathedral, as large as an island, and its pillars were great peaks, soaring into the nave of the sky. Clouds formed in the curvèd apse, purest canopy to the tabernacle; and the veil of the temple was mist. Its walls were the buttressed cliffs, rising in serried grandeur; and foaming ribbons of waterfalls dropped their Gothic windows into the deep dark chapels of forest pools. The congregation of the faithful was one of kneeling shrubs and prostrate ferns, in the rapt genuflections of grace, in perpetual adoration. The music was the exultant fugue of bird voices, sounding against the counterpoint of wind-song, praising God.

In this green sanctuary I stood for a long time, alone. Around me I heard the sounds of peace. But within me I did not know the stillness of peace. One thing more I needed to know, before I could be stilled, and this last benison was the one I was denied. But Damien had warned me that I could not hurry him. "When he is ready for us to know," the priest had said, "then will he send to let us know."

But how can I wait? I asked the wildly beautiful, the hurtfully beautiful land. My time is growing short. Unwillingly I lifted my gaze to the sky above the mountain peaks, to search for the tropic birds, the messengers of death. They were not there, in the morning of the world's rebirth: they were far out to sea, hunting fish, bringing death to the creatures of the sea that they themselves might live, and their fledglings. But the memory of their crying haunted me, as the gift of their pain haunted me.

It was the cry of my heart, the pain of my soul, crying, Why? into the empty heaven of my fearfulness. I was afraid of them, those tropic birds, because I was afraid of Death. Fear of Death, not love of it: this has been the secret of my life. And now, when Death was come so close to me, I had not yet made my peace with it. The lesson which Peter Kahekili learned so grievingly, the one which Father Damien accepts so easily, I was desperate to avoid.

I fought against Death because I could not be ready for it until I knew its meaning. I knew the meaning of Life: Life is a cheat, an eternal hunt, in which the hunter becomes the hunted, and even the carcass of the tropic bird becomes food for the fish. And if Life is a cheat, what can I expect of Death? Who will rid me of the body of Death?

Ah, Caleb, you would smile at Death, and welcome her, if God would but let you see his face, his foot, even the smallest of his toes. . . .

When he is ready for us to know, the bell of Damien's church rang out, joyous in the freshness of the morning, *then will he send to let us know.*

Moving slowly, Newman came out of the house to join me in the yard. His wounded arm was supported in a sling I had fashioned from part of an old sheet. The uniform, once so dazzling white, was stained and frayed, and it hung loose upon his thin body. But at least it was clean, and fragrant with sunshine and fresh air, after the boiling and scrubbing I gave it while he lay in his sickbed.

Nor would he ever be the unmarked man again. His body, too, had paid its toll, as the body of each of us who comes to Kalawao must yield up its tribute to the dominion of death. Grave and graven now with suffering, his was the countenance of a man who has crossed over the threshold of knowledge. His trying was not yet ended, and his wisdom was far from gained; but in the way he looked at me, and from me to the scape of Kalaupapa falling away from the hillside where we stood, I saw that he was no longer afraid to take his place in the enormous world to which he was returning.

The distant church bell was quieted. He stood with me in the stillness, looking with me at the loveliness we could not see before the morning of revelation. "It is beautiful," he said. "Beyond denying. This is how I want to remember it."

Together we started down the path to the church, two cripples scarred and hurt, two men who did not easily die. Halfway down the path he put his hand upon my arm. "Why are you so sad? I have not seen you this way before."

"Is this not a reason for sadness?" I pointed to the lepers' village spread out below us. " 'Lingering perdition, worse than any death can be at once, shall step by step attend you and your ways; whose wraths to guard you from—which here, in this most desolate isle . . . is nothing but heart-sorrow. . . .' "

"There are other lines in the play—better lines—which I commend to you."

"You have read it, too?" I asked foolishly. In all my life I've not met another person who has read *The Tempest*.

"Yes, a long time ago. And, as with so many Englishmen, only after I left England. Parts of it have stayed with me. And last night, while I lay awake thinking of all you have done for me, I brought some of them back to life again, from the corner of my memory in which they are stored. I did not expect to employ one of them so soon."

"If it fits, let me hear it."

" 'I saw such islanders . . . who, though they are of monstrous shape—' " He did not spare me the ugly word, but he softened it in such a way that even I could not take offense. " '—yet, note, their manners are more gentle-kind than of our human generation you shall find many, nay, almost any.' "

"You are more generous than we deserve. We have behaved toward you like a pack of dogs. And I have been the most hateful Caliban of all."

"Oh, no!" he protested with a genuine laugh. "That is my role, the part of Caliban. You cannot take it from me. You—I have worked this out, too—you are Ariel."

"Ariel?" I hooted it, robbing the lightsome name of its grace. "How could you make such a mistake?"

"Yes. And why not? I cannot imagine Ariel better played. But I am Caliban, I insist: let us have no argument about it, else I'll drag out my string of curses to heap upon you."

For once I, the very inventor of cursing, the most voluble practitioner of talk, was left speechless. Not that I agreed with him. It was just too stunning a proof of how each one of us looks at the world only through the little holes of his own two eyes.

"And Damien," he continued gaily, "who else can Damien be than the Prospero of this magical island, sending an Ariel like you to tame a Caliban like me."

"On Damien I must agree. This place would be a hell without him, a desert island. But for the rest of your players upon this stage—" After its brief rest the imperative bell sent out its call once more. "Well, we must talk about them later. Church is about to begin." Yet I was so flattered by his opinion of me that I could not keep my silly smile hidden away where in decency it belonged.

The steps of the little church were covered with people, and others were clustered outside the open windows to be near the service. Through the windows we could see the parishioners who were standing in the aisle of the near side.

In the place where the path met the road Newman stopped me. "Another idea came to me last night, too." He was forced to shout in order to be heard above the clangor of the bell. "I would like your lawyer's opinion upon it."

"Gladly," I said, enjoying my role as confidant to this cultured man, going more than halfway toward him in my willingness to accept the role of Ariel as well. "What is it?" Oh, the reeking unction of my soft answer! Oh, the toothful complacency of my smirk!

"Do you think that—if I asked him to do so—the King would release Keanu into my care?" His face was bright with hope. In the mirrors of his irises I could see the tiny images of myself, reduced almost to nothing. "I would take him away from Hawaii, of course, to a place where he could make a new start in life."

I could feel myself going pale, whiter than the streak of dead flesh in my cheek, as the blood drained out of my head. It was leaving my brain, the organ of my thought, suddenly disowned for having failed me. In the awful instant I saw how it had played me false, and I understood why the shamed blood should abandon it. It was sinking, this blood, into my empty bowels, where it was turned into the very aliment of dread. And this dread was quickly dispersed into every one of my wicked body's wretched parts.

No! I wanted to shout, No! You can't do this to Keanu! Have you thought of him? Of what he wants for his happiness?

"What's wrong with this idea? Don't you think it has merit? Don't you think he'll let me have my boon, after all I've done for his damned Board of Health?"

I was trapped: trapped in my lies, tied up in the rope of deceit and cynicism I had so irresponsibly woven for him, for his misery's sake. I thought I had fashioned for him a life line, with which he could pull himself back to sanity. But he had grasped it as a leash with which to bind his fate to him. I had given him the rope, grandly tossing it to him when I thought I was done with using it. But I forgot that it was a line with two ends, and he was using the loose end as a whip on me, as a tether, from which I could not get away.

"I don't know." I hated the weak smile with which I tried to keep him from knowing how perilous was our position, tied together like two blind men upon the edge of the sea cliffs. I hated myself because I could not look at him.

"Why not?" he snarled. "What can he gain by saying no? I will go to him direct, I'll not ask him through that cheating Gibson." In the clenched fists, in the bright fanatical eyes, his madness lay very close to the surface. It was by no means driven out of him, as I had so casually concluded; nor was it held in great restraint. I saw then how much the deceiver had been deceived by the devil who lived within him. I should have known, I mourned when it was too late, I should have remembered about that other kind of love. I should have known, by looking into myself, how difficult it is to exorcise the morbid monstrous selfish self.

Desperate to pacify him, I managed to mumble: "I am not sure. Let me think about it for a while." Even then I could not give up my pretension to powerful intelligence. Wrinkling my brow, gazing in a philosopher's abstraction at my boots in the dusty road, I acted out the part of a wise man deep in thought. But only one thought was in my craven brain: to bargain for time, until I could find an answer which could save us all. "Perhaps during the service something will come to me," I whined. "Let us talk about this afterwards."

"Good," he said, smiling again, putting the mask up over his need.

Just within the gate of the churchyard Eleu met us. Dressed in the black cassock, he was like a shadow on the wrong side of the wall. He held a handful of bright green fern fronds to his brow, shielding his eyes from the sunlight.

"Caleb?" he called, squinting at us across the wall. "Is it you?" The reflection of the doctor's uniform made Eleu's eyes seem to be already dead.

"Ae, Eleu. The kauka and I: we are here." It was a relief to escape from the doctor's grasp, to shout at Eleu above the pealing of the bell. "Are we too late?"

"No. Kamiano has saved places for you. I will take you to them." He gave us a slow smile, the message of the forbearing who have come too soon to resignation. This was not the Eleu I remembered. "Please. Come with me." He started toward the back door of the church, making his way carefully among the black stones lying in the grass.

Newman held me back. "What has happened to him? Is it his eyes?"

"Yes. A few more days, and then he will be blind."

"Ahh, those damned greedy devils!"

We caught up with Eleu at the vestry door. The handful of ferns was lying on the tread beside his swollen foot. A trickle of bright red blood wept from a sore in the soft flesh above the heel.

Against the green delicacy of the ferns the blood seemed a thing alive, infinitely beautiful, infinitely precious. But it was only the lifeblood of Eleu, dripping unnoticed into the dust. Above us the bell was crazy with glee at this sign of God's most recent triumph.

"Eleu!" I cried, unable to hold myself any longer apart, unwilling to let him go another step alone in this world of misery and madness. His hand upon the doorknob, Eleu turned his head, not sure that he had heard me call.

That damned bell! How could I speak while it clamored and boasted? Bursting with rage, I raised my fist against it, wanting to beat it into silence, but knowing, even as I did so, how futile my rebellion would be.

In that instant, Iokepa the bell ringer released his hold upon the bell rope. But I did not think of Iokepa then: to me, overwrought as I was, it seemed that God had ceased his laughter, the better to hear what I was going to say.

"Eleu!" I called again, loud in the stillness, as the waning music of the bell made it seem that all the choirs of Heaven stopped their singing to join with God in the listening. "Did Kewalo give you my message?"

"*Ae*, he told it to me, as you said it to him. I thank you, Caleb. Your heart is kind, and it makes my heart to feel good. But"—he spoke now to the closed door, not to me—"I am thinking I will be too much of a burden to you."

"A burden? No, not a burden!" I rushed up the stairs to stand at his side, to take him by the arms and force him to look at me. "A friend, Eleu." A better word came to me, one he would understand. "A brother, of whom I am in need. How can you be a burden, when you will be a help to me, even as I will be a help to you?"

He thought upon this new relationship for a moment. "Then let it be so. I will like this new way." He put out his hand. "We will shake hands on it. Then nothing will happen to spoil it."

As we sealed our covenant he asked: "When does this new life begin for us?"

"What is wrong with today? This afternoon, after the *kauka* has gone to the boat, we will begin it."

Something of the old Eleu was in his nod of approval. "Good. I do not like these people who are always starting things tomorrow. They have not learned, how sometimes tomorrow does not come." Then he opened the door and went in.

"You're doing a very generous thing," said Newman, coming up to me. "I shall use your fine example to support my request, when I go to see the King."

I think he meant his praise sincerely, that he had no idea of using it as a threat. But I, who knew all the secrets of devious men, I could only groan helplessly as he stepped past me into the church. The tether was pulling tighter, and I did not know how to loosen it.

"O God!" I prayed, lifting my face to Heaven, hoping that he still leaned out to listen. "Help me! Show me the way . . ."

In the tiny vestry we pushed past the three acolytes, crowding around Father Damien as they helped to robe him for the Mass.

"Good morning," he greeted us above the dark heads of the boys. "Happy Easter to you." His hands were busy tying the bow at the throat of the long white gown the boys were straightening over his cassock. "Please go right in. Eleu shows you the way."

When we passed through the door into the church I could almost feel the wave of silence rising up from the congregation. Worried over their reaction to the doctor's presence among them, I hurried him to his seat. A quick nod and a fleeting grimace from Dr. Pietsch made us welcome next to him. We were in the front pew, in the same place where I had sat the Sunday before.

The altar was ablaze with candles, the vessels were made of gold. The purple veils had been removed from the altar-table and from the objects of mystery standing at either side of the church and above the center of the altar itself. I found, with something of a shock, that they were statues: I did not expect to see such idols in a Christian church. The ones at the sides were cheap things of colored plaster, representations of creatures vacuous and ungendered. But the one who rose above the altar: ahh, *she* was different.

Mary the Mother looked down upon us, her slender body, beneath the weight of the royal blue mantle, slightly bent to hold the Holy Child upon her hip, her slender neck arched beneath the weight of a golden crown. Lovely and immaculate and serene, she was near and comforting, and strong because she was so full of love. That was not sadness in her eyes: it was the certainty of peace. That was not a crown of sorrows bending her head: it was the crown of a Queen.

In the golden vases at her feet were clusters of creamy white *kukui* blossoms, soft and mellow against the large dark-green leaves. White and gold and green, plucked from the Tree of Life, they were the signs of spring, the colors of the rebirth of the world and of the renewal of hope. As once they were a manifestation of all the ancient gods of birth and of growth in the thousand tribes of man, now they were the symbol of the Christ reborn, of the Son triumphant over death and despair. Honeybees crawled from one flower chalice to the next, in their unending search for nectar. They were like people, always stirring, always striving, searching for nectar as people search for happiness, for Heaven. It was a kinder world they drew me into, than the one of Momona's lice . . .

I lifted up my eyes to her, to the Lady of Peace. Why have I not known of her before this time? I marveled. The missionaries, Damien: they have not told me about her. But to her could I bring my devotion, as those bees are doing. Upon my knees would I crawl before her—

"What are these for?" Newman whispered, pointing to the holes piercing the boards of the floor.

I was impatient with the interruption, annoyed because he did not know. "For lepers. . . . To spit through."

"Oh my God!" He shuddered, closing his eyes. I felt better, to see that he still kept some of his weaknesses. I might have to play upon them yet, when we had our talk after Mass.

Half-heard, from beyond the door of the vestry, came the tinkling of the little bells. The door was thrown open, the bells rang louder, and, as the congregation rose to its feet, a choir in the rear of the church burst into song:

> *Introibo ad altare Dei,*
> *Ad Deum qui laetificat juventutem meam.*

The music took my breath away. It made the hair upon my head to rise, the tears to come to my eyes, the harassed spirit in me to thrill at such beauty. Rich with the voices of men and boys, deep with the organ's noble surge, it sounded forth in glory:

> I will go in to the altar of God,
> To God, the joy of my youth.

To this music of angels the acolytes came in, shining in their white surplices, soft on brown feet, swinging the smoking censers, preparing the way for Father Damien. Resplendent in vestments of white and gold touched with traceries of vernal green, he entered in, walking slowly. In the vestry he had been his ordinary self, a man bidding good morning to other men. But now he was transfigured: his eyes were closed, he wore the look of serenest peace.

> *Adjutorium nostrum in nomine Domini,*
> *Qui fecit coelum et terram.*

> Our help is in the name of the Lord,
> Who hath made Heaven and Earth.

While the choir finished its singing the priest stood before the altar, bowed in prayer, or moved before it in his stately ritual. In the hush, when the music was done, he lifted his clear voice:

> I arose, and am still with Thee, Alleluia: Thou hast laid Thy hand upon me, Alleluia: Thy knowledge is become wonderful, Alleluia, Alleluia. Lord, Thou hast proved me and known me: Thou hast known my sitting down and my rising up. Glory be.

More consuming than the pain which burned in my bones and in my rotting flesh; more clamorous than my fright over Newman and what he might do, was the hunger in me for the knowledge Damien had won. Why does he have it? I asked in envy. And why is it withheld from me?

At the glowing table the priest lifted his hands. "*Kyrie eleison,*" he sang. "*Kyrie eleison,*" chanted the choir, imploring the mercy of God for us sinners here below.

But not even in my extremity would he answer me. Only the blind bees could I see, crawling among the wilting flowers. And the black flies clustering upon the heel of Eleu, drinking blood from the chalice of his sore.

The Mass came to its end, with a last swelling of music from the choir, accompanying the departure of Father Damien and the acolytes from the sanctuary. The singing was jubilant, with the voices of women and girls lending their soaring purity to the ground bass of the men, raising up their intricate edifice of sound, with its pinnacles and spires of praise, its vaulting arabesques of exultation, thanking God for his goodness to us, magnifying his name.

For me, usually so comforted by music, it was an exercise in hysteria, meaningless and futile, a screeching accompaniment to my own cracked voice, crying out in prison. My miracle had not come to pass. Others in the congregation, judging by their moist cheeks and rapt expressions, had found solace in the Mass. But I had not: I was the same Caleb of the unquiet heart. Doubting and waiting, I was still the man left out.

The *Kyrie*, thrice repeated, had beat down my supplications, reminded me of my unworthiness; and the rest of the Mass was merely a deeper descent into ugliness. The votive lamps before the painted idol of Saint Philomena smoked and stank; the great lesion in the hem of her robe revealed to me how in the crumbling plaster of her body there could be no haven for the Holy Ghost. The congregation stirred and yawned, coughed and spat, fidgeted and fouled the air. The holes in the floor jeered at me: o o o o, they mocked, their round black mouths opened to scoff. During the Offertory the jingling of money, the brisk crassness of the collection, made the House of God a desecrated temple, where we sat forever entombed, spitting coins into a *kahuna's* calabash.

Only the image of the aloof Mother held its beauty. But its power over me was gone, vanished with my hope.

Kie! I might just as well have gone to see Kaupea, she who told me how my guardian dead were kind from love when they spared me for yet a while. Spared me for what? I wanted to know. For this? I asked, looking with disgust at the dingy fetid church.

I was sick of waiting, sick of pretense, sick of lies. To hell with Keanu, I said, and with this mad doctor, and with the troubles of *pupule* gullible Caleb the Leper. All this nonsense about God, all this foolish talk about love: it is nothing but a monstrous lie, a shouting in the fearful night, to keep ourselves from being sore afraid. All, all is vanity.

There is nothing now but Death, I knew, as I stared full into the face of Death. There is no escaping it: it is all about me, in the skulls' holes bored in the floor, in the bodies of my fellow patients, my brothers and my sisters, in all of us who are the children of Leprosy, the first-born daughter of Death. And why should I fear my Mother, to whose bosom I shall soon be pressed?

Broken in my will I was, and beaten down in my spirit. Empty was I, as is one who is dead.

Thus did I make my peace with Death.

While most of the congregation moved into the yard, a few people, led by Kewalo and Makaio, came forward to say farewell to Dr. Newman. He and I and Dr. Pietsch were standing at the front of the church when the delegation came to our rescue.

"*Kauka*, we hear that you are going away from us," said Kewalo, bowing awkwardly, not remembering what next to say. "We wish to tell you Godspeed," Makaio added piously, getting full credit on earth and in Heaven for the message Kewalo could not think of in time. Then others came pushing in, shouldering the first two aside. "We wish to thank you for your studies to help us," they said, and "We pray to Iehovah that they will bear good fruit," while behind them shyer ones bowed and smiled and called out "*Aloha*" to him. But, remembering how he had kept his distance from them, they did not come close, nor did they offer to shake his hand. Knowing them as well as I did, I could tell that affection did not bring them forward. It was Father Damien's appeal, passed among them by Kewalo, which made them attend upon the *kauka*.

And yet it was not entirely a performance of duty which drew from them the soft words of parting. Nor was it a sense of duty which made them exclaim, "*Auwe!* See how thin he is with his sickness," and ask, "Why is it that he must wear his arm in a sling? Is it because the arm bone is broken?"

When I whispered how his arm suffered from a boil, they were eager to share with him their remedies for so understandable an affliction. "A poultice of the *popolo* berries," claimed some. "No," said others, "of the *laukahi* leaf," while still others proposed the salt of the sea, the spittle of dogs, the sour cud of a red cow, as the only cure. They had as many different remedies for the treating of a boil as of the *lepera*, and no more proof that the medicines would work for the one than for the other.

They were content with their delusions; and as it was with the simples for such ordinary things as a boil, so it was with their recipes for such things as Heaven. To them there were many different ways by which a man could get to Heaven. But, by whatever route he might approach it, God, the Great Physician, would always be at the Gate, to see that he entered clean and whole into Paradise. No wonder doctors will never learn how to treat pimples and cure boils. I pitied my neighbors their stupidity, while I also envied them their simplicity.

Pale and uncomfortable, Newman stood beside me, murmuring his thanks, trying to smile. He was touched by their gentle kindness, but he was also made very unhappy by it. Now, as never before, he would know how much he had lost, and how much he had failed himself as well as them, when he shut himself off from them.

For him it was an ordeal, almost worse than no farewell at all. But for me it was a good thing, recognized even as I experienced it. It made me one of them again, by putting me where I belonged, in touch with my people. For too long had I been growing apart from them. In lifting my head to search for the way to Heaven, my feet had lost their touch with the muddy paths of reality. But now my feet were set upon the earth again. I had been upon so many foolish journeyings, in wild alternations of bounding and rebounding, bouncing like a rubber ball between the floor of Heaven and the roof of Hell. Now I was at rest again, and this time, I promised myself, I would remain at rest.

The last patients were still with us when Father Damien came from the vestry. The heavy robes of the Mass were removed, and he was wearing the black cassock which was his usual habit. Beaming with approval of the courtesy his parishioners were showing, he waited to one side with Dr. Pietsch.

Although I stood with Dr. Newman, translating whenever he could not understand the patients, I was thinking less of him than of myself. I was impatient for the afternoon, when the two doctors would have departed at last. My only plan was to keep Newman so busy with company, with breakfast, with starting upon his way across the beach of Kalawao, as to leave him no time for lawyer's talk. Once he was gone I would be free of him and his problems, and I would not have to live in terror of the lies I had told, mostly for his sake.

Then—*eia ka!*—how quickly I would run off to my own house. I was looking forward to my new life with Eleu. I was eager to read in my books again, and to introduce Eleu to their company. I longed to take up my flute once more, to be the solace of my liver and of Eleu's discouraged one. I would watch the seedlings grow, of every plant in the Settlement, not in greed for the fruits of their age, but for the pure delight of seeing them in the beauty of their growing, of seeing them as they are. I wanted to walk across the green and lovely land, with Momona for company, and Eleu, seated upon the slow-paced nag I had bought for Akala. We would lie in the shade of *ohia* trees to drowse; we would go swimming in the stream at Waileia. We might go to call upon Malie and Keanu; and on our way we would peer into the bottomless pit of Kauhako, which the people say is the birth-hole of Hell, filled with black rock, black water, and blackest darkness, which nothing can purge, where nothing can live.

When the last of the patients were going away, Father Damien limped across the sanctuary to Dr. Newman. "What they say they mean," he said gently. "I hope you know this?"

"I will never forget it," replied the doctor, close to tears.

"Now let us go to my house," Damien called to the rest of us. "I have some colored eggs for our feast, just as they are made at home."

In the background Eleu waited to put out the candles upon the altar. Supporting himself upon the long pole of the candlesnuffer, tipped with its little flower of brass, he was like a young warrior leaning upon his spear.

"For me I hope you have a dozen eggs," said Pietsch, fussing over his jacket, his tie, his mustache, like a man taken with the itch. "I have such a hunger. And I should eat now, ven I can. The ocean out there—*ach*, it vill make me sick, now, for a veek."

"*Na, na,*" Damien chided him. "Today the water is so smooth. You have no excuse to get seasick."

After the long service, and the even longer time of my concern over the doctor, I was so hungry that I was giddy. Sourness was burning holes in my stomach, as empty as a fish-head picked clean by the crabs; and where Pietsch demanded eggs I was ready to eat seaweed from the reef and raw fish still wriggling from the net. I was enjoying the thought of their *haoles'* horror, if ever they saw me doing such a thing, when Newman offered his share of comfort to the delicate Pietsch. "Father Damien's unique coffee will be the best preventive, I think, against the mal-de-mer. And with eggs, and *kanaka* pudding, to sustain you—"

The suspicious *malihini* raised his eyebrows. "*Kanaka* pudding?"

Laughing over the experience in store for him, we were preparing to leave when we heard footsteps entering at the front of the church. The light tapping of a woman's heels, the heavier tread of a man: the little building trembled with their approach. We turned, all in the same moment, to see who came so late into the church.

Beside me Newman gasped, as a man would who has been pierced through with a spear. He clutched my arm to keep from falling.

Go away, I wanted to shout at them, *Go away!* But I could not. I could only stand there, a support for Newman to hang upon, while my mind wailed helplessly, Why now? Why must they come now?

Slowly, in what seemed an eternity of time, in a great stillness in which all sounds were hushed, they walked toward us. The church grew larger with each step they took: it became so enormous that I thought they could never reach us. In the infinity of waiting there was time to think a lifetime's thoughts, to see every detail of feature and of dress in the approaching pair, every minute part in the swelling church and in the entire universe beyond its growing walls.

Slowly they came toward us, she leaning upon his arm, alight with happiness, smiling gently upon us, upon him, as she turned her gaze from him to us and back to him again. Her eyes were soft with love, for him, for all the world. Her smile was a blessing, making lovely all things upon the earth. She was dressed in a gown of softest blue touched with flecks of white: it was as if she were clothed in a piece of the morning sky, or in a foam-tipped wave pulled from the encircling sea. The locket of silver floating in the cloud of lace at her breast was the moon, tamed by her loveliness; the little blue gems shining in her ears, the flowers in her hair, were the attendant stars. Never had she been more beautiful. Never had I known that such beauty could walk in the world of men.

He was a man reborn: dressed in a white shirt and white trousers, he was a pillar of bright light coming toward us, supported by the darkness of his unshod feet upon the earth-stained floor, topped by the darkness of his handsome head, rising from the open throat of the shirt. Smiling upon each of us in turn, he was superbly in command of himself, and of us, as he drew her

with him, her body leaning toward his, her head, heavy with its
crown of dark hair, almost resting against his arm. His smile was
the gentle greeting of a man who knows no malice and no envy,
and who, in the innocence of his goodness, expects no harm from
other men. Never, since the dawn of the world, in Eden's garden,
has a man of such glory walked upon the earth.

All of the meaning of creation was coming into the church with
them: the meaning to love and to hate, to hope and to despair, to
life and to death, all was gathering in the all-embracing room.
There was no imperfection in them: there was only love and
beauty. And in the presence of such perfect love fear fled, and
hate and despair were cast out, and Death ran in frenzy to hide
herself away.

As darkness lifts at dawn, before the rays of the sun, so did
the silence move away, to make room for the sounds of life.
Beyond them, above them, I could hear the tears of mankind's
grief drying, as mist leaves the peaks of the mountains to vanish
into the sky. I could see mankind's pain drawing away, as a wave
falls back from the shore. The yellowing leaf turned green and
young again, in the time of the world's new morning. The whimpering demons of evil cringed in fright and faded away. In their
place came the high shimmering music of celestial choirs, proclaiming the goodness of God.

Softly, beginning as a whisper scarcely venturing to suggest itself, came the awareness that my emptiness was being taken away,
that I was being filled with an ineffable joy. And then, as the
angelic music grew in power and in exaltation, the thought
swelled in me until it grew into a certainty, that my joy was
being given to me as a gift from the Mother of God.

He is here, She said, in a voice I did not need ears to hear. I am
here, with them and with you, He said, in a voice coming from
within me, filling my emptiness, delighting my heart, setting my
spirit to singing hosannas of thanksgiving.

Trembling with the sense of His presence, thrilling with the
perception of His Grace, I knew at last the knowledge of God,
coming with the blessed pair into the immensity of the light-filled
room. Not the punitive Father was there, not the Lord of Might
and of Wrath, Who flashed lightning from His glance and Who
broke men beneath His heel for their pride, but Christ the Gentle
Son of the Gentle Mother. Not cruel Jehovah, the God of Fear,

but Jesus the Sacrificed Man, the God Who is Love, Who gives Mercy as His gift.

The beautiful pair stood before Father Damien, the man who had told me of this gentle God, the man who in my stubbornness I would not believe.

"*Aloha oukou,*" said Keanu in his deep voice.

"*Aloha* to all of you," said Malie, giving her benison to each of us.

The spell was broken. The music of Heaven ceased, the universe assumed its proper space, the little church shrank into itself again. But it was still flooded with light. And the grace of God: it remained with me, it was not taken away. Reeling with the wonderful knowledge, I closed my eyes to hold in my joy.

Here is the end to the long fugue of my flight and my desiring: here is the reward Paliku did promise me on the first day of my trying. I have found the way! This is the answer of Kailiki to his sorrowing daughter, in the long night of my terror. It is the fulfillment of Damien's test of me, and the goal of Kaupea's signs along the way. They have foreseen it, all of them, out of their knowledge, and only I have not believed that a leper's road can be a way to Heaven.

Father Damien moved toward them. "Malia, Keanu. We are happy to see you here today." In his voice there was not the marveling which I expected to hear from one who has witnessed a miracle. I opened my eyes, to see if he was sinking to his knees in awe before the holy couple. But no: he was giving a hand to each of them, drawing them closer to him.

"Kamiano," said Keanu. "We come to ask of you a boon. We wish to marry. Will you do it for us?" Over the priest's head he sent us apology for imposing his personal affairs upon us.

The fingers of Newman's left hand pressed like hooks of iron into my arm. Even though he did not understand Keanu's speech, he moaned, the moan of a man who is in mortal pain. No man who has found favor in the sight of God could make this sound of a heart's breaking.

Wondering why they were denied what I was receiving, I looked at my companions. Pietsch had backed away from us: he was staring at Keanu as if he were the Devil himself, and not a man of glory. Eleu, bearing the candlesnuffer before him like a chamberlain's staff, was coming forward to join us. Newman, deathly pale, was biting his lips to keep closed up within him the shrieks of his despair.

My heart faltered within me. Am I the only one who has seen the miracle? Then how can I believe in it, if I am the only one? And how can I endure to live another instant, if I can no longer believe in it? I began to tremble, as a mountain trembles when the earth beneath it quakes, praying for my doubts to be taken from me before my faith was shattered. Eagerly I sought within me for the remembrance of the presence which had come to fill my emptiness. I reached out my hand, that I might touch the light of God.

"But of course," the priest was saying to Keanu and Malie, joining their hands with his own before his breast. "I am delighted to do this. Nothing I can do will give me more happiness."

It was still there within me, my joy: it had not gone away. It was like a flame which, once lighted, cannot die out. And the light from it was passing into the very structure of my body, into its darkest parts, taking away the despair from it and the weariness, leaving a core of peace where once there was only pain. Finding it there, I knew that my doubts were forever ended. If I am the one chosen on this morning to be the receiver of His gift of grace, then who am I to question the wisdom of God? It is my time to know.

With this knowledge my doubts were thrown away. I ceased my trembling.

"There is something you must know," said Malie. But she could not go on, because of us who stood behind the priest. She touched her forehead to Keanu's arm, asking him to speak for her.

"She is with child, we think," he said proudly, drawing her close to him. "Only now have we learned it. Does this make a difference?"

Newman twisted the flesh of my arm, until the soft skin broke. "You lied," he accused me through his teeth. I turned away from the sight of his torment. "You knew it all the time!" he rasped, putting the strength of hate into his fingers until they pierced through my shirt and dug into my flesh. But I would not cry out, knowing how much greater was the agony he was suffering. I could bear any pain, now, any affliction.

Father Damien did not hold back his answer. "If this is so, then it is God's Will, and His Will is not for us to question. With your child He is saying to you that your life will go on. This is a blessing in which we can rejoice. And He will rejoice because you give your child as a covenant to Him."

In him was the same faith which glowed in me, the same great love which illumined them. Then I understood that I was not the only one to see the miracle: those three, they knew of Jesus and His Mother, and of Their Grace; and they walked accustomed in the world of Love into which only now I was entering.

"We thank you, Kamiano," Keanu said. "We are glad because God is so good. We know this, because He has brought us such great happiness when, in our hearts, we had lost all hope of happiness. For this reason have we come to ask His blessing upon us."

And Malie said softly, "Because He is so good to us, we will name the child John, when he comes."

With a cry of desperation Newman flung himself forward, thrusting the priest aside, to stand before Keanu. "Your arm!" he croaked at the man he had used as an animal. "Tell me! What has happened to your arm?"

From my wounded arm the warm blood was seeping out, dyeing the sleeve of my shirt. I looked upon it in gladness: it was my covenant with Him.

Keanu looked down from his height upon the little doctor. "'Scuse me, *Kauka*," he said simply, "fo wat I wen' do. My love fo Malie: it was too big."

The doctor stood before his victim, staring up with his heart in his eyes at the man whose victim he had become.

"You like—you want look 'um now?" asked Keanu.

"No, I cannot!" Newman cried, drawing back. "Yes!" he wailed, leaning forward. "Yes! I must see it. *I must know!*"

Gently Keanu withdrew his hand from Malie's hold. Calmly, as Father Damien and Dr. Pietsch and Eleu and I gathered around, he pulled back the white sleeve, bright against the warm dark skin.

Bending over Keanu's extended arm, the doctor was the first to see it. With a terrible cry he put his hand to his face and wept, staggering out of the circle we made around him. The blood which mingled with his tears was not only my blood: it was his blood, and Keanu's, as well as mine.

While Keanu held out his arm for us to see, the four of us leaned closer to examine it.

Father Damien was the first to find words for his thoughts.

Straightening up, he lifted his hand to make the sign of the cross before Keanu. "All things work together for good, to them that love God," he said softly. "He will not leave you comfortless, my son."

For the testimony of Keanu's arm could not be denied. He, too, was now a leper.